THE WAR PLANNERS
BOOKS 3-4

PAWNS OF THE PACIFIC & THE ELEPHANT GAME

ANDREW WATTS

POINT WHISKEY PUBLISHING

ALSO BY ANDREW WATTS

Books available for Kindle, print, and audiobook. To find out more about the books or Andrew Watts, go to andrewwattsauthor.com.

The War Planners Series

1. The War Planners
2. The War Stage
3. Pawns of the Pacific
4. The Elephant Game
5. Overwhelming Force

Max Fend Series

1. Glidepath
2. The Oshkosh Connection

PAWNS OF THE PACIFIC

BOOK 3 IN THE WAR PLANNERS SERIES

The world is in a constant conspiracy against the brave. 'It's the age-old struggle: the roar of the crowd on the one side, and the voice of your conscience on the other.
—Douglas MacArthur

1

Langley, Virginia

"What is this place?" David asked.

They had arrived at a high-ceilinged room that reminded David of a NASA command center. Dim lights. High-tech. Lots of people with headsets on, each neatly spaced throughout rows of computer screens. The people in the room were a mix of what David assumed to be CIA and uniformed military.

David had been showing up to Langley every day for the past few weeks. Each day, he was taken to interrogation rooms or conference rooms, where he was asked repeated questions about the Red Cell, China, and Iran.

But they never took him to a setting like this. Chase and the other man stood silent, waiting at the entrance of the room.

An enormous wall of monitors stood at the front of the large room, each screen showing different bits of data. Many of the men and women in the room were gathered around a screen that showed the live feed on one of the monitors.

It showed an aerial view of a small land mass, surrounded by water. The land mass looked familiar to David. It had a large runway that barely fit on the island. A few scattered buildings next to the runway. Beaches that were several shades darker than normal. The rest of the island was covered in green vegetation, right up its mountainous center.

A flash of recognition hit him. David was looking at the Red Cell island.

David looked at his brother, confused. Chase had that same knowing look in his eye.

David said, "What are these people working on in here?"

Chase replied, "What's it look like?"

David took in the room once more. Some of the screens showed tactical displays of the South China Sea. Others monitors were zoomed out to focus on the entire Western Pacific theater.

Tiny blue and red digital shapes covered each map. David knew that these were the ships, submarines, and aircraft. Blue shapes for allied forces. Red for enemy forces.

David observed a man sitting nearby. He monitored three computer displays. Thick headphones covered his ears. The man typed furiously, and David noticed that the text looked to be Chinese characters.

"It looks like they're taking the Chinese threat seriously after all. They're monitoring the Red Cell island, at least."

Chase nodded.

"You aren't surprised. You've known about this? Why the hell have I been led to believe that we weren't doing anything about it?"

He leaned in close to David's ear. "Keep cool and try not to be pissed off. You can yell at me all you want once we get to the car. But the fact that they've invited you here means that you're going to get read in. That's a good thing. Don't spoil it."

David looked at his brother a moment. Part of him was angry that he had been kept in the dark. But he understood that it couldn't have been a choice. Secrets were the norm for Chase's line of work.

The automatic doors let out a whoosh as they opened behind them. The room got quiet as about half of the personnel turned to look in David's direction. There was a brief moment of panic as he mistakenly thought they were looking at him. They weren't. They were all looking past him.

David turned around and saw two men. One, David recognized right away. He had seen the face on TV. Director Samuel Buckingham—head of the CIA, in the flesh. The other man was military. An Army three-star. Starched uniform and gleaming medals.

A woman with an air of authority said, "Director Buckingham, we're ready to start whenever you are. We have seats for you over here."

"Thanks, Susan." The CIA director checked his watch and frowned. "Alright, ladies and gentlemen. As you all know, business is booming around here right now. I need to brief the president on Iran later this morning, and that conflict is using up the majority of our resources. But I want you all to know that the work you're doing here is vital. Please don't misinterpret my lack of time for you this morning as an indication of the importance of your mission."

He looked at the Army general. "I've asked General Schwartz to step in and serve as the sponsor for this task force. He'll be briefing me every day on your progress. Now I've got thirty minutes free and I need to use two of them. Susan, I beg your forgiveness. Please give me a moment."

"Of course, sir," the woman said.

The director and the general turned to look straight at David. He walked a few steps, closing the distance between them, and stuck out his hand. He lowered his voice. "Gentlemen, I'm Bob Buckingham. This is General Schwartz." The men all exchanged handshakes and then sat down on couches facing each other.

The general said, "You're Art Manning's boys?"

"Yes, sir," said Chase.

"He's a good man. We were at the Navy War College together."

The brothers smiled politely.

Director Buckingham said, "Let's get a little privacy for a minute before the briefing begins. I'm afraid every goddamn person in this room will be eavesdropping on us. You'd think I was surrounded by spies." The CIA director had the broad smile and easy manner of an experienced politician.

They climbed a narrow set of metal stairs to an enclosed room that overlooked the larger space. The room reminded David of a box seat at a football game. They were above the worker bees here, and the chatter from below was being piped in by a speaker somewhere.

There were seats in the room, but no one sat. The director said, "Gentlemen, I would first like to thank you for your service to our country. Without the brave acts each of you performed over the past few weeks, we would be completely in the dark on the Chinese Red Cell, and the role that the Chinese played in Iran."

Chase didn't say anything.

David, still feeling his way around the situation, said, "I appreciate that."

"Now, I will ask you both to serve your country once again. General Schwartz and I have been directed by the president to put together this task force in hopes of…well, in hopes of preventing World War Three. If we can't stop it, then we're to ensure that we're at least prepared for it."

Sounds familiar, David thought to himself.

"David, I'm going to be frank. I always am. I find it saves me time, my most precious commodity these days. There are some members of the government that expressed concerns that you may have compromised your nation."

David was very familiar with the charge. Over the past few weeks, he'd been through countless classified debriefings and interviews with various agencies, including closed session hearings with congressional intelligence committees.

There were also news stories on him, which he was still getting used to. He wasn't allowed to comment, of course. But that didn't stop the damn press from speculating on what had really happened. Some of them came pretty close to the truth. Others—at some of the extreme ends of the journalistic spectrum—thought he was a traitor and should be shot.

Everyone—government and press—wanted to try and get to the bottom of David's allegations that the Chinese had tricked twenty Americans into disclosing classified information.

The director said, "These people would have me believe that you gave too much information to the Chinese and were an unwitting agent of a foreign adversary. What say you?"

David clenched his jaw. He could see Chase giving him a look as if he were ready to hold him back from socking the director. It took all the patience David could muster to respond calmly.

"I would say that I did the best I could under the circumstances. I never willingly gave classified information to the Chinese. And as soon as I discovered that the Red Cell was not what it appeared to be, I made every effort to organize an escape."

The director seemed satisfied with that answer. He looked at the general. "General Schwartz has recently been assigned to us. He is the Associate Director of the CIA for Military Affairs. I've asked him here because the four of us need to discuss a part of Operation SILVERSMITH that might become very important. I've known General Schwartz here for over two decades. I trust him implicitly. He tells me that he knows your father. He swears to me that you're from good stock."

"Thank you, sir."

"I will also note that I think it's very easy to second-guess someone if you haven't walked a mile in their shoes," the director continued. "So—if anyone gives you a hard time David, you just let me know. I, for one, think you're a fine American. I think what you did showed ingenuity, and tenacity. And I need scrappy, intelligent fighters on my team."

David looked at his brother, and then back at the director, not sure what to say.

Director Buckingham went on, "I also need someone who's seen what we're up against. Your experience will be an invaluable asset. And I'd rather have you helping us here than sending my interrogators to try and tease out bits of information that may or may not be the most relevant. I can't think of anyone who would be a better contributor to Task Force SILVERSMITH than you. You not only have the knowledge of what these bastards are up to, but you've also got the motivation to disrupt their plans. So, what do you say?"

"What do I say, sir? I'm sorry. About what?"

"I would like you to join us here at Langley for the foreseeable future. We'll work out the admin details with In-Q-Tel, but it should be manageable. We'd like you to work as an analyst and advisor for us as we evaluate the Red Cell and any potential Chinese war plans. Do you accept this request?"

He blinked. "Um. Yes. Yes, of course."

"Excellent. I apologize for the inconvenience of all those Q&A sessions we've been putting you through. But as you'll see, we're putting the information to good use. Now let's go back downstairs and get this show on the road."

Marching down the steps behind the other three, David felt dozens of eyes on him. He caught a few of their gazes. Not all were friendly. He wondered what they thought of him being here, given that he had been part of the Red Cell.

The director said, "Ladies and gentlemen, as most of you now know, we have been directed by the president to form a joint task force to defend against the Chinese threat to our national security. If you're in this room, Operation SILVERSMITH is now one hundred percent of your work plan. Drop everything else. Don't talk about what goes on here to anyone. What we do over the next few days, the next few weeks, and the next few months is crucial to the security of our nation. I have no doubt that each of you will give it your very best. Alright, that's my pep talk. Susan, I understand you're going to bring us all up to speed?"

"That's correct, sir."

"Alright, hit it. I've got..." He looked at his watch. "Twenty minutes."

They all sat. The lights dimmed. The woman whom the director had referred to as Susan spoke. Her voice was amplified through a small microphone attached to her collar.

"Director Buckingham, General Schwartz, good afternoon. My name is Susan Collinsworth and I'm the staff operations officer lead for this team. This is the introductory brief for Task Force SILVER-SMITH. Our objective is to identify and counter the Chinese threat to our nation, with a specific emphasis on the recently identified plans of Cheng Jinshan and the Chinese Red Cell. The following is a brief timeline of relevant events."

David looked over the room. The scattered audience sat in rows, many behind computer terminals. They each looked up at the big screen, where a presentation showed a timeline of events and pictures.

Susan said, "On October second, twenty Americans are flown from various locations in the continental United States to a small airport in California—Half Moon Bay Airport, just south of San Francisco. From examining satellite feed and FAA records, we have determined that nine private aircraft were used in all. Each of these aircraft was owned and operated by a shell company connected to Cheng Jinshan—more on him later in the brief."

She took a sip of water, then continued, "These aircraft then refuel and fly the twenty Americans to what we shall refer to as the Red Cell island—it has another name, but frankly, it's a bear to pronounce. The Red Cell island is located north of the Spratly Islands in the South China Sea. We assess that none of the Americans knew their true whereabouts or who was planning and operating the Red Cell."

David saw a few questioning glances in his direction. "We *assess*" was not the same as "we *know*." He wondered what the others in this room were thinking. Perhaps that he and the others in the Red Cell were fools? Or worse…traitors? The thought made him sick.

"From October third until October twelfth, these twenty Americans participate in a Red Cell operation on the island. There they're told that China is planning to attack the US, and that the goal of the Red Cell is to plot out ways in which the attack might be conducted. As many of you know, the group of twenty Americans was comprised of military and intelligence experts, as well as civilian experts in technology, communications, utilities, and several other fields."

Groans could be heard throughout the room. There was David's answer about how people felt.

The director said, "I've heard much of this before, but let me ask the obvious question. How were these people duped?"

Susan glanced at David and cleared her throat. "Sir, this was a legitimate Red Cell roster, jointly owned by the DoD and CIA. We are still working out how the Chinese were able to obtain the roster and personnel activation codes. But multiple messages went out over a forty-eight-hour period which notified participants. Most were activated by the Pentagon. In many cases, there was a legitimate source within their chain of command that triggered the participation request. It was quite an elaborate operation. Everyone involved at the Pentagon or CIA thought that someone else was running the show. Part of the problem when there are so many chefs in the kitchen."

"But who were the people who actually signed off on this?"

"Sir, we've identified at least five personnel that we think were responsible for triggering the travel and participation requests for the Red Cell participants. These five people had positions of authority in various defense and intelligence agencies. For example..." She looked down at her notes. "A GS-15 in the Defense Intelligence Agency used a contract with a Boston-based consulting firm to send one of their consultants on the trip. This consultant was a former Army officer and held a TS/SCI clearance. She had expertise in multiple classified Army weapons systems."

"So to be clear, this looked legitimate to the members of the Red Cell."

"Yes, sir."

"And where are these five people who triggered the travel and participation requests? What happened to them?"

"Four of them are missing. Each appears to have fled the country or gone into hiding."

"And the fifth?"

"Tom Connolly turned up dead on the shores of Bandar Abbas the day of the Gorji assassination."

The director nodded. "Ah, yes. Tom Connolly. *Delightful*. Please proceed."

David thought it was odd that the CIA director would have asked these questions today. David had been home for weeks. He had been interviewed many times by various government agencies, and especially the CIA. So the investigation into the Red Cell would have been going on for at least that long. The director must already know these things. *He does know*. He's just trying to give the members of the Red Cell credibility. To show that while they were duped, they should be considered loyal Americans.

"On October twelfth, the jig is up. Chinese military personnel storm the island and—we assume—take all the Americans into captivity. In the confusion, David Manning and Henry Glickstein escape from the island on a small Chinese watercraft. A few days later, the two men are picked up by an Australian fishing trawler. They spend fourteen days at sea and arrive in Darwin, Australia, on October twenty-fourth.

"This is the same day that two other events occurred. First, the Iranian politician, Ahmad Gorji, was killed, along with his wife, on the highway outside Bandar Abbas, Iran."

The screen changed to show an overhead drone's video feed of a highway near the ocean. A freighter truck was parked at an odd angle, blocking the highway. Three black cars stopped in front of it. A gunfight erupted. Then the screen went bright green as an explosion flattened the whole scene.

Susan continued to speak as the video played.

"The attack was extremely well executed. Our own analysis corroborates the Iranian claims that US- and Israeli-made weapons were used. About a dozen armed men emerged from the truck here and began attacking the politician's convoy of cars. We think that these men were a diversion. Hired Iranians who didn't know too much about their target. Once the firefight ensued, Claymore mines and a very talented sniper finished everyone off.

"The former CIA employee, Tom Connolly, was found dead near the beach, one mile away. This is the same man who had worked at In-Q-Tel and convinced several members of the Red Cell to attend a few weeks earlier. Also, Lisa Parker—aka Lena Chou—sent an unclassified email to several CIA employees indicating that she was a part of the mission.

David flushed at the mention of Tom's name. Flashbacks of his face under the foaming waves.

"It was an obvious framing. But because of these US connections, the Iranians think that we really were responsible for the assassination. Our analysts also stress the personal connection between the Iranian leadership and the people who were killed. Emotional responses are not usually rational ones."

The lights were dimmed, but David could see a few people were shaking their heads.

The director said, "Tell me about this Parker woman."

"Lisa Parker, aka Lena Chou. Graduated from the University of Maryland. Division 1 track athlete there. The Agency recruited her out of college. She's been with the CIA for almost fourteen years. Started out in Central America. Spent a few years there working anti-narco-terrorism operations. Top evaluations got her a slot in Iraq in 2007. She's done some work in Japan for us, but most of her time has been in either the US or the Middle East. She's a Political Action Group officer, but she's also reportedly an expert at unarmed combat. Her file says that she spends a lot of her personal time training in martial arts."

"Married?"

"No significant others or kids."

"Family in the US? I'm assuming that she's US-born?"

"She was raised by an aunt in the San Francisco Bay area. Her birth certificate says she was born there. And records show that the people that were supposed to be her parents were killed in a car crash in 1997. In San Fran. That's what the file says, anyway. And that's what all the background checks have stated, but…a recent investigation indicates otherwise."

He cocked his head. "Please elaborate."

"We now think she arrived in the US as a teenager right around the time the people she claims were her parents died in the car crash. Our analysts have been evaluating pictures of Lena Chou both before and after her parents' death. They don't match. Immediately after the car crash, the daughter went to live with an aunt in the suburbs of Baltimore. But no one who knew the daughter in San Francisco could identify Lena Chou when we showed them pictures. Granted that it would be fifteen years later—but still."

"Meaning what?"

David couldn't believe what he was hearing.

"Meaning that we think Lena Chou was swapped for this daughter of the car crash victims," Susan said. "The aunt took her and God knows what happened to the real daughter after that. But then the aunt picks up Lena Chou and takes her to Maryland. Then she starts working for the Agency, and her cover name becomes Lisa Parker. But the big news is that we now think she took the girl's identity as a teenager."

"How sure are you of this?"

"We're still investigating. We should know more by next week."

David watched as video on the screen changed to an image of Lena Chou looking up at the sky. The camera was overhead, so it was easy to make out her features. An official CIA photograph of her was displayed on the screen.

Susan said, "Lena Chou/Lisa Parker was involved in the Iranian assassination. We know that from this drone feed. Only weeks earlier, she was a CIA employee with a sterling record, working in Dubai. When word of a mole in Dubai Station was received, a counterespionage team was sent over to investigate. The team flagged Miss Parker for inconsistencies and asked her to fly back to Washington. She was told that she had been cleared of any suspicion, and that the flight back to D.C. was for training purposes. Apparently she knew better."

"Why was she allowed to travel back to the States by herself?" the director said.

Susan squirmed. "Sir, this is obviously not standard procedure, and we've reprimanded the counterespionage team member who made that decision. Apparently, he had a prior relationship with—"

The director's hand went up. "Alright. Please see me about that detail later. Continue."

"The second big event on October twenty-fourth, none of you need reminding about. The Blackout Attack. We have with us Mr. Diaz from the NSA to go over what happened."

A squat man in a V-neck sweater took the small microphone in his fingers. "Thank you, Susan." The screen changed to a map of the US. "The Blackout Attack, as people call it, was actually two distinct attacks. Each was executed simultaneously on October twenty-fourth. The first, we now know, came from the ARES cyberweapon. The transmissions emanated from several locations in Southeast Asia and affected approximately seventy-five percent of all satellites in orbit. I can't emphasize enough how complex an attack this was. The GPS satellites are beyond repair. This alone has caused massive problems. Estimates on getting replacements launched are at six to twelve months."

Chase whispered, "That's insane."

The NSA man continued, "What's worse—Internet and telecommunications have been greatly damaged by attacks on data centers and root servers."

"What are root servers?" the director asked.

The NSA man cleared his throat. "Yes, sir…uh…think of root servers as the decoder keys for the Internet. Instead of typing a sixteen-digit number into your browser to take you to a website, you can type Walmart dot com, for instance. But in actuality, the website is really identified by a sixteen-digit number. Thanks to the root servers, when you type Walmart dot com, it automatically syncs those letters to the correct number identifier and takes you to the correct website. But with these root servers down, there is no longer a decoder key. So technically, the Internet still works. But it's rendered useless to ninety-nine point nine nine percent of the population."

"Anyone but people like you?"

Nervous chuckles.

"Yes, sir, I'm afraid so."

The director said, "So why are we able to use Internet now? It went down for, what, thirty-six hours? It's slower, but it's back up. What happened?"

"Director, it appears that the ARES cyberweapon was effective in bringing down several of these data centers and root servers, but the Internet has just become too big and strong. It's developed immunities, if you will. Technology companies have built so many redundancies into the network that, unless the attack was perfectly coordinated with the physical destruction of undersea cables and other backup data centers, it was only going to be a partially successful attack. What we're living through now is a damaged Internet. But the tech companies are working hard each day to get it back to full strength. Effectively, we're going to have another one or two months at low performance before we get back to where we were."

General Schwartz said, "It's still killing my IRA. Stock market's down lower than in 2009."

"Yes, sir. The psychological and economic impact of the disruption are very real."

"Thank you, Mr. Diaz," Susan said.

The man nodded and returned to his seat.

The director looked at his watch, then back up at Susan. "Tell me more about Jinshan."

"Cheng Jinshan has multiple roles—he's a Chinese national, the billionaire head of multiple Chinese Internet- and media-related companies. His companies make up a large portion of the cybersecurity and censorship wings of the Chinese technology industry. We also have strong evidence that he started off as, and continues to be, a covert agent within the Chinese Ministry of State Security. The confluence of these two positions has made him a major power player in the Chinese government. To put it another way, he has his hands in everything. Jinshan has a personal relationship with the Chinese president, who recently appointed him head of the Central Commission for Discipline Inspection. This is the Chinese agency intended to *root out* corruption in the government. But the CIA's Chinese bureau thinks that Jinshan may have been using the CCDI to insert loyalists across the government."

"Sounds like a busy guy," said General Schwartz.

"Yes, sir. Our sources tell us that Jinshan has been trying to prepare China for what he sees as a coming collapse of their economy. Our own analysts agree that a Chinese economic downturn is inevitable."

The general said, "I thought the Chinese economy was booming. They make everything over there."

"Sir, while Chinese manufacturing is robust, their manufacturing boom occurred between ten and twenty years ago," Susan said. "Now, the money from that economic boom has made many Chinese citizens wealthier. People have moved from the poor rural areas to the wealthier and more congested cities. While it is still a communist nation, the Communist Party has been propped up by the furious pace of economic growth. But that rate of growth is now slowing. The low-hanging fruit has been plucked from the tree, so to speak. China has effectively put off the bubble bursting by using artificial currency manipulation. But even that can only do so much to keep reality from taking hold."

The director said, "So is that what all that Dubai Bitcoin stuff was about? Currency manipulation so that China could keep its economic advantage?"

Susan nodded. "We believe that's part of it, sir. Cheng Jinshan had a team of hackers that was trying to manipulate the value of bitcoin. He then helped to influence the Chinese government to partially adopt backing its own currency with bitcoin. But the hacking and criminal manipulation of the Dubai Bitcoin Exchange became public thanks to the work of our CIA team in Dubai. Now, proper safeguards are in place, and that artificial manipulation cannot take place. However, the Chinese economic situation is looking more dire by the day."

"So the bubble is about to pop, and the owner of the largest army in the world, a communist nation, will have hell to pay if it can't make its citizens happy." The director looked at General Schwartz. "You have any questions?"

"What else do we know about Jinshan's background?" Schwartz asked.

Susan looked down at her notes. "He is highly intelligent. He was a competitive chess player in college. He's charismatic—a gifted orator, when out in public. But he prefers his privacy. We've only recently been made aware of how deep his influence goes. He has no family—never married. No vices that we know of."

The director looked skeptical. "Everyone's got something. Keep looking."

"Sir, there is one thing, although it's not a vice. It's his health. Our investigation in Dubai uncovered that he may have visited a cancer specialist while he was there."

"Really? That's interesting. Any chance this situation is going to resolve itself in the near future?"

A few laughs from the group.

"We aren't sure, sir. That's all we've managed to find out thus far."

The director looked at his watch again and then stood up. "Alright. The general and I need to run. I want updates twice a day, and anytime there is any urgent news. Is that clear?"

"Yes, sir."

* * *

One Hour Later

The Situation Room, The White House

The president sat at the end of the long conference table. "Please proceed, Admiral."

"Mr. President, at twenty-two thirty local in Tehran today, electronic surveillance aircraft picked up a conversation between the Iranian Supreme Leader and his head of the Iranian naval forces. In that conversation, he told the Iranian Navy head to prepare two Iranian Kilo-class submarines to deploy under what we in the US military would term as a weapons-free ROE."

"Mr. President, under the weapons-free rules of engagement, a military asset would fire at anything not identified as friendly," the chief of staff said.

The admiral continued, "Sir, for a submarine—especially an Iranian submarine that doesn't have the sonar capabilities and training that our subs do—this would mean that they would start sinking just about everything they see. This order is in addition to movement we have witnessed indicating that the Iranians are preparing to lay mines, sir."

The president shook his head. "Now what in the Sam Hill is that madman thinking?"

Finishing the thought, the chief of staff said, "He likely intends to shut down the Straits of Hormuz, sir."

The president waved for him to keep going.

"Sir, we have a location of all of their subs right now. One is at sea. The other will take twenty-four hours to get underway. The mini-subs are all on alert. We recommend a preemptive strike on all Iranian submarines and mini-submarines within the next twelve hours. We also recommend striking all SAM sites, surface-to-surface missile sites with ranges greater than ten miles, and a cluster bomb strike on their go-fast gunboats. This will neutralize their medium-range and submarine threat."

"What about their aircraft?" the national security advisor asked.

The admiral said, "We feel confident that our combat air patrol would be able to neutralize any Iranian air threat on short notice if they take off and show any indication of hostile behavior. The ROE we agreed to last week gives our CAP aircraft that leeway. In short, we don't feel the need to attack their air force—yet. And we'd rather minimize our strikes, per the president's instructions."

The president looked at the CIA director. "Do you still think China may have been behind the attacks in Dubai?"

The CIA director chose his words carefully. "Mr. President, I believe that there are people working for the Chinese government and/or military who were at least partially responsible for the attacks over the past few weeks. Both the attacks in Dubai and the cyberattacks in the US."

The president said, "And what do you base this opinion on?"

The CIA director spoke up, "Sir, multiple sources, including information from the two gentlemen who escaped captivity in the South China Sea—"

"Yes, I'm quite familiar with those two," said the president.

There was audible laughter from the others at the table, particularly from the national security advisor, Charlie Sheppard. The director tried to ignore it.

The story of the Red Cell was controversial. Half the media thought it was just a miscommunication. An understandable cross-wiring of information during the confusion of the past few weeks. The other half of the media thought that it was a crazy conspiracy theory.

The US government leadership was also split on their feelings about David Manning and Henry Glickstein's Red Cell claims. Some in the government believed that David and Henry were lunatics, and that the whole story was some type of hoax. The NSA fell into this camp.

The more extremist news agencies were calling it a conspiracy theory. The national security advisor loved to quote these reports, when it suited him. The CIA director had his suspicions why that was. The NSA had done lobbying work for a lot of different firms. Some with heavy ties to China. That was something that he was quietly looking into.

Director Buckingham was on the other side of the fence when it came to the Red Cell. He had seen enough to know that there was a good amount of truth behind David Manning's story.

These extremist news agencies, Director Buckingham knew, sometimes got tidbits of news from sources that *originated* in China. Some NSA reports even showed that Cheng Jinshan's cyberoperations center pumped up these extremist news networks by using millions of fake social network accounts.

But there was just enough doubt in David Manning's Red Cell story to cause the US to go soft in its objections to China. A few of the eighteen "missing" personnel had contacted their loved ones, for instance. They had left messages that supported the idea that they were on legitimate personal or business trips. Director Buckingham's CIA analysts thought that these messages were coerced or outright faked. But the CIA's own intelligence reports in China had found that no one in the Chinese government leadership circles knew *anything* about the Red Cell. And that was very odd.

The aligned US strategy was to use trusted Chinese back channels and organic intelligence to gather more information on the Red Cell. Only then would they present options to the president.

The Iran-US conflict was the bigger issue, the argument went. The problems with China were considered second-tier.

The CIA director knew better. So too, he thought, should all the members sitting at this table. But there were too many politicians in this room. Men who should have been chosen for their nonpartisan expertise in military, intelligence, or international relations. But these days, many elected officials were mixing up their politics with national security policy. And so men like the NSA were now advising the president, relying on information stripped from partisan news columns, and downplaying the US intelligence agencies' daily briefings.

The thought infuriated Buckingham, who himself had been both a politician and a military officer in his past careers. But when he had sworn the oath taking this job, one hand on the Constitution of the United States, he'd promised himself that no matter what, he would always put country over party affiliation.

The president held up his hand at the laughter. "Gentlemen, that will be enough of that. Director Buckingham, please continue."

The CIA director took the slide clicker and advanced to his section of the brief. On the screen at the front of the room, a zoomed-in image of the Red Cell island appeared. There was a long runway with a dozen aircraft visible on the line. Several hangars. A few helicopters. A scattering of buildings in several locations.

"This is the island where we believe the American Red Cell operation was held."

The screen changed from a satellite image to an infrared image. Dozens more jets and helicopters were visible under the hangars. On the opposite side were several areas of intense heat.

A red circle came up around the heat signatures. "From our interviews with David Manning and Henry Glickstein, as well as our recent intelligence collection efforts, we believe this is where all eighteen Americans are *still* being held. The island is getting daily heavy transport flights in from several mainland air bases. And we've confirmed at least one submarine is in the island's pen."

"The island holds a submarine?" asked the president.

The director nodded. "The island is constructed to hold at least one submarine in a protected pen. Our reconnaissance analysis showed several design features on the island intended to shield submarines and aircraft from EMP attack. We've seen this feature at other Chinese military bases, including their submarine base at Yulin. It's essentially a big cave in a mountain—big enough to fit multiple vessels inside. Our theory is that the Chinese would neutralize US military assets in the region with a large-scale EMP attack and come out relatively unharmed themselves."

"Would that really work?"

The chairman of the Joint Chiefs of Staff said, "We have modeled a few scenarios, sir. In theory, it could provide them with a distinct advantage. Especially if they were privy to the timing of the attack, and we weren't."

"Wonderful. Continue, Director Buckingham. I've got about five more minutes. Let's get to the part where you tell me what the hell you think they're up to, and what you want my approval to do about it."

The slide changed to show several images of US ships, aircraft, and troops. There were also insignia for a few military units on the bottom of the slide.

"Sir, I understand that we can't ignore the threat of war with Iran," the director said. "While the seeds of this war may indeed have been planted by the Chinese, the continued threat from Iran is very real. You've been briefed on this, and we're committed to a strong military response. This may, however, play into the hands of the Chinese if they did intend for an Iranian conflict to tie up our military. General, if you would." The director handed the clicker to the Army general.

General Schwartz said, "Sir, this is Task Force SILVERSMITH. Each of the military units on this slide is in one of two camps. Either they're special operations units that have not yet been activated for the Iranian response plan, or they're units that are so new, they're not yet operational."

"What does that mean, not yet operational?"

"Sir, for example—the F-35 units depicted here are brand-new. They're conducting their initial training and readiness qualifications. We didn't expect to deploy them for at least another year. But the men are capable, and the equipment works. The same goes for the aircraft carrier, the USS *Ford*."

"Understood."

"Mr. President, our request is this: we want to activate these assets in secret, moving them to strategic locations that would allow them to respond to an imminent Chinese military threat, if needed."

"So you're just going to move everyone over to West Coast bases?"

"No, sir. We're going to move these assets to places where they wouldn't normally be stationed. Based on the Red Cell debrief, we're worried that staging these assets in regular locations could be too risky. If the balloon goes up, they could be taken out. We will treat these alternate locations with the utmost secrecy. These units will be used as insurance in case the Chinese really do attempt an attack on American forces."

The NSA said, "Sir, I'm not sure about this. Shouldn't we slow down and think for a moment? The Chinese have denied having possession of these Americans. We have reports that some of these guys are just on business trips, and have actually called their wives and families. I think all this talk about China is just a distraction. Let's be more deliberate. Iran is the obvious issue that needs to be dealt with. For crying out loud, they attacked us in the Persian Gulf. We have *evidence* of that. The China evidence is tenuous at best."

The president rubbed his chin, looking around the table. "Director Buckingham, I think it's always prudent to buy a good insurance plan. Your request is approved. Admiral, if the Iranian submarines sink anything, then I want a swift and immediate response. Until then, no preemptive strikes. Clear?"

"Yes, sir."

"Understood, sir."

"Anything else?" the president asked.

The general said, "Sir, we're going to modify the communication procedures as discussed earlier, due to concerns that the Chinese cyberoperations teams may be intercepting our movement orders."

"Alright. Anything *else*? What about the Americans on that island? Do you have a plan to rescue them yet?"

"Yes, sir, but as the national security advisor correctly pointed out, the Chinese have been refuting any claims of participation in the Iranian attacks, as well as denying that the Red Cell island holds any American citizens."

"So what help is needed there?"

"We'll have something for you soon, sir," the chairman of the Joint Chiefs of Staff said.

The president stood. "Good. Tell me when you've got more."

"Yes, sir."

2

Victoria said, "You have twenty minutes of fuel left."

"Roger. Can you tell me what you see below us?"

She craned her helmet to the left, looking through her night vision goggles. The dark Pacific Ocean that lay five hundred feet beneath their helicopter didn't give her much, but it didn't matter.

"There's a family of three down there," Victoria said. "The father is injured. Their boat just sank. The child looks to be about eight years old. None of them have flotation devices. They're treading water."

Juan gripped the cyclic stick a little tighter, scanning the horizon through his own night vision goggles—a constant side-to-side sweeping motion. But he too saw very little out there in the green abyss. There just wasn't enough light for the goggles to pick up. A flash on the horizon from a far-off thunderstorm. But nothing else.

His trained scan shifted to his cockpit instruments. Airspeed—eighty knots. Altitude—five hundred feet. Fuel—about one thousand pounds.

Juan said, "Is he ambulatory?"

"Yes."

"Water temperature?"

"It's warm."

"How far away is the ship?"

"Thirty miles."

"That's about fifteen minutes at a max range airspeed of one hundred and twenty knots, so that gives me five minutes to rescue them."

The lone enlisted man on the aircraft, AWR1 Fetternut, spoke into his helmet's microphone from the back of the aircraft. "Sir, we'll need ten minutes to be able to do the rescue."

"Uh...well, I could go single-engine and save more fuel," Juan said.

He knew as soon as the words came out of his mouth that it was a stupid thing to say. He could feel his boss, Lieutenant Commander Victoria Manning, shaking her head in disappointment.

"Sir, remind me not to fly with you when you make aircraft commander," came the sarcastic voice of the aircrewman over the internal communications system.

Fetternut was both a rescue swimmer and a sensor operator for the MH-60R Seahawk helicopter. He was a petty officer first class— lower-ranking than the two pilots, who were commissioned officers. But he had much more experience than Juan, who was the junior pilot.

Lieutenant Junior Grade Juan "Spike" Volonte could feel his blood pressure rising under the evaluation of his aircraft commander. She was not only the senior pilot on this flight, but the air boss on the ship's aviation detachment. That meant she was the senior officer of all thirty members of his helicopter squadron who were embarked on the USS *Farragut*. She was the third-highest-ranking person on the ship, with only the captain and the XO above her.

Juan raised his eyebrows to try and get the sweat to stop beading down from his helmet and into his eyes. He hated being grilled by his boss.

It was true that she could be patient. Her style was to be a teacher —not like one of those instructor pilots from flight school that got off on making the student look like an idiot for not knowing the answer. Still, when you flew with her, you always had to be *on*. She never stopped training. And oftentimes it was in the form of these pop quiz scenarios. That's what flying as a junior Navy pilot on deployment was: one continuous pop quiz.

She said, "You would take one engine to idle?"

"No. Sorry. That was dumb."

"Why?"

"Because I would need to go into a hover to rescue those people. And I would need both engines to do that. Otherwise we wouldn't have enough power to hover, and we'd start sinking towards the water." Sweat dripped down from his soaked hair under his helmet and onto his forehead.

Air Boss said, "Okay. Just checking."

He could practically hear her breathe a sigh of relief that her copilot wasn't a total idiot. She wouldn't recommend him to go to his HAC board unless he could consistently prove himself as a competent decision maker under pressure.

Then she said, "Maybe you can make up for it. *Simulated.*"

Simulated. Every pilot attached a special meaning to that dreaded word. It was used to denote that whatever happened next was a simulated emergency induced by the other pilot.

The ENGINE FIRE light illuminated on the master caution panel in front of him.

"Engine fire in flight procedures..." His voice increased an octave as he began announcing each step in the emergency procedure from memory. "Uh...confirm fire..."

He instinctively used his right hand, which was gripping the cyclic control, to place the aircraft into a steady turn.

Victoria said, "AWR1, you see a fire?"

"I don't know, ma'am, it's pretty dark out. I don't see any smoke."

Dammit, what was this? Now they were teaming up on him.

"Okay, Juan, now I want you to keep troubleshooting the engine fire emergency as if this scenario with the three survivors in the water below you was still going on. What's your plan?"

He had inadvertently put too much forward stick in the turn. The helicopter's AFCS computers had reacted by increasing the target airspeed for the autopilot system. *Autopilot*. Now there was a bullshit term. It was more like cruise control—it would help you out, but you sure as hell better keep driving.

Now they were going ten knots too fast. Not a lot, but it showed shoddy airmanship…and they were still in a turn.

Juan couldn't believe how dark it was, flying over the water on these moonless nights. It was much easier to fly during the day. Then he could use the horizon to determine the aircraft's pitch, roll, and yaw. But now, at night and over the dark ocean, he was completely reliant upon his instruments.

Instruments. Shit. He was still turning, and he didn't mean to be.

The digital readouts in front of him glowed a faint green. A collection of numbers and shapes. Airspeed indicators and altitude. Columns of pixels and an artificial horizon. Engine oil pressure and transmission oil pressure. And fuel. He *couldn't* forget about fuel.

Goddammit, was he still turning? She was still waiting for him to answer her question. This flight was not going well.

"Juan?"

"Yes, ma'am."

"Aviate, navigate, communicate. Check your airspeed. I've got you ten knots fast and twenty degrees right wing down."

Juan found himself fixating on his gyro, the round center of his digital display. It was what was telling him up from down. He had a twenty-degree turn in still. But he felt like he was straight and level.

He realized that he was tilting his body and neck to the left. *Dammit*. He was getting a case of the leans.

Vertigo. Spatial disorientation. His body had grown used to being in the turn and had begun to consider that normal. It had to do with fluid in the inner vestibular of his ears or something.

All Juan knew was that it took every ounce of concentration for him to shift his stick back to the left and get wings-level. Of course, he couldn't talk during that effort. So there was an awkward silence before he was able to answer his boss's question.

"You alright?"

"Yes, ma'am."

Now he was sweating profusely. It was humid, but it was more than that.

"So you've got three people down there waiting and an engine fire light with an unconfirmed fire. What's your next move, HAC?" Her voice was calm, but firm.

HAC stood for helicopter aircraft commander. It was the qualification that Juan hoped to achieve after they returned from deployment. A grueling multiyear process to get there. Once achieved, he could then sign for his own aircraft as the pilot in command.

Then he would go to work every day with his name as the primary pilot on the flight schedule. Uncle Sam would lend him his very own thirty-five-million-dollar helicopter, complete with his own copilot and aircrewman. *He* would then be in charge of the mission. It was essentially the equivalent of reaching adulthood in the naval helicopter world. But he had to get there first.

"Well, the fire is not confirmed, so I should land as soon as possible," he said.

"Let's say that the fire light just went out," said Victoria.

Juan said, "Okay. Then I'd contact the ship and tell them the situation and let them know that I will be conducting search and rescue and to make best speed for my position."

"But with the fire light on, you would go home? You would fly back to the ship?"

"Yes, ma'am."

"Even with the three people down there? And twenty minutes of fuel?"

"Uh…"

"Don't let her trick you, sir."

Victoria said, "AWR1, you shut your trap, please. Let the man talk. Juan, I still have you in a turn. Level off and check your speed."

"Sorry, Boss," said AWR1.

Juan said, "Roger, leveling off. Getting back to eighty knots." He gritted his teeth and fought his body's telling him that they were leaning to one side. He lined up the instrument wings so that they were straight and level, got the airspeed to exactly eighty knots, and trimmed it in.

Victoria said, "So would you turn back to the boat with three people in the water and twenty minutes of fuel, with an unconfirmed fire?"

Juan said, "Yes, ma'am. If the light stayed on, I would declare an emergency and land as soon as possible on the ship."

Victoria said, "But with the fire light out, you'd stay on station and rescue those people."

"Yes."

"Why? Either way, the fire is unconfirmed. What does NATOPS say?"

NATOPS. The Naval Air Training and Operating Procedures Standardization Manual. The bible for all naval aviators. It had all the checklists, emergency procedures, systems limits, and diagrams that Juan had to memorize to become qualified in the aircraft. Juan and the other copilot spent at least six hours each day studying from that manual, quizzing each other and memorizing every minute detail. For it would help them reach HAC, and potentially save their lives if they ever needed the knowledge to get out of an airborne emergency.

"NATOPS says if the fire is unconfirmed, to land as soon as possible."

"So the fire is still unconfirmed, right?"

"Yes...but—"

"Are there 'buts' in NATOPS? Sorry, I haven't been flying for very long. Explain to me when it's okay to violate NATOPS."

"Well...I...uh...well, operational necessity..."

"And what's that? Don't quote me fancy words unless you want me to ask you what they mean."

"Well...uh...ma'am, the instruction says that operational necessity is a mission associated with war or peacetime operations that justify risking the loss of aircraft or crew."

"That's not what it says. Not exactly. You need to know what it says *verbatim*. Keep going with the problem."

Juan said, "Is that twenty minutes until bingo or twenty minutes until the low fuel light?"

AWR1 piped up, "Ah, he's getting smart!"

"Until bingo."

She was being nice. Giving him more fuel—and more time—in the scenario. Bingo fuel was the point at which the helicopter had to turn back to the ship, lest it run out of fuel prior to landing.

"Alright, then. AWR1, let's set up for SAR."

"Sir, my rescue swimmer is all ready to go. Our checklists are complete."

The enlisted man spoke like he had said this a thousand times. He probably had. A senior petty officer, he was up for chief this year. He had probably helped to train hundreds of junior officers as they went up for their HAC qualification.

"Cutlass 471, *Farragut* Control, the ship is setting flight quarters." The radio call came from the external communications system. It was broadcast over the UHF radio from the ship to the helicopter. *Farragut* Control was one of the ship's enlisted personnel who manned the radar scope and acted as a controller and tactical operations relay between the ship's combat information center and the helicopter.

Juan responded, "*Farragut* Control, 471, roger."

The ENGINE FIRE light came on again.

"Simulated."

Juan said, "Is the fire confirmed?"

"Yes."

"Roger, engine malfunction in flight procedure—perform." His tone of voice uncontrollably increased in pitch under the stress of remembering the steps of the emergency procedure.

"Go ahead."

"Control Nr. Contingency power on. Establish single-engine conditions. External cargo/stores/fuel jettison/dump. Identify malfunction—okay, we have an engine fire."

AWR1 said, "Ahhh, sir, it's really hot back here."

Juan said, "Engine power control lever of affected engine—simulated off." He used his leather-gloved finger to wipe sweat from his eyes.

Victoria placed her hand up on one of the engine power control levers. "Okay, I'm ready to take off engine number one, do you concur?"

Juan glanced up quick, barely able to see her leather-gloved hand in the dark. His bulky NVG set, two black plastic tubes, protruded from his helmet outward from his eyes.

"Roger, engine number one…oh, wait! Ma'am, that's the wrong engine."

She had her hand over engine number two. In a real emergency she would have been pulling back the only functional engine. That would have been a pilot-induced disaster.

Victoria said, "Alright, Juan, you're done for tonight. Good catch. Take me home. And don't drop the pack. You're landing and you better stick it."

He let out a sigh of relief. He had a lot more of that emergency procedure to regurgitate. But they had been flying for almost three hours, and much of the flight had been like this. Constant training. Constant questions. He knew it would make him better, but he longed for just a quiet flight.

Now for the hardest part: landing on the back of a boat at night.

Juan repositioned himself in the seat, trying to get psyched up. They ran through their before-landing checklist, flipping switches and changing the lighting configuration. The night vision goggles became useful again as Juan began to make out lights on the horizon. The ship was still about twenty minutes of flying away. But the powerful NVGs could—

A flash of bright light in front of them bloomed out his vision through the NVGs. Lightning.

Victoria said, "*Farragut* Control, Cutlass 471, are you guys going through a storm?"

"Uh, stand by." Deep in the hull of the ship, he probably had no idea if it was raining or not. He would need to get someone on the bridge to let him know.

AWR1 said, "You kidding me? They found the only storm cell within fifty miles. They probably went towards it knowing that we'd be coming in for landing now."

Victoria said, "AWR1, what do you see on radar?" Their radar was meant for picking up surface contacts. And while it was not technically certified to detect the storms, it *was* sensitive enough to detect a submarine's periscope and did a pretty decent job at telling her which clouds to stay away from.

"I have the controls," Victoria said.

"You have the controls." Both pilots had their own set of pedals, cyclic, and collective sticks. The pedals controlled yaw, the cyclic controlled pitch and roll, and the collective controlled the power of the aircraft.

Free from flying, Juan typed a few keystrokes into his multipurpose display and saw the radar image that AWR1 was bringing up.

The crew of three was flying an MH-60R helicopter about one hundred and fifty miles off the coast of Central America. The deployment was supposed to have been a counternarcotics operation —they should have been looking for speedboats full of cocaine and other drugs on their way to Mexico. Instead, the Navy had seen fit to assign them to an international training exercise. Most of the participants were from Central and South America. *Farragut* was the only US Navy ship.

Most of the last two hours had been spent performing over-water surveillance—flying circles in a pitch-black sky that could only exist over a hazy and humid ocean. The dark night sky was occasionally lit up by lightning from a band of thunderstorms that had been steadily getting closer throughout the flight.

While Juan normally loved watching summer thunderstorms roll over his home in Atlantic Beach, Florida, he was significantly less comfortable tonight. Watching thunderstorms from the comfort of your covered porch was one thing. Dodging them at a few thousand feet over the water was another.

AWR1 Fetternut made calls from his radar scope in the back of the helicopter. "Come left to two-two-zero. That should get us through these two cells, and it should be clear on the other side."

"Okay, that looks good, left to two-two-zero," responded Victoria. The aircraft veered left and then leveled out.

Juan sucked back water from his CamelBak straw. After three hours of flying in this heat, he was very dehydrated. The heavy gear, constant concentration, and late hour were all taking their toll. He just needed to nail this approach and get it in the trap. That combination of efforts had proven elusive to him on many nights this cruise. To put it bluntly, he sucked at landings.

"Cutlass, *Farragut* Control, the ship is at flight quarters."

"471, Deck. I've got numbers when you're ready." That was the voice of one of the other junior pilots on the ship. Now that they were landing, he had manned his station behind the protective glass overlooking their landing spot on the rear of the ship.

"Stand by," Victoria said. She said internally, "Juan, your controls."

"I have the controls."

"You have the controls." The three-way positive change of controls was one of the many safety precautions aviators took. Most mistakes were made when everyone assumed that someone else was doing a very simple task. Bad things often happened when something taken for granted stopped working for a moment. The three-way change of controls made sure that one of the pilots was always responsible for controlling the aircraft.

Juan said on the external radio, "Deck, 471, ready for the numbers."

"Seven-one, Deck, roger. Ship's course and speed is one three at ten, winds one-niner-zero at two, pitch one, roll three, how copy?"

"Ma'am, you got it?"

"Yup," Victoria replied, penciling the numbers down on her kneeboard.

"Copy all, Deck," Juan said, and then took a deep breath. He looked at his distance measuring equipment. It gave him a distance estimation to the ship, accurate to the tenth of a mile. He also had twisted in the ship's course. A needle on the compass in front of him centered up as he maneuvered the aircraft to be on centerline while flying his approach.

The needle used information from navigational instruments on board the helicopter combined with a beacon on the ship. The needle started sliding away from centerline as Juan began to stray off course.

Staying on course required constant adjustments from the pilot. He had to make these adjustments based on barely noticeable changes from his instruments. All the while, he had to lower the aircraft's altitude and reduce speed on a specific profile. Failing to do this would cause them to crash or wave off.

Victoria said, "I've got you a little left of course." He could feel his stick move in his hands as Victoria made her own inputs on her controls, "helping" him to make the correct control input.

"Roger," was all he could say. His tired eyes were racing from one gauge to the next. Altitude. Airspeed. Ball. Fuel. Distance to the ship. Repeat.

"One point two miles, starting the approach. On instruments." He lowered the lever in his left hand that decreased the power and collective pitch of the aircraft. The radar altimeter began ticking down.

"Passing three hundred feet…" He blinked away a drop of sweat. It blurred the vision through his NVGs. As they got lower and closer to the destroyer, more and more detail came into view. Now he could make out the wake of the ship.

"Still a little fast, Juan. I have you at eighty knots. Start bringing that airspeed back."

From the back, AWR1 Fetternut double-checked the altitude and distance. He said, "One mile."

Juan pulled aft on his cyclic with his right hand and continued to take power out with his left hand. The faint glow of the green flight deck lights was now visible on the aft end of the ship.

Juan still felt dizzy. He realized he was cocking his head to the left.

"Two hundred feet," he said.

"Point four miles."

Victoria said, "You're high and still fast. Take out some more power. Aft cyclic."

He tried to do what she said. His scan of instruments was all over the place. He fixated on his airspeed, which started getting really slow. There was that dizzy, sliding feeling again.

He tried to look out the chin bubble, the glass floor of the helicopter, at the ship. They were way too high. He needed to get lower. Dammit, how had they gotten so high on the approach?

"Juan, aft cyclic."

"Point one mile." They were almost there.

Juan said, "Radalt hold off."

Victoria reached down and depressed the button that would turn off the radar altimeter, an autopilot function. She must have only taken her eyes off what Juan was doing for a split second.

"*Power, power, power!*" came the call from the rear.

The helicopter was descending behind the ship. Juan looked in horror at his airspeed—now reading zero.

Airspeed was life. His vertical speed indicator, which told him how fast he was descending, was below five hundred feet per minute. He gritted his teeth and pulled power, pushing the nose forward. The altitude warning was going off in his helmet with a series of loud beeps. They were below fifty feet, and he was staring at the stern of the destroyer growing larger in the window.

"I have the controls," said Victoria calmly, but loud enough that everyone was sure to hear.

He didn't let go, but he could feel her forcing the correct inputs through her controls. She immediately pulled in a lot more power, gained altitude, then adjusted the attitude of the helicopter so that it floated neatly over the center of the flight deck.

"Deck, 471 waving off," Victoria said.

Juan felt ashamed. He had nearly put them in the water.

Victoria climbed and accelerated, turning in a racetrack pattern to reset for another approach. She said, "Juan, shake it off. You alright?"

"Yes, Boss. I…I think I just felt a little dizzy."

She said, "Do you have vertigo?"

"I don't know. Maybe."

"Alright, you've got to say something if you start feeling that way, okay? We do not play 'I have a secret' up here. If something is wrong or doesn't feel right, speak up. Understood?"

"Yes, ma'am." He wanted to crawl into a hole.

Victoria turned the helicopter again and lined it up behind the ship. "On final."

"Roger."

Her approach was flawless. She hit every number—altitude, airspeed, distance.

Once over the flight deck, she smoothly hovered the center of the aircraft over the steel square known as "the trap."

AWR1 called, "Over the trap."

Then a sudden drop, and the twenty-thousand-pound, thirty-five-million-dollar aircraft sunk onto the flight deck, its robust suspension and thick tires cushioning the impact.

"471, Deck, you're in the trap. Nice one, ma'am."

"Chocks and chains," called Victoria.

Juan wasn't moving. He was too embarrassed and horrified that he had almost just put the aircraft into the water...or into the stern of the ship...to comprehend that he was supposed to do something.

"*Juan*, chocks and chains."

He snapped out of it and grabbed his green flashlight from the calf pocket of his flight suit. He turned the light on and moved it in a side-to-side motion. The plane captain, the enlisted man who stood outside in front of them on the flight deck, made a series of motions with two glowing wands. Then several more enlisted men were running with their heads down under the rotor arc, placing the chocks and chains on the aircraft.

"Air Boss, Deck."

"Go."

"Ma'am, the captain's been asking for you. He requests you to swing by as soon as you're done."

She didn't say anything for a moment. Then she double-clicked her radio to acknowledge the request.

She flipped up her goggles. "Keep with me, Juan. Are you alright to do the engine wash?"

"Yes, ma'am." He knew he had really screwed up. That was a truly awful approach. Thank God she was a good pilot.

"Alright. Let's shut down and then you've got it."

* * *

A few minutes later, Victoria Manning approached the door to the captain's cabin. She stunk, and was sweaty from the flight. Her hair was a mess. Not that she cared how she looked right now. She would have liked to grab a shower, though. But if she showered first, she wouldn't have an excuse to leave the captain's cabin. She hated these nightly sessions.

Each night the captain called his XO, the air boss—Victoria—and the ship's master chief into his room and had them sit there while he regaled them with stories about his past, and complained about how hard his current assignment was. No ship captain should do either of those things, in her opinion. Leadership was about others, not self.

Victoria's opinion of the ship's captain had not improved over the last year that she'd been assigned to his command. Now she stood outside the captain's cabin door, eyes closed momentarily, summoning the patience to put up with this bullshit for another night. She could hear the voices inside. She opened her eyes and saw that the red light was on. Like a traffic light, the captain had a light installed outside his door that would switch between green and red, to signify when it was acceptable for ship's personnel to enter. He always kept it red.

The silly part of that was that he couldn't bring himself to delegate. He demanded that his personnel update him constantly. He had standing orders to be informed of every minute detail of the ship's activities, wanting to make as many decisions as possible. As a result, his officers grew used to not making decisions themselves, and the captain almost never slept more than an hour at a time and was perpetually in a bad mood.

Dealing with this ship's captain was part of the job, however. She took a breath and knocked on the door.

"Sir, it's the air boss."

"Enter."

She walked in to see the captain slouched in his chair behind his desk. He wore his khaki uniform. His cheeks drooped, and when he looked at you, his neck hunched down at an angle, so that his eyes were looking up. He rarely left this spot. Victoria had heard some refer to him as the ghost captain. He rarely ventured out to the many parts of the ship, preferring instead to be at the comfort of his desk in the captain's cabin.

The XO and the master chief sat next to each other on an ugly grey couch. She nodded to them and they nodded back. Polite, respectful smiles. She liked them both.

The XO was reasonable, and sharp. A good listener, he knew what he didn't know. He was constantly asking Victoria questions about helicopter operations, wanting to make sure that the ship operations ran smoothly while seamlessly integrating the required flight operations.

The captain said, "Well, nice of you to join us, Air Boss. You have fun flying?" He turned to the couch with his forced sidekicks. "XO, I bet you'd like to get off the ship tonight, but we surface warriors actually have to work on deployment, right?"

The XO forced an awkward smile.

The captain said, "Air Boss, it looked like your landing got a little tricky out there tonight."

She looked up at the small black-and-white TV screen situated in the corner ceiling of the small room. It showed the helicopter, strapped to the flight deck. Her young copilot was shutting down the engines, the routine postflight wash complete.

The captain watched all of their landings. Partly for entertainment, she suspected, and partly out of worry. Flight operations were one of the riskiest evolutions conducted on Navy ships. An aviation mishap could ruin the career of a ship captain. And he wasn't about to let that happen. The most important thing to him, she knew, was his career.

She gave a courteous smile, careful never to give away her utter distaste for the man, "Well, sir, it was a bit of a rough approach, but it was a dark night. Good training for my 2P."

"Hmph. I've certainly trained my share of junior officers how to drive ships in bad weather. Some people just don't have the skill like you and I do, huh, Air Boss?" He grinned.

"I guess so, sir."

The phone rang. "Captain," he answered. "Well, alright. Thank you, CS1. Yes, send them right up. Coffee too. Yes." He looked up at the XO. "XO, how are you feeling about our preps for this weekend?"

"I think the ship's ready, sir. We've been drilling hard. Two GQs a day." The XO had assumed that the captain was talking about the anti-submarine warfare exercise with the Colombians. They were sending one of their diesel subs out here to partake in the training. The group of international ships would play cat and mouse, trying to find the Colombian submarine before it could get close enough to "shoot" them.

The captain rolled his eyes. "Not that. What about *the Crossing the Line ceremony*? Are we ready for that? This is big, XO. *This is big*. Think you can handle this?" He smiled and winked at Victoria. He tried to be charming, but it just came off as creepy.

Victoria should have known. The captain wouldn't have been so excited about ASW training. But the Crossing the Line ceremony… now that was right up his alley.

Crossing the Line was a tradition that dated back at least two hundred years. It celebrated the first crossing of the equator during that crew's underway period. It was a ceremony that reminded Victoria of a fraternity initiation. Lots of gross and physical trials for the first-timers, known as Pollywogs. And lots of laughs for the already-initiated, known as Shellbacks.

This would be Victoria's fourth time. While she was happy to allow her men to partake in the ritual, it was starting to get old for her. She had more pressing things to do.

A knock on the door. "Sir, CS2 with—"

"*Enter*," bellowed the captain.

An enlisted woman brought in a tray with a pot of coffee and a plate of cookies. The captain looked it over, rubbing his hands together. "Alright! Now this is…wait. Now what the hell is this? These are *chocolate chip*. Now SUPPO told me that CS1 was making me *sugar cookies*." He looked at the young enlisted woman, who was clearly terrified to be in this room with the most senior officers on the ship. "*Where are my sugar cookies?*"

"Sir, I'm not sure...um...if you want, I can..."

The captain frowned and waved her off. "No. Forget it. You're dismissed."

When she was gone, the XO said, "Sir, in answer to your question, the master chief and I have gone over the schedule for the Crossing the Line ceremony. We've reiterated to the chief's mess to make sure that safety and respect come first."

The captain ignored him and picked up the phone. "CS1, this is the captain. I thought you were making me sugar cookies. Where are my sugar cookies?"

Victoria's face reddened. She looked at the XO and the master chief. They were looking down at the floor, expressionless. This was embarrassing behavior for a ship captain. He was supposed to be an example for all the ship's officers and crew. Above reproach. Instead, he often behaved like a child king.

One of her life's greatest disappointments was when she'd realized that not all commanding officers were like her father. He had surrounded himself with similar leaders, so she had never seen the bad ones. To her, every military officer was a gentleman and a scholar. The type that put his men first and worked hard to get the job done right. Victoria had assumed that all leaders in the military were like this. Then she'd finished flight school and gone on her first deployment.

It was like finding out that there was no Santa Claus. They didn't always put the smartest and most capable leader in charge. Just the highest-ranking. And while the US military's bureaucratic personnel system did well in selecting many great leaders for promotion, many subpar ones also slipped through the cracks.

In his famous novel about the Civil War, *The Killer Angels*, Michael Shaara had written that there was "nothing quite so much like God on earth as a general on a battlefield." She wasn't sure about generals on the battlefield, but she had seen ship captains at sea. Their power was absolute, and often unchecked. They had absolute control and absolute responsibility. They were held accountable for everything, but only if it was made known to their superiors. When mistakes were made public, commanding officers were often fired for "lack of confidence." Many commanding officers became extreme micromanagers to ensure that their men didn't make any errors. That was when one would encounter situations like the captain who insisted on being notified of every change in status, no matter how minute the detail.

Oftentimes, the ship captain's bosses were hundreds if not thousands of miles away. Everything the ship captains did was private. If they screamed at their subordinates like madmen, no one would know. If that got the best results, it became a part of the culture. Many times, junior officers not used to making their own decisions would replicate this leadership style, because that was what they had "grown up" with.

With that absolute power, and the Navy's long tradition of hierarchy, tradition, and etiquette, came a sense of entitlement. Absolute power corrupts absolutely. Ship captains in the Navy needed to be strong-willed and determined not to succumb to the temptation to behave like a tyrant. While it could be effective and gratifying in the short term, it was also demoralizing and counterproductive in the long run.

The captain said, "Alright, fine. Next time." He hung up the phone and shook his head.

The master chief said, "Excuse me, Captain, XO, Air Boss. I must attend to something."

The senior enlisted on the ship, the command master chief was well respected by all the officers and crew. Victoria had only known him for a few months, but she knew the type. He had seen it all, and dedicated his life to the Navy. She had instantly liked him. He was also adept at getting out of these sessions with the captain, a skill Victoria needed to improve.

The phone rang again. "Go." He looked surprised at what he heard. "What. Now? Alright, tell him I'll call him immediately." The captain hung up. "You two will have to excuse me. The commodore wants me to give him a call."

The commodore was the captain's boss. He was deployed on an

aircraft carrier in the Middle East. Due to the time differences, meetings were often at odd hours.

The news that Victoria would be able to get out of this room earlier than expected was a welcome surprise. "Alright, sir, thanks." Both she and the XO left the captain's cabin and went their separate ways.

Victoria walked back to the hangar. Her men had finished the engine wash, and both helicopters were now folded and stuffed in the two hangars. The flight deck was quiet. The ship must have been traveling slowly, as she could hear the waves gently lapping the hull.

A bright white moon began to rise over the horizon, washing the calm Pacific Ocean with its light. She stayed for a few moments, enjoying the tranquil view. Victoria needed these moments. The pressure that she placed on herself was enormous. She recognized it, but wasn't able to stop it.

She was incredibly self-driven. The type of person who had to be number one at everything she did. Even now, she couldn't relax. For someone like her, relaxing was a chore. Another self-imposed task that she thrust on herself in hopes of some type of productivity improvement.

Still, she tried. Victoria had seen the statistics on the effect of prayer and meditation on performance. She had read up on the habits of other successful people, and many of them included time for this in their daily routines. So every day, she scheduled time to meditate alone for twenty to thirty minutes.

That time slot had once been allotted to prayer—until her mother had died. She didn't pray anymore. Like having conversations with her father, it only made her resentful.

The 1MC announcer came on. "Taps, Taps. Lights out in five minutes. Stand by for evening prayer." She rolled her eyes. Evening prayer on Navy ships was a nightly ritual. It was nondenominational, of course. Or multidenominational. Whatever. To her it was just a reminder of her own complicated relationship with God.

The XO's voice came on. The XO was a good man. He had a tough job—cleaning up the messes of the child king. "Shipmates, as we sail in calm seas, and prepare to cross the equator in a few days, we are reminded of how lucky we are. Lucky to be born in a free-dom-loving country. Lucky to serve alongside such great shipmates. As we all know, right now our nation is facing a growing conflict in the Middle East. So it is important for us to remember that many of our brothers and sisters in arms are *not* in calm waters like we are. It is with this in mind that I will read part of the Navy Hymn. The original hymn was written in the 1800s by an Englishman named William Whiting. When he was thirty-five years old, he was in a violent storm. He believed that God had spared his life by commanding the raging seas to calm. The hymn is thought to have been inspired by a passage from Psalm 107, in the Bible. With that, I'll read…"

Victoria smiled. The XO was a devout Evangelical Christian, and a historian. It was probably hard for him not to say too much.

"Eternal Father, strong to save,
Whose arm hath bound the restless wave,
Who bidd'st the mighty ocean deep
Its own appointed limits keep;
Oh, hear us when we cry to Thee,
For those in peril on the sea.
Amen.
Goodnight, *Farragut*."

* * *

Plug spoke while furiously pressing the buttons and moving the directional pad of his controller. "It's a long story."

"Come on," Juan pleaded. He was the odd man out, the only one without a video game controller.

The pilots were playing a World War II multiplayer shooter game. One of the 2Ps (the term commonly used for second pilot or copilot) had brought his PlayStation on the ship. On nights when they weren't scheduled to fly, the junior pilots took over the unused wardroom and played for a few hours, using the big screen on the far wall.

The wardroom was the eating and gathering place for the officers on the ship. A few of the surface line officers played cards on one of the tables. A few others were about to go on the midwatch—the zero dark thirty duty section that controlled the ship while everyone else slept. They chowed down on midrats. Midnight rations. The fourth meal of the day, where sailors standing the midnight watch grabbed leftover grub to get them through until sunrise.

"It's pretty tragic," Ash "Caveman" Hughes said. He was one of the two other 2Ps.

"Come on. How'd you get it?" Juan pressed. He was just glad that he didn't have to keep talking about his awful flight. He needed a funny story to cheer him up.

Plug never took his eyes away from the screen, but he told the story like a man who had told it many times before, and usually at a bar.

"So there we were. A few dozen miles off the coast of Colombia..."

"You did your first cruise here too?" Juan was surprised. It was pretty rare for ships to come down to do Eastern Pacific deployments nowadays, with the cutbacks and all. Pretty much everyone either went to the Middle East, to the Eastern Med, or to the Western Pacific.

"Let me tell the story, alright?" Plug paused for effect. "So there I was, starting up the engine for maintenance rotor turn, when out of nowhere comes this freaking little seagull—"

"I heard it was an osprey," Caveman said.

Plug glared at him. "Don't interrupt, 2P. Like I was saying, the seagull came out of nowhere, flew through the rotor disk, and miraculously didn't get chopped in half..."

"That's such bullshit."

"No way."

"'Tis true, my friends. We have video—"

"Do you?"

"Well, actually, now that you mention it, in the video it is hard to see. Some say that the avian in question may have just been blown by the rotor wash and then slammed into said hangar. But one should never ruin a good story with the truth, so…the osprey…it gets injured—"

Juan said, "You said it was a seagull."

"Whose story is this? The *bird*…it gets injured. And I, having studied zoology and biology at one of the great academic institutions in the world—"

"I thought you said you were a general sciences major. Isn't that for guys who flunk out of—"

"Hold your tongue. I studied a lot of female biology."

The group in the wardroom, all paying attention to the story now, laughed.

"And I watched the TV series *Planet Earth* about fifty times. Plus, graduates of the Virginia Polytechnic Institute like myself are held to a higher standard than you mere mortals. A general science major there is like a PhD at most schools. The point is, I was the only person *qualified* to nurse this animal back to life."

Juan looked at the other 2Ps. They were smiling, but also not taking their eyes off the video game screen as they tried to kill each other.

Plug said, "So for the next two weeks, we kept the albatross in a cage in the hangar—"

"Did the captain know?"

"Yes, the fucking captain knew. How the hell could the captain of a goddammed ship at sea not know there was a fucking pelican on board in a cage? Come on, junior. Listen up. So the albatross was nursed back to health by none other than yours truly. I fed him little bits of fish from the galley. I filled his little water bowl with…well, with water." He turned his head from side to side, emphasizing the greatness of his achievements.

"Until one day, when that cute little bastard was ready…when he looked healthy and could flap his wings in a strong and vibrant fashion…we released him—triumphantly—into the wild."

Caveman took his eyes off the screen and raised his eyebrows. He coughed to signal that there was more to the story.

Plug said, "And to our delight, the great winged beast flew up into the sky and lived happily ever after..." He finally took his eyes off the screen and looked at Juan.

"So how'd you get your call sign, then? I thought this was the story about how you got your call sign."

"Ah, well—perhaps I left out one minor detail. You see, the ship drivers—"

One of the surface line officers listening smiled and said, "Now don't go blaming it on the SWOs, Plug."

Plug sighed. "But it was their *fault*. You see, Juan—may I call you Juan? Of course I may, I'm a HAC, and therefore I can call you whatever the hell I want. You see, Juan, one thing you'll learn about these goddamned SWOs is that, for all their prowess in nautical navigation, they don't always think about the bigger picture. Like, for instance... if you take an injured bird onto your ship, and you're near land, then travel west one thousand miles into the freaking Pacific for two weeks straight, and *then* release the bird, you're pretty freaking far away from *land* at that point. You're a pilot, Juan. How far can you fly before you need food or water? Or a freaking break from flying."

Juan smiled. "How far were you from the coast?"

"When we picked up the seagull, we were about fifteen miles from the coast."

"And when you released him?"

"I want to say it was about two hundred and forty nautical miles out to sea. So there was no freaking way that bird was making it to land. The SWOs had condemned him to a short life of starvation and panic."

Caveman said, "Dude, take responsibility. Seriously. We haven't even gotten to the good part."

Juan said, "What's the good part?"

Plug said, "Well, this seagull must have had its own navigational instincts. Because we let it go, and I shit you not, the thing just circled around the boat for a couple of days. Like a poor old puppy, coming back to its master. He kept coming down to the flight deck, and people would give it crackers or a piece of their dinner. Come to think of it, everyone probably fattened him up so much I wonder if he wasn't over his gross weight limits. Didn't anyone do a weight and balance on that thing before he flew?"

Caveman said, "And *then*..." He motioned for Plug to get to the point.

"I'm getting there. Easy, son. *And then*...I was starting up the engine on our helo one Sunday morning. And there he is...the albatross...flying around. I swear he was looking at me. He was gliding there, into the wind, just off the starboard side of the ship. I can still see him. That magnificent orange beak. Those puffy white and grey feathers. He was such a noble creature. Full of pride and wonder. But he kept getting closer. I thought it was awesome that he was showing so much affection for me. Gratitude, even? Not like you shit 2Ps who don't know what the word means."

Caveman held up his middle finger.

"He was grateful that I was able to nurse him back to life. Until he came over the flight deck and tried to cross to the other side. The rotor wasn't turning this time. But the engine was. And he must have gotten too close because..." He shook his head for effect. Mock sadness.

Juan said, "He got sucked up in the engine intake?"

Plug nodded. "I could see it happening and pulled back the engine power control lever into the off position. But it was too late. A poof of white feathers, and he was gone. We scraped up his remains and had a short ceremony. I mean *very* short. Okay, we pretty much just threw pieces of that damn bird overboard as we found them. But I will tell you this—every bar we hit at every port stop for the rest of the deployment, I swear to you that we toasted that damn bird and his unwavering dedication to duty. He was fearless..." Plug feigned wiping a tear away from his eye.

Juan said, "And the call sign?"

"Well, you know the soft cushiony engine plugs that we put in the intake and exhaust ports to keep them clean of debris, right?"

"Of course."

"Well, the guys on my last deployment kept making jokes about how I used the bird as the engine plug. So, there it is. Plug."

Juan slapped his knee and nodded. Big smile. "Ah. I finally get it. Good story."

Plug said, "Yup. How'd you get Spike as your call sign?"

Juan shrugged. "The senior pilots thought that my hair was spikey."

"Huh. Well...that's a good story, too."

The door opened and the air boss walked in. "Good evening, gentlemen."

The pilots paused the game and sat up a little straighter. "Evening, ma'am."

She looked at the screen and then at the three 2Ps and one HAC. "Plug, did you get done with the maintenance plan for next month?"

"Uh..."

"The one that I asked you to have on my desk tonight?"

He put the video game controller down on the table. "I was about to get started."

She looked at her watch. "Please have it on my desk within the next hour."

"Will do." He got up and walked towards the hangar.

Victoria turned to the junior pilots. "You guys don't have anything more productive to do than play games?"

The three 2Ps stared at her, each looking slightly scared of what she was about to say. "Which one of you am I flying with tomorrow?"

Caveman raised his hand sheepishly.

"You have all your emergency procedures memorized?" The 2Ps were required to know all of the helicopter emergency procedures verbatim.

Caveman nodded.

Victoria looked at each of them in the eye. "You know, if you three were studying right now, and you made a mistake on your emergency procedures, or couldn't draw out the electrical system from memory, or couldn't name all nineteen functions of the automatic flight control system by heart tomorrow when I ask you...I could be okay with that. But if you *can't* do one of those things—and I *will* ask you tomorrow—if you *can't* do one of those things and you've been playing video games while you have enlisted men performing maintenance on your aircraft—well, that would *piss* me off."

After a moment of silence, all three of the junior officers quickly got up, turned off the video game, and went back to their stateroom to crack open the books.

Once in their room, with the door closed, Juan whispered, "What's up Boss's ass tonight?"

Caveman said, "That's just her, man. She's intense. But I think it's gotten worse since workups last year. After the accident."

* * *

One Year Earlier

Victoria Manning gripped the galley table as the ship rolled to a very unpleasant angle. Sea spray and rain pelted the tiny black porthole to her right. They'd been at sea for two weeks on the USS *Farragut*, an Arleigh Burke–class destroyer.

The bad weather had begun as a tropical storm down near Cuba. The warm waters of the Caribbean and a lack of wind shear had fueled the system into a massive hurricane, which was now moving northeast over Georgia, and out to sea.

While the path of the storm was predicted to miss the two carrier strike groups that were training in the Atlantic, the winds and low-pressure system still made for some of the most horrendous seas that Victoria had ever encountered in her eleven years of naval service.

The phone rang in the wardroom. She picked it up, saying, "Air Boss."

"Boss, can you come down to the hangar? We've got news on the bird."

She could tell by the sound of his voice that it wasn't good.

"Sure, I'll be right down," she said and hung up the phone. She began the balancing act of marching down the ship's passageway as it rolled from side to side.

Aside from the weather, the helicopter's maintenance had been the other disaster of their time at sea. Helicopter squadrons worked year-round to get their thirty-five-million-dollar helicopters in top condition for their underway periods.

There were thousands of complex parts in each of these aircraft. It was up to the twenty-somethings turning the wrenches and checking the electronics every day to keep each aircraft flyable. But in an isolated and harsh saltwater environment, with so many moving parts and almost no way to get spares, things often went wrong.

The USS *Farragut* had a single helicopter on board for this training period. They would deploy with two helicopters—one in each hangar—in a few months. The ship had been at sea for two weeks now. The weather had made it impossible to fly during at least seven of those days. And a plague of maintenance issues had kept them grounded for another five. It was embarrassing.

She arrived back in the hangar. The glum faces of her maintenance chief and maintenance officer stared back at her.

The maintenance officer, a lieutenant, said, "Boss, it ain't looking good. We had to replace the AFCS computer."

"So we'll need a maintenance flight?"

"Afraid so."

She left out a defeated sigh. Maintenance flights were not just flights. They were long diagnostic checks that took place both on deck and in the air. These events had to be completed before any other type of mission was permitted. It was as if they had just replaced a piano and now would have to spend the next few days tuning it before they were allowed to play any songs. Meanwhile, the ship's captain and the admiral's staff would have their arms crossed, asking for status updates every hour until they were ready.

The ship took another roll, and the three of them each grabbed hold of something sturdy, bending their knees and trying to stay upright. If she didn't feel so sick from the never-ending motion, it would be fun. But the constant rolls of the ship got old after a few hours of heavy seas. After a few days, it became torture.

She thought about the problem. The automatic flight control system provided stability to the aircraft when flying. Without it, it would be very hard to hold a steady hover or maintain altitude with precision. Some of their missions required them to hold a steady hover only a few feet above the water. On nights like this, the fifteen-foot swells would cause the flight deck to pitch and roll violently. Because of the clouds, there was no visible horizon to hint at which way was up. Flying in this weather would be hard enough. Flying without an AFCS computer at night would be near suicidal. That's why it was forbidden by the manuals.

Victoria said, "Okay, let's plan to start the maintenance turns tomorrow. Hopefully the weather improves. Are you going to order a backup in case this computer doesn't work?"

"Yes, ma'am. We should be able to pick it up from the carrier when we get in range."

Because of the hurricane, the fleet had been scattered over an area of several hundred square miles. They were well out of range of any supply ships or carriers right now.

They looked shamed. She realized that her men took maintenance setbacks as personal failures. Victoria smiled and said, "Gentlemen, you're doing the best you can in a lousy situation. This isn't your fault. Tell the team that it isn't their fault either. We'll get the bird up. With any luck, this godforsaken weather lightens up soon—maybe we can even get her fully mission-capable tomorrow."

The men nodded.

The 1MC speaker announced overhead, "Air Boss, your presence is requested in the captain's cabin." It was like getting called to the principal's office.

She was a lieutenant commander, and an O-4 in the Navy. Destroyer captains were O-5s, holding the rank of commander in the Navy—equivalent to a lieutenant colonel in the other services.

Victoria had been promoted early to lieutenant commander and been made a department head. She had leapfrogged many of her more senior peers to get this assignment, which was considered prestigious.

While she would never admit it to anyone else, she had expected nothing less. Victoria had been on the fast track ever since she'd set foot on the hallowed grounds of the US Naval Academy, fifteen years ago.

Victoria had not always wanted to go into the military. Quite the opposite. While her father was an admiral, she had been turned off to the idea of military service. This was partly due to the natural teenage need to rebel against one's parents, and partly because the military career track had just never seemed that interesting to her.

That is, until she had gone to a college fair in the fall of her junior year in high school and heard the word *no*.

Her grades and high school resume had been exemplary. But the man behind the US Naval Academy desk didn't seem impressed. Victoria didn't even know why she had stopped at the table. Maybe she had just wanted a USNA brochure so she could tell her parents that she had at least given it a look.

But when she asked the aged alumnus behind the booth for a brochure, he didn't immediately hand her one. A disapproving frown on his face.

"Honey, maybe you should look at one of the other schools instead. No offense, but the Naval Academy can get pretty rough."

That was all it took.

Victoria was an excellent athlete. Always had been. She had broken her nose playing lacrosse, but she joked with her brothers, "You should have seen the other guy."

She worked just as hard at her studies as she did on the athletic field. That work ethic came from her father, she knew. As did her inability to *accept* being told no.

Ironically, her father had tried many times to convince her to look at one of the service academies or ROTC programs. Nothing her father said had ever swayed her thinking. But this sexist old dinosaur, passing judgment on her with one look...*that* lit a fire under her ass.

She hadn't even applied to any other colleges. She'd aced her exams, received a nomination from her senator, and been recruited by the Navy women's lacrosse team.

Victoria had accepted her appointment in the fall of her senior year. Early admission.

When she arrived on campus, Victoria discovered that she actually kind of liked the military lifestyle. It gave her a sense of purpose. And she liked that the military rewarded disciplined, hardworking, and capable people like herself. She excelled in all aspects of Academy life, earning top marks, starting on the lacrosse team all four years, and being selected for Navy pilot upon graduation.

Flight school was a continuation of her successes. She was a natural pilot. Victoria suspected that her talent came from the coordination and ability to judge relative motion that she'd developed playing sports. But what really set her apart from her peers was her intellectual ability. Everyone there was smart. They had to be. Still, Victoria was better than ninety-nine percent of her fellow flight students at memorizing all the books filled with numbers and procedures. She could then rattle them off under pressure, and—most importantly—she was able to make sound decisions based on her newly learned knowledge.

Once in her fleet squadron, Victoria was ranked as the number one pilot of more than thirty competitive junior officers. While many of her fellow pilots went barhopping on the weekends, she dove right back into work. She didn't have a personal life. Nor did she want one. She had goals, and nothing else mattered.

Victoria knew that some thought she was judged favorably because she was a woman, and she deeply resented that. It was hard work and ability—anyone who said otherwise was just jealous. Her success earned her a sterling reputation among her commanding officers, and she was rewarded with the most coveted assignments. After finishing her tour as a junior officer, she'd spent several years as a flight instructor, then as an admiral's aide.

She was promoted early to lieutenant commander and sent to a HSM-46 in Mayport, Florida, to become a department head. She was to get her own helicopter detachment—to be sent off with two helicopters and thirty men somewhere halfway around the world.

Her early promotion and selection to department head were both her reward and her expectation. Stepping stones to someday becoming a commanding officer—and, hopefully, well beyond. They were not a surprise.

The surprise came after she began her work in the new leadership role.

Prior to becoming a department head, she had only had the opportunity to lead small teams. Now, she was the third-highest-ranking person on a ship of over three hundred. She was in charge of thirty highly trained aviators, rescue swimmers, and mechanics. And for someone who was used to being judged and rewarded based on her individual performance, it was a challenge to constantly be held accountable for the sometimes-substandard work of her men. And in the short time she had been on the destroyer—the helicopter detachment had only just joined the crew a few weeks ago—she had grown frustrated working with the captain.

The captain was a surface warfare officer. A ship driver. While he had worked with aviators before, his career had predominantly been spent aboard ships that did not have helicopter detachments. So the constraints of working with an aviation unit caused a lot of consternation between his young, newly minted O-4 air boss and him.

Every time they wanted to fly—even many of the times when they just needed to do maintenance and move or start up the helicopter—it required the captain to drive his ship a certain way. A certain direction, or a certain speed. It was limiting. And the captain had a schedule to keep. A *busy* schedule, written by the admiral's planners on the carrier.

It infuriated the captain that Victoria's helicopter had been grounded for maintenance for so long. She was having a major negative impact on his ability to meet the ship's daily schedule of events.

The captain made sure that Victoria understood his disappointment. The captain's boss was on the carrier, and he was putting pressure on the captain to get it fixed. The captain made sure to let her know that he was writing to Victoria's own helicopter squadron commanding officer, who was on the carrier, letting him know of how bad it was going.

There were also personnel issues to deal with in her own air detachment that were so numerous she couldn't keep them all straight. One of her young sailors was about to lose his security clearance over financial problems. Another had a pregnant wife at home who had just sent him divorce papers. One of her junior officers couldn't land the helicopter without almost crashing—which might be normal for this stage in his career, but it was still scary as hell to deal with.

Pressure in the aircraft had never gotten to Victoria. But the pressure of command—and the feeling of helplessness that accompanied it—was the hardest obstacle she had yet faced.

Thank God she had her own stateroom with a satellite phone—and her mother's calming voice. She kept the calls very short, never completely sure that there wasn't some crewmember in the communications office listening in. Victoria's mom was her only confidant. Her mom knew the Navy, having been a Navy wife for several decades. And she knew Victoria, and the amount of pressure she placed on herself. Her mother calmed her down, restored her self-confidence, and acted as the sounding board she knew her daughter needed. Thank God for her.

Now, walking to the captain's cabin, Victoria took a deep breath. She could get through this.

"Air Boss?" The chaplain poked his head out of the wardroom door. "May I speak with you a moment?"

"I'm sorry, Chaps. I need to run up to the captain's cabin. Can it wait?"

He looked apprehensive. "Yes. Sure. But please come find me when you're finished there."

She was curious, but simply said, "Will do. Sorry."

Victoria climbed up a ladder and kept walking down the passageway, swaying with the waves. She wondered if her father was feeling these seas on his carrier.

Admiral Arthur Louis Manning IV, the commander of the *Harry S. Truman* Strike Group, was about two hundred miles from her right now, she knew. This was the first, and likely the only, time they had been in the same area while acting in their official capacity in the Navy.

He was on one of the two carriers that were out here. His carrier was not supposed to be in charge of Victoria's ship. However, due to the hurricane, with the ships being sortied into irregular groups, Admiral Manning actually had tactical control of her ship for the next week. Her mother would get a kick out of that.

Victoria knocked on the door to the captain's cabin. "Sir, permission to enter?"

The captain opened the door and waved her in. He was on a phone.

"Yes, sir. Yes, sir, I'm about to discuss it with my helicopter officer in charge. I'll get back to you in five." He hung up the phone, then picked up another and said, "TAO, this is the captain. How far away is the *Porter*? Alright, let's make best speed there now. No, hold off on calling flight quarters." He hung up the phone.

"What's going on, sir?"

The captain stood up. "I understand that your aircraft is having maintenance issues. But I need a no-shit best effort here, Air Boss. The USS *James E. Williams* just had their helicopters go down. Since the fleet is so spread out, we're the only ship that has a helicopter in range."

Her face went white. "*Down*, sir? Should we go into the CIC? Look at the tactical picture? I can—" CIC was the combat information center. Also known as Combat, it was the central command and control space on the ship.

"Now, hold on. The admiral read our ship's daily status report and knows that your helicopter is not flyable due to maintenance problems. He only wants you to launch if you have those issues fixed. He was very clear on that point." The captain looked uncomfortable. "And he said he wants to speak with you directly about it as soon as you're available."

Victoria went over the scenario in her mind. By the book, it was an absolute no. There was no way she should allow her aircraft to fly with an AFCS computer that hadn't passed a maintenance check flight. Especially at night, over water, and in horrendous weather.

But she *knew* those pilots. The helicopter detachment on the USS *James E. Williams* were from her own squadron. Those were her brothers in arms. They would do anything for her, and she needed to push herself, her men, and her aircraft to their absolute limit if at all possible.

She said, "Sir, I think I can do it. I'll fly it."

The captain nodded. "Alright. I'll let you explain it to the admiral. We're supposed to call him back in five minutes."

The operations officer knocked on the door and entered. "Sir, you asked for an update?"

"Yes, what is it, OPS?"

"Sir, the suspected crash site is about ninety miles to our north. We've confirmed with Strike Group that we're the only ship with an air asset that would be able to get there in time. But we would need to launch soon, sir. With the water temperature and heavy seas, the SAR planners say we need to get there quick to give them a chance of survival."

The captain waved OPS away. "Very well." He picked up the phone and pressed a button, connecting them by satellite to the aircraft carrier.

As the captain waited to be connected, Victoria cursed herself. Who was she kidding? The winds were out of limits. The seas were out of limits. She didn't know if the AFCS would work. She would be risking the lives of whoever she took with her.

"Yes, sir. My air boss says that her aircraft is flyable, sir. Excuse me, Admiral?"

Victoria just realized something. She had assumed that the captain referred to the admiral on the IKE. But now that they were under the *Truman* Strike Group's control...God, was that *her father* on the line?

"Uh, yes, sir. Here she is." The captain looked torn as he handed her the phone.

Her father's voice was garbled. "Lieutenant Commander Manning, good evening."

Her face was turning redder by the minute. The captain watched her. "Yes, sir?"

"The captain tells me that you want to do the search and rescue, is that true?"

Her father had used her rank when he'd addressed her. He was speaking to her in his official capacity. She was dizzy. Was he second-guessing her? He was an aviator. Not a pilot, but a Naval flight officer. It didn't matter. He knew how it worked. He understood how strict the Navy was with its aviation safety protocol.

"Sir, our helicopter had a bad AFCS computer. We just replaced it with a good one. Technically we're supposed to test it before we fly. But in this situation, I'm willing to accept the risk."

Silence.

Finally, he said, "So you're saying you do *not* have a good aircraft?"

Victoria said, "Sir, that's correct. But in this situation—"

"This is a yes-or-no question. Is your aircraft maintenance up or down?"

She hesitated. "Sir, technically it is down, but I request that you waive—"

"No, Commander. I do not give my consent. You stay where you are."

A wave of fear washed over her as she realized what that would likely mean for the aircrew. If they were alive, she was their only hope of rescue. If her father didn't let her take off...

"Admiral, with all due respect, I can handle this. I would be flying the aircraft during a maintenance flight tomorrow anyway. What's the difference? People's lives are at stake. Please, sir. Allow me to launch."

A pause. "Commander, I don't want to lose these men, but there are limits to how much loss...how much risk is acceptable." His voice was emotional. A higher pitch than normal. A part of her brain couldn't believe it. This wasn't like her father. It was...inappropriate. He needed to weigh the two sides impartially, and he wasn't doing that. He was making this call because it was her, not because it was the right call.

"Sir, are you ordering me not to go?"

"That's correct." She heard a click as the line went dead. Her mouth was agape.

She said, "He said no. We are not allowed to launch."

The captain looked at her like she had leprosy and he might catch it. He took the phone and hung it up.

They both stood there a moment, swaying with the heavy seas. "That will be all, Commander," the captain said, disappointment in his tone.

She walked back out of the room and headed for her stateroom, trying to hold herself together. When she reached her room, the chaplain was standing outside.

The Lord works in mysterious ways. She could probably use a little chat with him right about now.

The chaplain said, "Air Boss, is it alright if we speak privately for a moment?"

"Sure, come in." She opened her door and attached the latch that would keep it propped open. "Would you like to take a seat?"

"Let's both sit down."

She eyed him. "Well, who is this about?" She sighed. Which one of her men had a problem now?

"Lieutenant Commander Manning, I'm very sorry to tell you that your mother has passed away. She died this morning of heart failure."

* * *

Present Day
USS Farragut
Eastern Pacific Ocean, 200 Nautical Miles West of Colombia

After lighting a fire under her pilots, Victoria retired to her stateroom. She looked at her watch. It was 2300. Time to start her evening routine.

She took out her notebook from her desk and flipped to the last written page. Victoria crossed off several items on her to-do list:

Sixty minutes of cardio exercise.

Listen to one of the TED talk podcasts (while working out).

Complete five personnel evaluations—finish reviewing the E-4s and below.

Improve aircrew training plan.

. . .

After crossing the items she had completed, she looked at the items that remained.

One hour of professional study.
Empty email inbox.
Meditate twenty minutes.

Getting those items done would cost her sleep if she wanted to wake up before 0500, which she did every day.

Victoria clenched her teeth and got to work. The more she got that feeling that she didn't want to do something, the more she pushed herself. There were two things that Victoria hated most in life: laziness and pity. Especially self-pity.

She spent the next hour studying from the helicopter manual. While she knew the three-inch-thick book by heart, the knowledge was perishable. She believed that as a leader, she must always hold herself to a higher standard than she did her men. After all, she had to be their example.

When she was done studying, she spent the next hour catching up on email. She responded to several work-related emails, and saved the personal ones for last. David, her brother, had written her. His note was short and to the point. Like the rest of the Manning family, he wasn't one to get overly emotional.

Victoria was glad to hear from him. It sounded like he was doing much better. But she worried that there were still several unresolved issues from his recent run-ins. She didn't have all the details, but between phone calls with David and reading the news, she knew that something terrible had happened involving the Chinese. He'd promised her he would fill her in when they could speak in person. But he had asked that she refrain from asking him any more over the phone or unsecured email.

Her reply to him was the typical deployment family message. Generic musings about the daily routine. A few humorous complaints. And the promise that she missed him dearly.

Ever since David had been on the news a few weeks ago, Victoria had become a minor celebrity among the officers and crew on the ship. At first, she had received a lot of questioning looks, back when the news was reporting that David was tied to criminal acts. But after his name was cleared, the questions had become less accusatory. And now, all the news was about the potential war with Iran. People had stopped asking about her brother.

There was one email she didn't respond to. Her father's. Admiral Arthur Manning was now heading up the USS *Ford* Carrier Strike Group. It was an unusual assignment for someone who had been transferred out of another carrier command only a few months prior. But the *Ford* was the newest carrier in the fleet, and not yet ready for deployment. It was, she assumed, a retirement posting.

Victoria's father had written her once a month for the past year. His emails always had the same formula. First, a vague message about what he was doing professionally. He would then recount a memory from their childhood. Sometimes it would be about Victoria's mother, which often pained her to read. She didn't like thinking about her mother. Lastly, he would write that he hoped to hear from her soon.

She hadn't replied to any of the messages since her mother had died. But her mother's death wasn't the reason.

Victoria couldn't speak to her father because she associated him with the worst moment of her life. The night that he'd refused to allow her to launch and rescue her downed squadron mates, a year ago. She partially blamed him, and partially herself, for their deaths.

She knew that everyone said it was just an accident. A one-in-a-million electrical failure. But when you fly a million hours, and many of those hours are at night and over water, that one time is deadly.

People also had tried to tell Victoria that her helicopter wouldn't have made a difference. That it was unlikely that anyone had survived the crash. But no bodies were ever found. So no one could know for certain that she wouldn't have made a difference.

She kept thinking about how she might have saved them, had her father not intervened. Yes, it would have been dangerous and against the rules to take her helicopter out that night, with its AFCS problems. But it would have been worth the risk.

The admiral had put his foot down, however. Victoria couldn't help but think that he might have chosen differently if it had been an unrelated male officer, instead of her.

When her peers looked at her in the squadron spaces, she wondered if they questioned her bravery. Or if they whispered that daddy's little girl was the reason that those three men never came home to their families.

It was a horrible thought. Partly because it made her feel guilty, and partly because she knew that her squadron mates were above that line of thinking.

She read her father's email three times, and her cursor hovered over the reply icon. She shook her head and hit DELETE.

Crossing off another item on her list, she looked at the last one. Meditate. She checked that the door was locked and put her headphones in. She played music from her favorite composer, Max Richter. The sounds of violins, cellos, and modern synthesizers filled her ears. She sat on her thin mattress, feet up, hands on her knees. As she closed her eyes and concentrated on her breathing, she tried to force all the anger, stress, and frustration out of her mind. It was not easy.

* * *

A few days later, Victoria was pleased to see that Juan's skills as an airborne tactician were much better than his ability to fly and land the aircraft.

Juan said, "Come right to zero-nine-zero."

"Roger, zero-nine-zero."

Juan typed a few keystrokes and manipulated the small stick on his multipurpose display. "Okay, I have waypoints for you to fly to for our first sonobuoy drop. Just follow the needle."

She looked over at his screen. "Nice job."

Juan called to the ship, "*Farragut* Control, Cutlass 471, we're ready to start the exercise. Any word from the Colombian submarine yet?"

"Negative, sir," the ship's enlisted air controller replied over the UHF radios. "But the captain says to proceed with the exercise."

"Roger."

Juan asked Victoria, "Is it normal for a submarine not to communicate when they said they were going to?"

"Not really. But I haven't worked with the Colombians much. I'm sure that someone just mixed something up. They gave us the coordinates and the start time, so we should be good to go."

"Okay. Well, please continue to fly to your waypoints that I put in. We'll lay down the first sonobuoy pattern with DIFARs."

"Sounds good."

When they reached the first waypoint, a *thunk* sounded throughout the aircraft as the first buoy flew out the port side. A small parachute slowed its descent into the water. Several more buoys were shot out shortly after.

"AWR1, let me know when you've got them tuned up."

A few moments later, he replied, "Sir, buoy number one's tuned up. Working on the others."

Once the sonobuoys were working, Juan hoped to be able to triangulate the position of the Colombian submarine and develop a track. The more information he got from the sonobuoy, the more he could refine the track's course and speed. Then they would simulate a torpedo drop. The goal was to attack the Colombian submarine before it could get too close to their own ship, the USS *Farragut*.

AWR1 said, "Sir, we've got a submarine. Sounds kind of funny, but here—you should be able to start seeing something on your screen."

"Yup. Okay, I've got it." Juan began manipulating his keyboard. A few minutes later, he said, "There. Okay, we've got the submarine twelve miles south of our ship, headed towards her at five knots."

"Not too shabby," Victoria said. "Send the information back to the ship."

Juan relayed the message to the *Farragut*'s controller.

"You ready to start pinging?"

"Yes, ma'am."

Victoria lined up the helicopter for the maneuver that would allow her to lower the dipping sonar into the water. They were in an out-of-ground-effect hover, the most intensive activity for a helicopter pilot. The heavy aircraft required just about maximum engine power to maintain altitude as the AN/AQS-22 Airborne Low Frequency Sonar lowered into the ocean.

"Alright, let's start pinging AWR1."

Victoria heard the off-key tone in her headset.

Juan began typing again. "Hmm. That's weird."

Victoria looked over at Juan's screen. "What is it?"

AWR1 said, "Ah, I think the Colombians are going crazy on us."

"Yeah...I'm getting multiple returns," Juan said. "Do they have a decoy? Or is this just bad data?"

"I think that's a system error, maybe."

"How could it be a system error? This dipper is supposed to be brand-new."

"I don't know, sir, I just work here."

Victoria said, "Guys, slow down. What are you seeing?"

Juan said, "The Colombian submarine is heading away from us at like...hold on...at like forty knots. That can't be right."

"Yeah, that's garbage."

"You said you're getting multiple returns?" Victoria looked out of the aircraft to the right, scanning the surface of the water for any sign of a periscope.

"No, I think that was just the old track," AWR1 said. "One looked like it was on the same course and speed, but I think...well, hold on."

Victoria sighed. As well as Juan was doing, she was ten times faster. It was frustrating to sit there in a hover and have a less experienced tactician feed her slow bits of information. Teaching a subordinate something new took a lot of patience. *But it pays off*, she reminded herself.

"Actually, I'm not getting that second track anymore," Juan said. "Alright, let's set up for our attack run."

Victoria frowned. This didn't sound promising. They reeled up the dipping sonar and began forward flight. She looked at her copilot. "Give me somewhere to go."

"Roger, Boss. Hold on. Almost got it. There."

Her needle spun around and she began heading towards the next checkpoint Juan had placed in the system.

"Alright, let's do the attack checklist." Juan began spouting off items, with the two other crewmembers responding every few seconds.

"Cutlass, this is *Farragut* Control. The captain wants you to return to the ship."

Victoria shook her head. "We're on our attack run, Control."

"Negative, ma'am. The captain wants you guys to return now."

Victoria frowned. This was ridiculous. It had taken them days to get ready for this rare and valuable training. "*Farragut* Control, please put the TAO on."

"Roger, ma'am."

The tactical action officer was the senior officer on duty in the ship's combat information center.

"Boss, it's OPS."

The operations officer was standing TAO right now. Good, he was smart. He would help sort this out.

"OPS, hey—can you tell me what's going on? We're about to go on our attack run of the Colombians, and we're being recalled to the ship. But we're scheduled to fly for the next two hours. The next crew is supposed to fly after us."

"Boss, the captain is cancelling the flight schedule." His voice sounded defeated.

"Why?"

"We just got sunk, Boss. The Colombian submarine radioed us a minute ago. We're dead."

* * *

Two hours later, Victoria and her crew stood in the ship's combat information center with a dozen of the ships personnel. The anti-submarine warfare officer, a lieutenant junior grade, was briefing the ship's captain on the results of the exercise.

The captain pounded his fist down on the chart table. "ASWO, you're telling me that a Colombian diesel submarine sunk our boat? Are you kidding me?"

"Yes…yes, sir," the young officer stammered.

Victoria couldn't believe this. It was training. Crucial training, rare training with an actual submarine. If she were the captain, she would have just asked the Colombian submarine to reset so that they could try again. But for some reason, the captain wasn't looking at this exercise as a training opportunity, but instead as some black mark that everyone needed to be shamed for.

The captain looked around the room. His eyes got to Victoria. "Air Boss, why did this happen? Didn't you guys find the submarine?"

"Sir, we had good contact, but then it appeared as if there were two separate tracks. They were diverging. So we went for the one that we felt was most likely the Colombians."

"And?" said the captain in an accusatory tone.

"And…it appears that we had the wrong contact, sir." She spoke without emotion. Better to get it over with and give the man what he wanted.

"Exactly. You were too late. Your aircrew, and everyone on this ship, failed me." He looked at his ASW officer. "ASWO, I take this as a personal insult. Let this be a lesson to you. Do not fail me again."

It was not often that Victoria witnessed a commanding officer treat his men like this. He was speaking to them as if they were children. The XO stayed silent behind the captain. His was a hard job. He was a good man, and his instinct was surely to say something constructive. But anything he said right now would be seen as going against the captain—as a sign of disrespect. Something that would hurt his ability to influence the captain behind closed doors.

When she saw that no one else was going to speak, she decided to see if she could salvage anything. "Captain. Sir, we had originally been scheduled to fly two bags of ASW today. With your permission, sir, I'd like to launch my second flight so that we can get some more training."

"*Your* second flight, Air Boss?"

She held her breath, trying not to show any of her exasperation.

"It's not *your* flight, Air Boss. It's *mine. I'm* the captain. *I* own these aircraft. Or did you *forget*?"

"Sir, I meant no disrespect."

He shook his head. "Fine. I don't care. XO, *you* take care of it." The captain stormed out of the room.

When he was gone, the XO spoke in a softer tone. "Alright, folks. Everyone, let's just learn from this. Air Boss, why don't you have your second crew go get ready to launch? I'll speak with the captain."

She nodded and made the call. The XO kept speaking with the team in combat, going over what they had seen. She called Plug and the senior chief, who were waiting back in the hangar. She told them to get the helicopter ready to fly again, and that they would continue the ASW training in a little while.

When she was off the phone, the XO called her over. "Sorry about that." He said it softly enough that no one else heard.

She shrugged. "Nothing you could really do."

He gave her a knowing look. "Yeah. Hey, on another note—I was just going over the tapes with our sonar tech and your AWR1. You got a sec?"

"Sure."

They walked over to the two enlisted men, who were standing next to the ship's high-tech sonar equipment. The XO said, "Tell her what you guys told me."

"Boss, we were looking at the tapes," AWR1 said. "You know how we had two tracks?"

"Yeah."

"Well, I had assumed that we just got some bad data back when we were pinging our dipping sonar, but we looked at the replay here. And it looks like the *Farragut* was getting contact on the two separate tracks as well."

Victoria frowned. "What do you mean?"

The ship's sonar technician pointed to his screen. "You see this here? This is the Colombian submarine. We know that because it corresponds to the location of the Colombians when they said they sunk us."

"Okay. What about that one?" She pointed to the obvious other marking on his screen.

"That's what we aren't so sure about."

"The second track we had was going ridiculously fast," AWR1 said. "Like thirty-five or forty knots fast. I just assumed that was fake. And I think I mixed them up. It was actually the other track—that turned out to be the Colombians—that was going five knots. The one that we were chasing was the second track. And that one really did appear to be going over thirty-five knots." His face was a mix of worry and skepticism.

Victoria looked up at the XO. "We don't have any US nukes around here, do we?"

He shook his head. "Not that I know of."

"What about the acoustic signatures? You get anything?"

The ship's sonar technician said, "Almost nothing."

"Almost?"

"Well, there was this one line here…but at that frequency it could have been a couple different types of subs, if it really was a sub."

"What types?"

"Well, it could have been a Los Angeles–class. Or…"

"Or what?"

"Well, supposedly the Chinese have a new type of nuclear fast-attack submarine that just came out that has the same characteristics at that frequency range."

"Chinese?"

"Yeah. But that would be kind of crazy for them to be operating out here, near the Galapagos."

Victoria nodded. "Alright. Let's make sure that we're looking at this stuff during the next flight. Let's see if we hear it again."

"Roger, ma'am."

Victoria remained in the combat information center for the second training flight. It went better than the first one, with Plug's helicopter and the ship both claiming to have successfully attacked the Colombians.

And this time, no more suspicious second track.

That evening, the XO checked with COMSUBPAC and verified that there were no US submarines in the area. It had to be a system error.

The only other alternative would have been that it was the new Chinese Shang-class attack submarine. That would have been highly unlikely. The Chinese didn't deploy their submarines to this area of the world. Plus, it would have been near impossible for them to operate out here in the vicinity of the USS *Farragut* and remain undetected.

After going over the data with the sonar experts on the ship, the XO and Victoria agreed that the second track must have been a fault in the sonar computer system.

3

Red Cell Island

Lena lay on the infirmary mattress. A window revealed the dark green jungle outside. She looked at her arm in disgust.

Natesh sat in a chair next to her. "You saw my report?"

She nodded. "I did. It was well done, as always." He too was looking at the grotesque burns on her arm and shoulder. Then he must have realized that he was staring and turned away, looking instead at the bare stone wall.

She hated him for making her feel insecure. It was a very rare emotion for her. The permanent burn scars that traveled up her side were hideous, she knew. But she had never cared about her looks. Or at least that's what she had thought until they were ruined. She had been beautiful. A fact that she had always taken for granted. But that beauty had been burned off by fire on a Dubai rooftop. Perhaps some of her confidence had been burned off as well. In its place was a growing anger.

Lena closed her eyes and lay back down on the bed. Her mind still a bit foggy from the pain meds. She would stop taking them today, she decided. A clear mind was needed for her role here on the island.

She said, "Your conclusion was not optimistic."

"When we drew up the plans, we expected six months to a year of preparation."

"You sound like you're complaining."

"When a project that is supposed to take six months to a year gets moved up by six months to a year—I think it's justifiable to complain."

"And the projects you worked on in corporate America were always on time? Every part always going to plan?"

Natesh tilted his head, annoyed at the remark. "Of course not. But it's one thing to switch to alternate plans. It is quite another to have no alternatives."

She opened her eyes and rolled out of bed. She walked over to the window. "Talk me through the problems."

"The container ships are not ready. The troops are not trained. Not only that, but we don't yet have the numbers of troops that I expected. Our initial landing spots in the Americas are just now getting their first infusion of Chinese Special Forces soldiers. And most of those units have no clue why they're really there."

He paused until she opened her eyes. He leaned forward to emphasize his words. "And the *psychological* operations have not yet begun."

"In China, you mean?"

"Yes, Lena. We can plan while we are on this tiny island. We can plan all we want to, but that only gets us so far. You know as well as I do that without the alignment of Chinese leadership, none of this is going to happen. All we have so far are *plans*."

"Look at me."

He looked, a pained expression on his face. "Do my scars look like we have been *just* drawing up plans?"

"No. I'm sorry. But Jinshan promised that we would have more by now. We need more *of everything*. More ships, more troops, more aircraft. The wheels need to start moving if he expects the timeline to move up as far as he does. I've been following the headlines in China. It's business as usual. This isn't what Jinshan said…"

"I know what Jinshan said."

"Well, will he follow through? We've identified the fixes needed to finish the network outages. I know that the Chinese military readiness has increased in the south, but everywhere else it's the same. But if we're going to stick to the schedule…we need manufacturing to shift from commerce to a wartime footing. I just don't see Jinshan's promised results happening on time."

Lena said, "He's asked to speak with us in person."

"He has? When?"

"After the Washington, D.C., operation is executed."

Natesh's stomach turned at the mention of that operation. He had been horrified to learn the details.

"Alright, so we can speak to him about this."

"Yes, in Guangzhou. He has asked us to come to him."

"Why?"

She looked at him, not wanting to reveal anything about Jinshan's health. "Because he is a busy man."

A knock at the door, and then one of the Chinese intelligence officers popped his head through. "It's time. You asked to be alerted when the Washington, D.C., operation was to begin."

Lena looked at the clock. Right on time. "Thank you. We'll be right there."

The man nodded and shut the door. "Natesh, things will work out. Cheng Jinshan has devoted the majority of his life to this cause. I have devoted my entire adult life to this cause. We will not fail. *I* promise you."

He sighed. "Okay."

She got up and said, "Alright, let's go watch the fireworks."

4

Tysons Corner, Virginia

"So you've known about this for how long?"

David Manning stared at his brother from the passenger seat. They were in heavy traffic on Chain Bridge Road.

Chase said, "I'm gonna take the Beltway."

"Don't take the Beltway. Traffic will be worse there."

"I'll take it to 66."

"They're both going to be parking lots."

Chase drove his Ford Mustang onto the on-ramp of the Beltway. David didn't say anything.

"Yes, I've known about it for a while. Come on, man." He took his eyes off the road for a split second, making eye contact with his brother. "You know that with my job...I can't talk openly about everything."

David stared out the window. The Beltway was a sea of red tail-lights, inching along slower than a person could walk. He looked over at his brother. A former Navy SEAL. Now an elite member of the CIA's Special Activities Division. But he was still human. Stuck in traffic, like the rest of D.C.

"I warned you," he said, looking at the logjam.

"It'll give us more time to talk," Chase said.

David's phone vibrated, and he scanned his new text message.

Lindsay: You on your way home yet?

David: Yeah in traffic

Lindsay: How'd it go?

David: Not bad I'll tell u more when home

Lindsay: K Love you

David: love u 2

David said, "On the one hand, I'm glad to hear that they're taking the stuff with China seriously."

"But?"

"When we were in that meeting today...the way a lot of those CIA guys were looking at me..."

"Relax," Chase said. "They wouldn't have asked you to be on the team if they didn't trust you."

"I don't think they *all* trust me."

Chase shot another look at his brother. "You passed the background check. You've had multiple polygraphs with some of the best analysts in the world. Your stories check out. And a lot of good people in the military and intelligence community have vouched for you."

"But some people still question whether I intentionally gave information to the Chinese...or if I was just too dumb to realize..."

"You gotta let it go, man. Forgive yourself. Focus on your new mission. Help save the people on that island. And help make sure our country is protecting itself from any Chinese threat. The director personally gave his approval to have you on the team. *David.* They believe you."

David shook his head. "So why are we still about to go to war with Iran? If they really trusted me, they would listen to my warnings. To your warnings too, for God's sake."

"Because it's hard to stop the drums of war," Chase said, "and Iran has killed Americans. Whether it was orchestrated by the Chinese or not, whether they were manipulated or not—they've killed Americans."

He referred to the Persian Gulf attacks a few weeks earlier. After Lena Chou had assassinated the Iranian politician near Bandar Abbas, Iran had retaliated by conducting a surprise attack on US military assets in the Persian Gulf. While the US Air Force and Navy had made quick work of the attacking parties, hundreds of American lives were lost. A tenuous cease-fire was declared. Things had settled down for now. But while Iran and the United States weren't technically at war just yet, American forces had been building in the region for weeks. And most of the American public was calling for retribution. War might be only days away.

David shook his head, looking back out the window. "We're playing right into Jinshan's hands."

"I don't disagree."

"Then why aren't you angrier?"

"Because Iran is a destabilizing force in the region," Chase said. "They're the largest state sponsor of terrorism in the world. There are lots of people in Iran who would relish a free and democratic government. Maybe all they need is a little help in getting there."

David turned to him. "You mean help from our military?"

Chase shrugged as he changed lanes. "Sure. Why not."

"Come on, Chase. You can't just bring democracy to countries. It isn't that simple. You of all people should know that. You've seen a lot of the results of that sort of thing."

Chase shot his brother a dark look. "You're right. I have seen a lot of the world. Where the American military has tried to bring democracy to other countries. And you're right. It is complex. It's not easy. But every country is different. Iran is not Iraq, and it definitely ain't Afghanistan. All I'm saying is, it sure would be nice if Iran had a free and open democracy. One where they weren't ruled by an extremist leader. It might be one of the keys to peace in the Middle East."

"Alright, I can appreciate that. But still, this whole Iran situation is a setup. It's been staged by the Chinese. We both know that."

"Right, but we can't prove it. Not to John Q. Public. And that's what matters."

"So then we just let China get away with it?"

"No."

"Then what?"

Chase looked at his brother. "That's what you're on the team for."

David sighed. "You're saying I need to be patient."

"Yes. You still have a lot to be briefed on. Trust me."

David said, "Alright."

A motorcycle puttered and snarled next to their car as its rider revved its engine, his feet touching the ground as the already-slow traffic came to a full stop.

Chase shook his head. "I forgot why I don't want to work an office job. It's this damn traffic."

David looked out ahead. Columns of cars, SUVs, and eighteen-wheelers stood still on the Beltway. David heard a few cracks that sounded like fireworks. He looked at the motorcycle next to them, trying to figure out if it was having some sort of engine trouble.

Then he saw Chase's face. His brother placed the Mustang in park and reached under his seat, moving fast. He pulled out a canvas black container about the size of a lunch bag and unzipped it.

"What is that?"

Chase didn't respond, just looked up out the window, scanning the horizon. His hands working the bag, reaching for its contents.

"*Chase*. What's wrong?"

Chase held up his finger. "Shhh." Then he removed a Sig Sauer P226 9mm handgun from the black bag.

"*Dude*. What are you doing?"

He was still looking forward, through the windshield. David turned to follow his gaze. An overpass stood about a quarter mile in front of them. A plume of black smoke began to rise up from the highway in front of it.

David said, "Chase, chill out, man. It must be an accident."

But as he watched his brother prepare his weapon, he began to suspect that it wasn't. Chase had been in war zones all over the world. He wouldn't have retrieved his weapon unless he knew something was amiss.

Chase shook his head. "You don't hear that?"

"What?"

"Gunfire."

* * *

"Hurry up," the first man said to the second over the sound of liquid splattering on the ground as he poured gasoline onto the highway. Horns blared at them. They had stopped the minivan in the middle of the Beltway, only a few dozen yards before the overpass.

"I'm going as fast as I can. It won't come out any faster." The two men had started pouring gasoline on either end of the minivan. They walked the streams of pungent liquid in a straight line to either side of the highway. Together, the line of gasoline and the minivan would form the blockade.

The third man stood with his rifle behind the minivan, out of sight of the jammed traffic. A few cars near them realized something menacing was occurring and screeched around the blockade. Engines revved up as they panicked and zoomed past.

"*Now.* Light it, light it!" The gasoline vapors ignited before the flame of the long gas grill lighter made contact with the liquid. The spreading fire engulfed the highway in one long strip, cutting off traffic and filling the air with black smoke.

"Good luck, brothers," the first man said as he raised his rifle. Both the retractable doors to the minivan were open. The three men hobbled through the opening and out to the other side, where the traffic stood motionless. They fanned out and began marching through the bumper-to-bumper traffic jam. In unison, they raised their rifles and began firing into the cars.

* * *

There were twelve of them in all. Divided into three groups of four. Three separate attacks conducted simultaneously on different parts of the Beltway. That was what the instructions specified.

Their leader, Javad, had been in the Iranian Ministry of State

Security. The others were mere foot soldiers, chosen for their loyalty and competence. But that was a long time ago.

They held only loose affiliations to each other. A few prayed at the same mosque, but most didn't attend anymore. Two of the men were roommates. None were married. None participated in any online activity that might get them flagged.

In truth, most members of the Iranian sleeper cell enjoyed living in America. The weather was nice. There was good food, and plenty of activities to keep them occupied. They enjoyed themselves. They were just good old Americans, who had been living in the United States for almost a decade.

Waiting for orders.

Most in the group had thought they would never be called upon. If he was honest about it, Javad had thought that too. Their sleeper cell was a nice weapon for Iran to have in its arsenal. But like other weapons of mass destruction, it could only be used once, and it would trigger swift retribution. So it was illogical, when one thought about it, that they would ever be used. Because that would mean... well, that Iran had reached a decision to irreparably harm itself, and sacrifice the lives of Javad and his men.

Javad and his men weren't terrorists. They were *soldiers*. *Patriots*. Few of them had any desire to be martyrs. They were too smart for that. But ideology, religion, and nationality were very closely related in Iran. And he had been briefed on the many ways his group might be used. Suicide missions and suicide attacks were very different in his mind. In a suicide mission, one still held hope that they might overcome all odds and make it out alive.

He reminded himself that suicide attacks had been used several times throughout history, often in military campaigns. Most notably, the Japanese had launched Kamikaze bombers at the end of World War II, sinking around fifty ships. It could be an effective weapon, Javad told himself. Iran must have a great need for it.

Over the past few weeks Javad had grown increasingly worried as he watched the news. Iran and the United States had already fired shots at each other in combat. While outright war still had not broken out, the media made it seem like it could happen at any time.

A part of him wished he could be in Iran, serving his countrymen. But another part of him was thankful that he was here, safe from the guided munitions of the deadliest military in the world. Despite what the Iranian propaganda machines would tell them, Javad knew the truth. No country on earth could make war like the United States of America.

The growing probability of war between the two nations brought his life's most important question to the forefront of his thoughts. Would they be called up into action? He'd made the rounds. He had spoken to his team leaders. And they had spoken to their team members. All twelve men had been told to be on the alert, but not to do anything that might raise suspicions. They didn't want the Department of Homeland Security or the FBI knocking on their door.

A few weeks ago, Javad had been almost certain that his network would not be activated. In the face of an almost certain military defeat, even the Ayatollah would know not to provoke America by using Javad's team. Javad was like one of the American soldiers that manned a nuclear missile silo. A highly trained overseer of a terrible, never-to-be-used weapon. This was the way he had thought of himself.

The activation order had come three days ago.

It was in the form of an email from a clothing company, and it went straight to his spam folder. His handlers—or, more accurately, the people they hired—could make any message appear as if it had originated from a different and innocent source. Javad was trained to check both his inbox and spam folder each day, looking for the right passphrase. The body of the email, to the untrained eye, would also look like a normal advertisement. But it contained coded instructions.

He immediately headed to the predetermined location and found the vehicle. It was an unmarked minivan. An older model. Blue. American-made. The keys in the glove compartment, inside a manila envelope. Also inside the envelope were detailed plans. A timeline with targets and locations. Where to get equipment. And a lighter, to burn the instructions.

The van was unlocked, parked in an alleyway and sandwiched

between two windowless brick buildings. A trashy apartment complex rose up across the street in front of him. He wondered if there was a team of FBI agents watching him behind one of its dark windows. He looked up as he read, knowing instantly that he was being watched. There was no way whoever had left written plans like this would allow them to fall into the wrong hands. If it wasn't the FBI in that building straight ahead, it was whoever had left these instructions. He could feel their crosshairs on his forehead.

When he finished memorizing the plans, he got out of the vehicle and lit the papers on fire, just as the instructions had prescribed. The alleyway kept any wind from blowing out the flame, and he didn't let go until the last morsel of paper was consumed. Then he got back inside the van and drove away.

That had been only three days ago, but it seemed like it had been a lifetime. The others were excited when they found out that they were to be activated. Their time had finally come. They would carry the sword. Strike at the heart of America. *Death to America.* They would show the West that Iran was not to be trifled with.

Javad hoped he could fulfill his duty without being caught. He gave himself about a one-in-four chance that he would execute his mission and get away alive. He had little confidence that his men would survive, but that was not something he would ever tell them.

When the day came, they found the minivans unlocked and parked behind a grocery store, just as the instructions had said they would be.

Javad's men wasted no time putting on the heavy protective vests that they were to wear. A phone was strapped to each of the vests, facing outward so it could record and transmit everything. Javad assumed that someone in Iran would then weaponize the footage, putting it out to the media and on social networks.

The vehicles also contained firearms. One semiautomatic long gun for each of Javad's men. Boxes of 5.56mm ammo. And several plastic five-gallon gas cans, each one filled.

For operational security, Javad hadn't told his men exactly what their assignment was until they were ready to execute. They only knew to be prepared for bloodshed.

When he told his team what they were to do, they grew excited. A few had fear in their eyes, but Javad quickly spoke words of confidence to them. At exactly the right time, just before rush hour, he sent the three vehicles away to complete their mission.

He drove a fourth vehicle. As he turned onto I-495, the Washington, D.C., Beltway, he wondered if there was really a God. After all the time he had spent in America, he now knew that the Americans were not the demons his government made them out to be. If there truly was a God, he wondered if He would forgive him for what he was about to do.

* * *

Chase kept looking forward through the windshield of the Ford Mustang.

"What is it?"

Chase's instincts were honed from years of experience on battlefields around the world. To the uninitiated, the sputtering of a motorcycle or the crack of fireworks might sound an awful lot like gunfire. But Chase's fine-tuned ears were the first defense of a highly trained operative.

"Stay here. Get in the driver's seat," he said to his brother. "We're in the outer lane, so if you see someone coming, drive off the road and get the hell out of here."

David looked aghast. "What are you gonna do?"

Chase opened the door and shut it behind him, walking forward with his arms extended, his weapon pointed toward the ground.

His eyes scanned down the lanes of traffic as he weaved in between vehicles, searching for the source of the gunfire.

A wall of black smoke rose up about fifty yards ahead. A few people honked their horns. Then he heard some screams, and more of the loud, unmistakable cracks of semiautomatic weapons.

The left side of the highway was a five-foot-tall median barrier. On the right side of the road rose a sloped area of grass. The grass ended at a twenty-foot wall—a sound barrier, separating the busy highway from suburbia. There was nowhere for people to run.

When the gunfire erupted and the screams began, Chase could see car doors ahead of him flying open, the passengers fleeing to either side of the stopped traffic, running away from the black smoke. A heavyset woman in heels ran right by Chase as he jogged toward the noise. She was panting and saying, "Oh my God, oh my God, oh my God," tears rolling down her red puffy face.

Chase side stepped to the left side of the highway and began making his way forward, faster now. He brought his weapon up, scanning the horizon by tracing the gun sight along his field of view. A yellow school bus motored in place a few cars ahead. He needed to find the shooters before...

Target.

The man wore blue jeans and a dark grey vest, and held what looked like an AR-15. He walked toward Chase along the highway shoulder. The same section of the road that Chase was using. Every few steps, the man fired into the traffic. A few more seconds and he would be at the school bus.

Chase opened the rear door of the bus and found himself staring at a group of middle schoolers. "Come on, hop down!" he called. A large man appeared next to the kids. Chase asked, "You the bus driver?"

The man nodded.

A woman in a sedan next to them saw what he was doing and got out of her car to help. Chase looked at her and the bus driver and said, "Help get everyone out the back door. Bring all these kids that way, away from the gunfire." He pointed back in the direction he had come from.

The woman and the bus driver nodded and started helping the kids hop down and run away from the screaming.

Chase left them and headed towards the gunfire.

* * *

Lena stood in the back of the room, watching the operation unfold. Chinese satellites were still effective. The ARES cyberattack had only affected US satellites—GPS and military birds, mostly.

With David Manning and Henry Glickstein escaping, she knew that there was an increased level of surveillance on the island. But now that the US network of reconnaissance satellites was inoperative, that greatly reduced the information they could obtain.

The biggest threat to the secrecy of this operation was US submarine and aerial reconnaissance. US Navy EP-3s and Air Force RC-135 aircraft routinely flew through the area. But the island had received several upgrades—electronic countermeasures, mostly—that would help shield their work. This island was still the best place for her. While Jinshan's power and connections protected him from the political scrutiny he faced after Dubai, *she* was a different story.

Officially, Lena Chou was not, and had never been, a citizen of China. She was an American, despite what the US intelligence agencies were now saying. That it had taken them ten years to realize her true identity was a testament to her ability, and the professionalism of Jinshan's operation.

"Ms. Chou?"

She looked at the Chinese military intelligence officer that was in charge of the room. "Yes?"

"Ma'am, it's time. You can now see our satellite feeds from over Washington, D.C., on screens one through three." He pointed to a set of displays strung out along the ceiling.

"Thank you."

The resolution was, surprisingly, good enough for her to be able to make out individuals. The video all came from a single Chinese intelligence satellite, in a permanent geosynchronous orbit above Washington, D.C. It was used to eavesdrop on the US government agencies and officials who ran them. But it also had great cameras.

All three screens showed different sections of the circular highway that ran around the capital of the United States: I-495, the Washington, D.C. Beltway.

She looked at her watch and did the math in her head. It was time. The afternoon rush hour was picking up. Exactly what they wanted. Maximum impact. Maximum casualties.

"Teams one and two have begun," said one of the Chinese intelligence personnel.

She saw two of the screens zoom in on the highway. Each showed similar scenarios unfolding. A minivan stopped on the Beltway, slowing and eventually blocking traffic. Then the third screen showed that the last of the teams had done the same thing with their minivan. At each location, men from the minivans got out and began pouring gasoline across lanes of traffic. Then they stepped back and lit the liquid, transforming it into a flaming barrier. The smoke distorted some of the overhead view, but it was still good enough for Lena to decipher what was happening.

In each scene, three men spread out across the highway. One man on either side, and one in the middle of the major road. Then they raised their black semiautomatic weapons to their shoulders and began firing into traffic.

She checked her watch. Right on time.

Lena heard a few muffled gasps from the Chinese personnel in the control room. She took a mental note of who seemed the most disturbed. She would have to give their names to the duty section head.

Loyalty and dedication were very important at this stage of the operation. Everything they did was still highly confidential. If word of their operations were to get out to the wrong people now, it could ruin everything.

It was understandable that some of these Chinese military and intelligence personnel were upset by this operation. This team hadn't participated in anything this gruesome before now.

Innocent women and perhaps even children would die. But it was necessary, Lena reminded herself. Was she rationalizing? Yes. But the ends justified the means, however horrible they were.

Lena watched one particular woman, manning her station. She looked to be about thirty years old. The woman covered her mouth as she watched the Iranian men on the screen, gunning down civilians stuck in the traffic jam.

Lena cocked her head. She wondered if this woman had a child at home. Unlikely, as the group assigned to this island was well screened. But this woman was quite upset. That much was clear. That was fine, Lena told herself. Let them be upset. As long as their being upset didn't transition into anything more dangerous, like dissent.

The Beltway attacks hadn't been planned by the Americans in the Red Cell. Jinshan's covert team from the Ministry of State Security had come up with this one.

The operation still fit the Red Cell's overall strategy—frame Iran as the most dangerous enemy of the American people. An enemy that needed to be dealt with immediately. Get the US committed to war with Iran. And while the Americans are focused on Iran, China will make her move.

Jinshan's group of Chinese spies operating in the US had been there for years. Some of his agents had even been there for decades. Lena herself had begun her work for Jinshan that way. A deep seed into the heart of America.

One of the objectives Jinshan had laid out for his team was to uncover agents from other nations who were also conducting espionage inside the US. All the major players had operatives in the D.C. area. The Russians, the Israelis, the British.

Jinshan's team had stumbled onto the Iranian sleeper cell a few years ago. At the time, Lena had been working as a mole in the CIA, stationed in the D.C. area. Jinshan had notified Lena of the Iranians and asked her to gather more information on the group. Information of that sort could be very valuable, should they ever desire to conduct a false flag operation in the future.

When the CIA had transferred Lena to Dubai, she'd handed off the work to another of Jinshan's men. Jinshan's team had continued to find out everything they could about how the Iranians conducted their communication. What were their methods of communication? Their chain of command structure? Who made contact with whom? How often? What types of missions were they intended to conduct? What were their standard operating procedures?

And, important to Lena's current operation, what activities would the Iranian sleeper cell perform on short notice, without having any in-person communication?

Lena had been surprised to hear how amateurish the Iranians were at some things, but how disciplined they were at others. They were great, for instance, at keeping low profiles. Out of the thirteen of them, including the group's leader, only one of them had ever shown up on a US government watch list. Lena had used the CIA's database to check.

But when Jinshan's cyberwarfare hackers had infiltrated the Iranian intelligence organization's computers in Tehran, they had been astounded to find out how many details were kept on file about the group. Everything was there. Their identities, their code names (which were comically unoriginal), and their method of communication.

Jinshan had been very pleased to find out that they would not use steps to double-verify orders if they were to be executed within one week's time. Double-verification of an action order was standard practice with Chinese sleeper agents. This prevented another foreign entity from exploiting the group.

Once Lena and her team had gotten their hands on the Iranian files, they'd begun to draw up plans for what they wanted the Iranian sleeper cell to do, and how they would anonymously communicate it.

The consensus was that an attack on a soft target—highly visible, easily achievable for this group of amateurs—would work best. But it would have to be done in a way that would tie up all loose ends.

"Sir, we're getting video feed from the phones on their vests."

"Please show it on screen," said the duty officer.

One of the large screens in the front of the room changed from overhead satellite footage to a cross-section of twelve video feeds.

"Why are we seeing only twelve?"

"The leader's feed isn't on for some reason."

Lena frowned. That wasn't part of the plan. "Is the cleaner crew ready if we need them?" She had a two-member group ready to take out any of the Iranians that survived the attack. But she didn't want to expose them unless she absolutely had to. It defeated the whole purpose of using the Iranians in the first place. The cleaner crews had connections to the Chinese.

"The cleaners are standing by, if needed," the duty officer said, looking at Lena.

The video feed from the phones was surprisingly clear, but not well focused. The gunmen were walking and jogging, shooting passengers as they sat in their cars or ran in the streets. Lena heard some more gasps from inside the room.

"It looks like one of them has been hit," the duty officer said, pointing to a video screen.

Lena saw the lone video feed that was no longer moving. The image was now half-covered by pavement. She looked up at the overhead satellite feeds until she found the one where the man lay.

A dark patch spread out on the ground next to his now-misshapen head. She searched and found the man who had shot him. A white man with dark hair and civilian clothes held a handgun and was taking cover behind a school bus.

Lena looked at the duty officer and said, "You know what to do." The man nodded and walked over to one of his men. The one who was able to send signals to the phones connected to the heavy vests the men wore.

* * *

Javad watched his men from the overpass. Every instruction had been followed to the letter, except for his own participation. His men didn't know any better.

Instead of four attackers at this location, there would be three. Javad was supposed to leave his own vehicle and get in one of the vans. He was supposed to take his rifle and do exactly what his men were doing. Firing at innocent civilians. But he couldn't bring himself to do it.

Instead, he had driven his own van and parked on the overpass next to one of the target locations. Javad had decided that he would watch the scene for a few moments, and then get a head start on his escape.

He'd arrived seconds before his men had stopped their van on the Beltway. Stopping their vehicle may have been enough to prevent traffic from moving, but the next step would ensure their success. Javad watched as they opened the five-gallon gas cans and poured them onto the highway, lighting it on fire to ensure that traffic stopped.

So many people, sitting in their cars. Looking ahead at the rising smoke. Long tongues of flame whipping up. It was such an eye-catching sight that most of them didn't even see the three of Javad's men fan out amongst them, wearing their protective vests and raising their weapons.

The cracks of gunfire changed everything. Screams erupted from the trapped bystanders. A few of them tried to slam on the gas and force their cars out of the traffic, but those attempts only served to make them the first targets of Javad's men.

The Iranian sleeper cell had been activated. Mobilized into a weapon of—he hated to use the word, but he knew it to be accurate —*terror*.

Spiderwebs of cracked glass appeared on windows and windshields. Dark red blood seeping out of the doors. Cars became coffins. The highway pavement and grass strip next to it became a slaughtering ground.

Javad had wondered if any of his men would object to the orders. Or perhaps they would become less interested when they found out the nature of their target? But it hadn't mattered. He wasn't sure if he should be proud of how efficient they were being, or horrified.

Javad had reminded his men that the greater the cost to the Americans here, the better chance they gave to the Iranian people in their homeland. If the Americans understood the cost of war, who knew how many Iranians they could save? They were defenders of their great nation, Javad had told his men.

He wondered if they had all believed it. They certainly hadn't looked like they had reservations. Once they had the rifles in their hands and moving targets in front of them, perhaps the killer's instinct had taken over.

Javad saw a man in a charcoal suit who lay quivering and bleeding next to his luxury SUV. One of Javad's men shot him in the head and marched on, firing at the fleeing passengers and into the cars.

Javad gripped the metal fence atop the overpass, his mouth

agape. He hadn't even bothered to put his own vest on. He didn't feel there was any need. The three men had walked fifty meters by now. Dozens of bodies lay strewn in their wake. Every few seconds, more cracks of gunfire. Changing of the magazines. Aim. Fire. Repeat.

Then one of Javad's men fell to the ground.

At first Javad thought he had stumbled, but then the second team member—the one who had been walking in the center of the highway—fell backward as well. That one's head turned into a bloody mess.

Javad should have expected it, but it still came as a shock. He hadn't seen any source of resistance. The surprise evaporated by the time he saw the third man killed.

The third man saw the second go down and began walking toward that direction, looking for the attacker. The third man went down in a similar manner. A single headshot. No clear shooter. All three of Javad's men had been killed inside of twenty seconds.

Javad had known that they would die. But he had expected a grand, televised shoot-out with police. After all, they were killing civilians. Who would be fighting back in this group? He didn't see any police cars. He supposed that it was possible there was an unmarked law enforcement vehicle out there in the sea of stopped traffic.

Javad suddenly felt the powerful urge to walk back to his van and grab his own rifle. From his vantage point, he could pick off his men's killer. But that would alert people to his position, and make any attempt to escape much less likely to succeed. Perhaps he could...

The section of highway where his dead men lay exploded into a mix of grey dust and yellow flame.

Javad felt the heat and pressure of the burst and dropped to the ground, alarmed by the explosion. What was going on?

* * *

Chase dropped the third shooter with a single shot to the head and continued to scan for targets. He found none on the highway. The shooting had subsided. Now the only sounds were of car engines, moans, and cries. Cries of anguish and cries of fear.

Chase had used the school bus for cover. Now he walked past it, around the flaming wall that lit up their section of highway.

He found his next target.

The man stood on the overpass, nearly hidden behind the green exit sign that read *Rt 7 Leesburg Pike Falls Church Tysons Corner*. He had a rifle in his hand. The same kind that these gunmen had. Was he a spotter? Or was there more violence to come?

Chase sprinted underneath the overpass and out of view of the man. Then he began to run up the grass hill behind the overpass, to where he would be able to jump the fence and get to the man with the gun.

It was during his climb that the highway behind him exploded.

* * *

The satellite feed had red dots that overlaid the locations of the phones the Chinese were using to activate the vest bombs.

Each vest was filled with a combination of plastic explosive and shrapnel material. They were designed to look and feel like bullet-proof vests, but the phones that were hardwired into them connected to the detonation switch.

The satellite feeds showed that two of the Iranian machine gun teams were still at it, walking their fire through crowds of screaming civilians, stuck in traffic. One of those two feeds now had the flashing blue lights of police vehicles arriving on scene.

But the third satellite feed showed the most "advanced" scenario. Once the gunmen were determined to have been killed, the Chinese duty officer here on the island sent the signal to detonate their vests. Red blinking dots overlaid the satellite feed with a reference number to be sure that they were detonating the right vest.

These explosions served two purposes. They increased the casualties and destroyed much of the evidence. The Chinese team that had put this mission together had used Iranian suppliers when obtaining their explosive materials.

The FBI and ATF would still undoubtedly uncover the identities of the Iranian team. That was expected and intended. But there would be no interrogation. It was always possible that the Iranians might have seen something that would lead a professional investigator to discover that Chinese hands were involved with this operation.

That couldn't happen.

Lena looked at the monitor. On the screen, all three of the Iranian gunmen had been killed before the vests were detonated. But in some of these other sections of the Beltway, where similar attacks were being executed, it was possible that the Iranian attackers might surrender or be captured. The explosive vests made sure that interrogations would not happen.

Lena walked closer to the screen where the vests had already been detonated. "You just detonated three of them. But I see four red markers on that screen. Why has that one not been detonated?"

The duty officer walked over to one of his personnel at their computer terminal and spoke rapidly to him in a low voice. Then the duty officer looked up and said, "Ms. Chou, it looks as if that one is not being worn. It is inside this van here, parked near the top of this highway overpass. We think that this man here is part of the team—one of the Iranians. He is standing on top of the overpass, watching. But he is not wearing his vest."

"Is he in the blast range?"

The duty officer again asked the man at the computer terminal something. Lena saw on the display that a cursor measured the distance from the unexploded vest to the man standing on the overpass.

"He's right on the edge of the kill zone. But if that vest is inside the vehicle, it could affect—"

Lena held up her hand. The duty officer followed her intense gaze back to the satellite feed.

One of the personnel in the room said, "Sir, in scenario number two, all three men have been either killed or captured. Permission to detonate their vests?"

"Yes, execute."

"Proceeding."

Lena said, "If that is indeed the Iranian not wearing a vest, it appears he is being taken into custody."

A white male jumped the fence of the overpass behind the Iranian. The man held up a handgun and walked towards the Iranian. Lena was pretty sure this was the same man who had killed the three attackers just a moment earlier.

The Iranian was much closer to the vehicle than the approaching man. Lena wondered if the Iranian would make a run for the van. That would be preferable, increasing the chances he would be killed the closer he got. But he didn't run. The Iranian kneeled down and placed his hands on the back of his head, obviously following orders.

"Ms. Chou, should we send the cleaner team?"

She said, "No. Detonate the vest immediately."

* * *

Chase walked toward the man, aiming his 9mm Sig at the guy's center mass. The man had dark brown hair and Middle Eastern features.

"Get down on your knees and put your hands on your head," Chase yelled.

The man was already on the ground. Chase thought it looked like he was deciding whether to make a run for it, but then he saw the gun and did as Chase commanded.

Chase took a knee and pulled out his cell phone, careful to keep his weapon pointed at—

The minivan on the other side of the overpass exploded into a burst of smoke and metal.

Chase fell to the ground, instinctively shielding himself from the explosion. He felt pain in his leg but ignored it, retraining his gun sight on the man ahead.

As he looked up, Chase pocketed his phone and huddled closer to the side of the highway, not sure what was going to happen next. He stayed low and hobbled towards his target.

The man was injured and unmoving. He lay on the ground about halfway between the exploded van and where Chase had been positioned. The man had been wounded in several places. Shrapnel from the explosion, Chase realized. It looked like a piece had torn through his arm. A few cuts on his face and legs. But his eyes were open, and at first glance he looked like he would pull through.

Chase huddled over him, keeping his weapon trained on the man. He looked at him, wondering what kind of sick bastard would take part in this sort of thing. There was nothing in his eyes that answered that question.

5

Contadora Island, Panama

Victoria lay on her beach towel, reading her book under the shade of a palm tree. She reached over, grabbed her coconut drink that was resting on the sand, and took a long sip.

She could hear the hollers of her tribe in the distance. Her four pilots had convinced her to come on this trip. A one-day excursion while the USS *Farragut* was in port in Panama City, Panama. They had taken the ferry to Contadora Island. Now, the four men were attempting to surf the endless swells of turquoise-blue water that drove into the bay.

She watched through her sunglasses as Plug got up on a wave, his legs shaking. Caveman pushed him off-balance as he went by and sent him cartwheeling and laughing into the water.

It was good that they were getting a break. She hated to admit it, but the sooner this deployment was over, the better. With the majority of all Naval deployments right now headed towards the Persian Gulf in preparation for a war with Iran, it was maddening to be stuck here in the Eastern Pacific. Everyone wanted to be "over there." The only saving grace was the excellent port stops that this deployment had. Like surfing on a remote island off the coast of Panama, for example.

Victoria wasn't quite the surfing type. Or the bathing suit type, for that matter. She was, however, more than content to place her toes in the sand and sip on her rum-based drink. A good book and a light breeze was all she needed. For once, she left work on the boat.

She actually had brought three books. The first one for fun—the latest by Rick Campbell. The other two books were more for self-improvement. One was on leadership, and the other was Tim Ferriss's *The 4-Hour Workweek*. While she wasn't sure she could get away with working for four hours on deployment, she had heard good things about his way of thinking.

She was a fast reader. She figured if she could get five hours of reading in today, that would knock about half her reading list out. Tomorrow, she was on duty and could probably finish the rest. But it was always good to be prepared in case she went fast, or decided she was in a different mood. As with everything she did, Victoria had a list of books. One of her favorite things to do was cross off items on her list.

Later she would attempt to call her brother David. While they had spoken briefly a few weeks ago, she wanted to catch up with him and make sure that he was alright.

It was incredible what he had been through, and troubling to Victoria that all of his claims weren't being taken seriously by the government. She had read a few newspaper articles that implied his allegations against the Chinese were considered conspiracy theory. But she knew her brother. He was an honest, reliable man.

Much like their father.

She closed her book and lay back against the towel, looking up into the swaying palm leaves and deep blue sky. She needed to reconnect with her father. It was time. It had been long enough. Almost a year since they last had spoken. Since her mother's funeral. Dammit. She needed to return his email. She just didn't know what the hell to say.

Victoria took another sip from her straw and got the slurping sound of a finished drink. She looked at her watch. Well, it was after noon. When in Rome, she decided, and walked barefoot to the tiki bar.

"Another?" the bartender asked.

"Yes, please." She placed her purse on the bar, shuffling through it to find her wallet.

The bartender thumbed up at the TV. "I am very sorry to hear about this. Is crazy, no?"

Victoria frowned in confusion.

"Sorry about what?"

"What is happening in the US. Did you not see?"

She squinted up at the TV, reading the scroll.

IRAN TERROR CELL ATTACKS AMERICANS ON WASH-INGTON D.C. BELTWAY

Over two hundred people confirmed dead. One suspect in custody.

The four pilots' boisterous voices grew louder behind her. "Hey, Boss, easy on the sauce. It's barely lunch!" one of them yelled.

She turned and waved them over to the bar, pointing up at the TV. "Check it out."

Seeing the serious look on her face, Plug said, "What is it?"

"Holy shit." The group called out other variations of the same as they saw the news.

Victoria heard a buzzing sound from her purse and pulled out the phone the ship had issued to all the department heads.

She answered, "Air Boss."

"Ma'am, this is Ensign Gorsky on board the USS *Farragut*. Ma'am, the captain has ordered all personnel back to the ship. Liberty has been rescinded until further notice, ma'am."

She closed her eyes. "Alright. Thank you." Hanging up the phone, she held up her hand as the bartender tried to give her another drink.

"Thanks, but we'll all need to close out. Can you tell me when the next ferry arrives?"

Plug said, "Aw, you've got to be shitting me."

"What is it?" asked Juan.

"We're getting recalled back to the ship."

Victoria looked at her men. "Let's keep things in perspective. A lot of people just lost their lives. Don't complain about liberty today, alright, gents? Especially in front of your sailors."

"Yes, ma'am."

"Come on, let's get our stuff. We've got a ferry to catch."

6

"They found something."

Chase looked up from his computer screen. He sat in one of the multiuse conference rooms that the SILVERSMITH team was using, scrolling through the *Washington Post* on his secure laptop. He had spent much of the day giving interviews to both FBI and CIA investigative teams.

"Let's have it," Chase said.

David and a man Chase knew to be an FBI agent came in, shutting the door behind them. The FBI agent's name was Peter Weese, one of the FBI's liaisons to the CIA. When the SILVERSMITH Task Force had been created, he had become the lone FBI agent on the team.

The Beltway attacks were being portrayed by the media as state-sponsored terrorism. All thirteen men were Iranian. It had been a little over twenty-four hours since they had occurred. FBI interrogators were going to work on the lone Iranian survivor.

Why that asshole hadn't been wearing his suicide vest was

unknown. Chase figured he'd just gotten cold feet. But what had triggered the device to go off?

Chase thought it seemed like he hadn't expected it. Did that mean that there were others in the area who might carry out more attacks on behalf of the Iranians?

Chinese threat or not, this was a new level of danger that Iran posed to the US. Most inside the CIA hadn't thought much of Iran's ability to strike within the United States.

While Iran claimed to have "thousands" of Hezbollah clones waiting around America, Chase had seen CIA threat assessments that those figures were greatly exaggerated.

With this latest attack, though…it had him nervous. It wouldn't be the first time the analysts had been wrong.

Weese looked around the room like he didn't want anyone to hear him when he spoke. "They've been interviewing the Iranian. And they have a few leads."

"And?"

"He gave up a few details that prove to be *very* interesting to our task force here. *Chinese* connections." He nodded his head as he spoke.

"Really?" Chase looked at his brother David and then back at the FBI agent. "Who knows about this?"

"Susan's briefing the director right now. You and I are about to go join her. But she asked me to come fill you in first. She said that we'd likely require your expertise."

"How so?"

"The Iranian received a communication a few days ago. Then they received minivans filled with weapons and the explosive vests. We were able to trace the vehicles, weapons, and explosive residue. The results are preliminary, but…it looks like it will be a dead end."

"Come on, Weese. Don't slow-play me. Give me the punch line."

He smiled. "Alright. It was the initial communication. They left some folder in a van in an alleyway in Maryland. There were no cameras in that area, so we couldn't see who put the van there. But there was only one building that had a view of it. The Iranian said he had to destroy the envelope. We figured they would want to be able to see that, to make sure it got done right. So we went over footage of the only building that had a vantage point on that alleyway. It's a big brick apartment complex. Lots of people coming and going every day. But only one of them showed up on our watch list."

David added, "The Chinese counterespionage watch list." Chase noticed that David was still a little awkward in his delivery. He was still finding his way in the conversation, getting comfortable in his new line of work.

Peter said, "FBI Counterespionage has been following a particular employee at the State Department for a few years. They're very confident that he's a Chinese plant. He feeds his handlers anything and everything he gets."

"How do you know?"

"We've had an ongoing blue dye operation. We provided specific details to single individuals. Single-variable testing. This allowed us to see which version popped up on the other end. Like I said, we're *very* confident he's working for the Chinese."

David hadn't thought about that part of the problem. He leaned forward, incredulous. "Wait, so you've known that this guy was working in our government, and you just kept letting him work there?"

The FBI agent looked at Chase and then back at David. "That's how the game is played, my friend. Sometimes it's more valuable to know who the spies are and leave them in place. It allows us to control the information flow."

David shook his head.

Chase didn't blink, saying, "And this Chinese spook was in the building across the street from the Iranian dead drop? The one that gave them orders to conduct the Beltway attacks?"

"Yes, sir."

Chase shook his head. "Why the hell would the Chinese have the Iranians go through with this? They have to know that eventually we'd get to the bottom of it."

David said, "You know why. It's the same reason that the Chinese have eighteen Americans in a prison in the South China Sea. The same reason they're staging a war between us and Iran. This is just one more piece of evidence for what I've been saying this whole time. We've got to wake up. The Chinese want us to go to war with Iran. It's in their best interests to keep us otherwise occupied..."

The FBI agent looked at Chase. "Susan said to join her in the director's office in ten minutes."

Chase stood. "Alright, well...let's go."

* * *

Chase and Special Agent Weese arrived at the director's office a few moments later. Susan, the CIA staff operations officer in charge of SILVERSMITH, was waiting in the chamber room outside the office. The director's administrative assistant motioned for Chase and Special Agent Weese to sit next to Susan.

"The director will be with you all momentarily."

"Thanks," Chase said.

Despite his confident demeanor, he was still a little uneasy about being brought into such a high-level meeting for the first time.

Susan leaned over to him as he sat down, whispering, "Has Weese briefed you?"

"Yes, just now."

"Do you have any questions?"

Chase gave her a look that said, *Of course I have questions.* "A few."

The secretary rose from his chair and opened the large wooden door leading to the director's office. "The director will see you now."

Susan whispered, "Just follow my lead. Try not to say anything provocative."

The three of them walked into the director's office. There were two leather couches that faced inward, and a small coffee table in the center. An older man in a suit sat on one of the couches. Chase thought he looked familiar, but couldn't place the face. The other couch was bare. The director sat in a wooden chair on the far end of the coffee table.

"Come in, folks."

The director of the CIA was a former congressman. He had been on the House Intelligence Committee for several years before the new president plucked him out of a safely red state. Before he had been a congressman, he had served as an Army JAG for twenty years. While Chase didn't like lawyers or politicians much, he respected the fact that the man had military service. And from what he heard, the director was one sharp cookie.

"Mr. Manning, I was reading the file you put together on what happened in Dubai a few weeks ago. A most interesting read. Especially the part about Miss Parker. Or should I say Miss Chou." Their eyes locked.

Chase reddened a bit. He had rightly included everything in his post-mission report, including his own relationship to the woman he now knew to be Lena Chou.

"Yes, sir" was all he could think to respond with.

"Well, I can't fault you, son. If the counterespionage group didn't know about her, we couldn't expect you to. And I'm very impressed with how you handled the situation. I'm sure that your brother is grateful as well."

"I believe he is, sir."

"And Susan tells me that his information has been quite a value added to our new China task force—SILVERSMITH."

"Sir, David is glad that people are taking action on his knowledge. Although he is concerned—and I share this concern—that there are still Americans being held captive by the Chinese on the Red Cell island."

Out of the corner of his eye, Chase saw Susan grimace.

The man on the couch said, "That has been vigorously denied by our counterparts in China. And some of our most reliable sources are not able to corroborate that information."

Chase had two voices in his head. One was Susan's, telling him to hold his tongue. He thought that might be wise, considering he didn't even know the name of this man on the couch who was challenging him. The other voice was his brother's.

"Sir, respectfully, if you were an adversarial nation who had just conducted an act of espionage—an act of war—I wouldn't expect you to be the most honest source of information on the subject."

Director O'Malley smiled. "Susan, Chase, please...have a seat." He motioned to the couch and sat back down in his chair. "Chase, this is the president's national security advisor, Charlie Sheppard."

Chase felt like an idiot for not recognizing who he was.

The director said, "Susan has just finished walking us through the update on a possible Chinese connection with the Beltway attacks."

"It's circumstantial," said the NSA. "Maybe this Chinese spy was in the building across the street for another reason. Or maybe he was even watching the Iranians, but he wasn't the one who had planted the orders to strike. We need to give the FBI more time to do their job and investigate."

Chase stayed quiet. The public fury over the attacks was like nothing he'd seen since September 11, 2001. There were over two hundred innocent civilians dead. Many of them were government employees or family members. Everyone in the D.C. area knew someone who had been affected. And the reports from the media all pointed to one source: Iran.

Chase wouldn't argue with that. It *was* the Iranians who had attacked. He had seen that with his own eyes. But just like the attacks in Dubai a few weeks ago, there was more to the story.

"Susan? Anything you want to add?" the director asked.

She crossed her legs. "Gentlemen, I agree that the FBI needs time to complete their investigation. But there are other things at play here, as you well know. Right now our military is preparing to strike in Iran. This is the second Iranian attack on US military or civilian personnel in a few weeks. Both times, there have been links to the Chinese. We can't ignore that."

"And we won't ignore it," Sheppard said. "But the president can't ignore that a radical Islamic nation that hates everything we stand for has just attacked our country. We need to strike back, and strike back *hard*. To send them a message—to send the whole world a message—that you can't mess with the United States and get away with it. And you know what, I don't care if the Chinese *were* involved. They didn't pull the triggers. The Iranians did. So don't you tell me that the Iranians were innocent."

"Sir, with all due respect, I was there on scene. I know that the Iranians weren't innocent."

The director spoke softly. "Chuck, Chase was driving home on the Beltway when it happened. He took down three of the terrorists, saving a lot of lives. And he helped capture the only one that was taken alive. Please cut him a little slack."

The NSA raised an eyebrow. "You did all that, huh? Well, I thank you for what you've done. But you must understand that these are tense times. We can't be playing games here. You of all people should realize that."

Susan spoke up. "Sir, I think what my colleague Mr. Manning is trying to say is that, if the Chinese were involved—if they triggered the attack somehow—then attacking Iran won't be the right response."

The NSA said, "Tell me how attacking the country that just attacked us isn't the right response."

Susan said, "Sir, the Chinese wouldn't have done this without a reason. We have evidence that they've been fanning the flames of a conflict between the United States and Iran for several weeks now, if not longer. If we attack Iran, we'd be playing into their hands. And with the intelligence David Manning has given us—"

The NSA scoffed. "David Manning. This is the guy that we arrested a few weeks ago for cyberterrorism with Iran?"

The director held up his hand. "Now, Chuck, that was a misinformation campaign. Which we also believe had roots in China. David Manning has been completely cleared. I can speak to that. His interviews and background checks over the past few weeks have been extremely thorough."

"But you know that not all the information he's given us checks out," Sheppard said. "Our own assets in China are saying that they have no idea about any Americans in captivity on an island, and that they had nothing to do with the Dubai attacks."

Director O'Malley held up his hand. "We're looking into that further." The director looked at Chase. "Chase, I apologize for any discomfort it causes you for us to discuss your brother like this. I assure you that we trust him; otherwise, I would not have invited him to be a part of the SILVERSMITH operation. And, quite frankly, you wouldn't be in this room. But there are, as Mr. Sheppard points out, *inconsistencies* with other bits of intelligence coming out of China."

Chase fumed but stayed quiet. He noticed that the NSA cast a glance at him when he mentioned his brother's name. Chase knew there were members of the government who didn't trust the information coming from his brother. But he hadn't seen such an overt questioning of the accuracy of David's word at this high a level.

Chase also began to wonder just why was *he* in this room. A high-level meeting like this wasn't something that someone in his community—the CIA's Special Operations Group—was normally invited to.

Director O'Malley said, "We have human intelligence coming out of China—sources in both the PLA and the Chinese government. And they don't match up with a large-scale Chinese military attack. For instance, aside from the military buildup at the Red Cell island, there aren't any indications of troop movements."

The NSA said, "It's the Central Committee that I care most about. The PLA wouldn't do anything unless the Central Committee okays it. And your sources in the Central Committee have always been good, right?"

"I'm familiar with these sources, sir. And that is correct, they've always been very reliable," Susan said.

Sheppard said, "And to be clear, the Central Committee sources have reported nothing unusual. No reports of military activity, buildups, increased training…"

"That's correct, sir."

"And no secret plans to kidnap Americans and bring them to the Red Cell island?" he persisted.

She shifted in her seat. "Sir, while that's accurate, our current hypothesis is that Jinshan's group in the Ministry of State Security might have—"

"Aw, that's bullshit, and you know it. There's no way an operation of that size and scope could have gone through Jinshan alone. Yes, I understand that he's got a lot of pull over there. But—and this is information coming from you guys"—he pointed at the three CIA members, leaning forward and raising his eyebrows—"there is no military movement that indicates the Chinese are going to attack American forces. Is that right?"

Susan sighed. "Sir, I admit that we have more work to do. The human intelligence sources in China don't fully corroborate David Manning's information. But I would point out that we still have eighteen missing Americans, some of whom are high-level-clearance types from our military and intelligence communities. These are the same people David Manning and Henry Glickstein say were on the Red Cell island."

The NSA raised his voice. "Well, it sure would be nice if you could get us on that island, or get the Chinese to give us a tour. But all our channels, including our military and intelligence back channels, have assured us that there are no Americans on that island, and that all that information David Manning gave us is conspiracy theory bullshit." He looked at Chase. "Son, I mean no offense."

Chase looked at the NSA. He clenched his fists under the coffee table. *I've killed better men than you.* He said, "None taken."

The NSA said, "I'm sure your brother believes he is telling the truth. And he might be. But the president needs to take action on real, hard evidence. Verifiable proof. And the Beltway attacks…the Persian Gulf attacks…ladies and gentlemen, I can say without a doubt that the Iranians were responsible in a *big* way. Let's focus on that."

Silence.

Chase now knew that any arguments he made would be falling on deaf ears with the NSA. This guy was a politician, and a certifiable idiot. He was reading the papers and reacting to the press and the fury of the people. What he needed to do was make smart, rational decisions based on intelligence information, even if they were hard and unpopular decisions.

But as Chase thought about the men, women, and children he had seen killed on the pavement of I-495, he realized that he couldn't blame anyone for reacting emotionally. Chase wanted to hit someone. To strike back, and take revenge. It was human nature.

However, if China and/or Jinshan had orchestrated these Iranian attacks on the United States, that would be the exact response they wanted us to take.

Susan said, "Gentlemen, we also now have a significant amount of evidence built around Lena Chou and Cheng Jinshan's involvement in the Dubai Bitcoin Exchange conspiracy—as well as Lena's espionage while within the CIA."

"I've read your reports tying Lisa Parker to the Chinese," the NSA said. "And I saw the footage of her in Bandar Abbas. The Chinese deny that she was ever in their country. They say she wasn't a Chinese citizen. We don't have much ground to stand on there either."

Susan was visibly annoyed. "Sir, we're very confident that she was a Chinese agent. And we know it was her in Bandar Abbas. She was the one who assassinated the Iranian politician, Ahmad Gorji."

"That may be true. But the president isn't convinced that Parker's actions in Bandar Abbas absolve Iran of any culpability in the Persian Gulf attacks. They actually killed Americans. They shot missiles at our Navy ships. That is real. That matters. Cold, hard facts. And I'll say another thing." He pointed his finger at the group. "You guys might not like hearing this, but the fact that you had a Chinese agent working in the CIA for years actually *hurts* your credibility. Not *helps*."

No one spoke for a few moments.

The director took a deep breath and said, "Susan, let's talk about next steps on the Chinese connection to the Beltway attacks."

Susan, red-faced and flustered, tried to regain her composure. "As I was briefing you earlier, we have a very high degree of confidence that there is a US State Department employee who is a member of Cheng Jinshan's espionage ring. He's the one who was spotted at the building across the street from the Iranian dead drop. We believe"—she looked at the NSA—"that there is at least a *possibility* that he activated the Beltway attacks."

The director said, "What would you like to do?"

"We've been going back and forth on this with the FBI." She looked at Special Agent Weese, who hadn't said a word this whole time. "We'd like them to take this Chinese operative in for questioning, and would ask that the FBI allow us to listen in on the interview and share information. We feel that there is a high enough threat to our nation that it is warranted."

The NSA shook his head. "Do you realize what a headache that would be if you're wrong? The president will never sign off on that. Like I said, your evidence is based on conflicting and circumstantial reports."

Special Agent Weese said, "Sir, we at the FBI feel that we would have support from the courts. We've gotten a FISA warrant on this particular person already. The evidence gathered there supports taking him in for questioning."

"I don't care about the courts, I care about what State and the president will say—do they already know about this? What are you going to say when they go on the news and say that the CIA just grabbed a US citizen on American soil because of China? Not *Iran*, who everyone knows just killed innocent Americans, but China?"

Chase glared at the man. "I would say that the Chinese are holding eighteen of our own citizens as part of an espionage operation. And that this State Department employee is a known spy, who may have contributed to one of the most heinous terrorist attacks ever to have been committed on US soil. And that we should go after the source of the attacks—the root cause—not just whoever pulled the trigger."

"Watch your tone, young man. I'll remind you that I'm the national security advisor. I outrank you by just a little bit."

Chase caught sight of the director placing his palm upward, signaling to Chase to tone it down. The director looked at Susan. "What do you hope to get from this guy—the Chinese operative that works in the US State Department? If he really did this…"

Susan said, "Our ultimate objective is to get hard evidence on China's connection to these attacks, and to find out why our human intel reports out of China aren't matching up with David Manning's information."

The NSA looked at his watch and stood. "I'm sorry, folks. But I haven't seen enough to sign off on that. And I know the president will feel the same way. Now if you'll excuse me, I've got a meeting in the Oval Office in about forty minutes, and I can't be late."

The group stood, and the NSA left the room. Director Buckingham walked him out, saying something that Chase couldn't hear.

When the door was closed, the director sat back down, this time on the couch across from Chase and Susan. He looked at each of them.

"What do you guys think?"

Susan said, "Sir, from my understanding, we have a matter of days before the US begins its shock and awe campaign on Iran. At that point, there'll be no turning back. If this is China's doing, they'll have achieved their goal. Maybe they already have, since we have such a high concentration of military forces redeployed to the Middle East."

Director Buckingham said, "You don't have to sell me anymore, Susan."

He looked at all three of them, a deadly serious expression on his face. "This Chinese spy in the US State Department—take him. Soon. Find out what he knows. And use our best interrogation team. The contractor."

Susan said, "But what about the—"

"*I'll* handle the national security advisor."

* * *

The next night, Chase and Susan arrived at Joint Base Andrews as part of a convoy of two CIA-owned SUVs and an ambulance. The area had been cleared of nonessential personnel. They used the same security procedures for moving the president during times of national emergency. No one wanted a wayward set of eyes to witness who they had on the stretcher.

The vehicles drove right up to the Gulfstream G-V, and people began moving. The ambulance doors opened, and three men transferred the man on the gurney, and his IV, up the stairs of the aircraft and into the specially designed back compartment of the cabin.

A group of five other government personnel sat in the forward part of the aircraft cabin. They were the customers. The notetakers. The ones who would have the interrogator adjust his line of questioning in the same manner that a marketing executive would ask the interviewer to change their questions with a focus group.

Only now the subject was a Chinese spy.

"Manning, right?" One of the five counterespionage agents shook Chase's hand.

"That's right."

"Thanks for joining us. I read about Dubai. Sounds like you were right in the middle of the action."

"I guess so." Chase nodded to the back of the plane. "You helped with the grab and bag?"

"Yeah. We picked him up about twelve hours ago. The IV's in, so he's getting in the right state of mind now. The Doctor's giving him a little bit of time to let the drugs do their work, and then we'll get started. The Doctor is something else. Interesting ideas, that's for sure. We had to conduct a simultaneous operation in Chengdu."

"What for?"

"Ah, you'll see, I'm sure."

"The Doctor," as he was known, was a retired warrant officer, who had effectively written the book on modern interrogation techniques. He was fifty years old and now performed his work as a contractor. The CIA and other US military and intelligence units flew him around the world whenever they had information that absolutely needed to be extracted. He was widely considered to be the single best interrogator in the Western world.

Chase had heard of the man when he was in Iraq. Whispers about this magician who was ten times better and faster than all the other interrogators. But he'd never seen him in real life. Until now.

One of the agents shut the door of the aircraft. "Alright, time to get started."

On the monitors, Chase could see that the Chinese operative was stripped down to his underwear and tied to a gurney. The gurney was tilted at an angle so that the Chinese man's head was about six inches lower to the ground than his feet.

"Are you cold?" the Doctor asked. He spoke in English, although he knew several languages. A CIA translator sat in the cabin of the plane, in case he was needed.

"Yes," the Chinese man replied in English.

The plane's engines began warming up. Chase looked at the men next to him.

"Are we taking off?" Chase asked. He spoke softly, even though he knew that the Chinese prisoner couldn't hear him behind the closed compartment in the back of the aircraft.

"Yeah," said the CIA man who had picked him up. "It's part of the theatrics—and since we'll be in international airspace when the interrogation is conducted, it allows us to get past some legal issues. Don't worry, though, we'll be landing back at Andrews."

Chase and the others put on headphones so they could hear the interrogation better.

The Chinese handler said, "What is that noise?"

"We're on a plane, my friend," the Doctor said. "We're headed to Cuba. Guantanamo Bay."

A twitch on the Chinese man's face. If he was a Chinese intelligence agent, he no doubt had training in counterinterrogation techniques. The Doctor would be earning his money today.

The Doctor said, "Let's start with what I already know. I know your name. All of them. I know where you're from. I know what you ate for breakfast this morning. I know whom you are sleeping with. And I know that you work for Cheng Jinshan, and the Chinese Ministry of State Security."

The Chinese man didn't move.

The aircraft began to shake as it rolled down the runway, the jet engines pushing it into the air, climbing upward.

"Your life is over. Everything that you ever knew is now gone. All the training they gave you to prepare you for this moment—just throw it away. You see, that counterinterrogation training presumes that somehow, someday, you will be freed. That the United States will let you out, or trade you back to China. But that will not happen. Because we will make it look like you are dead. It is a certainty that you will stay in Guantanamo Bay Prison for the rest of your life, however long or short that may be. But no one outside a small group of Americans will ever know that you are still alive. The only thing you can do now is to affect the quality of your life in that prison."

The Chinese man stared back, slightly shivering. He didn't say anything.

"Are you willing to discuss Cheng Jinshan, and matters that relate to him?"

The man said nothing.

"Alright. I want you to see something. Think about a life in prison, with no outside contact. Think about that while you watch and listen to this."

The Doctor placed headphones on the Chinese man's ears and pressed a button on a device. A video appeared.

The man's face contorted. After a few seconds, he began crying. Slowly at first, but as the video played, the crying turned into uncontrollable sobs.

On one of the monitors, a cute little girl, probably about age three or four, stood cuddled next to her mom's leg. She was speaking to the camera, smiling and laughing.

Chase said, "What is that?"

"Recordings from his family. The guy has a wife and daughter in Chengdu. We had our agents in China reach out to them at the exact same time that we bagged this guy. Our agents posed as a holiday greeting card company. They got the daughter to answer a few questions about her father. Our agents told them that they were sending him a loving message. The one from the daughter is especially touching."

On the other monitor, Chase saw the Doctor as he removed the Chinese man's headphones. He stayed quiet for a few moments. The occasional sniffle from the Chinese man was the only sound from the interrogation room.

"Would you like me to play it again?" asked the Doctor.

The man shook his head no. The altitude of the aircraft leveled off.

"We know that you aren't the one that ordered the Beltway attacks."

Silence.

"And I promise you that you won't be blamed. But you were part of it. You passed on information to the Iranians. We know that, too."

No response.

"You will need to go to prison for the rest of your life. Here. Please watch the video again. I want to make sure that you understand what this will mean for you."

The video of his wife and daughter appeared again. They answered more questions, laughing and smiling. The video lasted a full minute.

When it ended, no one spoke for a few moments. Then the Chinese man said, "What do you propose?"

"I will not ever lie to you," the Doctor said. "I want you to know that. As a testament to that relationship of honesty, I will tell you something that you will not be happy with now. You will need to go to prison for the rest of your life. That will not change. But your punishment could be much worse. And there are many different types of prisons. You see, I can also promise you that if you help us get information that we need, you'll be able to get more videos and recordings of your daughter and wife. That surely would be a more desirable alternative than any other circumstances, would it not? It is better to have something to look forward to. Better than decades of looking at a wall, in between interrogations."

The man tried to control himself, but he kept crying.

"But this is a onetime offer. You only get one chance at this. Again, this is the honest truth. I will always be honest with you. I know from experience that honesty between me and my subjects is the only way to get a mutually beneficial exchange."

The Chinese man did not reply.

"Are you uncomfortable? Can I make you more comfortable?"

The man was upside down and mostly naked. On the high-definition video, Chase could see goose bumps on his arms. But he said nothing.

The Doctor said, "I will now be honest with you about the consequences of not accepting this arrangement. We're airborne now. It will be several hours until we reach our destination. Guantanamo Bay, Cuba. When we get there, our relationship will end. I will be forced to hand you over to another interrogator. He is not kind like I am. He believes in pain. He will hurt you. For the rest of your life, he will hurt you. And once you are his prisoner, I will have no control over what happens to you. He doesn't make offers like I do. He only threatens and punishes."

The man sniffed.

"Let's watch the video again."

The video played again. The man cried some more. Chase realized that the Doctor was using a form of emotional waterboarding. It was like he was dunking his mind into and out of the only thing that could really get to the man—his wife and child. The interrogator was using the video and audio to immerse him in that environment. Over and over and over. It was breaking him down. Forcing him to consider a life of misery, without the only thing that truly made him happy.

When the video was over, the Doctor said, "Let's start with something simple. I will ask you a question. If you tell me the answer, which I already know, then I will let you put your clothes back on. Another truthful answer, and I'll let you sit up while we finish our discussion like civilized men. Will that work?"

He nodded. "Alright. Alright. Please."

It took them a full five minutes to get the Chinese man upright and clothed. He looked groggy. Probably from whatever was getting pumped into his bloodstream. They conversed for over an hour. About little things at first. A lot of questions about the Chinese man's family.

Chase marveled about the ease with which they talked. If this man was really a Chinese spy, he would know what to do and what to expect when being questioned. But the Doctor had found the single weak point in his defenses and exploited it masterfully. His emotional reaction to his daughter cut through everything else.

When the Doctor finally got to the questions about Jinshan and China's part in the Beltway attacks, he became very cooperative. The CIA men furiously typed notes and sent information in real time to the SILVERSMITH team at Langley.

When the interview was done, the Doctor made a hand gesture as if he was ready for the check at a restaurant. That was the signal to take the aircraft back to Joint Base Andrews.

The CIA team had been hopeful that they would find evidence of a connection between the Chinese and the Iranian attacks. Even so, none of them could believe what they had just heard.

* * *

Within two hours of landing, Chase and Susan were once again in the office of the director of the CIA.

The director said, "Let's hear it, folks. What did you find?"

Susan gave him the important points, providing details when asked. After speaking for about ten minutes, she finished with, "Sir, to summarize, it appears that Cheng Jinshan has been micro-managing this all himself. We believe that he has someone in the People's Liberation Army Navy—probably the South Sea Fleet Commander—working with him. That's the only way he could have pulled this off. Jinshan has his own intelligence network—a team of spies that he has been grooming and working with for decades. Many of them, including Lena Chou, have apparently infiltrated US government agencies and institutions."

"Do you have more names?"

"A few, sir, yes. The counterespionage teams at the CIA and FBI are both on it."

"Good."

"Sir, on the issue of providing evidence to American and Chinese leadership—a lot of this won't be provable. It won't be the smoking gun that we need to prove it to the Chinese president."

"Why not?" the director asked.

"If the Chinese don't accept that Lena Chou was a spy, we wouldn't expect this guy to be any better leverage. Jinshan likely operated his network of spies in such a way that almost no one in the Chinese government had access to their names."

The director stood up and paced around his office. "I see. What next? Folks, we need something clear-cut."

Susan replied, "We're working on that, sir. Our best lead is that the Chinese spy seemed to think that there might be some Chinese military movement in Latin America—he called it pre-positioning. The interrogations are continuing. And we're following up on all the leads that we've developed so far. We've started to look into this Vice Admiral Song—he's the South Sea Fleet Commander of the PLA Navy. So far it looks like he's the senior military conspirator aiding Jinshan. This guy was stationed in the same locations as Cheng Jinshan on several occasions of the past few decades. Our contacts in Guangzhou are telling us that they've been seen together several times this year. This lead shows promise."

The intercom on the table came on, with the secretary's voice saying, "Director, General Schwartz is here to see you."

"Send him in, please."

The Army three-star general marched in. He had close-cropped grey hair and wore his Army service uniform.

Chase glanced over the uniform. One thing he appreciated about the military was that you could learn a lot about someone just by looking at their chest candy. The RANGER tab, the Master Parachutist Badge with two Combat Jump Devices, the United States Special Operations Command Badge, a Silver Star, a Bronze Star with four oak leaf clusters, Afghanistan Campaign Medal and Iraq Campaign Medal—both with multiple campaign stars. This man was the real deal.

"Good evening, team."

"Thank you, Susan," the director said, "that will be all."

Chase and Susan both got up to leave.

The director said, "Chase, please stay seated."

Susan and Chase looked at each other, and then Chase sat back down. Susan departed the room.

When it was just the three of them, the director said, "The general needs to provide you with a new set of orders."

"Yes, sir."

The general looked at Chase. "Let me ask you a question, son. Do you know why we named this Operation SILVERSMITH?"

"I must confess that I don't, sir."

"There was a famous silversmith in our nation's history. That man rode through the night on horseback, warning of an impending invasion by soldiers cloaked in red."

"Paul Revere."

"The one and only. You see the symbolism there, don't you? Don't ever say that a West Point grad can't be a poet."

Chase smiled politely.

"You're our Paul Revere, son. The analogy isn't perfect. We don't yet know if we're about to be attacked by the largest standing army in history. Paul Revere was warning of an impending attack. Your role will be to warn certain elements of the American military and set them into motion."

The director chimed in, "Chase, we're going to need you to act as a messenger for a select group of military and intelligence assets. Ones that we need to get moving now, in case we need them later."

The general lowered his voice. "Your actions will allow Operation SILVERSMITH to fulfill its two main objectives. One, to confirm the threat we're facing. And two, to move some of our chess pieces on the board in a way that will counter that threat."

Chase said, "Understood. What do I need to do?"

The general handed him a file. "Some light reading. We'll go through it quick. You've got a plane to catch."

7

80 Nautical Miles East of Norfolk, Virginia

The two grey MH-60S Seahawk helicopters flew in a loose trail formation, two hundred feet over the water. Chase was in the first aircraft. He wore green digital fatigues, a large black cloth Trident sewn onto his left breast, above the US NAVY lettering. MANNING was on the right breast, a Velcro American flag on his right shoulder, and a small dark suitcase handcuffed to his right wrist.

Upon landing, the aircrewman shuffled him to someone wearing the white shirt and headgear of the air transfer officer. Everyone on the carrier deck had a distinct color that was associated with their role on the flight deck. The man in white motioned for Chase to follow him under the spinning rotors and into the superstructure of the enormous new aircraft carrier.

Moments later he stood at the door of the captain's cabin. His father sat on the couch. Another man, who he assumed to be the captain of the USS *Ford*, sat in the dark brown leather chair next to him. A small coffee table was in the center of the room, on top of a rug with the ship's crest.

"Chase, this is Captain Chuck Stewart."

They shook hands. The door was closed, and Chase unlocked the handcuff and opened the briefcase. He handed a single envelope, marked with the purple TOP SECRET/SCI stamp, to his father. There were several pages in the orders, and his father looked up at Chase a few times while he read.

When Admiral Arthur Louis Manning IV, commander of the USS *Ford* Carrier Strike Group, was finished reading, he handed the orders to the captain. He read the first few paragraphs and said, "You have *got* to be shitting me." He kept reading and then looked up.

Admiral Manning said to his son, "What these orders tell us to do...there is only one reason for that."

Chase nodded.

"Why the hell are they sortieing all our military assets to the Middle East and having *us* do this?" Captain Stewart said. "If they're worried about China, why don't they strengthen the Pacific theater?"

The admiral raised an eyebrow. "Why, indeed?" He stood up and walked to the back corner of the room, looking out a porthole that revealed the flight deck.

Chase said, "CINCLANT wants me to reiterate that this is for your eyes only. No one on your staffs can know about these orders right now—not until authorized."

His father snorted.

The aircraft carrier captain said, "That's ridiculous. Now how the hell are we supposed to get aircraft, parts, and supplies on board? It's our staff that's gotta do all the work and planning to make this happen." He held up the papers. "This won't happen unless we tell our staffs what to do."

"Yes, sir, I understand that you'll need to communicate what to do. The request is that you don't inform them why, until it becomes absolutely necessary."

"Chase?" His father spoke gently.

"Yes?"

"How many people know about this?"

"I asked the same question."

"And?"

"Fewer than one hundred. It has the highest level of classification."

"I see." The admiral walked over to the couch and sat back down. "I'm going to speculate here. There could be two reasons for secrecy of that magnitude. One, they want plausible deniability. That just doesn't fit here. We're talking about taking protective action, not about launching a strike."

"Not yet," said the captain. "But those orders say to be prepared to—"

"Yes. But still—they aren't keeping this a secret because they're afraid of the public finding out. That's my point."

The captain said, "Why, then?"

"Because they don't trust the normal channels of communication." The admiral stopped. He looked at Chase and said, "Why on earth are you delivering this to me?"

Chase smiled. "General Schwartz is working at the CIA. I'm on Task Force SILVERSMITH with him. He made the connection and thought that my going here might be appropriate. Yours is not my only stop."

The admiral nodded.

The captain said, "We're going to have to break a lot of rules to get this done."

"Yes, we are," said the admiral.

"And we're going to have some coconspirators. Who's gonna tell the USS *Michael Monsoor* and the F-35 guys about the plan?" He looked at Chase.

"Sir, I briefed the *Michael Monsoor*'s skipper yesterday. They'll be at the rendezvous in a few days. And as soon as we're done here, I'll be headed to Eglin Air Force Base and then to Yuma to round up the F-35 support. Most units already have an activation order, but they don't have all the information. I'm to provide that on a need-to-know basis to the unit commanders."

The admiral shook his head. "Look at you. Secret agent man. You try to get out of the Navy, and the CIA throws you back at us."

Chase smiled. "Sir, do you have any further questions about your orders?"

His father smiled. "No, son. That will be all. Come on, I'll walk you back down to the flight deck."

* * *

A few days later, Admiral Manning stood on the admiral's bridge, watching a flight of four F-35Cs conduct the break overhead. One by one, each aircraft banked hard left, then came around and landed on the carrier.

It had been a whirlwind few days, and there were many more to come. The USS *Ford* had pulled back into Norfolk for a day. Thousands of personnel immediately had come aboard from the air wing and spent hours furiously unloading parts and supplies.

Families—and the ship's personnel—were told that it was a last-minute additional training mission. But the admiral suspected that many of them knew better. Modern carrier strike group movements were planned years in advance. To conjure one up out of thin air—in a week's time—was unprecedented.

Two days later, the USS *Ford* joined up with her surface ships. Two destroyers, including the latest of the Zumwalt class, the USS *Michael Monsoor*. A supply ship, two littoral combat ships, and a Los Angeles–class submarine. Although only a select few knew that the submarine was tagging along.

"Afternoon, Admiral." Captain Stewart was all smiles. He loved getting aircraft aboard. That was what this ship was meant to do. He was tired of all the training and certification the *Ford* had been doing.

"Hello, Chuck. Anything new?"

"Sir, I triple-checked the Panama Canal for you. I'm now one hundred percent sure that even with the widening they just did, we still can't fit through. We're gonna have to go the long way."

The admiral shook his head. "Unbelievable. The United States made the damn canal, and we're the only navy in the world that makes ships that are so big that they can't fit through it. How long will it take to get to the other side?"

"Sir, the trip around South America will take several weeks."

"How many?"

"Well, the *Ford* can do it in two. But we've got to wait up for the slowest ships in company."

"I'm familiar…how many weeks, Chuck?"

"We think we can do it in three weeks at seventeen knots. We'll have to plan for about four replenishments at sea during that time."

"I know I don't have to tell you this, but just in case there is any confusion—we aren't stopping in port."

"Yes, sir. I've made that clear to the navigator."

"Alright. Thanks, Chuck."

"Yes, sir. Oh, and the supply officer told me to tell you that we're having steaks tonight."

The admiral smiled. "Well, now you've done it. Every Tom, Dick, and Harry on board will know that something awful is about to happen if we give them steak."

"Yes, sir." The carrier captain smiled and left the space.

Admiral Manning resumed watching the jets land. The F-35s had all been retrieved. Now it was time for the Growlers. A pair of F-18s zoomed overhead, the first one entering the break…followed shortly by the second.

He could see an Arleigh Burke–class destroyer several miles away, pitching and rolling in the sea. A Seahawk helicopter was landing on her. The admiral sighed as he thought about his daughter. She was right where they were headed. He prayed that this all turned out to be nothing.

8

Beijing, China

The Chinese president, general secretary of the Central Committee of the Communist Party of China and chairman of the Central Military Commission, was not having a good day. He placed his elbows on his large oak desk, closed his eyes, and rubbed his temples.

"Would you like some more tea, sir?" the stewardess asked.

The Chinese president waved the woman away without looking up. "No. Please give us privacy. No calls or visitors."

It was just the two of them—the president and his most trusted member of the Politburo, who was also one of the few members of his National Security Commission.

The Chinese president said, "You must understand the sensitivity of this matter. If it appears in any way that there is dissent among the party…that I am not in complete control of the military or intelligence community…then that would not bode well for us."

The Politburo member said, "I agree. That is why I have asked to speak with you alone."

The Chinese president shook his head, holding out his hands.

"Why do the Americans keep pressing us on this? They *must* know that we are being truthful."

"As I said, Mr. President, they have a very sophisticated intelligence apparatus. For my contacts in Washington to be reaching out to me for a third time and speaking to me in this manner is very unusual. *Unless there is something to it.* Something that you and I are not aware of."

The Chinese president looked up. "The Americans are getting paranoid. They have been attacked and are about to go to war in the Middle East again."

"And you think that explains this line of accusation, even through back-channel communications?"

"I truly don't know. I just don't understand why these rumors of Chinese meddling persist. There is too much for us to lose if we were to behave this way. The Central Committee would never jeopardize trade with the United States by allowing the kidnapping of American citizens. And for what, they say? For a few bits of classified information? And the American suggestion that we would support an Iranian attack on the United States is nothing short of preposterous."

The Politburo member hesitated. He knew from previous conversations that the president trusted Cheng Jinshan implicitly. He had known Jinshan, a successful businessman and member of the Chinese intelligence community, for over two decades and had even appointed him as the head of an agency that would root out corruption in the Chinese government.

Most members of the Politburo considered Jinshan a patriot, someone who would always put the Chinese people first. But everyone had enemies. Some in Beijing would like nothing more than to see Jinshan gone. He had grown too powerful, they argued. The president was oblivious to this notion. To the president, he was an invaluable asset.

Jinshan's work in the business and intelligence worlds often overlapped. His businesses were mainly information technology related. They created and operated data tracking software for China's Internet-based companies. Some of Jinshan's companies also oversaw the control and censorship of Chinese media. Many considered him a puppet master. He controlled the strings that influenced peoples' thoughts.

"Mr. President, my US counterpart apologized to me for asking again. But many of us—our diplomats, intelligence operatives, and government leaders—are getting the same inquiry. So it is with great hesitation that I broach this subject with you. The Americans want to know if there could be any possible truth to the rumors that Cheng Jinshan has organized Chinese participation in the Iranian cyberattacks, and the holding of American citizens in the South China Sea island. They say that they have information leading them to believe that Cheng Jinshan is indeed involved."

The president frowned. "How many times must we tell them? This is insulting."

"I understand, sir. I apologize for bringing it up again."

"We have gone to Jinshan and to our PLA generals. They were upset at the questioning."

"Are you satisfied with ending it there, sir?"

The president locked eyes with the Politburo member, a trusted advisor, and whispered, "They would never keep anything like that from us. It would be *treason*." The president sounded like he was trying to convince himself, more than anything.

The president looked out the window of his office. A peaceful scene outside. A well-trimmed garden. Giant goldfish making ripples in the surface of a quiet pond. The Chinese president sighed and said, "I am going to ask you a question that must never leave this room."

"Of course, sir."

"Do you think that there is any chance I am being lied to by my own people?"

The Politburo member noticed that he couldn't bring himself to say Jinshan's name. He chose his words carefully. "Sir, I think that… after this much consternation by the Americans…it would be prudent to have an outside party look into the matter."

The Chinese president did not respond, so the Politburo member took that as a sign to continue. He said, "This would have to be done in a way that would not lead to us. But I find it most concerning that eighteen Americans are still reported missing, and that two more claim to have been abducted by Chinese forces. It is very unlike the American government to make up such a claim."

"Many of their newspapers are calling it conspiracy theory —lies."

"Yes, sir, but my sources tell me that many in the American intelligence circles do not put stock in these media reports. They are still investigating the matter."

The president nodded. "Without the situation in Iran, this would be dominating their newspapers."

"I agree, sir."

"In that respect, we are lucky."

"Sir, do I have your permission to look into this some more? Outside of our normal channels?"

The president didn't reply verbally, but he looked into the man's eyes and nodded.

* * *

Just outside the president's office, the steward pushed the teacart into a small kitchen area. She picked up her phone to check her messages.

Her phone was very warm. She hated when it was like that. It was almost hot. She tried to tell her husband that the battery must be broken and that he needed to fix it. But her husband just shook his head at her, saying that it was normal, as if she knew nothing about technology.

Her husband had texted her, telling her to pick up some pork at the market on her way home tonight. He was going to make dinner. She smiled, as he seldom cooked. Only on special occasions. She wondered if he had finally gotten the promotion at work that he so desperately wanted.

A jingle at the door told her that the Politburo member was leaving. She walked back in to see if the president needed anything else, leaving her phone on the cart.

* * *

Two Hours Later

The software program on the phone was one of the latest and most sophisticated in the CIA's arsenal. A joint project with the NSA, the program could turn any phone into a very capable listening device.

The challenge hadn't been placing the program on the phone. That had been relatively easy. What had been harder was finding the right phones to listen to. The stewardess had left her GPS location information active on her phone, however. While all the high-profile members of the Chinese government had secure phones that were protected from this type of surveillance, she did not.

It was easy for the NSA to cross-reference GPS coordinates with important government locations around the world. They used this information to identify which phones would serve as the best candidates to allow them to listen in on military, intelligence, and political leaders. It took a lot of juice to record and send all that data, which was why the phone was so warm to the touch.

While the CIA's technical experts had to do a lot of ambient noise cleanup on the recording, they found—incredibly—that they could usually pick up the voices of the Chinese president from the next room when surveilling this stewardess's phone.

Susan Collinsworth handed over the transcript. "Mr. Director, something interesting from one of our NSA collection reports."

He took the purple folder stamped TOP SECRET/SCI and reviewed the printout of the translated conversation. He looked it over for a full minute.

"So, they really don't know."

"And they're beginning to suspect the same thing we are."

"That Jinshan isn't the loyal Communist that he says he is?"

She nodded.

"Alright. I'll see if I can get this to the president today. It might be hard to slow down the wheels of this thing right now, but this will certainly help if we can find evidence that links Jinshan to the Iranian attacks. Keep at it."

"Yes, sir."

9

Guangzhou, China

N atesh fought back another wave of nausea as their minivan curved around a corner. Everything in this godforsaken city made him sick. The food, the weather, the driving.

The strange food they served him at the Chinese military base was awful. The Chinese security men who brought them their meals must have thought it would be funny to give Natesh a local delicacy —cow brain. Natesh didn't eat it, but just watching them go to town on it, and then eat actual chicken feet, disgusted him. The odd taste of their tea made him want to vomit. He gave it a try, but then decided to stick with bottled water, not trusting what might come out of their tap. He missed the sushi houses of Silicon Valley.

A constant smog filled the Guangzhou air. It was so thick that it limited visibility to a few hundred yards. It was like being stuck in a bad dream—the world fogged over in toxic brown. By the end of each day, he grew nauseous, and a massive headache consumed him.

The pollution was much worse this time of year, he was told. During the winter months, the coal factories kicked into high gear to provide electricity and heat for the burgeoning population. People walked around in it, coughing and complaining. Many of them wore little white masks over their noses and mouths. Many locals even had an app on their smartphones that told them how intense the pollution was that day. For Natesh, breathing that crap in just made him want to puke.

It didn't help that he had to be taken to and from his living quarters in the back of a dark-windowed van. Security precautions, they were told. Driving in Chinese cities was like a mad derby race. Lots of honking horns and unexpected braking. Angry passengers.

Natesh and Lena had arrived on one of Jinshan's jets the night before last. They were kept in hiding at a local military base until called upon. Finally Jinshan had summoned them for this strategy session, and their handlers had sped them through the crowded city streets.

The van came to a halt outside what Natesh now recognized as Jinshan's residence here in Guangzhou, the third-largest city in China. A guard conversed with the driver, and then the entrance gate rose.

As they moved forward, Natesh glanced at the seat behind him. Lena stared back, that same cold look on her face. He turned back around to face forward.

The elevator was cramped. Tiny by Western standards. Lena, Natesh, and their three armed escorts squeezed in for the ride up. No one spoke. The escorts disappeared when they arrived at the penthouse.

The décor was similar to what Natesh had seen in high-end hotel suites. Modern furniture and paintings. Well decorated. No personal effects.

Natesh was glad that they were having these strategy sessions in Jinshan's penthouse, rather than the godforsaken military base Lena and he were holed up at. The air in the penthouse smelled cleaner, and the food wasn't the local cuisine. It was high-quality gourmet dining—fit for the billionaire that Jinshan was. Plates of steamed dumplings, but also Western-style sandwiches and salads. Two glass bottles of carbonated water in an ice bucket. A stocked liquor bar was off to the side, although no one approached it.

"Mr. Jinshan will be with you in a moment," said one of the assistants.

"Thank you," Lena said, unconsciously rubbing the burn scar that ran up the side of her neck and face. She did that a lot, Natesh noticed.

Jinshan had summoned Lena and Natesh to discuss the current state of their operational planning and make changes where needed. Natesh had previously made a living consulting for some of the best companies in the world. He had been around the block enough to recognize a nervous executive when he saw one. Jinshan was worried—with good reason. It wasn't all supposed to happen this way.

The bitcoin mess was not one of Natesh's ideas. He'd tried to tell Jinshan that it wouldn't work. Frankly, it wasn't necessary. If the Chinese Army was going to conquer the West militarily, why did they need to attempt economic warfare?

But Jinshan didn't like putting all his eggs in one basket. He had argued that if enough nations began using the bitcoin-backed currency, and Jinshan was able to manipulate the value, it would be an enormously powerful tool in their arsenal. But that idea had fallen apart before it could get off the ground. The CIA had uncovered the plot. And when David Manning and Henry Glickstein had escaped from the island, that had triggered a chain of events that moved all their plans up by several months.

Natesh had explained how critical it was to conduct all the information warfare attacks at the same time—the cyberattacks, the EMP attacks, cutting the undersea cables, destroying the US satellite communications. But they had not executed that way. Instead, some of these information warfare tactics were used for diversion. Jinshan and his planners were worried that the two escaped Americans— Manning and Glickstein—would shine a light on Jinshan's entire operation.

Perhaps Jinshan was right. One thing Natesh had to admit was that he knew how to manipulate the media, and as a result, people's opinions. When David and Henry had escaped, Jinshan had insisted that they use a few of the weapons in their arsenal immediately. *Months* earlier than Natesh had recommended.

So Jinshan's cyberwarfare team had used the ARES weapon to disrupt the American Internet and permanently damage many US satellites. The results were mixed. US-owned GPS satellites were out of commission until they could be replaced. Most military satellite communications were damaged to a similar level of harm. But the US Internet, as Jinshan had warned, was a self-healing monster. It had grown so large and interwoven that attacking only some data centers and root servers would only create a temporary setback.

Still, Jinshan's foresight into the behavior of the media, and the minds of the people, proved incredibly accurate. The Chinese intelligence team had inserted false information to several media centers about David Manning and Henry Glickstein providing the Iranians with a classified cyberweapon. Couple this with the Blackout Attack, and a media disinformation firestorm soon erupted.

The next few days were days of record-setting ratings for the TV news stations. First, Iran and two American traitors were implicated. Then, the Americans were captured in Australia. Then, they escaped captivity somehow. Then, the Iranian politician was assassinated. Then, the Iranian military attacked US forces in the Persian Gulf region. With the Internet down, everyone was glued to their TV.

With so much confusion, there was almost no coverage about China. Even after it came out that David Manning and Henry Glickstein had nothing to do with the Iranians, their claim that the Chinese had kidnapped Americans wasn't widely believed. The US government's own penchant for secrecy helped there. The two men weren't allowed to do interviews.

When news that China might have been involved did break, it was widely discredited. Many of the more extreme media outlets cried cover-up—claiming that certain political and media groups desired to appease Iran, and blame China. Jinshan's cyberwarriors fed this, of course. They paid third parties to write and publish articles that pointed to David and Henry as Iranian sympathizers. Spies. Traitors.

This disinformation strategy prolonged the time that the US

government spent investigating and questioning the two men, and reduced their credibility. It also gave Jinshan and China enough cover to deny any involvement in the Iranian incidents, or the "ludicrous" idea that the Chinese could actually be holding American citizens on an island in the South China Sea. With all the Iranian-US hostilities, the Chinese connection was soon buried.

Jinshan's plan had worked beautifully. Even with the two men escaping, Natesh admitted that there was still a very high probability that their war plans would succeed. However, Natesh was frustrated that Jinshan's team had lost their most important advantage—the element of surprise. But he also knew that surprise often couldn't be counted on. Competitive advantage needed to be about much more than just being a first mover. And it would be.

Natesh and Lena sat in silence on thick-cushioned chairs, on opposite sides of a large glass coffee table. He looked at his watch. They had another ten minutes before Jinshan was supposed to see them.

He glanced outside. Shadows of skyscrapers rose up through the smog. A part of him wondered if his efforts would do nothing more than expand China's problems around the globe.

No. Jinshan was not the cause of China's missteps. He reminded himself of why he had chosen to go down this path.

In his Silicon Valley job, Natesh could create and improve businesses. It was entertaining, but not fulfilling. But in this role, Natesh was truly changing the *world*. While Natesh had some disagreements with Jinshan on tactics, he firmly supported the man's big-picture strategic objective. At first, Natesh was seduced by just the size and scope of the challenge, and the promise of power as payment.

Now, though, he saw the same thing that Lena saw in Jinshan. Greatness. Vision. Jinshan was what those in Silicon Valley referred to as a thought leader. He was one of those rare men who envisioned a plan to change the world for the better, and made it happen.

After all, Jinshan was right. Democracy *didn't* work. Natesh had seen it with his own eyes. It led to populism. Populism meant that every common person was in control. Regular people. *Uneducated* people. Commoners who were too stupid for their own good.

Natesh believed that a group of elite experts were needed to carve out the best path forward. Jinshan believed that as well. But what Jinshan also believed, and had convinced Natesh of, was that a strong and forceful enforcer was needed to control it all, lest men fall victim to their own imperfections.

It sounded frighteningly like a dictatorship. It was, Natesh realized. But in his talks with Jinshan, Natesh had come to understand that there was one crucial difference. The goals of this new world order were utilitarian. Jinshan argued that you couldn't please all the people, and that you shouldn't try. Decisions shouldn't fall to the people *or* to the politicians. There was another choice. Decisions should be made by the *experts*. But who would decide who the experts were? And who would keep them in control? That was the crux of Jinshan's plan—there had to be a strong and just enforcer.

The challenge, as Jinshan saw it, would be to make sure that this all-powerful leader was acting in the best interests of the society. Guiding principles needed to be followed, and subsequent leaders would need to be groomed and chosen to follow those guiding principles.

The world had outgrown democracy, Jinshan preached. It was the duty of the great and capable few, like Natesh, to gift the next great form of government to the world. The hard part for Natesh to come to terms with was the cost of this transition. If their guiding philosophy was Act Utilitarianism, then the greater good would be worth the pain and suffering of those lost in the war to come.

Natesh took deep breaths of the clean air inside Jinshan's building. He closed his eyes and breathed out through his mouth in long, deliberate blows. Stress breathing. He had been doing that a lot lately.

Lena saw him and said, "Are you alright?"

He opened his eyes. "Yes. Just trying to relax."

Her scarred face stared back at him. He wondered if *she* had ever felt stress, or if she was immune.

The double doors opened, and in walked Cheng Jinshan and a man in a military uniform. Both Lena and Natesh rose.

Jinshan said, "Good afternoon. I hope that I have not kept you waiting too long."

"Not at all," replied Lena.

"This is Admiral Song. He is our closest ally in this endeavor. Please feel free during this discussion to share with him anything that you would share with me."

Natesh noticed the "during this discussion" qualifier. Jinshan was a very secretive person. He had to be.

The group sat, and a woman came to pour them each tea. When she left, Jinshan said, "The two of you will be leaving the island soon. Tomorrow for you, Mr. Chaudry. Lena, you will remain on the island for a few more days and take care of any remaining details there. Then you will follow."

Natesh looked at Lena. He tried not to look surprised. He looked back at Jinshan and said, "Where will we be going?"

The admiral said, "Manta, Ecuador. I believe that you are both already aware, but we have begun deploying a small number of our forces in South America. We have many assets there that have been pre-staged over the last few years. Under the guise of foreign arms sales. These groups will partake in consolidating our military assets in the region and preparing for the arrival of Chinese armed forces en masse."

Natesh was familiar with the location and plans. After all, he had helped to draw them up. Manta, Equador, was supposed to be the first of many bases at which the Chinese would begin massing troops in preparation for an invasion. The bases would be throughout Central and South America, and some would even be in Canada. These locations were still months away from seeing any Chinese forces, however. According to the plans, they weren't even supposed to head to Manta for another month.

Lena said, "Admiral, if I may be so bold, how does this match up with our timeline of increased military readiness? The plans called for troop transports and increased training beyond current levels."

Admiral Song looked at Jinshan, and then back at Lena. "Our plans are at different stages in different locations. Chinese leadership is not fully aligned yet."

Or aware, Natesh thought. Jinshan looked tired. His eyes had a yellowish tint. Natesh thought he looked like he was losing weight. Hmmm. Was he doing alright?

Jinshan said, "I must confess that not all of our political changes have been implemented yet. It is regrettable. However, a good plan is one that must be continuously modified. For now, Admiral Song has provided the capable assets of the PLA Navy's South Sea Fleet to serve our needs."

Lena glanced between the two men. "And senior PLA leadership? Are they aware?"

Jinshan didn't bother looking at the admiral, who shuffled in his seat. Jinshan said, "They are not."

Lena said, "Mr. Jinshan, you know that I have great respect and admiration for you. But...is this *wise*? How will we reach the levels of readiness and—"

Natesh said, "Mr. Jinshan, to be frank, we need bodies. We need truck drivers and logisticians. We need planners and button-pushers. That is the stage we're at right now. If we are to move millions of personnel across the Pacific Ocean, we need to get prepared for their arrival on the other end. And that means stocking warehouses full of food and materials, building barracks. I've drawn up the flowcharts —right now, I'm capacity limited. I need bodies, sir."

Jinshan took a sip of his tea and nodded. "Yes. I am aware, Mr. Chaudry. That is one of the things I would like to discuss here today. I believe the minimum number of personnel you said you would need for this part of the plan was twenty thousand workers, is that right?"

"That's correct."

Jinshan said, "Admiral, would you be able to provide that many people?"

The admiral shook his head. "I'm afraid that would be hard to do at this time. Not without alerting my superiors, which we don't want to do yet."

Jinshan said, "What kind of people do you need?"

"They can be unskilled," Natesh said. "Educated, preferably. And able-bodied. We can teach them what they need to do, but I need workers who can help to participate and manage supply chain and logistics work."

Lena said, "What about Junxun?"

The admiral frowned. "What about it?"

"Could we send some of them? Call it training?"

"If you will excuse me saying so, that doesn't seem like a good idea. It would be very unusual to send students like this away. Junxun is supposed to be held during the summer. It is still wintertime. And Junxun is normally held at local schools or military bases. What would we tell the students and their parents? There would be much complaining, I think."

Lena said, "We already have a way of hiding the movement of our military assets from our leadership, do we not?"

The admiral again looked at Jinshan. "We do."

"We could enact a special Junxun during the winter months, and say that we are flying them to the Red Cell island," Lena said. "That would allow us to switch the flight to where we really need them, would it not?"

Jinshan nodded. "Yes, that could work. By the time the complaints get serious, we will have come to an agreement with our political and military leadership on the way ahead. But this personnel transfer will ensure that we are ready for our large military movements across the Pacific when the war begins in earnest."

"What of the Americans on the Red Cell island?" Lena asked.

Jinshan took a sip of tea. "Are you still able to get information from the Americans that you consider helpful?"

"Yes."

"Then keep them where they are. My men on the island can oversee them now."

Lena nodded.

Natesh said, "I apologize, but I'm confused. What is Junxun?"

10

Guangzhou, 1997

L i stood at attention next to her classmates. Most were older. But while she was only seventeen, she had also just graduated from secondary school. Her stellar marks and off-the-charts scores on aptitude tests had helped her gain early acceptance into one of China's most prestigious universities a year early. It didn't hurt that her father was a colonel in the PLA.

Like all incoming university students, Li was expected to participate in the two-week military indoctrination course known as Junxun. Each summer in China, over seven million students gathered at their schools or at a nearby military base. Students were taught by members of the People's Liberation Army how to march, salute, and perform basic military drills. There were different levels of rigor at the various training sites. Most students considered it a rite of passage. A patriotic boot camp.

Li was in her third week of Junxun, and she had several more to go. While she had started out at her local high school, the military drill instructor there had picked her out as an overachiever right away.

Always a gifted runner, she had lapped the fastest of her male classmates in the five-thousand-meter race, and her academic test scores were all perfect. That, too, had raised eyebrows.

So after the first week at her hometown location, they had plucked her out of her class and sent her to a *special* Junxun location near the city. Guangzhou in the summertime was sweltering. When she got off the bus, she quickly learned that she was the only girl in her class. And the boys were all gifted. The military men who trained them here carried clipboards, marking down notes on each student as they went through the training.

This Junxun was not a two-week summer camp. It was something very different. The boys—and they were all boys, aside from her— were much bigger and leaner. They didn't joke around in class, and each had an intense look about him.

On the first day at the Guangzhou camp, there were over one hundred of them. Those numbers were whittled down fast. The physical activity picked up and many of them couldn't take it.

Their instructors woke them up each day before dawn to start physical training. Push-ups and other calisthenics. Long, arduous runs. They attended classes during the day and got tested each afternoon on what they retained. The classes were a mix of military recognition and academic aptitude. Those who did not score above a ninety percent on any given test were sent home.

Most quit. After the first week, there were only forty of them. The ones who were still here at the completion of camp would be promised entry into a special government program. If they could make it that long. No one was told what that program was, but they all wanted to be chosen.

Now they stood at attention in the hot gymnasium.

"Li!"

The instructor, a short, red-faced man, liked to yell in her ear.

"Yes, Sergeant?" she answered.

"Step forward and put on the boxing gloves and headgear."

"Yes, Sergeant."

She raced forward, throwing the smelly equipment on over her head and hands. She took a mouth guard and washed it off in the sink, then scurried to the center mat.

Today was her first day of live hand-to-hand combat training. They had been taught technique for the past three days but hadn't actually fought each other yet. As with most new endeavors, Li had mastered it right away. The PLA sergeant who taught the class tried not to show favoritism, but he was clearly thrilled at how much promise Li showed.

The instructor called on another pupil to face her on the mat. She could feel all the students' eyes on her, wanting to see what would happen to the girl who embarrassed them on the track and in the classroom.

Her classmates treated her differently. Some respected her for her exceptional ability. But most showed disdain. She deemed their attitudes a product of jealousy or sexism. Many of them teased her at meals. During exercise, some gawked at her body, the sweat causing her clothes to cling tight.

Her chosen opponent walked out onto the mat in front of her. His name was Fang. He was one of the ones who called her names. Not to her face. In whispers, in the cafeteria. Out of earshot of *most* of the military instructors.

One of the military instructors, however, was quite aware of her treatment. A lieutenant in the People's Liberation Army. One of the heads of this camp.

It was this lieutenant, by the name of Lin, who began causing her real problems. He saw what the boys were doing by making fun of her, and instead of stopping it, he actually encouraged it. Perhaps he didn't think she deserved to be there with the rest of them. Perhaps he knew her father from the military and didn't like him. Whatever the reason, Lieutenant Lin and his favorite student, Fang, made Li's life a living hell.

Lunch earlier that day had started like any other. She sat at her table, alone. A group of boys, including Fang, sat at the next table. Fang had used a derogatory term for female genitalia and nodded in her direction. The other boys laughed. She had pretended not to hear it.

Now he smiled. She knew a little English and thought his name appropriate. He had the smile of a wolf. He was a bully. She had dealt with bullies before. She tried to ignore him, but that wasn't going to work here.

They had hand-to-hand combat class after lunch. In the gym. When she arrived, she glanced at the rows of her male classmates. Their eyes were alive with excitement, their fists clenched and legs locked at attention. She fell in line in the back row, wondering why everyone was so quiet.

She darted a glance behind the rows of students and saw something she didn't expect. Two of the instructors were speaking with a man in a suit. One of the instructors was Lieutenant Lin. The man was nodding and listening. The instructors were pointing at her and making gestures. The man in the suit was looking at his notepad and made a face that implied he approved. Lieutenant Lin shook his head vigorously, frowning and speaking to the man in the suit. Li realized that the man was watching her and she quickly faced front.

Lieutenant Lin walked in front of the group. He called out two names: Chou and Fang. The sergeant quickly echoed his commands.

Lieutenant Lin walked to the center of the mat and smiled at her, whispering so only she could hear, "Let's see how *exceptional* you really are."

He stepped away from the two students, now standing in the middle of the mat, and exclaimed, "Fight!" The voice of the lead instructor broke her spell and she focused on the boy in front of her.

Li looked at Fang and felt a rage swelling up inside her. Her heart beat faster as she bobbed lightly on her feet. He came at her fast, his gloves rising to the fighting position, but she was ready.

Li had always been an exceptional athlete. While growing up, she had run track at a local running club for girls. She swam competitively, but she had never played a contact sport. She had never really fought anyone. As the bully crept closer to her, the anger inside her mixed with the familiar excitement that she got during her most competitive races. The thirst for victory pulsed through her veins. She desperately wanted to teach this boy and the lieutenant a lesson.

Fang was a foot taller, at least fifty pounds heavier, and much too confident. He started in on her with a left jab. It was quick, but not as quick as Li. Using the lessons her hand-to-hand combat instructor had taught her over the last week, she ducked under and snapped her hips to the right, using the motion to drive her clenched right fist into his undefended stomach. It was a quick, twisting movement, and a powerful, targeted blow.

He doubled over, eyes wide, unable to breathe. Fang's mouth came open and his mouth guard fell out just as her left knee came up into his face, her kneecap crunching into his nose and teeth. A mix of blood, saliva, and two teeth spilled onto the floor, and the boy fell like a sack.

Li kept bobbing, light on her feet. She watched her opponent, waiting to see what would come next. But he didn't get up. The instructor, alarmed at the blood, called off the training and sent one of the other pupils to get the nurse.

Lieutenant Lin began yelling at her. "What did you do that for?"

She didn't know what to say. She shrugged, saying through her mouth guard, "Because you told us to fight."

The man in the suit kept watching her, a wide smile on his face.

* * *

The man in the suit watched the girl from the other end of the gymnasium. She had just put down a much larger male candidate. "How has she been doing?"

Lieutenant Lin was back over with him now. Begrudgingly, he admitted, "She has received high marks, Mr. Jinshan. She has excelled in each evaluation that we have given her. But I don't think she has the fortitude for the People's Liberation Army."

Jinshan looked at Lieutenant Lin with skepticism. "Fortitude?"

"Yes."

"Are we talking about the woman who just embarrassed a much larger man in physical combat?"

Lin scowled. "She got lucky. That boy was complacent."

Jinshan asked, "How does she get along with the others?"

"She is an introvert. We have not observed her speaking much with the other candidates beyond that which is required."

The boy who had just been pummeled was walked off to the side by a nurse. She held a bag of ice and a blood-soaked gauze pad to his mouth.

"That boy won't be happy when he heals. She just humiliated him."

Lieutenant Lin didn't reply.

The annual Junxun programs for China's rising college freshmen served several purposes. They helped serve as a method of drilling a sense of discipline and patriotism into an increasingly pampered generation of teenagers. They registered the best and brightest of China's children for the military, in case there ever came a time that a dramatic military expansion was needed. And they served as an excellent recruiting tool for China's military and government agencies.

Many of these students would be sent around the world to foreign universities. Those students were flagged by China's intelligence organizations. It was crucial for the well-being of the motherland that these students brought back what they learned to benefit China. Some of them were asked to perform *extra* work on behalf of China's intelligence agencies. Refusal was not permitted.

In some cases, Junxun was used to identify students who were not already planning to attend a foreign university, but who showed all the qualities that Jinshan's special team of spies would want in a sleeper agent.

This Junxun location pulled all the top recruits from the Guang-dong region. The group that started with more than one hundred would eventually go down to about ten. All but one of them would be sent on to various government programs.

Every year, Cheng Jinshan came and got the pick of the litter. This year it looked like it would be this girl named Li.

Lieutenant Lin said, "Her father is a colonel. Did they tell you that? He has asked to be notified if she is selected for any particular government programs."

Jinshan said, "Give me this colonel's name."

Lin wrote it down and handed him the paper, which Jinshan stuffed in his pocket. He looked at the girl. She had gone back in line and stood at attention. Two other boys were fighting on the mat now.

This girl was special, Jinshan could see that. He wanted her on his team. This would be one of the ones that he sent to America. She would need to modify her identity. No ties back to China. The work she would be doing would be too important. This girl wouldn't just be a student there. Jinshan wanted her to become a US citizen. To stay there and infiltrate an agency of his choosing.

He would decide what role she would play later. For now, he needed to find a way for she and her father to part voluntarily.

He looked over at the boy being tended to by the nurse. The one she had just dispatched in short order. The boy's eyes were ablaze. He looked straight at the girl. There was a great deal of anger there. That could be useful.

* * *

Li's room was the only one occupied on her floor. The male candidates all slept in the dorm rooms one floor below. So when she heard the footsteps that night, it not only woke her up, it alarmed her.

Mosquito netting covered her bed. They all had it. They slept with the windows open, as there was no air conditioning. A luxury for the rich. The bugs were something awful this time of year. She lifted up the net and checked her alarm clock. It was just past midnight.

In the three weeks she had been at the camp, no one had come up to her floor at night.

Her relationship with the other candidates had remained poor. After defeating Fang in front of the others a few days ago, she had temporarily thought that she might have won increased respect. She had been sadly mistaken. The chiding at meals had increased, and Lieutenant Lin glared at her. After hours, when the other candidates would gather to socialize, she retreated to the solitude of her own floor. It was a lonely existence, but there was an end in sight. She only had to do this a little longer. Then she would find out what, if any, government assignment she would get, and head off to university.

The footsteps grew closer. Was it an instructor? Was this part of the training? The hard floors of the hallway carried the echo. Just one person, by the sound of it. But her door was locked, and only the instructors had the keys. So she need not worry about...

A jingle of keys, and the sound of the door handle turning.

Her pulse began pounding. The door opened and she sprang out of bed, flipping on her light.

Fang stood in the doorway, holding the keys.

She attempted to cover herself with her arms. She wore only a thin tee shirt and white cotton underwear.

"What are you doing here?" she demanded.

Fang looked back at her, anger and lust in his eyes. He closed the door behind him.

"I *asked you* what you are doing here."

"I came to see you," he said, the wolf's grin on his face.

"How did you get the keys?"

He took a step toward her. She wasn't sure whether to continue covering herself or get in the fighting stance. She wanted to scream for help, but her pride wouldn't let her.

He smirked. "You won't catch me by surprise this time."

"If I scream, the instructors will be here in an instant. They'll punish you and kick you out of the program."

Fang laughed. "Who do you think gave me the keys? Lieutenant Lin said you needed to be taught a lesson. No instructors will come."

She shook her head. "I don't believe you."

His eyes wandered over her body. "It's true. They told me to teach you a lesson. They said that you needed to be humbled."

He took another step toward her. "We don't have to fight, you know. I won't tell anyone. We could just..."

She gritted her teeth. "Stay where you are."

If he was telling the truth...the thought made her sick. To think that one of the instructors would betray her trust in such a way. She wanted to serve China, like her father. She had done nothing but excel in the program. She wished only to perform with honor.

She had admired the instructors. They served in the PLA and had always been professional and courteous to her, except for Lieutenant Lin. But the others had treated her fairly. A few times they had even given her words of encouragement as she'd bested her classmates in the various evolutions.

Li didn't want to believe that one of them would have given him the keys to her room—even if it was Lieutenant Lin. If Lieutenant Lin had handed Fang the keys, he had done so with the knowledge that he would do something reprehensible. That made Lin complicit.

She looked at the larger boy approaching her.

"I said to stop. Don't take another step."

"What can you do to stop me?"

She might win again if she fought him. But he would have his guard up this time. She was getting better at the martial arts they were teaching her, but it had still only been a few weeks of training. If she screamed, they might not hear her. If they did, her reputation would suffer. Or maybe Lieutenant Lin would hear her scream and just ignore it. Either way, everyone else would see her as weak. The colonel's daughter who couldn't take care of herself. What if they kicked her out of the program? What would her parents think?

Whether she fought him or screamed, she did not like her options. Then she thought of another alternative. The idea disgusted her to no end. But if she could get through the worst of it...

"Fine," she said. Her eyes conceded defeat.

Fang, approaching her with caution until now, stopped in his tracks. A confused look on the bully's face.

"What do you *mean*, fine?"

"When we are done, you will leave immediately. And speak of this to no one."

His eyes grew wider. His smile faded. His words were shaky now. A nervous teenager. "Yes...of course."

She turned out the light. "Then hurry up and get it over with."

* * *

When Fang left, she remained in her bed, silent. Stewing. Humiliated and defiled. She waited a few moments and then went to the shower down the hall. She kept the lights off and turned the water on hot. She scrubbed and tried to get his stench off her. Steam filled the room. She wanted to cry. If there ever were a time to cry, it would be now.

But the tears wouldn't come. She wouldn't be defeated. She wouldn't feel sorry for herself. Li focused all the emotion into anger.

Like the races and the fights and the physical competitions, this was just another challenge to overcome. Li must win it. And after what Fang had just done to her, the only way to win was vengeance. Li dried herself off in her room and put on her clothes. It was one o'clock in the morning now.

She worried that he would still be awake. Or worse, awake with the other boys. Telling them about his conquest. So she waited another full hour before making her move. She needed to be sure that he was asleep.

In her desk drawer there was a long, sharp pair of metal scissors. She fit it neatly into her pocket and walked out into the hall. No shoes. She wanted her entrance to be as quiet as possible.

Li crept down the stairs and then along the hallway where all the other candidates slept. The lights were off. She waited outside Fang's door for a full five minutes. Listening.

Nothing. Just the sound of two men breathing in their sleep.

She cursed herself as she realized that his door might be locked and she didn't have a key. She tried it anyway. It twisted open. A bit of luck. Either he didn't lock it at all, or he had forgotten to when he came back into the room.

Bullies didn't worry about their prey coming after them in the night. This one would, soon enough. And for the rest of his days.

Her footsteps were silent on the linoleum floor. There was barely enough light from the window to discern which of the two boys was Fang. It would be a shame to make a mistake. Like a surgeon amputating the wrong leg.

She figured out which one was which. Li crept up to his bed and stood over him, watching his chest rise and fall. Deciding how to do it. There would only be one chance. Then she would need to be quick.

Fang slept with his mouth open. Big mistake.

She lifted up the thin mosquito netting over his bed, removed the scissors from her pocket, and held them firm in her right hand. With her left hand, in one quick movement, she reached into his open mouth and grabbed hold of his tongue with the tips of her fingers. She pulled up on his tongue as hard as she could. With her right hand, she sliced the scissors hard and fast, pushing them forward into the tongue muscle and squeezing.

His eyes shot open as the top inch of his tongue was sliced off like a thick rubber band being cut in half. Warm dark blood splattered over the scissors and both of her hands.

Then the screams began.

Blood-choked, gargling screams. High-pitched and terrified. Shocked in pain, Fang screamed loud enough to wake up everyone in the building.

Li raced out of the room and up the stairs before the roommate awoke and realized what was going on. The lights behind her flicked on, but she was already out of sight. She kept her bloody hand and scissors in her pocket, making sure that no drops fell to the floor as she ran.

Once on her floor, Li first darted into the bathroom and threw the tongue piece into one of the toilet holes on the floor. She flushed it down several times, and then began thoroughly scrubbing her hands, arm, and the scissors. She scrubbed using the same pair of pants that were already bloody. She only gave herself a minute to finish. If anyone had seen her, they would be up here soon. If not, she would have longer. But she wasn't sure exactly how long.

She looked out the bathroom and into the dark hallway. No one was there, so she sprinted into her room and placed the now-clean scissors back in her desk drawer. She took the bloody pants and climbed up on her desk. She lifted a ceiling tile and shoved them up top, into the unused space above. Later, she would have to get rid of them. She then scurried under her sheet and pulled the mosquito netting back over her bed.

She could hear the commotion downstairs. Yelling from one of the instructors to get the nurse. Fang's continued screams of agony. Li listened for the footsteps down her hallway, but they never came. She kept imagining a trail of blood droplets leading up the stairs and to her room. She told herself that there wasn't one. That she had been careful.

The noise died down an hour later. It was the middle of the night. Only a few more hours until dawn. She smiled to herself. A deep feeling of content filled her, and—as she thought of the moment when she had cut off Fang's tongue—an excitement that she had never known until now.

* * *

Two days later, Jinshan marveled at the girl sitting on the other side of his desk. Had he known what would happen, he might not have suggested that Lieutenant Lin give Fang the keys to her room. No one would ever know the details of that particular transaction. Even Fang didn't know of Jinshan's role.

Jinshan had thought that Li would give Fang a black eye, or vice versa. Either would suit his purpose. The fight would be grounds for dismissal or even legal trouble for Li. Jinshan would be able to use this as cause to have her removed from the school, and she would join his own team. He would then talk to her father, the colonel, insisting that it was the only way to keep her out of trouble. Eventually, with the influence of Jinshan's contacts in the PLA, the father would give his approval.

But all had not gone as planned. This girl was quite unpredictable.

As soon as Jinshan had become aware of what had happened to Fang that night, he'd had Lieutenant Lin transferred to another district. Anything Fang said—or wrote, since he would never speak again—would be denied by Lin. Jinshan had made sure of that.

But Fang wasn't communicating anything. The investigative team, who were reporting through Jinshan, said that Fang didn't write anything about the keys, or paying the girl Li a visit in the night. His story was that he didn't know who had sliced off his tongue, or why. And he didn't want to know.

The poor boy was a neutered animal without his tongue. He just wanted to be left alone. And Jinshan didn't want anyone to find out that one of the instructors had a hand in this mess.

Jinshan had made sure that Li was not questioned about the incident. Fang's roommate had said that Fang had left his room for an hour earlier that evening, but that was all he knew.

So this interview, in the office of the supervisor of the Junxun camp, would be the first time that Li was confronted about the incident. Jinshan wasn't sure exactly what had happened that evening between Fang and Li, prior to Fang's tongue being sliced off, but he had his suspicions.

"Are you comfortable?"

"Yes, sir, thank you," said Li.

She looked calm. Jinshan was surprised at that. He thought she would be terrified to be in his presence.

"Do you know who I am?"

She said, "No, sir."

"But you have some idea of my role here?"

"Yes, sir."

"Tell me what you think I do."

"I think you are evaluating us. For which role we will go on to next."

Jinshan nodded. "This is partly true." He looked down at his notepad. "You've done exceptionally well here."

"Thank you, sir."

He watched her eyes as he asked his next question. "What happened the night that you cut off Fang's tongue?"

Li's composed demeanor shattered, but only for a microsecond. She then stared at the wall and remained silent.

"You heard my question," he persisted. "What is your answer?"

"He came to my room and…"

"And what?"

"He attacked me."

"Did he?" Jinshan let the question hang in the air.

He expected her to fill the uncomfortable silence with an excuse, or with an apology. But she offered none.

"If he attacked you, why don't you have any scars or bruises?"

She stopped looking at the wall and faced Jinshan. "Sometimes an attack is not easily recognized."

Jinshan pursed his lips. "Why didn't you bring this information to the attention of the instructors?"

"After he lost his tongue, that seemed unwise."

His mouth formed a slight smile. "What shall we do with you now?"

She didn't reply.

"I am of two minds. One, Fang was the aggressor and I would say that he got what he deserved. Two, you took matters into your own hands and committed an illegal act of violence."

She said nothing.

"Punishable by prison."

No response.

"Your father is a colonel in the People's Liberation Army. You would bring much dishonor to your family if it were to get out that his daughter was the psychotic girl who sliced off the tongue of the university student in Guangzhou."

At that, she looked worried.

Jinshan's instincts were right. She was selfless. Service and sacrifice, devotion to family, to country. These were her motivations. Jinshan could work with them.

Her eyes moved as she was thinking of what to say. "I am sorry."

Jinshan said, "Your father's career would be over. Your family name would be associated with this violent act for decades. Instead of university, you would be behind bars. These are all things that a thoughtful person would have considered before taking such drastic action."

Her head was down. Looking at the floor now. Shame was a powerful drug.

Jinshan held up his hand. "There is an alternative, however. Li, you have performed brilliantly here. I would hate to lose such a talented young woman to one careless act. An act that could be perceived by many as *justified*."

She looked up at him, her eyes watery.

He reached down for her file, thumbing through the pages. "Like I said, you've done quite well here. With training and discipline, you could learn to harness your talents. You could help our nation in extraordinary ways. But the path that I am thinking of...it requires a great sacrifice."

She nodded. "I am willing to sacrifice."

"I am sure you are. But would you be willing to sacrifice everything you have? The life you know? Even your identity?"

She looked confused. "If it meant that I would not dishonor my family. If it meant that I could serve my country, yes. Of course. I will sacrifice anything."

Jinshan smiled. "Then I think there is a way to remedy this unfortunate situation. I can take care of Fang and the incident here. I think you would be a valuable asset to my team."

"Your team?"

"Yes, Li. You see, each year, I look for the best recruit at these types of camps. Some years I don't find anyone suitable. This year, I have found you. The personnel that I select go on to serve China in ways that are dangerous but extremely crucial to our national security. We export many students to overseas assignments each year. Many of them do work for the Ministry of State Security while they are there."

At the mention of the Ministry of State Security, Li raised her eyebrow. "The Ministry of..."

"Yes. We work with students before they travel, to ensure that they keep their eyes open while they are abroad. We use these Junxun camps to identify the best candidates for this type of work. They will go for a few years. Perhaps they will be asked to make a copy of a particular file, or sometimes to take certain pictures. Tens of thousands of these types of activities funnel in to my office each year. The Ministry of State Security is able to use all this information to improve China's standing in the world."

"I see."

"But while it is very helpful to have so many temporary personnel performing these activities, we need to have a long-term presence as well. This allows us to better position ourselves for the bigger pieces of work. Long-term human resources, living and working alongside our adversaries. These are the type of people that I recruit."

Li nodded, understanding. She said, hesitantly, "Spies?"

Jinshan smiled. "In a word, yes."

"And when you say that I would need to sacrifice my identity…it is because I would become a…*spy*?"

"I am offering you the opportunity to serve your nation as a covert operative."

"What types of things would I be doing? If I may ask?"

"Of course you may. The Ministry of State Security has many arms. We engage in counterintelligence, the collection of our adversaries secrets and technology, and if needed, a variety of special activities that we don't need to go into right now."

"It sounds…*exciting*."

"It can be. It can also be incredibly boring. For every exciting day, you will have two hundred days of the mundane. But the work is very fulfilling. And there is no greater way to serve China with honor."

She took a deep breath. "I accept. What do I need to do now?"

A wide smile crossed Jinshan's lips. "Excellent. Tomorrow you will leave this camp to begin your training. It will be different from anything you have done in your life. Much more rigorous. Military training. Language schools. Schools in espionage tradecraft. We must prepare you, Li. You will remain in China for another year or so. Then you will move to the United States and live under your new identity. You will become an American citizen. You will attend an American university and get an American job after you graduate. We will help with that."

He slid over a manila envelope.

"What is this?" She reached for it.

"Open it. This is your new identity."

She looked down at the sheet of paper. "A new name?"

"Yes. A more *American-sounding* first name. I thought it was similar enough."

She looked down at the name and the life summary beneath it. The name had a nice ring to it, she thought.

Lena Chou.

11

Langley, Virginia
Present Day

Susan walked over to David's desk. "I just sent you a link. Check it out."

David searched his email for the message from Susan and clicked on the link. It took him to a top-secret portion of the share drive where recent intelligence data was stored. He pressed his thumb up against the biometrics reader to open the folder and began scrolling through the imagery.

David said, "What am I looking at?"

He scrolled through pictures of...

"Is that the island? Who took these?"

The profile was not an overhead view. All he had seen so far were images from reconnaissance drones. But these pictures were taken from the surface. As if someone had taken them from a boat.

Susan said, "Your access just went through, so now you'll be able to see all our surveillance intel on the Red Cell island. This one comes from the USS *Jimmy Carter*. It's a Seawolf-class submarine. Ultra quiet. She's orbiting around the island, gathering as much information as she can. But since almost all of our satcom is down, we're only getting her reports and data sporadically. You'll also get electronic eavesdropping information from our surveillance aircraft in the area. The updates come in about every hour."

David kept scrolling through the files. "This is great stuff."

She said, "Yes, it is. Anyway, take a look. We're meeting at two p.m. to go over the latest information. Can you join us?"

Until now, David had been asked to provide information almost solely based on his experience on the island. This was different. Now they wanted him to help out with the analysis of the collected intelligence.

Part of this change in his treatment might be due to being short-staffed. Some of the men and women who had been assigned to the SILVERSMITH project were reassigned to the Middle East desk after the Beltway attacks. The war with Iran was going to happen. It was no longer a question of if, but when.

This China theory, as some called it, was becoming a lower priority, despite interest from the director. While it frustrated David, he found that the more noise he made, the less credibility he had. Chase kept telling him that he needed to earn their trust first, and then give his opinions. This seemed to be the first evidence that the strategy was working.

"I'll be there."

She nodded. "Good."

He sipped on his coffee and resumed scrolling through the images on his screen, taking notes.

* * *

The next day, David watched an interrogation of the Chinese operative with a mix of intrigue and frustration. He sat next to Susan and a few others on the SILVERSMITH team, in a darkened room behind a two-way mirror. Some of them wore headsets so they could hear the interrogation through the speakers. Two video monitors showed the Chinese spy's face at different angles as he answered questions. But the man's answers didn't help David get any closer to the answer to his problem.

For the past twenty-four hours, David had been studying the data from the Red Cell island that Susan had granted him access to. His job was to look at the data coming from the USS *Jimmy Carter*, which was surveilling the Red Cell island, and compare it to other bits of intelligence.

Thinking he might have found something, he decided to look at the tail numbers of the large Chinese transport jets that were now landing on the island every day. Among the information they had access to were the details from the flight plans that the Chinese pilots filed before takeoff. Each of these files contained the tail number and takeoff time of the aircraft.

Next, David used the imagery and written summary provided by the USS *Jimmy Carter*. Its mission was to monitor everything that happened on that island, using its high-tech sensors to gather a variety of information. They were able to get pictures of almost every aircraft that landed on the island.

What David found interesting was that the tail numbers and the time stamps provided by the USS *Jimmy Carter* didn't match the filed flight plans. He was about to tell Susan about his find when the director stepped in.

"Morning, Susan," the director whispered, not wanting his voice to carry through the two-way mirror. While the rooms were supposed to be soundproof, they weren't perfect. "I've got about ten minutes. What have you got for me?"

"Sir, we're starting to hit a wall," Susan replied quietly. "He's confirmed his own role in instigating the Beltway attacks, but links to China are tenuous. We have a list of potential personnel within the US who might have assisted him. None of them have any ties to the Chinese, though. They're just third parties he's used."

"So where did he get the orders from?"

"He claimed that they were verbal orders, from Lena Chou."

"Another person the Chinese don't claim to own."

"Correct, sir."

"Anything more on Latin America and Chinese military movements?"

"No, sir, just that they are taking place. No distinct locations yet, although we're working with US Air Force and other reconnaissance assets to narrow down a few possibilities."

"What about the Red Cell?"

"He claims not to know much about the Red Cell. Our interrogator told us he would be digging more on this today. It seems the initial shock of being captured has worn off. Now he's sticking to his script more, and giving us less."

The director nodded. "Alright. Anything more from our friends in Beijing?"

He was referring to a human intelligence source within the highest levels of the Chinese Politburo.

"Sir, our source has triple-verified that the Chinese president and top generals in the PLA know nothing of any Chinese participation in the Beltway attacks. They aren't convinced one way or another about Jinshan's participation."

"How is Jinshan doing this? How is he able to use so many Chinese military and intelligence assets without the consent of Chinese leadership?"

Susan said, "Sir, we now believe that one of Jinshan's main allies within the Chinese government must be the South Fleet Commander of the PLA Navy. He would be the one in charge of the Red Cell island, based on the island's location. He would also have been able to grant access to the types of military assets that are supposedly supporting Jinshan's operation."

The director leaned in. "So you're telling me that Jinshan and one rogue general are really the ones doing all this?"

"An admiral, not a general. But, yes, sir. That's what we now think."

"Unbelievable. The president wants to show the Chinese president proof. Assuming that we think his reaction would be favorable."

"Our China analyst team thinks that the Chinese president would consider Jinshan's actions high treason, if confirmed, sir. And our China station is doing everything they can to help find out more and bring it to the attention of the Chinese leadership. But to be honest, sir, we still have very little proof, other than our word against theirs."

"But what about all the military buildup on the Red Cell island?" the director said.

"That particular military buildup is approved by the PLA leadership, sir. As you know, part of the Chinese military strategy is to build up military outposts and bases in the South China Sea. This extends their territorial claim and defensive capability."

The two were quiet for a moment, watching the interrogation going on in the next room, and David went back to looking at the Chinese flight records for the transports taking off and the images taken from the *Jimmy Carter* off the coast of the Red Cell island.

"Something doesn't match up here," David said to Susan.

Susan looked at him. "What do you mean?"

"I'm looking at the records of the Chinese military flights to the Red Cell island. Not all the planes are actually landing there."

The director overheard this. "What do you mean?"

"Sir, the submarine that's monitoring the island has been taking pictures of just about every aircraft that lands on that runway. I've been comparing them to the Mainland Chinese flight records. Only about a third of the jets are actually landing at the island when they're supposed to be."

Susan's voice was skeptical. "The submarine probably can't monitor everything. Maybe some of the aircraft were missed because it had to submerge or something."

David shook his head. "I thought about that. But I looked at the timestamps. That can't be the only explanation. At least two-thirds of these Chinese Air Force transport jets are supposed to be landing at the Red Cell island, but they aren't."

The director asked the obvious. "So if they aren't landing on the island, but that's what their flight plan is filed for, then where are they going?"

David said, "That's an important question. But what I think we also need to know is...well, I heard you talking about the Chinese leadership denying knowledge of Jinshan's Red Cell program. But they know that there's a military buildup there. What I can't understand is how these aircraft could be landing anywhere else and not alerting Chinese leadership."

The director said, "Say more."

"Well, sir, at In-Q-Tel, I worked with a lot of military technology from around the world. As I'm sure you know, network-centric warfare has been the big trend since the late nineties. The Chinese are following that trend with all their military equipment modernization. Military leaders want to be able to go to a tactical screen and see every asset they own and where they are at any given moment. In order to accomplish this, the Chinese have always used a system of transponders and GPS antennas."

Susan said, "So...you're saying that the Chinese military leaders would have been alerted to their aircraft not going to the Red Cell island."

David nodded. "Yes. Military leaders in Beijing should be able to look at a map and see if they have transport aircraft flying to...let's say, South America."

The director said, "Is there any other explanation here?"

"It's possible that this is part of another covert operation. But for"—David looked down at his notes—"twenty-two brand-new, massive military cargo jets to disappear without the top generals knowing about it, that seems pretty odd to me. And for that to occur when their destination is Jinshan's Red Cell island—that seems like too big a coincidence."

The director said, "How do we find out where these aircraft are going? And how they're hiding it?"

Susan said, "Give me a few hours. I think I know who might be able to help."

* * *

David and Susan sat in a windowless meeting room at the NSA Headquarters in Fort Meade, Maryland. David remembered the man sitting across from them as Diaz, the NSA person who had briefed them at Langley.

Diaz said, "So I was able to look into what you asked."

Susan raised an eyebrow. "And?"

"Actually, I found something quite interesting. But first let me explain. Chinese military aircraft—as well as many of their other assets, like ships and submarines—all use encryption for their communications."

David said, "What about location information? Do their military assets broadcast their location to each other?"

"Eh. Some of them. Aircraft all do, sure. That's called IFF. Identification Friend or Foe. Some ships have transponders of sorts. Submarines don't. Tanks don't. Soldiers don't. At least not normally. The reason is obvious. If your enemy were to gain access to your network, they would be able to locate all your assets. And that would mean they could target you very precisely. It would be a huge advantage. But it's also important for battlefield commanders to know where their units are, right?"

"Right."

"So, modern military forces encrypt all their data. We often shorten the word *encryption* to *crypto*. But we in the signals intelligence world don't need location-transmitting technology to find your location. We just need you to communicate. If you're broadcasting any electronic signal, that gives away your position."

Susan said, "So if the Chinese are operating a secret army in places that they haven't told all of their military and political leadership about, you would be able to use their communications broadcasts to prove their whereabouts?"

Diaz said, "In essence, yes."

Susan said, "Well, this is great! Do it."

Diaz cracked his knuckles. "Right. Well, two things. One, I've already found your secret army. They're in Ecuador."

Susan said, "Ecuador?"

Diaz held up his hand. "And two—this is the interesting thing that I've uncovered—they aren't using the same crypto that the rest of the Chinese are using. Their communications and location information is hidden, even to the regular Chinese military."

David said, "What do you mean?"

"This secret army of yours is using a different crypto key. A piece of hardware with their codes for encryption. There are a whole slew of Chinese aircraft, ships, and submarines, as well as many land-based units in Ecuador, that are using this unique crypto key. It's the same technology that the PLA is using. But the codes are separate. I've looked at it, and I can tell that it's being changed every ninety-six hours. But we can't break it. The technology is state-of-the-art."

"So what's next?"

Diaz said, "We need one of those crypto keys."

Susan said, "What do you mean, we need one? Why?"

Diaz said, "You told me that you need evidence on what the Chinese are up to, right? Evidence that will prove to the Chinese leadership that there is a rogue element—a secret army—operating without its approval?"

"That's the idea, yes," said Susan.

"Well, we can't very well show them our own signals intelligence that they're operating in Ecuador. But if you get me one of those crypto keys, that's China's own technology. It would allow me to show the Chinese hard evidence of their own creation that would be easier for them to understand. Plus, it wouldn't divulge any of our own closely guarded secrets."

David said, "So we need to get one of the crypto keys from the Chinese?"

Diaz said, "Yes."

"That doesn't sound easy."

"I imagine it wouldn't be. But there's something else. You know how I said that it operates on a ninety-six-hour reset?"

"Yes."

"Well, that's another obstacle you're going to have to worry about. It's a security measure. Every ninety-six hours, they change the codes. So if you steal one of these suckers, the codes it's holding will only be good for ninety-six hours. After that, it turns into a big, heavy, useless black box."

David said, "Oh. Good. So we have to steal one of the Chinese crypto keys, but it'll expire ninety-six hours after we steal it?"

"Yes."

* * *

Susan, David, and the director met with General Schwartz as soon as the interrogation finished.

"Sir, we hit the jackpot. It appears that the Chinese have been sending transport aircraft to Manta, Ecuador. Air Force reconnaissance drones just confirmed the location, and our friends at the NSA confirmed the method of hiding the military assets. We believe that they're sending troops and supplies there. Some of the transport jets remain on the Red Cell island. When the aircraft that are headed to Ecuador overfly the island, they're changing out their identification, using special crypto keys. These are the pieces of hardware that identify the military asset on the Chinese network. We now believe that the military assets working for Jinshan and Admiral Song have their own unique crypto keys. They can use these to talk with and locate each other, without the rest of the Chinese military leadership knowing about it."

The general said, "Why would they do that?"

"Because they aren't telling everyone in their chain of command what they're up to," the director of the CIA said. "We don't yet know how many of these Chinese military and intelligence personnel are aware that this is a rogue operation. But it *is* a rogue operation. We know that Cheng Jinshan and Vice Admiral Song are in on it. They're not being forthright with their leadership."

The general shook his head. "Unbelievable. So what, then? We just need proof to show the Chinese president? They'll execute Jinshan and the admiral tomorrow, right? My God...does this mean that we're about to go to war with Iran all because of these two men?"

No one spoke.

Finally the director said, "We need to get hard evidence to show not just to the Chinese leadership, but also to our own politicians. I'm facing some fierce resistance in our own government whenever I broach the subject of China. There is so much intensity on Iran after the Beltway attacks, it's hard to sway opinions. So, general, we'd like your help in drawing up plans to get that hard evidence."

The general said, "Of course. What do you have in mind?"

Susan said, "We want to steal one of their new crypto keys from their base in Manta, Ecuador. They must have one there. These crypto keys would have the unique data, which our folks at the NSA can then clone. It would provide irrefutable proof of what they're up to. It would also provide us a snapshot of where all these Chinese assets really are. We can then show this both to our political leaders, and to the Chinese leadership. If we can do that, our hope is that the Chinese hostilities would cease immediately, and we might even be able to scale back what's going on with Iran."

12

Two Weeks Later
USS Farragut
In port, Panama City, Panama

A loud whistle sounded over the 1MC throughout the ship, followed by, "Liberty call, liberty call. All hands, liberty call." A muffled cheer could be heard below decks.

Victoria stood on the fantail, looking out on the pier. Seagulls flew over the vendors' shops. The vendors were the local salesmen from Panama City who would sell trinkets and cigars to the throngs of sailors about to go out on liberty.

They had left port shortly after the terrorist attack on the D.C. Beltway, two weeks ago. It was a security precaution, ordered by the Navy. Victoria agreed that it had been the prudent course of action. But after several months at sea with only a few port calls, everyone was pretty upset that they had only been able to get away for a few hours before being recalled.

She had given the same speech several times now. *We need to be thinking about the lives of the men and women who were just taken from us. Our job is to protect and defend. No one should complain*

about something as petty as going out on liberty at a time like this.
The speech rang true. She could see it in her men's eyes.

But after two more weeks at sea, when Big Navy had reset the
threat level in Panama, they had been allowed back in for another
port stop. The captain had given his own speech about how the crew
needed to represent the values of our nation, especially after something like the Beltway attacks.

She wondered what was going on in the world. There were too
many "Attacks" lately. The Dubai attacks. The Blackout Attack.
Now, the Beltway attacks. Was everyone losing their minds?

Victoria walked through the wardroom and found her pilots
already in civilian clothes, chomping at the bit to get into the city.
She shot them a crooked smile. "Where the hell do you guys think
you're going?"

Plug smiled back. "I'm taking Juan here into Panama City. He's
my liberty buddy. And he also happens to be a native Spanish
speaker. Might come in handy."

Juan rolled his eyes. "I don't technically think you would call me
a *native* Spanish speaker since I was born in the US, but my mother
is Mexican and I can speak Spanish."

Plug said, "Did you acquire your Spanish speaking skills at an
early age?"

"*Sí.*"

"Are you able to produce fluent, spontaneous discourse in said
language?"

"*Sí.*"

"That's native enough to make sure I don't get ripped off by the
bartenders."

"*Sí.*"

Victoria chuckled. "Don't do anything I wouldn't do."

Plug said, "You sure you don't want to go out on the town with
us, Boss?"

You could hear a pin drop as they waited for her to answer.

While they had invited her out with them the last time they
pulled in, that had been the appropriate thing to do. She had
accepted, and the polite "hanging out with her men" box had been

checked, even if it had ended early. But she knew that the last thing any of them *really* wanted was for their boss to be out on liberty with them today. Especially Plug.

She said, "Well…I could have one of you guys stay here on duty tonight instead of letting you go out, now that I think about it…"

She looked at the expressions of the four junior officers. She made a face like she was thinking about it, trying to inflict as much pain as possible before declining.

The four pilots held their breath at the threat of losing the only thing that really mattered to them right now. Liberty was more than a meal and a few beers. On ships with little to no Internet, liberty was often the only time they could speak to their wives, families, and significant others. And *that* was the fuel that kept spirits alive during military deployments.

She waved her hand. "Nah…you guys go. I'm going to get some work done."

A simultaneous exhale from the group. "Okay, well, we'll see you tomorrow." They bolted. She had never seen them go so fast.

The 1MC speaker announced, "Air Boss, your presence is requested in the captain's cabin."

Hmm. Now it was her turn to try and avoid dinner with her boss. That was a much taller task. Oh, well. She would be the good lieutenant commander and take one for the team.

She marched down the passageway, turning the corner to the captain's cabin. She nearly fell down when she saw who was waiting for her.

The captain had a broad smile on his face, standing behind Victoria's brother Chase. Chase wore a sly grin, happy to surprise his sister. They embraced, joy in her heart.

"What the hell are you doing here?" she asked after finally giving him room to breathe.

His expression didn't change, but the captain's did, she noticed. The captain looked serious.

Chase said, "It's a work-related trip."

She nodded. "I see." There was another man—a Navy commander—sitting in the captain's cabin. She didn't recognize him.

The captain said, "Air Boss, your brother has a very interesting job. He's done briefing me, so I'll let you two catch up. He and his colleague said they'd only be able to stay for a few minutes, so I can't invite them with us tonight. But when you guys are done talking, come find me. I'm dragging you and the XO out for dinner."

She smiled politely. "Yes, sir."

She motioned for Chase to follow her. She decided to take him back to the hangar. "Come on, I'll show you the seventy million dollars in helicopters the taxpayers are trusting me with."

"Well, there's a mistake," he joked.

She didn't bother introducing him to her men, some of whom were in the hangar working on the aircraft. Victoria didn't want to be rude, but she knew that Chase's work was very sensitive stuff. And while she knew that she might be fanning some rumors with her wide smile and the good-looking man at her side, she wanted to do her part to protect his privacy.

"So you can only stay a moment?" she asked.

"Yeah, I've got to keep moving."

They leaned on the metal railing of the flight deck nets, overlooking the water that fed into the Panama Canal. Passenger jets flew overhead every few minutes, landing at the international airport.

"How's David?" she asked.

"Honestly? He's been better. You spoke to him, right?"

"Yeah. I called him a few weeks ago. He sounded scared and frustrated. He couldn't say too much over the phone."

She looked around to make sure they were out of earshot. "Anything you can fill me in on? The last thing I saw was what the news put out—saying the whole thing with them being apprehended on cyberterrorist charges was a misunderstanding at Interpol. Then this shit with Iran started happening and the news didn't care anymore."

Chase looked at his sister. "Can I tell you something that's going to sound crazy?"

"Yeah."

He whispered, "It's not *Iran* that we need to be worried about."

Victoria frowned. Half the US Navy was being deployed to the Persian Gulf. Shots had already been fired between Iran and the US.

Her father had debarked the USS *Truman* only days before it had been attacked by Iranian cruise missiles. The news was nonstop coverage about an Iranian terror cell attacking American civilians on the D.C. Beltway. Now the United States was getting ready to put an end to the extremist Iranian regime once and for all. The military buildup in the region was similar to the Iraq wars. Any day now, the balloon would go up, and a US-led invasion into Iran would begin.

"How is *Iran* not what we need to be worrying about?"

He shook his head. "I can't go into it."

"Come on, little brother, you can't say something like that and not give me any more."

He looked at her. "Your captain just got orders—he knows what he needs to do. He's got a sealed mission brief that he'll give to you if we need you. Otherwise, I can't go into it."

She crossed her arms. "What the hell are you up to?"

Chase looked at the helicopters, folded and stuffed in the hangars. He said, "What type of mission are you doing here?"

Victoria said, "What do you mean? In the EASTPAC? Counternarcotic, mostly. Some training exercises with the UK and some South American countries."

Chase looked grim. "That could change."

She didn't like this. Chase never got rattled. A former officer in the SEAL community, he had been on several deployments in the Middle East. Her brother was, although it was still hard for her to fathom, a decorated war hero. When he'd left the teams a year and a half ago, he'd smiled as he told her that he was going to be working for the Department of State.

She knew that men like Chase didn't take jobs like that. Not that there was anything wrong with working in the diplomatic community. But serving in that capacity wouldn't have scratched the itch for him. He was an operator, and an adrenaline junkie. She knew that Chase was involved in something more...*exciting*.

The night of their mother's funeral, the three siblings had drowned their sorrows at McGarvey's Pub in Annapolis. Chase always had loose lips when he drank. That was when Victoria usually pressed him about his relationships, so she could report back to Mom. Back when Mom was still around. But that night at the pub, Chase had admitted to her that he was going to work for the CIA as a member of their Special Operations Group. It would be similar work to what he was already doing, but it would open up a host of other opportunities within the CIA.

Victoria thought about the reason the CIA would send him here, to her ship. It was highly irregular. She tried once more. "What are you doing here, Chase?"

He shook his head. Then he looked down at the water. A school of fish were causing ripples on the surface, going after bugs. "I can't tell you what I'm doing here. But you saw me meet with your ship captain. If you guys are needed, we delivered a mission packet to the captain of your ship. Even he isn't supposed to read it unless you get the call. And, Victoria, if you *are* needed..." He looked up from the water and into her eyes. "Just be careful. Okay?"

"My God, Chase, you're starting to scare the shit out of me. *Something* must be really wrong. Does this have to do with the Beltway attacks?"

He looked at his watch. "Time for me to run." He reached over and gave her a great big bear hug. "Love you, sis. Good luck."

She watched him walk down the pier, hop in a cab and disappear. The executive officer, the number two in charge on the ship, walked up next to her on the flight deck. He was already wearing his civilian clothes.

"Air Boss," he greeted her.

"XO."

"Just had a talk with the captain. Seems like we're going to be changing our operating area for this international exercise next week."

"Oh? Where are we headed?"

"Somewhere in between the Galapagos and Ecuador."

"The captain say anything else? Like what the hell those two men just briefed him on?"

"Not really. Just that we need to go into a geographic box next week and stay there in case they need us."

"Need us for what?"

He shrugged. "He didn't say."

The XO pulled out a cigar. They were selling Cubans on the pier. He probably got it there. He looked up the dock and saw that they were getting ready to fuel the ship. He cursed and placed the cigar back in his breast pocket. "Come on, Victoria, I ain't got all day. Get your civvies on. Let's get out of here. We all need to have a stiff drink tonight."

She rolled her eyes. "Alright. I guess it's time for our mandatory fun."

* * *

While Victoria wasn't excited about hanging out with the captain, she had to admit that the meal was excellent. Steak and lobster at one of the best local restaurants, and as an appetizer, the most delicious ceviche she'd ever tasted. They hadn't stayed out long. The duty van brought them back almost as soon as their meal was done.

Now, the captain, Victoria, and the XO sat at a picnic table about one hundred yards down the pier from where the USS *Farragut* was parked. The captain wanted to smoke his cigar before they got back on the ship.

She had no objections. There was a distinct pull that all seafaring men felt. Whenever in port, it was best to be off the ship.

The captain removed two more cigars and handed them to the XO and her.

"No, thank you, sir."

"Suit yourself."

She was a little tipsy from the wine from dinner. "Oh, what the hell. Pass it over. I don't think I've had a cigar since college."

The XO smiled. "This stuff is the secret to happiness."

The rich, pungent aroma of Cuban tobacco filled the air.

The captain began, "Alright, folks, here it is."

She had wondered when he would get down to business. It had been all small talk and football over dinner. A few sea stories. But oddly, nothing about what was coming up. And nothing about the mysterious visit from Chase and the other commander.

"We're going to get underway tomorrow afternoon."

The captain turned to the XO. "When we get back on board in a few minutes, tell the officer of the deck to cancel all leave and liberty starting at zero eight hundred tomorrow. Once people return, they're to stay aboard. I don't even want people getting off the ship to go to the vendors. Air Boss, you're to start drilling your aircrew for multimission operations. XO, I want a general quarters, unannounced, right at lunchtime tomorrow."

"While we're ashore, Captain?"

"Yes."

Victoria said, "Sir, what exactly does 'multimission operations' mean?"

The captain shrugged. "Hell if I know. Everything, I guess. You're the aviator."

Victoria wasn't sure if she should admit that Chase had given her any hints, but she had to try and get more information. "Sir, is there a mission packet for me?"

The captain eyed her. "There is. But my instructions were to leave it in my safe unless we get told to open it."

Victoria said nothing.

The XO said, "Sir, may I ask what's going on?"

The captain took a puff from his cigar and slowly exhaled. "I wish I could tell you, XO, but to be quite honest, other than the geographic box they want us to stay in, I don't really know."

* * *

Juan watched in amusement as Plug lost his shirt. The night started off innocently enough. The four pilots had gone to their hotel—the Marriott—in Panama City. The other two junior pilots were both married and immediately attempted every possible method of communicating with their families. With much of the Internet's functionality still seriously damaged from the attacks of a few weeks ago, all video chat options—normally a mainstay of liberty stops—were out of the question. That meant that they had to call via good old-fashioned telephone.

Juan would have been happy to just grab a meal and hang out by the hotel's outdoor pool, relaxing in the seventy-five-degree December weather in Panama.

But Plug had other plans. He wasn't married, but he was always looking. And he was a HAC. A helicopter aircraft commander. Aside from Victoria, Plug was the only other HAC on this deployment. So inside the aircraft, he was in charge when flying with one of the junior pilots. He was a rank higher than the three junior pilots but treated them as peers when they were out of the cockpit. Unless it suited his needs to pull rank—say, for instance, if he wanted to go out drinking, and others didn't.

In a way, the social structure resembled high school. Juan and the other junior pilots were like freshmen, and Plug was like a senior. It was cool to hang out with a senior, if given the opportunity. So Juan agreed to go "out on the town" with Plug.

What could go wrong?

When Plug finished off a twelve pack of beers before they even left the hotel room, Juan began to wonder if perhaps he had made the wrong decision.

Several hours of bars, "exclusive nightclubs," and casinos later, Juan sat nursing an ice water, exhausted. They were in a private poker room at the Casino Panama. Throughout the night, it had become apparent that Juan was going to be Plug's babysitter. As Juan saw it, Plug was going to drink, smoke, and hit on as many women as he could until he either self-destructed or passed out.

Juan looked at him and shook his head. Plug had just reraised the ante at his table before they had even dealt the cards. This was a faux pas in a friendly game of poker, let alone the high roller table he sat at now. Plug had finagled his way into a seat at this private game.

"Sir, please wait until it is your turn," said the dealer in heavily accented English.

Plug scraped his chips back to the pile in front of him.

The other players all seemed to know each other. Juan could tell because they were having friendly conversations in Spanish together. Plug could barely understand English in his current drunken stupor, so he was at what one might call a disadvantage.

Juan was pretty sure the other players were colluding, although they didn't have to. Plug was quite capable of giving away all his money without any help. Several times he had even shown his cards by accident. A mix of groans and laughter erupted from the table each time.

"Sir, are you with him?" The man who spoke to Juan looked like the manager.

"Unfortunately."

"I'm afraid that we'll have to ask him to leave after this hand."

"I understand. Thanks," said Juan.

Juan went up and tapped Plug on the shoulder.

He turned and looked surprised. "Juan! What are you doing here?"

"I've been with you all night."

"Tremendous! Have a seat. We were just playing cards. Me and my new buddies."

Juan glanced up at the table. A few waved at him. Juan said, "Plug, man, listen, we need to go after this."

Plug looked serious. "Got it." He turned to the dealer and said, "All in."

"Señor, you just folded."

"Okay, next hand, then."

The dealer shot Juan a look.

Juan tried another tactic. "Hey, Plug, I know a place where we can get some *really* good pizza near the hotel."

"*Really?*"

"Yeah, come on."

He turned back to the dealer. "Sorry, guys, I gotta run."

Smiles and waves. Card sharks loved drunks and amateurs more than they loved aces.

Once outside the casino, they ran into a horde of enlisted sailors from the ship. They were hailing cabs, about to head back to the pier. Only the E-5s and above were allowed overnights.

Plug yelled, "Hey! I know you guys! Say, you guys wanna have some fun?"

Juan tried to steer Plug away, but it was too late. Some of the sailors, happy to laugh at a drunken officer and pilot, replied in the affirmative.

As the sailors got into their cabs, Plug took out a wad of cash from his wallet, handing what must have been two hundred American dollars to each cab driver.

He turned to Juan. "Okay. Now this is important. I need you to tell them something in Panamanian—or Mexican. Your choice. Tell the drivers that the money I've given them is for a *race*." He said the word *race* loudly and slowly, while looking at the drivers. "They're to race each other back to the boat, and to show these men a good time."

Plug swayed while he spoke. Then he looked at his shipmates, already packed into the two cabs like sardines. He held up his finger high in the air. "It is a race to the death!" The sailors cheered. Plug then looked at Juan, trying to focus on his face. "If they need more money, I can go back to the poker table. Tell them. Tell them in Spanish this time."

Juan patted Plug on the shoulder. "Sure thing."

He stood in front of the cabs. Both cab drivers leaned out their windows, smiling. They looked thrilled to get the extra cash.

Juan said loudly in Spanish, "My friend said to tell you to drive really fast until you get around the corner, and then to slow down and drive safe. Have a good night."

The drivers gave a thumbs-up. One of them revved his engine, and the other followed. More cheers from the passengers.

Plug turned to Juan. "Did you tell them?"

"Oh yes." He smiled as the first car sped off for the first fifty feet and then began driving normally. The second car followed suit. Boisterous cheers from both cars.

Plug slapped his knee. "Awesome."

Juan smiled. "Come on, we've got to get back to the hotel."

Plug nodded and held up a finger to wait. Then he turned and vomited on the sidewalk.

Juan sighed. He turned out to the street. "Taxi!"

Plug screamed at the top of his lungs, "*Whooo!* Glad I got that out of my system." He looked at Juan suspiciously. "Did you put something in my food?"

Juan held up his hands and shook his head.

"Alright, well, it's time for us to go start drinking."

A taxi pulled up.

Juan said, "Plug, I really think we should go back to the hotel."

A group of the ship's officers stuck their heads out of a cab driving by. They screamed the name of another well-known bar. "Meet us there!"

Plug gave a thumbs-up. His eyes were out of focus. He dove into the waiting taxi and yelled. "Follow that car!"

Juan sighed and got in the passenger seat. He checked his watch. This would be the last time he would make the mistake of babysitting Plug.

* * *

Plug awoke to the sound of knocking. Each knock struck his head like a hammer. His surroundings came into focus and he realized that he was in a hotel room.

He looked to his left and saw two women in his bed. One wore a bright red thong. The other was buck naked. Both were stunning Latin women. Dark hair, tan. Lots of makeup.

They were a beautiful sight, but he didn't care. He only wanted his head to stop hurting. He wondered if he would make it to the toilet before he threw up. Thankfully, he did, barely. He turned the faucet on, washing the sour taste out of his mouth, wondering what god he had upset to deserve this horrible feeling.

Images of the night before flashed through his head. Through the pain of his massive hangover, he knew that they had started off in a hotel room. Those pansy-ass married 2Ps didn't even want to go out. They just wanted to talk on their phones and make kissy noises with their wives. So he ended up going out with their most junior pilot, Juan. He was kind of a nerd, and a truly awful pilot, but a nice enough dude.

Plug remembered that they had gone to a casino. He was pretty sure that he lost money there, but he remembered they had a good time…then he didn't remember much after that. He thought they might have gone to a nightclub. Some of the ship guys were there.

Plug looked over at the bed. The two sleeping beauties were still there. He honestly had no idea how the three of them had ended up here. Or for that matter, where they *were*.

Knocks at the door again, and he remembered what woke him up. The room was spinning. God, he was still drunk. He threw his clothes on, hobbling over to the door. He cracked it open.

The three 2Ps smiled back at him.

Caveman, with the biggest shit-eating grin ever, said, "Have a nice night, HAC?"

Juan said, "Thank God. I was gonna be pissed if you were dead in a ditch somewhere."

"*Dudes*. Why are you knocking? What time is it?" he asked.

Plug opened the door a little more, and the 2Ps looked beyond him. They saw two pairs of bare legs lying on the bed and their smiles got wider.

Juan said, "You're not going to like this, but we have to go. We already packed up your stuff."

Plug was confused. Maybe it was the alcohol. "Did you say we have to go? We have this hotel for one more night, I thought. What are you talking about?"

"Shore patrol's been coming around. Everyone's getting recalled to the ship. *Again*. We have to go now. Ship's leaving today. Come on."

He looked back at the women on the bed. One of them sat up, a coy smile on her face. She partially covered her chest with one arm.

Plug looked back at the 2Ps. "Have I ever told you how much I really hate you guys?"

* * *

A few hours later, Plug sat on the flight deck, leaning up against the hangar door, as the ship began to pick up speed. The breeze felt good. The rolling did not.

His head pounded. He wore sunglasses and a fitted dark blue squadron cap to hide how hungover he still was. His flight suit was zipped down a bit too low. A rim of sweat formed on his brow. He had a large plastic water bottle that he sipped from every few minutes. He needed some Advil.

"You alright, Plug?"

Air Boss walked over, a sympathetic look on her face. Of course she knew. She never missed anything.

He tried to sit up a little straighter in front of his boss. "They got me good on this one. Telling us that we're going to have several days in port like that and then rounding us all up while we've been..."

"Drinking?"

"Relaxing."

She smiled and pulled up a fold-up chair. "I'd like to tell you that you can hit the rack and recuperate, but there's a reason we left port this morning, instead of three days from now."

He sipped more water from the water bottle and then got off his ass and stood up. The combination of the ship's increasing rolls and his blood alcohol mix not quite being back to normal made him almost fall down. He grabbed hold of the flight deck railing.

Plug said, "What's the story?"

She told him what little she knew.

"So...multimission operations. What does that mean? Like—be ready for anything?"

Victoria nodded. "That's the way I understand it. Can you gather up everyone and have them here for a quick meeting?"

Plug knew that by everyone, she meant the members of the aviation detachment. His eighteen enlisted maintenance men, the two enlisted rescue swimmers, and the three junior pilots.

"I can have them here in ten minutes, boss." A part of his brain was fighting through the fog, telling him that her mannerisms signaled something big was going on.

"Thanks." She smiled, crossed her legs and opened her notebook.

Plug walked carefully down the shadowy port hangar, squeezing through the narrow space between the helicopter and the hull, stepping over the chains that tied the helicopter down.

Plug found the man he was looking for. "Senior Chief?"

The senior chief was typing on one of the computers they used to keep track of all the maintenance done on the helicopters. The senior enlisted man in the aviation detachment, he was approaching his twentieth year in the Navy, and compared to most of the crew, he'd seen it all. This was his twelfth deployment. He'd spent a total of eight years of his life at sea. Two of his children were born while he was away.

When Plug had been selected by their squadron's commanding officer to be the maintenance officer on this detachment, the first thing he'd done was go introduce himself to his new chief. Junior officers could go far if they were talented. But they went a lot farther with a good senior enlisted to serve as a partner and guide.

"Sir, how may I be of assistance?"

"Boss wants everyone on the flight deck in ten minutes."

He grunted. "I was wondering when that was gonna come."

Plug said, "I'll go tell the pilots and aircrew. Can you send someone to round up the guys?"

"Sure thing," he said. "This about why we left Panama so soon?"

"I reckon it is."

He grunted again. A man of few words.

Plug walked through the ship and into the junior pilots' stateroom.

All three of them shared a space that was about the size of a large walk-in closet, a triple-bunk on the far side. Juan was reading a novel on the top bunk.

The room was dark, just like every sleeping space on the ship. Ship life was twenty-four hours, and some people had to sleep during the day. It drove Plug crazy that the surface warfare officers were always running their freaking drills and making noise in the middle of the day when people on the night shift were trying to sleep.

The SWOs saw any complaint about lack of sleep as an admission of weakness. Their argument was that SWOs, like surgeons, needed to operate on very little sleep. And that pilots were all pampered prima donnas who slept too much and saw the ship as their personal cruise line.

Pilots considered the ship more of a helicopter barge than a cruise line and argued that while one might be able to drive a ship at twelve knots while fatigued, it was another matter entirely to be tired and try to land a helicopter on the back of a single-spot ship in the middle of the night. Also, pilots required more beauty rest in order to keep their great looks.

Plug actually had a lot of respect for the surface navy. It was, like almost every other military community, a group of hardworking and dedicated men and women. SWOs had long hours, tough living conditions, grueling deployments, and very little recognition compared to other members of the military. They were technical experts and nautical masters. But he would die before admitting as much to any of those bastards.

"Where are the other 2Ps?" he asked Juan.

"Working out."

"Go get 'em. Boss wants us on the flight deck for a meeting in five."

"Yes, sir."

"Shut up, 2P."

He smiled and slammed the door. While Plug was a HAC, and senior to the 2Ps, the pilot culture had an unwritten rule that none of the officers under the rank of O-4 were ever to be referred to as sir or ma'am. That meant that on this boat, only Lieutenant Commander Victoria Manning would be called ma'am by the pilots. And it was still more common in this environment to address her as "Air Boss," or "Boss" for short. This was because she was the officer in charge of the helicopter aviation detachment on board.

Plug went to his stateroom and swallowed two ibuprofen pills, then walked back to the flight deck. He checked his watch. At least he would be able to sleep off his hangover after this meeting.

The twenty-six men who were part of HSM-46 Detachment Two were gathered around the air boss. It was a little funny having an all-male detachment and a female air boss. Not that anyone lacked respect for her, but a group of twenty-six military men led by one woman sounded like the premise for a sitcom. She was like their mother in some ways. A very smart, driven, whip-bearing, micro-managing mother.

Minutes later, the group was gathered on the flight deck. Boss stood in the middle of the circle, making light-hearted jokes with the men. She took good care of them. They respected her and worked hard to impress her. Plug had never heard her raise her voice. But she didn't have to. She had the ability to say things in a certain tone, to give you a certain look, which made whatever she said become your life's goal.

Boss said, "Everyone here?"

Plug, sunglasses still on, nodded. "Yes, ma'am."

"Good. I'm not sure how much more time we'll have. Rumor has it"—she looked around to make sure no one aside from her air detachment was in earshot—"that we may be doing some training this afternoon. As in, general quarters type training." Groans from the group.

She held up her hands to silence them. "Gents, I need you to suck it up." She spoke in that serious tone that got things done. The group went quiet. "We got word yesterday that we may be participating in some pretty high-priority assignments over the next few weeks. If I could tell you more about it, I would. But here's what you need to know. We're going to be training. Hard. And flying a lot. From here on out, I want to always have an aircraft on the Alert Fifteen. We're also going to need to have two flyable aircraft, with as little mainte-nance downtime as possible. No self-inflicted wounds. If we need parts for maintenance, let's order extra now. Plug, Senior Chief, you have my permission to order stuff that we might not even need, but that might be nice to have. If we need extra space, I can get it. If you run into any pushback, let me know. But we need to have two flyable aircraft, with all our mission systems working. Any questions?"

No hands were raised. Finally, the senior chief said, "Ma'am, what type of training will we be focusing on?"

She smiled. "I'm glad you asked, Senior. We're going to start practicing torpedo loads once per day. Hellfire loads once per day. It's also possible that we'll need to transport Special Warfare operators, so I need us to think about whether we would make any different configuration choices there."

A lot of raised eyebrows at that. Victoria had given herself an exercise the night before. She'd brainstormed on all the most important missions that someone like Chase—who worked for the CIA—might be involved in. While her helicopter detachment's obvious roles were anti-ship and anti-submarine warfare, her one clue had been that he was a former Navy SEAL. She imagined that his work with the CIA was related. So if he was involved, her theory was that they might need their helicopters to provide transport. It was just a hunch, but it was something to prepare for nonetheless.

The ship's alarm sounded, and the 1MC let out a whistle. *"General quarters, general quarters, all hands man your battle stations. Set condition Zebra throughout the ship. This is a drill."*

Curses amongst the group. They looked to Victoria. Her men were clearly anxious to get to where they needed to be but were torn between that and their respect for her, not wanting to leave until dismissed.

She said, "Alright, folks, we'll continue this later. Get going."

The group quickly scattered. The pilots walked back to Officer's Country. They stopped in the wardroom. Plug said, "Special Warfare pax transfers?"

She looked at him and nodded. "We need to be ready for anything right now."

As if on cue, the 1MC sounded off with another whistle. This time the announcement was for flight quarters.

The air boss said, "Juan, who have you got on the schedule right now?"

He looked nervously around the group of pilots. "Uh…Boss, we didn't have a schedule. We were supposed to be in port."

Plug said, "It's going to take us an hour to get one of the aircraft ready." His splitting headache was only getting worse.

She looked at her watch. "You've got thirty minutes. And when they're done with the maintenance inspection, tell Chief that he will need to get ready for a torpedo load. I want that done this afternoon."

Plug opened his mouth to complain, but decided not to say

anything. A torpedo load had taken them *forever* the last time they'd tried it. Boss was acting crazy.

She turned to Juan and said, "Are you good to fly?"

"Yes, ma'am."

"Alright, you're with me. Go get us an air crewman and have one of your sidekicks here"—she pointed at the other 2Ps—"write a flight schedule. We need a twenty-four-hour watch bill. Plug, you and whoever's on tonight should hit the rack soon."

That was the first good news Plug had heard all day.

The phone rang in the wardroom. Boss picked it up. "Air Boss. Yes, sir, I'll be right there." She turned to the group. "Alright, get your asses in gear, gentlemen. Vacation's over. Juan, follow me. The captain's going to have the TAO give us a mission brief. He wants it incorporated into their GQ exercise."

They left, and Plug looked at the two remaining pilots. "This is ridiculous."

The noise of the ship's engines increased as they left the channel. The high-pitched whine grew higher still. The white wake of the ship threw thicker and longer as they gained speed.

13

Manta, Ecuador

L ena clutched the overhead bar of the jeep as the vehicle bounced around on the weathered mountain roads. They passed several small villages. The sunburned faces of the poor looked back at her, their tired eyes squinting.

The villagers always stared at her longer than they did the soldiers she was with. At first, she thought it was because of her race. She had grown accustomed to those types of stares. When she had worked for the CIA, she had spent much of her time deployed to regions of the world where she looked nothing like the locals.

But that was not why they gawked at her. Not anymore.

Her fingers traced the ugly river of red skin up the side of her face and to her right ear. It was blotchy and wet looking. She was still beautiful, if you looked at her from just the right angle. But the frightened look in the children's eyes told her all she needed to know.

She thought of *him* when she touched the scars. *Chase*. A part of her longed for revenge. To humiliate him. To make him feel the same pain she had felt. The pain of fire igniting her clothing and melting away her skin. The pain of lifelong stares and humiliation.

She regularly had to shake herself out of her daydreams now. They always led her mind back to that horror-filled and helpless moment up on the rooftop of the Burj Al Arab hotel in Dubai. They were close to getting away when Chase Manning had thrown Molotov cocktails at the helipad. She had lain pinned down by gunfire, helpless as the hellish bath of flame erupted around her.

There was the other part of her inner psyche that was equally infuriating. The part of her that *longed* for him. All those nights they had spent together in Dubai. He was just a plaything at first. But then, oddly enough, it had morphed into something more.

Lena had looked in his eyes and seen a courage and conviction that demanded respect. She had slept with him. For professional reasons, at first. Her physical beauty and sexuality had always been a powerful weapon. It clouded men's vision and gave her access to a wide set of information. But if she was honest with herself, she knew that Chase was different.

Chase had amplified the clash of two emotions within her. Love and hatred. Beauty and ugliness. Her face had become an outward expression of who she truly was. Her lust for violence. The fulfillment she received from killing and maiming others—that was the ugliness. Something she could never explain. The quality had been with her since the incident at Junxun years ago. Logically, her euphoric reaction to inflicting pain on others—especially men—must have had something to do with her ability to control her own fate. To exact revenge and inflict pain upon the stronger sex, who had tried to harm her.

But what of the other side of the coin? Her beauty—what was that a symbol of? Goodness? Righteousness? That was what drove her each day, was it not? Serving China with honor. Creating the picture of the better world that Jinshan had painted for her so many years ago. That vision was now being executed.

And Lena was his chief executioner.

The jeep drove off the pavement onto a reddish muddy road. Jungle branches towered overhead. She could hear the troops conducting live firearms training. It sounded like fireworks. The jeep rounded another corner and pulled up to the range. A mile of cleared-out fields stretched in front of them. Wooden huts and tables. A makeshift military gun range. Dozens of men fired on paper targets. They trained on several different types of weapons. Two different-style uniforms.

The Chinese Special Forces soldiers were training the Ecuadorian soldiers to use the weapons. She observed one of them demonstrating how to change the magazine on a QBZ-95 rifle.

She thought about what Natesh and the Chinese intelligence analysts had told her. Using standard Chinese weapons meant needing standardized Chinese ammunition. And that meant a long supply chain across the Pacific. Natesh's solution was to get the factories in South America working on parts and materials so that when the war began, the supply lines were shorter.

He had set about accomplishing that as soon as he'd signed on to join Jinshan's team, over a year ago.

"Good morning, Lena."

Speak of the devil. "Hello, Natesh."

He dabbed at his sweaty brown skin with a handkerchief. "Warm day."

"Yes." Her voice was calm. Inside her mind was the pain and burning of ten thousand battles. Outside she was composed. "How are things coming?"

"Alright. I'll have a status report on your desk later today."

"Very well."

She looked down the firing range. About two platoons' strength, by the looks of it. Ecuadorian regular Army. They were being instructed in how to use their newly purchased weapons by Leishen Commandos.

The Leishen Commandos were an elite Chinese Special Forces unit. They were part of the People's Liberation Army Air Force. For the past few years, this particular unit had been taking part in several training exercises a year in Central and South American nations. It was part of China's national security policy to strengthen relations with Latin America through training and education.

Lena walked over to a tarped area about twenty yards back from the firing range. The gunfire had ceased for the moment. A mixed group of soldiers—both locals and Chinese—were going over weapons-cleaning procedures. She approached one of the Leishen Commando officers. His head was shaven. His face looked gaunt and tanned. Glossy with sweat and oil.

"Good day, Captain." She spoke in Mandarin, her words measured. "Perhaps you have a few moments to spare?"

He looked up, a suspicious frown on his face. "Who are you?"

"My name is Lena Chou, and I work—"

Recognition hit him, and he nodded and spoke rapidly. "Of course, of course. My apologies for not recognizing you. They told me you would be coming. If you please." He held out his hand to direct her to the far side of the covered area. Out of earshot. "How may I be of service?"

Lena said, "How many of our men are now on this base?"

"As of today, we have two battalions of Leishen. And about two hundred support troops for support and logistics. More are coming in every day now, including the Junxun recruits. Almost fifteen hundred in total."

"How are the preparations going?"

"We have been working with the same two Ecuadorian battalions for the past two weeks. Some of them are making good progress in weapons proficiency. Obviously, their knowledge of the local area is very good. But they have very limited knowledge of strategy and tactics. And..." He frowned, looking concerned.

"Yes?"

"They are lazy. And undisciplined. Not the same quality of soldier we are used to dealing with. These men have never seen combat."

"We don't need these men to win the war for us. We do need them to help support our supply chain as we begin to mass our forces. Do you foresee any problems with that?"

The captain shook his head. "I don't think so." He looked back at the gaggle of men cleaning rifles on the wooden counter on the other side of the covered area, then looked back at Lena. "If I may ask, ma'am, when will it all begin?"

"Soon," she said.

* * *

The captain took her to his commander, a lieutenant colonel who recognized Lena on sight. It wasn't hard. Just look for the half-beautiful, half-scarred Chinese woman who was almost six feet tall.

Still, the Chinese officer showed her nothing but respect, and Lena thought to herself that he must have been briefed by his superiors. She wondered how that conversation went. *There will be a woman coming. Do whatever she says. She has the ear of our leadership. And a penchant for violence.*

"Good day, Colonel."

"Good day, Miss Chou. I am pleased that you have joined us. I have been instructed to make myself and my men available to you. I assure you, whatever you need is yours."

They sat at his desk, situated in the corner of the command post tent. Dim artificial lights. The sound of a generator running outside. Cables and wires ran along the floor. There were very few computers. Charts were sprawled out over a large center table. Half a dozen Chinese soldiers were working on them, with a few Ecuadorian officers in tow.

A light rain fell outside. She could see it through the tent's open entryway, and could hear the pitter-patter of the raindrops on the tarp overhead.

"Colonel, what are your standing orders?"

He looked around the room, taking in who was in earshot. "My orders are to train our partners in Ecuador, and make preparations for a large influx of reinforcements on this base." He smiled. "Reinforcements beyond these young college students who I am told will start arriving soon."

He was referring to the thousands of Junxun candidates who were to begin arriving today. He continued, "I am told to expect heavy military reinforcements at any time—by sea and air."

She nodded. "And after the reinforcements arrive?"

He stared back at her, not saying a word.

"Good. That is the correct answer, if anyone asks. I take it that the Ecuadorian military is in the dark."

"That is correct. As are many of my own men."

"How is the training with the locals going?"

He took in a breath. "I have been a part of several cross-training evolutions over the past few years. As you likely know, our nation has begun supplying several Latin American countries with weapons and military systems. These pieces of hardware are not simple. They are quite advanced and require much training to become proficient."

She caught movement outside the tent. About fifty yards away, Natesh was headed toward them with a few Ecuadorian soldiers. One had a bright silver star on the center of his cover. She turned back to the colonel. "And?"

"And there is not the same sense of urgency and professionalism here," he said. "It's just a job to them. They don't think they will ever use these skills in combat. The Ecuadorian soldiers arrive in the morning, they do the minimum, and they are home each night. We've worked with the Venezuelans, the Ecuadorians, Bolivians and some in Argentina. I don't have confidence in the ability of these men to fight. They just don't have the motivation."

"I understand. What is their role at the Manta base?"

"They still see it as *their* base. So they are standing perimeter security. We are only just now beginning to get our defenses operational. Surface-to-air missiles, radar, and such."

Natesh and the party of Ecuadorian soldiers entered the tent. Natesh had a worried look on his face. As he made eye contact with Lena, he mouthed, "Sorry."

She raised an eyebrow and shook her head. *No problem, my friend. This is what I want.*

The Chinese lieutenant colonel Lena had been speaking with rose to his feet. He saluted the Ecuadorian man with the star on his cover. "Good morning, sir. How may I—"

Red-faced, the Ecuadorian general spewed forth spittle as he screamed. Lena's Spanish wasn't as good as it had once been, but she understood what he said. "Who the hell is this Chinese *puta* who dares to summon me on my own base?"

All the people working in the command post tent stopped what they were doing and turned. No one spoke.

The general looked Lena up and down. He contorted his face as he saw her scars. "What the fuck happened to you? Are you the *puta* who thinks she can tell me what to do?"

He walked up to her, standing a foot away. "I am the commanding officer on this base. I am a *general*. You have no authority over me. I let you Chinese onto our base because our country has agreements with yours on training and weapons sales. But I can make you leave anytime I want. Don't you *dare* send your Indian servant to come get me ever again. Do you understand me?"

His men stood behind him, smirking at the dressing-down. They were fat, Lena noticed, and their uniforms were sweat-stained. One of them was eyeing Lena's chest.

Lena had come to her feet when they entered. She did so out of habit, more than out of respect. She said, "General, do you speak English? I assume that you don't speak Mandarin, and my Spanish is not very good."

He glared at her and said, "I speak English."

She spoke softly. A subdued tone. She wanted him to think that he had power over her. "General, I would like to apologize for any appearance of impropriety. Surely I did not mean to imply that you were subservient to me. Clearly, you are a great military leader. I expect that you are an accomplished strategic planner. A brilliant tactician who can teach our Chinese soldiers many things."

The Ecuadorian general narrowed his eyes at her. "I could teach the Chinese many things if I had the time. But I am a busy man. This is not my job. You Chinese are here to teach my men how to use the weapons that you have sold us. That is *all* we need."

She nodded respectfully. "Of course, of course."

The general said, "I don't know why we need so many of you here. But if that is what our military leaders have agreed to, then so be it."

She walked over to the large map spread out on the center table.

The men who stood there, silently staring, moved out of the way. "Now, General, as you are in charge of this base, I hope you don't mind walking us through the security positions that you have set up? Natesh, the colonel, and I wish to be well versed in what—"

The general held up his hand. "I told you that I don't have time for this. I do not answer to you. Now you listen to me, *puta*, this is the last time I will be speaking with you. Who are you? Are you with the weapons manufacturer? The Chinese government?"

She said, "I represent the interests of China."

He spat on the floor. "You will work with someone on my staff. Unless..." He smiled and examined her body, then turned and said something in rapid Spanish. Laughter from his entourage. "No, I think this Chinese *puta* is not good-looking enough even for that. Perhaps with a bag over her head to cover those scars?" He stood over her, smirking.

Lena could see Natesh flush, and the Chinese lieutenant colonel tense up, looking to her for direction. She didn't flinch. She just stared silently into the eyes of the Ecuadorian general.

Uncomfortable with her gaze, he looked away and said, "Do not waste my time like this again." He turned and walked out, followed by his smirking underlings. One of them, while looking at her scarred neck and face, make a comment, and the others laughed on their way out.

She stared at the Ecuadorian men as they left the tent. Then she gestured to Natesh and the Chinese lieutenant colonel. Lena said, "Colonel, could you clear the room for a moment? I wish to speak with you two alone."

The officer looked at the Chinese soldiers in the tent and waved for them to leave. A moment later, the three of them were alone, standing over the large map on the center table.

"So that man is what you have been dealing with here?" She looked back and forth between the two of them.

"Unfortunately, yes," Natesh said.

"Is he impeding your progress?"

Natesh sighed. "We have a host of impediments. He's just one of them."

"Give me your update, Natesh. I don't want to wait any longer."

Natesh wobbled his head from side to side. "You need a supply chain created from scratch. That is what Jinshan has asked me to work on here. I've done the math. Do you know how big your inventories will need to be to support the flood of troops that you will have arriving?"

"How big?"

"In dollars, the inventory level is equivalent to that of the entire North American automobile industry. Enormous. But the automotive companies have had *decades* to put their supply chain in place. They have teams of *thousands* of expert purchasers and material supply managers. Men to plan the manufacturing, so that they have the right quantities of materials produced and available to them at the right time. Men to manage the transportation, so that it's delivered to the right warehouse at the right time. Men to manage the warehouses themselves, so that when one is filled up, the excess inventory gets moved to a backup location and doesn't clog up the trucks and trains."

She tapped her foot. "And you are saying that we do not have this in place?"

"I'm saying that there is a complicated network that needs to be set up, and no one has started filling those roles until now."

The lieutenant colonel frowned and said, "The Chinese military has an enormous group dedicated to logistics—"

"The Chinese military isn't fully on-boarded to this plan yet," Natesh said. "You know that. And more importantly, the Chinese military has been static on Mainland China for *generations*. They have neither the experience nor the expertise to do this."

The officer said, "I don't see why it is so complicated. Just order the supplies. Get the fuel and bullets. We will do the rest."

"You are kidding, right? These Chinese military and intelligence men I've been working with know *nothing* about what is needed. They can plan for how your army will attack just fine. But then they will run out of bullets and fuel and it won't matter. You will need a river of supplies constantly flowing to feed your army as it marches through Central America and Mexico. The moment this Slinky of tanks and jeeps expands and slows, your chances of success will as well. Trust me, I've read every book on war that I can get my hands on, and I know modern supply chains. The logistics and supply chain is quite possibly the most important factor in a military victory. And *this* one has yet to be created."

Lena observed him. She knew just how intelligent he was and took his words to heart. "What is your solution?"

Natesh held out his hands. "I mean…" He half-laughed in exasperation. "I mean, you are asking for a miracle. This timeline wasn't supposed to be so near-term. I was told—"

Lena raised her voice ever so slightly. "You were told what you needed to know. Do you have a solution?"

"I will need help. Assistants. Ones who have experience in this sort of thing."

"What do you need?"

"I need a team that can support me. A competent team. Not just college students from China. I need the members of my consulting firm to assist me in this."

"From America? You can't be serious." She thought about it. "We will get you help. Chinese consultants versed in the Latin American supply chain. We cannot risk using Americans."

He paced back and forth over the map, his words rapid. "Fine. Just make sure they are good. And get them here quick."

Lena crossed her arms. "Done. But we'll need them under close observation. And there will be strict rules on what they can communicate and with whom. You'll need to make that clear. I'll have some of the colonel's men overseeing things to make sure there are no security breaches."

Natesh nodded. "I understand."

Lena said, "So do you have any good news?"

"The tent camps on this base are being set up quickly and efficiently. The Chinese soldiers that are already here have prepared well for the imminent arrival of the Junxun students. The students will live in these camps. They will be trained by the Chinese commandos who are already here. The first step will be military indoctrination. After the first week, I will begin using them in logistics roles."

"Good. What else is working well?"

"I have been pleasantly surprised by how many Chinese-made weapons and weapons systems are already in place."

The Chinese colonel nodded. "We have built up a sizeable amount of Chinese weapons and military vehicles in Latin America these past few years. It is being used by different national governments. Different pieces of hardware are in different locations. For instance, many of our armored personnel carriers are at a single base in Venezuela. But there are several hundred anti-aircraft missiles located in Ecuador. And we have done a great deal of military trade with Bolivia, as well."

Lena said, "How long will it take to transport all those supplies here?"

"To Ecuador?"

"Yes."

"About two days by rail from Venezuela," Natesh said. "But it's through the mountains, and out of the way if the convoys will be heading north. What the colonel and I had discussed was sending a contingent of our men—those with experience using the vehicles that would be requisitioned—to Venezuela. They would meet us just north of the Panama Canal. The Bolivian convoy would be traveling about three days up the coast before meeting us here."

Lena saw the nervousness in Natesh. "What's wrong?"

"These movements would be open and obvious. They could only be safely executed after a total communications blackout occurs. And we would need air defense to ensure no reconnaissance flights picked up what was going on."

"Colonel?"

"He's right. That will be a major challenge. We will need to protect multiple large convoys from US air power. Once we get to Mexico and the continental United States, their aircraft won't even need tankers to refuel. They will then be able to rapidly and continuously target our land forces at that point. How will we prevent this from occurring?"

Natesh looked at Lena.

"Colonel," Lena said sharply, "that will be enough for now.

While I respect your expertise and the work you are doing for us, you are not yet privy to the entire scope of our operation. When we are ready to divulge further information, you will be informed of our plans. For now, please continue to train your men and prepare this base for the imminent arrival of our troops. That information in itself is highly confidential, and I implore you to keep it to yourself."

"Yes, ma'am. Of course."

Lena looked at the map and then up at the two men. "Soon this base will become the first military outpost in China's expansion into the West. Keep working to make that a success."

* * *

The colonel drove Lena around the base in his jeep, making sure that she was aware of the perimeter defenses, as well as the plans for growth.

A giant grey transport aircraft flew overhead, landing on the runway.

The colonel said, "Ah, so they have begun to arrive."

Lena said, "Are those our new recruits?"

"Indeed they are, ma'am."

She shook her head, amazed that Admiral Song had been able to get it done so fast. He had organized a voluntary winter Junxun for all first-year university students and those who would be attending university the following year. The deal was sweetened by promising highly sought-after government jobs. Jinshan's cyberoperations team had amplified the message over Chinese social media, and over two thousand students had volunteered so far.

While they'd thought the special winter training would take place at an island base just off the coast, the Chinese military transports actually took them across the Pacific Ocean to Manta, Ecuador. That was one piece of information that the students had not been aware of when they'd signed up. The other was that their military service was indefinite.

The whole world would know soon enough, Lena thought.

The jeep stopped near one of the hangars. A PLA captain walked up and saluted the colonel. Lena squinted as she realized that she knew the man.

Lieutenant Lin.

Now promoted. Captain Lin. She was rarely surprised, but she found this shocking. Her face betrayed nothing, however.

"Good day, Captain," the colonel said. "What do you have for us?"

Lin looked at Lena and Natesh, but it appeared that he didn't recognize her. Perhaps it was the scars. Or the two decades of age. "Sir, we are filling up the hangars with supplies, and sending out clothing and other materials to the new personnel."

"Very well. Is everything on schedule?"

"Yes, sir."

Now Captain Lin paused when he looked at Lena. She was unsure if he recognized her or if he was just staring at her scars.

"Something wrong, Captain?"

"No, Colonel."

"Very well, that is all."

"Yes, sir."

The man saluted and walked back towards the hangar, where they were unloading the contents of a pallet onto the back of a truck. She saw him turn and glance back at her as he walked.

Lena said, "Is he one of yours?"

The colonel said, "You mean is he one of my commandos? Oh no. He is just a logistics officer. One of the ones who came over with us. Why?"

"No reason," Lena replied.

14

Panama

C hase and the US Navy foreign affairs officer shared a cab back to the US embassy after they finished the *Farragut* briefing. The Naval officer was only needed to make sure that there was Navy involvement when providing orders to the Navy ship captain.

Chase then traveled to a CIA safe house on the eastern side of Panama City. Several members of Task Force SILVERSMITH were already there, including specialists from the NSA and military cryptologists. There were also two US Marines wearing plain clothes.

Chase shook hands with the Marines, a senior enlisted by the name of Darby, and the unit's commanding officer, Captain Calhoun.

Gunnery Sergeant Austin Darby and Captain Jake Calhoun were members of the US Marine Corps Special Operations Command. The outfit had recently been renamed the Marine Raiders, an homage to the elite Marine Corps units of World War II. In 1942, Raider battalions were involved in combat action against the Japanese in places like the Solomon Islands and Guadalcanal. Today, the Marine Raiders were the Marine Corps's own elite unit within SOCOM, the US Special Operations Command.

Chase had worked with Marine special operators in Iraq. They were used there to train and fight alongside Iraqi Special Forces in battles against ISIS. Chase considered the Marine Raiders among the elite soldiers of the world. They were much like the SEAL teams he had been a part of.

The CIA briefer sat them down at a table and opened his laptop. After typing a few keystrokes, he brought up a screen that said OPERATION SILVERSMITH.

"Who comes up with this stuff?" asked the gunnery sergeant.

The CIA man replied, "Actually, for this one...I did."

"Ah."

"Alright, gentlemen, we now have approval to move forward with this portion of SILVERSMITH. Some quick background..." He tapped a key and the screen changed, showing a bar graph. "Over the past decade, China has sold an increasing number of arms to nations around the world, including Latin America. It started off with just nonlethal supplies. Uniforms. Medical aid. But in recent years, they have switched to some more advanced weaponry..."

An image of two Chinese Z-9 helicopters appeared. Then an image of an armored personnel carrier. Then a tank.

"And that has raised some eyebrows. There are two main concerns. First, the Chinese are arming nations that have sometimes-adversarial relationships with the US, like Venezuela, Ecuador, and Bolivia. Also—many of these financial deals didn't make sense."

"What do you mean?" Chase was familiar with parts of the operation but hadn't been a part of this brief preparation.

The CIA briefer said, "We looked at the finances of these transactions. The Chinese didn't make a profitable deal, in many cases. They sent Venezuela way more APCs and tanks than they were paid for. Now, the Chinese, as a rule, are good businessmen. They don't make mistakes like that, unless it's on purpose."

"What are you saying?"

"We think they saw it as an investment."

Chase frowned. "You mean, like foreign aid? In order to have a good relationship with these countries, so they would be partners in the future?"

The CIA briefer shook his head. "Not just that. We think that they were pre-staging their arms. Putting military equipment over on this side of the pond so they would have easy access later on."

Gunnery Sergeant Darby said, "Clever little bastards."

"A week ago we received signals intelligence that Chinese military units were conducting operations near Manta, Ecuador. Reconnaissance images"—the CIA briefer flipped through a few screen shots of an air base—"showed an increasingly large presence of Chinese personnel, weapons, and transport aircraft. These are Chinese construction companies plowing the fields, Chinese defense contractors selling the arms, Chinese troops training the Ecuadorian armies.

"Stuff like this has been going on for years, but not in concentrations like this. China is the largest arms seller in the world today. And much of it goes to nations unfriendly to the US. But the number of troops here is abnormally high. And it's raised a lot of concern in Washington. We now suspect that there was at least some Chinese involvement in recent attacks on US interests around the world—this includes the Persian Gulf attacks, the US cyberattack known as the Blackout Attack, and possibly even the Beltway attacks."

Chase watched the reaction of the two Marines. He wondered how long it had been since they'd been able to catch up on the news. The mainstream media was a twenty-four-hour billboard for the Beltway attacks and the imminent US war with Iran, but there was almost nothing about China. That secret was being tightly controlled by US intelligence.

But Chase knew better. And now that Jinshan's operative was spilling his guts to Langley interrogators, others would too. The Chinese—or Jinshan and his allies—were planning a major military attack on the United States. The wheels were already in motion. The cyberattack on the US satellite and communications network last month, while not crippling, had done an incredible amount of damage.

The American GPS system was still down. Military satellite communications were still down. The US Internet was just now recovering, with billions of dollars of data lost from tech companies' data storage centers. And perhaps the biggest impact—the US economy was plummeting from the shock to the markets. People no longer had confidence that the Internet would be there for them. Perhaps they never should have had that confidence to begin with...

David and the American members of the Red Cell had unwittingly been planning a Chinese invasion of America. If the Red Cell plans were being implemented, then the Iranian attack on the US a few weeks ago was just a diversion, created by Jinshan. And Chase had seen with his own eyes that Lena Chou had been a part of that operation near Bandar Abbas.

After the Beltway attacks, nearly eighty percent of Americans, according to the latest polls, supported a war with Iran. But they were being misled. And if Jinshan succeeded, it would be one of the greatest head fakes the world had ever seen.

The CIA briefer tapped his keyboard and brought up a grainy image of what looked like a trailer with a bunch of antennae.

"This is a PLA mobile communications unit. We took this picture last week."

Chase said, "Where?"

"At the base in Manta."

Chase said, "I thought the satellites were down."

"This picture was taken from an Air Force drone. But once we saw the SAM sites get erected, we stopped sending aircraft overhead. That's when we placed the MARSOC team nearby."

Chase looked at the two Marine Raiders. "Have you got eyes on them now?"

Captain Calhoun said, "We've got a recon team positioned north of the base near Manta."

"What have they seen?"

"A total of twelve aircraft drop-offs that we've witnessed so far."

"What airframe?"

"Chinese Xian Y-20 military transports. Long-range, big suckers. They look just like Air Force C-17s."

Chase said, "Twelve aircraft. That's a lot of supplies. If they were selling arms to Ecuador, it would be a lot more economical to transport by ship."

"That's what your CIA guys told us in Colombia."

"So what did they take off those planes?"

Gunnery Sergeant Darby said, "Not just *what*. *Who*."

"Excuse me?"

"They took a lot of pallets of stuff off those planes, that's for sure. But that wasn't what the big stink has been about. It's *who* they've been unloading off those planes."

The captain reached down into his backpack and produced a small tablet device. He held it for all to see and scrolled through the pictures.

Chase said, "That's a lot of Chinese soldiers. How many?"

"Almost fifteen hundred by our last count."

Chase whistled. "Do we know what unit they came from? Specialty?"

"The CIA guys we've been working with in Colombia think some of them might be Leishen Commandos. PLA airborne Special Forces."

"That's a lot of Special Forces."

"Yup. They've also started sending planeloads of very green-looking troops. New recruits, it looks like."

Chase said, "Really? That's odd. Why would they do that?"

The CIA briefer said, "We still don't know."

"There were also a few other interesting faces in the mix," the captain said, showing another image.

Chase's world stopped. He tried not to show any outward change in expression, but he felt his face getting hot. He saw the CIA briefer watching him and wondered how much backstory he had gotten.

It was Lena Chou.

The photo showed her walking down the ramp of one of the aircraft, her dark, flowing hair draped over one side of her face. Covering the burns that Chase had left.

"When did she arrive?"

"Two days ago."

"Has this been sent to Langley?"

"No clue. That's you guys' job, remember? As far as I know, you spooks are having just as many problems with comms as we are."

The CIA briefer said, "I'll make sure to take these latest images back. Thank you, Captain."

Calhoun handed over the tablet.

The CIA briefer said, "Gentlemen, there is a piece of hardware that we will refer to as the crypto key located inside that mobile comms unit. This crypto key could help us unlock a lot of mysteries. Right now there are competing theories on China's level of aggression towards the United States. We believe that the Chinese president and highest-level leadership are unaware of what some of their military assets have been doing to cause harm to the United States. By taking this crypto key, our team of experts here in Panama will be able to provide the Chinese president with infallible proof that there is a contingent of rogue operators in the Chinese military and intelligence community. This could help prevent war between the US and China, and possibly stop war between the US and Iran."

Gunny Darby said, "So if we steal this piece of equipment... that's going to tell you what the Chicoms are up to? That what you're telling me?"

Chase nodded. "That's about it, in a nutshell."

"And what are we stealing?"

The CIA briefer said, "A piece of crypto. A big black box. Their key that lets us cut through all their encryption on the Chinese military datalink network. It's a new system, but we've got an NSA team that can hack into it, if we get that crypto key."

Darby said, "Alright, so we go in, kill all fifteen hundred of them Chinese Special Forces, plus a few Ecuadorians for good measure, and steal that trailer. Maybe I could drive my Ford F-150 down there and hook her up? Then you send down a C-130 and pick us up, and we'll be out of there lickety-split. That it? Damn, I'm good at this shit."

Captain Calhoun smiled at his gunnery sergeant. "Please excuse this old man. He's growing senile in his old age."

The CIA briefer said, "ROE—no use of force with deadly weapons, unless in self-defense."

The Marines went silent for a moment.

Captain Calhoun said, "Sorry, maybe I'm missing something, but why is that?"

Chase frowned. "Because they aren't sure if the Chinese are really bad guys yet. Sorry. I know this won't be easy. I'll be coming with you. We'll have nonlethal weapons to take out the men manning the comms unit. The point of this mission is to prevent World War Three. If we go in there with weapons blazing...well, that kind of defeats the purpose."

Calhoun said, "Seems to me like this mission isn't to prevent World War Three, it's to confirm whether it's already started or not."

"Probably an accurate statement," Chase conceded.

The Marines looked at each other. "Alright, how are we stealing it, then?"

Chase said, "I've been trained on how to remove the crypto key box. I just need your help getting into the trailer."

"Sir, I'm from the Deep South," Gunny Darby said. "I got lots of experience sneaking up on trailers to get to my girlfriends without their dads knowing. You don't have to worry about a thing."

Chase smiled. "Glad to hear it, Gunny."

He winked back. "What's the plan for extraction?"

The CIA briefer said, "It will be a delayed extraction after the mission is accomplished. We recommend a small team of about four of you to go in. You'll steal the device without being noticed. We'll have a way for you to incapacitate the men manning the comms trailer. Their shifts are for four to six hours each, so if you go in during a shift change, you should have about that long before they're discovered."

Captain Calhoun said, "That sounds like wishful thinking."

"It may be. But we'll have a local asset on the base with a small supply truck going by the comms trailer when we're ready to get out of there. Once you get the crypto key, you'll ride in the back of a supply truck for about a mile. That will get you far enough away from the scene that you won't risk capture. The truck will stop some-where along the road that no one will be able to see—and drop you off back into the jungle. That team will then hike it back to your larger team's recon position on the mountain, north of the base. It will then be another few miles to the extraction LZ. We will have a pair of Army helicopters waiting in Colombia, assigned to pick you up."

Chase turned to the briefer. "I thought we talked about this. It can't be a delayed extraction. It puts us all at unnecessary risk. And the timing might be off."

The CIA briefer sighed. Chase could tell that he didn't like giving him this information. Don't shoot the messenger.

He said, "Mr. Manning, we looked at every option. In this situation, the enemy has air superiority and is likely able to prohibit air and water extraction in the immediate area. As long as you're able to accomplish the mission undetected to begin with, you'll still enjoy the jungle terrain's cover and concealment. You and your team are to travel back up the mountain, undetected, and reconnect with the rest of the MARSOC unit. You'll then travel on foot to an LZ that's a safe distance away. It will be out of range and hidden by terrain—so the anti-aircraft batteries they have at Manta won't be able to shoot down the helicopters."

"What if they get on foot and chase us? And maybe bring some RPGs? Or MANPADS?" said Captain Calhoun, using the term for shoulder-mounted surface-to-air missiles.

Chase said, "And you said we've got…what, four days before the codes are switched on this thing, right? This plan kills a lot of that time. I'm sorry, but this seems too risky. Who the hell thought this up?"

The CIA briefer said, "You'll have ninety-six hours to get it to us once you remove the crypto key. After that, we don't think the data will be usable, as the codes will reset. Gentlemen, the JSOC planners have been over all the options. This is the best we've got. You'll have to stay undetected and move fast. We did the calculations and expect you to travel on foot for approximately eight hours. The air extraction process will then get you to Panama City three hours later. It should be enough time."

Calhoun looked at Chase. "We'll have to come up with something to help with escape and evasion if we run into resistance. Let's talk offline." He didn't look happy.

* * *

A few hours later, Chase left his hotel and spotted Darby waiting for him across the street. Darby leaned casually against the black metal streetlight pole. A light grey hoodie covered his shaved head, and he had his hands in his pockets. Wraparound sunglasses. Khaki shorts and hiking boots.

As Chase walked outside his hotel lobby, Darby locked eyes with him and gave a slight nod. They joined up in silence and began walking down the street.

"Gunny."

"Mr. Manning."

"You ready?"

"Yup. One of my guys is parked around the block. He'll take us to the airport. We've got a small plane that'll fly us down the coast."

"Sounds good."

It was a two-hour plane ride south, into Colombia. Darby slept the whole way. Calhoun looked like he was going over things in his head. They landed on a tiny little dirt strip in the middle of the night. Glow sticks lined the runway.

The three men got out of the aircraft, and it immediately turned around and took back off, its engine noise fading into the night. They walked through long grass to the end of the makeshift runway. Four Chevy SUVs were parked in a column. The windows were rolled down. It was December, but still a humid seventy-five degrees Fahrenheit in this part of the world.

There were about four men in each vehicle. Chase could see that they all wore jungle camouflage. In the moonlight, he could tell that most had on camo face paint. White eyes stared at Chase.

"Gunny, you guys can change over here." One of the men pointed to the lead vehicle, its rear hatch open. "We've got his stuff ready too."

Someone took one of the glow sticks off the runway and placed it in the trunk of the lead vehicle so they could see their gear better.

"You need boots?" Darby asked.

"No thanks." He had learned the hard way never to break in a pair of unused boots when on a mission. It was the one article of clothing he had on that wasn't really civilian attire. Darby and Chase hurriedly threw on their gear. Then Chase got in the same vehicle as Darby, and the convoy began rolling.

It was bumpy, mountainous terrain. The car smelled of mint chew. Dip. Every few seconds he could hear someone spitting into an empty plastic bottle.

Darby said, "Mr. Manning, you want some of this?" He held up his tin.

Chase shook his head. "No. Thanks anyway."

Darby shrugged.

"How long until we get there?" Chase asked.

"Shouldn't take us more than an hour to get to where the helo will pick us up," Darby said. "About an hour in the air after that. They'll drop us off in some pretty thick rainforest. It'll be another day's hike after they drop us off. Don't want to get too close, you know."

The vehicles came to a halt. An H-60 was spinning in the field about one hundred yards away. The other Marines got out of their SUVs. They threw on their gear and marched in a column toward the aircraft.

* * *

Two days later, Chase saw the Y-20s with his own eyes.

"Goddamn, those things are big."

One of them was on a slow final approach. Dark grey, wings sloped downward. Four engines and a T tail, just like the C-17. Its flight path took it about even in altitude with their mountain location. Chase's chest reverberated as the jet engines drowned out all other noise. The freaking thing was a monster.

They lay in thick jungle brush, watching the airfield from a mountain several miles to the north. Everything was wet, and a light mist hovered above the trees. The sounds of jungle birds and bugs filled the air.

Chase looked through a sniper spotting scope, examining the

base. The two Marines who had been serving as the recon team on the hill for the past week lay next to Chase and Gunnery Sergeant Darby. The other dozen men on the MARSOC team were spread out in the forest around them, forming a defensive perimeter.

One of the Marines said to Chase, "Two days ago they started putting up sandbag pillboxes stationed at all four corners of the base. Today was the first time we saw them place anti-aircraft weapons inside. The SAM units were unprotected before that."

Chase looked at each of the pillboxes. "Looks like they've got two 35mm twin guns on the eastern side. And I don't see anything on the western pillboxes. Just personnel."

"MANPADS."

"Got it."

"Saw them doing training on them earlier. My guess is once they unload some of these recent cargo arrivals, they might put something in there more sophisticated."

Chase said, "Alright, thanks. What else?"

"Take a look about a mile to the east of the airfield. You'll see bulldozers and a tent city going up. They've got a few semipermanent structures, but most of it's pretty mobile."

"Strength?"

"That's where they all are. About fifteen hundred, I'd say. But they go out in groups into the fields and forest farther over to the east. Lot of training, that's for sure. We hear small-arms fire about round the clock right now. Three days ago they even were firing off mortars."

"How much participation from the Ecuadorians?"

"Oh, they're there alright. They got some general or something who has a nice car and an entourage."

"Communications center?"

"Just south of the airfield. About three hundred yards from the runway."

Chase looked at the gunnery sergeant. "Sounds like it would be pretty hard for us to get access to that."

"I agree," said the gunny.

"What were they hoping to get in there?"

Chase said, "An important piece of hardware."

Captain Calhoun said, "When do you want to move?"

Chase said, "The longer we wait, the better their fortifications are going to get."

Gunnery Sergeant Darby said, "And to be clear—if we can get you into the communications center, would you know what you're looking for?"

Chase nodded. "Yes. They gave me training on how to identify it and remove it." He patted a zipped pouch near his waist. "They gave me something that looks like a bottle opener to unlock it. And I've got wire cutters."

"How often do they change out personnel in the comm center?" Chase asked the Marine who had been watching the base.

"About every six hours. Something like that. I've got it written down."

"And how many are in there?"

"Just two at a time."

"So for watch turnover, when the door gets opened, we've got four to worry about."

The gunny gave him a look. "And anybody who sees us walk up to it. Remember, you got a couple of bunkers down there. Those guys have got nothing better to do than look around and see what's out of place."

Chase said, "Then we'll need a distraction."

"We're Marines," the gunny said. "We'd always be happy to blow something up for you."

Chase smiled. "I appreciate that." He frowned. "Do we still have access to the drone?"

"Yeah, but they told us not to use it. Too risky."

Chase rubbed his chin. "You know, maybe I do want you to blow something up after all."

The gunny smiled. "Now you're talking."

* * *

They waited until the next night. The day was spent pulling in extra help from the remaining Marines in the Raider unit and carefully watching the patterns of the base.

There were two valuable bits of work that any reconnaissance unit performed. One was to report precisely what they saw. How many enemy troops? What type of vehicles? Pictures and video were even better. It allowed the experienced analysts at the DIA, CIA, and other agencies to extract information that the untrained eye would miss.

The other important thing recon units did was to take note of *patterns*. How many hours *between* aircraft arrivals? What *times* were the watch turnovers? How *long* did the watch turnovers take? Were there different numbers of guards at night versus during the daytime?

Since the Blackout Attacks of a few weeks ago, military communications had been severely hampered. That meant that there were no pictures or video being instantly streamed back to the collection and analyst teams.

This was why the CIA had sent Chase down here to participate in this operation. He had been trained on what to look for. And based on what he witnessed, he had been briefed on what action to take.

The Marines in this unit were excellent observers. Chase suspected they had a lot of experience over in the sandbox doing just this.

Captain Calhoun had placed two of his Marines near the extraction landing zone to the north. He moved the rest to the top of their observation mountain. From there, they had access to a nearby dirt road that led to the base. This would be where the small group would get dropped off after stealing the crypto key.

The MARSOC team also had the option of humping it down the other side of the ridgeline and sprinting to the extraction LZ in about an hour if things got too dicey.

Four men infiltrated the Manta base. What could have been a thirty-minute journey took seven hours. Chase, Gunnery Sergeant Darby, and two of the other Marine Raiders walked, crawled, and slid down from their elevated observation point through the jungle brush. Once down the mountain, they stayed concealed while following a stream that ran around the airfield.

It was a balmy eighty-two degrees. The light mist that covered the top of the ridge now grew thicker. This would reduce visibility between the Marines on top of the mountain and Chase's small team of infiltrators. Chase silently cursed himself. As was often the case, the weather would negatively impact their plans.

They didn't speak over radios. If the adversary had been a third-world military unit or some wannabe ISIS group, they might have used headsets and encrypted comms, but the Chinese were a different story. Any radio communications, whether encrypted or not, might alert the Chinese communications personnel that a military unit was operating in close proximity. And that could signal doom.

So they synced their watches and agreed on a timeline. If Calhoun saw that Chase had infiltrated the communications center without any trouble, then he didn't need to do a thing. Just wait for the team of four to make it back, and then they would all head to the extraction point. The four Chinese communications personnel would hopefully not be found until the Raider unit was loaded onto the Blackhawk and headed north to safety. That was the best-case scenario.

If, however, either Calhoun couldn't see Chase's progress, or the time was after 2300 local and Chase hadn't entered the comm center, Calhoun was to use the drone for its special purpose.

Crawling through the tall grass next to the stream was painfully slow. The sun had set around 1830. That had helped. But there were freaking Chinese and Ecuadorian military all over the place.

Chase's team had made gradual progress once they had gotten near the airfield. If they moved too fast, they risked being spotted. If they moved too slowly, they wouldn't make the timeline.

He looked at his watch. It was 2240. They still had about a one-hundred-yard crawl through the brush until they got close enough to the comm center. From the right angle, they could make it to the communications trailer without being seen by the watch team. The Chinese communication center's duty section turnover the past few nights had been at 2250 local time, plus or minus a few minutes.

The gunny risked a whisper. "We're gonna have to pick up the pace. If we don't make their watch turnover, it will be a lot harder to get inside."

Chase nodded.

They could hear the faint echo of voices in the distance. Laughter. Probably some of the soldiers shooting the shit while on the night shift.

They reached the edge of the jungle brush, to where it fed into the grass cutout of the air base. A few hundred yards away stood the communications center. The building was nothing more than a trailer on cinder blocks. A coil of razor wire about three feet high surrounded the structure. Dozens of antennae and a few dishes protruded up from its roof.

Two Chinese soldiers caught Chase's eye. They spoke in a loud, casual tone and headed for the communications trailer. He looked at his watch. Time: 2251. He glanced up at the ridge. The glare of base lighting made it hard for him to see anything but darkness now. He looked through his observation scope, but its night vision revealed only the layer of mist returning green and black twinkles of scintillation. Chase had no idea if Captain Calhoun was able to monitor their progress. *Shit.* Unless they hurried, Calhoun was going to switch to plan B no matter what. If the "distraction" occurred *too* early, that would make it much harder for Chase and the men.

The two Chinese soldiers approached the entrance of the communications center.

Chase whispered, "Let's go."

The four men rose up from the brush. Each of them carried an MP-7, fitted with a suppressor and a forty-round magazine. Chase and the gunny had their MP-7s secured, however. They brandished suppressed shotguns that were specially designed for the use of US special operations.

The group of four walked up silently behind the two unsuspecting Chinese men who were now knocking on the door of the mobile communications center. Chase and team timed their approach so that they were just behind them at the moment that the door opened.

The Chinese soldier who opened the door saw the two Chinese men who were about to relieve him and his comrade. He also saw four men in dark tactical uniforms jogging towards them, each holding black weapons pointed in his direction.

In the split second before the shotguns began firing, a confused look appeared on his face.

The suppressed shotguns barely made any noise while firing. The silencers were modular units, which added about ten inches to the end of the weapon. They were bulky, but not heavy. The rounds were subsonic. But the quietness of these shotguns wasn't the reason that Chase and gunny Darby were using them. It was the ammunition.

The ammunition was a type of Taser, developed from an earlier prototype called the Wireless Extended Range Electro-Muscular Projectile (XREP). Taser International created the XREP to be fired from a twelve-gauge shotgun at ranges beyond twenty-five meters.

Chase and Gunnery Sergeant Darby fired their suppressed weapons from less than three meters away. The two oncoming watch standers each took two projectile rounds in the back, while the man who had opened the door took two in the chest.

The shotgun-like shells delivered a powerful blunt impact as their small metal prongs dug into the flesh and triggered the release of electronic energy. The three men's muscles locked up, and they fell to the ground twitching as thousands of volts of electricity ran through their body.

Darby hopped over the man in the doorway, careful not to touch him, and found the fourth man walking towards them inside the trailer, saying something unintelligible. Darby fired two more wireless Taser rounds and the man hit the floor, shaking. Behind him, Chase and the Marines were dragging the incapacitated bodies of the men into the communications center, using special rubber gloves to remove the Taser rounds.

The trailer had a single walkway, wide enough for one person to move at a time. Chase quickly worked his way over the rows of electronics, communications equipment, and displays. Dials and knobs, all labeled in Chinese characters.

"There." Chase found the section he was looking for. The crypto key was a large rectangular box made of dark green metal, the size and shape of a DVD player. He took out his tools and began removing it as the Marines bound and gagged the Chinese men on the floor.

Chase checked his watch once more: 2304 local time. Calhoun's diversion could be any moment now.

* * *

Captain Calhoun looked through his observation scope once more, knowing he wouldn't see anything useful but hoping he would be surprised.

The fog had become so thick that it robbed him of his ability to see the base below. It would take too long and be too risky to move to a lower elevation. And it would take away the Marines' ability to make it down to the road, which the plan stipulated they must maintain access to.

He looked at his man holding the drone. "Launch it."

One of his Marines flipped the switch to turn on the small propeller and then hurled the drone like it was a giant football. The RQ-11B buzzed off into the night, a pound of C-4 strapped to its undercarriage.

They had pre-programmed its flight path. It would travel at five hundred feet above ground level and then make its way down to the runway. The C-4's detonator was set to go off on impact.

Calhoun sighed. "Alright, let's hope this works."

* * *

Chase had just finished placing the crypto keys in his pack when they heard the explosion. The comm center had no windows, but the radio chatter increased dramatically.

Darby said, "Was that it?"

"Yeah. Must have been."

"What should we do?"

"Look out the door window. Do you see a supply truck nearby?"

"I don't see shit."

Chase walked over to the door and cracked it open, looking around. There was no sign of any vehicle waiting for them like the CIA briefer had promised.

Chase stared down at the Chinese troops. They had all regained their ability to move, but the restraints, gags, and blindfolds kept them docile. He looked up at the gunny. "What do you think?"

"I say we go right back the way we came."

"In the bush? Back up the hill?"

"We'll have about five seconds of vulnerability. If they see us, we can make a run for them jeeps. They're fifty meters away, and one of my Marines here can hotwire it if he has to. But that's not a good option. You know it."

"Crawling up through the brush and jungle while they're alerted doesn't sound great either."

The gunny looked at the men. "You sure we shouldn't..."

Chase shook his head. "ROE. No shooting unless it's in self-defense." He frowned. "Hold on, I've got something we can use." He reached into his pack and pulled out a small case with a syringe. It took him about two minutes to inject each man in the ass with a dose of the stuff. The men's eyes began to flutter and close shut.

The gunny said, "What is that?"

"It's enough drugs to keep them out of it for several hours. That should buy us time."

The four men stood at the door, ready with their weapons. Chase said, "Just walk normal until we get into the brush. If we move fast, it'll catch more attention. Walk normal, and anyone who sees us might not get a good view and overlook us."

They opened the door and walked through the opening in the razor-wire coil, then around the trailer and back into the long grass. As they crouched down into the prone position, Chase looked out over the runway. A fire truck sprayed water onto the flames. About a dozen men stood around it, staring. He could see the Chinese troops in the nearest anti-aircraft bunker. There were three of them, each watching the flaming wreckage on the runway.

"Psst. Hey."

A short Hispanic man stood near the trees, outside the illumination near the mobile communications trailer.

The man whispered, "You guys looking for a ride?"

Chase nodded, "Yes, where is it?"

"Come." He waved. The four men followed him around the group of trees. In the darkness, Chase hadn't seen it. But there, parked in grass, was a small covered pickup truck, bags of laundry in the rear.

"Please. We go right now."

The four men piled in back.

"Put the bags on top. They won't check us on the way out. The Chinese are not guarding the gates. Only the Ecuadorians. They don't look at us when we leave. But we must go now."

A minute later, the four men lay in the back of the pickup truck, bouncing as the truck drove through the base, big white laundry bags covering them.

"Okay, we're off the base now. I will drop you off in a few minutes. There is a road up here that will take us near the mountains. That is where I am to leave you. Will that be okay?"

Chase said, "Yes. Thanks."

Ten minutes later, they were once again in the jungle, heading up the mountain. The sound of the truck fading in the distance.

Chase couldn't believe their luck. The distraction had worked perfectly. No one was looking for attackers after the explosion. There were no alarms. People were just watching the flames, curious. Like they didn't know that they were about to be at war…

15

The following morning, two battalions of Chinese Special Forces soldiers stood at attention on the flight line outside the Manta base hangar. The Leishen Commandos looked like statues, Lena thought. Strong, tall and disciplined. Everything that a warrior should be.

A company of Ecuadorian regular Army stood at attention next to the Chinese. Behind them all, a few hundred of the new Chinese Junxun recruits rounded out the audience.

A small platform stood in front of them. If not for the investigative team around the drone wreckage, one might mistake this for a parade or decoration ceremony.

It was Lena's idea.

There were a few important lessons that Lena had learned from what happened the night before. One of which, was that the soldiers on the base were woefully unprepared for the conflict that lay ahead. That needed to be remedied.

The Chinese base commander had no question as to who was in charge when Lena showed up. His leadership had given him strict orders to do whatever she said. He had wanted to disperse his men immediately and begin looking for the team that raided the communications compound.

But the Ecuadorian general had intervened. He wanted an investigation completed first. Lena had been in the field, training with the Leishen Commandos. They had sent for her immediately, but it was hours before she arrived back at the base. Hours of lost time.

She needed to contact Jinshan, and inform him of the lost crypto key. She needed to track down the Americans—she assumed it was the Americans—and attempt to retrieve the stolen equipment. But first, she needed to send a message to the soldiers on this base.

Lena walked up to Natesh. "Are the swarm drones ready?"

"They arrived yesterday afternoon. We're working to unload them now."

She looked in the hangar. Captain Lin was there, overseeing some of the logistics personnel as they unpacked the cargo. He stared back at her, a suspicious look on his face. A part of her wanted to walk over there and take care of him right now. But he was not a priority.

The base commander walked up to her and Natesh. "Ms. Chou, I don't think we have time for this gathering. We need to go after the men who raided our base."

She raised her hand. "Please be patient, Colonel. We will."

"But they *stole* our cryptologic key. We must gain it back. If that got into the wrong *hands*—"

"Colonel, have you heard any aircraft? Have your radars picked up any aircraft?"

"No."

"Then they are on foot, and we have the advantage. We will find them, but first I need to make a statement to the men."

Two jeeps screeched through the gate and came to a halt just off the platform. The Ecuadorian general and his staff got out. He was fuming, screaming and swearing as he looked at Lena and the colonel.

Lena just watched him, a serious expression on her face. *Perfect timing.*

"What is the meaning of this? Who called my men here like this?

You do not give orders to my men. First you crash an airplane on the runway last night, and now you have...what is this, an award ceremony?"

Curious eyes snuck quick glances among the hundreds who stood silently at attention, eager ears waiting to see how the normally restrained Lena would respond.

Lena said, "This is not an awards ceremony, General. Quite the opposite."

He approached her, standing below the platform, suddenly aware that close to a thousand well-trained Chinese Special Forces troops stood very close to him. His voice grew much quieter. "Well, then, *what* is this?"

* * *

By sunrise, Chase's team was joined up with the others under Captain Calhoun's unit.

"We probably didn't need the drone diversion."

Calhoun cursed. "Sorry. I was worried about that. But I figured it was better to stick to the plan. We couldn't see shit up here."

"What's been going on since we left?"

"The sky's cleared up, as you can see. They had a repair crew working on the runway, patching it up. And they moved the drone wreckage over to one of those hangars. The Chinese have been inspecting it all morning. Your girl is with them. The one you said is important."

Chase said, "When did she arrive?"

"Early this morning. Take a look. I have to admit, I wasn't expecting this...*ceremony*. I thought they would have a search party out for us by now."

"Ceremony?" Chase looked through his scope. "Damn. They must have a thousand men there. What the hell are they doing formed up like that? Why aren't they coming after us?"

Several companies stood at attention in front of a small stage. Lena and a Chinese officer stood on the stage, facing the men. Then a couple of jeeps rolled up and came to a halt right next to the stage.

"Who's that guy?"

"It's the Ecuadorian general," one of the Marines on the recon team answered. "He's been in and out of the base several times since the Chinese have been here."

The Ecuadorian general stood very close to Lena. Neither looked happy. The general crossed his arms, a smug look on his face. Lena turned and began to address the men in formation.

Chase wished he could hear what she was saying.

* * *

Lena stood with her fingers touching while she spoke, as if she was in prayer. Her voice was strong and carried well over the windless morning.

"Last night, a military special operations team infiltrated our base. They stole something very important. They then set off an explosion on the runway and made their escape."

Lena watched their faces as she spoke. The Chinese soldiers were stoic. The Ecuadorians and the young Chinese Junxun recruits were squinting and fidgeting in the morning sun.

The Ecuadorian general looked surprised at her words. Perhaps this was the first time he was hearing all the details. Well, it was too late for him now.

Lena continued, "If we are to accomplish our mission here, there can be no mistakes like this again. The time for training is nearing an end. As many of you Leishen must suspect, you would not all have been sent here if this were only a simple training exercise. So what is it, then? Why are we here? And who has infiltrated our base?"

She pointed at the drone wreckage, laid out on a sheet like a crime scene. "That is an American drone. They *attacked* your brothers in arms. Just as the Americans attack peaceful nations all over the world."

She looked at their faces as they listened. The general was quiet now. Confused, but listening.

Lena said, "China has been oppressed by the West for too long. The

Americans cripple us through unfair trade, leaving our families poor and helpless. They invade countries in the name of national security, all the while making their own nation rich by stealing natural resources. The Americans encroach on our territorial boundaries in the South China Sea and fail to recognize all of our territory. They promote religions of hatred. They worship violence and materialism. They demonize our Chinese society that only wishes to bring peace and equality to all of its citizens.

"But China will stand for this no more.

"You soldiers are here because China is seizing its destiny as a great global power. *You* men have become the instrument of this great evolution in our national expansion. You are our *warriors*. Our *pride*. You are the sword that will bring peace to the world, and make China the dominant global force."

The Chinese commandos didn't move. They just took it all in. Lena could see the pride in their eyes, though. Every soldier…every *man*… liked hearing that he was *important*. That he was special. *Elite*. Destined for greatness.

Napoleon was right. It was amazing how much one would go through to earn a little piece of ribbon on their chest. Pride was a powerful tool in the commander's toolbox.

So too, however, was fear.

Lena looked at the Ecuadorian general. "*Unfortunately*, there is not yet the appropriate level of professional attention being paid to our daily duties. Let what happened last night serve as a reminder. Training is over. From now on, everyone here should consider us at *war*. Conduct yourselves appropriately."

The Ecuadorian general stared at her, confused. She said, "General, I asked you a few days ago to show me your perimeter security posts. You *declined*. You said that you did not have time."

He gulped. "I…" He kept shaking his head. Gone was the machismo.

Lena knew that a few thoughts were making their way through his inferior brain. He was wondering if he had misjudged what level of authority Lena held. He was asking himself to reevaluate why the Chinese needed so many troops here on this base. And he was beginning to feel afraid of what this tall, scarred Asian woman who stood before him might *do*.

"General, this morning your president—the president of Ecuador—pledged allegiance to our cause. In doing so, he promised that Ecuadorian armed forces would serve under the oversight of Chinese military. You should now consider yourself under my command. So I ask you, why were your base security measures so lax? Why did you fail us last night?"

The general's face reddened. He didn't speak.

"What's the matter, General? I will give you all the time you want to answer."

He cleared his throat, gathering his courage. Looking back and forth between Lena and the rows of Chinese commandos. Some of their eyes were no longer looking straight ahead, but at *him*.

The general said, "You are not in charge. I am the general. You are—"

She marched off the platform and slapped him, open-handed, across the face.

He brought his hand up to his cheek, staring back at her in disbelief. Then anger came. He raised his right hand and, in the slowest windup Lena could ever recall witnessing, attempted to strike her face.

It was child's play for her. She stepped to her right and with both hands grabbed his right bicep and the upper left section of his uniform. She gripped, twisted, and turned forward, using his momentum against him. The overweight general was flipped over onto his back, landing faceup on the pavement.

He lay gasping for breath on the ground.

Lena looked up at the Chinese colonel. "Sidearm, please" was all she said.

The colonel's eyes widened, but he complied. His fingers fumbled around at the holster, but then he handed her the weapon.

Lena said, loud enough for everyone to hear, "General, you have chosen to reject the authority of China, and of your own president. As the senior representative of the Chinese government on this base, I hereby find you guilty of treason."

At the sight of Lena holding a handgun to the general's forehead, the Ecuadorian staff began to object. But Lena was too quick.

A single gunshot rang out.

The Ecuadorians' mouths opened. Blood drained from a single hole in the general's forehead.

She then turned to the Ecuadorian staff. "Who's the next in command?"

Two of them actually pointed at the other. She looked at one of them and smiled. "Excellent. Congratulations on your promotion. A warning. *Don't* let this happen again. Now, your government has pledged that your men will report to us. We can confirm with them on the phone later today. But from now on, your men will report up through the Chinese base commander. Is that understood?"

The scared Ecuadorian officer nodded quickly.

"Good."

She turned to the Chinese base commander. "Colonel, if you could please see to it that none of our new Ecuadorian conscripts have second thoughts."

He nodded, still in shock that she had just executed the Ecuadorian general.

Lena turned to the lieutenant colonel in charge of the Leishen Commandos. "Give me two platoons of your men. We have some hunting to do."

* * *

"Good God."

Chase took his eye away from the spotter scope and looked down at the dirt. His breathing was heavy. Who was this woman? She was a monster. How could this be the same person he'd been with in Dubai?

As Chase watched her, she handed her sidearm back to the Chinese officer, turned from the group she was with and began walking with a thin, brown-skinned man.

Chase searched his memory for the name. Natesh Chaudry. That had to be the American consultant David had worked with on the Red Cell island. The one who was working with Lena and Jinshan.

The pair walked over to the adjacent hangar, where a different group of Chinese soldiers were rolling some type of covered platform out onto the flight line. They threw off the tarp cover, revealing several dozen machines spread out across a flat white surface.

"What are those?" asked Calhoun.

They looked like giant metal spiders. Or...

"They're drones," said Chase.

One of the soldiers next to Lena typed on a laptop computer. All twelve quadcopter drones rose in unison, hovering twenty feet above the pavement. Each of the quadcopters had several round protrusions underneath. Chase had received briefs on these things. They were the newest iteration of weaponized drones. Small quadcopters, controlled by ground troops. They could be used to hold a variety of items. Cameras. Sensors. Bombs.

The drones spread out and began heading toward their mountain.

"Oh shit."

Chase said, "I don't know what kind of sensors those things have, but if they start looking around over here, they could find us pretty quick."

Captain Calhoun called out, "Alright, folks, let's get a move on. We're heading to the extraction LZ right now." The Marines leapt up from their positions and began moving.

Chase kept watching through his scope. They were rolling out a second drone platform, lining it up next to the first.

The last thing Chase saw before he high-tailed it out of there was the second set of drones taking off.

Lena stood fifty meters behind the drones, but she paid them no attention. She was looking through a set of binoculars. They were pointed up into the jungle-covered hills, where Chase and his team were located.

16

The drone swarm buzzed overhead, sounding like giant wasps. Chase hoped that the canopy of rainforest might provide some cover. The noise made the group tense.

The Marines were spread out in a column about fifty yards long, half-walking, half-jogging. The men in the front cut through the vines and thick jungle brush with machetes every few feet.

They came upon a muddy road. The first few Marines hunched down on either side, only a few feet into the vegetation. They used hand signals to cross. Quick and quiet. The sun was still high overhead. The mist had cleared away.

But always, that buzzing noise. The drones were up there. Watching.

Captain Calhoun said, "Gunny, how we doing?"

Gunnery Sergeant Dalby tapped the Marine next to him and they both stopped. Darby spread out the map on the second Marine's back.

"Sir, we have about another hour, and we should be at the LZ."

"Alright, I'm gonna make the call."

Darby nodded.

Chase was staying quiet, keeping up while carrying the heavy pack that contained the crypto key.

Calhoun took out his radio and extended the antennae. He typed in a preplanned code. The two US Army H-60s were spinning on a small grass landing strip just over the Colombian border. The Blackhawks were part of the Army's First Battalion, 228th Aviation Regiment. They were part of Joint Task Force Bravo, out of Central America. General Schwartz had requested two of their aircraft to participate in this highly classified mission.

The crew chief in the lead H-60 had been waiting for the Marine Raider radio signal, notifying them to head to the extraction zone. Within one minute of receiving the notification, they were flying to the landing zone at one hundred and twenty knots. The crew chief also sent a signal back, indicating that they were on the way.

Calhoun heard the reply in his earpiece. He then removed the earpiece and tucked the radio back into his pack. "We're good. The Blackhawks should be at the LZ in about nine zero mikes."

They were all breathing heavy. Chase was covered in dirt and grime from crawling through the woods for the past few days. Sweat soaked through his camouflage utilities. He took a swig of water from his CamelBak as he walked.

Chase said, "These drones sound like they're sticking over us, right?"

Darby said, "Sounds like it."

"We just need to make it to the LZ," Calhoun said.

They reached the grass cutout, and the Marines stayed hidden in the trees and brush. The landing zone was only about the size of a large backyard in the suburbs. Barely enough room for the Army helicopter to land, Chase thought.

"How much time?"

Calhoun looked at his watch. "About ten more minutes."

Chase took out his own map. The LZ wasn't marked, but he had memorized where it was. The nearest road was about one mile to the east. There was another road about five miles to the west, along the coastline.

Unless the Chinese had access to helicopters of their own, they would have to use the roads to get to them. And they hadn't seen any helos on the Manta base.

The Marines simply had too great of a head start from their initial position on the hill outside Manta. He tried to reassure himself that they were going to get out of here unscathed.

Chase checked his watch again. The bird should be here any moment. Chase could still hear the damn buzzing overhead, but couldn't see any sign of drones when he looked up.

Gunnery Sergeant Darby knelt down near Chase. "If the drone had eyes on us and you were the Chinese commander, what would you do?"

Chase thought about it. "I'd first want to make sure that we didn't escape."

"Right. Which means you'd want to deny air coverage and roads, right?"

"Yeah."

The familiar *whomp whomp whomp* sound could be heard in the distance. It was the Army Blackhawks.

Chase said, "Sounds like our ride."

"I don't like it," Darby said. "If they've had drones overhead this whole time, it means they know where we are."

"If they know where we are, then why haven't they come at us? Cuz we have a head start?"

Darby said, "I don't think so. There are too many roads around here that they could have used to catch up."

"So what, then?"

"Son, I like to hunt in my spare time. I'm a good ole southern boy at heart. You know, during hunting season, before I get my buck, there's only one reason I won't take a shot at a deer."

"And what reason is that?"

"Because I plan to get a better shot by waiting."

Chase didn't like the sound of that.

The H-60 Blackhawks came into view. The first aircraft did a single pass, north to south, just above the trees, and then banked hard right, slowing itself down in the turn. The second aircraft followed. The Marines ducked down as the rotor wash blew through the field.

The first Blackhawk hovered at about one hundred feet, its nose pitched up slightly. The second circled behind it.

And that's when the hunters struck.

A lightning-fast trail of smoke shot out from the east, and into the first helicopter. The Army aircraft exploded in a yellow-and-orange fireball. Pieces of shrapnel and parts rained down on the forest. The Marines underneath hunkered down, trying to get out of the way. The centrifugal force of the spinning rotors, and the violent explosion, shot out a wave of hot shrapnel in every direction.

The second aircraft began to move forward, expending dozens of bright flares. Then two more missiles shot up towards it, and it too burst into flames, falling to the ground below.

Then there was only fire, scattered throughout the landing zone.

* * *

Gunnery Sergeant Darby and Chase were up on their feet as soon as it was over. While the shock of death and destruction incapacitated most people, members of the military's special operations were trained to compartmentalize and react.

The Raider team, which had been hidden and prepping for an air transport, sprung to life. Their heads popped up, searching for enemy threats. They broke into separate teams, fanning out and forming a protective formation based on the most likely threat vector.

Finding no immediate enemy in sight, they turned to Captain Calhoun and Gunnery Sergeant Darby for direction. Calhoun had been struck in the arm by a piece of shrapnel, but he was still mobile. Miraculously, the rest of the Marines were uninjured.

Darby said, "Check for survivors."

A few of the Marines ran over to the helicopter wreckage to see if they could rescue anyone or recover any remains. After a few moments of inspection, the Marine next to the flaming crash site looked at Darby and shook his head. The gunny frowned and waved them to follow him.

Darby said, "We need to go west, now. Those SAMs looked like they were launched from about a mile away to the east. If we go west, there's a road in that direction, and a small village about a mile to the north once we get to the road. We might be able to get vehicles there."

Chase said, "I agree. The Chinese must be on the road to our east. It's going to take forever to hump through this jungle to the west, but it's our only option."

Calhoun nodded, wincing in pain. "Let's move."

Once they were traveling, Calhoun began getting treatment for his shoulder wound. It looked to Chase like something had sliced right through the muscle tissue, about an inch deep. He looked to be hurting pretty bad. But the man working on his shoulder cleaned it and poured a clotting agent powder on it, then taped it up well enough for the bleeding to slow.

Chase said, "Even if we get vehicles, I don't like the idea of being on the roads for too long. I'm going to activate our second option for air extraction."

Calhoun nodded. "Good idea." His face was covered in sweat and dirt.

Chase took Calhoun's radio and made the call, using the code word AUDIBLE in an otherwise innocuous phrase. He repeated the phrase several times until he heard a three-tone reply transmitted back. That indicated that the NSA relay station had picked up the signal. The NSA relay team would then send a message to a US Navy destroyer, the USS *Farragut*.

The USS *Farragut*'s orders, which Chase had personally delivered to the captain only a few days ago, were to remain in a defined geographic box, a little more than one hundred miles off the coast of Ecuador. They were to loiter in that position in case they were needed as a backup transportation option for Chase and the Marine Raider team. Chase had thought the chances of them actually being called upon were less than five percent.

Turned out he was wrong. He thought about his sister, getting in her helicopter. Would she realize that her mission was to come rescue him? Probably. She'd always been the smartest of the three siblings.

Chase looked at his watch. "Now that I've sent that signal, we'll have about six hours to make it to the backup landing zone."

"We'll have to acquire a few vehicles if we're going to make it there on time," the gunnery sergeant replied.

"Yup."

Chase thought that he would never be as happy to see his sister as when she picked him up in her helicopter today. Then he thought about the chances that someone would have a surface-to-air missile near the next site.

"We're going to have to set up a perimeter of a few miles around the next LZ, to make sure the same thing doesn't happen."

"Got it. There's only one road. We'll separate into three fire teams. One will stay at the LZ. The other two can separate along the road and make sure it stays secure."

They came to a shallow stream. The group crossed it all at once, the water getting only ankle-deep. As the group began to help each other up the bank on the other side of the stream, Chase heard a snap.

The sound could have been confused for a breaking tree branch —except for the fact that one of the Marines collapsed into the stream, facedown. A blur of dark red blood poured out of his back.

Yellow muzzle flashes from the forest behind them, followed by bursts of automatic gunfire. Chase grabbed onto a branch overhanging the stream and pulled himself up the embankment. He then turned around and lay in the prone position, taking stock of their attackers.

A single loud crack to Chase's left turned into an outbreak of return fire. One of the Marines began firing his M240G squad automatic weapon, or SAW, and the tropical forest erupted in noise. Tracer rounds sliced through the air in a flat line over the shallow stream, and into the dark jungle on the other side.

Thunk.

Thunk.

Chase turned at the noise. Two of the Marines fired grenade launchers toward the attackers and then moved positions.

One of the Marines ran to the stream and grabbed the corpse lying in the water. He slung it over his shoulders, then turned and ran back to cover.

Darby jogged up next to Chase. "Why aren't those bastards

moving in on us? They're just sitting back there, trying to pick us off from far out."

"I don't know. But we can't stay here and fight. We'll need to keep moving. What are our options?"

"I could leave a team here, but I'd rather not do that. I could..."

Movement out of the corner of Chase's eye. Airborne. Chase looked up and tried to make sense of what he was seeing. It looked like a dark grey square, hovering in the air. At first he thought it was a single object. But then he realized that it was the swarm of drones. They had collected together, about a dozen of them flying in close formation.

The drone swarm moved in unison, which created the illusion that they were a single object. The object appeared to be growing larger, and the buzzing grew louder. The drones were flying towards them, Chase realized.

Like they were about to attack.

"*Darby.*"

"What?"

He pointed at the drones.

As Chase looked again, one of them raced towards them and released a cluster of small objects. As each object impacted the surface, it exploded.

The explosions started in the stream. Spouts of water and rock lifting up into the air, and then walking up the bank and into the forest.

The drone was dropping some type of bomblets. Chase covered his head and ears and lay as tight to the ground as he could. Trees exploded and splintered all around them. Two more drones made similar bombing runs. When the cluster bomb attack stopped, Chase looked up and saw men running on the other side of the stream. It was the Chinese attackers, regrouping. Trying to flank them.

A ringing in his ears. He could barely hear anything. *Shit.* He should have put in his earplugs. It was stupid of him not to.

The Marine with the SAW began firing up at the drones. He walked the tracer rounds into the area where they were flying and began shattering them into pieces. Then the rectangle spread out, as if on command. Either they were programmed to do it, or one of the Chinese controlling it had spread them out as a defensive measure.

Chase looked at Darby, who was surveying his men. He crawled back to Chase. "Two dead. One injured. The captain's in bad shape."

"We need to get the crypto key back to the US. The data that's on here"—he patted his bag, where the crypto key was stored—"is going to save a lot of lives."

Gunnery Sergeant Darby looked across the stream. In the shadows of the forest, small groups of soldiers advanced to nearer positions.

Chase said, "Let's go now. If we run, we can make the village…"

"Do you know where you're going?"

"What do you mean?"

"I mean, do you know how to get to the LZ on your own?"

Chase shook his head. He knew what the gunny was thinking. "*Don't.*" Even as he said it, he knew his words would have no effect on the gunnery sergeant.

"If you go now, and we stay and hold them off, you'll make it. If we all run, they'll start picking us apart. We'll be slow and ineffective. The mission comes first."

"If you guys stay here, you could be killed." Chase regretted saying it as soon as it came out.

"Son, don't be stupid. I'm a US Marine. *They'll* all be killed. Now go."

Chase turned to go and then stopped. "Listen, just give me a head start. That's all I need. Then you get your team out of here. Head to one of the villages northwest of here and hunker down near the road. Monitor guard frequency. Once I get to the helicopters, we'll come pick you guys up."

"Oorah." The gunny yelled out the common cheer of the Marine Corps.

"Shut up."

The gunny smiled.

Chase began running.

17

USS Farragut
200 Nautical Miles Northeast of the Galapagos Islands

Victoria held the fingers and palms of her glove so that they just barely touched the controls of the helicopter. Her heavy steel-toed flight boots were poised with their heels on the deck, angled to be ready to step on the helicopter's foot pedals at a moment's notice. She did this because she wanted to be able to grab the controls instantly, but still needed to let her copilot be the one doing the flying.

Her head moved constantly on a swivel. Looking forward to judge the distance between the hovering Seahawk helicopter and the ship's hangar. Looking down through the glass floor—known as the chin bubble—to judge the altitude to the flight deck. And looking from side to side to gain better awareness in determining their drift.

They were hovering a mere ten feet above their destroyer, the USS *Farragut*. A gigantic USNS supply ship pitched and rolled alongside the *Farragut*. She guessed it was maybe fifty yards away.

They had shot lines only a few moments ago, using guns that reminded her of what they used to shoot free tee shirts out at football games. Her ship had fired, and a soft cloth-covered ball, attached to a line, had traveled in an arc from the *Farragut* and landed on the supply ship.

The two ships were now connected. The supply ship was able to use that first line connection to begin connecting the bigger fuel lines and sturdier supply zip lines. Deck hands moved pallets and net around the ship with practiced efficiency.

Beneath her twenty-thousand-pound aircraft, several enlisted men scurried about the flight deck, nervously hooking up the netted pallet to the bottom of the helicopter with a line and hook. It must have been a nerve-wracking job to be those men on the flight deck.

The flying pilot was Lieutenant Junior Grade Juan "Spike" Volonte, her inexperienced copilot. It was his first real vertical replenishment, or VERTREP, evolution. His face was a mess of sweat, and he was making constant overcorrections. As a result, the helicopter looked like it was constantly shaking and shimmying.

Up one foot, and then rapidly down two feet. Sliding to the left three feet, then surging quickly back to the right one foot. Their aircrewman, looking through the floor hatch in the rear of the aircraft, was attempting to make gentle correction calls. But he knew that with a pilot this inexperienced, it was almost useless. The kid just needed more practice.

Victoria's job was to make sure Juan got enough hands-on experience so that he could learn and get better, yet be ready to jump in the split second he made too big a mistake. Basically, she needed to do the same thing she did every other time she flew with these nuggets. Get the mission done without killing anyone.

The way young Juan here was squeezing the black out of the stick, he would be exhausted after a few more minutes.

"Need a break?" she asked.

No response.

"Juan."

"Yes..." He was grimacing. "Yes...Boss?"

"Here, let me have the controls for a minute."

"Roger, you have the controls."

"I have the controls."

"You have the controls."

Two things happened. First, the helicopter, which had been lurching all over the place and scaring the shit out of the men below, instantly stabilized into a near-motionless hover. Second, Juan's body sagged into a gelatinous sack of sweat and limp muscle, held to his seat by five tightly connected straps.

"Alright, ma'am, you're hooked up," said her aircrewman in the back of the aircraft.

"Roger, coming up and aft."

She pulled up with her left hand—just a touch. At the same instant, she put in a tiny bit of forward pedal with her left foot and pulled aft on the cyclic with her right hand. Three distinct movements that got the helicopter to move the way she wanted. But they weren't a conscious set of actions. With her years of flying experience, the control inputs just came naturally. Victoria just knew what she wanted the aircraft to do, and her body moved in such a way that the helicopter's nose came up and began moving backwards and gaining altitude.

The aircraft floated up and drifted aft until they were about one hundred feet high, and perched directly in back of the *Farragut*. Two heavy pallets filled with supplies swung from a net below the helicopter. She kept pulling up with her left hand, getting more and more power from the engines as they came out of ground effect. The rotor wash blew a sphere of white sea spray around them as they hovered over the water.

Victoria next moved the cyclic forward an inch to arrest their backward drift. They were now essentially flying in formation with the destroyer, which was itself driving in formation with the large supply ship at her ten o'clock.

Victoria pushed forward with her left foot, and the nose of the aircraft yawed to the left. She moved the cyclic forward and left and pulled a bit more power. Now the helicopter began drifting left, maintaining altitude, and sliding from its perch behind the destroyer on over to a similar spot behind the supply ship.

She maneuvered the aircraft closer and lower to the deck of the supply ship and came to a hover ten feet above the deck.

The aircrewman said, "Okay, you're in position. Come down. Load's on deck."

"Releasing the load." She pressed the button on her cyclic that opened the cargo hook, allowing the pallets to remain on deck.

"Load's free."

Victoria said, "Well, there goes our snail mail. Any bets on how long it takes to reach our families?"

The aircrewman said, "Come up two...one...steady. Okay, they're hooking up the next pallets now."

"Roger."

"Alright, you're hooked up. Ready to come up and aft."

She performed the same maneuver as before, effortlessly bringing the helicopter up and then sliding it over back to her ship. This time she transferred four pallets, bundled up in dark green netting, over to the *Farragut*.

They had several hours of this work to do, and it was one of the more fun exercises in helicopter naval aviation.

"Cutlass 471, *Farragut* Control."

"Go ahead, Control," Victoria responded. She checked the paper attached to her kneeboard, where she logged the current time and fuel. This allowed her to calculate the aircraft's fuel burn and calculate how much remaining flight time they had. They were burning eight hundred and fifty pounds of fuel per hour—about normal.

"Ma'am, OPS just came over and gave me a strange request."

She sighed. Whenever the ship communication began with a warning, it always ended badly for the aircrew. "Let's hear it."

"Boss, I overheard them talking, and it sounds like they want you to fly to South America."

"*What?*"

"Hold on, ma'am."

She looked back down at her fuel gauge and did the quick math. "We'll need to land. When do they need us there? And what are we picking up?"

"OPS says he'll brief you when you land. We're clearing our flight deck of all supplies right now."

"I assume the captain has given his approval?"

"Air Boss, this is OPS."

Victoria paused. It was very odd for him to get on the radios to talk to them while they were flying. "Go ahead."

His voice sounded tense. "Boss, we just got an emergency message telling us to open up the sealed mission brief in the captain's safe. We're to execute these orders as soon as possible."

"Roger. Can you give me any more details?"

"The captain asked that you please head in for a landing so we can discuss."

"Copy that. We're inbound as soon as the deck is cleared."

* * *

Twenty minutes later, Victoria walked into the port-side hangar, where the operations officer was waiting for her.

She held her helmet under one arm. Her hair and face were wet with sweat. "What's it say?"

OPS said, "Come with me. Captain's on the bridge. He wants you to see him first. XO had me tell the pilots. Plug and Caveman read the orders and are in the wardroom getting ready."

She was happy to hear that. No wasted time. *But ready for what?*

She walked up onto the bridge. The captain was on the port bridge wing, watching the replenishment at sea. The supply ship was still only a few dozen yards away, still hooked up and pumping fuel into the destroyer. Waves crashed into the hull between the two ships, splashing up white water every few seconds.

"Sir, OPS said that we have the go order?"

He turned to face her. "Yes. It sounds like they need you to go be a bus driver for some special operations troops. It didn't say what for. Just gave a time and a place to be. But they want us to send both helicopters. That going to be a problem?"

"*Both* helicopters?" She thought about that. Dual-helicopter operations from a single-spot ship, like a destroyer, were tricky. Only one aircraft could fit on the flight deck at a time. This meant that when both aircraft returned to the ship, only one of them would be able to land. That helicopter would then need to shut down, fold the blades and tail, and then be traversed into the hangar. That process could take thirty minutes to an hour—during which time the other aircraft would be burning precious fuel, without the ability to land.

She told the captain, "Sir, we can do it. We'll just have to make sure that one of the other ships in company is designated as our alternate landing spot—I recommend the supply ship since she's right here and has a big flight deck."

The captain said, "Fine. OPS, make it happen."

"Yes, sir."

"Any questions?"

"Sir, I still haven't read the mission orders."

"Your other pilot has them."

OPS said, "Plug. In the wardroom. I'll show you, Boss."

Victoria said, "Alright, thanks, sir."

The captain nodded, looking annoyed.

She and OPS left. OPS said, "It's been one of those days with him."

"Great." She'd never met such an emotionally unstable man as the captain. It was unbelievable to her that he had risen this high in the officer corps. "Any idea why?"

"Beats me. I guess because this is changing his plan of the day. He doesn't like change."

When they arrived in the wardroom, Plug and Caveman were waiting. They had aviation charts of South America. The Colombia and Ecuador charts were spread out on the tables. The two pilots had rulers, pencils, and yellow highlighters and were quickly marking up the charts.

Plug handed Victoria a manila envelope. "Mission orders are in here."

She took out the two white sheets of paper and read over them. "It gives us a few checkpoints to hit, and a time to be at the LZ. Other than that, it's not very detailed."

"Nope."

"It says we have to be there in three hours. Can we make that?"

Plug said, "We just got done doing the math. As long as we don't have any mechanical trouble with the second aircraft, I think we'll be in good shape."

She shook her head. "This is crazy." She looked at the charts. "Show me the landing zone."

Plug pointed to a spot on one of the charts that showed her the location of the landing zone in Ecuador. It was about fifteen miles inland, just east of a mountain range. It looked like it was in the middle of the jungle.

Victoria read the orders. "It says we're supposed to shut off our transponder and lights and not make any external communications once we get within fifty miles of the coast. We're not even supposed to notify Colombia or Ecuador that we're coming. Expect up to fourteen SOCOM passengers." She looked up at her maintenance officer. "We're going to need to get rid of all of our extra weight."

Plug nodded, a rare serious look on his face. "I already asked Senior Chief and AWR1 to see what they could do to make us lighter and clear out any extra space for passengers. Boss, this sounds like more than a training mission, huh?"

"I would say so." Victoria turned to OPS and said, "So do you have any idea what this is about? We're picking up some special operators in the middle of the Ecuadorian jungle?"

"Pretty much. We didn't get anything else in the radio notification. Just to open up the mission brief and execute as planned. And that it was urgent."

"Ever seen something like this before?"

"No. But I heard a story once where they sent a helo from a cruiser into the middle of the desert in Saudi Arabia. It picked up some CIA guy wearing a suit and brought him back to the ship. Once they landed, he gave them a time and location in the middle of the Red Sea to drop him off. Sure enough, a submarine popped up, and they did the *Hunt for Red October* thing where they sling him down to the sub."

"So you think we're gonna be doing that? Dropping these guys off in a submarine?"

"Well, I don't think you're going to be picking up my newest group of ensigns, let's put it that way."

"Plug, how far is the trip?"

"One hundred and twenty miles. I told OPS that we'll need to head east to make sure you're good on fuel."

She realized what he meant. "Christ, we don't even know if I can get fuel there?"

OPS shrugged.

She closed her eyes. "This is so messed up."

OPS said, "I'll make sure we close the distance so you'll burn less fuel on the return leg."

"And have the TACAN on high power. I'll be climbing up high to get comms and a good navigational lock once I head back from the beach. But if I don't find you guys by the time I get to my bingo, I'm turning around and taking an all-expenses vacation back in Colombia."

"Easy there, Air Boss."

"I'm serious about the bingo fuel. Don't screw with me. Close the distance. I don't mess around with fuel."

"Yes, ma'am."

The wardroom phone rang. Victoria answered, listened, and then hung up. "Alright, gents, everyone still safe to fly? Any questions?"

They each shook their heads, excited looks in their eyes.

Victoria said, "My aircraft just finished fueling up. Juan's on his way here. Let's see if we can wrap up our mission brief in the next ten minutes. Then we'll roll."

One hour later, Victoria was headed east over the Pacific at two thousand feet, with Plug's helicopter in trail.

18

Lena watched the American Special Forces soldier fall after her bullet hit its mark. She could have taken out many of the others in their unit, but then a few of the Leishen Commandos began firing their automatic weapons, costing her the element of surprise.

That had frustrated her. Lena preferred to work alone. Especially when conducting this type of work. She tapped her ear and spoke into her headset. Now that the Americans knew they were so close, there was no reason to hold off on the drone strike.

"Send the drones to drop their bomb clusters."

The Leishen commander crouched down next to her. "Ma'am, my men are ready to cross the stream upon your command."

"We have air support coming in. Let's soften them up first."

"Yes, ma'am."

She looked through her scope again, searching the far embankment for a target.

There. Two of them were lying down speaking to each other. She had a clear view of one of them...

Him. How was that possible?

Of all the people they could have sent here, why would they have sent Chase Manning? Did they know she would be here?

Her mind raced. She hated coincidences. She didn't believe in them. In her line of work, there were no coincidences. Coincidences were often really preplanned events, and things to be investigated. Or they were timed to have a psychological impact on one's prey. So, was she the prey here?

The thought angered her. Her finger began to depress the trigger. She could end it here by killing him. No compromising emotions. No more thoughts of him in her bed.

But he had let her live.

And burned her, she reminded herself.

She could still see the white curved architecture of the Burj Al Arab, the rotors of the Iranian UH-1 helicopter, about to take off. She could still smell the disgusting smell of her own skin cooking, burned from the Molotov cocktails Chase had thrown in her direction. As he had climbed up the stairway of the helipad to save his brother, he'd had a clear shot. He could have ended her life. She knew that a man of his talent would not have missed her from that range.

But he had.

It was for the same reason she had spared his life only moments earlier. She had met him in the Skyview Bar and had told the Iranian she was with not to harm him. She had just wanted to see him one last time.

So were they now even? It didn't feel like it.

The water in the stream began exploding up again as the drones came in to attack the Americans. The explosions moved from the stream and into the forest. Rapid blasts filled with shrapnel rang through the forest, violent and merciless. They ripped through the trees, where the Americans were firing back at her platoon of Chinese commandos.

When the dust settled, she tried to find Chase again. She moved her telescopic view throughout the area, but couldn't find him. A part of her was...what? *Worried?* She cursed herself. Her emotion was a crutch. She needed to control it better. There was no logic or honor in letting Chase survive because of their past relationship. Too much was on the line.

She tapped the button on her headset. "Hold fire on the airstrike. Hold fire." She looked down at her map. There was a road about two kilometers behind the American position. If she could get there with reinforcements, they could surround them.

Lena turned to the Leishen commander. "A change of plans, Major. Move your men forward immediately. I will fall back and gather the other Leishen Commando platoon. I will take them around in jeeps and flank the Americans. If they run, keep following them and forcing them to me. Let us finish this."

* * *

Victoria sucked more water through the straw of her CamelBak. "Cutlass flight, come down to two hundred feet."

"Two," came the response from Plug's helicopter.

Their transponders were already off, fifty miles out from the coast, as stipulated in their mission brief. The two-helicopter formation flew in low—two hundred feet above ground level. It was still daylight, but the hope was that by staying low over uninhabited jungle terrain, they wouldn't be seen.

She was the lead aircraft. Plug's helicopter was formed up on her right side, with a fifty-foot separation in altitude and several rotors' diameter separation.

Victoria looked at Juan, her copilot. He had that deer in the headlights look. When she had briefed them all on the mission, both 2Ps had been excited. Victoria and her crew had gotten back into their helo, which was already spinning on deck, and flown around in circles for thirty minutes above the ship. That was how long it had taken Plug to have the maintenance team get the second bird out of the barn, spin it up, and get airborne. Once both aircraft were flying, they'd quickly formed up and headed to the coast.

They crossed over the coastline and turned south over the triple canopy jungle. A lot of the terrain was mountainous. Nothing crazy, but a lot more hills than Jacksonville, Florida, where their squadron was stationed. They used the navigation charts to keep track of various landmarks and maintain their position.

The navigation wasn't too bad. They flew close enough to the coastline until the town of Esmeraldas, Ecuador. Then they followed the river south.

"Watch out for power lines," she said to her copilot. "It would be a shame to fail on our first covert mission with Special Forces because we crashed into electrical wires."

"Roger" was all Juan said back.

The kid was scared shitless now. Before he had been head down in the chart. Now he was about twenty percent in the chart, and eighty percent looking ahead. That was fine with her. It would help keep them alive.

Victoria said, "There should be a bend in the river up ahead, you see it on the chart?"

"Yup."

"Is there a bridge next to the bend in the river?"

"Yeah."

"What direction does it head?"

"The road heads south, then there's a fork. Looks like a major road according to the map."

"Yup, that's the one. We'll be following the road and taking the fork to the west."

She leaned forward and looked out her right window. She could see the second MH-60R, hugging her right side. Normally she would tell Plug to give her some space, but she didn't want to break radio silence. And she knew that for all his faults, he was a damn good pilot.

"There's the bridge, Boss."

"Looks like major roads in some countries are less impressive than in others." It was a tiny, single-lane road. But it was paved, and the trees were cut out around it well. So it would be easy to follow.

Victoria banked the large grey aircraft around sharply to begin flying over the road, careful to stay just above the treetops.

"What's the time?"

"Fourteen twenty-three on the clock."

"Alright, we need to shave off a little time. I'm going to head due west. The road bends around to the north, but if we head west we'll be able to intercept it again. Should save us about five minutes. I don't want to be late. We're supposed to be at the LZ at fourteen forty-five. Set the timer on the clock on my mark."

"Roger."

"*Mark.*"

"Clock set."

She banked the helicopter hard left and skimmed the dark green treetops. The forest flew by.

This close to the jungle, it felt like they were traveling incredibly fast. They *were*, she reminded herself. The illusion was when they were higher up and appeared to be traveling slowly.

Juan said, "Should be a river, running north south, before we get to the—"

"There it is."

"Roger."

"There's a town to the north, but I think we're too low to see it."

"Let's keep it that way."

They flew on for another two full minutes, and Victoria was starting to get worried that she had missed the road. Low-level navigation was hard enough. It was harder when you missed a checkpoint or made a mistake.

"There it is."

She looked at her airspeed indicator. One hundred and twenty knots. They were running late. Only a few minutes, but still. Operations like this were supposed to be right on time.

One hundred and twenty knots was her max range speed. It would use her fuel in the most efficient manner and give her the best chance of making it back to her ship without running out of gas. They would need to travel over one hundred miles to the ship once they picked up their passengers. They needed all the fuel they could get.

Fuel was going to be tight just based on the distance alone. But if the Navy—or whoever had activated this mission—was going with their backup plan, Victoria wondered what kind of trouble they might encounter at the landing zone. The only hint at that was the note on the mission orders to ensure that the helicopters were armed.

"AWR1, is your weapon ready?"

He had a .50-caliber GAU-16 mounted to the rear cabin door. "Locked and loaded, ma'am."

"Roger."

She looked at her fuel gauge again. Victoria pulled the collective lever with her left hand and pushed forward on the cyclic with her right. The nose dipped down a bit, and they gained another ten knots of airspeed.

"Picking up the speed a little."

"Roger." She loved how agreeable junior copilots could be. She could tell this guy that they were going to fly through a train tunnel and he would probably reply with "Roger."

Ten minutes later, the landing zone was in sight. It was just an open field near a bend in the road, a dozen or so miles from the coast.

Victoria gradually dialed back the speed by pulling back on the cyclic and letting out power with her left hand. She didn't want to decelerate too fast. If she did, it risked her wingman overshooting her —or worse, collision. The two aircraft overflew the empty field once, surveying it for obstructions and potential hazards. Victoria took them around and into the wind, landing on a flat spot about twenty yards from the tree line.

As soon as she landed, a man wearing jungle utilities emerged from the forest, running towards them and waving.

It was her brother.

She had suspected he would be one of the ones here but had been afraid to let herself think about it. She was sure as hell glad to see him.

* * *

When Chase got into the helicopter, Victoria told her crewman to hook him up to the comms.

"Victoria, is that you?"

Victoria noticed that her copilot was giving her a funny look. Probably wondering how the hell she knew their new passenger. She had violated the safety brief, failing to mention that she had a conflict of interest on today's mission.

"It's me, Chase. Are you alright? Can we get out of here? Is anyone else coming?"

She looked down at her fuel gauge. Only sixteen hundred pounds of fuel. That was way lower than she was comfortable with, but she could probably have the ship maneuver to get closer once they got high enough to communicate with them.

"We need to go pick up a few others."

She turned around to face him, her expression of worry visible in the section of her face that wasn't covered by her helmet or tinted visor.

"We don't have the fuel."

"Victoria. We *have* to. It's close. The men who were with me are going to get killed or captured if we don't go."

She didn't say anything.

"Your door-gunners are going to need to lay down covering fire. I can help."

Fuck it. "Alright, I can give you about ten minutes. But that's all. And just so you know, we might get wet later because of this."

"Ten minutes should do. It's two miles down the road."

"Where's the landing site?"

"The road."

She shook her head and made sure her external comms were switched to the right frequency. This was more important than radio silence. "Seven-six, seven-one."

Plug came over the radios. "*Go.*"

"We need to make a quick detour."

"Boss, I'm real low on fuel."

"Me too. Ten minutes…and tell AW2 to lock and load."

Another double click of static on the UHF radio told her that he would comply.

As she pulled in power and they gained altitude, the nose dipped forward and they stayed low to the ground, following the road.

Chase said, "Oh, Victoria, one more thing. If you see any helicopter drones around here, let's try and shoot those suckers down. Okay?"

She shook her head. What the hell was her brother involved in?

19

Lena's jeep pulled up to the platoon of Leishen Commandos near the Ecuadorian town. She had gone back to the additional platoon of Chinese commandos and directed them along the road to the other side of the forest, near the town. The idea was to surround the Americans. It had taken the second Leishen platoon much longer than expected to get to the road on the other side of the woods.

She appeared to be too late.

"What happened, Major?" she asked the first platoon commander.

"Ms. Chou, the Americans set a trap for my men. Once we were over the stream, they set off explosives and cut down many of us with automatic weapons fire. We were eventually able to push them back, but our forces were greatly slowed. We pursued them through the jungle and to this town. When we arrived, they were getting into two US Navy helicopters."

She cursed, then looked up at him. "You are sure they were Navy?"

"Yes, several of my men are fluent in English. They saw the markings on the side."

"Then what happened?"

"The helicopters picked them up one at a time. The other helicopter was circling and began firing with high-caliber weapons onto our positions in the jungle. We were unable to stop them."

"Which direction did the helicopters head?"

"West, ma'am."

"Out to sea?"

"I would assume, yes. We are very close to the coastline."

She frowned. "This is troubling. I will need to get to the communications center immediately. Let's go."

* * *

Lena's jeep came to a screeching halt right outside the communications trailer.

She knocked hard on the door. An armed guard inside the trailer opened up the spy hole and verified who was on the other side. Improved security measures, she noted. Too little, too late.

She entered the trailer and looked for the senior man. "I need to reach the island. Please patch me through."

It took about five minutes for her to be on the phone with the duty officer in the Red Cell's operations center. "I need to speak with Jinshan. Can you connect me?" she asked.

"Please wait."

Another five minutes until she heard the old man's voice. "Lena, is this you?"

"I'm afraid I have bad news, Mr. Jinshan."

"Lena, what is it?"

"Sir, it appears that the equipment we have been using to track our military assets without alerting Chinese leadership may have been compromised. The hardware known as the crypto key has been taken from the mobile communications center in Manta."

"Taken by *whom*?" Jinshan said.

"We believe that they were Americans. A Special Forces unit."

"Are you *sure* that they were Americans?"

She thought of telling him how she knew. That she'd had Chase

Manning in her sights. Then she changed her mind. She would never admit that to anyone.

"I'm sure, Mr. Jinshan. I saw several of their faces, and their equipment. And they were picked up by US Navy helicopters. Their first attempt to escape was several hours ago, on another set of helicopters. We were able to shoot those two down."

The other side was silent. Then Jinshan said, "So it has begun. I had hoped for a more deliberate start."

"I apologize, sir. But it appears that we must now take action."

"Please wait one moment, Lena. I must confer with Admiral Song."

It was a full ten minutes before Jinshan got back on the line. "Admiral Song and I will take care of this from here. You were right to inform me of this, and right to take extreme measures to prevent the crypto key from falling into the hands of the Americans. We are not ready for that level of information disclosure yet."

"Sir, is there anything else I can do to help?"

"Not now, Lena. Admiral Song is sending a message to his naval units in the Eastern Pacific as we speak. We have an idea of where the crypto key has likely gone. And we will take steps to ensure that it does not go any further."

20

"Captain in Combat," yelled one of the petty officers on watch in the *Farragut*'s combat information center.

The destroyer had just finished conducting its underway replenishment with the supply ship. The "breakaway" song was playing on the 1MC. One of the modern traditions on board many Navy warships was to play a popular song over the ship's speakers as a way to celebrate the successful completions of the replenishment at sea. Today's song was from the Doors.

"Turn that damn song off," said the captain.

"Aye-aye, sir."

"OPS. Where the hell is OPS?"

"Here, sir." The ship's operations officer stood behind one of the sonar stations.

"What's the status of the helicopters?"

OPS walked over to one of the computers and changed the display in the center of the CIC. "Sir, they checked off with us about one hour ago. They were out of communications range…here." He moved the cursor from the symbol that represented their ship over to an X with the tag "HELICOPTER OFF STATION."

"And how far from the coast were they?"

"About fifty miles, sir. Air Boss told me that she expected to be back up with us"—he looked at his watch—"any minute now."

The ship's communications officer burst into the room, holding up a clipboard. "Sir! HF radio transmission…" He was out of breath, like he had been running.

"Not now, COMMO." The kid was still trying to make it up to him that none of their satellite communications ever worked. Ever since the captain had chewed him out in front of the wardroom at dinner that night, he had worked around the clock to try and improve their HF systems, as well as retrain his men. This was probably some incremental fix he had just made, the captain thought.

"Sir, please forgive me, but this is critically important."

The captain turned. He hated the way this kid talked. Like he'd gone to some snooty Ivy League school. "What is it, COMMO?" he asked, annoyance in his voice.

"Sir, the helicopter, sir. They're on their way here. Some of their passengers have been trying to reach us with their HF radios since they're so far away."

The captain rolled his eyes. "Well, what did they say? Come on, I don't have all day."

"Sir, they've been *attacked*. They say that Chinese military forces shot at them. They have wounded inbound."

There were almost fifteen people in the CIC, working at various stations. There was a good deal of chatter on a normal day, but as busy as today was, it was loud.

Until the COMMO made his statement. At that, heads turned, and everyone stared at him.

The captain's face contorted. "*What?* I thought that they were just supposed to pick up some SEALs or something. What are you talking about? They flew to South America, for Christ's sake. What the hell are you talking about with *Chinese?*"

The young communications officer shook his head. "I don't know, sir. The transmission was garbled. They had to use a radio from one of their passengers. It was the aircrewman who sent the message."

The captain looked at his XO, confused. "What the hell is going on, XO?"

The XO said, "Sir, I'll have medical personnel standing by for when they get here. Do you think it would be wise for us to increase our weapons posture?"

The captain shrugged. "I mean...I don't understand what the situation is...I'm not sure that's needed."

The XO said, "Sir, I recommend that we increase our weapons posture, until we know more. Perhaps we should go to general quarters, sir?" The XO looked alarmed. He scanned the room, thinking about what they needed to do.

The sonar operator had his earphones on and was staring at his screen, away from the group. He hadn't heard the commotion. He held up his hand and said, "TAO, sonar."

OPS was the standing tactical action officer and had taken off his headset when the captain had arrived in Combat. He didn't hear the petty officer calling for him.

The captain waved his hand at the group, as if he was annoyed about the unwelcome news. "Fine, XO, if you want to increase our weapons posture, fine. But don't go to GQ. That's too much. I'll be up on the bridge."

"TAO, sonar!" the young enlisted man called out.

The group of senior officers turned. "What, sonar?" OPS asked.

The petty officer's face was white. "Sir, I'm not sure, but I think..."

OPS said, "What is it?"

"Sir, I think I hear...a *torpedo*..."

* * *

The Chinese submarine had been following the Americans for several weeks. These attack orders had come much earlier than expected, but the captain had been told to be ready. They were constantly given times and locations of potential attacks, but the orders had never been given. Until now.

"Sir! The orders are from the South Fleet Commander. We are to execute our attack immediately of American destroyer 099 and ships in company."

He grabbed the paper document. "You are sure?" He read it over. It was indeed time.

The Type 093 Shang-class submarine was one of the newest in China's fleet. It was longer than a football field, displaced seven thousand tons when fully submerged, and carried a crew of one hundred and ten enlisted and twelve officers. This particular variant was the G model, which meant that it had a vertical launching system for its YJ-82 anti-ship missile.

The captain had thought those missiles a nuisance when he had watched them being loaded onto his submarine at their home port of Yulin Naval Base. There were many extra safety and security precautions that he had been responsible for once those missiles were aboard. Now, about to launch four of them, he thanked the heavens that they were aboard.

"Torpedo tubes one and two flooded and doors open, captain."

The captain had personally checked on the accuracy of the targeting solution. While the Colombian diesel submarine was no match for them, removing it from the theater first was the best way to ensure his success.

"Explosion in the water, sir. The Colombian submarine has been hit, sir. We can hear it breaking up and sinking."

The captain nodded. "Good. We must move quickly now."

There were four surface targets he needed to sink. One of them was a highly formidable American Arleigh Burke–class destroyer.

A single-dimensional battlefield was much easier to fight than a multidimensional one. That was what he had learned in countless exercises off the coast of Hainan Island.

The captain pointed at his weapons control officer. "Fire torpedo from tube one. Standby on two...*Fire* torpedo from tube two."

The sound of his men repeating his orders and completing their tasks echoed throughout the small space, followed by a reverberation as the torpedoes launched out of his vessel, and then the high-pitched noise of the running torpedoes, changing frequency as they increased their distance.

He looked at his missile operator. He pointed at him and nodded. "Fire missiles one, two, three, and four."

Now he would see how good this American destroyer really was.

* * *

"TAO, sonar, torpedo in the water bearing two-six-five."

The captain looked up from the emergency message. "What did you just say?" He looked at the sonar operator like he had two heads. They had just finished a resupply with the USNS Supply. They were closer to the Galapagos Islands than any other land mass. The most dangerous thing out here was the hippies who wanted to protect the whales and sea turtles. What the hell was this man talking about a torpedo for?

"Explosions in the water, sir," said the sonar operator. A senior enlisted man sat down next to him and put on a headset. "More torpedo noise, sir!"

The XO was not so slow to react. He had been standing behind the captain. Now he said, "OPS, set GQ immediately. And for God's sakes, make sure all our air defense is up and operational."

The captain turned and looked at the XO, annoyed that he was speaking out of turn. "Come on, XO, let's get up to the bridge."

The alarm sounded throughout the ship. Steel-toed boots ran on deck plates as the men and women of the USS *Farragut* ran to their battle stations.

As they climbed up the ladder to the bridge, men were yelling and moving quickly throughout the space. The captain walked out to the bridge wing, where the officer of the deck was pointing to something and shouting.

The captain said, "All ahead flank."

"All ahead flank."

The captain and the XO joined the OOD on the bridge wing. "What is it?"

"Sir, we just saw what looked like a submarine explosion about six thousand yards out."

The first indication that missiles were inbound came from the ship's vertical launch system as it automatically fired three SM-2 surface-to-air missiles. Guided by the ship's SPY-1D radar, they attempted to destroy the incoming Chinese YJ-82 anti-ship missiles.

But the YJ-82s had a very low radar cross-section and skimmed the surface of the water at only a few meters of altitude. It took only a few seconds for the YJ-82 to increase its speed to over four hundred knots. Because it was fired from a distance of only two miles, the total time of flight was just over six seconds. Barely enough time for the SM-2s to get off. Only one SM-2 found its target, exploding and sending the Chinese missile into the water.

The last line of air defense for the American destroyer was the Phalanx Close-In Weapons System (CWIS). The giant Gatling gun sounded like God had just zipped up an enormous zipper. The sound shocked the captain. But the CWIS did what it was intended to do, launching a barrage of armor-piercing tungsten penetrator rounds at the rate of three thousand per minute.

Unfortunately, it only was able to fire for two seconds before impact. That meant that one hundred rounds were fired at the now-nearly-supersonic Chinese anti-ship missile. Only two of the missiles were designated for the Americans. The *Farragut*'s SM-2 surface-to-air missile took out the first. The CWIS exploded the second. But at that range and speed, the shrapnel from the Chinese missile still traveled with an enormous amount of kinetic energy.

Right into the bridge wing of the USS *Farragut*.

P lug saw the smoke first.

"What is that?"

Caveman looked up from the tactical display. "What the…?"

It reminded Plug of a volcano. Or maybe more like the footage of all those oil wells burning in the Iraqi desert. A deep black smoke billowed up into the sky and trailed off to the east.

"You hear from the ship yet?" Plug asked.

"No. I'll call again." Caveman switched to the UHF external frequency that he would be able to reach the ship on.

"*Farragut* Control, Cutlass 476, how do you read?"

Nothing.

The single column of smoke became two. Then four. Plug made a call to the other helicopter. "Boss, you seeing this?"

"Affirm." Her voice sounded strained. "We keep heading there for now."

Plug could see the ships now. A sickening feeling formed in his stomach. The way they sat in the water was all wrong. He counted four ships, each tilted at an odd and deeply disturbing angle.

"Oh my *God*."

Plug aimed his nose at the closest warship. The bow protruded up out of the water. Violent whitewater foamed and bubbled around it as the innards of the hull traded air for seawater. A scatter of lifeboats gathered around it. Frantic, shocked crew looked up at the helicopter as it flew overhead, tilting in a turn.

The FUEL LOW light illuminated on the helicopter's master caution panel. Plug was expecting it. But the feeling of dread only increased.

"Anybody see *Farragut* yet?"

AW2 Ross, their aircrewman, said, "I don't see her, sir. I only count four. Maybe she got outta here before...?"

Caveman replied, "Or she sank already. Plug, we might want to think about—"

"The needle just swung." He nodded towards the TACAN needle on the digital compass readout. It was tuned to their ship. It was now picking up the navigational beacon from *Farragut*.

"Nine miles. Coming right to three-one-zero. Thank God. I really didn't want to have to ditch this far out."

"You see that FUEL LOW light, right?" Caveman asked.

Plug turned and looked at him, lifting up his visor so the junior pilot could see his expression.

"Just checking."

Plug made the call to the other helo. "Boss, we're picking up Mom on TACAN. Nine miles on a heading of three-one-zero."

"Roger, we've got her on FLIR," came Victoria's response. "She looks like she's going pretty fast, and has damage near the bridge. We'll keep trying to reach her. You land first and get off deck. We'll drop our pax off after you, then I'll let you land and stuff the bird in the hangar."

Plug could see the USS *Farragut* now. "Boss, we're at five hundred and fifty pounds of fuel. You can't be much better."

"Plug, no arguments, please."

Plug said, "Ma'am, we're not going to have time to shut down and fold and stuff one of us in the hangar."

"Yes, you will, Lieutenant. That's going to be the plan."

Lieutenant. She had never called him that before. Aviators went by first names and call signs. She wanted to emphasize that she was in charge. Plug realized that she was afraid he might come up with his own plan.

That got him thinking.

Caveman said, "Two miles, conducting landing checks. Jones, everyone okay back there?"

"Aside from the bleeding, fine, sir."

"Roger." He flipped a few switches and then said, "Landing checks complete."

Plug kept the aircraft at one hundred and twenty knots until a half mile. He didn't look at any of his instruments. He just used feel. The site picture of the ship. The rate of closure of the deck. A grey smoke drifted overhead, and it smelled like burnt rubber and chemicals. His hands were slippery with sweat, but the leather gloves gripped onto the controls well.

"*Farragut* Control, Cutlass 476, declaring an emergency. We're low fuel and have not been able to get you on comms. We'll be landing and dropping off pax. Some need medical attention."

He was slow now. Just fifty knots indicated. But with the ship going so fast, it felt much slower.

"Over the deck."

"Roger." He kept the helicopter drifting forward in a gentle hover. The flight deck rolled underneath, but he didn't wait. He knew that the other aircraft was burning fuel above them. Every second longer he took meant a little bit less of a chance that they would survive.

The helicopter dropped into the center of the flight deck with a crunching jolt.

"Whew! That was ugly. Jones, Caveman, get everyone in the hangar. I've got the controls. Don't bother waiting for chocks and chains."

One of the hangar doors opened up, and one of his mechanics waved at them, his mouth open as he saw the aircrewman carrying a wounded soldier toward the hangar.

Moments later, Plug was alone in the aircraft, rolling side to side with the ship, the rotors turning. The fuel gauge was now less than five hundred pounds. He knew that he would only have a moment.

He pulled in power and slid the aircraft up and aft. Then he pedal-turned to the left and nosed it forward.

"Boss, I'm sorry, but I'm going to have to disobey you here."

"Stay near the ship, Plug. You'll land after I drop off my pax."

"I'll try, but I'll probably need you guys to drop a smoke or—"

"Plug, you listen to me. Keep airborne. I will drop off my pax and then let you get fuel."

"Not enough time, Boss. You know it. One of us is going in the drink. Just do me a favor and pull me out after you guys refuel, okay? I promise I'll get you one of those girly drinks you like next time we're in Panama."

There was only silence for a moment. Then she came on with a quick, resigned reply. "Remember your training."

He smiled. She was such a machine. He knew how much she cared about her men. It drove Plug crazy that she was unable to express it. *I mean, life isn't hard. You love someone, you say it. You hate someone, you punch them in the face. You work hard, you play hard.* Plug had done both.

Life had been fun while it lasted. His heart was beating faster. *Shit…*

He found himself talking out loud. "Well, better get this over with."

He turned off the radar altitude hold and slowed his aircraft to a crawl about a mile to the port side of the ship.

"One hundred feet. Ditching checklist. Windows—jettison."

He pulled the red-and-yellow handle, breaking the safety wire. Then he punched the Plexiglas and let it fall to the sea. He looked at the other helicopter. They were on short final now. Just coming over the deck. Good. That meant they would make it. He hoped that this was all worth it.

He was just about to bring the aircraft into a five-knot forward hover when he ran out of fuel.

The noise level decreased dramatically as the number one engine flamed out. His left hand instinctively dropped down the collective lever to preserve the rotational energy of the rotor, and get closer to the ground before the number two engine…

Ah. There it went. Total flameout.

The digital cubes that told him the status of his engines plummeted. He let the helicopter fall, holding the nose slightly forward to retain his forward speed.

It was the quickest autorotation of his life.

"Fifty feet. Flare." He gritted his teeth and clenched his stomach and he brought the nose up, trading off his airspeed for rotor turns—this slowed his rate of descent.

The rotor wash kicked up salt spray over the front window. He looked out the empty side window, watching the dark blue water. Then he looked back at his radiant and moved the cyclic and collective to level himself and squeeze out all of the potential energy of the rotors.

"Twenty feet. Fifteen feet. Ten knots. Ten feet."

The impact was about two seconds before he expected it, and hard. He jolted forward in his seat, restrained by his harness. The force was similar to a ten-mile-per-hour car crash. The helicopter's fifteen thousand pounds crashed into the ocean and immediately filled with water.

To his horror, he felt his feet and legs getting wet. It seemed strange to see the familiar electronics suite get covered with rising dark blue water. Plug reached up and pulled off both engines to the OFF detent. Then he pushed the rotor brake all the way forward. For a second, he thought the helicopter might maintain its upright position. Then the terrible rollover began.

Helicopters were very top-heavy. Once in the water, the engines and transmission weighed it down, causing the aircraft to roll completely upside down as it sunk underwater. The cool seawater rose up his waist and chest. He remained strapped in to his seat harness. The water kept rising as he tilted sideways, and it covered his neck. Then one final breath before the water covered his mouth and nose and scalp...

Plug held his breath as the world turned upside down and dark. Victoria's last words to him over the radios replayed in his head.

Remember your training.

It didn't seem so silly now. *Grab hold of a reference point. Put your breathing device in your mouth now.*

As the helicopter's generators kicked offline, only a few lights remained on. The world was quiet. He quickly put the underwater breathing device into his mouth with his free hand. He blew out to clear the water out of the mouthpiece and breathed in precious air. Holding on to his seat with his left hand, he felt around for the seat belt latch, which would unlock the five harnesses that kept him strapped in. He didn't feel upside down now. Now, he had no idea which way was up.

His eyes stung from the salt water and whatever oils were leaking out of the helicopter into the sea. He began to panic because he didn't think he was moving fast enough. If the helicopter sank too deep, he could get the bends.

Click.

He released himself from his straps and began floating to his right, but held his place with his left hand. He reached out where the window was, gripped the empty metal edge, and pulled his body through, kicking for extra propulsion.

A moment of panic as his boot got stuck on the rim of the window, but then he kicked free. Wriggling out of the sinking aircraft, he pulled the black beads around his vest and felt himself rising up to the surface as it inflated with air.

* * *

"On final."

Victoria leveled off from her turn and aimed her helicopter directly up the long white wake of the destroyer. A grey smoke from the bridge area trailed up into the sky.

"Roger, on final," came the voice of her young copilot.

They were landing on a smoking, damaged vessel, which had yet to respond to their communications. Not that they had a choice. The bright yellow FUEL LOW light shined on the master caution panel, demanding attention.

Victoria pulled back on the cyclic with her right hand and

lowered the collective lever with her left. The speed began to bleed back. She made a radio call over the external comms.

"*Farragut* Control, Cutlass 471, on final, no comms, declaring an emergency. We see that you have received damage. Request you maintain course and speed for five mikes." She turned and looked out her right window. "And if anyone hears this, we need fuel and our other rescue swimmer."

Victoria switched frequencies to the VHF channel that Plug and her helicopters were using to communicate. "476, 471."

Nothing. Plug was in the drink. God, she hoped they were alright.

"Point five miles, landing checklist."

Juan was already flipping switches and rattling off the steps of the before-landing checklist.

The airspeed indicator slipped below forty knots, but it felt like they were barely closing in on the ship.

Juan said, "They're booking it."

"Yeah." She pushed the stick forward and pulled in more power to close in on the ship.

The ship rolled hard left, white salt spray shooting up and covering part of the flight deck. The rolls were much more intense than normal due to the speed the destroyer was traveling at. They must have been going close to thirty knots.

"Over the deck."

She caught a glimpse of one of the hangar personnel doors opening, and a face peeking out. Whoever was in there must have heard the sound of the aircraft as it made its way over the back of the ship. Then the face disappeared back in.

She positioned the helicopter over the center of the flight deck and held it hovering. The ship was in another big roll, this time to the right. It was a pattern. Every few seconds, the pendulum swung back and forth in opposite directions. She timed the pattern in her mind, holding the helicopter in a perfect hover, waiting. She kept the aircraft just high enough that the wheels wouldn't get caught by the moving surface beneath them.

There it was.

The roll started coming back in the opposite direction. Victoria timed her power reduction to drop the aircraft right on her landing spot at the exact time that the roll would make the ship even with the horizon. The result was a perfect landing.

They immediately began rolling hard to the left, but the helicopter weighed about seventeen thousand pounds, and physics would keep them in place. Unless the rolls got too severe...

The man who had opened the hangar door came running out, holding the dark metal chains they could use to tie down the helo.

"Fetternut, go help him out please."

Her aircrewman immediately unstrapped and grabbed one of the chains, hooking it to a metal tie-down point on the helicopter and fixing that to a tie-down point on the flight deck.

"Juan, you have the controls. I'm going to go get us fuel."

"Roger, Boss. I have the controls."

She unstrapped, carefully moved out of her pilot seat without hitting the flight controls, and slammed the cockpit door shut. Then she walked back to the cabin and looked at the group of wounded soldiers.

She scanned the faces. Chase wasn't among them. He must have already walked into the hangar while she was unstrapping. She gripped the side of the helicopter as the ship rolled back and forth.

"Do they have a doctor on board?" one of the soldiers yelled over the noise of the rotors. His face was caked with dirt and dried blood. His eyes were tired but alert.

"No, but we have corpsmen." Victoria tried to sound out her words so that the man could read her lips.

He frowned. "So do we," he yelled back. "Let's get us to somewhere we can treat the wounded."

There were now several men from Victoria's maintenance crew running out from the hangar wearing headgear and vests, ready to help.

Once inside the hangar, her maintenance chief was waiting at the door, blocking her view. "Ma'am, the command master chief's been looking for you. We got hit, ma'am." His eyes were wide. The younger petty officers next to him watched them both, eager to hear the conversation.

The hangar door flopped open as the ship rolled. Whoever had come in last hadn't secured it. She stood with her legs spread apart wider than normal, her knees bent. It helped her to balance as the ship rolled so much. Why were they still going this fast?

The group of soldiers spread out, sitting in the empty hangar and treating their wounded. One of her younger petty officers ran to go get the ship's corpsmen and more medical supplies.

Victoria said, "Chief, we need fuel now. We need to go back up. 476 just ditched." She tried to say it as calmly as possible.

"They *ditched*? Holy shit." He turned and said, "AD1, go get the fuelies now! Get 471 refueled." He looked back at Victoria. "Ma'am, it might be hard to get all the ship guys, but we'll take care of it."

"Why can't you get the ship guys?"

"Some of them are still doing damage control. They had a fire around the bridge."

"I saw that. Was anyone hurt?"

He didn't answer. "Ma'am, the CMC needs to talk to you. He asked to speak with you immediately when you land."

"If the master chief needs to talk to me, he can come here. I need to take off again. We need to go…"

Then she saw her brother. He was talking to the same soldier who had been in her helicopter asking about corpsmen.

She tried not to run. A quick walk. They made eye contact and then Chase stood and gave his sister a hug.

She stepped away, nodding, fighting back tears and smiles. "Glad you're okay."

Chase grinned. "Glad you came in time."

"Are you going to tell me what this was all about?"

"I need to, yes. And I need to speak to your ship captain." He held up a backpack. "We need to get this to Panama as soon as possible. Within the next few days, or it becomes useless. It's extremely important, Victoria."

She looked at the bag and then back at her brother. "Alright. I'll—"

"Airboss." The ship's command master chief hurried into the hangar. "A word please, ma'am."

She looked at her brother and said, "Can you give me a few minutes?"

He nodded.

Victoria and the master chief walked to the corner of the hangar, out of earshot of the others. Enlisted men and women hurried in and out of the hangar, providing aid to the wounded.

Victoria said, "What happened?"

"About an hour ago, we got hit by an anti-ship missile. It struck the bridge and a few spaces forward of the bridge."

"Was anyone hurt?"

He had a funny look in his eye. "Ma'am, it is my duty to tell you that you are now the senior line officer on board. The captain and XO were both killed in the attack."

She shook her head. "*What?*"

"The captain and XO were killed. I checked the lineal numbers. You are now the senior line officer on board. Per Navy regulations, you are now in command of the ship. Ma'am, I suggest you appoint one of your junior pilots to handle any immediate concerns here and follow me to the combat information center, where we can get you up to speed."

Victoria couldn't speak.

Several hours ago, her biggest problem of the day had been hauling cargo beneath her helicopter from the supply ship to her own.

Then a simple radio call had changed everything. She had flown her helicopter into a jungle combat situation, rescued a group of what she presumed were Special Forces, and flown back to find out that her ship and the ships in company had been attacked.

Now she was being thrown into command of a surface ship. She was a helicopter pilot. She wasn't even high-ranking enough to be a commanding officer in her own community.

"Master Chief, are you sure? I mean, am I really the one who—"

The CMC didn't give her time to contemplate it any further.

"Ma'am, respectfully...we're in the middle of an emergency. I assure you that I am doing this by the book. Now I need you to come with me."

She had let her guard down when they'd landed. In the air, she had automatically compartmentalized. She'd blocked out any thoughts that might distract her from making good decisions and completing the mission. She realized she would need to treat this situation the same. She could think about it later. Right now, she needed to take charge.

"Yes, of course," she said.

Aviate. Navigate. Communicate. The mantra of all pilots. While it took a literal meaning in the air, it applied to everything in life as a metaphor. She needed to prioritize. There were several vital things she needed to accomplish in short order. And she didn't need to be the one to do them all herself.

She looked up and saw her rescue swimmer. "AWR1, go hold the controls for LTJG Volonte and tell him I need to speak with him immediately. Send him to Combat. That's where I'll be."

The rescue swimmer looked at her like she was crazy. He would normally never sit in the pilot's seat, let alone as the only person at the controls of a spinning helicopter. Despite the fact that it was tied down, it was still highly irregular. "Yes, ma'am."

She called to her brother, "Chase, I'll be right back." She left him with a confused look on his face.

"Let's go, Master Chief. Bring me to Combat."

* * *

Everyone in Combat was wearing their general quarters gear. White fireproof cloth over their heads. Gloves. Sleeves rolled up. Victoria took in their faces. They each looked drained and shell-shocked.

The command master chief began, "OPS, I've informed Air Boss of her new...*status*."

Victoria realized that she had just been part of the most informal change of command she'd ever witnessed. OPS had been the senior officer on the ship until she had landed. He had been in command. Now she was.

He nodded at her. "Welcome back, Boss." He looked like hell.

"Can you bring me up to speed?"

"The fires are out, and there is no more flooding. But we lost fourteen personnel, including the captain and the XO. Another ten are injured. We suffered a steering casualty when the bridge got hit. Had some trouble transferring control to Engineering. That's been resolved."

She looked up at the displays. They were traveling at twenty-eight knots. "Why the speed?"

"At first, it was because the captain gave the all head flank order. And then we had the steering casualty, so keeping this course and speed was our best method of evasive maneuvering."

"And now? Why are you still going this course and speed?"

OPS didn't like the question. "Because a fucking submarine just sank all the ships that were next to us and hit us with a missile. And I'm trying to make sure it doesn't finish us off."

She didn't like the attitude but understood the stress that he was under. That they all were under. She took a deep breath. "Okay. What are your intentions?"

"I'm getting as much distance as I can between us and the location of the attack. I've put out distress calls, but satcom is still down and we haven't reached anyone on any other channels. I *intend* to keep us from getting sunk. We're headed west right now, but I'll turn us north and slow us down soon. We'll listen and try to get a fix on the sub—"

"What do you know about it? Did you have any warning?"

OPS turned to the sonar station. Three sonar technicians were looking at their displays. Two wore headsets covering one ear while they talked. "They can give you a better idea of what they heard. But it happened quickly. We had about two minutes' notice. They picked something up. Transient sounds—torpedoes. We think they sank the Colombian diesel boat first. Then the next thing we knew, we were being attacked. Damage control parties were running around the ship, the lights went out for a bit, and all hell broke loose. Look, I don't need to be judged, alright? I did what I thought was right and got us out of there. As far as I know, none of those other ships made it—"

Victoria said, "We flew overhead. They have people in the water in lifeboats. We'll commence rescue operations once the helicopter gets refueled. And I'm not judging you. I just want to know what happened and then we'll decide what to do next."

He looked surprised to hear that there were survivors.

"Ma'am?" One of the junior officers held out one of the phones.

She took it. "Air Boss." She wondered if she should keep calling herself by that title. She didn't feel comfortable calling herself the captain.

"Boss, it's Juan. What's up? AWR1 said you wanted to talk to me."

She turned from the group in Combat and lowered her voice a bit. "Juan, I need you to be in charge back there right now. Get Caveman. Listen, you two are going to be doing the SAR flight to pick up Plug as soon as you're fueled up."

Silence on the other end. Juan and Caveman were junior pilots. They had never flown a Seahawk helicopter without an aircraft commander. But Victoria needed to get things done, and her normal procedures and precautions were out the window right now. Despite the dramatic chain of events, she realized that it still came as a surprise to the young pilot.

"Juan, do you understand?"

"Yes, ma'am."

"Can you handle it?"

"Yes, ma'am."

"Tell me what you're going to do when you take off." She decided it might be worth making sure that he wasn't in over his head.

"Uh...I'll...I'll fly opposite direction of the ship's heading. We dropped a smoke. I'll use the SAR checklist to calculate a starting point and then execute a search pattern and—"

"Okay, just checking. You'll do fine. Go pick up our other HAC. We're going to need him. Just ask for green deck when you're ready to take off. I'll get the ASTAC at his station again so you'll have someone on the radio."

"Yes, ma'am."

She handed the phone back to the junior officer and walked over to the three sonar technicians. "Tell me what you know, gentlemen."

The chief sonar tech spoke. "Ma'am, we went over the tapes. It looks like a Han- or a Shang-class. A Chinese nuclear fast-attack submarine. She launched four torpedoes and several surface-to-surface missiles. We've been trying to listen for her now, but with all the noise we're making at this speed, it's kind of hard."

"What would you expect a Chinese sub to do now, Chief?"

"Probably trail us. With as much noise as we're making, she'll be able to track us from pretty far away. She'll probably slow down once we do, so we can't hear her. But my guess is that we've created some pretty good distance. It'll be harder for her to sneak up on us like that again now that we know what we're looking for."

"Sounds right to me. See if you can get air support. We need P-3s or P-8s doing ASW for us immediately."

OPS nodded.

Victoria said, "Here are our priorities: One, stay at a safe distance from where we think the Chinese submarine is. Two, rescue Plug and any survivors from the other ships that were attacked. Three—well, we'll get more on that once we talk to the special operations team that we just pulled out of Ecuador. Where's the navigator?"

OPS looked down. "She was on the bridge when it happened."

Victoria turned her head, a pained expression on her face. "Sorry. Who's taking her place?"

OPS looked pissed. "I haven't gotten around to staffing yet—"

The junior officer who had handed her the phone earlier picked it up when it rang again. After a moment, he said, "Ma'am, the helicopter is fueled and requesting green deck."

"Granted."

She watched one of the TV screens as her two young copilots, officially unqualified to conduct the mission they were about to embark on, took off, then turned back to OPS. "We need to figure out how long we'll need to pick up all the survivors. And we need to figure out how much time it'll take to get in helicopter range of Panama City. We have to get a piece of equipment there as soon as possible. Any gap in time is going to be taken out of our on-station time in rescuing the survivors from the other ships. Is that clear?"

"Clear."

"Good. You guys crunch the numbers. I need to go talk to the troops we just pulled out of the jungle."

22

D avid sat in his cubicle at the CIA headquarters building, waiting for the latest update from the USS *Jimmy Carter*. He had grown accustomed to getting updates every hour on the hour.

There it was.

The files in the top-secret share drive began filling up with photos and other data. He scrolled through them, looking for anything of immediate interest.

A few cubicles down, Susan stood up at her desk. The look on her face was alarming. David hadn't seen her look like that, even after the Iranians had attacked the D.C. Beltway.

"What is it?"

"Did you see the latest information from the *Carter*?"

"I saw that it was uploaded. I haven't gone through all the data yet." He wondered how it was possible that she had.

"They sent a flash summary. Alerting us about something specific. I'm looking at it now. Oh my *God…*"

She raced over to his desk, stopped and turned her head back and forth, looking in each direction. She was trying to decide what to do first. She said, "*Come on.* We need to see General Schwartz."

They walked down the Langley hallway until they reached General Schwartz's office. Susan told his secretary, "I need to see him now."

The secretary nodded. "Go ahead."

They opened the door. He was on his computer. He stood, seeing the urgency on Susan's face. "What is it?"

"Sir, the USS *Jimmy Carter* just intercepted a communication from the Chinese South Sea Fleet."

"What'd they get?"

"Sir, it was sent only to ships that were using the Red Cell crypto key. We believe that the Chinese are in the process of attacking our units operating in the Eastern Pacific. They specifically mentioned US Navy Warship 099, which is the hull number of the USS *Farragut.* We're still verifying, but I would consider this information highly accurate."

The general held up his hand. He dialed a number on his secure phone and put it on speaker.

"Director Buckingham."

"Sir, this is General Schwartz. I have Susan Collinsworth and David Manning in here. We just got an important update, sir. You're going to want to hear it."

The director said, "I hope it's good news. I just heard from our Colombian station chief—the Army Blackhawk that was sent to pick up the MARSOC team hasn't reported in. The MARSOC group had to activate the backup plan—two Navy helicopters from a destroyer off shore."

Susan said, "Sir, if the MARSOC group was able to get the crypto key and is headed out to sea, that may explain the information we just received. The USS *Jimmy Carter* just made some electronic signals intercepts that originated from the Red Cell island. The Chinese South Sea Fleet—this is the command we think is working with Cheng Jinshan—has just commanded a surface action group and a Shang-class submarine to find and sink the USS *Farragut.*"

The director said, "So PLA Navy ships and submarines have orders to sink the USS *Farragut*?"

"That's affirmative, sir."

"That doesn't make sense. It would take them a month to travel across the Pacific. How—?"

"Sir, from the intercepts we received, it appears that these units are already located somewhere in the Eastern Pacific."

The director didn't respond at first. After a moment he said, "How did we not already know this?"

Susan said, "With our reconnaissance satellites down for the past few weeks, it would have been relatively easy for them to make that voyage undetected, sir."

The director sighed. "I'll contact the president. General, please make sure that our SILVERSMITH military units get this information as soon as possible."

"Will do."

The director said, "Hold on. As I think this through…General, this should *not*, I repeat, *not* be put out wide yet. I don't want to start a shooting war between the US and China if it turns out that this is all the work of two rogue Chinese men. If we can still contain this and prevent World War Three from breaking out, I'd like to do that."

The general nodded. "I agree. I'll speak to Pentagon leadership as soon as we're off the phone. We'll keep this information compartmentalized to just the SILVERSMITH Task Force and leadership."

* * *

USS Ford
500 Nautical Miles West of Chile

FM CNO WASHINGTON D.C.
TO TASK FORCE SILVERSMITH
SUBJ / EMERGENCY WARNING NOTIFICATION
RMKS/1. US MILITARY FORCES IN EASTPAC SUFFERING COMMUNICATIONS OUTAGES. POSSIBLE ATTACK IN

PROGRESS ON USS FARRAGUT AND ACCOMPANYING ALLIED VESSELS.

2. SIGNALS INTELLIGENCE COLLECTION INDICATES CHINESE SURFACE ACTION GROUP (STRENGTH UNKNOWN) BELIEVED IN VICINITY OF EASTPAC AND TASKED WITH ATTACKING USS FARRAGUT.

3. SIGNALS INTELLIGENCE COLLECTION INDICATES CHINESE SHANG-CLASS SUBMARINE BELIEVED IN VICINITY OF EASTPAC AND TASKED WITH ATTACKING USS FARRAGUT.

4. FORD CSG SHALL CONTINUE NORTHBOUND AT BEST SPEED AND RENDEZVOUS WITH USS FARRAGUT. MAINTAIN APPROPRIATE WEAPONS POSTURE AND OPERATE IN ACCORDANCE WITH PREVIOUSLY SPECIFIED RULES OF ENGAGEMENT.

Admiral Manning sat at his desk, reading the high-priority message that his chief of staff had just handed him.

"What do you think, COS?"

The admiral's chief of staff stood across from his desk.

"Sir, it sounds like a shit show up there."

"That's what I think too."

The COS said, "Sir, I understand that your daughter is on the *Farragut*."

Admiral Manning looked up at the Navy captain. "That's right."

The COS looked uncomfortable. "Sir, just let me know if—"

The admiral stood. "I appreciate your concern. I'll let you know if my emotions get in the way of performing my duties."

"Oh hell, sir. I didn't mean it like that. I more just meant—well, if you need anything, sir, just let me know."

The admiral nodded. He realized that this was just one emotionally challenged military man attempting to comfort another. "Sorry. Thanks, COS. I appreciate the gesture." He took a deep breath. "Everyone ready?"

"Yes, sir, they're all waiting."

"Alright, let's get started."

The chief of staff opened the door that led to the large conference room next door.

"Attention on deck!" A group of thirty or so officers jumped to attention.

It was packed. At the long wooden conference table sat no fewer than five Navy captains and a host of commanders. The CAG, who was in charge of the air wing, and the commodore, who was in charge of the surface and subsurface warfare, sat closest to the admiral. The COs of the ships in company were teleconferenced in, their faces on the projector screen forward of the conference table.

An outer row of chairs surrounded the table. In them, the squadron commanders and staff officers sat shoulder to shoulder, many with notepads in hand, ready to start scribbling at the first hint that their boss would task them with an order.

"Seats," called the admiral as he sat down at the head of the table. Everyone immediately did as commanded.

The admiral looked at their faces. "Ladies and gentlemen, as many of you now know, we may soon be in open hostilities with Chinese warships in the Eastern Pacific. I've been briefed on three scenarios. The first, which seems out of the question now, was that China is completely friendly to us and this whole exercise was a waste of time. As of a message I read just a few minutes ago, I now consider that scenario to be ruled out."

Many of the faces staring back at him nodded. A few looked confused—those were the ones that the information hadn't gotten to yet.

"The other scenarios are as follows. Either there is a contingent of rogue Chinese military and intelligence personnel who have, without orders from Beijing, executed an attack on United States interests...*or*, there is a far larger and more comprehensive Chinese attack in the works. Because we do not yet know which scenario we are facing, and because we wish to avoid triggering the worse of the two, we must act in such a way to avoid unnecessary hostilities with the Chinese military."

Admiral Manning watched the faces of the men and women in

the room as they digested his words. "Simply said, we do not yet know whether to shoot some of them, or all of them."

The room was dead quiet. He held up the message in his hand. "They've just attacked the USS *Farragut*. And there are now several ships and at least one submarine headed to finish her off. That can't happen, team. Not on our watch."

He looked at the group. "Alright, I want options. When will we be in range with our aircraft?"

CAG said, "Sir, with tankers, we could be in range tomorrow. We've got about another forty-eight hours before we'll be in range without tankers. We're working with the Air Force to get support for that as we speak."

"Could we launch the air wing onto shore somewhere and let them operate from there?"

CAG nodded. "Yes, sir, but the intelligence reports we've been given are now suggesting possible Chinese surface-to-air missile defenses set up in the area of Manta, Ecuador."

The admiral rubbed his chin and thought it over. At least thirty faces looked back at him from around the room, waiting for him to speak. Their looks were eager. They all wanted to get in on the fight. He wondered how many of them knew that his daughter was aboard *Farragut*. He smiled inwardly. They all knew. This was a Navy vessel. Nothing was a secret around here.

"CAG, tell me what you're thinking."

"Admiral, the warfare commanders and I were just discussing this. We suggest launching an E-2D and keeping them out of missile range of Ecuador. We'd be able to set up a link connection with the *Farragut*. We'll be able to talk with them, share data, and get a sitrep."

"Approved, what else?"

"Once we either get tanker support or get in range—whichever comes first—we can then launch a pair of Growlers and a pair of F-35s. We could use the Growlers for electronic attack on the Chinese surface ships. This would help prevent them from detecting or launching their missiles on the *Farragut*. The F-35s will be armed and ready to drop bombs and conduct strafing runs on the Chinese ships if needed."

"Bombs and strafing runs?"

"Correct, Admiral."

"The F-35s don't have any anti-ship missiles?"

"There are some prototypes in development, sir. But we don't have any on board."

The admiral kept calm. While the news was extremely frustrating, it would have been counterproductive to show anger in front of his men. "Understood." He turned to the commodore. "Any thoughts, Commodore? What's the best way to fight those Chinese surface ships from your perspective?"

"Admiral, the *Farragut* has anti-ship missiles it can use. We're working on getting an Air Force JSTARS to conduct a mission to the area and help us locate the Chinese, without getting too close as to alert them. Once we do that, we'll be able to go over attack options, if it comes to it."

"Alright. What about the submarine? What are our plans for that?"

"Sir, I've been in touch with the P-8 squadron in El Salvador. They've been brought into the fold on SILVERSMITH. They've promised to provide as much ASW coverage as possible over the next few days, until *Farragut* gets to Panama. There is a problem, however."

"What's that?"

"Sir, the P-8 skipper told me that they don't have any live torpedoes. Their mission in the area was ASW training and counternarcotic surveillance only."

"So I have fighters with no anti-ship missiles, and ASW aircraft with no torpedoes. Very well. I assume that they'll be able to work in concert with the *Farragut* and her helos?"

"Yes, sir. We've had intermittent HF communications with *Farragut* today. We think some of her communications equipment may have been damaged in combat. Once we get the Screwtops up and airborne, we'll be able to relay all this information and confirm plans. It's been easier to speak with the land-based assets, sir. But we're working on it."

The Screwtops was the call sign of the airborne early-warning E-2 squadron, VAW-123. They had recently transitioned from the E-2C to the newer model, E-2D.

"Alright. Get the aircraft launched as soon as possible." He turned to scan the eyes of the men and women around the room. "Make sure everyone on board knows that they aren't to share any of this information with anyone on shore. No unauthorized phone calls, email, or Internet. This place is on information lockdown unless it's official business. That understood?"

"Yes, sir."

The admiral stood up and walked out. In silence, everyone in the room stood at attention until he left.

23

USS Farragut

Victoria walked into the crowded wardroom. No one called attention on deck, but she could feel that pause—that tension that occurs when the seniormost person enters the room. All eyes were on her, as if asking permission for whatever would come next.

She had called for a department head meeting as soon as OPS had come off duty. They had one of the junior officers standing tactical action officer in CIC.

Chase and the soldier she'd been speaking to in the helicopter—she learned he was actually a Marine captain, and would probably detest the term *soldier*—ate sandwiches prepared by the wardroom's CS2. The rest of them sat, waiting for her. A recently retrieved Plug stood in the back of the room.

Juan had picked up a total of thirty-two officers and crew from the various international ships, but they were all recovering in the empty hangar, now converted into an infirmary.

Victoria began, "COMMO, you said you had something to tell me about getting our datalink network up and running."

"Yes, ma'am," the ensign said, "we actually just got a good

connection a few minutes before I walked in. We're now linking with an E2-D to the south of us. We still have to set a few things up, but we should be able to have encrypted chat capability with them, and some voice channels, ready within the hour."

She raised her eyebrow. "Did you say E2-D?" That was the newest carrier-launched radar plane. It provided early-warning and networking capabilities to fleet ships and aircraft. If one of those was flying around in range of them, that meant that a carrier was almost certainly nearby.

"Yes, ma'am."

"To the south? That doesn't make a whole lot of sense. Are you sure?"

"Yes, ma'am. We're trying to get more information, ma'am. We'll have something for you shortly."

"Alright. Let me know the minute you get any comms. We need them to relay our ASW help request and send more air assets to check for any more survivors near the attack site."

"Roger that."

The chief engineer spoke for a bit about the status of bridge repairs and damage. Then OPS filled everyone in on new staffing, replacing those who were lost in the attack. No one said a word while he spoke. She could see the looks on their faces. People were exhausted from the stress of the last twenty-four hours.

When it grew quiet again, Victoria said, "Listen, I know that everyone is tired and stressed out. Make sure when you aren't on watch, if you don't have anything vital to the mission going on, that you're taking care of yourselves and getting rest. You'll be no use to me if you're so tired that you type in the wrong numbers when we find and attack that Chinese sub. And don't give me any shit about the pilot always being concerned about crew rest." She smiled.

The group smiled back. That was a good sign. People were nodding their heads.

"Plug."

"Yes, ma'am."

"Are you good to fly?"

"Yes, ma'am."

"I only have one more helicopter, so please try to keep this one dry, okay?"

"I'll do my best."

"I need you to make sure that the bird is fully outfitted for ASW."

"We're loading MK-54s now, Boss. Should be done in another hour."

"Good." She turned to the ship's combat systems officer. "CSO, how is *Farragut*'s ASW readiness?"

"We're using our passive systems to see what we can turn up, ma'am. All of our weapons are ready. No issues."

"Except for the undetected hostile submarine in the area," replied Victoria. She didn't mean to sound sarcastic, but it came out that way.

"Yes, ma'am. Except for that."

"Very well. Keep sharp, everyone. Plug, OPS, please stay. We need to have a conversation with our guests here." She looked at her brother. Victoria hadn't bothered to tell anyone on board that Chase and she were related. A few of them had probably seen the hug they'd exchanged in the hangar. But everything else had been strictly professional. She didn't even have to say anything to Chase. It was just something that they both understood. The environment they were operating in required total focus. Emotion and relationships would have to wait.

When the room emptied, Victoria said, "Chase, what can you tell us?"

He placed the backpack on the table. "We have a very important piece of equipment in here that we need to get to Panama. If you can get me to the international airport there, I can do the rest. But we have a finite amount of time. This thing has an expiration." He looked at his watch. "We have about seventy-two more hours before it's no longer useful. I need to get it to members of my team in Panama City with enough time to do something with it. They told me they need about a day. So if you add an hour for me to secure transportation…that gives us a little under forty-eight hours to get me on the ground in Panama City."

Victoria looked at OPS. "How far away are we from Panama City?"

He said, "I can double-check to give you an exact distance, but roughly eight hundred miles if we go straight there."

Victoria did the math in her head. "Alright, so we'll have to steam forty hours at twenty knots. Plug, how far would you be willing to launch at? Three hundred miles away okay? Consider this an emergency."

"Three hundred should work if the winds aren't in our face too much."

She tilted her head. "Okay, let's call it three hundred miles. That puts us down to a five-hundred-mile trip. Is twenty knots a good assumption?"

A few of the more senior surface officers nodded.

Victoria said, "So we need to head straight toward Panama for twenty-five hours. Then there'll be flight time. Plug, what's that?"

"Let's call it a three-hour flight for simple math."

"Alright—so you guys would be on deck in Panama City in twenty-eight hours. Will that work?"

Chase said, "It should, yes."

"This supposes that we don't have to fight off the submarine on our way there. If that happens—"

The phone rang, and the person closest to the phone answered it. He looked up at Victoria. "Air Boss, it's for you."

She walked over and picked it up. "Manning." She looked up at the group. "OPS, please come with me. The rest of you stay here and keep working on the details of a plan. I'll be back shortly."

"What is it?" Chase asked.

She looked him directly in the eye. "The USS *Ford* is contacting us. They're driving up the western coast of South America."

Chase smiled. "I was wondering when they'd show up."

* * *

Victoria walked into the CIC with OPS in tow. The communications officer stood over the central chart table. "Good evening, Air Boss."

"Good evening. Sounds like you've been busy. What have you got?"

"Ma'am, about an hour ago we started getting a datalink connection request. We went through all the procedures, and everything checked out good. Long story short, it was an E-2D Hawkeye, launched from the USS *Ford*."

"Understood. Now, how is that possible?"

"The USS *Ford* Strike Group is several thousand miles to the south of us. But they've launched their airborne early-warning aircraft. We're now sharing our tracks over datalink via the E-2."

Victoria looked at OPS. OPS said, "When will they be here? It's going to be several days at least. Call it a week."

"We just started chatting with them now, sir. We don't have voice up yet—it's all on chat." Chat was the term for the encrypted instant messenger system the military used to communicate on.

"So? What are you waiting for? Ask them," OPS said.

"Sir, uh...*Ford* CSG Actual is on chat. He wants to speak with *Farragut* Actual. I...I assume that is the air boss? Is that right, ma'am? I wasn't sure what to say."

Victoria nodded. "That's fine. Show me where to type." They walked over to one of the computer monitors.

FARRAGUT TAO: This is FARRAGUT Actual. Status: Air Boss had to take over as FARRAGUT Actual after CO and XO were KIA in missile strike. FARRAGUT casualties were 14 Dead, 10 wounded. Four ships in company were sunk. 32 personnel from ships in company have been rescued and are on board. All FARRAGUT systems have been restored and are operational. We have taken on 10 personnel from a MARSOC unit, including high-priority cargo. Are you familiar, over?

FORD CSG BWC: FARRAGUT Actual, this is FORD CSG Actual. Sorry to hear about your KIA. Am familiar with MARSOC mission and cargo. Understand priority and destination. State intentions, over.

FARRAGUT TAO: Intend to proceed to Panama City at best transit speed and launch cargo with one member of MARSOC unit as soon as we reach helicopter range.

FORD CSG BWC: Roger, stand by.

Victoria took a deep breath. This was a surreal experience. She looked around the dark, high-tech room. She was commanding a US Navy warship, and sending messages to her father, who was commanding an aircraft carrier strike group.

"What ships are with the *Ford*? I mean, what type of ships? Do you have that up on the board?"

"Yes, ma'am. Looks like they have the DDG-1002, the USS *Michael Monsoor*, riding shotgun. They also have the USS *Mason*, the USNS *Henry J. Kaiser*, and the USS *Detroit*, a littoral combat ship. It's like a Navy recruiting commercial—they've got one of everything."

Victoria just nodded, too tired to smile. While she waited, she wrote down a list of questions that she had for when FORD started talking again. The chat window became active a few moments later.

FORD CSG BWC: FARRAGUT, until further notice, FORD CSG takes tactical control of your unit.

FARRAGUT TAO: Roger, understand FORD CSG has TACON of FARRAGUT.

FORD CSG BWC: FARRAGUT, be advised, Chinese surface action group headed your way from the west. Additionally, Chinese Shang-class attack submarine believed to be in your vicinity. BOTH surface action group and sub have orders to sink your unit.

Victoria looked at the screen, whispering, "Well, no shit, there's a Chinese sub. Thanks."

OPS said, "Do they have a location or number of Chinese surface ships?"

Victoria typed.

FARRAGUT TAO: Interrogative position of hostile units?

FORD CSG BWC: Unknown. Working with reconnaissance assets to search the area. Will pass updated track information to you when able.

FARRAGUT TAO: Roger.

FORD CSG BWC: FARRAGUT, your orders are to stay at current location until FORD CSG gets to your position.

Victoria looked at the screen in disbelief. What was her father thinking? Didn't they know that the crypto key had to get to Panama City as soon as possible? Plus, if there were ships and submarines out here trying to find her, the last thing she wanted to do was sit around. She needed to plow through and head to Panama.

FARRAGUT TAO: FORD CSG, respectfully—this will not allow us to complete our mission. VIP and Cargo needs to get to Panama ASAP. Waiting at current position not an option. This will also expose us to submarine attack.

FORD CSG BWC: Understood. Was not aware of cargo transfer requirement. Stand by.

* * *

Admiral Manning sat in a chair on an elevated platform in the rear of a room the size and shape of a movie theater. Yet instead of normal seats, the room was set up similar to NASA mission control. Rows of highly trained Navy personnel worked on computers, gathering information from sensors and eyeballs around the fleet. This room was where the admiral's watch team ran the carrier strike group. It was the brain. The central command center for billions of dollars of high-tech warfighting equipment and thousands of personnel.

A Navy commander was the head watch stander, the battle watch captain. He stood behind the admiral while the admiral typed from the battle watch captain's chair.

The battle watch captain's assistant came up to him, whispering, "Sir, we just got voice communications good uplink and downlink. The admiral can call and speak to *Farragut* on voice, if he prefers."

The admiral, his ears used to trying to listen in on the whispers of underlings, turned and said, "Yes. I want voice. Which one is it?"

The commander handed him the black plastic phone. "You just press this button here, sir. They should be the only ones on that channel."

"Thank you."

He paused, realizing who he was about to be speaking with. "Gentlemen, could you give me a moment?"

The watch standers and his aide stepped out of earshot. He closed his eyes and took a deep breath.

"*Farragut*, this is *Ford* CSG Actual, over."

"*Ford* CSG Actual, this is *Farragut* Actual, over."

It was her voice. He wasn't sure how many people would be listening to the conversation, but he didn't care. This was the first time he'd spoken to his daughter since his wife's funeral.

"It's good to hear your voice, Victoria, over."

A pause.

"*Ford*, this is *Farragut*, Thank you, sir. You too, over."

That was the most affection either of their proper etiquette-based personalities would allow.

"*Farragut*, this is *Ford*. I understand that you disagree with the decision to remain on station until *Ford* CSG arrives, over?"

"*Ford*, this is *Farragut*. Affirm, sir. I understand that it would be several days until you are within range of us. The MARSOC team and the intelligence officer with them have a very time-sensitive mission. Their cargo will expire and become useless if it doesn't reach the shore as soon as possible. This cargo is crucial to bringing an end to this conflict." She paused, letting that information sink in.

"*Farragut*, this is *Ford*. Understood, over."

"*Ford*, this is *Farragut*. We've done the math, sir. We can't wait, over."

"*Farragut*, this is *Ford*. You have four Chinese surface ships and one submarine bearing down on you. We're still several thousand miles away, but are working on plans to provide air support. The odds are against you. I don't like the risk level, over."

"*Ford*, this is *Farragut*, sir. Respectfully, sir, I understand the risks involved. But this is the only way to accomplish the mission. I request that you allow us to proceed to Panama at best speed. We will take proper precautions and use the P-8 for air cover, over. Request CSG assistance in setting up air support."

Admiral Manning stood silent for a full twenty seconds, mulling it over in his mind. What would he do if his daughter were not on that ship? He sighed, knowing the answer, and hating it.

"*Farragut*, this is *Ford*. Proceed as requested. Will work on air support plan, over."

"*Farragut*, Wilco, out."

As the admiral hung up the phone, he looked up at the tactical display, showing red units surrounding the single blue icon that represented the USS *Farragut*. He hoped he had made the right choice.

* * *

Victoria and OPS reentered the wardroom and sat back down in their chairs. She got everyone up to speed.

Chase said, "So you're saying that you've got a bunch of Chinese ships and one submarine out there, all looking for us, with orders to blow us out of the water?"

Victoria said, "Unfortunately, that about sums it up, yes."

Chase looked at the ceiling and whistled. "Can you fly me back to shore?"

"I'll do it," Plug volunteered.

A few smiles from the group. Everyone knew the two were trying to make a somber situation more light-hearted with the attempted joke.

Victoria said, "While I appreciate your noble gestures, we need to head northeast. Getting close enough for a helo transport to shore is the only realistic option of getting the cargo to Panama City fast enough. I've instructed the TAO to start heading to Panama City at twenty knots."

She looked at her watch. "What I want to do with the next twenty minutes or so is brainstorm on what tactics we can use to get through unscathed. Thoughts?"

OPS said, "We could turn off all our radars and go completely dark. Try and hide from the Chinese surface ships. As long as they don't have some other way of getting our location, like satellite or something, then that should be good enough for them. But it won't hide us from the submarine. If we're traveling at twenty knots, and the submarine is in between us and Panama, we're going to stick out like a sore thumb."

The ASW officer said, "Ma'am, OPS is right. We need a way to find the submarine."

"Well, we're calling in maritime air support. There is a P-8 deployed to El Salvador that should be out here as soon as possible. That should give us protection against the submarine."

Plug said, "I don't think they'll have enough buoys to protect us for five hundred miles."

"Well, have you got a better idea?"

Plug sat on the couch in the corner of the wardroom. There was a small TV and a bookshelf filled with DVDs. One of the DVDs was a 1996 film starring Kelsey Grammer.

He said, "What if we hid from the submarine?"

The group turned and looked at him. Lots of skeptical eyes. OPS said, "How the hell are we gonna do that?"

Victoria said, "Plug, say more, please."

"Well, at the risk of admitting that I'm the village idiot...I mean, no one else has any ideas, so..."

OPS said, "Spit it out, man."

"You guys ever seen the movie *Down Periscope*? You know that scene where the submarine goes right up under the merchant ship and uses it to hide and slip through undetected?"

The group's skeptical looks got even worse.

Plug persisted, "Look, I mean...I fly over merchant ships all the time out here. This part of the world, about half of 'em are headed east...and if they are, they're going to the same place we are. *Panama City.* So, well...what if we just, what if we just 'encouraged them' to travel really close to our ship? At the same course and speed. Like, *really* close to us. Maybe we could hide from the Chinese then?"

Victoria frowned. She probably had the most ASW experience in the room. She thought it sounded nutty. Her impression was that submariners were like trained K-9 units. They could pick out a million different scents and wouldn't get thrown off just because two ships got real close together. But she had to admit that she wasn't *totally* sure that it wouldn't work…

Victoria said, "Can someone call our sonar tech senior chief in for a moment? If I remember correctly, he started off as a submariner, right? Let's ask him what he thinks." One of the junior officers close to the wardroom phone picked it up and dialed a number to get the senior chief.

OPS said, "We'd have to run it by the *Ford* Strike Group. They have tactical control of us now."

Victoria said, "For the sake of argument, let's say for a second that this plan would work. How would we execute?"

The chief engineer said, "We could fly prize crews to each of the merchants, and have them make sure that they're doing what we want."

Victoria said, "We don't exactly have a lot of people to spare to become prize crews. And what about the legality of it? Hell, this might be construed as piracy."

Chase said, "I think we've got a bunch of Marines who would love to participate. Right, Captain?"

"Ma'am, I believe the terminology you're looking for is 'safety inspection,'" the Marine Special Forces officer said. "It just so happens that the Marine Raiders on board have been trained in these safety inspection procedures. I think that with the right encourage-ment, we could get a few merchants to happily comply with our navigational recommendations while conducting these safety inspec-tions. Now, some of my men are wounded. But anyone who's up to it would be able to go. Now, our navigational recommendations will be identical to your ship's course and speed, offset by…well, by what-ever spacing you give us." The Marine gave a charming smile.

She felt like a substitute teacher who was getting taken advantage of by an unruly group of students. "Alright, let's keep this as a hypo-thetical for now. But…Chase, Plug, and Captain Calhoun, please make your way up to Combat and start looking into potential merchants that might be good candidates."

The three men got up and left the room—a little too quick for her taste. Like they'd succeeded in getting away with something and didn't want her to change her mind. But while there was humor in their excitement, there was nothing funny about a potential Chinese submarine waiting in their path.

* * *

Juan said, "I still can't believe we're doing this."

Plug was flying the aircraft. Juan manipulated the FLIR—the infrared camera in front of the helicopter—so that they could see the merchant ship that they were approaching.

It was a giant.

The hull was painted light blue, with big thick black letters announcing that it was owned by MAERSK LINE. Stacks and stacks of shipping containers filled the deck, six stories high. A long, thin glass walkway towered one hundred feet above the water. It was the bridge. And their target.

Plug said, "Honestly, I'm surprised that we're doing it too. But we asked the only guy on the ship who had any idea whether it would work, and he thought there was a chance. I mean, no one had any better ideas on how to hide from a submarine. I really just got the idea from a movie. But Senior Chief ended up throwing some big words in there, like broadband acoustic interference and all that. Next thing I know, everyone thinks I'm a genius. I think I'm going to start asking Senior Chief to sit next to me at bars when I talk to chicks. He can make me sound good."

Juan shook his head. "A genius? Is that what you think you are?"

"No way, man. After today, I would describe us as more like *pirates*."

Juan shook his head again. "I can't believe we're going with your plan. If we don't get sunk, I owe you a beer."

"Amen, brother. Alright, I'm coming into a hover right above the port bridge wing. AWR1, are the Marines ready?"

"Yes, sir. I'll send them down with the rescue hoist once we get into position."

Plug said, "Alright, I'm making my call. Here goes nothing." He flipped his communications switch to the external frequency known as bridge-to-bridge, which all mariners used to communicate on.

"Maersk *Atlanta*, Maersk *Atlanta*, this is US Navy helicopter 471, come in, please."

After a moment, the reply came in a thick New England accent. "Navy helicopter, this is Maersk *Atlanta*, we read you loud and clear. How may we be of assistance, sir?"

"Maersk *Atlanta*, it is my duty to inform you that under the Merchant Marine Act of 1936, your vessel has been declared an asset of the US Navy. Please prepare to be boarded. We'll be sending down a few advisors on your port bridge wing. Thank you for your help."

Plug then unkeyed the mike and said on his internal comms circuit, "Arrr, mateys. Commence the boarding."

AWR1 said, "Sir, you're in a good hover. Come forward two... one...steady. Alright, lowering the hoist."

After a few moments, three members of Captain Darby's MARSOC team were standing on the top of the container vessel's bridge. They began climbing down a white metal ladder.

Juan saw a door to the bridge open, and the Marines entered. A few moments later, the radio came on again. "Navy helicopter, this is the captain of Maersk *Atlanta*. We have just had a conversation with the Marines. I don't think that the Merchant Marine Act covers this particular situation. However, I have decided to alter my navigational heading to match up with your Marines' recommendation."

"Roger, Captain, your country thanks you."

Juan kept shaking his head. "I can't believe this is happening."

Plug nosed over the helicopter, gaining airspeed. "Alright, let's head back to Mom and get our next batch of pirates."

* * *

Victoria walked down the passageway from the wardroom to Combat, carrying her thermos of strong coffee. It was five in the morning. She had only gotten about four hours of sleep, and even that had been interrupted by several phone calls from the tactical action officer.

As she passed various members of the crew, she noticed the different way they looked at her. A new level of respect.

"Morning, ma'am."

"Good morning."

"Morning, ma'am," said the next.

"Good morning," she replied as she continued to march along in her steel-toed boots.

Vigorous nods, solid eye contact. The way they used to treat the captain, she realized.

The first time she heard them refer to her as captain was when she entered Combat.

"Captain in Combat."

For a brief second, she thought to chastise the junior officer who had said it. But she found herself instead saying, "Status update."

The TAO walked over to her. "Hey, Boss."

"Hey. Have our friends snuggled up next to us yet?"

"Affirmative. We now have two US-owned merchant ships in a very tight screen next to our ship."

"Excellent. Any pushback so far?"

"Nope. I think it helps having armed Marines over there. You sure you don't want to inform Strike Group?"

Victoria thought about that. She shook her head. "I think this is one of those 'better to beg forgiveness than ask for permission' moments. Besides, we already did it. No point in asking now."

The anti-submarine warfare officer stood over nautical charts next to the chief sonar tech. The ASWO was an ensign who had been a college student at Notre Dame a year ago. Now he was tasked with overseeing a division of enlisted men who would locate a Chinese submarine and prevent it from sinking their ship.

The ASWO said, "Good morning, ma'am. Long story short, we still don't have contact with the sub. We had a few sniffs last night, but they turned out to be false alarms. The helo launches at zero six hundred, and they'll begin spitting buoys in certain areas, performing passive searches for us here, and here." He pointed to a few locations on the chart.

Victoria said, "Alright. What else?"

"OPS asked me to tell you that—"

"Ma'am, Pelican 434 just checked in. On-station time is six plus zero zero."

"Copy, thanks." Victoria looked at the tactical display. She turned back to the ASWO. "You were saying?"

"OPS asked me to tell you that he was trying to get us a P-8. Looks like it just checked in."

"Good, let's have the P-8 clear out a path for us."

The P-8A Poseidon was the Navy's newest maritime patrol aircraft. Primarily used for anti-submarine warfare, it had replaced the aged P-3C Orion. The P-8 was essentially a Boeing 737 outfitted for Navy missions. It could carry thirty percent more sonobuoys than the P-3, as well as torpedoes, infrared cameras, electronic sensors, and even anti-ship missiles.

Most importantly, it was reliable. The 737 airframe was one of the most successful of this generation. The older P-3 had been notorious for breaking down in the chocks. But if the P-8 was scheduled, it would show up ready to fight.

One hour later, the P-8 had placed sonobuoys all along the *Farragut*'s intended track. In addition, the destroyer used its own sonar to listen for the Chinese submarine.

She nodded to the team in Combat and walked up to the recently repaired bridge. The repairs were being conducted all day long, but only a skeleton bridge team was up there now.

The bridge crew stood in a pitch-black environment. Dawn wasn't for another few hours. Their eyes were adjusted to the low light. They needed to be able to see the most minor detail on the horizon, and any light on the bridge would hurt their night vision, diminishing their ability to see contacts.

"Air Boss on the bridge!" someone yelled. That announcement was normally reserved for the captain. The ship's new navigator, who was standing officer of the deck, walked up to her. "Morning, ma'am."

Victoria looked at her watch. It was 0200. She needed sleep. Her head was groggy. "I guess it is morning, isn't it? How's the ship?"

"Doing better, ma'am. They've got all the navigational and bridge helm controls fixed. But there are still a lot of electronics, windows, and parts of the hull that need repairs."

The sound of billowing wind filled the spacious bridge, as many of the windows and doors had yet to be repaired from the missile attack.

"Alright, NAV, thanks. You call me if you need anything."

"Roger, ma'am."

The bridge tactical communications circuit came on with, "Bridge, Combat, is the air boss there?"

"Affirm."

"Please have her rejoin us in Combat. Penguin 434 just got a sniff. *We may have found the Chinese sub.*"

24

———

J uan shot up out of his bed as the alarm went off.

"*General quarters, general quarters, all hands man your battle stations.*" The voice on the 1MC didn't sound bored like it had during training a few weeks ago. Now it was alert. Intense. Angry.

Juan had been sleeping in his flight suit. He looked at his watch. Three a.m. One hour before he was supposed to wake up.

He threw on his brown leather boots and began tying the laces.

Plug opened his door and said, "Yo. Dude, we're launching. Boss just called me. They found the sub. Get your shit on and meet me back in the hangar in five. Boss wants us off deck ASAP."

"Got it."

The announcement for flight quarters immediately followed the call to battle stations. He wondered how they had found the sub.

Juan ran through the main passageway of the destroyer until he got to the hangar. AWR1 Fetternut saw him and threw him his helmet. He put it on and fastened the chinstrap, then grabbed his heavy survival vest.

Caveman ran by, giving Juan a thumbs-up. "Hey, man, the bird's already preflighted. External power's on, and I made sure everything is set up in the cockpit. You guys should be ready to go. I'll be down in the LSO shack."

Plug stuck his head outside of the cockpit. "Hurry up!"

The ASWO ran up to Juan, handing him a sheet of paper. "Here! It's the latest we got on the submarine. It's them. The P-8's tracking it now, but they don't have a torpedo."

"*What?* Why not?" Juan shook his head. "Whatever."

"Good luck." The ASWO jogged back out of the hangar.

Juan saw members of the crew walking in through the hangar door, carrying the engine plugs that kept out seawater.

A minute later, Juan and Plug both strapped into their pilot seats, with AWR1 checking the sonobuoys one last time. Their hands raced over switches and circuit breakers, making adjustments and checking for proper positioning.

Juan went through his checklist. "Seats, belts, pedals, and mirrors —adjusted?"

"Adjusted."

"Cockpit window emergency releases—aft and shear wired?"

"*Let's go, let's go.* We don't have time for all this," said Plug. "Shut your door. I'm starting up number two." Plug slammed his door shut and gripped the number two engine power control lever, thumbing the silver starter button.

Everything happened fast. The high-pitched whine of the General Electric T-700 engine spooling up. The plane captain pointing at the engine and spinning his free hand as he did. Plug started the number two engine, then he removed the rotor brake and throttled the power control levers forward. The rotors began spinning with ferocious speed, and Juan's heart beat faster as he realized that they were about to go into combat.

"471, Deck, you have amber deck for breakdown, green deck for launch."

"471 copies."

Out of the corner of his eye, Juan saw the blue ocean water rising and falling with the ship's movements. The ship heaved and tilted wildly. The destroyer was racing at twenty-two knots, finishing its turn into the wind.

Plug, gripping the controls, called, "Chocks and chains."

Juan used hand signals to communicate with the plane captain that they were ready to remove chocks and chains. The plane captain pointed at the two enlisted men standing next to him and signaled them to go in. They sprinted in from each side of the helicopter and removed the chocks and chains as fast as a NASCAR pit crew. Juan could hear the heavy steel chains dragging on the deck as they brought them back in front of the aircraft for inspection. The pilots gave them a thumbs-up, and the enlisted men disappeared inside the hangar.

Juan looked through the windscreen and saw his fellow 2P, Caveman, standing in the LSO shack with his headset on, ready to open the steel trap that held them in place on the deck.

"Deck, 471, ready to lift."

"Roger, 471, beams open."

Plug said, "Coming up and aft."

The power pull was aggressive. Much more than Juan was used to, or comfortable with. The instruments that measured engine power and torque rose up into the yellow zone, even flickering red for a moment. But Plug knew the limits of the bird. The MH-60 shot up and aft, paused for a nanosecond, pedal-turned to the left, and then nosed over, climbing and accelerating. The blue ocean water and grey steel of the ship's hull raced past them.

Plug said, "Get the P-8 on the horn. Check in with them and get the latest info. AWR1, you too—both of you, get all your combat checks, sonobuoy launch checks, and torp launch checks out of the way now. I want to be ready to drop our torpedo the second they tell us they've got a target."

"Roger," said Juan.

"Roger, sir," said AWR1 Fetternut.

"Pelican 434, Cutlass 471, standing by for your updated sitrep."

The P-8 began reading off information on all of its sonobuoys and the latest details of the submarine track.

"Cutlass 471, Pelican 434, how many torpedoes do you have?"

Juan said, "471 has two Mark 54s aboard."

"Roger, Cutlass 471, we are ready to prosecute the sub. We're tracking her passively right now, but she probably knows it. We intend to go active as soon as you're on scene. We'll vector you in for the torp drop."

"Roger, Pelican. ETA twelve minutes."

The double click on the comms was all the response he got, letting him know that the P-8 understood.

Juan triple-checked that all his torpedo launching checklist items were complete and that all of his switches were in the right place.

Plug said, "AWR1, are you listening to their buoys?"

"Yes, sir, I've got 'em tuned up."

"Have you got a track?"

"Yes, sir. You can see it on your screen…*now.*"

Juan switched to his ship communications frequency and related all their information back to the ship.

The ship's ASTAC said, "Roger, sir. We're copying everything from link. Good hunting."

Plug said, "Traffic, twelve o'clock high, no factor."

Juan looked up and saw the grey P-8A flying straight and level. Every few seconds, a barely visible cylindrical object would drop from its underbelly. These were the sonobuoys. Brightly colored mini-parachutes slowed their descent towards the ocean.

When they were within a few miles of the target, Juan made his call to the P-8. "Pelican 434, Cutlass 471, we're ready for your vector."

"Roger 471. We just put our DICASS sonobuoys in the water. We'll be going active shortly."

A few moments later, Juan turned up the knob to hear the sound from the sonobuoy through his helmet audio. An electronic-sounding high-pitched noise emanated from the speakers in his ears. It was the pinging noise from the active buoys.

* * *

The Chinese submarine captain stood watching his team of young officers and crew as they did their work. The captain had ordered them to rig for red lighting so their eyes would adjust prior to going to periscope depth. The dim red lighting fit the tense mood of the men.

These men had worked on very little sleep for the past week. Stalking their prey. Executing the previous attacks flawlessly. And now, finishing the kill.

After their initial attack, they had gone deep and silent, listening to the breakup of the hulls from the sinking ships, and tracking the lone American destroyer that had gotten away. The captain had expected the orders to follow it, and destroy the US Navy warship. It had been the primary target, after all. But he hadn't expected the urgency.

Twelve hours after the attack, he had gone up to periscope depth, which had allowed them to establish a satellite link with South Sea Fleet. He had updated the fleet with the battle damage assessment. The response had been immediate.

SINK US NAVY DESTROYER 099. CRITICAL AND TIME-SENSITIVE CARGO ON BOARD MUST NOT REACH MAIN-LAND. SINK US NAVY DESTROYER 099 PRIOR TO REACHING 200 MILES OF SHORE, AND WITHIN 48 HOURS OF RECEIVING THIS MESSAGE.

Before receiving those orders, they had been following the destroyer to the northwest, but allowing it to open distance. The captain was worried that if they traveled too fast, the submarine would make so much noise that the destroyer would hear them. The US Navy warship had a helicopter on board. One with a dipping sonar. He wanted nothing to do with it.

But after the orders from South Sea Fleet had come in, the submarine captain had commanded his men to sprint ahead and change course to due north. They lost time while reeling in the towed-array sonar, as that activity limited their speed. Once the towed-array was in, however, the captain was able to use the nuclear-powered submarine's impressive speed advantage to cut off the destroyer's path to land. The US Navy warship's initial travel direction put them farther away from land. If they had cargo on board that they needed to take to shore, they would surely have to turn back east at some point.

During the six-hour sprint to the north, his sonar men had lost contact with the destroyer. When they slowed down, they once again brought out the towed-array.

The initial readouts from the sonar room were confusing. None of their sonar contacts had the obvious signature of the destroyer. There was one very suspicious contact that was heading east at high speed, however. The sonar technicians had informed the captain that the contact sounded like a group of ships, with characteristics similar to both a warship and a large merchant.

Without visual confirmation, the captain couldn't be certain that this was his target. The captain didn't want to fire on it until he knew.

Attacking that group of ships would hurt him in several ways. One, it would help the Americans to learn his position. It would also waste his valuable anti-ship weapons. With the war that had obviously just begun, they were now worth their weight in gold. Also, firing his weapons without seeing his target would mean that his chances of success were greatly decreased. And lastly, he didn't want to risk sinking an innocent merchant ship.

The captain instead had positioned their nuclear attack submarine almost directly in the track's path, offset by only a few thousand yards. If all had gone according to plan, that would have allowed him to fire his torpedo right off the bow of the target. It would have been a very easy kill. He sighed. *Would have been…*

The first reports of sonobuoys being dropped had come about an hour ago.

"Conn, sonar, buoy splash bearing zero-two-five."

The buoys kept coming. Rows and rows of them, spread out for several dozen kilometers ahead of his target. No surface contacts were nearby. And his sonar operators had not reported hearing any aircraft noises. That could mean only one thing. A maritime patrol aircraft had arrived on station. One that was capable of dropping many buoys and operating at a high enough altitude that the submarine couldn't hear it. One of the new American P-8s.

The thought was chilling.

Their submarine was now right in the middle of this giant

sonobuoy field. It was like treading water in the middle of a school of Portuguese man-o'-war jellyfish that were attracted to movement. As long as his submarine stayed quiet and still, there was a very good chance that they could remain hidden. But if they moved, the deadly sensors would detect the submarine, bringing great pain and danger.

The US warship, or at least the track that he assumed included the US warship, was now only twenty-five kilometers away. Soon the submarine captain would be able to see it with his periscope.

If he was willing to risk getting that shallow.

The only thing worse than a submarine being detected by sonar was a submarine that was visually spotted by an aircrew. He decided to wait. Just be patient, he told himself. Let them get closer.

The executive officer shot the captain a worried look. "Sir, we will need to make a decision soon."

"Yes. But not yet. We need to—"

The sonar supervisor said, "Captain, buoy splash. *Very close to us this time.*"

"How far away?"

"One is less than one thousand meters, sir."

The captain swore to himself, but his face remained calm. If they were dropping them that close…

"Come hard right to zero-four-five. Increase speed to all ahead full."

The echo of repeated commands sounded throughout the space. The captain stood over the tactical chart, one of his junior officers updating it with the latest reports from the sonar team.

He wiped sweat from his forehead. The game had just moved to the next phase.

* * *

The DICASS sonobuoys began sending pulses of sound energy out into the deep ocean water. The sound waves expanded in every direction, and bounced back to the buoy when they hit something. That data was then sent from the buoy to the P-8 and MH-60R by radio.

Both of the aircraft had sophisticated onboard computers that would analyze the sound data from the buoys, and turn it into valuable information: target distance, course, and speed.

"It's a good ping, sir. We have solid contact." The AW manning the sonar station was the first one to say anything after the pings had gone out.

The O-4 standing over him patted the enlisted man on the back. He then turned to look down the narrow passageway of the aircraft. He pointed at one of the junior officers. "Vector in the helo for torp drop."

The junior Naval flight officer nodded and adjusted his lip microphone. He took a breath and said, "Cutlass 471, Pelican, come left to two-six-five."

* * *

Plug said, "Left two-six-five." He yanked the stick to the left, banking the helicopter and watching the heading indicator. Then he leveled it off on a new heading of two-six-five. Plug snuck a look over at Juan's tactical display, checking that they were indeed flying toward the hostile submarine track.

"Cutlass, Pelican, standby for torpedo drop."

Juan said, "Roger, Pelican."

Juan wondered what the Chinese in the submarine were going through right now. All he could see was the same blue ocean racing along a few hundred feet below his feet. But that sub was down there. He shook the thought from his mind. Now he only had one job. Press the button.

"Cutlass, Pelican, come right to three-one-zero."

"Right three-one-zero."

The helicopter banked sharply and then leveled off on the new heading. Adrenaline was pumping through his veins. Juan's eyes scanned all his instruments and then gripped the hand control unit that would allow him to launch the torpedo.

"Stand by for torpedo drop. On my mark. Three...two... one...mark."

His breathing quickened. Pulse racing, Juan lifted up the small plastic protective cap and pressed the torpedo release button. Immediately, he felt the aircraft shudder with the sudden loss of over six hundred pounds of weight.

AWR1 yelled, "Torpedo away! Good 'chute!" There was a brief pause, and then he said, "It's in the water."

Juan made the radio call. "Torpedo is in the water."

He again listened to the noise from one of the passive buoys, wanting to hear the sound of the torpedo—and what they all hoped would be a good hit.

AWR1 said, "She's pinging. Executing her initial search."

Juan could hear it. The Mark 54 torpedo began diving into the water, turning and pinging, looking for its contact.

Plug said, "Alright, Juan, where to now?"

Juan looked at him in confusion. "Huh?" They had just dropped the torpedo. Now it was time for them to wait and listen for it to hit the target.

"Tell me what to do, man. Let's not sit on our ass."

Juan thought about it. Plug was right. What if the first torpedo didn't hit the target? Or what if it was only slightly damaged? They shouldn't just assume that everything would go according to plan. There was always something they could be doing.

"If I was the submarine, I'd want to get out of there—to change my location. But I would still want to maintain the ability to attack the *Farragut*."

"Okay, so where does that put him? Where's he going to go if that torpedo doesn't sink him?"

Plug looked at his tactical display. If the submarine moved too far to the rear of the *Farragut*, it would have trouble catching up. So that meant...

Juan moved his cursor to a certain spot and placed a waypoint in the system, then tapped a few keys. "*There*. Let's fly to this waypoint and get ready to drop a buoy."

"Sounds like a plan."

* * *

"*Captain*, torpedo in the water, bearing one-two-zero, range less than two thousand meters!"

The captain replied, "Begin evasive maneuvers! Launch countermeasures."

The cascade of voices rang out through the room. Men were yelling and sweating. They sounded afraid. They *were* afraid. So was he.

The crew leaned to one side and held on as the submarine began turning sharply and changing depth.

The XO said, "Captain, I'm afraid we've lost the array."

He winced. "Understood." The maneuvers had exceeded their speed limits and torn off the towed-array. This was extremely bad news, as it would reduce their sensor capability. But he couldn't dwell on that now.

The first torpedo pings were several seconds apart. They sounded different than the sonobuoys that had been bouncing off their hull moments ago. These were a different pitch. With each noise, the tension in the crowded compartment grew.

"Captain, the torpedo is pinging faster. It appears to have acquired its target."

The captain said, "What is the status of the countermeasures?"

One of his junior officers looked up. "Sir, countermeasures away. They just launched, sir."

The captain watched the navigational readouts. They were racing away from the torpedo, but it was much faster. Still, if they could put enough distance between themselves and the decoy...

The pinging noise grew quieter, and its frequency changed.

"Sir, the torpedo appears to be going after the countermeasures! It is no longer following us," the sonar technician said, practically gasping with joy. Some of them grinned like silly boys, having evaded death.

"Gentlemen, please mind your stations," the executive officer bellowed. "This is not over."

But after a few minutes, it appeared to be. For now.

"Sir, I no longer hear the torpedo. It has run out, sir."

The captain stood over the tactical plot. They would try to attack him again. He needed to get off his shot.

"Range to target?" asked the captain, his voice slightly above a whisper.

"Sir, the contact is now at ten thousand meters."

Ten thousand. A lucky number.

"Come up to periscope depth. Flood torpedo tubes one and two. Plug in a solution."

* * *

"Sir, the torpedo has stopped running. No explosion noises heard."

The flight deck of the P-8 was deadly quiet.

The mission commander stood arms extended, his hands on the sonar tech's chair. He said, "Do we still have contact?"

The lead AW listening to the sonar replied, "Stand by, sir."

About thirty seconds went by with nothing but silence. "Well?"

"Sir, we will need to reacquire the target. It appears that we have lost them for now."

The mission commander said, "Alright, let's keep listening, then. Don't let these guys slip through."

He looked at his tactical display. If the Chinese submarine had evaded towards the *Farragut*, it would be getting dangerously close to its torpedo range.

* * *

The submarine captain said, "How long until we're in range?"

The XO said, "Captain, we'll be at the maximum effective range of our torpedo soon, but because the towed-array came off, our track estimate is no longer accurate."

The captain sighed. "Very well. Raise periscope. We will have to confirm visually and use that for our target solution."

Surfacing with aircraft overhead was extremely risky. But it might be their only chance of successfully attacking the American ship.

"Understood, sir."

* * *

"Cutlass 471, *Farragut* Control, request status of ASW prosecution."

"*Farragut*, Cutlass, we're about to spit a DIFAR and try to reacquire the sub."

"471, Roger. Pelican, *Farragut* Control, say status."

The P-8 voice came over the radios. "*Farragut* Control, Pelican, we have negative BDA, and we have lost contact with the sub."

"Roger, Pelican."

After a moment of silence, the voice from the P-8 said, "*Farragut*, Pelican, our passive buoys are still picking up noise consistent with the Chinese submarine. Trying to reacquire the track now."

* * *

Victoria heard the call. She said, "Where is the helo?"

The ASTAC pointed his finger to the radar position. "Right here, ma'am."

"Is he dipping?"

"Negative, Boss. They were going to put a passive buoy there and see if they could reacquire the sub."

She looked at the helicopter's position on the chart. If the submarine had evaded by trying to get closer to the destroyer, that meant that the Chinese submarine captain was trying to get off another shot. If he thought he was about to be detected, he would probably fire his weapon soon. She didn't want that to happen.

It was a chess game. Each one of her moves determined what her opponent might try next. She needed to think several moves ahead, and limit his options.

Victoria walked back over to the sonar table. "ASWO, show me your plot." She looked at the nautical chart, all marked up with notes from the young officer. Grey pencil marks filled with where they thought the submarine was, based on the latest information.

She looked back at the radar screen, doing the mental math to superimpose where the helicopter was on this nautical chart. She pointed to a position on the ASWO's plot. "The helicopter is right about here."

The *Farragut* was barreling right toward that position.

She liked the location the helicopter crew had chosen. If she were the Chinese submarine captain, that's right where she would have gone after being attacked.

Juan and Plug must have had the same thought. Now there was a good chance that their buoy location would be right on top of the sub. They were going to drop a passive buoy. But what if they went active here instead? They could use the helicopter's dipping sonar. It was one of the most powerful tools in her arsenal. If they started pinging, they could get a great torpedo shot at the submarine again.

But what if she was wrong? What if the submarine had departed away from the destroyer, on the other side of the previous attack location? She thought about that. Then the pinging would still deter it from turning and closing on Victoria's ship.

Victoria said, "Tell the helicopter to dip and go active. *Right now.* And be ready to drop their last torpedo quick if it's right under them."

"Roger, ma'am."

Victoria said, "OPS."

"Yeah, Boss?"

"Turn the ship around."

OPS looked confused. "Uh…Boss?"

She said, "Reverse the ship's course. *Now.* If that submarine is headed towards us, we're going to walk right into their torpedo. I want to keep our separation. The P-8 and the helicopter are right on top of it. If we can give them more time to hunt, we'll have a better chance of success. If we keep going this direction, we're putting a time limit on how long our air assets have."

"Don't we have to reach the Panama coast by a certain time?"

"OPS, if we don't sink this submarine, we won't reach the Panamanian coast."

＊ ＊ ＊

"Cutlass, *Farragut*, Air Boss wants you to dip and start pinging."

"Roger, setting up for dip."

"And she says be ready to drop your torp right away."

Juan said, "Roger, *Farragut*."

The helicopter came in to a hover, lowering its AN/AQS-22 Airborne Low Frequency Sonar (ALFS) into the water. The MH-60R had the most advanced dipping sonar in the world. It was incredibly sensitive, and its detection ranges were greatly improved compared with previous models.

Plug said, "Are you all set up for the second weapon drop?"

Juan had been ready this time. "Checklist complete. Just waiting to get target confirmation."

Plug said. "Uhh…I think you've got confirmation."

"Cutlass, Pelican, we have visual contact! Periscope just off your right side."

Plug said, "Drop it. Drop it now!"

Juan, surprised, hit the button and again felt the shudder of the aircraft as the torpedo let loose.

＊ ＊ ＊

"Conn, sonar, torpedo in the water, bearing two-three-zero!"

The submarine captain yelled, "Evasive maneuvers. What's the range?"

"Less than one thousand meters, sir."

The captain could hear the pinging through the hull. The pinging came loud and fast. It must have been right on top of them.

＊ ＊ ＊

"I didn't see the 'chute," said AWR1.

Plug said, "Alright, just listen." He shook his head. "Shit, I mean, I guess just watch. We can see it right—"

Juan said, "*Farragut* Control, we just dropped our torpedo. We have visual of the sub."

AWR1 said, "Torpedo's pinging. Pings getting faster. I think she's acquired her target. I hear… holy shit. That's gotta be a hit."

"471, *Farragut* Control, roger. Please provide BDA."

The ocean around the periscope transformed into a white web as wide as a football field. The white circle rose into a surge of white water, erupting into the air.

"My God," said Juan.

The area of water glistened as it became covered with an oil slick, bubbles of air breaking the surface every few seconds.

"*Farragut*, Cutlass, we have visual. Torpedo has hit the sub."

"Roger, Cutlass. Bravo Zulu."

25

USS Ford

A dmiral Manning stood on the admiral's bridge of the USS *Ford*.

The phone rang. "Sir, this is the battle watch captain. Our Growlers have just finished tanking and are en route to *Farragut*'s position. The F-35s are about thirty minutes behind them. Also, sir, the JSTARS is on station."

"Thank you" was all he said in reply, hanging up the phone.

He looked over at the Zumwalt-class destroyer to their starboard side. It was heaving up and down in the water as they steamed north at close to twenty knots.

The admiral commanded thousands of personnel, and controlled billions of dollars in military assets. Some of the most technologically sophisticated war-fighting machines on the planet. But now, with his daughter in trouble, he felt powerless. All he could do was wait.

* * *

The E-8C Joint Surveillance Target Attack Radar System, or JSTARS, had taken off from Robins Air Force Base in Georgia early that morning. Their mission was supposed to last for twelve hours, with a concentration of the work being done in the Eastern Pacific, just west of Panama.

Two members of the crew were not US Air Force. One was NSA, and one was CIA. Both sat next to each other, the US Air Force major watching their screens. One of his airmen sat next to the two men, managing the inverse synthetic aperture radar.

The airman said, "Sir, we have four surface tracks bearing two-six-zero for about"—he moved his cursor to measure the distance—"two hundred nautical miles. Based on the ELINT, sir...yup, that's the Chinese."

The NSA and CIA men had sophisticated surveillance equipment that canvased huge swaths of the Pacific for electronic signals. The CIA had provided intelligence that there might be a group of Chinese Navy ships headed towards the Panama Canal region, and that they might have had orders to open fire on the US Navy destroyer that was also in the area. The aircraft carrier USS *Ford* had a whole strike group but was still far to the south, so the *Farragut* was pretty much on her own. But no one had been able to pinpoint the location of the Chinese ships.

Until now.

It was a huge game of cat and mouse. Thousands of square miles of ocean. Hundreds of ships headed to and from the Panama Canal Zone at any given time. Both the Chinese and the Americans had their radars off, likely trying to remain hidden from the other until the last minute.

It was a sound strategy. If the ships kept their military surface search radars turned off, the adversary ships would not likely be able to use their passive electronic surveillance equipment to identify them.

Once those military radars were flipped on, however, one could cross-reference the radar track with the knowledge that the military radar had originated from it, then the cat would have found the mouse.

As soon as the JSTARS aircraft had gotten into range, it began operating on the same encrypted datalink network that the E-2 connected to the USS *Farragut* with.

JSTARS, however, had certain highly classified sensors on board that went well beyond normal electronic surveillance measures.

The NSA man said, "Alright, move your ISAR to check out this group here."

The Air Force man did as requested. Sure enough, the screen showed a pattern of pixels that resembled a group of warships.

"That them?"

"Certainly looks like it to me."

"Major, recommend you vector in one of those F-18s to take a look."

A few minutes later, one of the F-18G Growlers flew near the group of suspected Chinese ships, using its onboard camera to take pictures and then transmit them back to both the JSTARS aircraft and the E-2D.

The CIA man on board JSTARS said, "Yup. Those are Chinese warships."

The major in the JSTARS aircraft began typing.

JSTARS: FARRAGUT, we have located the four Chinese surface vessels—transmitting their position now.

FARRAGUT TAO: Roger, JSTARS, copy tracks.

The major made a call to the pilots flying the aircraft. "Gents, how are we on fuel?"

"About another hour on station, sir, then we're going to have to return to base."

The major typed.

JSTARS: FARRAGUT, JSTARS has 1+00 on-station time remaining. Interrogative intentions, over?

* * *

Victoria sat in the captain's chair in the Combat Information Center of the USS *Farragut*. She could read the chat messages between the JSTARS aircraft and OPS, who was again standing TAO. The man had barely slept in the past few days. None of them had. *They can rest when this is over.*

"What's the range between us and the four Chinese ships?"

One of the sailors standing surface watch replied with the bearing and range.

OPS said, "That's within missile range."

Victoria had to make her choice. Normal rules of engagement would prescribe that she not attack, unless in self-defense. But while war had not been declared, the ROE had changed. That much was clear.

The Chinese submarine had attacked them, and sunk three friendly ships. It was a hostile environment. And they now had intelligence that these four Chinese warships were on orders to intercept and attack the USS *Farragut*. Until further notice, all Chinese warships, submarines, and aircraft in this geographic area should be considered hostile.

"OPS, what weapon do you recommend?"

"We're outside of the SM-2 range. But we have eight SM-6s that are set up for surface-to-surface. They're new. We could launch them at this range. But unless you want to illuminate the Chinese ships with our radar, we're going to need help from the JSTARS in making sure that we hit the right target. I'd hate to attack some merchant ship by accident."

Victoria nodded. "I agree. We've got one more hour with the JSTARS on station. How long until we're close enough to Panama City to launch the helo?"

"Based on the three-hundred-nautical-mile range, we've got another three hours at this speed."

Victoria stood and looked at the charts. This was now about how much risk she wanted to take. If they could make it another three hours, she could launch the helicopter and they might get lucky.

If the Chinese kept their radar off, they might never know that the helicopter had taken off, and might never know where the *Farragut* was. Even if they did turn on their radar, the Chinese might confuse the *Farragut*'s radar signature for the numerous other ships that were approaching Panama.

Unless the Chinese had some other means of locating the *Farragut*. If they somehow located the destroyer, they could begin their attack right now.

The Chinese could also fire on the *Farragut*'s helicopter after it took off. Again, that would require them turning on their radars. But if Victoria didn't fire on the Chinese now, that was exactly the risk she faced.

She thought about that for a moment—the Chinese ships turning on their air search radar, and firing God knows how many surface-to-air missiles at their helicopter. It would be a sitting duck.

It was her move. Keep hiding, or attack with the advantage. Kill or risk being killed.

"TAO, aft lookout reports a helicopter off the port beam! It's not one of ours, sir. Lookout says it's got a red star on the side."

"*Shit*," Victoria said. That forced her move. "OPS, get an updated location of the tracks from JSTARS, and fire the SM-6s at will." She had to remind herself to remain calm in front of the men. "Make sure our air defense is ready to go if we get any ESM hits that their missiles are coming."

"Everything is ready, Boss."

That helicopter was from one of their ships. It had to be. The *Farragut* had just been located. Now it was a race between the Chinese ships and the *Farragut* to see who could get off their missiles first. Her heart started beating faster as she thought about a slew of Chinese anti-ship missiles heading towards them.

The combat information center was a flurry of activity. Tense officers and crew sprang around the room, going through checklists and double-checking settings.

Then the entire ship quaked as the SM-6s roared out of the vertical launch system, one after the other.

* * *

Chinese Destroyer Lanzhou

The *Farragut* launched eight missiles in all, columns of bright white smoke shooting up and arcing away into the distance.

The SM-6, or RIM-174 Standard Extended Range Active Missile (ERAM), was very new to the US Navy's surface-to-surface arsenal. A semiactive missile, it was originally designed for extended range anti-air warfare. It was used to shoot down fixed-wing, helicopter, unmanned aerial vehicle, and anti-ship cruise missiles. But the Navy needed a more modern, farther-reaching anti-ship missile. And the SM-6 was it.

The Chinese surface fleet was made up of one Luyang II–class destroyer, the *Lanzhou*, one Luda-class destroyer, and two Jiangkai II–class frigates. All four were controlled by Admiral Song's South Sea Fleet.

The helicopter that spotted the USS *Farragut* was attached to the *Lanzhou*.

Victoria was right. As soon as the helicopter got a visual on the *Farragut*, the aircrew immediately passed that information back to the *Lanzhou*. The captain of the *Lanzhou* then passed the coordinates on to his ships, with orders to open fire.

As soon as that order was given, he received the first indication that the *Farragut* had beaten him to the punch.

"Captain, we have a missile warning!"

"Battle stations!" the captain shouted. Alarm bells rang and men began running throughout the ship.

"Enemy acquisition radar bearing one-five-zero."

The captain said, "Bring all radars online, and activate our air defense missiles."

The powerful air search radar took a full minute to warm up. When it did, the men in the *Lanzhou*'s control center were horrified at what they saw.

* * *

The naval flight officer in the rear seat of the F-18G Growler had been communicating with the JSTARS aircraft as they flew towards the Chinese ships at just under four hundred knots. It had been only a few minutes since they had passed on the imagery of the Chinese vessels, confirming their identity.

His screen lit up as he saw indications of the USS *Farragut's* starting their attack.

"*Farragut* just launched missiles."

The pilot said, "Roger."

The NFO's hands raced over his tactical controls, as he anticipated what the Chinese ships would do next. Their best bet would be to try and shoot down the American anti-ship missiles. To do that, they would need to turn on their air search radars, identify and track the incoming missiles, and use their own surface-to-air missiles to shoot them down.

The Growler crew wasn't about to let that happen.

"Activating the ALQ-99s."

"Roger."

The AN/ALQ-99 was the airborne integrated jamming system. Upon activation, the NFO began jamming the Chinese warships' air search radar. With any luck, they would be helpless in defending themselves from the incoming missiles.

* * *

"Captain, we have four…six…no, eight missiles inbound!"

"Shoot them down!"

"Air search radars are still trying to track them…there seems to be interference."

The captain walked over to his air defense station. "Well?"

"Sir, something is wrong. I think we are being jammed."

No one else had time to speak.

Through its datalink, the JSTARS had provided the USS *Farragut* with precise coordinates on the four Chinese ships. The *Farragut's* crew had done the rest. They fed in the exact coordinates of each ship, dividing up the ships so that each one would get two missiles a piece.

The anti-ship missiles traveled at over three times the speed of sound. As the SM-6s got close to their targets, they switched on their semiactive radar homing, finding their targets and "pinging" them to ensure they each got a precise hit.

Making them even more deadly, the eight missiles used their networking capability to communicate with each other, making sure that each missile had the most precise targeting information possible, and that the targets remained evenly divided up among them.

While the warhead on each missile was only one hundred and forty pounds, the kinetic energy of such a high-speed missile did enormous damage. Two blasts fragmented throughout the center of each ship, one after another. The entire event took a little over forty seconds.

One of the missiles struck the weapons hold on board the *Lanzhou*. It triggered a chain reaction that caused a massive explosion to rip the destroyer apart. The backbone of the ship rose thirty feet from the sea in a surge of white water and then plummeted back down. The *Lanzhou* sank within minutes.

The other three ships were "mission kills." Many of their crew survived, but the weapons systems and power plants were out of commission.

26

USS Farragut

Victoria walked back into the hangar. Behind the closed hangar doors, the helicopter spun on deck, waiting for its lone passenger.

"You alright, sister?" Chase said quietly.

She was a mix of energized and numb from the action. She tried not to think of the lives lost, but of the potential lives saved.

"I'm good. I hope this is all going to be worth it."

He patted her on the shoulder, careful not to embarrass her in front of her men. "I think it will be."

"Be safe. Good luck."

Chase grabbed his pack, which contained the Chinese crypto key, and walked over to the helicopter's aircrewman.

The two of them opened up the small hangar door and walked into the rear of the helicopter.

Victoria watched them take off through the hangar door's small porthole. As the MH-60 Seahawk flew into the air, she said a silent prayer that they would land without incident.

"Captain."

One of the ship's ensigns stood behind her.

"Please don't call me that."

"Sorry, ma'am. Um, Air Boss, OPS asked me to tell you that the USS *Ford* will be within helicopter range of us by tomorrow afternoon. They're asking that we close their position, and provide status updates."

"Alright, thanks. I'll be right there."

27

CIA Safe House, Panama

Chase sat in the kitchen as NSA and CIA team members worked on their computers in the next room. They had a lot of sophisticated gear. Big servers. Lots of wires. When Chase arrived, they immediately hooked up the crypto key and got to work.

One of the CIA guys walked into the kitchen and sat down at the table across from Chase. He had a slight smile on his face.

Chase said, "So? What's the verdict? Have you guys been able to get anything from it?"

He nodded. "Oh yes. They're sending it all up to D.C. now."

"What's the story?"

The guy looked behind him and then back at Chase. He leaned in. "The short of it is that it looks like our rogue theory was right on. They've got Chinese military assets from the south region that are a part of this thing, but that's *it*. It's limited to them. So we can deduce from that information that, aside from Jinshan, the only other bigwig who is involved is this Admiral Song."

"So that's good, right? So now what?"

"I'm afraid that's above our pay grade, buddy. For you and me, we sit and wait."

Chase took a swig from his plastic water bottle. He got up and walked over to the window, looking at a small patch of Pacific Ocean.

* * *

Director Buckingham stood in the Oval Office. The president, the national security advisor, and the chairman of the joint chiefs were each there.

Sheppard was fuming, pointing his finger at the chairman of the Joint Chiefs of Staff and the CIA director. "That ship should have requested permission to fire before attacking those Chinese naval vessels. This is outrageous. Only the president can authorize something like this. Now you people have opened up a real can of worms."

The chairman of the joint chiefs said, "I would remind the national security advisor that the USS *Farragut* was attacked first, and that several friendly naval vessels were lost in that attack. The *Farragut* acted in self-defense, which is her right."

The NSA said, "How do we know that the Chinese ships weren't there for peaceful reasons? And you don't know that the Chinese submarine was the one that attacked. That's speculation."

Director Buckingham said, "Charlie…"

"Don't start, Sam. You've wanted this to be about the Chinese this whole time. Mr. President, this is outrageous. It's Iran that we should be worried about. This nonsense about China has gotten out of hand. And now they've finally gone too far and started a shooting war. With no proof of Chinese wrongdoing."

Director Buckingham said, "That's where you're wrong. The SILVERSMITH team was able to recover one of the crypto keys from Manta, Ecuador." He handed the president a folder. "Sir, we now have hard evidence that proves that two Chinese nationals are responsible for this, and several other hostile acts over the past few weeks. Cheng Jinshan and the Chinese South Sea Fleet commander,

Admiral Song. Together, they've organized a rogue military and intelligence operation that included the Red Cell, instigated Iranian-US hostilities, and attacked the US in multiple instances."

The NSA's mouth dropped. "When did you get a crypto key? Why wasn't I told about this?"

The director shot the NSA an icy gaze. "It was determined that you didn't need to know."

Sheppard nearly exploded. "What? How dare you? Mr. President, I demand that—"

The president held up his hand. "That'll be enough, Charlie."

The NSA said, "Sir, this just doesn't feel right. I don't think you should trust this information. The director..."

The president stood and the NSA grew quiet. "Charlie, what do you mean when you say it doesn't *feel* right?"

"Uh. Sir. It just...the Chinese wouldn't do this. It just doesn't seem like they would—"

The president said, "Charlie, first of all, you aren't listening. Director Buckingham just said that this wasn't the work of Chinese leadership. This was the work of two rogue individuals. And secondly, I have no use for people that come to me and tell me that intelligence doesn't *seem* right or *feel* right. I want *facts*. Not *feelings*."

"Mr. President, it's just that—"

"Charlie, let me give *you* some facts. I've just read the most interesting report from the FBI. It seems that prior to accepting this post, you've done extensive work for companies with ties to Mr. Cheng Jinshan. Were you aware of that?"

The NSA went white. Director Buckingham had been wondering when the president would do this.

"Who told you that? Mr. President, did the CIA tell you that?" The NSA glared at the CIA director. "Mr. President, you can't believe everything you hear. There are people here who would like nothing more than to see you go down in flames. But I'm one of the loyal ones. You can't listen to them—"

"Charlie, we're done. You've been moving forward your own agenda and ignoring the professional intelligence services for too long. At the very least, you've been giving me advice that's less than stellar. At worst…well, I'll let the Department of Justice handle that. But either way, your services are no longer required. Please vacate the White House."

The NSA's mouth was open. It took him a moment, but he finally got up and walked out the door.

The president read through the rest of the report on Jinshan. He looked up at the CIA director and said, "You're sure about all this? There's no way that this could be wrong?"

The CIA director nodded. "Sir, we have excellent intelligence. This was all the work of two people: Cheng Jinshan and Admiral Song. The Chinese president, and Politburo leadership as far as we can tell, were all left in the dark. The crypto key that our Special Forces team recovered shows historic data for all of Admiral Song's rogue military units. That includes communication signals from a Chinese submarine in the Persian Gulf, right at the time of the attacks there. We've corroborated this with other signals intelligence, and it looks like the rogue Chinese elements have been trying to push us into a war with Iran. They've been building up troops in Ecuador. All these factors together point to the veracity of David Manning's testimony about the Red Cell."

The president shook his head. "Unbelievable."

The chairman of the joint chiefs said, "Sir, I've spoken with my counterpart in the People's Liberation Army. He's assured me that China has no hostile intent towards the United States. He couldn't explain why any Chinese South Sea Fleet units were located in the Eastern Pacific. He's agreed to stand down Chinese military assets' defensive postures. We've seen corresponding activity that verifies that. Ships pulling into port, fewer fighter aircraft flights. That sort of thing. Our Pacific theater assets are all on alert."

"So we're not at risk of starting World War Three, after we just sunk a sub and four Chinese Navy ships? Is that what you're telling me?"

"Sir, from what I can tell, the Chinese want very badly to de-escalate. They were shown the preliminary evidence that Director

Buckingham mentioned, and they realize that this was their fault. The Chinese don't want any further aggression."

* * *

CIA Director Buckingham and General Schwartz sat in a private meeting room at the embassy of the People's Republic of China in northwest Washington, D.C. The official communication would take place between the US president and the Chinese president and include high-level State Department personnel. But that official meeting was still being set up. This was the unofficial communication. And it couldn't wait.

Their meeting was with the Chinese ambassador in D.C., and by secure video feed, with a Politburo member they were certain was loyal to the Chinese president. Director Buckingham went out of his way to ensure that no Chinese intelligence representatives were invited into the room. He was too worried that Jinshan would influence the proceedings.

The discussion took about an hour. It was late at night in Washington. The Chinese Politburo member asked for a ten-minute recess when the Americans were done speaking. He did his best not to sound upset, although it was easily the most difficult conversation of his professional career.

After the recess was over, they re-joined the call.

The Politburo member said, "We are gravely concerned about this matter. I am to assure you that China's senior leaders were quite unaware that this was taking place. We are very upset that military action has been taken. These military actions occurred without the knowledge or consent of the Chinese military leadership, including the president."

The CIA director said, "The United States would like to keep our relationship with China positive. We understand that these actions were not the result of Chinese-sanctioned activities."

The Chinese Politburo member said, "I have been authorized by the highest levels of my government to ask if there is any way that we might find a mutually beneficial resolution, and keep these conflicts...confidential?"

Director Buckingham said, "I'm afraid *that* is not possible. You can hang that on Jinshan if you like, but lives were lost. We will not keep this conflict secret from the American people, or from the world."

"I understand."

"Good. Now, what about Iran, and any Americans who might be on the Red Cell island? We want resolution on those matters as soon as possible. We request that China immediately contact the Iranian regime and enlighten them on Jinshan's actions there. Specifically regarding Jinshan's part in the assassination of Ahmad Gorji. We want China to pressure Iran into standing down its military, and ensuring that no further hostilities occur."

The Chinese Politburo member nodded. "Yes, of course. We will contact the Iranian leadership immediately."

"And the Red Cell—the Americans that are being held on your island base in the South China Sea? We demand that they be released immediately as well."

"Please give us a day to look into this. Again, this is most disturbing for us. A complete breakdown of trust in our chain of command. We need to take these rogue leaders into custody and then ensure that the personnel under their command conduct no further illegal actions. That will take a matter of hours. Once that occurs, we will ensure that any Americans that they had in custody are released."

The CIA director nodded. "That sounds acceptable."

"The president of China will call your president tonight. He wishes to personally pass on this message. He wishes no harm to our relationship. These actions were not the actions of the Chinese people. They were the misguided actions of...as you have said, rogue persons. If there are truly any Americans on that island, they will be released immediately."

* * *

Guangzhou, China

Jinshan and Admiral Song were in the middle of their lunch when the call came. They sat on the enclosed balcony of Jinshan's tower penthouse. The view of the hazy cityscape stood in front of them as they dined on seafood and white wine.

"Mr. Jinshan, you have an urgent call."

He waved over his assistant, taking the encrypted phone and putting it to his ear.

Admiral Song had been discussing their military options. Song was nervous. It had been almost twelve hours since they had heard from the four ships and one submarine that were to attack the USS *Farragut.*

Jinshan listened to the voice on the call. "You are sure? When?" Jinshan looked at his watch. "That was more than *two hours ago.* Why am I just getting this information *now?*" He looked at Admiral Song in disbelief. He held his hand to cover the receiver and told the admiral, *"They know."*

"Who? The Americans?"

Jinshan shook his head. Song's eyes went wide.

The front door burst open and commotion erupted in the next room.

A group of nearly a dozen uniformed military police stormed into the dining area. Jinshan's own three bodyguards looked at him nervously, not sure of what to do. They were clearly outnumbered and outgunned, and likely wanted nothing to do with a confrontation with the People's Liberation Army.

The highest-ranking officer in the group of military police looked at the two men eating lunch and announced, "By order of the general secretary of the Communist Party of China, you are both under arrest."

Admiral Song stood up. "What is the meaning of this? This is preposterous. What is the charge?"

Jinshan didn't say anything. The military police quickly surrounded the two men and placed them in handcuffs.

The military police officer said, "Treason."

* * *

The Chinese Y-20 jumbo transport plane landed at the Manta airport runway just like all of the others, with one exception.

This one wasn't expected.

The Chinese PLA captain who was in charge of the airfield's flight operations called his superior, but he couldn't be reached. So the captain cleared the aircraft for landing and sent out a team to taxi it in to the nearest hangar. He and his men watched it from the control tower with curiosity.

As the rear ramp went down, he was surprised to see a platoon of fully armed military police walk off and begin separating into groups, heading to different parts of the base, their leader shouting and pointing as they marched.

"Sir, there is the colonel," one of the men said, the only one in the control tower to speak.

Indeed, the base commander had driven up to the aircraft in a jeep, with two other vehicles behind it. The military police filled them, and the small convoy raced off to the other side of the runway, where the barracks were located.

The military police were to arrest only one person on the base. The others were to stand down and await further orders. They were all to be recalled to China within the week, according to the senior ranking officer of the military police unit.

"*Where is she?*" the military police captain asked the base commander. His men had searched her quarters, but they were empty.

"The last report that I received on Lena Chou was that she was in her quarters with the Indian man."

The base commander spoke the truth. Just like he was told, he had kept a close eye on her as soon as he had received the call from Beijing. One of his trusted lieutenants had been watching them this morning, and he was told to notify the base commander of any unusual activity.

They called the lieutenant over. The one that had been watching her from his own office window.

"Where are they?" demanded the military police captain.

"Sir, Miss Chou and Mr. Chaudry were in Captain Lin's trailer this morning. I saw them go over there about an hour ago. I have been watching them as instructed. I did not see them leave."

"Captain Lin?" the military police captain said.

The colonel said, "What of him?"

The military police captain was thinking that a Captain Lin was the one who had contacted them, letting the PLA military police know that Ms. Chou was the one they were after, and where she was located.

"Nothing. Where is his trailer?"

The man pointed to another trailer fifty meters away. "The last one in that column. He bunks with three other logistics officers."

The military police vehicles raced over there, and a team of them entered. One of the men who went in came out a moment later. He looked like he would be sick.

The military police captain said, "What's wrong with you? Are they not in there?"

The man shook his head.

Furious, the military police captain pushed by him and into the trailer.

Captain Lin lay on his bed. Blood running out of his mouth. A knife jammed into his chest.

The military police captain swore profusely and walked outside. After a few more minutes of arguing, the military police force was instructed to fan out and search the base.

Their efforts were fruitless. Lena Chou was gone.

* * *

David read the headline of the *New York Times* with delight.

IRAN-US Stand-Down as China Negotiates Truce

At the bottom of the front page, which would have been below the fold on an actual print version of the newspaper, was another headline.

China returns 18 Americans, apologizes to US—Rogue Chinese intelligence mastermind arrested

Chase walked up to his brother's cubicle. "Pretty wild, right?"

David said, "There will be massive repercussions."

"When does it say that the Americans are coming home from the island?"

"They're in Korea now. It says that they'll be transferred to the States within twenty-four hours."

Chase looked proud. "You did great, David."

"Thanks. You too."

"Are you going to go back to In-Q-Tel?"

David looked around his CIA office space. "I don't know if I can."

"What, like they won't let you?"

David shook his head. "No, I mean—there's nothing that compares to the work they do here. It's invigorating, being a part of something like this. The work the people at the CIA do…it really saves lives, and protects our country. It's just so…"

"Fulfilling?"

"Yeah. Exactly."

Chase nodded. "I get it. You don't feel like the research you were doing was the same."

David looked over at the group of CIA analysts a few desks down. Their normally serious faces were all smiles. They were gathered at a single desk, enjoying their morning coffee and basking in their recent victory.

The intelligence collection and analysis that they conducted led to massive global decisions. The SILVERSMITH team had, in less than a week, stopped a war. It had freed American hostages. And it had saved American lives from a Chinese attack.

Most importantly, the intelligence community, including the NSA, DIA, and CIA, had illuminated the *truth*. In a world of ever-increasing moments of espionage and disinformation, it was these dedicated patriots that had saved the day.

David knew that preventing the US-Iran war was only part of it. Jinshan's group had tricked the US and Iran into attacking each other, yes. But their real objective was much larger. By uncovering Jinshan's plot, millions of lives might have been saved.

David still wasn't sure if it would have been possible—but Jinshan was going to launch a Chinese invasion on the United States. Many of the other members of the SILVERSMITH team laughed at the idea. It wouldn't have been achievable, they had argued. But a few weeks ago, they might have said the same thing about Jinshan's other terrible achievements. David knew in his heart that his CIA team had prevented a large-scale invasion on the United States of America.

Chase nodded to the *New York Times* article on David's screen. "Does it say what's going on in the Persian Gulf now?"

David read, "American and Iranian forces are both being ordered to stand down, as it now appears that many of the recent regional hostilities were triggered by a massive deception. Sources close to the White House are saying that rogue CIA agent Lisa Parker is now believed to have been working with Chinese billionaire Cheng Jinshan. These same sources say that there is now credible intelligence pointing to Jinshan as the one who ordered the assassination of Iranian politician Ahmad Gorji, the event that provoked the Iranian attacks on US military assets in the region. Incredibly, Jinshan also appears to have been the primary communicator responsible for the Iranian sleeper cell's attack on the Washington, D.C., Beltway. Chinese diplomats have apologized profusely for these actions, which they claim were conducted in secret, without the knowledge or consent of Chinese leadership."

Chase shook his head. "This is crazy."

"I know."

The brothers sat in silence for a moment. Finally Chase said, "You said you might not be able to go back to In-Q-Tel. So what, then?"

"I've actually been talking to Susan about sticking around here."

"As an analyst?"

"Yeah."

"Cool."

"But first, we plan on taking some vacation. Lindsay, the kids, and I."

"Nice. Where at?"

David shrugged. "Henry Glickstein has a beach home near Destin, Florida. He's down there now and offered to let us stay there. We might take him up on it."

David could see his brother reading the article in the paper. "You're looking for her, aren't you?"

Chase glanced at his brother. "Did it say anything?"

"No. She's still missing."

"They won't find her. Not if she doesn't want to be found."

Susan walked over to David's desk. "Good morning, Mannings. Congratulations again on saving the world."

* * *

Victoria felt good getting back into the cockpit again. It had only been eight days since she had last flown, but that was too long for someone like her.

She aimed her aircraft straight at the giant grey floating city on the horizon. She could see two helicopters in orbit on the starboard side of the carrier. They were in between cycles, she knew. The brief window for helicopters to take off, land, and refuel before the jets needed the flight deck.

She adjusted her lip mike and checked that she had the right frequency before she made her call.

"Tower, Cutlass 471 is five miles on your 170, inbound for pax drop-off."

"Roger, 471, we got ya," came the full southern accent on the other end. She presumed that it was the air boss on the carrier. He would be a Navy commander, most likely a jet pilot. His job was to oversee every aspect of active flight operations on the carrier's flight deck and close-in airspace.

She checked her airspeed. One hundred and twenty knots. "Coming down to two hundred feet."

"Roger, two hundred feet," replied Juan.

He had a renewed confidence in his tone—and why not? In the last week, he had gotten more actual over-water SAR rescues than any Navy helicopter pilot she'd ever met. He'd also sunk a nuclear submarine in combat.

He was a little upset by that, he had confided to her. She would need to pay attention there. There was no glory in killing, she had told him. But there was honor and justice in protecting others. He had done the right thing.

The external radio circuit came on with the tower voice again. "Cutlass 471, Charlie spot three—you're cleared to land on spot three. Just follow the wands, Princess."

"471, Charlie spot three." Well, she guessed everyone knew she was coming. She shouldn't be surprised that he used her call sign, Princess.

Victoria also noticed that he gave her extra instruction since she wasn't one of the helicopters based on his carrier.

Helicopters from single-spot ships that weren't used to operating around aircraft carriers were like rural persons who found themselves driving through New York City. It was a busy, shocking atmosphere, and there was little room for error. The air bosses on the carriers usually didn't have any tolerance for helicopters that weren't familiar with their procedures. But most helicopters weren't piloted by their boss's boss's boss's daughter.

They landed on the carrier's flight deck, and two flight deck personnel wearing yellow shirts and head gear came running in from each side to tie the aircraft down with chocks and chains.

Victoria said, "Unstrapping. You have controls."

"I have the controls," Juan echoed.

She got out of the helicopter and followed one of the white shirts over the carrier's expansive flight deck. Everyone who worked on the flight deck wore different-color shirts and helmets, which denoted their job type. White shirts were part of the air transfer officer's unit, responsible for logistics flights and passenger transfers.

She was always surprised by how large and stable the carriers were. She could barely tell they were at sea. It was just flat, huge, and motionless. Compared to one of the small destroyers that she landed on, it was like landing on a real airport on land.

They entered the superstructure door and she took off her helmet, holding it by the sweaty chinstrap as they climbed up the stairs.

"If you'll follow me, ma'am, I'll take you to see your fath—um...the admiral."

Victoria smiled. "Thank you."

Her legs were cramping by the time they reached the admiral's bridge, nine flights of stairs up from the flight deck. The white shirt opened the door, and Victoria saw her father for the first time in a long time.

The admiral's bridge was an expansive room with shiny blue laminate floors. Bright daylight shined in through the Plexiglas windows that wrapped around on three sides of the room. Almost no furniture, save a few treadmills and an admiral's chair.

The admiral was surrounded by a small group of men. The admiral and a Navy captain next to him both wore khaki flight suits. The captain's name tag just said "CAG." Victoria knew that to mean Commander, Air Group. He was the head of all aviation units on the ship. A commander wearing a khaki uniform stood next to them. He had on a SWO pin. Victoria surmised that this would be the replacement for the USS *Farragut*'s late ship captain. A submariner lieutenant stood a few feet behind the group.

"Gentlemen, please excuse us," Admiral Manning said quietly.

The group of officers thanked the admiral, and nodded in respect to Victoria as they walked out of the room.

Victoria's face was like a stone, save a lone tear that streaked down her cheek.

Seeing the tear, her father pulled her close, embracing her. They didn't speak for nearly thirty seconds. The only sound was her sniffles.

When they separated, he held her shoulders, looked at her in the eyes and said, "I'm so very proud of you."

She gave quick nods, regaining her composure but not yet trusting herself to speak. She wiped away a few more tears, smiling and embarrassed.

"You saw the commander who just left. He'll be your new ship captain for now, until Big Navy can tell us what the long-term plan is."

"Alright. Thanks." A part of her was disappointed that her brief tenure as a ship captain was over. Another part of her was relieved. She might finally be able to get more than two hours of sleep without getting an emergency phone call.

They spoke about nothing for a few moments. He asked about the flight over. About the performance of her crew and helicopter detachment over the past week. She didn't tell him that Chase had been the one she'd flown off the ship. She would, eventually—if he didn't find out on his own first. But now didn't seem like the right time.

She looked at her digital watch. "I should probably get going. The cycle will be starting up again, right?"

Her father nodded. "I could always tell them to go land somewhere else. My daughter's visiting."

She laughed. Then she looked serious. "I love you, Dad."

They embraced one last time, and he said, "I love you, too."

She left and found the white shirt and the SWO commander waiting outside the room for her.

As the group marched down the stairs, Victoria felt an incredible satisfaction. She had been faced with the ultimate test of a military officer. She had led men in combat, and proven herself up to the task. And the pride in her father's eyes told her that she had served with honor.

THE ELEPHANT GAME

BOOK 4 IN THE WAR PLANNERS SERIES

China is a sleeping giant. Let her sleep, for when she wakes she will move the world.

— NAPOLEON BONAPARTE

1

"They're coming for you," the base commander told her as he returned the phone to its cradle.

Natesh watched Lena for a reaction. Nothing. Stoic. But he knew that there was more behind the emotionless eyes. Lena was trusting everyone around her even less than usual after the recent failures.

It was probably over, Natesh knew. His life's defining moment—and his biggest mistake—was coming to an end. Cheng Jinshan had been taken into custody. And now a plane full of Chinese military police was secretly flying to Manta, Ecuador, with orders to apprehend the criminal Lena Chou.

Criminal.

It was amazing how quickly things could change. Lena was the best covert operative China possessed. Natesh had seen the results firsthand. And they were sometimes hard to watch.

Lena stood next to him now. Her long black hair ran down her tall, muscular frame. She had been wearing her hair down more lately. Natesh suspected that she wanted it to hide the recently acquired burn scars that ran from her right ear down to her leg. He had seen her looking in the mirror at the scars, when she thought no one was watching. That was a remarkable sight in itself. It proved that even the robotic killer queen wasn't immune to human emotion.

What was going on behind those eyes? Was she contemplating the recent turn of events, and how it would affect her? Would she become a survivalist, turning on Jinshan as others in China must have?

"When was Jinshan taken?" Lena asked the base commander.

"Several hours ago."

She turned to Natesh. "What have we heard from the island?"

"Nothing since the Americans attacked our ships. Admiral Song's operation has gone dark."

Their failure was still raw. One Chinese ship had been sunk in the Eastern Pacific, as well as one Chinese submarine. Three Chinese navy ships were limping into a port in Panama.

The American Navy had responded swiftly when one of their destroyers, the USS *Farragut*, had been attacked by a Chinese submarine. Three US-allied ships were sunk, but the *Farragut* had survived. The *Farragut* had then gone on to recover a team of US special operations commandos who had raided the Chinese base in Ecuador and gotten a vital piece of Chinese cryptologic equipment into the hands of the NSA.

That was what had gotten Cheng Jinshan arrested, Natesh knew. The crypto key had uncovered Jinshan and Admiral Song's secret military movements. With that evidence, the Americans had shown the Chinese president and a few politicians that Jinshan was plotting a war. While the Chinese leadership had likely been horrified to learn that one of their most powerful citizens had been able to orchestrate a Chinese military operation without their knowledge, that wasn't what scared them the most. The Chinese politicians were most terrified of what their *exclusion* from Jinshan's inner circle meant for them. He must have been planning a coup. And there is nothing like the fear of losing one's throne to motivate action. Cheng Jinshan and Admiral Song had been arrested within hours.

Lena let out a breath of frustration through her nostrils, looking at the floor. Slowly turning her head. Thinking. "Colonel, do you know when the aircraft filled with military police will arrive?"

"My source tells me to expect it sometime today. This information didn't come from normal channels. It is likely a matter of hours."

She nodded, her eyes racing from side to side as she thought. "Very well. Thank you for the notice. We bid you farewell for now. When they do arrive, this conversation never happened."

"Of course."

Natesh followed Lena out of the office. He knew enough not to ask her any questions right now. Natesh had seen her eyes like this before. She was on the warpath.

Their first stop was at one of the barracks buildings. They were nothing more than a series of trailers, recently set up to house the influx of Chinese military personnel that had been flown over from Guangzhou.

This trailer held a single resident. From his uniform, Natesh saw that he was an officer. When he saw Lena and Natesh enter, he sat up in his bunk, a surprised and frightened look on his face. Lena and the officer began speaking in rapid Mandarin. Natesh couldn't understand them, but the Chinese officer rose to his feet and began to protest whatever Lena was saying. Her eyes were narrowed, and the tiniest of smiles crept over her face. Natesh took a few steps back.

The fight didn't last long. As soon as the Chinese officer realized what she was here for, he tried to move past her. But she blocked his path down the narrow corridor of the trailer, sliding gracefully in front of him and cocking her head.

He would have to go through her.

The officer's face grew red. He glared at her, then struck. A right hook that would have connected with her head, had she not ducked. The miss angered him, and he yelled and walked forward, on the offensive.

Lena's movements were fast and controlled. Her fists shot out in a series of rapid strikes to his torso and neck area. The captain doubled over and fell to his knees, writhing in pain. He made a choking sound, one hand covering his throat and the other his stomach.

Lena removed a knife from her belt.

"Lena," Natesh said, "what are you—"

She jabbed the knife up into the officer's chest. The man's eyes widened as the gleaming blade penetrated his heart. He collapsed onto the floor, a steady flow of blood pouring out of the wound. Lena grabbed him by the shirt and pants, her muscles rippling as she dragged him back over to his bed and heaved him up onto the mattress. She walked over to a sink, cleaning the blood off her hands. The knife remained in the man's chest.

Natesh stared in silence, his eyes wide. For a moment, the only sound was that of the running sink.

She scrubbed off the blood with soap and water, not looking up as she spoke. "You are wondering why I have done this? Well, here is your answer. I knew this man. I had a debt to settle with him. And I suspect that he may have been the one who notified the authorities that I am here. If he is watching us, I don't want him to see us exit the camp."

Natesh didn't reply immediately. He just looked at her and the dead body behind her, the knife protruding from the man's chest cavity.

A wave of questions filled Natesh's mind. Was this something he wanted to be a part of? What had he fallen into? These methods weren't what Natesh had agreed to with Jinshan. Modern war was to be quick and decisive. Jinshan had lured Natesh with the opportunity to design a new and better society. But first, he had to help orchestrate a war. The allure of power and the challenge of writing history —even if that history began with a war—was what had drawn him to this path. But seeing the violence up close...this wasn't at all how he'd thought it would be.

She glanced at him. "Are you alright? I'm sorry that you had to see this, Natesh."

He nodded. "I'll be okay."

She dried her hands and arms with a towel. "Come. This way."

* * *

As they walked out of the dead officer's trailer, Lena could see that

Natesh was upset. He had every right to be. A few weeks ago, he had been a promising Silicon Valley entrepreneur. CEO of his own boutique consulting company, working with some of the world's largest firms to solve problems and create new products.

Now, he was a witness to murder, each one bloodier than the last. He was likely questioning himself. Natesh Chaudry was one of the chief architects of the Chinese invasion of the United States. A brilliant mind, and a valuable asset. One that Jinshan thought highly of. She couldn't have him getting cold feet.

"Wait here, please." She went into her own quarters, leaving him outside. She dug around in the trunk under her bed. Beneath a false floor was a hidden compartment. She opened it and removed a satellite phone that worked through an encrypted connection, routing calls through a special network of Chinese military communications satellites. Lena powered up the phone and dialed a number from memory.

The operator on the island picked up within seconds.

After providing her passphrase, Lena was transferred to the duty officer. Their conversation lasted five minutes, as Lena received her instructions, interrupting only twice to clarify the information. When the call ended, she stared at the phone. Then she shook off the feeling of surprise and placed the phone in her bag. She dug around in the trunk and retrieved other items as well—clothing, a silenced pistol, cash, and false IDs. Passports for both her and Natesh.

She walked back outside and handed him his passport. "Is your travel bag ready?"

"Yes."

"Let's go to your quarters and retrieve it. Quickly. I want to be gone in the next few minutes."

Natesh nodded and they both walked over to his trailer. He was in and out in a matter of seconds. They walked over to the fenced area that stored the military vehicles. The guard saw Lena and nodded to her. Everyone knew and feared her. There would be no questions. Not until the team arrived from Beijing.

Lena had toyed with the idea of having the Leishen Commandos on the base take the military police prisoner, but she didn't want to test their loyalty. Besides, now she had a new set of orders.

She threw her bag into the back of a jeep. "Put your stuff in here."

Natesh did as commanded. "Where are we going?"

"We're going to Portoviejo. It is a city about an hour from here. Now get in."

She started up the jeep and drove them out of base. The guards nodded at her as she left. Lena could have had the private jet pick them up from Manta, but there would be too much risk that it would be tracked by the Americans or Chinese parties not loyal to Jinshan.

Green jungle trees arched over the dirt road, providing shade from the hot sun.

Lena glanced at Natesh. "You are worried."

"Yes."

"Don't be. We've planned for this."

"For what?"

"For the possibility of Jinshan being taken into custody. For the possibility of…things not going well."

"Lena, four Chinese navy ships were defeated by the Americans. A Chinese submarine was sunk. Now the Chinese government is coming to Manta to apprehend you." He looked exasperated. "If Jinshan has been taken into custody, that means that the American government has exposed him. The Chinese president must know about the Red Cell now…"

"Yes?" She looked over at him while driving. "What of it?"

He sighed, looking into the dark rainforests that whipped by.

"Have faith, Natesh."

"Lena, you need to think about your own well-being. *We* need to think about—"

"Stop it. Listen to what I said. We have *planned* for this."

Natesh shook his head. "We need to figure out a plan to hide. Maybe we should consider reconstructive surgery. I have cash. At a bank in Barbados. It's an untraceable account. I've been putting some away ever since Jinshan told me about—"

"Natesh, please. Nothing has changed."

She reached over and grabbed his shoulder with one hand, making sure to hold his eye for just the right amount of time. Then she placed her hands back on the wheel.

"How can you say that? So much has gone wrong."

She decided to change tactics. "Is this *really* about Jinshan being captured?"

He bristled. "What else would it be about?"

"I know that you have been uncomfortable with things."

He pouted, not responding immediately. "Well, this was supposed to be a war of *deception*."

"It is. It will be."

Natesh scoffed. "Jinshan had promised me that there would be minimal casualties. In the past few days, I watched you execute an Ecuadorian military commander in front of thousands, and you just stabbed a Chinese officer to death."

Her grip on the wheel tightened. "I understand your frustration."

He was still staring at her as she drove. "Things are out of control."

"I'm sorry that you feel that way. But you knew that this wouldn't be easy. Great achievement requires great sacrifice."

They didn't speak for the rest of the trip.

An hour later they drove through a small town. Most of the homes were shacks. She parked her jeep outside the airport and they both hopped out.

"This airport doesn't look open," Natesh said. Bits of grass were growing up through segments of the runway pavement. The hangars and parking lot were empty, and the central terminal looked abandoned.

"It's not."

"Excuse me?"

"It's not open."

She walked over and stood in front of him, taking his hands. He was frowning, still angry.

"I'm sorry, Natesh. You are right. Things have gotten out of hand. This isn't what Mr. Jinshan or I intended to happen. But you must keep trusting him. He is a visionary. And I suspect that you joined him for many of the same reasons that I did. His grand idea of what the world could become, if we can win."

"I appreciate you admitting that."

Lena nodded, doing her best to show empathy. "Part of the allure of our great task...for people like you and me, Natesh, is the challenge of sculpting the world into greatness."

Natesh folded his arms.

Lena continued, "I know that you have now seen me do some horrible things. Truth be told, I am not proud of everything that I have done. But I won't lie to you and tell you that it is going to stop. *Many* more will die. It *has* to happen. The world has become entrenched in political systems and power castes that won't relinquish control without a fight. You must have known this when you accepted Jinshan's offer to join us."

Natesh took a deep breath and nodded. "I was optimistic. Maybe naïve."

"Natesh, when I take someone's life, I do it for a reason. That Ecuadorian general—he was a barrier to our progress. And his death, however gruesome, served as an example for the others. They will be better soldiers now that they understand the seriousness of their job. Now that they understand the realness of this war."

"And the Chinese officer?" Natesh looked skeptical. "Why did he need to die?"

"I told you, I was worried that he might turn us in. We had history, and—"

"Lena, you didn't have to kill him."

Her face darkened. "Listen. That Chinese military captain that I just..." She looked away for a moment. "If you knew what he did to me when I was a girl... Natesh, I was but a teenager. Trust me, if you knew what he did to me, you would be fine with his death."

Natesh's expression changed. "I didn't know. I'm sorry."

She nodded. "There is a lot that you don't know, Natesh. Cheng Jinshan is a good man. He wants to bring about a better world. We are his instruments. You need to trust that in the end, it will all be worth it."

Their eyes met, and Natesh nodded.

A propeller plane buzzed low overhead, circling the runway.

"There they are. Right on time."

Natesh said, "That sign says the airport is closed. And I can see some tents and containers on the far half of the runway. Where is the plane going to land?"

"I spoke with them before we left. They assured me that they would be alright."

"Them?"

"Colombians. Contractors. They're going to fly us to the coast of Colombia. From there we will take a boat."

"To where?"

She didn't answer.

The small propeller plane landed on the near side of the runway, which was clear of debris. The plane taxied over to Lena and Natesh's jeep. The pair got out and threw their things into the plane.

Moments later, they had taken off, headed north.

Over the loud noise of the plane's engine, Natesh spoke into Lena's ear. "Can you please tell me where we are going now?"

Lena leaned over, her long black hair flowing down over Natesh's arm and shoulder as she spoke. "Back to the United States."

2

Han-class submarine
90 miles west of Panama

Captain Ning read the email for the third time, shaking his head. Ning had taken his submarine across the Pacific as fast as possible, per Admiral Song's orders. Their original mission had been to support the other Chinese naval forces in the area.

But a lot could change during a journey across the Pacific.

A week ago, the Americans had sunk a Chinese submarine and destroyer and severely wounded three other Chinese warships in the Eastern Pacific. This was the naval group that Captain Ning was supposed to assist. Ning *knew* the men aboard the submarine that was lost. The captain's wife was friends with his own. He clenched his fist, thinking about the loss.

The email was from the senior PLA Navy commander. It came as background information—an addendum to the submarine's official orders. Their official orders were to stand down and cease all further hostile activity towards US Navy warships. There was no further explanation about what they were to do after that.

But the email from the admiral contained extra information.

Ning was to continue into the Eastern Pacific and await further instructions. He wasn't sure why this was but had hypothesized that it might be to escort the wounded Chinese navy vessels on their way into Panama. After discussing the matter with his XO, however, he had become convinced of an alternative reason. Ning had precious cargo on board his boat—highly trained naval commandos.

Captain Ning rose from his desk and headed to the bridge.

"Status report."

"Sir, the American carrier group is to our north. We haven't noticed any active sonar activity in the past day. One unknown submerged track is coming in and out of contact in the vicinity of the American carrier group. We believe this to be either a Los Angeles–class or a Virginia-class attack submarine."

The captain nodded. "Keep working to identify who it is. We must be very careful here. We cannot afford to be detected."

"Yes, Captain."

The communications officer entered the bridge. "A message from the island, Captain."

The island. Those two words were spoken with a hushed reverence now. Or was it worry in the young officer's voice?

The captain nodded and followed him to the communications room, where he hunched over the computer and adjusted his reading glasses. He read over the message and sighed. "Please fetch the executive officer."

"Right away, sir." The young officer scurried off.

The captain wasn't sure what was going on in Beijing now, but at least this message answered one of his questions. His XO had been right about using their special cargo.

Admiral Song had warned him that something like this might happen. The fog of war spreading into the hallways of government. Confusion and misinformation were byproducts of such a radical body of work. Jinshan's operation must have been rejected by Chinese leadership.

Was a coup underway? But if Admiral Song was behind bars… would Ning be imprisoned when he returned to home port? Maybe there was still a way out of this conspiracy. He shook off the thought. Ning had already picked his side.

Admiral Song had chosen a dozen of his most trusted and capable commanders, and Ning was among them. Song had brought them into Jinshan's inner circle and explained what would happen to China if they didn't make war upon the United States.

The operations that they were to participate in would be classified at the highest level. Even members of the Politburo would not know the truth. The loyal and patriotic officers of the South Sea Fleet had pledged to do whatever needed to be done, and Admiral Song had begun deploying them in clandestine operations around the world, in preparation for Jinshan's war.

Captain Ning's boat had been training near the island, practicing with the elite naval commandos before traveling across the Pacific Ocean. While Captain Ning didn't know Cheng Jinshan, he trusted Admiral Song implicitly. Admiral Song was a brilliant strategist, and an outstanding officer.

Still, he wondered how the charade was being kept up in Beijing. Were the political and military leaders there still so confused as not to know where their military units were, or what they were being told to do? If Song and Jinshan had been arrested, why was the island still sending them orders? Orders that appeared as if nothing had changed.

Could it be a test? To see if Ning was loyal to Beijing or the island?

Or maybe Jinshan and Admiral Song *hadn't* really been arrested. Perhaps that was a ruse, too. But then why had Beijing sent out their message last week after the naval battles—the one that told all Chinese military forces to stand down and cease further hostilities?

He read the computer screen again, shaking his head. The island had just sent him orders that directly conflicted with the stand-down instruction. Now he would have to decide which instructions he would follow.

"Captain, you wanted to see me?"

The captain nodded toward the screen. "Read."

His executive officer was the number two officer on the submarine. His subordinate, but also his closest and only confidant. Captain Ning thought highly of the man.

"What do you think?"

The XO looked him in the eye. "Very odd, after what the PLA Navy high command sent us last week."

"My thoughts as well."

The captain turned to the bulkhead, thinking. "Tell the conning officer to head us towards these coordinates. See if sonar is picking up anything that matches this description. If it's there, we'll follow these orders."

"Yes, Captain."

The executive officer left the communications room and began issuing orders to the different members of the crew.

The captain picked up the phone and dialed a three-digit number. The commander of the South Sea Fleet's naval special operations detachment answered from his stateroom several spaces away.

"This is Lieutenant Ping."

"Lieutenant, please have your men get ready for immediate deployment."

A moment's hesitation. After two months at sea, and the news of the last week, the young officer was as surprised as anyone. "Yes, sir, of course."

"And come see me as soon as you are ready. I'll provide instructions. We have received an urgent message from the island."

* * *

Chinese special operations forces are very different from the United States' own units. The PLA has almost two and a half million active-duty members, and an estimated thirty thousand special operations personnel. The United States active-duty military is about half that size, although its numbers of special operations personnel are comparable.

But while the Chinese special operators are high in quantity, they are low in experience. United States special operations forces have been sharpened by decades of war around the globe. Their units are made up of experienced veterans, and they are often integrated with organic specialized aviation units.

Chinese special operations forces, on the other hand, are comprised mostly of two-year conscripts and first-tour lieutenants. Chinese commandos are known for being extremely tough and capable, but young and inexperienced.

Lieutenant Ping was one of these young lieutenants. He was four years into his service as a naval officer. A graduate of the newly formed Special Operations Academy in Guangzhou, he was one of only fifty officers in the South Sea Fleet's Special Operations Regiment, one of the few Chinese naval SOF units.

While his unit spent most of their time training, Chinese military leadership had recently stepped up SOF deployments. Lieutenant Ping's regiment had sent teams to various parts of the world in order to better project power and protect Chinese interests. Ping and his group of peers had competed fiercely with one another in order to be selected for one of these coveted deployments. When Ping was chosen, he relished the opportunity to prove himself in a real-world situation.

Ping had been deployed aboard a PLA Navy destroyer and sent to the Middle East on a counterpiracy deployment in the Gulf of Aden. Their mission was to escort cargo ships transiting the Internationally Recommended Transit Corridor in between Somalia and Yemen. Merchant shipping companies had learned from the rash of pirate attacks over the past decade and often hired private security to escort their valuable ships. But acts of piracy still occurred.

Lieutenant Ping had led a team of naval commandos as they retook a Chinese-flagged merchant ship from a band of Somali criminals. Ping had received many accolades from his superiors and earned the respect of his enlisted men. Ping's men appreciated his cool demeanor and quick decision making. But more than that, the young officer looked out for his troops and demanded from himself a level of performance that exceeded that of his men. He was always the hardest-working, the first one to meetings and the last one to leave the training areas.

But as Ping listened to his orders now, he had many questions.

Some of them he would voice to the captain. Others he would keep to himself. In the PLA Navy, a few questions would show intelligence and preparation. Too many, and he might show a lack of comprehension, or worse…that he was questioning the wisdom of his orders.

"Terminate all personnel with extreme prejudice, it says."

"You have read the orders accurately," replied the submarine captain.

"Who are these men?"

"Criminals. Drug smugglers, from what the description says."

Ping looked at his watch, then back at the orders on the screen. "We have two hours to prepare."

"Correct."

Ping read over the instructions once more. "May I use the wardroom to go over our mission brief with my men?"

"Of course. Just let me know what you need."

"Very well. We will study this and spend the next hour planning. This will be an unusually quick reaction time, but we will be ready, Captain."

"Excellent, Mr. Ping. I wish you good luck." The captain extended his hand.

The young special operations lieutenant shook the captain's hand, his eyes fierce.

Ping hurried to the different sections of the submarine where his men were located. Some were working out, others sleeping. Within five minutes of notification, they were all dressed and in the wardroom, looking over a chart. Planning took an hour. They looked at the type of vessel they would be assaulting, how many personnel were on board, expected armament and skill level of enemy forces, and optimal entry points.

Preparations for their underwater exit took another forty minutes.

They divided into four groups of two for the exit. They used the submarine's two escape trunks, built just inside its hatches.

The outer doors were flush with the body of the submarine. The chamber just inside the outer hatch was the escape trunk. They could fit two people at a time. A submarine crewman operator stood just inside the inner hatch. His job was to make sure that the inner and outer doors were both locked, that the pressure was equalized with the ocean outside the door, and that the hatch was flooded with water and refilled with air at the appropriate times.

Moments later, all eight members were swimming outside the submarine, breathing with the help of their scuba system. Ping and his team swam over two hundred yards to the boat. They broke the surface once, about fifty yards away, to check their bearings.

The moon and starlight reflected glimmers of white off the ocean surface. The smugglers' boat was a black shadow, pitching and rolling in the sea. The ship was dead in the water—engine off. Ping could hear the occasional sound of voices over the lapping of the waves.

His team was silent, swimming fast with their scuba gear and silenced submachine guns strapped to their wetsuits. Once they were underneath the vessel, Ping had a decision to make. They could use grappling hooks and rope, climbing about five feet above the water-line. But that might be noisy, and it would take a little longer than the alternative. The second entry possibility was a small ladder at the aft end of the ship. The problem with that was its proximity to where the boat's crew was likely to be. They would have to climb up one man at a time. If the smugglers were armed and had numbers, it could end badly for Ping's men.

Not to mention that there was a propeller right next to that ladder. The motor was off for now, but Ping wasn't sure how long they would have until the cigarette speedboat arrived. The submarine captain had estimated one hour. Would they start moving once it was within radio range? Or would they stay quiet, afraid to draw the attention of coast guard and navy vessels patrolling the area?

Ping's men would follow his lead. Sometimes it mattered less whether one made the best choice than whether one made it in a timely manner. He chose to go up the aft end of the ship and signaled his men. They began removing their weights and tanks, tying them off on the ladder.

Ping grabbed on to the metal ladder and pulled himself up, step-ping and climbing fast. He was heavy, his tactical gear weighing him down as soon as he was out of the water. He threw himself over the stern of the ship and unstrapped his weapon. He then brought his mask down around his neck, looking and listening for any sign of opposition.

His team was only seconds behind. Each of them followed his movements, preparing their equipment and aiming their weapons forward, trying their best to be quiet in their bulky black wetsuits.

The lights were all off on the ship, and voices could be heard coming from the bridge. Ping and his men each removed a clip-on night vision goggle apparatus from a waterproof chest pocket and snapped it in place. A flick of the switch, and the unit powered up. Night became day, and his men broke into preplanned teams, each silently making their way throughout the vessel.

Ping walked along the port outer deck of the boat. There was a covered bridge ahead. Another team would be walking along the starboard side, and yet another would be heading down the ladder and into the berthing area. It wasn't a large vessel. This would only take a few seconds.

He heard a shout and rapid Spanish ahead, then the familiar rattle of one of his men's silenced submachine guns. Then there were many shouts.

Movement ahead. *There.*

A smuggler appeared in front of him. The man backed out of the bridge, his hands to his sides. Ping pressed his trigger and fired a burst from his machine gun. His target's body convulsed and then fell to the deck.

"Clear," said one of his men from the bridge.

More gunfire. This time from belowdecks. Bullet holes in front of him as the floor was peppered from below. Ping ran backwards to get out of the line of fire, his heart beating. More gunfire. Ping could see two of his commandos advancing down the stairs, their weapons glued to their shoulders, firing in short, controlled bursts. Then, silence.

"Clear belowdecks."

Ping went to the bridge and checked the radio. He keyed the mike three times on the bridge-to-bridge frequency. The submarine, at periscope depth, would hear this and know that the first part of his mission had been a success.

He turned to his men. "Stow your diving gear and get ready. The speedboat should be here any moment now. When they arrive, we need to fill it up with gas. We will then board it and head inland. We must be ashore before dawn. Does everyone understand?"

"Yes, sir." Nods from his men.

So far, so good. Ping wondered what the island would have in store for him once they reached the Americas.

She would know.

Lena Chou. Ping had heard of her—most of them had. Ping had even seen her once, when he had attended training on the island a month ago. But he had never spoken to her.

She was a shadow. An elite blend of intelligence operative and special forces warrior. One of Jinshan's special spies. Rumor had it that she had been embedded with an American intelligence agency until recently. Her cover blown, she was now operating as Jinshan's personal cleaner, fixing and improving their espionage and special operations capability at the tip of the spear.

"There it is, Lieutenant. The range finder says two thousand meters." One of his men was looking through a night vision telescopic lens.

Ping checked his watch. "Excellent."

When the long cigarette speedboat finally pulled up alongside, Ping's men threw out bumpers and tied it up. They began pumping fuel from the mothership to the go-fast.

Lena Chou stepped across to the mothership. "Who is in charge?"

"I am Lieutenant Ping, Miss Chou. My men and I are now at your service."

"Thank you, Mr. Ping. We'll need to get to shore before dawn. Once there, we'll be able to get your men into civilian attire before we journey north. How much have they told you about this assignment?"

"I know that we will be traveling through Mexico and into the United States. My men are prepared for anything."

"I'm sure they are, Mr. Ping. This won't be hard. But we'll need to keep a low profile. How many of your men speak Spanish or English?"

"All of them speak English, ma'am. But some better than others. Two are fluent in Spanish."

She nodded. "That will do."

Ping noticed a dark figure in the speedboat, lying in a heap. He seemed to be groaning.

"Who is he?"

"He is with me."

"What's wrong with him?"

"Seasick."

Ping smiled.

One of Ping's men walked up to them, balancing himself on the rail as the waves rocked them back and forth. "We're finished fueling, sir."

Then Lena walked over to the radios on the bridge. She tuned up a frequency and began transmitting. She spoke several times, but nothing she said made any sense to Ping. It was gibberish. Or code.

"Miss Chou?" Ping knew that it was not smart of her to make any radio transmissions. The US military would be able to triangulate the transmission. The American intelligence collection agencies would be able to match her voice to their data. They would surely be looking for her voice...

Lena continued speaking for one full minute. Then she turned off the radio and faced him. "When investigators evaluate this vessel, they will likely take fingerprints and see that I was here. Intelligence agencies will match my voice to the radio call I just made and know the transmission location. There are those who would like to see us fail. They are looking for me. This will throw them off my scent."

"I see." He looked over towards the speedboat. "We should not waste time, then."

Lena nodded at Ping, who said, "Everyone on the speedboat." He then asked Lena, "Do you think we should do anything with the bodies?"

She said, "Dump them over the side. That should be good enough."

Ping barked orders to his men. The corpses were dumped unceremoniously into the black ocean. Splashing sounds echoed every few seconds. Then the rumble of the speedboat's engine announced their imminent departure, and everyone hopped aboard.

Lena pushed the throttle forward, and they raced to the northeast.

3

Destin, Florida

David Manning sat on the beach under an oversized umbrella. The clear greenish-blue water of the Gulf Coast lapped gently against the sugar-white shore. His three-year-old daughter was building a sandcastle near the surf with his wife, Lindsay. Their baby slept in the shade next to him.

Henry Glickstein walked up, smearing his face with thick globs of sunblock. He wore a gardener's straw hat, oversized sunglasses, and a Tommy Bahama tee shirt.

"Sorry you had to come down when the water's still a little chilly. You'll have to come back when the weather warms up. But don't come in April—that's when all these young college kids get here and ruin everything."

David said, "Oh no, this is still great, Henry. Can't thank you enough for letting us stay here for a few days. It's warm enough for Maddie to play in the sand. That's all we need."

"Sorry about the drama last night. I should have known better than to let the riffraff in when you guys were here."

The prior evening, Henry had had a visitor show up unexpectedly at his home. Apparently, she was a waitress at one of the less-than-reputable establishments in nearby Pensacola.

David's wife Lindsay had smelled stripper on her from the moment she'd walked in the door. Bleach-blond hair and fake...well, everything. While David had been amused, Henry had been embarrassed at her often inappropriate and less-than-intelligent additions to the conversation. But David suspected that Henry hadn't been interested in her intellect. Lindsay's eyebrows were permanently raised and her chardonnay glass permanently full for the evening.

The young woman had stayed for the barbecue they were having, but then left abruptly after dinner when Henry had said that he wasn't going to be able to go out with her that night.

"She was, ah...nice?" It was the best David could offer. She couldn't have been more than thirty years old.

Henry smiled, as if it were a compliment. "Yeah, she loves that I was on the news." Glickstein shrugged, then sat in the empty beach chair next to David. "So you hear from any of the group? The Red Cell folks, I mean?"

The Americans who'd been freed from Chinese custody in the Red Cell had been transported to a US military base.

"They're being given medical treatment and doing interviews with government officials. I've seen some of the debrief reports."

"The interviews with our government this time?" Henry smiled.

"Let's hope so." David snorted. "We've flown their families out to be with them. They should all be arriving back home soon, I think."

"*We*, now, is it?"

"Yes, sir. I guess it is." David was now working full-time as an analyst for the CIA. He had only been working in the job for a few weeks and was still getting used to it. He was assigned to the interagency SILVERSMITH team—a program created in response to China's increased hostility towards the United States.

David was part of the reason the SILVERSMITH operation had been started. He had been an unwitting participant in a Chinese espionage operation. Twenty Americans—Henry Glickstein among them—had been led to believe that they were joining a CIA-sponsored

Red Cell. The Red Cell was made up of US defense, intelligence, and technology experts whose mission was to create a plan for China to invade the United States.

But as David had quickly learned, the Red Cell was actually part of an elaborate Chinese intelligence operation, designed to uncover classified American secrets and bolster China's own soon-to-be executed attack plans. The Red Cell was the brainchild of Cheng Jinshan.

Cheng Jinshan wore multiple hats. A Chinese national, he had risen to become the head of several Chinese Internet and media-related companies. His firms made up a large portion of the cybersecurity and censorship wings of the Chinese technology industry. All throughout his career in business, however, he was also employed as an operative within the Ministry of State Security—the Chinese equivalent of the CIA. His business roles had begun as a mere cover. But Jinshan's power had grown tremendously.

The influence he wielded in each of his positions—the private sector and the Chinese intelligence world—had served to rocket him into the stratosphere of China's elite power brokers. The Chinese president had even been friendly with him, and had appointed him as the head of the Central Commission for Discipline Inspection, normally a cabinet position, reserved for a politician.

The CCDI was the Chinese agency intended to root out corruption in the government. But Jinshan had wielded his authority like a sword. He had used the CCDI to consolidate power, installing loyalists in key positions within the Chinese government. His political views were quite unique. Jinshan was obsessed with Chinese dominance of the West and envisioned creating an idealistic form of government, led by an inner cadre of technocrats.

Jinshan had attempted to bring his vision to life through a global conspiracy. Admiral Song—a Jinshan loyalist and commander of the PLA Navy's South Sea Fleet—had secretly organized the military wing of Jinshan's campaign. Through a complicated network of spies and secret communications, Jinshan and Admiral Song had engaged in deception and covert operations against the United States in various parts of the globe.

This conspiracy had culminated in a series of naval battles in the Eastern Pacific Ocean, off the coast of Central America. David's sister, Victoria Manning, had commanded the USS *Farragut* during the hostilities, ultimately leading the US Navy to victory.

The director of the CIA and the American president had contacted the Chinese president after they had gathered verifiable evidence of Jinshan and Admiral Song's treachery. They had informed the Chinese president that he was only days away from an attempted coup, and that Jinshan and Admiral Song were the chief instigators.

The Chinese president, embarrassed and surprised by Cheng Jinshan's rogue activities, had taken swift action. He had called upon all Chinese military forces to stand down and promised no retaliation against the US Navy. The Chinese had fired the first shots in the skirmish, and the US actions had been defensive in nature. The members of those Chinese naval units had been under the impression that they were following legitimate orders, and were considered innocent. Jinshan and Admiral Song were the criminals. And Lena Chou, wherever she was…

For now, the two nations were at peace. But the citizens of both nations were furious at the loss of life, and each felt that they were the victims of a grave injustice. The peace was fragile.

Henry reached into the cooler and pulled out a sparkling water. "Want one?"

"No, thanks."

He opened the bottle and took a sip. "Seems to me that things quieted down kind of quickly, don't you think?"

David looked at him. "What do you mean?"

"I mean, our country was attacked. I know the Chinese have publicly apologized and everything, but…"

"You're not one of those crazies who's saying we should go to war with all of China now, are you? I thought that was just for the political websites. I mean, where's that going to get us?" Much of the country was still in an uproar over the Chinese-American naval battle that had occurred. David knew it wasn't fair to characterize Henry as crazy and immediately regretted saying it.

Henry said, "Well, you've got to admit that they have a point there, David. Hundreds of lives were lost. What was the total count?"

"Including the Chinese ship, I think they said eight hundred and seventeen people died. Mostly from the initial Chinese submarine attack."

Henry flung up his hands, shaking his head. "Well, that's what I mean. They can't just get away with that. They apologize and that's it? Now our president is just acting like it's not a big deal. Like we can bury the hatchet and blame it all on one guy."

"I don't think that's what the president is trying to do. But he doesn't have very good options. And they're supposedly working on a new bilateral agreement that's going to make China pay for what they did."

"Right. The new bilateral agreement. What's the president going to do? Slap a tariff on them? They'll just do the same thing to us. Look, I mean, I don't want anyone else getting hurt. But that was an *act of war*. That wasn't just Jinshan. China's military did that. They were responsible too."

"It wasn't a sanctioned military activity."

Henry folded his arms and cocked his head in protest. "*Come on.*"

This same argument was being played out on radio shows, podcasts, and news rooms across the world. What it all came down to, David knew, was that China had crossed the line. And the American people wanted them to pay.

"Have you seen all the funeral footage? They had a big one in Bogotá. From the Colombian navy ship that was sunk. And the poor kids of those US Navy men. The ones from your *sister's* ship, for crying out loud."

David looked at his daughter sleeping next to him. She was less than a year old and was starting to stir from her nap. David held his finger up to his lips.

Henry got the hint and began to whisper. "All I'm saying is that people are *angry*. They feel wronged. I mean, the stock market has crashed since all this stuff came out. GPS isn't working, and the Internet is half of what it was…"

"Things are being restored. And Chinese sailors lost their lives too."

"So you're defending them now? This was all just one big misunderstanding, is that it?"

"Henry, what do you want, World War III?"

Henry frowned. "I already said I didn't. But they deserve to pay. An apology isn't enough."

"Jinshan and the admiral he was working with are on trial. They will pay the price."

"Says who? China's president? Can you trust them after what they did?"

"You *do* sound like the talking heads."

"And you sound like one of those hippies who just wants to make peace everywhere. Don't be so naïve, David. You saw what they're like. *You* were on the island. You of all people should know."

"What does that mean?"

Henry took another swig of his sparkling water. "I have a hard time believing that it was really just one person, and no one else is to blame. What about Lena? What happened to her."

"They're looking for her. She'll be caught. It's only a matter of time."

"You think China really *doesn't* know where she is? They know, believe you me."

David couldn't be completely sure that Henry wasn't right on that point. The CIA had had some of the same discussions about Lena. If the Chinese government found her before they did, would they let the Americans know? She had been a double agent, embedded in the CIA for over a decade. They would want her for themselves—even if she *had* been part of Jinshan's unsanctioned operation.

Lindsay and Maddie strolled back up the beach to where the two men were sitting.

"Daddy, Mommy says I can have a snack."

"Sure, honey. Want a peanut butter and jelly?"

"Yes, please." She held out her sandy hands. David brushed them off, took out a quarter of a PB&J sandwich from the cooler, and handed it to her.

Lindsay pointed to Henry's drink. "Can I grab one of those?"

"Of course, madam." He handed her a sparkling water, and Lindsay sat next to David on the towel.

"She still sleeping?"

"She's starting to move, but yes."

Lindsay sat on the towel next to David, their knees touching. She said, "Henry, how long have you had this home?"

The three-story beach house was stunning. A large open floor-plan, great views. Lindsay had been talking about getting a beach house for years.

"I got it a few years ago. After I began working for myself. It's nice to come out here whenever I want."

"It's beautiful."

"Yup. Retirement is nice."

She said, "So are you still getting interviews with three-letter agencies, or are they done with you?"

Henry glanced at David. "Not sure I'm supposed to say this, but yes, I still get calls occasionally. But I think they feel they've sucked everything out of my brain that's going to help them for now. I didn't get a job offer, like some." He smiled at David.

"Well, some of us don't have beach homes, so we still need jobs," David shot back, also smiling. Henry laughed.

"I mean this, folks—you guys are welcome down here whenever you desire. Even if I'm not here."

They lay on the beach making small talk for another twenty minutes, until the baby woke up. Then they collected their beach gear and went back into the house. Maddie got cartoons on the iPad. "It's vacation," Lindsay said, justifying the extra screen time.

Henry put on Fox News in the kitchen, and the adults made lunch from last night's leftovers. The volume on the news channel was low, but David could still read the headline. It was all anyone was talking about.

CHINA TENSIONS STILL BOILING AFTER HIGH SEAS COMBAT

One of the talking heads was the recently ousted National Security Advisor. He was making arguments for something he called "strategic patience."

The other talking head was a China expert from a D.C. think tank. He claimed that the Chinese political scene was like the novel and TV series *Game of Thrones*, with power struggles and deceptive tactics throughout. His argument was that only time would tell who was really in control, and what China would do. David agreed.

Henry handed David a beer. David opened it and took a sip.

"David, something has been bothering me and I'd like to get your take on it."

"What's that?"

"Jinshan is a master planner, right? A billionaire, a genius. Everyone agrees."

"Right."

"So why didn't he have his ducks all lined up in a row when they were attacking our Navy off the coast of Ecuador?"

David furrowed his brow. "Well, I think they were acting in a panic. The Chinese were surprised by a team that we sent down there. I can't really say more than that."

"I know. And I read about it online. Some black ops group infiltrated their base in Manta. Blink twice if I'm close."

David smiled. "I can't say."

Henry continued. "But what I mean is…Jinshan must have been planning a coup, right? The Chinese president wasn't in on it. Otherwise, he wouldn't have arrested Jinshan when the United States showed their evidence on what he was up to. Right?"

David nodded. "I think it's generally accepted now that Jinshan had intended to stage a coup."

"*And?*"

"And what?"

"That timeline doesn't strike you as odd? Jinshan, a master planner, a genius, was in the process of staging a coup, but doesn't strike while the iron is hot? What was he waiting for? I mean, he must have a ton of support. Otherwise it wouldn't work. Jinshan doesn't plan something without a lot of preparation. Just look at the island."

David felt a tickle in his brain. Henry was on to something. "Say more."

Henry looked at the wooden blocks that David's three-year-old daughter was now playing with. She had built them up into a tower. "So Jinshan is building this castle, right? He's been working for years at this. Building it piece by piece. The military forces are starting to be sent overseas. He's got schemes going on in the Middle East to tie up our forces there and hurt our economy. And he's got his cyber forces starting to cripple US communications—like how they've taken out our GPS satellites. Now to me, it sounds like Jinshan is pretty darn close to completing this castle. But one major piece seems to be missing. *He isn't in charge of China.*"

David sipped his beer. "And what you're saying is that he must have been ready to execute the coup, if he was this far along in all his other plans."

"Exactly. Which brings me to my real question—why didn't he? *Why didn't he* execute the coup on time?"

"I see what you mean." David looked out at the ocean. "I guess if Jinshan was planning a coup, and he had everything set up, it might still be pretty easy to move forward with it. But he didn't. Why?"

Henry tipped his beer towards David. "Yes. That's been bothering me something fierce. From what I saw in that Red Cell, everything was raring to go. If they stayed on schedule, that means that their military exercises have been prepping for an attack that should take place right around now. And their industrial capability should be shifting over to wartime production. Shipping containers should be specially outfitted for military uses. Undersea cables would be cut. EMP attacks. Everything we talked about over there. The works. But when we were in the Red Cell, we didn't much talk about convincing the Chinese *leadership.*"

"No," David admitted. "We pretty much took that one for granted."

"Right. Instead, we talked about winning over the Chinese people. Hearts and minds. Popular support for the war. That was what the Shrink kept talking about. And Natesh, the bastard."

David glanced over at his wife, who was eyeing them, the children right next to her.

Henry said, "What?"

Lindsay walked over from the kitchen, smiling, and whispered, "You said *bastard*."

"Sorry. Not used to the little ones being around." Henry reddened.

She waved it off. "We're just busting your chops. You guys want a sandwich?"

"Sure. Thanks, honey," David said.

Lindsay nodded and walked back into the kitchen.

David turned back to Henry. "What if those two things are related somehow? What if Jinshan can't gain control of China's leadership until he successfully motivates the Chinese citizens towards supporting war against the United States?"

"That might solve the puzzle." Henry rubbed his chin. "So what, then—a big event that causes all of China to hate the United States? We *did* sink their ships. Is that the catalyst?"

David shook his head. "Nah. I don't think so. We've been monitoring their news and Internet. The Chinese version of events doesn't place total blame on the United States. They say it was a training accident related to Jinshan and Admiral Song. Chinese media is saying that they were arrested for crimes against the state. But they don't list what those crimes against the state actually are."

"You're kidding."

David shook his head. "Nope."

"Don't their people know? Can't they read about it on the news?"

"State-controlled news is all they're broadcasting now. They've tightened up which TV and Internet news sources are accessible even more than normal. Even in places like Hong Kong, which are traditionally more lenient in that department. The great firewall of China is alive and kicking."

Henry said, "But their leadership is cooperating with us, right?"

"To an extent. But they're looking out for themselves above all else. The government news agencies have said that Jinshan and

Admiral Song's trial is going to be live-streamed, if you can believe it."

"No shit? Why would they do that?"

"Someone in the Chinese government must want to make sure that the coup is totally squashed."

"Well, that's good news at least. Gets rid of the loons."

David picked up one of the blocks and placed it carefully on top of his daughter's tower, studying it. "You know, my grandfather was at Pearl Harbor."

"No kidding?"

"I know. Pretty incredible, right? He was on duty on one of the ships when the bombs began falling. I always thought it was amazing that one major power could surprise-attack another like that. I remember asking him about it when I was a kid, when he was still alive. I said, Grandpa, didn't you *know* Japan would attack? I was just a kid. I didn't know you weren't supposed to say stuff like that."

"What did he say?"

"He said there were plenty of signs that war with Japan was coming, but—how did he say it?—he said the people with the best view of a tsunami are usually the ones who are sitting on the beach."

Neither said anything for a moment. Then David added, "Henry, here's what bothers me most about this—if Jinshan was waiting for one big planned event to happen, something that would motivate the entire nation of China to want to go to war with the United States, what's to say that this event isn't still in the works?"

* * *

Susan Collinsworth didn't have a good feeling about the message she was reading. She was the CIA's senior operations officer in charge of the SILVERSMITH program—the interagency task force set up to counter China's recent increased aggressive behavior. Susan was privy to a variety of restricted-handling materials being collected in the Western Pacific area of operations.

Her concern stemmed from the most recent message sent from an Agency asset placed high inside the Chinese government, code name

GIANT. GIANT was the long-time assistant to Secretary Zhang, one of China's powerful Central Committee members. His real name was Dr. Jin Wang. A Chinese citizen, he had been sent to school at UC San Diego in the late 1980s. He had been permitted to stay in the US to finish his education and received a PhD in economics from Berkeley, just before returning to China.

While in his PhD program, GIANT befriended an American—another Berkeley student in a program similar to his own. Unbeknownst to GIANT, this American student was also an operative of the CIA. CIA recruiters were looking for Chinese students who might one day flower into quality sources.

In 1989, just before GIANT finished his PhD program, Chinese troops with assault rifles and tanks killed several hundred demonstrators in Tiananmen Square. GIANT watched the American press coverage and was deeply disturbed.

When GIANT returned to China, he was not shocked by the stark difference in Chinese press coverage of the Tiananmen Square incident. But he was motivated by it.

His friend from Berkeley met him in Beijing a few months after he'd returned. The meeting, while appearing coincidental to GIANT, had been meticulously planned by the CIA. The friend had been hired by the US State Department, GIANT learned. He would be stationed in Beijing for the next few years.

The men continued their friendship. Over several private meals, the CIA operative carefully teased out GIANT's strong feelings of distaste for the Chinese government. Eventually, the CIA man proposed that GIANT and he work together. Men like GIANT were needed, he was told. America needed back-channel communications. Windows into the minds of Chinese leadership. GIANT could help China to become a free and just nation, by becoming a confidential advisor to the American diplomatic and intelligence communities. Help create a China where another Tiananmen Square could never happen, he was told.

GIANT began spying for the US government shortly after, and continued to do so as his reputation and job title increased in prominence.

Because he had risen to such a high level in the Chinese government—the chief of staff of one of its most powerful policy makers—and because of the fierce counterintelligence operation in China, his reports were restricted to only a handful of personnel within the US government. That level of classification would protect him, and it would protect the uninterrupted flow of information from a reliable and well-placed source.

"Shit," Susan muttered to herself, reading over his latest message.

Secretary Zhang and President Wu fear Jinshan's coup and hostile operations may still be in progress. There is an ongoing power struggle as many Jinshan loyalists remain in important positions. Have heard rumors of unknown military training throughout regions in Guangdong and Liaoning provinces. Of particular interest is Liaoning training. Have recently learned that this covert camp holds special operations units conducting unique training. Intercepted communications have revealed that Jinshan held this camp as crucial element in his plans.

Susan tapped on her desk, thinking. GIANT's information was always helpful in understanding what the hell was really going on inside the Central Committee. But this was not what she wanted to hear. Jinshan was in prison. He wasn't supposed to be able to influence anyone there. Were things really so bad that President Wu was losing his political clout? This wasn't something that her analysts had expected. Then again, neither was a Chinese false-flag operation that had conned twenty unwitting American defense experts into giving up national secrets. But *that* had happened...

She looked at her meeting schedule for the day. She had to sit in waiting during a Senate Intelligence Committee briefing while the deputy director for clandestine operations gave them an update on SILVERSMITH. Her role was to feed him information on any questions that he couldn't answer.

The intelligence world was flipping out about their reduced satellite capabilities. Backup satellites were being launched, and patches were being installed to encrypted datalink networks. But it was a slow healing process—America could only launch so many satellites so fast. And many of the datalink networks were still considered security risks. The Chinese had crippled space-based reconnaissance and communications for months, if not years. Monday morning quarterbacking and cross-departmental finger-pointing were in full swing. And since SILVERSMITH was "the CIA's special China program," as one senator had put it, *Susan* was under a lot of pressure to fill in the intelligence collection gap.

Her desk phone was blinking. The special light. The director.
Double shit.

Since she had been put in charge of SILVERSMITH, the director had taken to calling on her at will for updates. That was understandable, given the gravity of the situation. But as a veteran of decades of fieldwork, Susan felt like a fish out of water here in headquarters. She hated the frequent in-person updates to leadership, the incessant worrying about political ramifications, and the chess matches between the massively egocentric career bureaucrats.

"Director Buckingham, how can I help you, sir?" she answered.

"Susan, you got a moment? Please come up."

"Of course."

It took Susan five minutes to reach the seventh floor.

The director had his jacket on and was standing behind his desk. "You read GIANT's latest?"

"Yes, sir. I was just going over it now."

"I'm speaking with the DNI and the president this afternoon. I'm going to include some of that intel in the brief. What help do you need?"

Susan liked the CIA director. He was the type of leader who looked to empower his people and break down walls.

She didn't hesitate. "ISR on Liaoning, sir." Intelligence, surveillance, and reconnaissance. She was asking for imagery on the Chinese military camp that GIANT had mentioned.

"Have you already requested it?"

"Yes, sir. I've been asking for ISR on various Chinese locations for weeks, but I'm hitting walls. The Liaoning camp is one of my new priorities. Technically I haven't asked for surveillance on that location yet, but I already know what response I'll receive. Satellites are depleted. Drones are vulnerable to Chinese countermeasures and cyberoperations. I even mentioned the SR-72 to General Schwartz. He floated it by the Pentagon, but they said that it wouldn't be a good asset to use. It's not ready for prime time yet."

The director buttoned his jacket, frowning. "I agree that we need intelligence collection on those camps. And I agree that we're low on ISR options. I'll mention it, but if the National Reconnaissance Office and the Pentagon are pushing back, then we'll need to come up with an alternative. Please work with General Schwartz on developing a few options. Be creative."

"Yes, sir," she replied as she followed the director into the hallway outside his office. Two escorts joined him, and Susan fell back.

Great. How the hell was she supposed to collect intelligence on a secret Chinese camp one hundred miles inland, with no ISR support?

4

USS Farragut
Eastern Pacific Ocean

While repairs normally would have taken place in port, the US Navy had decided that these were exceptional circumstances. The *Farragut* had pulled in to Panama City for only seventy-two hours, then left to continue an East Pac patrol. Repairmen and contract maintenance crews had stayed aboard to fix the sections of the ship that had been damaged when the shrapnel from a Chinese submarine-launched missile had torn through parts of the bridge and forward compartments.

Lieutenant Commander Victoria Manning stood on the flight deck, watching the Panama City skyline sink below the horizon. Their single helicopter was in the port hangar, a daily maintenance inspection underway.

Lieutenant Bruce "Plug" McGuire wandered up to her. "You know why they made us leave, right?"

"Why?"

"The Chinese ships—the three remaining ones—are supposed to pull in tomorrow."

Victoria shot him a skeptical look. "Where'd you hear that?"

"Rumor mill."

"Rumor mill isn't always that reliable. Is that the same rumor mill that said we were going to go home through the canal today instead of back out to sea?"

"Maybe."

"Hmph," she said triumphantly.

"It'll be on the news," Plug said, using his best "you'll see" voice. "They won't be able to hide it. I heard that they couldn't make it back to China, so the US government agreed to it. And they didn't want us in port causing trouble."

"You really think that our sailors would go over and do something to them?"

Plug shrugged. "Fourteen of our shipmates were lost, Boss, including the captain and XO. Forgiving is pretty hard after something like that."

Victoria said, "Amazing, if it is true. This whole situation is like a dream. Nothing makes sense. I can't believe that China is so dysfunctional that one rogue billionaire and an admiral could do all that damage."

Lieutenant J.G. Juan "Spike" Volonte walked out of the open starboard hangar wearing workout clothes, sweat dripping down his shirt. He saw Victoria and Plug and walked over. "Hey, guys."

"Spike." Plug mock-saluted.

"What's the good word?"

Victoria said, "I spoke with the captain."

"The new guy?" Plug asked.

"The *captain* of the ship, *Lieutenant*," Victoria said.

Plug pointed his thumb at her and said to Juan, "She's been pointing out my rank a lot lately. Ever since I crashed one of her helicopters. Sometimes I think she doesn't appreciate me."

Victoria glared at him. "We're clear to fly tomorrow evening. I want to do deck landing qualifications. It's been a while."

"How many hours?" Plug asked.

"Why?"

"We could use a five point oh to get into the next maintenance window."

"I'm not sure the captain will want to do DLQs for that long, but I can ask."

"If not, can we throw another flight on the back end to get it in the window?"

"I don't see why not." Victoria smiled.

* * *

The next evening, Juan felt like maybe he was finally starting to get the hang of this Navy helicopter thing. The twenty-thousand-pound Seahawk helicopter hovered over the rolling flight deck of the USS *Farragut*. He moved the stick in much smaller increments than he used to. The result was that the helicopter needed smaller corrections when he inevitably overshot his intended hover location.

"Good. Good. Nice, easy inputs. You're getting much better, Spike." Victoria sounded like a proud mother.

"Thanks, Boss." Juan had trouble sounding normal under the stress. He was still flexing all his muscles and sweating profusely.

The aircrewman said, "Easy right two…one…over the trap."

Juan lowered the collective down with his left hand and made rapid tiny adjustments with the cyclic in his right hand, doing his best to keep the helicopter over the same spot on the back of the destroyer as it rolled in the ocean. The aircraft came down from its five-foot hover at a steady rate and landed on the steel deck with a bouncing jolt. The heavy-duty wheel suspensions were built for the rough landings, Juan knew. He was learning that he needed to come straight down faster than he was comfortable with, lest he give the rolling ship enough time to slide him out of position.

"In the trap. Nice one, sir."

A wave of relief washed over Juan.

Over the radio came the words, "In the trap, beams coming closed. Trapped."

Caveman, the other junior pilot who was manning the LSO shack, was controlling the hydraulically operated metal contraption just beneath the aircraft. A foot-long metal probe protruded out of the bottom of his helicopter. Juan had just landed so that the probe would end up in the three-foot-by-three-foot metal rectangle on the flight deck. Then Caveman had flipped a switch that closed the beams, locking the probe in with its jagged metal teeth.

"Chocks and chains," Victoria called, making the proper hand signals as the enlisted men ran out on deck, securing the helicopter further. With the ship constantly rolling in the sea, a big enough swell could cause a rolling movement that would tip a helicopter right over, with catastrophic results—thus the need to heavily secure it whenever they were not actually in the process of taking off or landing.

And right now, they were conducting a crew swap.

"Good flight, Juan. Much improved from last month. You'll make HAC no problem."

"Don't jinx me, Boss."

She smiled as she began unstrapping. "I'm out." She unplugged the black communications cord that ran from the ceiling to her helmet.

Plug was coming in next. Juan would fly with him. It was a welcome change. While Juan enjoyed flying with his boss—he admired her as a pilot and an officer—she was a tough trainer. His flights with her were nonstop question-and-answer sessions. She was constantly trying to make him a better pilot and decision maker, throwing scenario after scenario at him to see how he would react.

Flying with Plug was quite different.

"Hey, fucker." Plug had just connected his headset. "You ready to play some movie quote trivia tonight?"

"Sure, I guess…" Juan smiled. "You mind if I pee first?"

Plug carefully got into the cockpit's right seat. "Sure, let me strap in." He fastened his harness and adjusted his seat from the Airboss's settings. "Man, Boss is tiny. How do they allow her to fly? She couldn't have passed the flight school medical exam. Probably wore lifts that day. Okay, I got controls. Go pee."

Juan unstrapped and walked out of the rotor arc and into the hangar. He removed his sweaty helmet and walked through the ship, weighed down by his heavy gear. He passed through the wardroom. There were a few people in there who had brought up plates from midrats.

"Hey, sir, did you get dinner?" the first-class petty officer in the wardroom's kitchen yelled to him.

"Not yet."

"You want me to put something in a box for you?"

"Sure, thanks. Appreciate that."

When Juan returned from the head, the petty officer had two white boxed dinners waiting for him. "There's metal forks and knives in there, so make sure you don't toss 'em."

"Hey, thanks, CS2."

"Anything for the guy who sank the submarine."

Juan glanced up at him, nodding, not knowing what to say to that. He left through the wardroom door and marched back along the ship's main passageway to the hangar, carefully holding the boxed dinners. After putting his helmet back on and walking out onto the dark flight deck, he entered the rotor arc and handed the food to the aircrewman in the back of the helicopter, who gave him a thumbs-up.

Juan opened up the left cockpit door, plugged the communication cord into his helmet, and strapped back into the bird.

"CS2 give you this, sir?" said AWR1 Fetternut.

"Yeah, why?" Juan said as he snapped down his night vision goggles and adjusted his gear.

"I was down in the mess with him earlier. You got a fan club now, you know."

Plug said, "Alright, let's talk after we get airborne. I don't want to piss off the Shoes for being on deck too long. Checklists." Shoes was the semi-insulting term that pilots sometimes used when refer-ring to members of the surface Navy. It had to do with the fact that traditionally, pilots wore brown shoes, and other naval officers wore black. Black Shoes, or *Shoes* for short.

The crew ran through their checks and contacted the ship to get takeoff clearance. Moments later, they were lifting off deck, sliding aft, and watching the ship slowly steam away from them.

"Nose coming left."

"Roger," said Juan. His visual scan was on the instruments now. Everything else around him was black. Even the green image through the night vision goggles was just a useless blur, with nothing to focus on.

"Pulling power. One…two…three positive rates of climb."

Juan could feel the nose dip slightly and carefully watched the radar altimeter, the barometric altimeter, and the vertical speed indicator as all three instruments showed that the aircraft was indeed climbing upward. When they were flying at night over water like this, almost everything they did was on instruments. There were simply too few visual stimuli.

"Radar altimeter on," Juan said, flicking the toggle switch.

"Roger," said Plug. "Leveling off at a thousand."

"Roger," said Juan.

"So, did Boss quiz you on your limits and emergency procedures?"

"Oh yeah," said Juan.

"She was merciless as always, sir," said AWR1 Fetternut.

Plug said, "Coming right to zero-four-five."

"Roger, zero-four-five."

"Okay, well, if Boss already took care of your training, let's just shoot the shit."

"Sounds good to me."

Juan knew that while Plug was trying to justify not asking Juan any questions, the truth was that Plug would much rather just chill out and have fun while they burned holes in the sky for a few hours. Every pilot was different. The way they flew usually fit their personality. Plug was carefree when he could be, and extremely detail-oriented and skillful when he had to be. Like the Airboss, he was a very talented pilot. Sometimes Juan wondered if he would ever get to their level. To some, it came naturally. Others had to work at it. Juan thought of himself as part of the latter group.

Plug said, "Okay, the game is 'would you rather.' Would you rather be twenty minutes early for every meeting for the rest of your life, or ten minutes late?"

Fetternut said, "Sir, you're already ten minutes late to everything."

"Okay, Fetternut, you've forfeited your turn. Spike?"

"No question. I'd rather be early. You can't be in the military without being early to everything. What's the saying? Fifteen minutes early, you're on time, on time, you're late, and late, you're better off not even showing up."

Plug said, "Okay, that one was easy. Would you rather be alone for the rest of your life or always surrounded by annoying people?"

Fetternut said, "How annoying?"

"Think of the most annoying girl you've ever dated."

"Okay. Hmm. I can handle it. I'd rather be around annoying people. Cuz if you were alone, you could never have sex. So really, that's a double whammy…"

"Spike?"

"Alone."

"Hey, sir, I have a radar contact at one-fife-fife for sixty. It's the only thing around."

Juan tapped a few keystrokes on his panel. "I just put in a fly-to, just follow the needle."

"Got it, coming right." The aircraft turned and leveled off on the new course. "Okay, would you rather have a horrible job for ten years and then be able to retire, or have your dream job but have to work forever?"

"Isn't that basically what the military proposition is?"

"Come on, don't say that. You don't love this?"

"Flying, yes. But being stuck on a boat with you guys…"

Laughter.

Juan said, "So, Fetternut, what were you saying about those guys in the mess deck?"

"Oh yeah. Sir, you got a fan club on the ship. They all know your name now. They're talking about you as the guy who killed the submarine. You're famous. You're like the guy who shot bin Laden."

Juan could see Plug glancing over at him, his eyes lit up by the green glow of the NVGs. Plug didn't say anything, but his expression was one of concern.

Juan hadn't felt good about what had happened. Watching movies and reading books about war was one thing, but actually pressing the button was another matter. Dropping a torpedo and seeing the white water of the exploding submarine rocketing up into the air. Knowing all those souls were gone. He had lost a lot of sleep since that day. He would do it again if he had to. But he hoped that he never would.

Plug turned back, looking out the windscreen, scanning back and forth through his goggles. "Fetternut, how far away is that radar contact?"

"We still got a little way to go, sir. It's over forty miles away."

"Okay. Let me think of another question…"

Juan said, "I got a joke. How about that instead?"

"Spike? A joke? Lord have mercy, are you feeling alright?"

Ignoring him, Juan began. "Okay, so there are a bunch of ISIS fighters in Iraq, and they're hiding in some mud hut. The leader says, 'Okay, guys, the Americans are closing in on us, and there are reports that the CIA might have even infiltrated our ranks. So, I tell you what we're going to do. We're going to double up the watch sections.'"

Plug said, "Sounds like this guy's a SWO…"

"'Two guys to a duty section instead of one. First up, Omar and Muhammad. Second watch, Rahim and Akmed. Third watch, Hamid and Bobby.'"

AWR1 Fetternut was laughing.

Juan looked over at Plug and could see him smiling underneath his NVGs. "Oh, I get it. Because Bobby was CIA. Funny." He let out a howl. "Alright, 2P, find me this boat. It's the only thing out here tonight."

Juan placed his hands on the control unit for the forward-looking infrared camera—the FLIR, as it was known. He pressed a few buttons and his display began to show the camera image.

The screen showed a green sea with a flat horizon and a few clouds. Juan used his thumb to turn the camera. "What's the bearing?"

"Should be about ten degrees right of where you're pointing it, sir."

"Okay. I think I see it."

A little white dot on the horizon of the screen was the only disruption to an otherwise symmetrical view.

Plug said, "How far from Mom are we?"

"Close to seventy miles from *Farragut*."

"Okay, let's check in with them. Let them know we might lose comms for a moment."

Juan checked his communications selector switch to make sure it was on the right frequency. Then he depressed the footswitch that allowed him to speak on the UHF radio. "Farragut control, Cutlass 471."

"471, Control."

"471 is investigating a surface contact seventy miles to your north. We might lose comms for a moment, but we should be back up in five mikes."

"Copy, 471."

Plug said, "Coming down to two hundred feet."

"Roger, leaving one thousand for two hundred."

"One thousand for two hundred."

Juan's eyes bounced from location to location as he scanned his various sources of information. He looked outside through his night vision goggles to see if there were any other air or surface contacts in the area. Nothing. Then he checked his instruments to monitor Plug's descent to two hundred feet over the water. It was crucial that everyone in the aircraft checked this. While it was a simple maneuver, being so low to the ocean could be deadly if the pilot became distracted and continued descending through his altitude. He checked the radar altimeter, the barometric altimeter, and the VSI.

Then, as they got close to their level-off altitude, he said, "Fifty feet prior."

"Roger." The altitude stopped on 200. "Two hundred feet, radalt on."

"Roger, two hundred feet." Juan glanced at the radar altimeter, the autopilot feature that served as the most precise altitude hold.

"Looks like a trawler or something."

"Yup," Plug said. "I'm going to circle it on the right."

"Roger."

Juan could feel them banking left and then coming back over to the right, making a wide arc around the boat. He manipulated the FLIR to keep the camera focused and locked on to the boat the entire time.

"What do you think? Fishing boat or drug trafficker?"

"We got any intel about drug boats out here?"

"No."

"I don't see anybody moving on deck."

"Me neither. Can you get a name?"

"Nah. Can't see it on her. Too dark."

"She doesn't look like she's making way."

Fetternut said, "Yeah, I show her at one knot on radar, sir. So she might actually be dead in the water."

Juan zoomed in and focused the camera. "Is that someone laying down on the back of the ship?"

Plug snuck a look at the screen underneath his goggles. "Looks like it. He moving?"

"No."

"He alive?"

"I don't know. This is creepy."

"Let's come up and show Mom."

"Roger."

"Coming up to two grand."

"Roger, two thousand feet."

Juan felt a flutter in his stomach and watched the numbers on his instrument panel rapidly begin rising as Plug pulled power and climbed. Now that they were higher, it would be easier to establish a communications link with their faraway destroyer.

"Farragut control, 471. We have video on the surface contact out here. Looks like a fishing boat, a trawler. But she's not making way, and we have one...uh, person...laying on the back of the deck. They aren't moving."

The *Farragut*'s air controller said, "Roger, 471, we're getting it on link now."

"Okay, they want us to do anything?"

"Stand by."

Juan said, "I mean, we're quite a ways from land. Kind of weird for a ship to just be hanging out around here, right?" The fishing arms weren't down, either.

Fetternut said, "They didn't look like they was fishing."

The *Farragut*'s air controller said, "We have video and took some screenshots. We're passing it up the chain to see if they want us to go check it out."

"Roger, control. We'll need to head back soon if we're going to make our landing time. Let us know if you want us to loiter here or not."

"Stand by." After a minute, he said, "Negative. TAO says to come back and land on time."

"Roger."

Juan said, "Don't they care about this? I mean, what if that's a dead body down there?"

"If it is," Plug said, "it isn't going anywhere."

They flew back to the ship without incident. During the debrief for the flight, Juan checked with the folks on watch in the combat information center. They had been told to investigate the fishing ship in the morning.

* * *

Victoria had been up since dawn. She had worked out while her men were conducting the freshwater wash-down of the helicopter on the flight deck. Thick sponges and a light soap to get all the salt off. It helped prevent corrosion. The deck was wet with small pockets of soap bubbles every few feet.

She sipped coffee from a metal thermos. "Morning, Senior."

"Morning, ma'am."

"You guys gonna tear it apart today?"

"Yup. We'll start the phase maintenance inspection today. And because I know you're gonna ask, we hope to be done in seven days or so, as long as you guys can get the rotor turns done quick."

Victoria smiled at the seasoned senior enlisted. "Don't worry, your esteemed maintenance officer has already been lowering my expectations on the timing."

The senior chief smiled. "He's learning." He placed his hands on his hips and yelled something at one of the enlisted men washing the helicopter. Then he said, "You hear any rumors about them giving us another bird from *Ford*?"

"I inquired about it. But I don't think it's gonna happen. *Ford*'s compliment of helicopters is light as it is. They were in a rush to get out here, apparently."

He nodded. "Hmm. What about any rumors on when we might be headed back? It'll be six months tomorrow."

"I know." She sighed. "Everyone's spooked right now, though. No one wants to lower our Navy presence in the area. I mean, can you believe that we're out here right now, after taking hits?"

"Ma'am, I don't know what to believe anymore. This is all crazy. I heard that the Chinese ships were pulling into Panama City."

"Oh, so *you*'re the one that Plug got it from."

"Chief's mess knows all, Boss." The seasoned Navy veteran nodded, a wide grin on his face.

A whistle went off through the ship's 1MC speaker system, signifying that it was 7 a.m. Morning meal had started. "Alright, that's my cue."

"You have yourself one of them good ones, Boss."

"You too, Senior. And stop telling the MO your secret rumors."

The senior chief laughed as Victoria made her way through the starboard hangar. She walked along the busy passageway, the smell of a mass-produced breakfast wafting through the air from belowdecks. The officers and crew were rushing through the passageway. Some had wet hair, just out of the shower. Some had red eyes, just off the midnight-watch rotation. Everything they did was on the clock. They hurried to eat, hurried to prep for their morning meetings, and hurried to go on watch. The packed schedule made the time go by faster. The repetition sharpened their skills.

Victoria loved the Navy. She was meant for this life, she knew. Her father, and his father before him, had served in America's Navy.

She had never *expected* to become what she now was—a battle-tested officer on a ship at sea. But as she saw the look of pride in the eyes of the men and women who passed her, she was so glad that she had chosen this path.

She opened and stepped through a door with a blue sign that read, "Officer's Country: Enter on Official Business Only." She remembered the first time she had seen that sign, many years ago as a US Naval Academy midshipman, on a destroyer as a part of her summer training. She had stood outside the door for five minutes, too afraid to open it without permission. "O-country," as it was known, was the part of the ship where the officers' quarters and the wardroom were located. When an ensign had finally seen her, paralyzed with fear, he'd chuckled and explained to her that she was part of the club. The sign was more tradition than actual warning. And besides, no one paid any attention to it except for brand-new seamen and midshipmen.

Victoria opened the wardroom door and stepped in for breakfast. She looked around the filled room and met the eyes of the ship's new captain, Commander James Boyle. She liked him so far. But while she respected the memory of the recently deceased previous ship captain, it didn't take much for an upgrade. And there was always a feeling-out period as you began working with someone new. Time would tell what Commander Boyle would really be like to work with.

"Permission to join the mess, Captain?"

"Have a seat, Airboss. Good morning." The half dozen conversations at the wardroom tables quieted a few decibels whenever the captain spoke.

"Good morning, sir," she replied.

"They getting ready for the phase maintenance on the bird?"

"Yes, sir, I was just back there in the hangar. They're set to begin taking her apart this morning."

There was a single long table in the destroyer's wardroom. A smaller table with only a few seats stood off to the side. This was the room where the officers ate, and where many meetings were held.

"Coffee, ma'am?" asked the petty officer over her shoulder as he laid out a clean set of silverware and a napkin.

"No, thanks. Just a water, please."

He placed a glass of ice water in front of her. "What would you like, ma'am?" The sailor had a pencil and paper in his hand.

"Could I get scrambled eggs and toast?"

"Sure. Any sausage? We have sausage this morning."

"No, thank you. Got any fruit?"

"Apples are still good."

"Oranges?"

"No, ma'am. We ran out yesterday. Should get more the next resupply."

"No problem. Thank you, CS2."

The petty officer nodded and went over to the window on the far bulkhead, where another enlisted man was waiting to take the order from him. They ran it like a high-speed diner. Fast, polite service. Get everyone fueled up quick so that they could get back to work. There were still remnants of long-held naval traditions in modern wardrooms. The silverware was a little fancier than in the enlisted mess downstairs, and the tablecloths were nicer. Officers were expected to eat here for most of their meals. Proper etiquette rules were followed. They were expected to ask the captain or the highest-ranking person in the wardroom permission to join and leave the mess. The enlisted mess a deck below was buffet-style. Hundreds of sailors flowing through the line every meal. Nonstop cooking and cleaning. The thick smell of grease in the air at all times. But everyone on board ate the same food—officers and enlisted.

Victoria made small talk with the captain and the other officers at the table. None of her pilots were there yet. Normally they crawled in five minutes before the meal hour ended, their hair embarrassingly disheveled, lines on their faces from just rolling out of their racks.

They didn't disappoint this morning.

First came Plug, then Juan, then Caveman. All in wrinkled green flight suits. Plug's hair was sticking up, and he needed a shave.

Victoria would have to talk to him about that later. She didn't want to piss off the new captain. First impressions were important, and he'd already screwed the pooch on that. Her pilots grabbed boxes of cereal and any of the leftovers that the CSs would provide. They gave them plates of sausage, toast, and hard-boiled eggs. If there was one group on board the ship that her aviators kept up a good relationship with, it was the cooks.

It was a bit of an odd relationship between Victoria and Captain Boyle. She had been the acting commanding officer of the USS *Farragut* for almost a week before he had arrived. She had taken command after the previous captain and XO had been killed in combat. While she would have given anything to bring them back, she had to admit that the thrill of command was everything she had been told about by her father. Admiral Manning had held many commands in his career. And even though he was a naval flight officer, his favorite job had actually been commanding ships. He had been the commanding officer of two deep draft vessels, including once as an aircraft carrier captain.

Victoria now understood why he had said that. To hold that awesome power and responsibility was unlike anything else in the world. The commanding officer of a ship at sea was all at once a town mayor, county sheriff, restaurant owner, and military commander. Command was the ultimate goal and the ultimate high of many military officers.

The wardroom began clearing out. The captain excused himself. The place settings were being removed and Victoria's pilots rushed to finish, shoveling food and gulping down their glasses of juice.

"You gentlemen plan on staying for OPS Intel?"

"Yes, Boss."

"Good. Next time, please make sure you shave before showing up in front of the captain, okay?"

Plug gave a sheepish grin. "Sorry, Boss."

The petty officer who was running the wardroom said, "Ma'am, gentlemen, would you mind getting up so we can clear off the table before OPS Intel?"

"Of course. Sorry, CS2."

"Oh, it's no problem, ma'am. I just see the ensign over there in the corner waiting to set up his PowerPoint presentation."

The communications officer waved. He was holding a laptop and a bundle of cables, each with a bright red sticker on them that read "Classification: SECRET." The pilots each went to their staterooms while the room was cleaned up. Victoria washed out her thermos and left it by her sink. She grabbed her notebook and walked back into the wardroom. The seats had been arranged in rows now, and dozens of people had entered the room. Many stood, swaying with the ship's rolls, not wanting to take the seat of someone who might be of higher rank.

At exactly 8:15 a.m., the captain and XO walked in.

"Attention on deck," one of the senior chiefs called out.

Most were already standing at attention when they saw him enter. A few tightened up. Plug got up from his seat in the corner, standing at attention a little too slowly for Victoria's taste.

"At ease," replied the captain. Those with seats sat down. All of the off-duty department heads and many of the senior enlisted were present.

"What have you got for us, COMMO?"

"Sir, this is the morning OPS Intel brief. First, OS2 will give the weather."

"Captain, good morning. The weather is predicted to be in the midseventies and partly cloudy for most of the week. A sea state of two until Friday, when a low-pressure front is moving into the area and we'll have a sea state of three, and some rain is possible."

"Thank you, OS2."

The brief went over the schedules for the next few days. Victoria looked at the screen and took note of when the RAS was. The replenishment at sea would bring them their much-needed parts and supplies. With her only helicopter going into a maintenance period, there was always a chance that some unknown problem would pop up. And the only way to solve it might be with a helicopter part that could be picked up on that RAS.

The operations officer spoke next. His slide showed a map of the Eastern Pacific theater. There were dozens of blue ships with three-letter name identifiers next to them scattered throughout the area.

Three red ship icons were near Panama City, with an arrow pointing towards the port location.

"Sir, Third Fleet has informed us that the Chinese ships will be in port, Panama, tomorrow."

Grumbles from the crew. The captain didn't say anything. Perhaps he would have told the crew to quiet down under different circumstances. But he hadn't been aboard when the Chinese had attacked them, killing some of their shipmates, so he probably was giving the crew a longer leash.

"The Bush Strike Group is now conducting a training exercise off San Diego."

"This early?"

"Yes, sir. They've moved up her deployment schedule by six months. And they've moved around some of the escort destroyer and cruiser maintenance schedules to increase the size of her strike group. Also, sir, the VP squadron is sending more P-8s down to El Salvador to work with us here."

Victoria had the phrase "too little, too late" in her head. The battle was over. *Or was it?*

Was the Pacific Fleet ramping up its operational tempo in response to recent Chinese aggression? Or in preparation for more? She shook off the thought. Three wounded Chinese warships were headed into Panama City. That was not where they would go if further hostilities were on the horizon.

The captain said, "Okay. Any word on where they want us after this week?"

"No, sir, but the guys at Desron are breathing down my neck about it. They want us home for our next maintenance inspection."

"Which Desron?"

"Not the one on the carrier, sir. The one in Mayport."

"They're actually called Surfron now," someone said.

"What the hell is a Surfron?" someone else said, and a few people laughed.

"The staffer who's giving you trouble at Surfron can go to hell," the captain said. "We've got more important things to worry about out here. This is a combat-ready warship. Our maintenance inspection will happen when it happens."

Pleased nods from the crew. The captain would win them over with that attitude. It made it appear as though he was sticking up for the crew in the face of "the man."

The captain looked around and held up his hands. "Well, now, don't tell anyone I told Surfron to go to hell or anything. He's still my boss when we get back to Mayport."

A few chuckles.

The captain pointed at the map on the display screen. "The Navy wants us here, patrolling the Eastern Pacific. An aggressor nation just launched an attack on us. So, this is where we should be. Our reason for being isn't so that we can pass maintenance inspections. We do maintenance and training so that we can effectively defend our country."

"Yes, sir," said OPS.

"That being said, if they do extend us here, let's look at the impact that will have on personnel, training, and maintenance. CHENG, OPS, please identify any risks you see and present your findings to the XO."

"Yes, sir," the two officers echoed. The XO nodded, acknowledging the request. Like the captain, he was also a new arrival.

The captain said, "Alright, now what about this mystery boat that the helo crew found last night?"

"Sir, it's about fifteen miles away now. Our VBSS team is standing by in case we need to go over there."

The captain nodded his approval. "Good. Anything from Third Fleet?"

"We don't yet have permission to conduct a security inspection, sir. I think they have their hands full with the Chinese stuff and they've been slow to get back to our requests. But we did see a message about some sort of signals intelligence in this area. Supposedly the office of naval intelligence is involved now. They want us to report on anything out of the ordinary."

"Well, I would say our mystery boat counts."

"Yes, sir."

"Alright, please ask again. I want permission to board this sucker by the time we get there."

They went through a few more slides. Meeting schedules, training for the week, and the joke of the day, something that the communications officer—who was also the Bull Ensign—had put together. The Bull Ensign was the most senior of the ensigns. As ensigns were the lowest-ranking officers, it wasn't much of a distinction. But it was a position of humor and tradition beloved by wardrooms around the world. His gold collar devices were oversized, and he was expected to mentor his junior peers.

"Alright, Bull Ensign, what have you got for us?"

"Sir, I just want to say that this joke excludes the Airboss."

The pilots all perked up at that. Plug was smiling. "Bring it, COMMO."

The ensign went red.

The captain said, "Let's go, COMMO."

"Sir, what's the difference between a pilot and their helicopter, sir?"

"What?"

"The helicopter stops whining when you shut down the engines."

Laughter and several "Oh's!" throughout the wardroom.

The Airboss kept a straight face. "COMMO, please see me for counseling later, even if you did exclude me from the punchline."

The captain stifled a laugh and stood to leave.

"Attention on deck," said someone from the back of the room.

The captain left, and the officers and crew of the USS *Farragut* began their day. As everyone was leaving, Victoria tapped Plug on the shoulder. "Got a minute?"

"Sure, what's up, Boss?"

"Let's get coffee."

The junior pilots, eavesdropping as always, echoed comments of "Uht-oh" and the like. Victoria headed over to the far end of the now-empty wardroom, taking an empty mug. She filled it up with a thick black version of coffee that she was pretty sure could only be served aboard Navy ships and administered to animals in scientific experiments—outside the US, of course.

Plug filled up an obligatory cup and sat at the cleared table, waterproof blue fitted cover on top with the ship's emblem in the center.

"What's wrong?" Plug turned his head slightly as he said it and had the tone of "What did I do now?"

"Nothing. Well—this is going to be a difficult conversation."

"For who?"

"Mostly for you." She put on a serious face. "You weren't chosen to be a RAG instructor." The Replacement Air Group was technically a retired term. The acronym "RAG" was deemed less politically correct as more and more women filled the ranks of naval aviation. The unit that Plug had applied for was now known as the FRS—the Fleet Replacement Squadron. But everyone still called it the RAG. Old habits died hard.

The RAG was the squadron that trained young nuggets fresh out of flight school on how to fly their fleet aircraft—in this case, the MH-60R Seahawk helicopter. Only the top pilots from each fleet squadron were selected for this assignment, which was seen as the first step along the "golden path" towards someday becoming a commanding officer.

Victoria watched his face closely. This was a job that he'd really wanted, and he would be very disappointed. The good thing about Plug was that he was what she liked to call emotionally expedient—he went through all five stages of grief at once.

He let out a big sigh. "Fuck."

"Yeah. Sorry, man," she said.

He looked back up at his boss. "You weren't a RAG instructor, right?"

"That's correct. I was an HT instructor." The HTs were the squadrons in flight school where student naval aviators learned to fly helicopters for the first time and earned their wings of gold. HT was the Navy designator for Helicopter Training Squadron.

Plug sipped some of the black coffee in his mug and tried to make a joke. "And you've already been a CO."

Victoria smiled. "Technically. Although I was relieved after a week, so..." They were referring to her brief stint as CO of the destroyer after the former captain and XO were both killed in a missile strike. She grew more serious. "Listen, I checked, and this slate of instructor pilots was already selected for the HTs."

His face fell in a second defeat in as many minutes. "Okay, Boss. What's next?"

"We'll keep looking. I've got a draft email typed up that I'll send to the skipper. We have a few other options lined up. But if you really want to get one of those instructor pilot slots, you may want to consider extending in the squadron, or taking a different set of orders for a short period of time."

Plug shook his head. "Dammit. Okay. Thanks for letting me know. Just tell me what I need to do."

"Just keep worrying about your mission out here for now. And keep having a good attitude. We'll figure something out for your orders."

* * *

A few minutes later, Victoria stood on the bridge wing next to the captain and the officer of the deck. The captain and OOD were looking at the fishing boat through binoculars.

"Ti-bu-ron Panama." The OOD turned to the captain. "What's *tiburon* mean? Is that Greek mythology or something?"

The petty officer next to him said, "Uh, sir, it's Spanish for shark."

"Ah. Thanks."

The captain said, "The helicopter crew said that they saw someone laying out on the deck last night. I don't see anyone. At all."

Victoria said, "It's been about eight hours since they overflew it. Maybe they're down below?"

The captain handed her his binoculars. Plug's instincts had been correct. Something was off about this boat. About one hundred miles from shore. No personnel on deck. Dead in the water. Looked to be about sixty feet long.

The voice of the TAO came over the radio buckled to the captain's uniform. "She's registered in Panama City, sir. We just looked it up."

He unclipped his handset. "Understood, thanks. Tell the VBSS team to conduct a safety inspection."

"Roger, sir."

The captain looked at Victoria. "Your helicopter already taken apart?"

"They've probably started that process, yes, sir. Sorry about that. If I'd known that we might be doing this today, I would have tried to hold off the maintenance for another day."

"Don't worry about it, Airboss." He began walking into the bridge. "Come on. Let's go to combat and start prodding Third Fleet to let us do our jobs."

* * *

Ensign Adam Kidd, like everyone on board a Navy ship, had several duties. His primary job was to be the USS *Farragut*'s communications officer. So just about everyone on board called him COMMO. But one of his collateral assignments was as a Visit Board Search and Seizure team leader. The VBSS team was essentially the US Navy's shipboard version of a SWAT team. This role was his favorite part of being in the Navy.

Ensign Kidd looked over his team. They were decked out in black tactical gear, snuggly fitted over their uniforms. Black Kevlar chest protectors and helmets. Thin waterproof communications headsets and protective eyewear. They carried a mix of M-4 carbines and M-9 handguns.

One by one, all seven of them climbed down the rope ladder extending from the USS *Farragut*'s boat deck down to the rigid-hull inflatable boat below. The RHIB was tied to the destroyer, its engine rumbling, the two personnel who were part of the boat team already on board.

"Careful. Watch out," the driver of the RHIB called out as his small vessel heaved in the ocean, the rope ladder swaying. Within two minutes, all members of the VBSS team were being driven towards the fishing trawler, pitching and rolling over the deep blue ocean. White splashes of salt water whipped in their faces. A small American flag waved on the aft end of the RHIB.

"We already got permission to board?"

"Yes, sir. Combat just confirmed." The OS1—Operations Specialist First Class—was the most experienced member of his team.

"Any reply from the fishing vessel yet?"

"No, sir. Nobody over there is answering."

All eyes were ahead as they clutched their weapons and held on to the RHIB. They sat on the inflatable outer rim of the watercraft, and their black helmets bounced up and down as it traversed the waves.

The six men and one woman on Ensign Kidd's VBSS team were well trained. They had done two of these on their deployment already—although the other times had been to inspect suspected narcotics traffickers. While this boat might very well be a smuggler mothership, the fact that no one was aboard or responding was very odd. Still, he was confident that his team could handle it. Many of his men had been on multiple deployments and conducted boardings around the world for piracy and security inspections. Their training and capabilities weren't anything close to Navy SEALs or other special operations units, but the VBSS teams were typically made up of some of the best sailors on board Navy ships. And they took their job seriously.

As soon as the RHIB made contact with the *Tiburon Panama*, the team rushed onto the deck, weapons pointed outward. The vessel wasn't very large.

It didn't take them long to find the bloodstains...or the body.

"Sir, come check this out!"

Kidd headed forward into the small bridge.

"Guy doesn't have a pulse. He's cold. But the bloodstains look like he's crawled all over the ship. Must have been looking for something."

COMMO nodded and reached for his radio. "Captain, this is Ensign Kidd, sir."

The radio blared, "Go ahead, Kidd. What's your status?"

"Sir...there's one dead body on board. But there are bloodstains on the main deck and in the berthing area. It's pretty bad."

* * *

The Coast Guard cutter *James* arrived later that day. She had been on patrol only fifty miles to the north when the USS *Farragut*'s VBSS team was conducting their boarding. While the *James*'s main mission was counternarcotics focused, she was one of the newer Legend-class national security cutters that the US Coast Guard had in service. They were larger and more capable than their predecessors and allowed the Coast Guard to effectively perform a wider variety of national defense–related missions.

A Coast Guard investigative team had joined the Navy's VBSS team on board the smuggler boat. The Coast Guard lieutenant had spent decades on these types of missions. He was speaking to both his captain and the captain of the USS *Farragut* over his radio.

"Looks like a mothership alright. Empty fuel drums, guns belowdecks. We just did some tests and there are traces of multiple chemicals here that indicate narcotics trafficking. But something definitely went down here. Pretty strange, really. We don't normally see this type of thing way out in the ocean. If it was a rival smuggling operation, I would expect them to fight it out on shore. Either way, we think there were five or six people killed here. We've collected seventy-four rounds of ammunition so far and we're just getting started. We'll send that back to the lab once we get into shore."

The CO of the Coast Guard cutter replied, "What about the dead body?"

"Sir, it looks like that person was part of the crew of this mothership. We think he was trying to hide in a small storage locker. There were bullet holes in the locker. The person must have been shot while hiding in there, but then made his way out when the attackers were gone. Then he just bled out. My guess is the other bodies were dumped overboard. Probably floating around here somewhere if the sharks haven't already gotten to 'em."

Commander Boyle said, "Alright. Thanks for checking this out, gentlemen. I assume you've got it from here? We were just informed that we have a rendezvous with the aircraft carrier *Ford* that we have to make."

"We've got it from here, Captain," replied the captain of the Coast Guard cutter.

Commander Boyle recalled his VBSS team to the *Farragut*. Within the hour, the destroyer was sailing away. The Coast Guard cutter *James* ended up towing the narcotics mothership back to Panama City. From there, special investigation teams would comb it for clues and pass on the intelligence to various international agencies.

It would be several days before forensic experts matched some of the spent rounds to Chinese military weapons.

5

General Chen threw his cover across the room with such velocity that it slammed into an unstable bookshelf, swaying it and knocking several volumes onto the floor. The noise was sufficient to cause his secretary to open the door and check on him. Through the small sliver that she dared to create, she could see that the general was quite upset, but physically unharmed. She quietly reclosed the door.

Chen knew that three members of this staff would be out there in the waiting area. The general's mood was the chief indicator of the quality of life of his staffers. General Chen had fifty-six staff members in all, but he only spoke to the most senior officers among them. The others were beneath him. But for those staffers who had daily contact with him, death would be a welcome comfort, providing a quick end to the general's daily verbal onslaught.

The general knew that he had a certain reputation among his staff officers, but he didn't care. They were tools for him to use. A good day for them was when the general sent them on a distant errand, usually to investigate the status of one of his units.

Today was not a good day.

Cheng Jinshan and Admiral Song had been arrested over a week ago. To the general's knowledge, no one in the president's circle had been aware that he too had been assisting Jinshan. But now he had been told that two Central Committee members were asking about him. Their staffs had contacted his own, asking for information on his schedule.

What if they were scheduling an inquiry? Given his high rank, they would want to be sure of his involvement before leveling any charges.

General Chen had *told* Jinshan that things were moving too fast. China was a massive country, and massive organizations didn't move with lightning speed. But Jinshan was notoriously persistent. He'd demanded that the Chinese military be ready for war by spring. How was that supposed to happen given the current presidential leadership? When was Jinshan planning on installing a puppet? If the coup was unsuccessful, any one of them could be rounded up and shot for treason. And now they were in a precarious position…

For the last fifteen to twenty years, the general had been of such high rank that he had grown used to unwavering support of his every idea. His belief that he was supremely intelligent and omnipotent was reinforced by subordinates that quivered at the thought of opposing him. He ruled with an iron fist. Any subordinate that voiced an opinion of dissent was sprayed with a verbal flame that left little doubt as to how to behave in the future. These years of royal treatment had served to reinforce the general's belief in himself.

Disappointment could be devastating to his psyche. His response was usually disbelief and a therapeutic lashing out at his favorite of targets—the staff.

Where were they? Did they expect him to come get *them*? *Fine.* He stomped over to his door and swung it open violently, hitting the wall and causing the secretary to jump in her seat for the second time in as many minutes. The general glared at his men.

"Well?" His voice boomed. "Get in here!"

They scurried in like scared dogs. Then the general slammed the door behind them, marching around his large wooden desk and collapsing in his chair. His staff remained standing. They were senior officers themselves, but the general's treatment of them was indicative of their place in his eyes. They were the lowest of cretins. They would stand because they were subservient to him. He would sit because he was their king.

"Well? What do you have to say for yourself, Mr. Li?"

Colonel Li, the general's chief of staff for the last two years, did not know *what* to say. The general was worried about being taken down with Jinshan and Admiral Song. The senior staff officers knew of Jinshan's plans. They had to know. It was the senior staff that did all of the work. For them, it was a risky proposition, being loyal to General Chen. That loyalty was a one-way street. But he was quite vindictive, if crossed, and the Chinese government wasn't known for its surplus of whistle-blowers. The last staff officer who had tried to lodge a complaint against General Chen had ended up getting demoted on the spot. Then he had been shipped off to the Russian border, never to be seen again.

Li could either attempt to show that he had nothing to do with today's cause of pain, or take responsibility for it himself. Either way, the staff would take a browbeating. The general was in one of his moods.

Li began, "Sir, I sincerely apologize that we have not supported you well enough. I will do everything I can to rectify…"

The general held up his hand. His face was contorted in disgust. "Li, do you know what this is? Failure. Each of you has failed me. Once, just *once*, I would like the support of my staff. But instead, this occurs. *Failure*. If I am accused of anything…"—he couldn't even utter the word *criminal*—"then I owe it all to you."

The three men, sweating and swaying in their stance, stood silently and tried not to make eye contact with their boss. There was no reasonable predictor for when the general would be in one of his moods. Each time the staff approached him, it was like sticking their heads into the mouth of a lion to determine whether it was hungry or not.

"Failure," the general muttered quietly. He was shaking his head now. "How many times did I say that we needed to keep ourselves separate from Admiral Song's operations?"

The staff nodded in agreement.

"Just get out."

The three staffers did not need to hear that twice. They walked in a line to the exit, closing the door behind them.

General Chen put his face in his hands. A dark cloud formed over him. He was sixty-two years old. He had spent over forty years in the Chinese military, and twenty as a flag officer. None of this was his fault. His talent and leadership went criminally underappreciated. Those bastard politicians didn't understand what it was to be a warrior like him.

He was confronted with his own mortality for the first time that he could remember. Over the years, each promotion had been another step on the ladder towards the highest title in the Chinese military. He was so close to it now. Jinshan had made promises.

But those would not come to fruition now.

General Chen thought about what might come next. If the politicians who were investigating him found him guilty of conspiracy, he could face imprisonment or even death. Even if they couldn't prove anything, he would likely suffer a reduced stature in retirement.

The general looked at a picture on his wall. In it, he stood in front of a military parade in Beijing as tens of thousands of troops and tanks went by. The Chinese president was next to him.

He shook his head. It couldn't end this way…

Jinshan had promised him title and power—supreme commander of the Asian theater. General Chen would take command of all five PLA branches during the war. His name would go down in history as the greatest battlefield commander in all of China. Perhaps in all the world.

The intercom on his desk interrupted his thoughts.

"Sir, I'm very sorry, but you have a call from Qincheng."

"Qincheng?"

"Yes, General. From the prison, sir." *What is this?* "Fine," he barked, pressing the flashing light on his phone and picking up the receiver.

"This is General Chen, who is this?"

"Hello, General. This is Cheng Jinshan. I hope you are well."

* * *

A few hours later, General Jin Chen sat behind his office desk, flipping through a brief on the American military's Pacific deployment schedule. He adjusted his glasses as he read. His three staff members were back in front of his desk, relieved at their sudden change in fortune.

"When do we leave?" he asked his chief of staff. Chen did not look up as he spoke.

"Your car is waiting, sir. The drive is only ten minutes, but the politicians will be arriving soon. Now would be a good time to go," replied the chief of staff, Colonel Li.

The general nodded and looked up at the colonel. "What are you hearing from your friends to the West?" He was referring to the other chiefs of staff that Colonel Li had spoken to at the behest of his superior.

"It is as Mr. Jinshan said, General. The wheels are still turning. And the politicians' staffers who inquired about your schedule were doing it to ensure that you would be at this meeting."

General Chen shook his head and smiled. A rare expression for him. "Cheng Jinshan is a remarkable man. Even in prison, he is in control."

"Where will the meeting be?"

"Mr. Jinshan will join you and the politicians in the warden's office."

"And Song?"

"Admiral Song will also be present."

Chen nodded. "Excellent. I must say that I am relieved. But I am glad to see this positive turn of events."

Colonel Li gestured with his arm. "Sir, if you are ready, it would be good for us to depart now."

The general handed the folder to one of his aides as he marched out the door to a black sedan. Three escort vehicles were in trail, two of which were part of a Chinese special operations security detail assigned directly to the general. The security men held light machine guns with slings over their shoulders. Their eyes took in everything.

The other escorts carried small briefcases with secure laptops inside. They had access to any information the general might need during the brief.

The general's motorcade stopped outside the gate of Qincheng Prison. A gate guard began to check identifications and then spotted the general. He gave a crisp salute and motioned them to head in. The cars passed under the traditional Chinese arch known as a *paifang*. Then they parked in the courtyard, where several more military guards were waiting.

Qincheng Prison had been built in the 1950s with the help of the Soviet Union. It was located in the Changping district of Beijing, an hour away from the city's center. The building was highly secretive, and the only prison that belonged to the Ministry of Public Security. Political prisoners, including those who had participated in the democratic protests in Tiananmen Square, had been imprisoned there. But more recently, Cheng Jinshan and the CCDI had used it as a place to send China's "purged" elite. It was cynically referred to in China as a "luxury" prison. Ironically, Qincheng Prison was where Cheng Jinshan himself had sent politicians he had deemed to be disloyal. The prison warden had been on the payroll for years. He was one of Jinshan's staunchest supporters.

Several weeks earlier, Cheng Jinshan and Admiral Song had been taken into custody by the PLA military police and sent to Qincheng Prison to await their sentencing.

But their stay hadn't been uncomfortable. They had been given number identification, just like all the other prisoners. Guards watched them. And they weren't allowed to leave the premises. But they *were* able to make phone calls whenever they pleased. And their rooms were filled with creature comforts. Jinshan had a bedroom, an office, and a couch. His personal secretary had even begun working there out of an office near the warden's own.

Admiral Song's staff, in disarray for the first day after his arrest, had quickly learned that they were expected to continue their operations on the island and update him several times a day by phone.

The wheels were indeed still turning.

"This way, General." The commander who was waiting for them

wore the uniform of the South Sea Fleet. One of Song's men; General Chen recognized him immediately.

Minutes later, the general sat upright in an elegant leather chair, sipping tea. Two politicians—the ones who had scared him half to death with their inquiries—sat across from him. They were engaged in a meaningless conversation about each other's families.

Cheng Jinshan walked through the door wearing the drab clothes of a prisoner. There were bags under his eyes, and his skin was tinted yellow. General Chen was reminded of the rumors that he was in bad health.

Jinshan looked at the guard who had escorted him in and waved the boy away. The guard followed orders and left the room. Probably the highest-ranking meeting ever to have occurred here. General Chen laughed to himself.

"Sorry I'm late, gentlemen. I hope I did not keep you waiting for too long."

The others dismissed the apology with nods.

"We are each glad to see that you are well," replied General Chen, unsmiling.

He had first met Jinshan years ago, when Chen had been a mere colonel. That unfortunate situation with his daughter. Chen still wondered about her sometimes. But he never asked. That was part of his deal with the devil.

Chen's wife had never been the same since then. Li had left with nothing more than a phone call for a goodbye. With Jinshan's help, Li had been chosen for a prestigious yet secretive program. The general and his wife wouldn't see their daughter for a long time, they were told. Perhaps never. But it was by far a better outcome than what could have been.

Li's actions at Junxun had been inexcusable. Criminal, even. She had mutilated another student in response to some sort of disagreement they'd had. Chen's conversation with his daughter had revealed it to be more than that, but the details didn't matter. It was her word against theirs, and no one would believe the girl. Besides, an opportunity had presented itself...

Cheng Jinshan had claimed to be a sort of *recruiter* for the

Ministry for State Security. He had explained that, from time to time, he could help wayward candidates to overcome their misfortunes—as long as it was in the best interests of the state, of course.

Li was an exceptional candidate, Jinshan had remarked to Chen. Her slate could be wiped clean. She would be placed in a special program. One where a person of her talents could pursue an honorable and noteworthy occupation. The sky was the limit for someone of her talent. She would be of great service to her country. And importantly, Jinshan would *surely* remember the sacrifice that *the colonel* had made as well. After all, he was up for promotion. And Jinshan was well connected to the PLA's flag officer corps.

A recruiter indeed. General Chen laughed at that claimed occupational title now. Chen knew that no mere recruiter for the Ministry of State Security would have been capable of what Jinshan had accomplished.

A part of General Chen was sad that Li had left them. But truth be told, he wasn't the fatherly type. The arrangement had been the best thing for all of them, he knew. In one fell swoop, Jinshan had allowed his daughter to retain her honor and ensured that Colonel Chen became General Chen.

Chen's career had quickly blossomed after that. He had *barely* made colonel before meeting Jinshan. That was his ceiling, he had been told by the PLA's human resources staff—idiots.

They hadn't recognized his talent. That had been four promotions and three decades ago. General Chen was now one of the five highest-ranking military members in all of China. It had taken a man of Cheng Jinshan's vision to see his talent and assist him up a promotional ladder fraught with politics.

Politics were Jinshan's strength, not General Chen's. Chen continued to receive visits from Jinshan throughout the years. They had quickly found that they shared two things in common: persistence and an unbridled ambition. Empires were formed by such men.

Now General Chen looked at the two politicians sitting across the room. The fact that they were here meant that they were loyal to Jinshan. He wouldn't have invited them otherwise.

But these politicians didn't yet know *why* they were here. Did they possess the ambition to become empire builders? Or would they wilt in the face of such a radical proposition?

Why did *they* think Jinshan had invited them? Perhaps they expected Jinshan to lobby for his release, or to have his sentence commuted? Both of the politicians were powerful members of the Politburo's inner circle—the Standing Committee. They had likely had to take many precautions in order to come here without being seen. General Chen knew that—like himself—they must expect that the return on this investment outweighed the risk.

The Standing Committee of the Central Political Bureau of the Communist Party of China was possibly the most powerful group of men in the world. Their *official* role in the Chinese government was to make decisions when the larger Politburo was out of session.

But their roles were so much bigger than that. The Standing Committee Politburo members were *always* the real decision makers. These seven men, which included the president of China as their senior member, were the key influencers of the entire government.

Cheng Jinshan's role as the head of the Central Commission for Discipline Inspection had allowed him to become very close to these political figures. While they might no longer feel indebted to him while he was in this faux prison, they still knew how useful he could be, if given the right tools. Jinshan had eliminated their enemies and helped them to consolidate power. What else was possible, given time?

Another thought occurred to the general. Everyone knew of how much research Cheng Jinshan did on his business ventures. Jinshan must have had *leverage* on all these politicians, should their relationship ever take a turn for the worse.

The general pondered all of this as he studied the faces of these men. How would they react? What *were* they expecting to hear? He doubted very much that they knew what Jinshan was about to propose.

War.

6

Lena's van drove onto the rural property in the early afternoon, tires crunching against the long gravel driveway. She had taken a few of the Chinese special operation team members with her. The ones who spoke the best English. They weren't trained for this, but she wouldn't be using them for much more than a little extra muscle, if need be.

An old pickup truck sat just outside an empty barn. Two of its tires were missing, concrete blocks in their place. A scattering of dirty children's toys throughout the yard. A giant black star adorned the house's siding. Rocking chairs under the front porch.

There were stacks on the grass next to the driveway. Lena read one of them:

REPENT SINNERS. THE FIRES OF HELL AWAIT ALL WHO TURN A BLIND EYE.

Lena knocked on the door, hearing someone stir inside. It was a Sunday, and the man had asked them not to come until their church service was over. His wife was inside, watching TV. For now.

He opened the door, looking suspiciously at the mix of Asian people at his door. Then recognition hit his eyes and a pleasant look formed on his face.

"Well, hello. Glad you all could make it."

"Thank you for having us," said Lena.

Natesh was playing the part of the cameraman. She had to keep an eye on him. His nervous attitude of late was concerning. She would have to speak to Jinshan about him when they arrived in China.

The American man said, "What program did you guys say you were with again? I was trying to look it up on the iPad, but I must have—"

"We're with the Chinese Christian Alliance. We don't have a specific TV program or channel. But our organization puts out documentaries like this one for TV stations to pick up. We aim to show viewers the persecution that Chinese Christians face. And we want to show like-minded Christians that there is something they can do. We want to bring stories like yours to as many people as possible, in hopes of helping Chinese Christians." She smiled at the man.

Charles Beulah let out a grunt in response. "Damn right. Them Chinese have been killing people in Tiennymen Square and persecuting people like us Christians for far too long. You see on the news what they did to them Navy ships? It's getting crazy. I mean, I can't believe we aren't at war after that. And now the president is saying we know it wasn't *really* China. Well, that's…" He looked over his shoulder. "That's just *bullshit* if you ask me. Pardon my French."

Lena nodded in agreement. "It really is incredible how the Chinese government has hurt our poor Christian brothers and sisters. But, Mr. Beulah, we're really excited for this opportunity to speak with you. We'd like to waste as little time as possible. I want to hear your story, and get it on camera. Where can we set up?"

"You mean, like, for the filming?"

She nodded and smiled, restraining her desire to strike him in response to his slow intellect. "Exactly."

"Well, we could go in the barn, I guess."

"The barn?"

"Don't worry, it's cleaned out. We just sold our three cows. There's plenty of space in there. Betsy don't want me doing this inside, bless her heart. She ain't been feeling well lately. Trying to quit smoking. She's on the patch. Makes her a bit irritable, if you ask me."

"Sure—no problem, Mr. Beulah. We can use the barn." Lena looked at Natesh. "Will that work for the lighting?"

"Sure, no problem," Natesh said, an uncomfortable look in his eyes.

"You can call me Chuck. Everybody does. Chuck Beulah, TV star." The man let out a laugh. Then his face darkened, remembering why the film crew had come today. "It really is a shame what them Chinese have done."

Then he narrowed his eyes, looking Lena over. "Now, excuse me for saying this, but you're Chinese, am I right? So…"

"Yes, but I'm one of the good ones. We're Christians, like you." She hoped he wouldn't test her Bible knowledge.

He made a face that implied her answer had just cleared everything up. "Ah, yup. Makes sense now."

Lena's "cameraman" took about five minutes to set up the lights, the background, and the folding chairs for their interview. She knew that both of the Chinese special forces soldiers were monitoring them from the back of the van. If she signaled them, they would be there in seconds, ready to clean up.

Natesh said, "Okay, we're ready." He gestured towards the folding chairs. After they both sat down, Lena said, "Are you okay? Remember, don't be nervous. Just speak slow and from your heart."

"Sure thing."

She looked at the camera. "Okay, I'm here today with Mr. Chuck Beulah. He's a strong Christian and a patriotic American. And he believes that people around the world should be able to practice their religion without fear of government interference. Isn't that right, Mr. Beulah?"

Lena had a few names on her list. Chuck Beulah was the first one they had tried. He started off a little shaky, but once he got going, Lena was sure that they would be able to use the footage. That was good. It would save her having to do extra work.

"Yes, ma'am. That sure is right. My church—and my country—are the most important things in my life. I believe in Jesus Christ and the holy God above. Now you look at what those Chinese are doing over there, and it's a mess. They're Communist baby-killers. And I think it's just awful."

Lena said, "And how do you feel when you hear stories of Christians not being allowed to go to the church that they want to go to? Not being free to practice their Christianity?"

"The Chinese government should allow all Chinese to practice Christianity. Only then, with the help of the Lord Jesus Christ, can China be saved."

"But what about the Chinese president? He has said that religion can be harmful. That only state-sponsored churches should be condoned."

"The Chinese president is flat wrong. He's against God and the people."

"Would you support removing the Chinese president?"

"Absolutely. If the Chinese president is against God, he should not be in charge of those people over there."

"Are you aware of the government-mandated abortions in Chinese law?"

The man's face contorted a little, as if searching which word he should grasp onto. But eventually he found it.

"I've heard about all the abortions in China. And that's what I am trying to make more people aware of. It's awful. They kill little baby girls just because they want a boy."

"What do you think should be done about that?"

"Someone should stop those guys! I mean, they're killing babies."

"What would you do if you saw someone trying to take one of those poor women and force her to abort her baby, against her will?"

"I would kill 'em. I think those Chinese communist bastards who do that deserve to die."

"Thank you for your passion, Mr. Beulah. Someone should put a stop to this madness. Tell us about what you do to help Chinese Christians and protect the persecuted."

Chuck scratched his beard. "I have a website where I blog about these things. And every second Tuesday of the month, me and a few guys from my church, we go up on the corner of Fifth and Main, in town. And we take a megaphone and signs and tell the whole wide world what we know about it. And I do believe that it makes a difference. Maybe not everyone, you know, but even if we can just illuminate a few people's brains—that's all I'm saying."

Lena said, "And what is your religion?"

"I'm a Baptist, ma'am."

"You are a Christian."

Chuck shot her an odd look. "Yes, ma'am, I am a Christian."

"And what do you think about the atheists in China who want to persecute Christians?"

"I think all atheists are going to burn in the eternal fires of hell. Especially those in China, cuz they're killing all them Christian babies. Atheism is one step away from worshiping Lucifer himself."

Lena had to be careful here. She wasn't sure if he'd say it exactly the way that she was hoping for. But editing would take care of the rest. "The president of China is reportedly an atheist. What do you think should be done to him?"

Chuck didn't disappoint.

"If the Chinese president is an atheist, then he is an enemy of all God-fearing Christians. He deserves to die, just like the rest of 'em Satan-worshippers. He's part of the problem then. Spreading atheism and killing babies. And now they're trying to sink our Navy ships and killing our brave armed forces. Damn those bastards to hell. Pardon my French."

Lena looked back at the cameraman, who nodded. "We're good."

Lena slapped her hands on her knees. "Okay. I think we're done here. Thank you for that, Chuck. You were *excellent*."

She turned back towards the van and signaled, and the doors opened. Two of the Chinese special forces soldiers walked toward them.

"Who are they?" Chuck asked, bewildered.

* * *

The charter aircraft flew from the US to Mexico, and then to China.

The Chinese special forces men had remained behind, meeting up with other operatives in Jinshan's network. They would be very busy in the coming months.

Dozens of special operations teams would be stationed throughout the United States. Training only at night, in secluded rural locations. Scouting out positions and targets. A gas pipeline. A highway intersection. A radar. So many undefended targets. It was only a matter of which ones to prioritize. But Jinshan had made that decision. The soldiers at the camp in Liaoning were training for their special targets even now.

But Lena didn't worry about that. She had other concerns. Lena sighed as she looked at Natesh, sitting in the seat next to her. Several rows forward of the drugged and sedated American. Chuck Beulah was a nutjob, as they say. But he would serve a purpose.

Lena had seen how upset Natesh had been after her men had killed Beulah's wife. But what was Lena supposed to do? The woman had *seen* them when she'd walked outside, her husband screaming at the sight of her men's machine guns. The wife had to be eliminated.

Natesh was a brilliant mind, but intelligence had no correlation with mental fortitude. Everyone had their limits, and Natesh was reaching his. It was time to see how bad he had gotten. From that, she would determine what her options were going forward.

Lena broached the subject delicately. But it was like placing a pin into the skin of a water balloon. Everything came tumbling out. Natesh was sobbing after five minutes. Lena tried to say all the right things. She even embraced him for a short moment. A robotic, empty hug. A check in the box, to let him know that she cared.

"You *have* to get me somewhere else. I can't keep doing this. I can't keep seeing all this violence. It's not what I wanted. It's not who I am."

Lena watched Natesh's chest heave. He wiped his red eyes and tried to regain his composure, realizing, no doubt, that he sounded like a pathetic child.

"Natesh, let me ask you something. Do you still believe that we're doing the right thing?"

He looked up at her, a flicker of instinctive worry in his eyes. Then, quick nods. Reassuring words. "Of course. Lena, I know that what Jinshan is trying to do is the right thing. I just…I'm not *made* for this type of work. Put me somewhere that I can help plan logistics and manage people. Give me a team and I'll optimize your workforce. But what we did to that man's wife…"

She fought the urge to roll her eyes. So they had placed two bullets in the forehead of Chuck Beulah's wife. *Get over it already.* Lena was glad to see that Lieutenant Lin's men could obey orders. When Lena had given the word, they had not hesitated to kill the woman. Then they had left the scene quickly.

Lin's team would need to be careful to keep a low profile on the American streets. Lena wasn't quite sure when Jinshan would call for the first wave of the strike on America. But until then, she must assume that American law enforcement investigations would proceed as normal. And she didn't want the FBI looking for groups of Chinese special forces who were killing the wives of crazed evangelicals.

Lena straightened her shirt. "Natesh, we all have to do things that we don't want to do sometimes."

"I understand."

"Natesh, I tell you what. Let me speak with some people. Maybe even to Mr. Jinshan. I know that there is a place for you, as long as you are still with us. Perhaps that place is a bit removed from the less tasteful aspects of our work. Hmm?"

He nodded. "Thank you, Lena. I'm sorry for asking, but thank you."

7

Cheng Jinshan began in a soft voice. "Gentlemen, I welcome you each here. We are about to embark on a great journey, and I hope that you will keep an open mind—and a strong conscience." The flat-screen monitor behind him showed a series of charts.

"This is classified data. Here you will find the most accurate economic indicators of our nation's likely future. You will *not* see these numbers in our newspapers or hear about them in your political meetings. These reports were commissioned anonymously by one of my private firms. There is no bias or fear of repercussion built into these numbers. These numbers, gentlemen, are as close to the truth as we can get. And our esteemed General Secretary of the Communist Party of China does not wish for you to see it."

Jinshan paused and saw both politicians frown as they processed the information. The numbers showed very sharp declines in Chinese production and GDP. The charts also showed very sharp rises in inflation and national debt.

China was changing. As money flowed into the country, a huge middle class was rising up in financial prosperity. This phenomenon detracted from what had once been China's greatest advantage—an endless source of cheap labor. With the increased economic prosperity came an increase in life expectancy. Government-subsidized benefits were getting more expensive.

The people needed more.

But once the poor switched from low-cost rice-based diets to more expensive poultry-based diets, they could not realistically be asked to switch back.

China was getting what it wanted—wealth—but with that came the problems of a wealthier nation. Cheng Jinshan had seen the writing on the wall. With an economic downturn and a populace that wanted a better life, the communist system was in danger. And unhappy citizens didn't bode well for the political lifespan of the Central Committee members here today.

A new slide came onto the screen. It showed American debt, and the percentage of ownership by each nation around the world. China was at the top of the list—by a lot.

This was not news to anyone. There was a very large trade imbalance with the US in China's favor. China was thus flush with cash and had been buying up US treasuries at a furious pace. It was the safest place to put their money when the markets got jittery. And it gave them a strategic edge in the economic cold war with the world's only other superpower.

"Our country has purchased an exceptional portion of US debt throughout the last decade. We have been saving up for a rainy day. Now if you look at this"—the slide changed to show US and European economic indicators and their projected impact on the value of American bonds over the next decade—"you can see that this rainy day is coming soon. In the free market system, the saying is 'buy low, sell high'—well, it may be time to sell."

The first politician spoke up. "Mr. Jinshan, we appreciate your information and advice, as always. These numbers are disturbing to say the least. This is something that our parliament must discuss and take action on soon. But I was under the impression that we were here to discuss your...*personal* situation."

"We will get to that, my friend."

The second politician said, "I notice that General Chen has joined us. I suspect that there is another reason for showing us these economic numbers. Perhaps this reason will explain why our esteemed military representative is present?"

"Yes, you are correct," Jinshan said, looking briefly towards Chen. The next slide showed a comparison of projected Chinese and American military capabilities every five years for the next three decades. Jinshan said, "Defense forecasts are hard to predict with certainty. National militaries are subject to national budgets. When we evaluate these military comparisons between the United States and China, we should do so with the economic forecasts of the previous slides fresh in our memories."

The first politician said, "Can you explain what you mean by that?"

Jinshan sipped his tea, and his face looked grave. "Over the past two decades, China has been strengthening its military might. We have been closing the military capability gap between us and America. We have built dozens of submarines, stealth jets, military satellites, and..."—he paused for effect—"most importantly, cyberweapons. We hold some advantages today. But I can't promise that we will hold those advantages in five years. And I can almost guarantee that with our budgetary constraints, we will begin to fall behind our foes in the strength and modernity of our conventional weapons systems."

A new picture appeared on the screen, illustrating how Internet-based computer attacks could be used against a foreign enemy.

Jinshan continued, "We have reached a new level of sophistication with our cyberweapons technology. The recent cyberattacks on the United States—what they have been referring to as the Blackout Attacks—have greatly reduced their satellite communications ability and completely destroyed their organic GPS satellite network. They are attempting to switch over to European-owned GPS networks, but that is no easy task."

"And the Americans are calling for our heads on stakes. For *one* of our heads in particular," commented one of the politicians.

Jinshan nodded. "I understand your frustration, given the current political climate. But that will be addressed. Please allow me to finish." There was a hardness to his tone.

The politician held out his hand. "My apologies. Please continue."

"We have the capability to strike American communications and utilities infrastructure and make the previous cyberattack look *minor* in comparison. We have implanted software into several key utilities in their country that allow us to disrupt the vast majority of their electrical grids, oil pipelines, and water pumps. Many of the key nodes to these networks cannot be disabled through software alone. So I have emplaced human resources at our disposal, assigned to destroy them if need be. In essence, we can turn off the communications and electrical grids of the United States—a country that is completely dependent on technology.

"Logistical supply lines for food, water, oil, and gas—lines that have become too reliant on technology—would crawl to a standstill. We estimate that their grocery stores would be bare within the first forty-eight hours of our strike. Cold winters and hot summers would turn deadly. The civilian population within the United States would begin looting and rioting in the streets, and law enforcement and hospitals would be overwhelmed. We estimate that it could be *months* before they would be able to get their systems back up and operational. *If* they are even able to recover."

The next picture was a rendering of the United States at night, the dense cities illuminated by masses of lights.

"As discussed, most of America's GPS and communication satellites—both military and commercial—have been impacted by the cyberattacks of last month. But there are several weapons that have yet to be used. The most important of which are our highly advanced EMP weapons."

Jinshan clicked and several red circles appeared, spread out across the map of the US. The lights began to go out on the map, simulating the effect of the EMP weapons on the US electrical grid. "These EMP weapons would further amplify our attack on utilities and communications infrastructure."

"This capability is very impressive," the first politician said.

"Gentlemen, we have reached possibly the only point in our lifetime when three things will be true simultaneously. We have a distinct military advantage over our main adversary, a distinct economic advantage over our main adversary, and the people's support of our capable political leaders. You see, gentlemen, I study trends. And the trends indicate rapidly approaching changes in our national health. If nothing is done, our unemployment will go up. Our per capita income, adjusted for inflation, will go down. And we will *lose* the support of our people. The Chinese citizen will demand change. After that occurs, history tells us that violent revolution will soon follow."

The politicians squirmed in their seats. "Is it really that bad?"

Jinshan nodded. "I liken the world of international relations to the jungle. As the saying goes, it is *kill* or *be* killed. Our leaders must show strength and choose aggression when that is the best option for our survival. China needs a change in *strategy*."

Jinshan read their faces carefully. The politicians looked alarmed, but attentive.

"Do either of you play Xiangqi?" Pronounced Shyahng chi, it was sometimes referred to as Chinese chess.

"Of course. I used to play a lot when I was in school," one of the men offered. The other politician, and the general, stayed quiet, waiting to hear Jinshan's point.

"I played when I was young as well. I enjoy it very much. It hones one's strategic skill. Do you know what the Western translation is? I will tell you. They translate Xiangqi into 'the Elephant Game.' Partly—for obvious reasons—because the first character for the word means elephant. And partly because the original pieces were carved from ivory. Taken from creatures of the jungle, who knew how to survive in the wild."

He paused for effect.

"But when explaining the game to Americans, I have always called it Chinese chess." He shook his head. "I think that explanation doesn't do the game justice. The Elephant Game is so much more nuanced than a simple game of chess. I bring up the Elephant Game because it mimics our own situation. In the game, soldiers normally do not support each other in the beginning. Because at that point, they are vulnerable. But as the game progresses, it becomes advantageous to form new alliances."

He met their eyes.

"We have always been your close friends, Jinshan," said the first politician.

"I know you have. But now, our bonds must become stronger still. Let me ask you a question. What do you think will happen in ten years, when our inflation is twenty percent and our GDP is negative four, as indicated by the chart earlier? More importantly, what will happen to your sons?"

Jinshan did not wait for an answer. "Do you think our political system will survive if unemployment increases to more than one in four? And if wages decrease by more than half? This is what we project in less than ten years. You will not hear these figures uttered in the halls of parliament. But I assure you, they are accurate. As a businessman, it is my profession to study these figures, for the benefit of my company. But as a servant of China, it is my *duty* to recommend action based on these figures, for the well-being of our country."

The politicians took in what they were hearing. Both looked concerned.

Jinshan spoke gently now. His eyes seemed to pierce those of his audience. "Our nation needs direction. We have the greatest country on earth, filled with peace-loving people. But our population needs more resources in order to sustain its growing prosperity. The United States clumsily throws its military around the world, killing civilians in the name of peace. Its citizens, too, yearn for direction. Chinese policy and law have transformed our nation into a dominating force. Today we have the ability, gentlemen, to transform the entire world into a unified and prosperous planet. Imagine a world without borders, without the threat of war, without the need to build up stockpiles of weapons and worry about whether our financial burden will support our potential ability to kill. Have you ever wondered what a united world would look like? It *could* look like *China*..." His voice was just a whisper now.

It wasn't just an act. Jinshan felt pride and excitement at the great things they could accomplish with one set of laws around the globe. He wanted to cement his legacy before it was too late. Before his sickness took him to his grave. This was the one choice that China had if it was to continue prospering. And it would cure not only China, but the world as well. Jinshan knew that they must act now to secure China's future with bold action, or they would slowly go down on a sinking ship.

Jinshan used altruism as his reason for action. He did this not because politicians were altruistically motivated, but because they wanted altruistic reasons to be *seen* as their primary motivation. Even in this small group, he knew that it was the best way to manipulate them. When he finished listing off how China's global "spreading" would better the world, Jinshan switched to his true pitch: appealing to their vanity and ambition.

"Each of our new Chinese states would need Chinese *governance*. And a new global Chinese government would need new and more powerful leadership—capable leaders with the foresight to plan for all contingencies. These leaders would no doubt be the same ones who had the foresight to take bold steps when others were happy with the status quo. You see, gentlemen, as we realize the dramatic shift in strategy our nation must make to ensure our prosperity, we also realize the internal reorganization that must take place —so it is not only your support that we seek, but your *leadership* as well."

Now they were both starry-eyed as they imagined their personal futures. A knock at the door snapped the four men back to the present. The general pressed a button on his remote and the screen went blank. He walked over to the door and let in a pair of servants with roller carts. Lunch was being served.

Jinshan spoke again. "Let us eat, gentlemen. We can discuss this more after lunch."

He was pleased.

He saw General Chen looking back at him, a knowing grin on his face. *With these two, the rest will go*, Jinshan had told the general on the phone. Jinshan sat back in his chair and refilled his teacup. They had done it. Over tea, they had just overthrown the Chinese government and cemented the start of a world war.

* * *

The meetings continued for the next hour. Then the Chinese politicians and military advisors departed. Jinshan looked to his assistant and nodded to bring his next guests in.

The Russians were only too eager to put the screws to the Americans. Jinshan's conversation with them had been ongoing for more than a year through back channels.

The Russian ambassador actually had a prepared message from his own president, which offered military cooperation with China in the Pacific. But that was not part of Jinshan's strategy. He needed the bulk of Russian military assets to remain near Europe. There, the Russians would force the Americans to keep valuable assets in the European and Middle Eastern regions. Jinshan needed the Russians to serve as a deterrent.

Russia had a fraction of the military power that the USSR had once held. But it still owned more nuclear warheads than any other nation on earth. And even today, its military was quite formidable compared to most of the West.

"Good day, Mr. Ambassador."

The Russian ambassador to China was all smiles. He walked up to Jinshan's desk and shook his hand, commenting on the strength of the proposed military plans. Jinshan preferred never to show his hand. But he knew of the Russian president's obsession with military and intelligence details, and he needed him to get on board. So he had given them a glimpse.

"Moscow is very impressed. And our leadership wishes to extend to you once again our warmest regards. Russia and China are strong strategic partners, and we want to continue this prosperous relationship in the future."

"Of course." Jinshan sipped his tea. It was cold now, but his voice was growing hoarse from talking. "That is why I have invited you here. I can't trust this message to a phone call or the written word. I need you to travel back to Moscow and deliver this directly to your president."

"What shall I tell him?"

"I need Russia to contact all the countries in the European Union and the Middle East. I would like your president to express his neutrality in this war, once it begins in earnest. But I also want him to pose to these nations an ultimatum. If *they* enter the war, or pledge allegiance to the United States, Russia shall do the same with China. And Europe shall be Russia's prize."

The ambassador listened happily, his jowls jiggling as he nodded. "I understand. You wish to keep this between the United States and China. And you want Russia to be the neutral deterrent. Standing by in case any of the European nations join the fight. Do I have that right?"

"Yes, Mr. Ambassador. I would like you to make these conversations happen over the next twenty-four hours, if possible."

"The people of Russia would like nothing more than for you to succeed, Mr. Jinshan."

Jinshan nodded. He knew that the Russians would cooperate. Europe was their prize, they had been told. Whether any of the EU nations joined the fight or not.

8

David took a bite of buttered toast and scrolled through the news headlines on his phone.

Coming off their vacation in Florida had been an adjustment. Even if they had only stayed for a few days, it had been great to get away. But now they were back to the grind.

It was dark outside, and the kitchen light was dimmed down all the way. He sat at their round kitchen table across from his wife. She was wearing a worn purple bathrobe. Taylor—their six-month old—lay sleeping in her rocker on the floor, bright-colored plastic shapes dangling over her tiny head. She had just fallen asleep after nursing, a look of pure satisfaction on her face.

Lindsay stole a sip of coffee from David's cup and whispered, "Between Maddie and this one, I was up five times last night."

He looked up from his phone. "I'm really sorry."

"I'm going to be a zombie today."

"Sorry."

"Stop saying sorry."

"So—okay."

"You men have it so easy."

David looked at his watch. "I have an early meeting."

"Get going. Leave your wife. She'll have a hot meal for you when you return."

"Hot wife, hot meal. Can't ask for more than that." He got up and smooched her on the cheek, which she held out for him.

He grabbed his keys and waved goodbye again, careful to shut the door quietly so as not to wake up either of the two kids. The drive to the CIA headquarters only took about twenty minutes at this time of the morning. It helped that David lived close by.

As he drove along the streets, flashes of the past few weeks rolled through his mind. While he still wasn't quite sure what a normal week would be like now that he was officially a full-time CIA analyst, he was liking the work so far. The last few weeks had been anything but ordinary.

As a technologist for In-Q-Tel, the CIA's private equity firm, he had traveled the country evaluating new software and hardware that might have military or intelligence applications. Now, he was evaluating Chinese technology, as well as geopolitical and military intelligence estimates, as part of the SILVERSMITH team.

David passed the security checkpoints in the CIA headquarters and began walking towards his office space. He wasn't sure if he would see his brother today. Chase, while technically part of the SILVERSMITH team, was a different type of CIA employee. He was one of the *special* ones.

Chase Manning was a former US Navy SEAL and had entered the CIA two years ago as a member of its elite Special Operations Group. But a few recent high-profile and successful missions had put Chase in very high demand. He wasn't an operations officer—he didn't have the training and experience of that world. But he had become a sort of hybrid agent—working with the operations officers and the Special Operations Group. Chase learned fast, and his ability to quickly solve problems and integrate seamlessly with special operations units made him a valuable tool of the SILVERSMITH program.

Alas, his desk was empty. They must have him out on assignment. David expected to receive either an email or an intel report over the next day, letting him know more about his brother's whereabouts.

"Morning, David."

"Morning, Susan."

Susan Collinsworth was pushing fifty years old, with strands of gray starting to overtake her otherwise short brown hair. She had the look of a stern elementary school librarian—she wore rectangular Coach glasses and a cashmere sweater vest over a white button shirt.

As far as David knew, she had no kids and had never been married. The Agency was her life. She was always in the office before him and worked like a dog.

Susan had taken David under her wing during his brief time here at Langley. In his conversations with her, he had learned a bit about her history. While she was modest in her self-description, David had learned that Susan had made a name for herself early on in her career. In the '90s, she had been running agents out of various European stations. Several of them had been former KGB operatives, struggling with how best to navigate the transition to the modern Russian spy game.

David was fascinated with that part of the work. While his brother was getting more than his share of it now, it was foreign to David. In his own section of the intelligence world, he was relegated to research and analysis. His little wins came while identifying the technical clues that made the geopolitical puzzle clearer.

Behind closed doors over half a dozen lunches, Susan had regaled him with stories of foreign agents and dead drops on dark city streets. Surveillance operations on diplomats. Hunting moles within their own agency. "In one European city, I was running this girl—a pretty little thing, a secretary—who was sleeping with the Ukrainian ambassador..."

She was careful about how much she gave away, even decades later. But it became clear to David that Susan had been there and done that. From her stories, David learned that the real goldmines weren't garnered from computer hacking or telescopic lenses. The most fruitful bounties came from long nights of note taking with reliable assets.

Assets with inside access to their own national intelligence organization's knowledge and plans. These bits of information allowed US intelligence to ferret out moles, to protect their own agents, and to continue the flow of valuable information into the hands of the policy makers.

David followed Susan into their meeting room and sat down at the long, glossy conference table. About six others were already sitting at the table. Most were typing on computers and sipping coffee, trying to achieve the proper level of caffeination.

Susan was all business, as usual. "Okay—let's begin."

They went around the room, each person responsible for a different part of the weekly update. This group contained a Chinese military expert, an NSA analyst, a representative who specialized in South America, and a nuclear weapons expert.

"We still haven't seen any change in Ecuador."

"*Still?* What the hell?"

"Yup. The Chinese troops have not returned to China, as promised. The planes have stopped bringing in more of them. So at least the numbers aren't growing. But the troop strength is still around two thousand."

David said, "What are they doing?"

"They're still training, as far as we can tell. Rifle shoots. Field exercises with the local military units."

Susan said, "Remind me. The State Department put that in the terms of our agreement with China, right? Full withdrawal of all military forces in Ecuador. I'm not making that up?"

The South America specialist nodded. "That's correct."

"Is State aware that they aren't yet in compliance?"

"We've made sure to share this information with our State Department rep on the SILVERSMITH team."

"Good. Let me know what happens there, please. What's the status of their naval vessels?"

"We got the name of the one that was completely sunk. It was…"—he checked his computer screen—"the *Lanzhou*. The other three ships have either sailed under their own power or been towed to Panama City for repairs. They're there right now."

The naval battle in the Eastern Pacific was only two weeks old. The resulting diplomatic chaos was expected.

Jinshan and Song were in jail, and China was retreating, begging forgiveness from allied nations in private, and spinning an acceptable story to their citizens on state media. Chinese citizens were told that the sunken ships had resulted from a tragic and *unauthorized* international training accident, with a jailed politician (Cheng Jinshan) and a navy admiral (Song) solely responsible.

Full details of new Chinese reparations and punishments were still being worked out by the diplomats. But the United States had announced certain requirements on Chinese military units in the Eastern Pacific immediately.

"Our inspectors are in Panama?"

"They are. They arrived last weekend. As stipulated, US State Department and DoD personnel are overseeing the Chinese naval vessels while they are in port. No Chinese sailors are allowed off the pier, except to go to the airport as they are flown back to China."

The door opened and a uniformed General Schwartz walked in. "Good morning, team."

Susan rose from her seat at the head of the table. "General, I didn't realize you were going to make it this morning. Would you like to sit here?"

"Canceled meeting. And no. I'll humbly accept the chair closest to the screen so that my old man eyes can actually see what we're discussing."

General Chester Schwartz was a US Army three-star, a Ranger, and now Associate Director of the CIA for Military Affairs. Director Buckingham had asked him to be the SILVERSMITH team's "sponsor." He was supposed to be informed of everything they knew and to empower them to cut through any bureaucratic barriers as they arose.

Over the past few weeks, he had also sent Chase Manning to several brand-new military commands to hand-deliver their orders. General Schwartz had worked with the Pentagon to preemptively deploy several special operations teams and high-tech military units in case they were needed for an immediate response to Chinese activity.

It was a good thing he had done so. Chase had ended up working closely with a MARSOC unit in Ecuador to steal a Chinese crypto key. This turned out to be the crucial piece of evidence that helped convince the Chinese president that Jinshan was really maneuvering PLA military units without his consent. Other military units that General Schwartz helped to activate included the newly formed Ford Carrier Strike Group. The Ford CSG proved instrumental in helping to defend the USS *Farragut* against the four Chinese warships in the Eastern Pacific.

Susan smiled and sat down. "We were talking about Chinese military status in Latin America."

General Schwartz said, "I read a report yesterday saying that the PLA numbers in Manta are unchanged. Is that still the case?"

"Yes, General. The Chinese are bringing back naval personnel from their wounded ships, now docked in Panama City. But there's no change to the ground troops in Ecuador."

The general frowned. "So why would they be following the agreement with regard to the PLA Navy ships, but not be recalling their troops in Manta?"

David said, "Those Navy ships are worthless now. They've suffered severe damage. And there are US inspectors monitoring everything in Panama. That isn't the case in Ecuador. Those PLA troops are still training. And their effectiveness hasn't changed over the past two weeks."

"What are you suggesting?" asked the NSA analyst. "That they are still up to something? The whistle's been blown, David. There's no element of surprise anymore."

Susan didn't look happy. "What level of readiness are we seeing across the rest of the Chinese military?"

The Chinese military expert said, "The coastal naval activity has subsided. Submarines and ships have been called into port. It's the lowest PLA Navy activity level we've seen in the past five years. Army and air force units on the coast have also hunkered down. Air force flights have all but stopped. We *have* noticed more strategic bomber activity further inland, near Chengdu. Some exercise, we think."

"Don't forget to tell her about the 41s," said the nuclear weapons expert.

"What's he talking about?" said Susan.

The Chinese military analyst said, "Before you got here, we were going over the Chinese land-based nuclear weapons movements. The Dongfeng-41 is their newest ICBM. They've recently started deploying them along the Russian border."

David said, "Isn't that a good thing? They're keeping Russia in check, and the nukes are farther away from us, right?"

The nuclear weapons expert shook his head. "That's not the way it works."

The Chinese military analyst said, "The Chinese have had ICBMs that were capable of reaching *all* of Russia for more than a decade. But these Dongfeng-41s are new. And the fact that they are stuck up there against the Russian border actually makes them *more* vulnerable to a Russian strike. But it *does* make it a lot harder for an *American* unit to attack it. Oh, and what makes the 41s special? The 41s are able to hit anywhere in the United States."

"Haven't the Chinese already had this capability?"

General Schwartz said, "The Dongfeng-5, right? Isn't that the name of the Chinese ICBM that could hit anywhere in the US?"

The analyst replied, "The Dongfeng-5 has been around since the 1980s, and yes, it could reach the US. But it was liquid-fueled. So that means it would have to go through a long fueling process before they could launch it. We would see that and respond accordingly. So the Dongfeng-5 wasn't a good first-strike weapon. Then they came up with the Dongfeng-31 in the 2000s, and its alpha version could hit the US. But it had a poor payload capability. Most of the members of my assessment team believe that the 41 is the first real game changer for them. It puts their land-based ICBMs on par with US missiles. Now they can finally hit anything in the US, and execute the attack on short notice."

General Schwartz turned to look at the map on the screen. It showed a flat display of the earth, with winding lines to show the different missile ranges launched from China. "So, you're saying that the recent deployment of this Dongfeng-41 to the Russian border represents an increased nuclear threat to the United States."

"Yes, sir, most certainly. Because they deployed these ICBMs far away from the coast, near the Russian border, it would take a long time for us to reach them."

"Long time, as in...?"

"Depends on the strike method, sir, but assuming that we were using ballistic missiles ourselves, twenty plus minutes to reach the target."

"And twenty minutes is a long time?"

"It's a long enough time for them to realize that we are attacking and respond accordingly, sir. Especially with their island bases and the air defense they've got stacked up. They have three islands in the Spratleys, and one in the Parcels, that they've converted into military bases, with runways long enough to land anything in their arsenal, fuel and munitions, and SAM batteries. They have the South China Sea dominated with anti-air capability."

General Schwartz looked at Susan. "I feel like I'm going back in time—back to the good old days of the Soviet threat. Thank you all for this warm feeling."

Susan looked at the analysts. "That's *one* aspect of their triad. What about submarine and air-launched-nuclear capability? Have we noticed any change in their strategic air and submarine missile boat activity? And how big of a threat are those assets?"

The nuclear weapons analyst said, "The Chinese nuclear missile boats aren't nearly as capable as our own. They only have a few type 94s. That's the closest thing they have to our Ohio-class subs. But theirs are noisy. We generally know where they are at all times. As for the air component, they do have over one hundred and twenty strategic bombers. But they aren't able to reach the continental US. The Chinese are reportedly working on a competitor to the B-2 Spirit, but we haven't seen it fly yet."

The Chinese military expert said, "Near the coast, as we previously went over, military activity has been kept to a minimum. But PLA Air Force activity is high at many of the inland bases. Susan, they're still training around the clock over there. Maybe the Chinese president's orders haven't trickled down yet, or…"

David said, "Or, maybe they're getting another set of orders."

* * *

David sat alone in the CIA cafeteria. He had brought his own lunch. Ham and cheese sandwich, a plastic bag of yellow corn tortilla chips, and a Tupperware container of carrot sticks.

"Mr. Manning, how are you liking the new job?" General Schwartz stood over him. Like the trained Ranger that he was, he had approached with speed and stealth.

David started to stand.

"Please, keep your seat. Mind if I join you?"

"Of course, sir. And the job is going well, sir, thank you." David wondered if he was using too many "sirs." Probably his Navy training, or his admiral father's discipline shining through.

The general sat in the empty chair across from David. They were the only ones at their table.

"Susan speaks highly of you. And you've caught the director's eye. I might not be a CIA guy, but I've learned a thing or two about upward mobility in my day. The director of your agency is probably a good one to impress."

David reddened. "I hope they are happy with my work. To be honest, it is somewhat similar to the type of research I had done at In-Q-Tel."

"Really? I thought you researched technology there." The general took a bite of his meal, a spring mix salad with slices of grapes, walnuts, and croutons. Everyone was a healthy eater nowadays.

"That's right, sir. I researched technology. Weapons and weapons systems. Sometimes cyberweapons. Sometimes aircraft or missiles. It was interesting. I got to be a jack of all trades. But in order to do the job well, we had to research what our adversaries were capable of —and what they were working on."

The general nodded. "I see."

"In a way, I'm doing the same job now. The only difference is the timeline."

"How's that?"

"At In-Q-Tel, I was looking at what our potential enemies might be doing in the next five to ten years. Here, I'm looking at what they might be doing in the next few days or weeks. It's the same game, just a different time scale that I'm looking out over."

General Schwartz smiled. "Strategy versus tactics. Some would argue that the two are the same, just on a different scale."

They ate their lunch and made small talk for a while. David told the general about his sister, Victoria, and how she was still deployed to the Eastern Pacific. "She isn't sure when they'll return home."

"No, I imagine she wouldn't be. My guess is very few people know the answer to that question right now."

David said, "I can't help feeling that we're all waiting for something, sir."

"For the other shoe to drop? I think a lot of us have the same feeling. We were just attacked by the only military on the planet that outsizes our own. Whatever the politicians say they intend to do, history would demonstrate that hostilities would increase, not decrease, after a string of events like we just had."

"I agree, sir. In my research, I've seen a few indicators that give me concern."

"Like what?" The flag officer checked his wristwatch. "Care to show me?"

The general was easy to speak to. He didn't have that stuffy, all-knowing manner of conversation that many senior leaders did. His speech pattern was no-nonsense. Gruff at times. But mostly friendly and down to earth. Like he hadn't forgotten what it was like to be working in the trenches.

David didn't want to overstep his authority. Susan was his direct superior, and she reported to the general. But since the general and he were already talking...

Schwartz smiled. "What's the matter?"

"Nothing, General. I just would have prepared something for you if I'd known—"

"Yeah, I know that. But we need to get away from that bullshit. I don't want you guys having three meetings of preparation before you have one meeting with me or the director. We just don't have the time." He stood up, using a napkin to wipe his hands. "Now let's go."

They walked back through the hallways of the CIA headquarters to the SILVERSMITH team spaces. David took a seat at his cubicle, and the general pulled up a chair from the empty desk next to his.

"Now you guys just told me that you think the Chinese might not be fully complying with their stand-down claims. That right?"

"Yes, sir."

"So what else might we look at to verify what their true intentions are?"

David said, "Sir, I've been looking at a few things. Leading indicators, I call them."

"Leading indicators for what?"

David looked uneasy. "I don't want to get ahead of myself, sir."

"Son, in the past few weeks, you have been on the receiving end of a Chinese espionage operation, and our nation has been openly attacked by Chinese military and cyber assets. You are not getting ahead of yourself. In my opinion, we're all playing catch-up."

David turned to his computer and opened a folder. He pointed to the screen. "This is something I've been looking at. When Susan and I briefed you earlier, we told you that we were seeing mixed messages from the Chinese military analysis. Some military assets are standing down. Some are increasing their levels of activity."

"Tracking."

It took David a second to register that this was Army slang for "I understand."

David said, "So I wanted to check out some leading indicators that might be *harder* to conceal. Leading indicators that would tell us if they were preparing for a large-scale war."

The general sat forward in his chair, looking at David's screen. "What am I looking at here?"

"Blood bags, sir."

"Blood bags?"

"Yes, sir. Chinese orders of blood bags." David moved his mouse and clicked on another file. "And this one is for a refrigeration unit. A specially made one that keeps blood and plasma at a specific temperature during storage. The NSA provided me with internal company documents that showed orders to the manufacturing plant. They don't match the company's sales numbers."

"So that means they are trying to conceal something?"

"Possibly, sir. That is my hypothesis. It's a Chinese medical device company that is making a huge quantity of blood bags and refrigeration units, and not reporting it. And what's more, this specific style of blood bag is one that their civilian hospitals *don't* use. It's only used in *military* hospitals, and in the field."

"Can you tell who made the orders?"

"No, sir. These orders are only found on the internal network at the manufacturing plant. No buyer is listed."

"Sounds fishy."

"Yes, sir."

"Am I reading these numbers right? It looks like the orders have increased dramatically over the past week."

"Yes, sir." David eyed the general. "You are reading the numbers right."

"How did you come up with this? What made you look at blood bags?"

"We—me and some of the people on my team—did a brainstorm session on what other items might need to be prepped if the Chinese were about to follow through on the Red Cell plans. When the US military began its surge in Iraq, and when we made several other large-scale troop increases over the past few decades—periods when this type of medical transportation technology was available—orders for blood bags went way up. We had a few mathematicians look at our data—American military data—and we came up with an equation. Now, there are several variables where we don't know if we have the inputs right. But we can extrapolate a range..."

"A range of what, Manning?"

"How many troops they intend to move into a combat zone, sir."

The general sat back in his chair, his face showing much more interest now. "And what number did you come up with?"

David lowered his voice, a bit embarrassed at the assessment and how crazy it might sound. "Sir, when we use the data from American military movements and input these recent Chinese medical device orders into the equation, we come up with ten, sir."

"Ten?"

"Yes, sir."

The general sounded confused. "Ten thousand troops doesn't sound like—"

"Ten *million*, sir. These numbers correspond with preps to place ten million Chinese troops into a combat zone."

The general frowned. He leaned back in his chair and didn't respond for a moment.

"General, I'm not saying this means that China is about to send ten million troops overseas. I'm just saying that there are companies that are making military medical devices in quantities that are astronomically high. And it corresponds with these levels of troop movements."

"Maybe it was part of previous plans, and the purchases just haven't been canceled yet? They could still be catching up with the fact that Jinshan is behind bars. Or maybe they manufacture them in bulk? I'm just trying to play devil's advocate, before we start spreading this around."

"Sir, we're with you. That's possible. But the odd thing about this is that these purchases really ramped up in the past week. *After* Jinshan was taken into custody. So I would think that these manufacturing orders could be our first indication of *current* military intentions. Our first window into the PLA mindset after recent hostilities."

The general nodded. "Okay. I'm done with devil's advocate for the moment. Now I'll play devil. Let's say that this is real. What would have to be true?"

"You mean what else would we expect to see?"

"Yes."

David didn't hesitate. "Shipping containers."

The general nodded. "Right. That's what I keep hearing you guys talk about. Specifically, though, what about shipping containers would you want to know?"

"The Red Cell plans called for specially made shipping containers to outfit merchant ships to easily become troop transports. They would also allow for quick and easy troop movements by rail, once overseas."

"So have you looked into the shipping containers angle?"

David nodded, a serious look on his face. He made a few more mouse clicks and another file came up. "Another leading indicator. We have human intelligence reports that several shipping container companies are now canceling orders."

"Why are canceled orders bad?"

"We think that they need to add capacity to their manufacturing lines. Capacity for these *specially made* containers."

"And how big are these shipping container orders?"

"We're still working on this one, sir. Right now, we're just hearing reports that some of these modifications might be being made."

"Understood. What do you need to confirm?"

David made a face. "Sir, that's not really my area of expertise."

"Well, who's the expert, then?" The general looked around the open office area. "Susan! Please join us for a moment."

The CIA operations officer walked over, flashing a look at David as if to ask, *Why are you speaking to my boss alone?*

"Thanks, Susan. Quick question. I asked David to take me through some of the work you guys have been doing on..." He looked at David. "*Leading indicators.* What do you need to confirm whether or not the Chinese are actually outfitting shipping containers for mass troop transports?"

Her face relaxed as it became clear what the conversation was about. "Sir, we're working on that. As you know, we've struggled with our human intelligence sources in China over the past seven years..."

Seeing the look of curiosity on David's face, Susan said, "The Chinese government cracked several of our networks in 2010. It was a very dark time for the Chinese desks. They began losing agents left and right. Over a dozen CIA sources were killed. One of our assets was shot in a public square in front of the government building where he worked. They made his colleagues watch. It was a message for the others. That was in 2012. It made the *New York Times*. You might have read about it."

"What happened? How—"

"There was a mole. At least one. That, coupled with some pretty sophisticated hacking into government databases, allowed them to piece together who our operatives over there were. From there, they did what any good intelligence agency does. They began surveilling all our operatives. Laying traps. Tracking who they spoke to and where they went. As some of our assets were taken prisoner, they began giving up information. Once enough of the puzzle is clear, it becomes easier for them. We still haven't fully recovered, David."

General Schwartz said, "Susan, I sympathize with the challenges you've faced. But we may not have a lot of time. So, what do we need to confirm some of these leading indicators that your team is starting to uncover? Particularly with respect to the shipping containers."

Susan said, "We have sources that may be able to help us with this. But we still need to find a solution to our other problem."

David frowned. "What other problem?"

The general and Susan glanced at each other. General Schwartz nodded, and Susan motioned them into one of the soundproof huddle rooms, closing the door behind them. She looked at David. "We have HUMINT that suggests Jinshan has a covert military training facility a few hundred miles north of Liaodong Bay."

David nodded. "I read your report on that. It was vague. Something about Jinshan holding that location as important."

"That's right. My report was vague to protect the source, and because we don't know what's at that location. But the asset who gave us the information is very good. If that person is convinced that it's an item of interest, then we need to be concerned. The cable we received said that Jinshan had considered the site to be vital to his plans. Based on everything we've seen, I can only assume that these plans were to wage war against the United States."

She glanced up at the ceiling as she recalled the exact phrasing. "A covert camp with special operations units conducting unique training. If Jinshan is still wielding influence and power in China, and these military units are still preparing for something, it is crucially important that we find out what they are training for."

General Schwartz said, "Susan and I have been working on ways to get a team in there. With satellite capabilities degraded, and it being in a location not suitable for drones or manned reconnaissance flights, we think a small, covert team might be best. Ideally, it would be an agent or agents already in country."

"But as we discussed," Susan said, "the CIA's HUMINT resources in China are less than stellar."

Schwartz said, "I have a small group of Delta operators that would be well suited for the job, but the problem is insertion. We think we have a way to get them out of the country. But we can't insert them the same way."

David said, "The camp is supposed to be about one hundred miles inland in China, right? And you need a covert method of insertion for a SOF team?"

"Correct."

David smiled. "You know, when I was at In-Q-Tel, there was one interesting project that I took a look at. DARPA came up with the idea. I think they might even still be working on it."

9

Chase walked out of the Kyoto train station to a blue sky, crisp air, and the sound of large tour buses. It was rush hour on a weekday. He wasn't sure if that made Kyoto more or less crowded, since it was such a huge tourist destination. The beautiful city was known for its tranquil and historic temples. Some of them were in the city, while other temples were tucked away in the mountains, accessible only by hiking along winding paths through quiet pine forests.

Crowds lined up outside to get tickets for their tour buses. The buses arrived along the curb and departed, an endless ferry to the temples.

Chase walked up to a standing map—the kind you saw in most indoor malls. Thank God they wrote in English under the Japanese descriptions. His eyes searched the restaurant section.

There. That was the one he was looking for. Ogawa Coffee.

After a brief walk, he arrived at the tiny cafe. Chase took in the rich smell of coffee. The little shop had wooden boxes filled with beans. The boxes had tiny windows so that you could see what you were getting. Plastic scoops and bags. It reminded him of the gourmet coffee shop his mother had loved in Tysons Corner when he was growing up.

"Mr. Manning?"

Chase turned to see a Japanese man standing behind him. Medium build, jet-black hair. He looked like the picture he had been shown two days ago in Langley. Then again, half the people here looked like that picture. Was it racist to think that?

Chase stuck out his hand. "I'm sorry. I'm going to butcher your name if I try to pronounce it."

"Hiramatsu. Hi-ra-ma-tsu. That's my last name. Tetsuo is my first name. Just call me Tetsuo."

His English was excellent. Zero accent. Which made sense, since he had been born in the US and had lived there most of his life. It was the CIA that had sent the second-generation American back to the home of his ancestors.

Tetsuo Hiramatsu worked in the US embassy in Tokyo. While he had an official title as an economic advisor, that was a cover. He had worked for the CIA in Tokyo Station for four years now. It was his third overseas assignment with the Agency.

A native of Seattle, Hiramatsu was an avid Seahawks fan, a third-degree black belt in the Japanese style of karate known as Shotokan, and a recent student of a type of car racing known as "drifting." He had paid for several lessons, when he could get away from his actual work.

Tokyo Station was one of the most important CIA locations in the world. All sorts of politicians and businessmen traveled to Tokyo for legitimate reasons. It was a great place to run an agent. And Tetsuo was running several important assets for the Agency.

"You can call me Chase."

"Pleased to meet you, Chase. I have to admit, I was a little worried. Kyoto has many tourists. And I've been here too long—all you white people are starting to look the same to me."

Chase laughed. Perhaps he had found a kindred spirit.

"Would you like a coffee before we head out?"

"I would, actually."

They ordered and took two coffees to go. Chase stirred in a sugar packet as he followed Tetsuo out of the cafe. A Toyota sedan drove up and stopped just in front of them. Tetsuo opened the door for Chase, and he got in the back seat. Tetsuo sat in the front.

The driver worked for Tetsuo, Chase learned. He was one of their CIA technical experts. His job was to do things like place listening devices in hotels when they were surveilling persons of interest.

"Where are we headed?"

"To one of our safe houses. Susan wants you to sit in on this." Tetsuo sipped his coffee, looking back at Chase from the passenger seat. "I'm told that you have made quite a name for yourself in a short period of time. You were a Special Operations Group member until recently, were you not?"

The Special Operations Group was an elite subset of the CIA's clandestine services. They were the shooters. The guys who helped to provide a more robust level of security where needed, and got sent in for the more kinetic missions. They were seen as a supporting element to the Political Action Group operatives—the more traditional agents who operated around the globe on behalf of the CIA.

"That's right," said Chase.

"So what are you now? You still SOG, or what?"

"I don't really think they've defined that. They just tell me where to go, and I go."

"Interesting."

Tetsuo seemed like a good guy. But a lot of operatives had massive egos. They had to, considering the balls it took to do what they did. Men like Tetsuo had been like gold miners in the 1800s. They would conduct painstaking searches for valuable locations of their precious commodity. They took many precautions not to be observed by the competition. And once they found a good mine, they would carefully extract every bit they could, until it was dry. But the competition was dangerous and ever-present.

Instead of gold, intelligence operatives like Tetsuo mined information, access, and influence. Tetsuo had an official cover. And by the code of intelligence agencies around the world, violent action against him was off-limits, as long as he was playing by the rules.

It was the lives of his agents—the ones that he was running—that were really at stake. If the Chinese, or the North Koreans, or the gangsters or crooked businessmen found out that Tetsuo's informants were providing him with secrets, things wouldn't end well for them.

Tetsuo was GIANT's handler and had been for the past four years. GIANT had had a myriad of handlers over his long career of spying for the Americans. But Tetsuo's reputation for street smarts and operational discipline had made him a top choice for the assignment. GIANT frequently made work trips outside China. From his station in Tokyo, Tetsuo was able to quickly and discreetly meet with him when he was in town. Every six months or so, they would spend long evenings in quiet hotel rooms, GIANT filling him in on insider information about the Chinese political scene and military advancements.

It was Tetsuo's job to protect his agents. And not just for their safety—if they were found out, that mine of information would be sealed off, and the CIA's collection capability would diminish. Not to mention, Tetsuo's career would take a tumble. It wasn't like Tetsuo's goal was to get promoted to GS-15 or anything. He had joined the CIA to serve his country, not end up a bureaucrat. But if his agent got made, and his career suffered, Tetsuo wouldn't get any more plum assignments—the ones that really made a difference. And he *did* care about that.

So when Susan Collinsworth had sent him a message two days ago, asking him to allow his most valuable agent to meet with Chase Manning—some new guy who was working out of Langley—he had rightly told her to go to hell.

It wasn't often that the director of the CIA got involved in Tetsuo's business—never, actually. But shortly after Tetsuo had told Susan Collinsworth to go to hell, Tetsuo's boss, the CIA's Tokyo station chief, had gotten a call from Director Buckingham himself. The director had ordered them to assist Susan with whatever she needed. SILVERSMITH was point on all things China. The message was clear: *Get on board.*

Tetsuo had done his homework on Manning. *Oh*, he realized. *That* guy. The Dubai guy. Rumor had it that Chase had been sleeping with one Lisa Parker—the Chinese mole who had sent earthquakes through the Counter Intelligence Center—before she had gone

AWOL. Poor Chase had had no idea that she was a Chinese double agent. No one had. Another interesting item in Chase Manning's file was his location over the past few weeks. On temporary assignment in Latin America. Right when all that shit in Ecuador was going down.

Tetsuo had seen the reports. A SOCOM team had been inserted into the Chinese camp in Manta, Ecuador. SILVERSMITH, the CIA's code name for the operation attempting to counter recent Chinese aggression, was assisting the SOCOM team. Susan was in charge of SILVERSMITH.

If Tetsuo was a gambling man, which he was, he would bet money that Chase Manning had been a part of that SOCOM group. Especially since Manning had been a Special Operations Group guy in the Agency. All of those fellas were taken from the SEALs and Army Delta. Tetsuo decided to give Chase the benefit of the doubt.

Chase eyed Tetsuo as the car swerved along the narrow Japanese roads. They raced past rows and rows of small attached homes, single-car garages on each one. A bike lane took up a lot of the pavement.

Chase said, "How long have you been running your source?"

Tetsuo glanced at him. "He's been with several handlers over the years. Let's leave it at that."

A few moments of silence went by before Tetsuo said, "When we go in there and speak with him, I want you to remember something. He trusts me, not you. I'll ask that you remain quiet while I'm talking to him. Don't interrupt us. He is risking his life by working with us. Chinese counterintelligence is quite active in Japan, and they usually try to monitor their own dignitaries when they visit. In other words, there may be Chinese operatives trying to look for him. If anything goes wrong, the minute I say the word, we leave. Just stick with me, don't talk, and leave. Understood?"

"Got it."

"If the Ministry of State Security finds out that we're using him..."

Chase simply said, "I understand." He knew how delicate the relationship was between handler and agent. It was the first time he had worked with Tetsuo. He still had to earn his trust. And this guy GIANT was a big-time agent.

The car slowed in front of one of the identical attached homes and pulled under the small car overhang. Chase was pretty sure that they had driven in at least two complete circles before parking.

Chase and Tetsuo got out, but the driver stayed in the vehicle. Tetsuo began walking along the sidewalk around the building. Chase followed him. "We aren't going into the house?"

"Not that one."

Surveillance detection, Chase realized, watching Tetsuo's eyes scan the streets. These guys weren't screwing around.

Chase continued to follow Tetsuo along a path that ran parallel to a thirty-foot-wide canal. An identical pathway lay on the opposite side of the water. Cherry blossom tree branches covered them overhead, reflecting in the still water. They were still another month from blooming, but the scenery was impressive. The walking path was made of square stone tiles and gravel. Wooden walking bridges arched over the canal every fifty yards or so. There were plenty of tourists posing for pictures.

"Nice area."

"This is called the Philosopher's Path. Very well known here. You should come back in the spring or fall. It is truly beautiful."

As Tetsuo talked, he continued to work. Scanning each passerby, each person on a bench, each tourist with a phone—looking for anyone who might be watching them.

"Are we black?" Chase was asking if they were clear of any foreign surveillance.

"I think so. We'll do this for another twenty minutes. I have a local team helping out with countersurveillance as well."

Eventually Chase followed Tetsuo as he veered off into a nearby neighborhood. Homes and shops were pressed up next to each other, just like everywhere in Japan's urban districts. Busy streets filled with tiny cars and pedestrians. Many were riding bikes. The two men walked up to an unremarkable two-story townhouse. Power lines buzzed lightly overhead.

They walked into the house through a back door, not visible from the street. A man stood waiting for them. Tetsuo introduced Chase and the man—another member of his team. One of the only ones with access to this safe house and knowledge of his asset's identity. The team member didn't smile; he just gestured toward a pile of shoes near the door. Chase frowned and wriggled out of his shoes. The man, Japanese or Japanese American by the look of it, rolled his eyes and picked up Chase's shoes, rearranging them neatly next to the others. More Japanese culture stuff. It was a country of obsessive-compulsive disorder patients.

"Tough crowd."

Tetsuo smiled. "There are a lot of etiquette rules here."

"I guess so."

Tetsuo gestured for Chase to head down the narrow hallway. "First door on the left."

Tetsuo opened the door, and a diminutive Asian man wearing a suit stood and bowed at them. GIANT.

"Dr. Wang." Tetsuo bowed and said something in a deep, rapid flurry of Mandarin. He gestured to Chase, who bowed awkwardly and then stuck out his hand.

The man looked like he was in his late fifties. Maybe early sixties. Gaunt features. Steady eyes. He bowed slightly and shook Chase's hand, then looked expectantly at Tetsuo.

Tetsuo said, "Let's have a seat."

On what? Chase thought to himself. The room was empty except for a little six-inch high coffee table and a small green plant in the corner.

But then they all sat down on the floor—a tatami mat, he realized. Tetsuo and the aging Chinese man sat gracefully, folding their knees underneath themselves and continuing their conversation in Mandarin with the slightest hint of a smile as they spoke.

Chase, an ex-lacrosse player and well-muscled man, forced himself to sit Indian style, his knees jutting up uncomfortably. It wasn't working. He rearranged himself up on his knees, but then he was a foot higher than the others. He finally sat on his butt, with his socked feet flat on the floor, holding his knees for balance—he felt like a kindergartener.

Tetsuo glanced at him, visibly annoyed. "You alright?"

"Fine."

He sighed and resumed conversing in Mandarin. Issuing an apology for his idiotic American friend, no doubt. Who the hell sat on the floor? And how were they both able to fold their legs so effortlessly? Didn't they have groin muscles?

A few times during the conversation, Tetsuo made audible changes to his tone, which indicated surprise and interest. It was killing Chase not to ask what the hell they were talking about. It had been fifteen minutes now, and he had yet to provide a translation. All Chase could make out was the occasional English-sounding acronym and once—he wasn't completely sure—he thought he'd heard them say "Jinshan."

Finally, Tetsuo turned to Chase, his eyes narrowing. "Do you speak Chinese?"

"No," Chase said. "Of course not."

Tetsuo leaned toward Chase, speaking quietly. "Then why haven't you said anything? What have you been doing this whole time?"

"You said to be quiet," Chase whispered back.

Tetsuo looked at Dr. Wang, who smiled. Tetsuo looked pained. "Forgive us. We will continue in English, if you please."

Chase reddened.

"Dr. Wang is here in Japan with a Chinese envoy, accompanying Secretary Zhang, whom he works for. President Wu has decided to make Cheng Jinshan and Admiral Song's trial public, as a way to provide maximum impact in reducing Jinshan's power."

Dr. Wang said, "He hopes this public trial will serve as a turning point."

Chase said, "The two are in jail."

"Yes, but unfortunately, Jinshan still wields influence. Jails for the Chinese elite are not the same as jails for the commoners, I'm afraid. Jinshan has many friends, even now. But Secretary Zhang and President Wu are working to curb that remaining power."

Tetsuo turned between Chase and GIANT. He said, "Dr. Wang,

we are concerned that some of Jinshan's military plans may still be in motion. What are you seeing on your end?"

Dr. Wang said, "Secretary Zhang and President Wu have been forced to send out inspection teams to various locations. Men that they trust. Because like you, we are also getting reports that Jinshan's men are still operating under his separate instructions."

"What have the inspectors seen?"

"Nothing that provides evidence of a continued conspiracy. Each place they go, teams loyal to Jinshan or Admiral Song are there already. Records have been cleaned up. Factories and military bases made to look appropriate. Without Jinshan tried and convicted, he is too powerful to entrap. All we have are rumors and secondhand reports."

"Well, what do those say?"

GIANT's face went dark. "That the island is still operational. That factories in Guangzhou are pumping out militarized shipping containers. That the air force has been training for a classified mission. That some of our most elite special operations groups are at a secret base in Liaoning—training for a mission that Jinshan commissioned."

Chase had read the reports while at Langley. This was what they were hoping to find out about.

"What are they doing at Liaoning?"

"We don't know. But my sources tell me that it is very important to Jinshan. There are two locations that seem to be central planning centers for his operation. The island is one. The special operations training camp at Liaoning is the other."

Tetsuo said, "Dr. Wang, how is it that you don't know if any of this is true or not? Why haven't your inspections identified—"

Chase saw a flash of frustration. "Excuse me, young man, but things are not so simple right now. The Chinese people are angry, and so are many of the politicians. There are some who say that Jinshan was the one who was protecting China from Western hostilities. Many military leaders and politicians are openly supportive of Jinshan, even now. Others pledge loyalty to Wu, but we suspect they are secretly working for Jinshan. It is difficult to know who can be trusted in this environment. As head of the Central Committee for Discipline Inspection, he helped to place many of these politicians in their current roles. And do not forget, Cheng Jinshan controlled much of the censorship for state media."

"Controlled or controls?"

GIANT shrugged. "Who can say for sure? But if you control the censoring agency, you control the message. You shape opinions. There is a great anti-Western sentiment among many Chinese right now. It is not easy to choose the unpopular path in a communist state. The populace gets their news and opinions from social media and state news on their phones. The 3PLA has programs that control what articles are posted and shared on these platforms. Guess whose company monitors those programs?"

"Jinshan."

Wang nodded. "President Wu was wrong to trust him. The Central Committee allowed Jinshan to become too powerful. Now, we are all paying the price." He paused. "But there is something else. Another reason that it is hard to know whether Jinshan's operations are still being conducted."

"What reason is that?"

"Cheng Jinshan practices compartmentalization to the extreme. He segments up his teams and decentralizes command. Apart from Jinshan, Admiral Song, and Lena Chou, there were almost no personnel—at least that we are aware of—who were versed in all of Jinshan's day-to-day operations."

"So you have Jinshan and Admiral Song."

"They are not cooperating."

"What about Lena Chou? Do you know where she is?" Chase said, leaning forward.

Dr. Wang looked confused. "You haven't heard? Lena Chou is dead."

Chase felt oddly numb. While he no longer harbored the same feelings for Lena Chou that he once had, the news was shocking.

Tetsuo glanced at Chase, then said, "This is the first we are hearing of this. Can you elaborate?"

Dr. Wang went on to tell of a Chinese satellite intercepting a radio transmission in the Eastern Pacific. The intelligence organization concluded that Lena Chou had attempted to escape from Chinese military police by hitching a ride out of the region with Colombian drug smugglers.

Wang said, "There was some sort of gang war between rival smugglers. A gunfight on the boat. It is our understanding that Lena was killed on board. This is the information we have received from the Colombians, and..."—he looked embarrassed—"and by looking at reports from your own agencies. Your Coast Guard is investigating the matter."

Tetsuo and Chase looked at each other. Chinese cyberoperations were reviewing US government reports in search of Lena Chou.

Tetsuo said, "Do you have any way to verify that she is really dead?"

"Chinese intelligence is attempting to do so now. Secretary Zhang and President Wu had seen Lena Chou as a potential 'star witness' in the case against Jinshan. Although she would not be likely to testify against him, the information that she knows could be very useful as we put a stop to any of Jinshan's ongoing plans."

"And now?"

"If Lena Chou is truly dead, this will be much more difficult, for reasons already stated."

Tetsuo looked frustrated. "Is there a way that you can get us more solid information on these rumored military training operations?"

GIANT looked unsettled. "I have given this much thought. If I were to go myself, under the authority of Secretary Zhang, perhaps I could inspect one of the two locations—either the camp at Liaoning or the island."

Tetsuo shook his head. "That sounds too dangerous. You shouldn't be the one—"

GIANT held up his hand. "The inspectors we are sending are turning up nothing. No one wants to stick their neck out because Jinshan is still too dangerous. But he will go to trial soon. His power will recede. If I could conduct a surprise inspection during Jinshan's trial, then I could provide you with the information which you desire.

I could tell you how deep his conspiracy goes. And whether there are any remaining military plans in progress."

Tetsuo looked at Chase, who nodded. "Okay. Thank you, Dr. Wang. I will speak with my superiors and get their thoughts. I will meet with you once more tomorrow evening."

* * *

After transmitting their reports to Langley that evening, Chase and Tetsuo ate dinner in Osaka.

"You drinking?" Tetsuo's mood was much more light-hearted now that the work was done. They sat on pillows on the floor, thin wooden walls on three sides giving them privacy. An open curtain revealed dozens of similar tables. Well-dressed Japanese businessmen and women, done with the day's work at the early hour of 10 p.m., were out on the town, ready for cocktails and fine cuisine.

Chase's legs were once again squeezed at impossible angles underneath the table—it couldn't have been more than a foot off the ground. Why didn't they use chairs in this country?

"I think I'll need some alcohol to get over the pain in my legs from all this yoga you people have been making me do."

Tetsuo smiled. "So I take it you've never been to Japan."

"Never been to Asia, actually. Well, not this part of Asia."

"You've been in the sandbox, though, right?"

"Yeah. Spent all my operational time there with the teams and then with the Agency."

"Teams? Like, the SEAL teams?"

"Yes."

"Nice. How does this compare?"

"This? This is very different. But it's interesting work, and I'm trying to learn as fast as I can."

The waitress came and Tetsuo ordered for them. Chase had looked at the menu, but everything was in Japanese. A minute later she brought two frosted mugs and filled them with bubbling golden lager. The bottle said Asahi. Chase took a sip and gave a nod of approval.

"Cheers. Welcome to Japan."

"Thank you. I was worried you were going to make me drink sake. I've had that. Don't care for it much."

"No, actually, we start with beer here. It is the Japanese way."

The waitress came back a moment later and laid down a cubic stone that looked like a miniature castle tower. She lit the gas flame in the center of the stone and placed a metal grate on top. Next she placed a plate of assorted raw seafood on the table. She then smiled, bowed, and left them.

Tetsuo said, "You gotta use your chopsticks and just place the meat on the grill. Let it cook for a minute and then eat. We'll have several courses, so save room. The best stuff is coming later. The Kobe beef is unbelievable here. They just give you little morsels, but the way they cook it, and the quality—it wins awards."

Chase fumbled around with the chopsticks and eventually got a few pieces of a translucent white meat on the grill. "What is this stuff?"

"It's the fin of a ray."

"No shit? Like a manta ray?"

"Yeah. Or maybe a stingray. I forget. But it's really good."

Chase sipped his beer while he let the ray cook. "How about you? What's your story?"

"I entered the Agency right out of college. My fluency in Japanese and Chinese helped. I wasn't sure what to expect, but I love it. There's nothing better than this game, I tell you what."

Chase gripped a piece of cooked ray with his chopsticks and brought it to his mouth, taking a bite. "Damn. That is pretty good. It's like salty beef jerky."

"That's a great description. Never heard that one." He took another gulp of beer, finishing his glass. He signaled the waitress to come over and ordered another round.

After she left, Tetsuo lowered his voice and said, "So we've shot off our reports to Langley. We'll wait and see what they want to do next. But my guess is that they're going to want exactly what we asked for. Details and verification."

Chase nodded. "Let me ask you something. You've had to learn about Cheng Jinshan, and you know the Asian geopolitical scene. What do you think is going on over there in Beijing right now? What's going to happen with Jinshan's trial?"

The waitress returned and brought two more beers. They waited until she departed before continuing their conversation.

Tetsuo said, "I've never seen it like this before. My sources in China say that they're cracking down on religious groups, and on the information that's filtering to their people, like never before. This anti-American, antireligion kick is pretty scary. They've always leaned atheist, from their communist roots. But China has a lot of traditional religions that influence their people as well. Taoism, Buddhism. This antireligion thing is different. It's more like a nationalist sentiment than anything. Our analysts say that a lot of it stems from a big social network and news media propaganda push. But it's hard to gauge how prevalent the feeling is without being on the street."

"But we must have a lot of agents there, right?"

"We do. And we do get reports. Anecdotal stuff. But honestly, China has spent the last decade purging our agents over there. It was pretty bad there for a few years. We've had to rebuild our network from scratch. And it's really dicey trying to gain access to their political and intelligence mindset."

Chase said, "What's your opinion?"

"Me? Shit." He took another swig of beer. "This could be the conflict that shapes the next few decades. America and China have coexisted and mutually benefited from each other. But now that China is becoming more wealthy and powerful..."

"And what about Jinshan?"

"I just don't know, man. But if they're dragging him out in front of everyone for a public trial, I would think that his time is coming to an end."

Chase felt a buzzing in his pocket. He pulled out his phone. It was a CIA-issued smartphone, with little capability other than sending and receiving encrypted phone calls and text.

CONTACT SILVERSMITH FROM SECURE LOCATION ASAP

Tetsuo saw his look. "What's up?"

"Tell them to hurry up and send the Kobe beef. We gotta go."

* * *

Susan and General Schwartz gave Chase and Tetsuo the details of the brief on video conference. A slightly buzzed Chase noted that his brother, David, was also at the table. An almost imperceptible nod between the two brothers was transmitted thousands of miles across the world on fiber-optic cables that had been specially laid by the NSA over a decade ago.

David looked good, Chase thought.

Susan looked worried. "I realize that parts of what I'm about to say will be highly unusual. But we commend you both on your recent operational achievements and are confident that you'll be able to make this work."

Outlining the plan took a little over an hour. It would involve coordination between an Air Force B-2 Spirit crew stationed at Guam, members of the 1st Special Forces Operational Detachment–Delta (known more commonly as Delta Force) stationed in Korea, and Chase.

Susan said, "We evaluated GIANT's proposal that he be the one to inspect the camp. Frankly, we thought that was too risky. We would use GIANT only as a last resort."

Tetsuo said, "Understood."

They spoke for a few more minutes, going over timing and some of the details of the plan. When the video conference ended, Chase turned to Tetsuo. "So I guess I'll be going to China."

* * *

Shortly after their video call with Chase and Tetsuo, Susan hit David Manning with a new assignment.

"The Chinese think Lena Chou is dead."

David nodded. "I read the report that they sent this morning."

"And if you believe that, I've got a used car to sell you."

"What are you talking about?" David asked.

"Come on, I'll show you." She walked into one of the enclosed huddle rooms in the CIA headquarters. One of the senior analysts was already in there.

"Last week we received a report from the NSA. They picked up a radio transmission matching Lena's voice ID."

David said, "Yeah. Near Ecuador. I remember."

The analyst shook his head. "Not near Ecuador. Further north. Several hundred miles north."

David looked at Susan, confused.

She was nodding. "Turns out that the most likely source of the radio transmission was a seized Colombian narcotics transport vessel. The Navy spotted it a few days after the radio transmission and conducted a boarding. A Coast Guard cutter came in to take over the investigation."

"What investigation?"

"Based on GIANT's report and what our NSA partners are saying, this incident has at least *some* in the Chinese government convinced that Lena Chou is dead. The Chinese knew she was on that smugglers' boat, from their connections in Colombia. The NSA matched her voice to radio calls in the area. If they did it, you can believe the Chinese 3PLA did the same thing. We also believe that 3PLA hacked into and read our Coast Guard investigation report. Here it is. There was a gunfight. Several dead. Most were found floating in the sea. No one was alive on board. Lots of blood, though."

David said, "So Lena was really there?"

The analyst said, "We do think Lena Chou transmitted from that boat. Yes."

"What the hell was she doing there?"

"We don't know. But as GIANT reported, the Chinese government now considers her officially dead."

"But *who* in the Chinese government?"

"Exactly. This report came from a source close to the Chinese president. We think that means that people aligned with him are being led to believe that Lena was killed on this drug boat, while trying to escape."

"But you don't believe that?"

"No. This is classic deception. Rule number one: if there is no body, consider your target alive." Susan stood.

David said, "What do you want me to do?"

She smiled. "Figure out where Lena went, and what she's up to now."

David nodded. That day, he connected with different members of the SILVERSMITH team—including representatives from the FBI, Homeland Security, and the NSA. He ran the facts by them, gathering their thoughts and asking them to put out alerts to their agencies.

The next day, they caught a break. David gathered Susan and General Schwartz to show them what they had found.

"Last week the US Navy and Coast Guard conducted a joint boarding on a vessel about a hundred miles off the coast of Central America. Drug smugglers use standard lanes coming up from South America and into Mexico, and we think this was a mothership. This particular mothership was empty, except for one dead body. But the forensics analysis now shows that at least five people were killed there. There is signals intelligence that suggests Lena Chou broadcast a radio transmission from that vessel."

Susan waved him on. "We know. We know. So…"

David held up his hand. "Here's the new news. You're familiar with a man by the name of Charles Beulah?"

General Schwartz and Susan both shook their heads. "Never heard of him."

"Did you hear about a religious fanatic in Oklahoma who is missing after they found his wife dead in their home?"

General Schwartz frowned. "I think I read something about that. Saw the headline…"

The NSA analyst in the room spoke up. "Chinese social network bot farms have been plastering this guy's name up—"

David interrupted. "Can you explain what those are, for those who might not be familiar?"

"Sure. Governments like Russia and China sponsor bot farms—"

David said, "Start with bot."

The analyst looked annoyed. "Bot. Robot. A bot is a software program that automatically performs a certain task. Like an automated response for your email. But bots can get a lot more advanced than that. Foreign intelligence services will create fake profiles on social media. They will program these bots to post or relay information from each of these fake social media accounts—this acts to amplify a certain message."

General Schwartz said, "Pardon me, I'm just an old soldier. Posting online for everyone to see isn't really my style. I don't have, nor do I want, a Facebook account. So my question is, does that really work?"

David said, "The bot farms can control millions of fake social media profiles. To answer your question, sir—yes. We've done studies that show how they really do influence people's opinions. These fake accounts look and behave like real people. And with the way these social networks are set up—especially in China, where the government controls everything—the effect is that your average user believes that an idea or article is very popular. This idea of appearing popular is very important in shifting people's opinions. I mean, why else would companies spend billions of dollars a year on marketing, if it didn't work?"

Susan said, "Marketing 101. If you want to influence people to think a certain way, convince them that everyone else likes what you're selling. So these bots in China are amplifying certain ideas?"

The NSA analyst nodded. "Yes. They have been talking a lot about anti-Western and, in particular, anti-religious themes lately. This guy Charles Beulah is a popular target."

"Why?"

"Because he's nuts. Or at least, that's the way the Chinese websites are portraying him. He's well known there in some circles. He proclaims to be pro-America and pro-Christianity. But some of his views are way out there, and he's obsessed with China. His website talks about how he wants the US to use drones to kill Chinese politicians, for example."

"Okay. And this guy just went missing?"

David said, "Yes. A local relative drove to Beulah's house and found his wife dead inside the home. Beulah hasn't been seen since. The SILVERSMITH team gets any news and intelligence bulletins that might be related to China. This one crossed our desk, but at the time we didn't think it was relevant."

"But?"

"I asked the NSA to focus some of their more sophisticated surveillance programs on that area, to see if anything pops up related to Lena Chou."

The NSA analyst tapped on his computer and an image appeared on the screen. It was a white van. The resolution was good, but the van was a bit blurry. "Sorry that the picture isn't perfect. This was taken from a home security camera one mile from the Beulah residence, the same day that the coroner's office says the wife was killed."

In the passenger seat of the van sat a woman. Long black hair flowed down from her head, covering half her face. From what was visible, she looked Asian.

"You think that's Lena Chou?"

"Yes."

"That would never hold up in court. It's not clear enough."

"I wasn't aware that was our standard."

"It's not. Good work."

General Schwartz leaned forward, his hands on the table. "Am I thinking about this right? What are we saying here? That Lena Chou murdered the wife of this religious activist?"

David said, "Correct. And she didn't act alone. The bullets found on the drug smugglers' boat were fired from weapons favored by Chinese navy special operations. And someone is driving her in that van. Looks like an Asian male, about twenty to thirty years old."

"So Lena and a Chinese *special operations unit* murdered people on a drug-smuggling boat in the Eastern Pacific? And this same unit murdered Chuck Beulah's wife—*inside* the continental United States?"

The FBI representative said, "That is one possible conclusion, yes. We don't have hard evidence that Lena Chou and/or any other Chinese nationals were involved in the Beulah shooting."

General Schwartz said, "But this Beulah religious activist guy is missing. And Lena Chou is still missing."

"Presumed dead by the Chinese." Susan added.

"So where the hell are they now?"

Susan shook her head. "This is sloppy. Why use Chinese weapons on the drug-smuggling boat? And why wasn't she more careful not to get photographed? The woman is a trained intelligence operative, wanted by both China and the United States. But she's driving around riding shotgun in the middle of Oklahoma?"

David said, "To be fair, no one was looking for her there. But that part concerns me too. My only thought is that she isn't worried about repercussions from the United States."

"But why? We'll bring this evidence to the Chinese. President Wu has been very cooperative. He's going to agree with us that—"

A sharp knock on the door interrupted the meeting.

One of the other SILVERSMITH team members cracked it open and stuck his head in. "Sorry to interrupt, but you guys need to turn on the news immediately…"

10

Lena Chou's caravan of vehicles came to a halt just outside a towering building in central Beijing. Her long black hair swung back and forth as she walked up to the chief security guard on the Chinese presidential detail. He recognized her on sight.

"Good morning, Miss Chou."

"Good morning. Everything set?"

"As you have instructed us, ma'am. The streets have been cleared for two blocks around this position. All security cameras have been shut off."

"Excellent work."

She turned back towards her vehicles and nodded her head. Doors simultaneously opened, and men in suits identical to the presidential guard's got out of the vehicles. The rear door of one of the SUVs was opened, and a body bag removed. Two men carried it tucked under their right arms.

There were more than a dozen of them in all. Each carried a black duffle bag filled with clothing, weapons, and equipment.

They stood in the lobby, waiting for the elevators to come down. No one spoke. The group was one of Jinshan's "wet" teams. They were the cleaners—the mechanics who sought out and killed informants and spies of foreign governments. They also took part in assassinating rival businessmen and politicians when Jinshan required it. They specialized in making it look like an accident.

But today was unique, even for them.

A ding announced the opening of the elevator door. Five of the men stepped inside and took the elevator up to the floor just below the penthouse suite.

Lena rolled her eyes. She was spoiled from years of work outside of this country. Elevators in China were known for being extremely small. Because the elevators were so tiny, and the building so tall, this process of getting her men up the building took several minutes.

Once gathered on the floor below the Chinese president, Lena and the others conducted their final stages of preparation. They retrieved specially tailored clothing from their bags and began putting it on—white tunics with a bright red cross painted on both the front and back. Matching masks with little slits in the eye and mouth areas.

"Everyone ready?" Lena asked.

Nods all around.

They looked ridiculous, wearing sheets over their heads. It looked like some type of cult. But from her time in the US, she knew that the outfit had been designed to resemble that of the KKK, a fanatical hate group that claimed ties to Christianity. In all of Lena's time in America, she had never met anyone in the KKK. And her experience with Christians had been unremarkable. But as Jinshan was always saying, truth was malleable. What mattered was what Chinese commoners would believe, after today.

"Follow me."

The group took the fire escape stairway up the final flight of stairs. Masks on. Weapons out. Lena was the only one who hadn't bothered with a mask yet. She might be caught on camera. But no one would be investigating the matter other than Jinshan's loyalists, and they would quickly find out, if they inquired, that Lena wasn't to be investigated.

The presidential guards in the hallway saw Lena coming. One

whispered something into his cuff, and they began walking away from their posts.

It was remarkable. Even she couldn't believe how Jinshan's fingers had infiltrated *that* section of the government. But everyone had a price, a desire, a fear. Everyone had a motivation—something that Jinshan the artist could use to mold the world into his vision.

The penthouse door opened and several more presidential guards left, hurrying down the hall, opposite Lena and her approaching troop.

Lena and her team of white-sheeted and armed men entered the penthouse.

"What is this?"

There he was. President Wu. His eyes widened as he saw the white-masked men fanning out throughout the spacious living area.

"Where are my guards?" His words were directed at her, the first hint of fear in his tone.

Lena said, "They left."

She stood in the center of the white marble entranceway, thick columns rising up on either side of her. She was a picturesque statue, all at once beautiful and grotesque. Her dark eyes and sharp features would be the envy of any runway model, but for the scars.

A flash of recognition hit the president as he stared at her. One of Lena's men grabbed hold of him.

Two screams came from the bedroom. Seconds later, her men emerged, holding the president's wife and daughter kicking and screaming in their arms.

Lena focused on the daughter. She was only fifteen or sixteen, by the look of it. An odd feeling came over Lena. Maybe it was that ridiculous discussion with Natesh, about how some people weren't meant to see certain things. But she felt sorry for the girl. Lena decided that the daughter didn't need to be a part of this.

"Tie the daughter up and place her down in my vehicle." No one questioned Lena's orders. Two of the men left with the teenager, who was whimpering now but didn't put up a fight.

President Wu said, "You are Lena Chou. Jinshan's agent…"

"I am." Her eyes were unblinking.

485

"Jinshan—is he what you are here for? Is his freedom what you are trying to accomplish? You are going to hold us hostage for his release? Miss Chou, this tactic is not in your best interests. Jinshan's fate and yours are not tied together. Please reconsider before..."

Lena's lips formed a thin smile as she studied the president. Leader of one point four billion people. And now that his life was in danger, he flew back to the familiar. Calculating and probing. The master politician. Trying to find weakness and motive in his opponent.

But Lena had realized long ago that famous politicians and celebrities were often nothing more than propped-up machinations, created by publicity studios and marketing firms. Without their makeup and their carefully crafted speeches, they were nothing. Lena was unmoved by his words.

"Sit them down," she said to her men.

They forced President Wu and his wife onto one of the couches. The wife was near hysterical. She wouldn't stop screaming.

Lena sighed. "Gag her, please."

One of her men stuffed a rag in the woman's mouth and used tape to keep it in there. The wife looked like she was choking at first but then calmed down, breathing through her nose, closing her tear-filled eyes as if she could wish this all away.

Several of her men began removing equipment from silver cases. They set up cameras and microphones. A tripod was placed ten feet in front of the couch, and then a camera placed atop it.

President Wu was red-faced. "I will not release Cheng Jinshan. And my guards will be here soon. They will—"

Lena stood tall in front of the president. "Your guards left voluntarily."

He stopped speaking at that. While he had seen his presidential security detail depart, he hadn't thought about the implications until now. His eyes lowered, a wave of defeat washing over him.

"We don't want you to release Cheng Jinshan, Mr. President."

He looked up at her, confused. "Then what do you want me to do?"

* * *

Lin Yu stood behind the counter of his uncle's small electronics store in central Guangzhou. He ate a lunch of reheated noodles with steamed vegetables. He used one hand to take another bite with his chopsticks while using the other to scan the social media feed on his phone.

His shop was empty, as usual. Beneath his elbows was a glass display filled with rows of cell phone parts. Memory cards. Screens. Microchips. Some of the big cell phone suppliers were located nearby. Lin Yu's store sold spare parts and secondary items from those plants. The manufacturers got rid of parts that they didn't need and reduced their overhead. Everybody won.

Except for Lin Yu, working in this dead-end job. Entire weeks would go by without a single customer. Then the floodgates would open as buyers came in from all over the world, here to find bargain prices for their companies. Lin Yu's uncle would show up on those weeks. He would take out his calculator and bargain with the men on prices and quantities. The purchasers would use the display cases to point to which item they were interested in. The quantities were often astronomical during those busy weeks. But during the dry season, as Lin Yu called it, manning the store was a dreadfully boring task.

However, Lin Yu needed a job. He couldn't go home during the day. He still lived with his parents. And the longer he was there, the more likely his mother would be to drive him towards insanity.

All the woman talked about was him finding a woman to marry so that she could have a grandchild before she was dead. She wasn't fifty years old yet and she was talking about her own death. More likely, she just used the all-powerful bargaining chip that all mothers possessed—guilt.

It wasn't Lin Yu's fault that he couldn't find a girlfriend. It wasn't like he was uninterested. It was just slim pickings.

One of his friends had forwarded him an article last year that said China had thirty-three million more men than women. His friend had meant for the article as a joking excuse for why they couldn't find girlfriends. But as Lin Yu had read the article, he had been fascinated—and horrified—at the conclusions. The article had been written by a Western journalist, and it had been deleted on China's Internet by the censors shortly after Lin Yu had read it. The article claimed that the one-child policy and sex-selective abortions had driven the gender disparity in China. At the height of the problem, in the early 2000s, there had been twenty percent more male babies being born than female.

"Hey, Lin Yu. Get any customers?" His friend who worked at a similar shop down the hall stood in the doorway.

"Nothing. You?"

"Nah. This week will be sleepy, I think. I'm off now, though. Done for the day. I have to go help my mom with something."

He grabbed a snap pea from Lin Yu's lunch.

"Hey, stop it—come on."

"Relax. Just one. I'm hungry. Hey, what are you reading? The stuff about the navy ships?"

Everyone was talking about the recent American attacks on their navy ships in the Pacific. It was a horrible accident. The PLA Navy ships had been on a training mission in the Pacific Ocean, but somehow an American ship had accidentally fired weapons at them. At least, that was the story he read on the state news.

"You know that news is all fake, right?"

Lin Yu frowned. His friend was always telling him that the news he read was bogus. He was one of the rule-breakers. He used a VPN to dig under China's government-censored Internet—"the great firewall of China." His friend would often check out foreign news websites. And just as often, dirty pictures of white women.

"What are you talking about?" said Lin Yu.

Feng brought up his phone and tapped a few times. "Here. See? The British news is saying that it wasn't an accident. They say that some of the Chinese ships were there on purpose. And that one of *our* submarines fired first."

"What? That's crazy. Why would our submarine do that? Tell me you don't believe that crap."

His friend grabbed a noodle from Lin Yu's bowl and held it up, slurping it down.

"Come on. Stop that. This is my lunch."

"It's a good lunch."

"What are you talking about with the navy ships?" Lin Yu didn't believe him, but it was still very interesting to hear about.

"Something's going on, Lin Yu. Something big. I can feel it." His friend tapped his heart. "You've seen all the signs about Junxun, right? When was the last time you ever heard about Junxun being held in winter? And the kids who volunteered—they *still* haven't come back." Junxun was the Chinese government-sponsored summer training program for all high school graduates. Each year, millions of Chinese teens were forced to attend a multi-week military basic training program that prepared them for military service, in case that were ever to be required.

"What are you talking about?"

"I have a cousin who volunteered for the Guangdong Junxun a few weeks ago. My aunt hasn't heard from him this whole time. She wrote to the People's Liberation Army office where they said parents can call, but they just gave her some line about hearing from him soon. But that was last week. Trust me, there's something mysterious going on, and they aren't telling us about it."

"You're a conspiracy theorist. You don't know what you're talking about."

Lin Yu's friend rolled his eyes. "Okay."

"Whoa. What is this?" Lin Yu held his phone so that his friend could see.

"Oh my. Is that the president?"

"What? Oh no."

"Is this live?" His friend tapped the volume button on Lin Yu's phone so that they could hear what was being said.

* * *

Lena walked out on the outdoor patio and waited until both cameras were set up inside. She savored the view, up here atop the city's skyscrapers. They had another camera positioned on a rooftop across the street. That one would pick up great footage, with maximum psychological impact. It would get a view of the open-air garden outside the president's suite, where she now stood, and of the ropes that were slung over the thick wooden beam atop the tall awning.

Her men had tested this part out for hours. They couldn't make any mistakes here—not today. Jinshan had worked with his cyberoperators to ensure the bandwidth could handle such a massive audience for this footage. It would be live-streamed on all of China's social networks and TV stations.

One of her men approached. "The cameras are rolling, ma'am. We're on CCTV. The newscasters have been informed. It's time, Miss Chou."

Lena thought about her pseudonym briefly. She could use her birth name, now that she was back in China. But she had grown fond of the name Lena Chou. She took in a deep whiff of the garden flowers and said, "Very well. Let us begin."

Her men began dragging President Wu and his wife out to the garden area. The two of them could see the nooses swinging now, and both were fighting mightily against their restraints. Lena walked back inside, out of view for the moment.

"Why would you do this? Why is Jinshan doing this? Whatever he has promised you, I can give you more."

She stayed inside the covered area, behind the glass wall, until her white mask was on. Then she walked back outside, speaking through the small cutout for her mouth.

"No. You *can't*, Mr. President. That's really why we are here, isn't it? Few are capable of leading us to the future that Mr. Jinshan has promised. They don't have the stomach for it. The world is changed not by mere politicians and statesmen, but by those capable few who build great things—who seize power and force drastic action. China has been moving too slowly, Mr. President. But no longer. You should know that your deaths here today will serve a greater purpose." She leaned in close. "I want to thank you for your sacrifice."

She picked up the gas canister and poured the pungent clear

liquid on top of his head. He coughed and then nearly vomited as it drizzled down his body. His wife tried to cry out in fits, muzzled by her gag. Then she too was doused with the flammable liquid. Lena was careful not to spill it on her own clothing.

The nooses were placed around their necks, and the men behind them pulled steadily on the ropes, which began raising the president and his wife in the air. Their hands tied behind their backs, there was nothing they could do as the ropes tightened and lifted them up. Their faces transformed into plums, veins nearly popping out.

One of her men handed her a small lighting torch. She clicked the metal starter, and it ignited. Their white masks and tunics, while designed to mimic the look of the American KKK, also served another purpose. They were made with flame-resistant material, to reduce the risk that they might accidentally burn themselves. Lena walked up to the president of the world's largest country, who was now swaying on his noose, the life squeezing out of him.

Fire would accelerate the process.

Lena held the torch to his feet and felt the familiar tingle that only violence could bring her. She tried to conceal her bloodlust as she raised the flame up and the gasoline ignited. She then walked over to the woman and repeated the process.

They didn't scream. They couldn't. Through her white mask, two flames reflected in her brown eyes. The burning bodies shook and then went still, flesh melting and turning black. A violent, horrific end.

The black smoke rose up into the air. One of the burning ropes snapped, and the president's flaming corpse fell to the ground.

She called out, "Time to leave."

But two of her men were coming in through the penthouse entrance, shoving the daughter along by her arms.

"What is this? I told you to place her in my vehicle."

One of them handed her a phone.

Jinshan's voice on the other end. "*Everyone*, Lena. The daughter is the most important piece." She began to reply, but the line was dead. Jinshan hadn't spoken to her in that tone in years. She wondered which of the men had reported her amendment to the plan to Jinshan.

Her demons twisted around inside her mind, one lusting for more blood, the other filled with sorrow and sympathy as she looked at the poor girl's tears. Unfamiliar emotions to Lena, but powerful ones. The daughter was on her knees now, reacting to the sight of her burning parents, the men trying to control her as she sobbed and fought and cried.

Everyone, Lena.

She found herself thinking about what she had said to Natesh, only a few days ago. *We all have to do things that we don't want to do sometimes.* Amen. So be it.

Lena walked over to the girl. Sixteen, Lena decided, not fifteen. A pink hair tie in her hair. A silver locket around her neck.

The fire was too large for them to hang the girl like they had her parents. Lena brought the daughter to the center of the outdoor garden, a spot she was sure was covered well by all the cameras.

"Stay," she said to the girl, who was looking into her own eyes. She no longer had tears. Just a numb look of curiosity, perhaps at hearing her voice and seeing that Lena was a woman, hiding under that white mask. Maybe the girl was wondering what sort of monster would take part in this. What sort of gruesome creature?

Lena pulled out a black handgun that had been holstered under her robe and stared back into the girl's face, feeling the cold metal weapon in her hand and reflecting. The fires of her dead parents burned in the background, warming them both.

You are wondering how I became this way? Scarred skin and full of bloodlust? I was like you once. Beautiful and innocent, filled with the hopeful dreams of the young. But then I was torn from my home and molded into this creature that you see before you. A spy. An assassin. A warrior, fighting for the cause. But the lies and violence have made me numb. What is good and evil, when I have to do this?

Lena raised up the pistol and fired a single shot into the girl's forehead.

11

David looked at the TV screen in the CIA conference room.

BREAKING NEWS: CHINESE PRESIDENT AND WIFE KILLED.

"This footage is coming to you live from Beijing. We need to put out a warning to all of our viewers that this may be disturbing video. There have already been two reported deaths. We're still trying to get audio worked out with our news bureau there, but it looks like this is some sort of penthouse—you can see the outdoor patio. It's a...okay, hold on. We now have our chief Chinese bureau correspondent with us. Tim, can you hear us?"

A British-accented voice came over the TV.

. . .

"Yes, we're watching this video with you for the first time. We do have confirmation that the president and his wife have been killed. We are about to see that footage. This area of Beijing is a very upscale section. And we are being told that the penthouse suite in this building was being occupied by the Chinese president and his family. It began as some sort of hostage situation. The streets are being cleared and the police are on scene. As you can see, it looks like there are several masked persons walking out on the patio with automatic rifles. All of them are wearing white shirts with red crosses on the front and back. And it appears that they've strung up some type of rope—a noose, it looks like—over one of the high wooden beams on the penthouse patio. Oh. Oh my."

"Holy shit. What are they doing? Are they going to hang her?"

Susan said, "I think so. My God. That's the Chinese president's wife. And that's the president."

They watched in horror as the two were strung up, hung, and burned.

"How could this happen?"

"Doesn't the Chinese president have security like ours?"

"Yes, of course."

"Then how is this possible?"

"I don't know."

David and his coworkers watched in shock as the violence unfolded on TV. The newscasters provided more dialogue, trying to make sense of what they were witnessing.

"I'm getting word from our producers that we need to cut to—okay, this video that we're about to show you is from a group that claims to be responsible for what is going on. They are calling themselves the American Christians Against China Coalition."

The screen cut to a white man of about sixty years of age. He was sitting in front of a bare beige background. His face was red as he spoke. The video was clearly heavily edited, but the quotes were from his mouth.

"Someone should stop those guys! I mean they're killing babies...I would kill 'em. I think those Chinese communist bastards who do that deserve to die... I am a Christian...I think all atheists are going to burn in the eternal fires of hell. Especially those in China cuz they're killing all them Christian babies...That Chinese president deserves to die, just like the rest of 'em. He's part of the problem then. Spreading atheism and killing babies. And now they're trying to sink our Navy ships and shootin' down our helicopters. Damn those bastards to hell."

David looked at Susan. "That's Charles Beulah."

General Schwartz said, "The religious fanatic?"

"Yes."

David shook his head. "This has to be set up."

Susan nodded. She walked over and picked up her phone.

"Who are you calling?"

"I want to have some of the NSA folks put some numbers behind this. I want to know what the Chinese media and social media are saying about all this."

David looked back at the screen. He covered his mouth, disturbed by the image of two bodies swinging from a noose, burning.

"I'm not sure that you need the NSA to tell you. They're going to be going crazy."

One of the people wearing a white robe walked out onto the garden area, dragging a younger-looking Chinese woman with them.

"Who is that? She looks young."

The person in the white robe lifted up a pistol from beneath the garment, aimed it at the head of the young woman, and fired.

"Oh my God." David winced and turned away for a moment.

Susan shook her head. "I think that might have been the daughter. We're going to need to put together a preliminary assessment of how this is playing over there."

* * *

Director Buckingham was in his office with one of his deputies when Susan and David arrived.

"What are your thoughts?"

Susan said, "It's too early to say who's responsible."

"Gut?"

David crossed his arms. "This sounds like Jinshan. Everything we've seen from him has been carefully orchestrated. He has a talent for manipulating public opinion."

Susan filled the director in on the information David and the team had uncovered regarding Lena and the religious fanatic, Charles Beulah.

"So this is the work of Lena Chou?"

"And by association, Jinshan. That's a guess. The evidence is sketchy right now, but we'll obviously dig further."

The deputy director of the CIA said, "You think Jinshan would have the balls to off his own president? He's in prison right now, isn't he? How the hell is he supposed to orchestrate anything?"

Susan said, "Sir, we have reports that he's still been active, even while awaiting his trial. Putting him in prison in China is like putting Pablo Escobar in prison in Colombia. He still has access to and communication with many of his loyalists."

The dark blue phone rang and the director picked up, glancing at his audience. "Director Buckingham. Yes, sir, Mr. President. I'm just speaking with my team now." He looked at his watch. "Very well, sir, I'll work out timing with the chief of staff." He hung up the phone.

"We need something fast. The president wants an estimate on what we think the Chinese reaction will be. I assume that Secretary Zhang is now in charge over there. Please confirm that and coordinate with State to make sure they're feeding you everything they know. Susan, you have one hour to prepare a brief. I want you two with me when we head to the White House."

"Me?" David said.

"You know Lena Chou better than anyone. You two better get moving."

* * *

David found the Situation Room utterly intimidating. He wanted nothing more than to leave, but the importance of the conversation kept him from letting his mind wander too much.

The president had just finished listening to Susan's geopolitical estimate—how China would react to the death of their president, ostensibly at the hands of an American religious fanatic.

"So, you think that this Cheng Jinshan might be responsible for this? And what—they decided to blame it on religious extremists?"

"Not just any religious extremists, sir. *Christian* extremists. Americans, specifically. We think that was very purposeful. This particular man who the Chinese are holding responsible has been vilified on Chinese news media sites for several weeks now. Just before this meeting began, I saw that the Chinese state-sponsored news is now showing an image of Beulah's corpse at the crime scene in China, supposedly shot by police. But based on our own initial investigation, we suspect that this may be a ploy. We think that Chinese agents may have taken that religious fanatic from his home and brought him to China. It's possible that this is another deception created by Jinshan."

The president raised an eyebrow. "Why? I mean, why a religious fanatic?"

Susan said, "Sir, it's possible that Jinshan's war plans are still being executed. In their Red Cell operation, when they created their set of psychological warfare plans, one of the objectives was to suffi-ciently motivate the Chinese people."

"Motivate them to do what?"

David said, "To want to go to war with America, sir. The Red Cell was looking for social or cultural issues that would help drive a wedge between the two countries. Religion was it. We looked at polling. In 2016, over seventy-three percent of the United States identified as Christian. Eighty-two percent identified as religious. In China, while religion statistics are hard to accurately measure, the polls we looked at were flipped. Between fifty and ninety percent of Chinese citizens were *not* religious. And only two percent were Christian. Those who do practice religion in China do so with the government carefully watching the churches."

"So what's the idea? Make the Chinese people hate Christians? Make America into a Christian boogeyman?"

"Pretty much, Mr. President."

He looked at the director of the CIA. "What's your take? Would that strategy work?"

"Mr. President, at this time, we're just trying to confirm whether or not Cheng Jinshan had a part in this. But it fits with his profile. He has enormous influence over the Chinese government's communications tools—its media messaging. This Christian extremism angle could be a very effective cornerstone for a propaganda campaign— one designed to rally a country to war."

The acting National Security Advisor said, "But Jinshan is supposed to be on trial, right? Is that still happening?"

"We believe so, yes."

The president said, "Let's pretend for a moment that Jinshan is continuing his war plans—are we seeing other signals that are consistent with a war drumbeat?"

Director Buckingham said, "This is the other item that we need to discuss. While we are seeing coastal military activity and Chinese naval activity decrease, we're still seeing a flurry of movement with the Chinese army and air force at bases located several hundred miles or more inland. Our analysts are in disagreement over what this means. It could be that the inland military activity is unrelated, and that the coastal and naval military activity is them complying with our demand that they stand down after last week's hostilities."

The president said, "I'm guessing that I'm not going to like the other theory, am I?"

"No, Mr. President," said Director Buckingham. "Sir, the other theory involves electromagnetic pulse weapons."

The president closed his eyes for a moment and then reopened them, turning to the Chairman of the Joint Chiefs of Staff. "Let's start talking about how we can prepare for the worst."

The attorney general said, "Look, gentlemen, my background is in law. And the evidence that you've presented is highly speculative. Bullets at a crime scene at sea as evidence that the Chinese military did it? A picture that shows an Asian woman with half her face covered as evidence that the Chinese kidnapped someone on American soil? Let's just slow down. Yes, there has been a tragic event that has occurred in China. But, Mr. President, if I may...this could present us with new opportunities. If Secretary Zhang is installed as their new president, that could be very good for US-China trade relations. And that would mean jobs, Mr. President..."

David could see the twinkle in the eyes of both politicians. Jobs. Approval ratings. *Votes*.

The president said, "General, what is your take? Give it to us straight. Is China preparing for war?" He spoke to the Chairman of the Joint Chiefs of Staff.

"With all due respect to Director Buckingham and the excellent work that his staff has done, I would urge caution against shouting that the sky is falling just yet. Yes, someone has just killed the Chinese president. Yes, there may be evidence of a continued conspiracy against the United States. But I find it hard to believe that China could be planning for a massive war without making a much more visible footprint. I agree it would be prudent to take precautions. But with all that's going on in the region—including options that we've discussed to tame North Korea—I don't want to over-stress our armed forces by taking unnecessary action. Our military is spread pretty thin as it is. And we have a strong presence in the region that serves as a deterrent to China."

The president said, "What's your estimate for worst-case scenario, General?"

"Worst case, Mr. President?" The general rubbed his chin. "Well, I was concerned about the report I read that they were purchasing equipment for up to ten million troops. Blood bags, I think it was. I even read one of General Schwartz's memos on the increased military recruitment they've been doing."

"So you *are* concerned?"

The general took his time. "Honestly, Mr. President, I just don't see the Chinese military capable of long-range power projection. There are strategic disadvantages they have, based on the makeup of their armed forces. It is possible that if they became truly belligerent, I would say that perhaps China finally makes a play for Taiwan. But anything beyond that is just not realistic, in my view. A large-scale war would be settled by the US Air Force and Navy in the far Western Pacific. Our bases in Korea and Japan, and our carrier strike groups in the region, simply have too much firepower for them to test us there."

Director Buckingham surprised David by speaking. "And, General, what if the Chinese *did* get past our fleet in the Western Pacific, and were able to neutralize US and allied military forces in Japan and Korea?"

The general said, "The Pacific Ocean is very large. And we have critical military strongholds on Guam and Hawaii. Those are very strategic locations. Our aerial refueling program allows us to project air power all across the Pacific. Our airborne early-warning aircraft and other radar assets provide us advance notice should anything go wrong. As long as we have Guam and Hawaii, and air superiority, China could never challenge American dominance in the Pacific."

The president said, "Thank you, gentlemen. General, please take precautions as you see fit. But let's not do anything that might provoke China during an unstable transition period."

Director Buckingham, in an unusual breach of protocol, spoke after the president. "Mr. President, excuse me. One more question for the general. What if, to play devil's advocate, China *were* able to find a way to neutralize all four of those locations—Korea, Japan, Guam, and Hawaii? What then, General?"

The general let out a snort, frowning and shaking his head. "It'd never happen."

"What if?" the director pressed.

"Well, then, we'd be shit out of luck, wouldn't we?"

12

L in Yu walked through the crowded marketplace. Carts of food and cheap goods were stacked along the curb. Young men carrying heavy burlap bags of produce on their shoulders hustled to restock the outdoor shops. Mobs of people moved in and out of the street like ants. Salesmen hawked their products. The old women bargain-hunters had made their way down from tiny high-rise apartments, eager for their daily entertainment. Young and old alike, their heads were buried in their mobile phones when they weren't actively doing anything else. The normal fast-paced bustle of life in Guangzhou, China.

But there was something new in the crowd today. A tension that hadn't been there the week before. Before the president and his family had been murdered on live TV.

People were kinder to each other. More polite to each other. More open in their conversations with perfect strangers. "That poor girl."

But there was something else. They were *unified*. Angry at foreigners, and at the religious zealots that would attack their peaceful leader.

Lin Yu's social network feed was a volcano of fury. People

wanted revenge on the man responsible for the terrorist attacks on their president and his family.

But it was too late.

The police had killed the Christian terrorists as they'd entered the building. Four white people. Americans, they said. The leader was a Christian advocate against the Chinese government. He had posted videos online, and everyone had been sharing them. The lunatic had called for their president to be killed. He was obsessed with abortions and religion.

Lin Yu stopped at the market to purchase some vegetables—his mother wanted them to make dinner. He overheard the conversations ahead of him in line. An older woman was speaking to the owner of the small outdoor shop.

"Our poor president. And those poor women. I just hate the people that did this."

The store owner was nodding in agreement. "Yes. Yes. Especially for what they did to the daughter. Crazies, all of them. Religious fanatics."

"Have you heard that the government has started to come down hard on the local churches?"

"Yes. I saw one two streets over. They had rocks thrown in the window. Now, I don't think people should throw rocks at them, but—"

"And why not?" asked the woman. "They're responsible for this. We shouldn't allow them to spread their hateful message."

The store owner shrugged.

Lin Yu said, "Sir, may I buy these?" He held up a pair of bell peppers.

The man and the woman both shot him a look for interrupting.

The woman, spurred on by Lin Yu's impatience, finally handed the shopkeeper her items. The owner rang her up as she continued talking.

"I hear that the daughter was being taken out of the building, but that the religious leader—the American man from the video—he called her back in because he wanted everyone to see her being murdered. He knew that the TV cameras were on."

The woman shook her head. "Despicable."

"And the only one who is standing up for the citizens of our country *is on trial*. Did you hear? Cheng Jinshan is going before the Politburo on TV next week."

"I have heard that. I've never seen them do this before. A publicly broadcast corruption trial. They must know how much people care about the outcome."

The woman paid for her things and left. Lin Yu handed the man his peppers. "Who is Cheng Jinshan?"

The store owner scoffed. "You young people need to pay more attention. Don't you read the news? He is a businessman who was appointed by our late president to root out corruption in our government. And now they want to try him for conspiracy."

"What do they say that he did?" Lin Yu had heard of Jinshan, but he wasn't sure about the charges against him.

"Something about the military. He and an admiral from Guangzhou were training to defend us against the American military. Some say that he didn't ask permission. And somehow the American training accident that sank our navy ships was related to this. It's complicated. Not so easy for a young man like you to understand, I think. But Jinshan is a good man. He wants China to be strong and protect itself from other nations that would see us become nothing but their workers. You should watch tonight. Everyone else will be."

Lin Yu paid for his food and thanked the man, heading back home.

* * *

Lin Yu sat on his couch the next morning, half-watching TV while he scrolled through his social network feed on his phone.

"Hey, you see this?" His friend was pointing to the TV.

"What?"

"The government is looking for new employees. It will help you get training in technology and pay for college. Good pay and benefits while you serve your country. I think it's some military job."

"What, as a soldier?"

"I don't think so. Why would they talk about training you in technology if they wanted you to be a soldier?"

Lin Yu cocked his head, looking at the TV advertisement. He searched for more information on his phone. "I found it online. They say you can start work immediately. Oh, wow. They pay twice as much as I'm making in the phone parts shop."

His friend said, "Are you really interested?"

"For that much money? Maybe. I'll check it out on the way to work today."

An hour later, Lin Yu was walking into the Guangzhou recruiting office of the People's Liberation Army.

A pretty woman in a green uniform greeted him at the door. "Hello! Are you interested in signing up for our new program?"

Lin Yu pretended to be disinterested. He shrugged. "Maybe. I just wanted to hear about it."

The woman gently grabbed him by the shoulder, bringing him further into the small office. There was a line of young men and women signing up at a table on the other side of the room. Two other uniformed men sat behind the table, smiling and helping the new recruits to fill out their paperwork.

The woman looked Lin Yu up and down. "You have graduated from school?"

"Yes, last year."

"You speak any other languages?"

"Just Mandarin and Cantonese."

"Are you good with computers? Do you know how to do any programming?"

"Not really."

"Why don't we have you take a short test, and we can tell you what type of work you would qualify for? It's fun, try it!"

Lin Yu frowned and checked the time on his phone. "I don't know. I need to get to work in an hour."

The woman pulled out a chair at one of several empty desks and grabbed a laptop that was already set up. "Here. It will only take a few minutes. We'll get your results and have you on your way. You might be eligible for a big bonus if you score well. Trust me, you will want to know. Here, type in your name to start, and your birthday. Yes. There you go."

Lin Yu shrugged and began the test. The first question was easy. Simple math. The woman was still standing over his shoulder. She said, "There's a timer in the corner. See that? That tells you how long you have to answer each question. Okay, I'll be back. Let me know if you finish and I'm not here."

She walked back to the entrance, greeting more kids as they came in. Lin Yu was annoyed. He didn't want to be taking a test right now. But if there really was a better-paying job that could help him pay for university fees, he wanted to know about it. And lately, he'd felt a sense of patriotism that he'd never really felt before—ever since President Wu had been killed by the Americans. And he was very tired of sitting behind an empty store counter all day, hoping to hawk leftover cell phone parts to American suppliers in for the weekend.

The recruiter was right; the test went by quickly. Ten minutes and he was done. He turned around and she was leaning over him again, looking at the results screen. He could smell her perfume.

"Oh, yes, this is very good. You have done quite well." She smiled and tapped him on the arm. "You should be very proud of this score. Ninety-five percent. You are very smart."

"So, what does that mean? Ninety-five percent?"

She took out a booklet and thumbed through the pages. "Hmm. Hmm. Okay, yes. I think we would most likely place you in our mobility program."

Lin Yu said, "What's that?"

"It is for most of our best-qualified candidates. Are you physically fit?"

"Sure."

"Okay. You will need a physical examination before we can give you any guarantees. But..." She turned to check who was listening, then whispered, "I'm pretty sure that this score will get you into our exceptional candidate program."

"Really? Do you have anything that I can read about what I would be doing?"

"Of course." She reached over to her desk and handed him a brochure, opening it to pictures of good-looking young men and women in uniform.

"You would do a few weeks of accelerated training here in Guangzhou. Then, depending on what you select after that, you might be able to travel. Many of our recruits are promoted right away out of training if they're smart like you. You would probably be promoted right away. Maybe you will be my boss someday?" She smiled.

"What's the pay?"

"Oh, the pay is very good. Very competitive. You can find all that in the brochure. And after you're in your job for two years, you become eligible for college tuition financial aid. This will help your career if you decide to leave the military."

Lin Yu checked the time again. "I think I need to go."

"Sure, no problem. Just sign this form first, please. You can come back to this address tomorrow and we can get your physical examination done. Once you do that, we'll know for sure about your signing bonus and how much that will be."

Lin Yu liked the sound of that. The only bonus he had seen in the past few years was when his uncle had given him extra hours of work during the busy season.

He signed the form and they said goodbye.

Lin Yu walked out the door and headed down the street.

The woman recruiter waited until he was gone and then headed over to someone else who had just finished their test. She leaned over and looked at their screen. She said, "Oh...this is a very good score! Ninety-five percent!"

* * *

Lin Yu had to hurry to work. He didn't want to be late. But he had an added spring in his step after acing the military aptitude test. He hadn't failed to notice that the woman who was recruiting him was somewhat attractive. Perhaps after he joined the military—if he decided to do so—he could ask her out on a date?

The wide road sloped down and curved around near a park, large green willow trees providing shade from overhead. It was warm and humid, even this time of year.

There were a lot more of the volunteers walking around, wearing those red armbands. The armbands had Chinese characters in yellow that said "Security Patrol." They were just normal people. But they acted like they were police. Stopping foreigners to check their passports. Telling people not to take their pictures. And standing outside the churches…

There were boisterous crowds gathered ahead. At first, Lin Yu thought he was just hearing the usual city noise. But as he passed the food carts and outdoor markets, filled with people hawking street food and trinkets, he noticed something else.

A temple. No, a church. There was a construction crane pulling and tugging at the top of the church. And the crowd was chanting below. Dozens of police were there, holding the crowd back. Even more of the volunteers in red armbands stood behind the police. Onlookers had clustered around the activity.

A snap from overhead, and a large wooden beam fell down to the ground. The crane had tugged the cross down from the top of the church. It landed with a smack and splintered into multiple pieces.

A woman thrust a pamphlet towards him. She said, "End the persecution of Christians. They say that we are free to worship, but we are not. End the persecution of Christians. Stop the…"

A police officer with a black club came over, grabbing the pamphlet. "What is this? Stop what you're doing. You are not allowed to give this out. You do not have permission. Who are you?" He pointed the club at Lin Yu.

"No one. She just…"

The woman screamed and pointed across the courtyard as two of the people wearing red armbands began beating a man wearing white robes—a priest, by the look of him. The police stood by, doing nothing.

Several people had their phones out. They were taking videos. Some in the crowd were yelling to stop, but it wasn't clear whom they were commanding—the police or the Christian group.

More police vehicles arrived, and the crowd spread out. Two cracks and then tear gas canisters plummeted from the sky. Lin Yu ran away from the scene, coughing, his eyes burning.

He arrived at work a few minutes later, out of breath and wondering what he had just seen. He went to the bathroom and washed his eyes out in the sink. Then he went to the shop and began speaking with the girl who was working the shift before him.

He told her what he had seen.

"I was just reading about it." She pointed to her phone.

"You were reading about it? Already?"

He looked over her shoulder. She was on her social network feed. There were hundreds of comments on it, streaming in real time. Images, videos.

"It says that the church priest was breaking the law. I'm not surprised. Those Christian churches are criminal organizations, most of them. They're money-making schemes. Passing around baskets for all those poor gullible people to give away their money. I heard in school that a lot of other governments will send missionaries here to try and hurt our own government leaders. They don't like how successful China has become, so they try to infect us with their religious groups."

Lin Yu said, "I don't know. I knew a man who was Christian. He worked in one of the shops here. He wasn't so bad."

"No way. They're all crazy if you ask me. The Islamists and the Christians. Anyone who thinks that some magic god is real and tells people to kill everyone in the train station with knives should be thrown in prison. If you ask me, I'm thankful that our police got rid of that church. I don't want people like that in our city."

Lin Yu knew she was referring to the Kunming Railway Station attack in 2014. Six men and two women with connections to a Uyghur Muslim group had stormed into a train station and begun attacking people with knives and cleavers. They had killed thirty-one people and wounded 143.

"I need to go. Bye."

Lin Yu waved and hopped onto his stool behind the counter. He thumbed through his social network feed and saw news articles on the priest who had been arrested. The article made no mention of the fact that the church had been shut down or the cross removed. It also made no mention of any tear gas or other arrests. It just said that the priest was a criminal and had been arrested.

Then Lin Yu saw that he had an email from the military recruiter. It was a confirmation of his appointment the next day. He looked up and down the hallway outside. It was empty. He would be lucky if he got any sales over the next six hours. He sighed. He decided that he would go to the military physical examination the next day. What could be the harm?

* * *

Lin Yu had never felt less human than he'd felt this morning at the military physical exam. The pretty woman recruiter had been nowhere to be seen. The military men who helped to corral the recruits like cattle were not smiling. They were stern and tough looking.

"What is your name, recruit?"

"Lin Yu."

"That's Lin Yu, Sergeant!"

"Lin Yu, Sergeant," he muttered.

"Here are your papers. Memorize this number—this is your serial number—and go follow this line until you get to the room that says 'Immunizations.' Wait there and someone will tell you what to do." The sergeant looked at him expectantly.

"Yes, Sergeant?"

"Go."

He hurried off down the hall, following a series of arrows that were painted on the floor. He didn't need this. He didn't want to be yelled at. Boredom in his shop was better than being yelled at. He decided that he would complete the physical—asking to leave would probably not be received well—and then go home. He would never call them again. He wouldn't return any emails. Screw that stupid aptitude test.

"Hey, you. You have your papers?"

A man wearing a white medical coat looked at him through a window.

"Yes. Here." He handed the thin envelope through the window.

The man looked at them and placed a stamp on the papers. Then he said, "Come on back."

Before Lin Yu knew it, he was rubbing his arm after getting four different shots. *Four.* They hadn't even answered him when he'd asked what they were for. They'd just stuck him and told him to keep moving. He kept going through different rooms and seeing different nurses and doctors. Some of them examined his hearing, some examined his eyesight. Others asked him to jump up as high as he could, measuring the highest place on a wall that he could reach. Others asked him stupid questions about whether he was happy or ever had thoughts of hurting people.

In each room were more exams, and his folder got thicker and thicker throughout the day. Finally, he went through a pair of double doors to the side of the building that he hadn't been to yet.

The sergeant was there. "Lin Yu, go stand on that yellow dot over in the corner." He looked around and saw that there were about twenty dots painted on the concrete floor. He went over to his. More recruits came in behind him, and before he knew it, all twenty yellow dots had people standing on them.

They were cattle. Being checked out for any medical problems. The sergeant was yelling at one of them for not standing up straight. Lin Yu rolled his eyes and then caught himself. He kept a plain expression on his face. Better not to draw the attention of this dim-witted sergeant. He didn't care what they were paying; he didn't want anything to do with this mess.

"Alright, recruits, I'm going to send the first row out this door. You'll get your haircuts next. After that you will get bags of clothing. Then you will be getting on a bus. Everyone understand?"

"Haircuts?" one of the boys in the front said. "I'm not getting a—"

Wham. The kid never saw it coming. The sergeant punched him right in the gut with tremendous force. Everyone stood up a little straighter, and the only sound was the wheezing of the poor guy who'd been hit. He was now on his knees, holding his stomach. Lin Yu's eyes were now wide.

"Everyone understand?" the sergeant repeated.

"Yes, Sergeant," the group replied in unison.

"Louder, recruits."

"*Yes, Sergeant!*"

Lin Yu's pulse was pounding now. Had there been a mistake? Did they think that he had volunteered for this? He had only signed a paper to get the physical examination. Not for anything else.

"First row, move."

Lin Yu was in the first row. He turned and entered the next room. There were six empty barber chairs, each with a man holding clippers standing behind them. Lin Yu sat down and was immediately covered by a smock. A click and then the dull buzz of the hair clippers. The feel of it shearing his scalp. Cold and hard. Fast and merciless. Clumps of black hair falling away to the floor.

"All done."

It was the quickest haircut he had ever received. He stared in the mirror, looking shocked at the bald person who was staring back.

"Move, recruits," said the sergeant from the door.

The next room had several other sergeants, each one louder and more ferocious than the last. They were handing out bags of clothing and supplies. Before Lin Yu knew it, he was lugging three heavy bags and one shoe box up the stairs of a bus.

The bus's engine was running. The candidates were all filing in, sheared heads and heavy canvas bags being stuffed into the seats. A recruit sat down next to him. It was the boy who'd been punched in the stomach. A tear rolled down his cheek.

"What's going on?" he whispered. "Did you sign up for this? They just told me that this was a physical exam. I didn't sign up for—"

"Shut up. You want to get us in trouble?" replied a voice from behind them. "Next time, read what you're signing. They got a lot of recruits that way. The paper that you signed at the recruiting station was the only one that mattered. That commits you to a minimum of two years. If you don't serve it out, you could face jail time."

Lin Yu went white.

"What?" said the kid next to him. He began crying into his hands.

The bus door squeaked shut, and a sergeant yelled, "Alright, recruits, I hope none of you get motion sickness. We'll be heading up into the mountains, and the road gets pretty bad. The last group puked all over the place. Okay, bus driver, let's go."

The bus left the parking lot, its silent passengers in shock, each contemplating their future.

13

Cheng Jinshan heard the keys rattling on the outside of his prison door. A click. Then the door swung open. A young officer flanked by two guards walked into the large cell. Jinshan didn't recognize the boy.

This must be it. The time had come. These weren't the prison guards who had ensured his stay was comfortable. These were military police who were here to escort him to his trial.

"Please come with us, Mr. Jinshan." The voice of a man who thought he was in charge.

"Of course."

He saw handcuffs in one of their hands, so he stood and turned around, making it easy for them. They slapped on the cold metal cuffs and walked him out through the prison hallways. Admiral Song, also handcuffed, and another pair of guards fell in behind them. They were marched into the military jeeps and driven away.

He had been told to expect the trial and had made sure to wear his prison attire—a simple gray tunic and pants. He needed to look the part. The next twenty-four hours would be immensely important.

That imbecile Zhang was Jinshan's last impediment. A strong showing today. A vote in front of the cameras. A speech to the people. They longed for a strong leader to get behind after a crisis. The Chinese people were like smoldering tinder. A gentle wind would ignite them.

* * *

Secretary Zhang looked out over the filled hall. A buzz hung thick in the air. The front row was still empty. The show hadn't started yet. But the audience—hundreds of politicians and Politburo members—was seated, sharpening their knives, waiting for blood. Zhang could feel it. He had a strong political intuition. It was what had allowed him to rise all the way to his current position.

Zhang, already a Central Committee member, had been made acting secretary of the Central Committee for Discipline Inspection by President Wu shortly before Wu had been killed. Ironically, this was the exact position Cheng Jinshan had held until a few weeks ago. Now Zhang's duty was to lead the corruption and treason investigation on Jinshan.

This was what President Wu had wanted, he told himself. Sure, there were calls to commute Jinshan's sentence. To sweep the events of the past few months under the rug. It was embarrassing, some of the other Central Committee members had pointed out. And Jinshan was a powerful man. He had many friends in the military and intelligence world. Was it wise to anger him?

Zhang ignored this talk. This was the right thing to do. Rules were rules, and they must be followed. Especially by the men at the top.

Besides, Secretary Zhang was worried that Jinshan was still up to his old tricks. There was still the matter of the secret camp in Liaoning Province. It was supposedly filled with special operations personnel, training for something—what, he did not know.

The camp had been a part of Jinshan's plans, Zhang knew. He knew it because Jinshan himself had told him when Zhang had gone to visit him in prison, trying to solve this mess. Jinshan had had the audacity to make a sloppy pitch to Zhang to join his cursed game.

Zhang had played coy, trying to fish for information. Feigning interest to see how deep the conspiracy went, hopeful that new information might uncover co-conspirators who still needed purging. Zhang, like Jinshan, was a strategist, so he had asked Jinshan strategic questions about his plans to attack America. How would China overcome America's military might, Zhang had asked Jinshan?

That was when Jinshan had told him about the camp. There were teams there, Jinshan had said. They were working on something very special. Zhang had asked for more details, and who else was involved. But Jinshan had seen through him. Jinshan had stopped wasting his breath, and Zhang had left the prison.

Jinshan's last grip on power would end with this trial. Then Zhang would uncover the rest of the traitors and shut down any further unauthorized military operations. It enraged him that it had to come to this. That he—the most powerful politician in China now that Wu was dead—couldn't fully control his country's own military. Zhang would finish off Jinshan—publicly—and send a message to anyone else who dared go against the Communist Party of China.

On the stage with him were several other key members of China's political and military leadership. The president's memorial ceremony had been held three days ago. Zhang had spoken with many of them there. None of these men were keen on the idea of a public trial. That had been President Wu's idea as well—at least, that was what Zhang presumed. It certainly hadn't been *his* idea. But the wheels were already in motion. Let the people see what Jinshan had done.

Cheng Jinshan and Admiral Song would be punished. Swiftly and publicly. Everyone in China and on the world stage was watching this. China as a country must separate itself from the acts of war that Jinshan had orchestrated. The attacks in the Persian Gulf. The submarine attacks in the Eastern Pacific. Hundreds of men and women killed. Lies. Subterfuge. Treason.

An example must be made of Cheng Jinshan. Much of it would be shocking to the citizens of China. They had been fed watered-down versions of his transgressions. Not all of it would be made known here, if Zhang could help it. But enough that they knew what kind of creature they were dealing with.

Like many government-sponsored public events in China, great attention was paid to theatrics. The massive hall was more than three times the size of the American congress's house chamber room. Members wore black suits with ties. A scarlet carpet adorned the floor. Giant Chinese flags surrounded a gold hammer and sickle behind the center of the stage.

The cameras were on. And although hundreds of people were present—most of them career politicians—the room had fallen eerily silent as the clock struck twelve. Everyone here knew Cheng Jinshan. He had been in charge of the Chinese president's quest to eradicate the "tigers and flies"—the anticorruption campaign that Jinshan had actually been using to install his own loyalists.

But now the tables had turned. Zhang would admit it to no one, but he relished this moment. He would vanquish Jinshan. A thorn in his side for so many years. He had always tried to position himself close to President Wu, to the detriment of Zhang.

The large oak double doors at the entrance to the chamber opened. At least a dozen uniformed military police marched Cheng Jinshan and Admiral Song down the aisle. Small gasps from the audience. A few bitter looks. Hungry eyes. The two were marched to the front row and forced to sit in between armed military policemen. It looked humiliating. Zhang loved it.

"The Politburo Standing Committee will now hear the findings from the investigation into Cheng Jinshan and Admiral Song. Both have been accused of crimes against the state. They are here today facing charges of high treason and corruption."

Zhang listened as one of the justice officials sitting on stage with him recited the crimes and dictated how the hearing would go. Several experts were called on to present findings. Normally this could take hours, but since they were on live TV, Zhang made sure that things moved along at a good pace. The audience gave their rapt attention to every word.

Finally came the part that everyone was waiting for. While a criminal trial could go on for weeks, Secretary Zhang felt that it would be in the country's best interests if this matter was resolved with extreme haste. The other members of the Central Committee had agreed that Secretary Zhang would have full authority to hear the summary of evidence and provide his recommendation to the others on the judicial panel.

The judicial panel was the jury. But their vote was more lip service, as designed. Zhang would make the recommendation of guilt or innocence first, and then the jury would vote unanimously as he did. There would be no dissent. After the judicial panel voted the way Zhang recommended, he would then ratify the vote and announce a sentence. Jinshan and Admiral Song would spend the remainder of their lives behind prison walls.

But first, there were appearances to keep up.

Zhang looked down from his perch high up on the stage. "Mr. Jinshan, do you have anything to say in response to the evidence presented here today?"

"I do indeed, Secretary Zhang."

Zhang frowned at the display of stubborn pride. But they were on live camera. Let the man get out what he had to say, and then get on with the rest of it.

"Proceed, Mr. Jinshan."

"Today we have all heard evidence that I have conspired to increase our military readiness, to incite war, and to defend China from our enemies…"

"The United States is not our enemy, Mr. Jinshan," said Secretary Zhang, annoyed.

"I disagree, Mr. Secretary. You ask if I have anything to say in response to my charges? I will tell you. I wholeheartedly embrace these accusations. I accept responsibility for my actions. And I suggest that the others here wake up to the threat that approaches."

Zhang was about to say something else into his microphone when one of the other panelists interrupted him. "Please let Mr. Jinshan speak, Secretary Zhang."

Surprised, Zhang frowned at the other panel member, but relented.

"China was once the mightiest empire on earth—and she will be again. But not under our current leadership."

Zhang rolled his eyes and spoke into his microphone. "That's enough. Shut off—"

There was something wrong.

He couldn't hear his voice being amplified over the speakers.

Zhang tapped on his microphone but heard nothing. His microphone wasn't working.

He jerked his head back to the side of the stage, where he knew the auditorium director was seated in case there were any technical problems. The auditorium director was there, sitting in front of his tablet computer, which controlled everything—the lighting, the stage curtains, and the microphones. But there was a woman standing over him. Zhang narrowed his eyes. He didn't recognize her. She was very tall and would have been quite beautiful, if not for the scars. She was watching him closely. Zhang tapped on his microphone and gestured for them to fix it. But the auditorium director wasn't making eye contact. And the woman just stared back at him, ignoring his plea for help, a defiant look on her face.

Jinshan continued to speak. "I suspect that I am here for a reason other than the well-being of our great country. I was in Secretary Zhang's role not long ago—head of the Central Committee for Discipline Inspection. It was my job to root out corruption, and I did that well. Indeed, many of you are here today because of my efforts."

At that comment, Jinshan paused and made eye contact with several of the politicians and military members on the judicial panel next to Zhang.

Zhang slowly looked to his right and left, feeling uneasy as he saw the appreciative nods of at least *half* of his panel.

"But there are some among us who are so entrenched in this world of backroom deals and conspiracy that even I wasn't able to stop them. As we all saw on the news recently, our beloved president and his family were the victims of a religiously motivated attack. Hard-right-wing religious zealots. We have suffered before at the hands of religious terrorists. But this is something different, I am afraid. This rash of religious extremism is a new pattern in the world. A global realignment, led by the West. These conservative religious groups come from all over. And not just one religion, as we saw when our president was so brutally murdered. While we once concerned ourselves primarily with Muslim terrorism, now radical Christian groups are infiltrating China."

Murmurs from the audience of bureaucrats and politicians.

"And now—Chinese politics. So let me ask you, Secretary Zhang, why am I really on trial today? Is it because I have worked with our brave military members to protect our country? Or is it because you are motivated by extremist religious views?"

The audience began to chatter louder.

"How many of you here know that Secretary Zhang once attended a *nonsanctioned* Christian church? It is true. And in my investigations, I have uncovered evidence that he has even met with *American Christian groups*."

Zhang threw up his arms and yelled for someone to silence Jinshan. But with his microphone off, his voice was barely heard. Zhang signaled the security guards to stop Jinshan from speaking. They looked up to the military general on the panel for guidance. The general next to Zhang shook his head in response.

"What are you doing?" Zhang shouted at the general.

"Please, Mr. Secretary," replied the general.

Jinshan's voice was raised now. "These religious extremists—led by America—will be our country's *downfall*. They have *attacked* us. Attacked our *leaders*. Attacked our *children*. They assault the very values that we hold dear. My fellow citizens, we must rise up and fight back."

The crowd was boisterous now. Cheers of approval. What was going on?

"I hereby call upon all members of the Chinese Communist Party to *denounce* Secretary Zhang and his extremist religious views. I call upon the panel to expel him from the Communist Party immediately, and to appoint someone who is not associated with these anti-Chinese groups as our new president."

People were smacking their seats and clapping. The audience

was with Jinshan. This was ludicrous. This was supposed to be *his trial*.

Jinshan looked at the woman standing just off the stage and nodded. The general sitting next to Zhang spoke first.

"While I understand that Mr. Jinshan may have not followed protocol in his actions, I share his concerns about the direction of our country." He looked at Zhang. "Secretary Zhang, I am horrified to hear of your connections to these radical religious groups. I cannot support leadership that is influenced by our enemies. I motion that Secretary Zhang be expelled from the Communist Party of China, and that he be taken into custody until further notice."

Immediately, several voices on the panel next to him spoke into their microphones, giving their support.

The audience was cheering.

Zhang said, "This is preposterous. *Ludicrous*. Surely you can't—"

The general continued, "And I call for the immediate release of Mr. Cheng Jinshan and Admiral Song, and a full reinstatement of their titles and duties."

More shouts of approval.

The tall woman with long hair stood behind him. Where had she come from? Zhang hadn't even seen her approach. He noticed that she was incredibly strong as she seized Zhang by the shoulders and lifted him up out of his seat, prodding him to walk off the stage, where military police were waiting.

Zhang was dumbfounded.

Everyone was looking at him like *he* was the traitor. What had just happened? Didn't they see? Didn't they understand that he was the only one who was looking out for what was right?

As he was taken away, he saw Cheng Jinshan speaking to the woman. They were on stage, speaking with the general and other members of the panel. Zhang passed by the auditorium director. He pointed his finger at one of his workers and said, "Cut camera feed and audio. Mr. Jinshan wants to see all the footage before it gets circulated."

"Yes, sir."

14

Two days later, Jinshan walked into the conference room and looked around the table. Dedicated eyes stared back at him. Politburo mostly, but some military men as well. Senior generals and admirals. Some were Politburo Central Committee members. The head of the Ministry of State Security was present. All were loyal to Cheng Jinshan.

The others had been purged.

Shortly after Jinshan and Song had been acquitted of all charges and Secretary Zhang removed, the Central Committee had held a vote on who was to be their next general secretary. The vote for Jinshan had been unanimous, and the subsequent consolidation of power had been swift.

Jinshan sat down at the head of the table. Everyone was quiet, waiting for Jinshan to speak.

"How much has changed with our military readiness over the past few weeks?"

The question was understood by the occupants of the room: how much progress had been lost because of his unplanned incarceration?

General Chen spoke first, which was only appropriate. He was now the senior military officer in all of China. Jinshan had asked his predecessor to retire a few days earlier.

"Mr. Jinshan, very little has changed. We have continued to train and prepare our army, navy, and air force for the next stages. While China's official response has been to apologize for the recent hostilities, we were able to convince the former president that we needed to maintain a high level of alert in case of a retaliatory response from the Americans. A separate order chain was used to keep up pretenses prior to…"

Jinshan smiled. "Prior to my public proclamation of my innocence?"

"Yes, sir." Uneasy smiling. Ambition and fear of retribution coated every one of their faces. But a culture of strong central control was needed during wartime.

Jinshan nodded. "Good. I am pleased to hear that our military forces are making progress. They should be ready to execute with little to no notice. Am I clear, General?" Cheng Jinshan's appointment as the general secretary also made him the chairman of the Central Military Commission.

"Of course, sir."

"The Americans will likely be unnerved by my freedom and newfound power. We will need to ease their worries, and distract them from seeing us as their primary threat." He looked across the room. Lena and Natesh sat in chairs along the wall. "How has the response been, domestically?"

Lena looked at Natesh, who was standing in the back of the room. He didn't speak Mandarin. She quickly relayed the question to him in English. Natesh cleared his throat. "Yes, Mr. Jinshan. The video of your…*speech*…is getting extremely high views on all Chinese social media. Our bots are amplifying the positive response. The message that Chinese citizens are receiving is that you were unjustly imprisoned for standing up to religious activists and wanting to defend China's military. Polls show most citizens believe that you desire our nation to grow stronger and stand up to oppressive Western regimes."

"Are the people with us, Natesh?"

"Yes, Mr. Jinshan. The data that my team has been looking at shows that the overwhelming majority of Chinese people fully support you and your agenda. They see China as being attacked by outside meddlers, and they see you as a savior, sir." Natesh's eyes darted around as he said it.

Jinshan held his gaze for a beat longer than normal, then turned to his generals. "We will need to act swiftly. The American military and intelligence community will understand what this means. They will be increasing their readiness levels. They will be making their own preparations."

Nods around the table.

"We have prepared for years. Soon we will act. A few more weeks at the most. Everyone must be prepared to execute our plans immediately, when the order is given."

* * *

As the generals and politicians were leaving, Jinshan said, "Natesh, Lena—please stay for a moment."

They gathered near him and Admiral Song. Jinshan waited for everyone else to leave before speaking.

"I thank you for the great work that you have done thus far. I fear that there will be much more to do before we are finished."

Neither of them spoke.

"Natesh, you seem concerned."

Natesh glanced at Lena and then said, "Our loss-of-life estimates have increased."

"Have they?" The old man sat back down in his chair. Natesh thought he looked awful. Tired eyes and sallow skin. More wrinkles and spots on his face than the last time Natesh had seen him.

Lena said, "Natesh, we don't need to bother Mr. Jinshan about this."

Jinshan held up his hand. "It is alright, Lena. Too often, I am only told good news. Perhaps if more people around me were brave enough to tell me the truth, I wouldn't have spent the last few weeks in a prison." He looked out the door as he said that, in the direction of the Chinese military generals and politicians he was working with.

Natesh said, "It's just that—none of this was expected. Our plans would have been much more effective if they had been executed all at once. But we aren't doing that. The GPS satellites were taken out a month ago, but the Americans are making progress towards fixing that. Their military readiness has increased dramatically in the past few weeks. We still don't have an active supply chain in Latin America. And we haven't even started our Canadian—"

Jinshan looked up at Lena. "But as you have said, the people are with us."

"From what I've seen, yes, Mr. Jinshan."

"Then we can overcome schedule setbacks, as long as our people are motivated."

Natesh said, "Those people are going to find out eventually."

"Find out what?" Jinshan's eyes grew dark.

Natesh hesitated. "That none of this was about religion. I understand the need to motivate them. But I worry that by not telling them the truth, we hurt ourselves in the long run."

Jinshan and Lena shared a look.

"Natesh, truth can be a dangerous thing."

"A moment ago, you told me that you wished more people told you the truth."

Jinshan's fatigue was gone now. He raised his voice. Just a bit, but enough that Natesh was taken aback. "Mr. Chaudry, nothing has changed since the moment when we met in San Francisco. Our objectives have not changed. Our methods have not changed. The only thing that is new for you is that you are witnessing with your own eyes what sacrifice truly means. Bloodshed. Death. Lies. All of these things will be necessary. If you can't stomach it, please let us know. Did you really think that a world war would be won in a few weeks? Did you think that a few blackouts in the United States would allow the Chinese army to stroll in and plant a flag in Washington? Ninety-day wars are campaign slogans. There is no such thing as a quick and easy war—not when you take into account the occupation and transformation of the populace. I hired you because this was a complicated, challenging task, and you were a worthy contributor."

Jinshan's flash of anger sent a chill down Natesh's spine. "I'm sorry…"

Jinshan recomposed himself, speaking in a softer tone. "There can be no second-guessing now, Natesh. You have committed yourself to this. Soon, my generals will give orders for a military strike the likes of which the world has never seen. After this order is given, much of the globe will be in darkness."

Lena said, "Mr. Jinshan, perhaps there is a way that Natesh can support us that is less—how shall I say—involved in the kinetic aspect of our plans?"

Jinshan looked at Lena, admiration in his eyes. "What would you propose, Lena?"

"We have an office in Japan. Your logistics supplier is out of there. The one who manages our shipping containers. Natesh's talents are best put to use in operations management. With his knowledge of our ultimate objectives, he would be quite valuable as an embedded advocate in Japan, would he not?"

Jinshan looked thoughtful. "He could join our Tokyo embassy personnel as soon as the war begins. To ensure his safety."

Natesh was looking between Lena and Jinshan, not sure if this was a good thing or not.

Finally, Jinshan said, "Go to Japan. Do our work where no one will be looking for you. We will get you a special military assistant. They will make sure that anything you need is done. I want you to continue to improve our logistics. The container ships must begin their journey across the Pacific soon. Convoys will need to start as soon as the EMPs detonate."

"Yes, Mr. Jinshan." His voice sounded shell-shocked.

"Now go. Both of you have a lot of work to do."

* * *

Jinshan's first order of business was to solidify alliances. To reassure worried leaders that he would look out for them. He would meet the

Russians again in Beijing. Their proxies could be trusted. But North Korea was another matter. There was only one decision maker there. And while Jinshan preferred not to step foot in the Hermit Nation, it was a necessary evil. Flattery went a long way with that one.

The jet landed in Pyongyang at night. Thankfully, he was met at the airport. As requested, the North Koreans did not have any sort of welcome party waiting. Only a seven-vehicle column of military jeeps and the Great Leader's personal limousines. Jinshan knew that one of the two limousines carried a body double, a man whose sole job it was to walk around and test the air for an assassin's bullet. He smiled at that. What a life.

The door to the second limousine opened up, and Jinshan was asked to walk over. He bristled at that, but obliged. Two of his body-guards and a translator followed. They were searched, and then Jinshan and his translator sat inside the vehicle. Across the cabin sat the North Korean leader.

The conversation was interrupted every few seconds with rapid translations.

"So you've done it, Mr. Jinshan. Or shall I say President Jinshan. I congratulate you."

"Yes, I have. And thank you."

"And now you are here to make sure that I stick to our agreement?"

Throughout his career, Jinshan had conducted many a business meeting with high-level foreign executives, often using translators. It had always amused him when he watched the other executives care-fully crafting their questions and answers in their native tongue, only to have those carefully chosen words butchered in the translation. Better to keep it simple.

"Yes. I have come to make sure that you are still committed to our arrangement."

"When do you intend for the first shots to be fired?"

Jinshan said, "That will come soon. But I would ask that you help me with something else first. A preliminary demonstration of power. Similar to what you are already doing."

The North Korean leader looked surprised. He leaned forward, his double chin becoming more pronounced. He nodded vigorously, a look of intrigue appearing on his face.

One of the North Korean generals—looking tiny in his oversized uniform—misdiagnosed the Great Leader's facial expression. One could never go wrong sticking up for the Great Leader, so the general began raising his voice in a high-pitched protest, directed at Jinshan. The North Korean leader looked at him, annoyed, and yelled for the general to shut up. While the scene was amusing, if not insulting, Jinshan remained quiet. One always found oneself walking on pins and needles in the Hermit Nation.

"Could you provide me with the details?"

"Of course. I propose that I leave a team of ballistic missile specialists here to help your men with the technical setup. Is that acceptable to you?"

"This will be acceptable." China had been providing materials and expertise to the North Korean missile program for decades.

"Excellent. With regard to South Korea, you should expect further word on timing within a few weeks."

"You will provide me with a target list?"

Jinshan shook his head. "I am sure that you already have military plans for such an attack on the South. I ask only that you execute the plans you already have. We will do the rest."

The large round-faced man nodded, a proud look displayed for his generals. "I will lay waste to the South. It will be turned to ash."

Jinshan could see through the act. But he wouldn't dare to challenge the young man. If an unstable man was doing what you wanted him to do, it was best not to introduce any new variables into his calculations.

"And after the war is won? Our terms remain the same?"

"Yes. You will have Korea. All of it."

15

Tokyo

T etsuo watched the woman at the other end of the bar. She was all dolled up. Carefully plucked eyebrows, lots of makeup, and full breasts pressed together by her tight-fitting black shirt, a hint of a bright purple bra showing underneath. High-heeled leather boots. She looked like she had a mix of Japanese and Caucasian blood, if he were to guess.

She laughed a little too loud and placed her hand on the shoulder of the white man next to her. There were a group of them, obviously American service members by their haircuts and loud mannerisms. Each of them stole glances at her bosom as they drank, just happy to be off base. If they only knew who she worked for.

This part of town was filled with bars that catered to the Americans. It could get rowdy, especially in the evenings and on weekends. Curfews were an on-again, off-again affair, the base commanders reacting to the latest incidents. But women like her would always be around, regardless of the military rear echelon's attempt to instill good behavior among the troops during their off-duty time. Hers was the oldest profession, after all.

But it wasn't her only profession.

Tetsuo's team had been watching her for a few weeks now. The orders to take her had come twelve hours ago. The CIA was getting desperate for information. No one knew what the hell was going on in China, and they needed leads.

He had been advised to approach her with extreme caution. His team had two vans outside around the corner. There wasn't any place to park on the street outside. A female CIA operative sat across from him, pretending to keep up conversation.

They heard another loud burst of laughter from the group of service members, and the woman and one of the men began walking out the door, her arm intertwined in his, with her free hand resting on his broad shoulder. She glanced back at the other men, giving them a wink as if to say, *Maybe you'll be my customer next time, boys.*

"You stay. Follow me after you pay," Tetsuo said to his colleague. Then Tetsuo whispered into his wrist microphone, "She's on the move with the tall white guy on her right side. They're walking out the front door now." He put his leather jacket on and walked out of the bar, about ten seconds behind them.

The whore and her mark walked up the road for a few minutes and then veered off into a massage parlor with pictures of attractive women plastered on the outer window. The man dug out his wallet and paid at the front door, then the two disappeared inside. Poor stupid kid. Tetsuo hung back, watching.

He could see one of his vans move into position at the nearest intersection. The driver made eye contact and nodded. The female agent he had been sitting with walked up behind him.

"How do you want to play it?"

"I'll see if I can pay off the woman working the front desk. If I give you the thumbs-up, get the vans right outside and use the curtains."

She nodded.

Tetsuo walked into the massage shop and approached the older woman sitting at the front desk. She barely glanced at him, her eyes fixed on her phone as she asked him to choose from a menu of services. Her Japanese was heavily accented—Korean.

"You the owner?"

She looked up at him suspiciously. "No. My husband is the owner."

He took out his wallet, thumbing through a wad of cash. "You know that woman that just came in? Is she a regular?"

"Yes," the Korean woman answered, taking a few bills.

"I need to speak with her."

"She is busy."

Tetsuo placed his hands on the counter. "I don't want to cause trouble. But I don't think that she'll come with me unless I make her. I need you to go in that room back there and close the door for the next five minutes. Can you do that for me? I promise you that I won't hurt her, and I won't get you in any trouble. But I don't want anyone to see it when my friend and I take her out. Okay?" He slid over a thick wad of cash.

She looked down at it, counting, and looked back up towards him, a curious smile appearing on her face. "Who are you?"

"What room are they in?"

"Room four. Upstairs."

"Is there a lock?"

"No locks. We've had problems with locks. Who are you?"

"Five minutes." Tetsuo held up his hand, thumb and fingers extended.

The woman shrugged. "Knock on the door if anyone comes. And don't get me in trouble with the police."

"I won't. Is that camera on?" He pointed up at the black orb hanging down from the ceiling.

She nodded.

"Let me see you turn it off. You can turn it back on when you come out."

She picked up her phone and tapped a few times, then showed him the screen as she selected OFF on the security camera's application. Then the woman disappeared into the back room.

Tetsuo waited until the door was shut and turned to give a thumbs-up to his agent standing outside. She turned and gave a nod to the van, which in turn made a call to the second van. Both pulled up close to the curb, only feet from the door.

Then the back doors of one of the vans opened and Tetsuo's team members set up curtains that shielded the short path from the parlor entrance to the vans.

"Room four, upstairs. No locks."

The three men who moved ahead of him were members of the CIA's Special Operations Group. Most of these men were former special forces guys. They had made a career of apprehending and killing terrorists. This operation was a little different, and they had been warned. If their information was correct, she was one of an elite group of Chinese intelligence operatives, and she could be quite lethal.

The team crept towards the door marked with a 4. Two held silenced pistols. Tetsuo and the other man gripped Tasers.

It happened in a flash.

The door opened, and the three professionals sprinted into the small room. The woman was in her bra and panties, straddling the American service member, who lay on his stomach, while rubbing oil onto his back. She jerked her head around as the door opened, hopping off the man and trying to respond, but they were too quick. Tetsuo's men grabbed her, separated her from the American man, who was yelling, and then zapped both of them on the side. Then one of the CIA operatives removed a pair of syringes from a case attached to his waist. Both the American service member and the Chinese spy were injected with a solution that would keep them unconscious for the next few hours.

The men quickly dressed the limp bodies and carried them into the back of the lead van, where they were tied down on stretchers and carefully monitored. The American would be dropped off with his military ID and otherwise empty wallet just outside of the base. Tetsuo wanted it to look like a robbery. The service member wouldn't remember much, but his buddies would know that he'd left the bar with a prostitute. They would assume that she had been part of the heist.

It would make sense that she would never show up around that area again.

* * *

The hooker was one of Jinshan's operatives, they had learned, but she wasn't anything like the highly trained Lena Chou. This one was straight honey trap, used to lure in men who might know something about American and Japanese military movements or technology.

After they'd interrogated her for a few hours, promising her the reward of a safe life in America, without the threat of retribution from her Chinese handlers, she finally talked.

And she had a lot to say.

The hooker had a prodigious customer list. It included low-ranking clientele, like the enlisted men in the bar, who had access to flight schedules and deployment status, but also higher-ups, including a colonel in the US Air Force who had bragged about the F-22s that were coming to his base. She had even worked her magic on a Japanese executive who was giving her access to AEGIS radar technology being sold to the Japanese Self-Defense Forces. Some of the classified information these men provided was knowingly exchanged for sex. Others were clueless as to the importance of the details they let slip—at least, according to her.

Under normal circumstances, each one of these clients would be investigated, questioned, and charged. But these were not normal times, and that wasn't what Tetsuo was interested in today. The woman was working for Jinshan's agents, and Tetsuo wanted to know any special instructions that Jinshan's office had given her in the last few weeks that might be related to the shipping containers being managed out of the Tokyo office.

"They told you to meet someone coming from China?"

"Yes, they wanted me to keep him company."

"Is that normal?"

"Not at all."

"Why do you suspect they are doing that?"

"They said that his confidence is low. This man is upset about the things he is doing. Stressed out. They thought that I might be able to help with that. And they wanted me to keep an eye on him."

The woman was sitting on the couch, drinking from a bottle of water. She observed her three interrogators with careful suspicion but seemed indifferent to the work she was involved in. As if it was totally normal.

Tetsuo said, "What were you supposed to do?"

"If the Indian-American man said anything that made me think he was disloyal, I was to notify my handler immediately. They told me that they were worried about him having second thoughts. They want to keep using him. Apparently, he's a boy genius or something. But if he's not able to keep working for them, they want to take care of the problem soon."

Tetsuo's face remained impassive at the mention of the man being Indian American.

"Does he have a name?"

"His name is Natesh Chaudry."

Tetsuo wrote down the name on his notepad.

The woman said, "He doesn't know me...yet. I'm supposed to make it appear natural."

"Tell us when and where you're supposed to meet him."

16

D avid's youngest daughter was staring at him from her baby seat, the tower of plastic that rolled up next to the kitchen table, ensuring that her head was slightly above theirs when she ate. Maybe that was where she had gotten the idea that she ruled over them.

He had stirred together a little baby rice cereal with warm water, placing the tiny spoon into her mouth. She just glared back at him, the sludge dripping back out and down her chin. *Not today, Dad. Nice try.*

The side door to the carport opened and his wife and oldest daughter came in. "Hello, Dad. How's the feeding going?"

"Well..."

Lindsay made eye contact with the six-month-old, who smiled wide at the sight of her mother. David used the opportunity to stuff a little more food into her mouth. She made a face, but he was pretty sure at least something got in there. Little wins.

"Have a good class?"

"Yeah, actually. Thanks for letting me go."

Lindsay had taken Maddie to the gym nursery while she took a class. David had stayed home with Taylor and made breakfast, catching up on a little Saturday-morning *SportsCenter* on ESPN.

"I made some eggs. They should still be warm. And the bacon is in the pan."

"Mmm. Thanks. I'm just going to jump in the shower. Can you see if Maddie wants any? She didn't really eat before we left."

David's phone began buzzing on the kitchen counter. Lindsay stopped walking and eyed him as he picked it up.

"This is David."

"David, it's Susan. We need you to come in. Sorry for the short notice, but something big is going on and we need you."

"Sure, what's up?"

"I'll see you when you get here. Actually—David, pack a travel bag. You'll be flying out tonight."

The phone call ended, and David gave his wife a look that she was beginning to know all too well.

She put up her hand, rolling her eyes. "Don't apologize. Just let me shower. Five minutes, then you can go."

* * *

"David, your debrief from the island says that you befriended him while you were there."

"Yeah, but then Natesh *betrayed* me. He betrayed all of us."

Susan folded her arms, looking at General Schwartz. "The psychological profile we have on him says he's susceptible to recruitment. You have a relationship with him. Our source says that he was showing signs of cracking up, and that's why he's being sent to Japan. To work with a logistics company that runs Jinshan's shipping operators."

David said, "Look, Susan. I'll do whatever you want, but I don't see how much I'll be able to help. I have zero training in this kind of thing."

"You would be surprised how much a friendly face can do when trying to turn someone. You'll have someone good there. Tetsuo is one of our best operations officers. He'll brief you. Just follow his lead."

David was incredulous. They were going to send him to Japan to meet with Natesh Chaudry. The Silicon Valley consultant who had partnered up with Lena Chou and Cheng Jinshan. The architect of many of Jinshan's war plans. David understood the value in recruiting him as an agent of the CIA. He would be able to provide insight and information that would be immensely valuable, especially given that Jinshan was now the most powerful man in China. But David knew nothing about how to play these spy games. His expertise came from watching a lot of James Bond movies when he was younger.

"Your flight leaves as soon as you get to the airport, David. A car is waiting outside to take you there right now. Sleep on the plane. You'll need to move fast once you get to Tokyo."

* * *

When Natesh arrived in Japan, he immediately felt a weight lifted from his shoulders. He felt free. It was the first time he hadn't had Lena or any Chinese soldiers looking over his shoulder in months. He used the payment cards and IDs that Jinshan's people had provided to check into his hotel. He wasn't back in America, but it was better than it had been.

Still, there was the knowledge that every person he passed on the street was at risk. He knew what Jinshan was planning to do with the nation of Japan. At least, he thought he knew. They would be given an ultimatum, just like several other Pacific Rim nations. Stay out of this, or be obliterated. Natesh's money was on Japan staying neutral. He hoped to God they would. He hated to think of the alternative.

In the morning, he was taken to the logistics company. He met the chief of sales, one of Jinshan's men. The executive provided Natesh a private office in a modern high-rise building, along with a staff that was sworn to secrecy. The technology was first-rate, and Natesh quickly had his team plugged into the supply chain, planning for the next year. Food, petrol, parts, men, tanks, aircraft, bullets.

Everything needed a demand estimate, a demand signal, and a corresponding product that it was tied to.

Each item was tagged with a reference code. A specific type of rifle was 80282071. Within that rifle were dozens of parts, each with their own reference codes. The Chinese reference codes were used. That was not suspicious, since the company already did so much business with China. The products formed little tree graphs, and through each branch, Natesh's demand signals flowed. The Chinese war machine's supply chain would be optimized, reacting quickly to any change in the battlefield.

After the first day of working with his Japanese team, he was pleased. They were able to take the information he had been working with, first at the Red Cell Island and then in Manta, and get it transferred over to the servers in Tokyo.

After a few days of this, Natesh might even forget that he was working to supply a war. They were just numbers. And he needed to make sure that demand never outstripped supply. If one ship full of parts and materials didn't make it to a destination, he would work on alternatives. Everything must be optimized for time and cost. He wouldn't think about why that ship hadn't gotten there, or about how many lives had been lost when it had sunk to the bottom of the Pacific.

He ate at the sushi bar in his hotel and smiled for the first time in a long time. The food was good. He was at peace.

A man next to him said, "You American?"

Natesh froze, not sure what to say.

"Sorry, I don't mean to interrupt your dinner. It's just that I used to work in Seattle. I think I might have heard you speak to my company once. Natesh Chaudry, right?"

Natesh flushed and shook the man's hand. "Oh. Sorry, yes. That was probably me."

"Man, small world, huh? I'm over here for a few weeks doing work and... sorry, where are my manners. My name's Tetsuo." He stuck out his hand.

Natesh signaled the man behind the bar to get his check. A blur of dark fabric as someone sat down in the seat next to him, on the opposite side of the talkative American.

Natesh turned to see who was sitting so close, when there were plenty of other open seats at the sushi bar.

He saw the face, but it didn't click in his brain for a half second. Then his mouth dropped open as he realized who was sitting right in front of him.

That was impossible.

"Hello, Natesh," said David Manning. "My friend here and I would like to buy you a drink. How about we go upstairs where we can talk in private?"

* * *

Natesh said, "You must despise me."

They were in a room on the third floor of his hotel. Tetsuo had rented it out earlier that day, just before he'd picked up David at the airport. The tech team had come in, checked it for bugs, and then installed their own video and audio equipment. CIA countersurveillance teams were scattered around the block and in the hotel. A large portion of Agency resources in Japan were on this case now. If they could get one of Jinshan's inner circle to turn and could extract what he knew, that could be a game changer.

Tetsuo said, "The important thing is that you're here now, and you're willing to help. Is that an accurate statement?"

"It is." Natesh looked down at the floor, defeated. "I can't go back to them. I don't know why I thought they were right. Their end state is inspiring. But I've seen enough death up close now. I've seen Lena Chou and Cheng Jinshan for what they truly are. And I don't want to be a part of that."

David tried hard to control his emotions. This guy had betrayed his country and nearly gotten David killed. He was complicit in conspiracy, and his contributions to Jinshan's operation had cost hundreds of lives, many of them Americans. David would like nothing more than to take him to the top floor and throw him off the building. But Susan and Tetsuo had convinced him of his value. If they could successfully recruit him to work for the CIA, then there was important work that Natesh could still do.

"I don't want to go to jail. I know what I've done is wrong, but I also know what the US government will likely do to me once I get back on American soil."

Tetsuo leaned forward in his chair and lightly slapped Natesh on the knee. Like they were friends, buddies. Like he was trying to cheer him up. He was, David realized. Tetsuo was working on him. Trying to establish a connection. Trust.

"We will take care of you. I'm not going to lie, I read about Lena Chou. She's very impressive. So is Jinshan. They could have convinced a lot of people. We don't blame you, Natesh, and you shouldn't blame yourself. And if you're worried about repercussions, then talk to us. It will go a long way back in Washington if you're cooperating. Give us a sign of good faith. Let's start a discussion—what can you help us with? What did you see over the past few weeks and months that we don't know about?"

Natesh's expression grew more positive the longer Tetsuo spoke. David could see that the Japanese-American man clearly knew his craft. He had simultaneously injected Natesh with a boost of confidence and begun the interrogation process.

Natesh said, "Plans. I know what Jinshan intends to do. I know where they plan to strike, what their strategy is. Excuse me for saying this, but Jinshan is way ahead of you. And if you are going to stop him, you'll need what I have."

David glanced over at Tetsuo, who kept staring at Natesh.

"Of course. We recognize your value. What…"

Natesh kept talking, looking down at the table, thinking while he spoke. "I suppose it would be impossible just to go back to my old life. I don't think any of us will be able to do that. I just want to be cleared of any wrongdoing. I want immunity in the United States. When this is all over, I mean. I'll feed you what I have. And you promise me that I can live in peace and quiet when I'm done. I'll just go somewhere in the countryside and live my life alone. I've made a mistake. An unforgivable one. I realize that now. And I'm trying to make amends. The only way I know how—by giving you the secrets that you need. By giving you the plans that I helped—that I am helping to design."

"You're still working for him now? In Japan? What are you doing here?"

Natesh said, "Do we have a deal?"

"Yes. We do. You start working for us, and we have a deal. I can get you immunity. We'll place you in the witness protection program or something similar. You'll live in the middle of nowhere, and no one will ever be the wiser. But you need to stay in place for now, here. We need you to continue your work for Jinshan and provide us with insider information. Now, what are you doing in Japan?"

"Logistics planning. I'm helping to manage all of the people, parts, fuel, and food that will need to transit the Pacific in order for Cheng Jinshan to wage war on the United States."

The two men stared at him, unable to speak for a moment. "So, Jinshan is still planning to go to war with the US?" Tetsuo asked.

Natesh nodded. "Yes. Of course. Nothing has changed for him."

David cleared his throat. "Why are you doing that out of Tokyo?"

"Jinshan told me to. I believe he wanted to create separation between the people American intelligence was monitoring and the work that needed to get done." Natesh's expression changed. "There's something that you need to know. Something immediately important, that I overheard when I spoke to Jinshan last."

"What?"

Natesh was biting his lip, his eyes shifting around nervously. "North Korea is going to test-fire an ICBM."

"Don't they do that all the time?"

"This time will be different."

17

J inshan sat at his desk, reading through his daily reports.

His assistant knocked at the door.

"Sir, the Americans are asking to set up a phone call between you and the American president."

"Are they?"

"I assume you want me to turn it down?"

Jinshan looked down at his notes.

"No. Let us speak with the Americans. Perhaps we can use it to our advantage."

"They can meet anytime, sir. What should I say?"

"Tomorrow morning, our time."

The timing would be just before the fun started. It would be the middle of the evening in Washington.

When the time came, Jinshan looked at the screen, a dark blue background with the American presidential seal. Then the screen changed to a view of the American president. He was sitting at the head of a long conference table. The view was zoomed in so that only he was visible, but there must have been advisors there. He wouldn't take a call of this importance without them.

Jinshan had a similar setup. He kept his gaze on the screen, the tiny camera above it capturing him unfiltered. Jinshan noted that his own image made him look tired. He felt tired, too. Just a little longer, he told himself. Then this whole endeavor would be self-sustaining.

"Mr. President," Jinshan said.

"Hello, Mr. Jinshan. Thank you for agreeing to speak with me this evening. I felt it urgent to hold this conversation face-to-face."

"I understand, Mr. President. How can I help you?"

"This conversation might not be easy, Mr. Jinshan. But I feel that it is necessary. I must strenuously object to your recent undemocratic ascendancy to the leadership position of the Chinese people. A week ago, you were on trial. We have evidence that you were involved in planning military action against our country. Now I must ask formally what your intentions are, and make my own intentions known."

Dark lines of fatigue lay under Jinshan's eyes. He coughed into a gray handkerchief, the deep, full cough of a sick man.

Jinshan began. "I understand that you did not expect to see me here today, Mr. President. Let us dispense with any diplomatic pretense of pleasantries. To be frank, I just don't have the time." He paused, then looked thoughtful. "Do you know what the biggest threat to the well-being of a society is?"

The president was thrown off by Jinshan's conversational tone. He frowned but remained silent.

"I will tell you. It's the proliferation of a free and open Internet. As the saying goes—the pen is mightier than the sword. A free and open Internet places pens and audiences in the hands of the entire global population. The consequences of which would be the *undoing* of modern civilization, if left unchecked."

"Mr. Jinshan, I would like to discuss—"

Jinshan cut him off with a held-up hand and spoke over him. "You can see the symptoms of this spreading disease in developed countries around the world. As more and more people use the Internet and social media to gain their information, democratic governments and large media companies are no longer capable of shaping the opinions of their populace. This is a dangerous thing.

"Information was once controlled by the powerful few. Words

were carefully crafted to convince people to believe what we—the *elite*—wanted them to believe. But if the elite—the great thinkers within a state—cannot shape the opinions of their simple-minded citizens, as they have done for ages, it will lead to the absolute worst form of government. Irrational, uninformed democracy.

"I have seen it happen in your country. Your citizens pick their poison—sources of information that serve to reinforce what they already believe. Your citizens are herded by paid manipulators and forced to the polar extremes."

The American president finally bit. "And you think this is worse than your propaganda machine? Citizens who must get their information from a state-run news channel? At least Americans can see all sides…"

Jinshan scoffed. "You think that they see all sides? They see two sides. A bipolar choice. Why? Because every vote in your congress can only have a yes or a no. So, your lobbyists and marketing machines get to work, coming up with campaigns to motivate the masses to serve their own purpose, and fill their own coffers.

"We're both manipulating people, Mr. President. I don't deny it. But in America, you are tearing yourselves apart. And the rest of the democratic world will follow. All because you have armed your citizens with a free and open Internet. But I won't let that happen to my country."

The American president said, "Americans are free thinkers. You have too little understanding of or faith in humanity if you think that my countrymen are such sheep as you describe."

Jinshan said, "If that is what you really think, then you are more naïve than I thought. Your country is becoming more and more polarized. You can't deny that. This leads to gridlock in the best of cases, and civil war in the worst. It is your American-run social networks that tailor algorithms to show people only what they want to see. The echo chamber of ideas, bouncing around cities with only like-minded people hearing them. Meanwhile, a frenzy of anger wells up on the outside of your city walls.

"Both sides are being misled, Mr. President. You know this. Politicians and businessmen, marketers and lobbyists—they're all manipulating the opinions of the Western populace just like we in China have shaped the opinions of our own citizens. But in China, the thought manipulation—let us call it what it is—is orchestrated by leaders who generally have the country's forward progress in mind. In the West, that is not the case. In the West, anyone can put out polluted information, regardless of its consequence."

"In the United States, we value free speech."

Jinshan scoffed. "You must see what is happening, Mr. President. Your institutions were once trusted. Just like feudal kings once were, before the printing press. But then ideas spread. Uncontrolled, unfiltered, diseases of ideas. These ideas infected the populace like a plague. These ideas spread throughout the countryside, attaching themselves to anyone who was searching for a reason to believe them. The ideas become reinforced with strings of intellectual thought. They gain rabid followings and evangelists. Before you blink your eyes, Mr. President, the ideas have taken over your kingdom. And the rioters are at your door, calling for your head. Now I ask you, what does this phenomenon remind you of?"

The president frowned. "I don't know, what?"

"*Religion*. An institution where people believe not in fact, but based on faith in the institution itself. Its followers need security and reassurance. In their crumbling world, they want to know that their time isn't wasted—that they are serving a higher purpose. And the ideas that have spread like a virus throughout society have morphed into just the religion that they desire. They would worship anything, as long as it supports them and reassures them. These religious groups have leaders that make proclamations, and soon after, the fervent followers will recite these words by heart, or perhaps act out violently on their behalf. Your religious leaders are no longer clerics —they are political talk show hosts and writers. But the end result is the same. Destruction. Free speech is a virus, Mr. President."

"Well, Mr. Jinshan, we value morality in America."

"Don't lecture me about morality. You Americans would bankrupt millions to save the life of one. And what good is that? I choose victory over morality."

The president said, "Mr. Jinshan, I need you to discuss our current crisis."

"I assure you, Mr. President, there is no crisis. The crisis has been averted. I have prevented it."

A moment of silence.

"I don't follow."

"I wouldn't expect you to. But I'm afraid this meeting must come to a close." Jinshan looked at his watch. "You are about to have a busy night, Mr. President. Good luck."

The screen switched to the Chinese flag. In the White House, a group of military officers entered the president's room.

"Mr. President, we have an emergency."

18

The North Korean missile launch was detected right away, with multiple countries tracking it. US reconnaissance aircraft and Korean human intelligence sources had provided notice that it was coming. The single missile had taken off from a mobile launcher.

Chinese intelligence agents and their nuclear weapons experts had helped train the North Korean crew manning the weapon. One of the Chinese agents had even helped to evaluate the missile's central processing unit...and made a few adjustments.

One of the Chinese Ministry of State Security operatives had thought of the plan. Jinshan had loved it. It would ratchet up tensions between North Korea and the West and shift away attention from China. As was typical during North Korean missile tests, all Chinese involvement was kept secret. The Chinese didn't want anyone to know. And the North Koreans didn't want to look like they needed any help.

The North Koreans only knew that they were to test-fire a missile at the precise time provided by the Chinese. They thought that the ICBM was supposed to fly more than two thousand miles before it was to land harmlessly in the water. That was what the North

Koreans expected, because that was what they had programmed into the navigational computers.

But Jinshan's team of operatives had reprogrammed them, unbeknownst to the North Koreans. It was not programmed to fly over Japan.

It was programmed to *hit* Japan.

There was no warhead in the missile. After all, it was only meant to be a test. To show off the military might of North Korea's strategic missile force. But it didn't matter that there was no warhead. The Chinese team "helping" the North Koreans had placed a small explosive charge on board. When the device exploded, the ICBM was traveling at over *ten thousand* miles per hour.

Some of the debris burned up in the atmosphere. But the larger pieces didn't. They fell on mainland Japan.

If the North Koreans had meant to be provocative, they had exceeded their wildest expectations. No one was hurt. The pieces of the missile landed in Japan's unpopulated mountain terrain. But the political damage had been done.

* * *

"Natesh provided us with good information. That much is confirmed."

Susan sat in the director's office with General Schwartz. The director had just been briefed on the North Koreans' ICBM test.

The director said, "So this missile broke up over Japan. And we're saying that it was *intentional*? Part of a Chinese plan?"

"That's correct, sir."

Director Buckingham said, "This Natesh Chaudry told us to expect this before it happened?"

General Schwartz said, "From what Susan just briefed me on, Natesh Chaudry told our team in Japan only hours ahead of the launch. He didn't know the details of how it would happen, but he knew that the North Koreans were going to test-launch an ICBM, and that it would break up somewhere over Japan. He wasn't sure if any pieces of the missile would actually land on mainland Japan or not. But he says that it was part of Jinshan's strategy."

"Part of his strategy? What the hell does that mean?"

Susan said, "We're told that Jinshan wants to shift our focus away from China to a more belligerent North Korea."

Director Buckingham said, "Well, it's working! The president is demanding response options from the Pentagon tonight. He wants immediate action. They crossed the line this time."

"Sir, if we escalate, we would be doing exactly what Jinshan wants us to do."

"I understand the game, Susan. The question is, what is our best next step?"

"If Jinshan was hoping that this would take pressure off China, maybe we need to do the opposite."

"I don't want to tip our hand that we knew this was going to happen. That needs to stay in this room, for now. We can't afford to expose Chaudry. He may be our best new source of information."

"Yes, sir. I'm not suggesting that we need to risk compromising our source. Just that it may be in our best interests to…well, I assume that the president will make a statement on this? In response to North Korea's missile test? What if he were to announce demands on China at the same time? Linking the two nations' recent hostile actions together?"

The director frowned. "I like it, but in my experience, the White House communications office doesn't take it well when we suggest what comes out of their mouth." He rubbed his chin. "But hell, I'll offer it anyway. It's not a bad idea."

General Schwartz said, "Please tell the director what *else* Natesh said."

Susan said, "Jinshan was—as we suspected—actively engaged, even from prison. Natesh says that there was a power struggle going on in the Chinese Politburo, with Jinshan on one side and Secretary Zhang on the other. But now Jinshan has imprisoned Zhang—or worse—we don't have confirmation. It's meant to send a message to anyone looking to oppose him."

Director Buckingham said, "Does Natesh know if Jinshan intends to attack the United States?"

"He says that preparations are still in the works, yes."

"Can we trust him?"

"Like you said, sir, his information on the ICBM was accurate. Tetsuo's gut is that Natesh is being open and honest with us now. He wants out."

The director said, "The president's advisors are urging him not to escalate. Some are calling our warnings about war overblown. A lot of intel supports that assessment."

General Schwartz nodded. "Their military activity on the coast has died down. And the most recent military communications intercepts show a drawdown of PLA activity. Recruitment is up, though. And some of their inland units—their strategic bomber units and several army divisions in particular—have continued to drill like crazy."

Susan said, "Without more reconnaissance satellites, it's been harder to get good data. Air Force reconnaissance assets are stretched thin right now."

"When are we supposed to have more satellites up?"

"The National Reconnaissance Office has fast-tracked its launches. They're saying another week and they'll have two more up that we'll be able to use in that area."

"Okay. I'll talk to the president. Susan, I think you're right. I think that he needs to lay down the law to China. Any new information on Chase Manning and his team?"

"They're on Guam. Chase and the Delta team have been training for their assignment there. He says they're ready to go, if needed. Also, we heard from GIANT."

"And?"

"GIANT had a conversation with Secretary Zhang before he disappeared and got approval to go inspect the Liaoning camp. Apparently, Zhang confided in GIANT that whatever Jinshan was working on there, it was *the key* to his strategy in attacking the West."

"How would Zhang know something like that?"

"We don't know, sir. Zhang is close with several Politburo members and military leaders that are in Jinshan's circle. Perhaps he saw or overheard something…"

"What could be at this camp that would be so important? General, any thoughts?"

General Schwartz said, "Perhaps they have a weapon there? It could be chemical or biological. I honestly don't know. But with recent events in North Korea, and Jinshan's rise to power, I think it's pretty crucial that we find out."

19

David watched from his hotel room. He was doing pushups with the news on in the background. The news commentators were chatting about how the president was under a lot of political pressure to push China harder after the recent revelations of hostile acts against the United States.

"Can't say I disagree with that," he said to an empty room. He turned over and began doing sit-ups.

The newscaster said, "In the White House's prereleased remarks, it looks like the president is going to address this criticism directly. He is not only going to address the missile test in North Korea, but he will also say that 'America will not be challenged by rogue persons or rogue nations.' To me, this is reminiscent of George W. Bush's comments on the 'Axis of Evil' after September eleventh."

The talking heads went on for several minutes, agreeing with each other ad nauseam.

The newscaster said, "Okay, here he comes. He's walking out along the red carpet in the East Room. This is very symbolic. Typically, presidents only do this when they have something of monumental importance to say. A big national security policy change, for example. Okay, I'll be quiet now as we hear the president speak."

The American president walked up to the podium, gripping it firmly with both hands. "My fellow Americans, I come to you tonight in the shadows of great sadness, but with the hope of a stronger and more secure future. Recent events have left us feeling anger and despair. I have been to several funerals in the past month. None of them were easy. I told the families that their sons and daughters did not die in vain. And now, I want to speak with you about how we must honor that pledge."

He took a sip of water. "Rogue actors and rogue nations have for too long been allowed to dictate their own destiny. But no more. We as a country saw what happens when irrational actors—such as China's Cheng Jinshan—get hold of military capability. While rogue members of the Chinese government were responsible for these recent tragedies, there are still elements around the world that pose a threat to America's interests and security. So, I say to these rogue actors and rogue nations tonight—be warned. To North Korea, know that America will no longer turn a blind eye to you. Be warned. If China will not act to quell the hostilities of its neighbors, then we will. And when our enemies test us, we must strike. We will not callously put our country in unnecessary danger. We will strike, *before* our enemies are able to act.

"If China wants to avoid further military conflict, they must do three things. One—in response to recent Chinese aggression, the United States demands that China implement a downsizing of military forces, to be agreed to in a treaty, and that they consent to inspection by international inspectors. Two—China must immediately begin its withdrawal from the Spratley Islands and end its land grabs of non-Chinese territory around the world. Three—and this is most important—China must fully support the nuclear disarmament of North Korea."

The president paused and took a breath, taking stock of his surroundings. "America will be a safer place. It will be a more secure country, because of our improved relationship with China. But we will enforce peace through the strength of our great military. God bless America."

With that, the president turned and walked back down the red carpet.

David was sitting up, holding his knees and sweating. That was certainly a different type of speech.

The news show host said, "So there you have it, ladies and gentlemen. The president is walking back down the red carpet of the East Room after giving his speech. It only lasted a few minutes. But the message was…well, let's hear takes from our panel…"

The first talking head, a white-haired man who was described as a professor at the Kennedy School, said, "Well, I must admit I am surprised at the list of demands that the president sent to China. Normally that would be done through diplomatic means…"

"Which means it was probably political?" came the host.

"Well, I don't know that it was necessarily political. But the fact that he used this forum—I think that at least means that China wasn't the only audience for this speech. The president wants the American people to know that he is responding to both North Korea and China with strength. This is a president who draws red lines and sticks to them. So, I think clearly the president wants to send a strong message around the world that the United States will not be trifled with anymore."

The host said, "So is the problem that it wasn't clear where the red lines are?"

"Perhaps. I mean, he did list off those demands for China to comply with. But aside from that, I don't believe I know where the red lines are for North Korea."

"Did anyone else feel that way?"

Another person on the panel said, "I completely agree. The tone was right. And that will silence some of the doubters and satisfy those who were calling for a stronger response to Chinese hostilities, but aside from that, it was very vague. I mean, he kept saying, 'be warned.' I wrote it down here, he said, 'If our enemies proceed to test us, we will strike…' Now, that's a very tough statement. But you can really interpret it any way you want, can't you? I mean, what does it mean to *test* us? Does that mean that North Korea can test-fire a nuclear missile into the ocean? As they have been doing? Is that testing us? Is he saying that we're going to strike North Korea for their accidental missile breakup over Japan? Is that against this new set of rules that the president has set down?"

"I think that may have been one of the things that he wanted to call out, yes."

Another panel member said, "I think that the president did a great job tonight. He was very clear, I think. Very clear. China is now on notice. North Korea, Iran, Russia. They are all now on notice. This president isn't afraid to fight back. I think that's what we should take away from what we saw here tonight."

The host said, "So where is the line drawn?"

The champion of the president said, "We are finally drawing a line. The recent hostile acts by China will not be tolerated. And our military responded with appropriate deadly force in the Pacific, when challenged. And now everyone else who wishes to do us harm should be warned as well. I think the president did a fabulous job in communicating that. And I'm pleased to see that he listed a clear set of demands for China. They can't just blame this on a rogue politician or businessman or whatever this Cheng Jinshan fellow is over there. Now the whole country is going to be held responsible. And I think that's a smart move by the president. I'll tell you what else I liked. I also liked that he tied in China and North Korea together. Because let's face it, folks, North Korea has their nuclear technology *because* of China. And it's about time that China began to police them the way they should."

David grabbed the remote and shut off the TV. He was halfway through another set of sit-ups when his phone let out an alert noise on his bed. David grabbed it and checked the number.

It was a text message from Tetsuo.

Meeting with Natesh. 30 minutes.

20

M ajor Mason sat in the auditorium with the US Air Force crew of seven other pilots and combat systems officers, all waiting to receive their mission brief. It was just two crews today. The doors were shut, as was normal. But their CO—commanding officer of the Ninth Bomb Squadron—was present, which was not normal.

Something big was going down.

"Good evening, gentlemen. Here is the plan for the sortie tonight." The intelligence officer had a somber look.

The briefing took an hour. There were a lot of raised eyebrows and exchanged glances. When it was finished, the commanding officer said, "Anyone has questions, now's the time."

There were a few questions about tanker positions and timing, and fighter cover. Then Major Chuck "Hightower" Mason, who was flying as pilot in command of the lead B-1B, raised his hand.

"Sir, I'm not sure if this is my place, but do we expect any repercussions from this?"

"Repercussions?"

"Yes, sir."

The commanding officer said, "I think we will need to be ready for anything, Hightower. Fly safe."

The room was oddly silent as they got up to depart. The pilots and combat systems officers all realized that this mission would be different. Many of them were combat veterans. They had dropped ordnance in Iraq and Afghanistan. But that airspace was definitely not the Korean peninsula. Spending hours loitering tens of thousands of feet over the mountains of Afghanistan, waiting until a forward air controller called in close air support, was one thing. There wasn't much in the way of return fire up that high.

North Korea was loaded with air defense assets.

Only two crews would go on this mission. There were squadrons of B-1Bs and B-2s currently deployed to Anderson Air Force Base on Guam. But this mission would only use the B-1s. A limited strike.

The major thought that sentiment was laughable. There was no such thing as a limited strike when it came to North Korea. They couldn't predict what might happen after the bombs dropped. While he appreciated that his target was a good one, he questioned the wisdom of upping the ante like this. If the United States was going to attack North Korea, his opinion was that it had to be all or nothing. But he was just a major. No one had asked him.

"You believe this shit?" His combat systems officer was the mission commander for his aircraft.

"What about it?"

"Come on. Don't pretend you aren't wondering the same thing I am. You were the one who asked the question on everyone's mind. What comes next? *After* we drop these bombs."

"Could be something they aren't telling us."

"Maybe. But I don't think so. The B-2 guys aren't briefing. Most of our squadron isn't briefing."

"I think the generals are trying to have it both ways by just sending us in. They're trying to blow up a little missile silo and hope North Korea doesn't get too pissed."

"That's a gamble, man. Dudes at the Pentagon must be smoking some good shit, that's all I can say."

"Yeah, well. Shit, I don't know. I just work here."

They walked into the base ops building in their green flight suits and jackets, their survival vests over top. They put their helmets and oxygen masks on for preflight. They took turns checking that their oxygen masks were working properly on a small gray box. Flipping switches, one at a time. The process was second nature. They did it before every flight. Fast hand movements, clicks, the swing of a needle, and on to the next guy. The sound of aircraft auxiliary power units cranking up outside on the flight line.

The birds were already preflighted. The "Bone," as the B-1 was called, was one of the largest and fastest bombers ever made. Originally designed as a high-speed addition to the nuclear triad, it had been brought into the world to drop nuclear weapons on the Soviet Union back during the Cold War.

The B-1B could fly over nine hundred miles per hour and carry more than seventy-five thousand pounds of munitions. Hundreds of support personnel had been deployed to Guam to keep the giant supersonic aircraft flying.

Hightower and his crew sat in the back of a golf cart, riding from their squadron building over to the aircraft. They were dropped off about fifty feet away. Hightower made one long walk, all the way around the Bone. It was sleek. It was aerodynamic. It was beautiful, and he loved flying it. Personally, he was glad that it no longer supported the nuclear mission. He didn't like the idea of training for something that he hoped he would never have to do.

Growing up outside the Houston area, Hightower had been interested in only two things during his high school days: football and girls. He hadn't been a star in either area, although he liked to say otherwise. But he had really wanted to play Division 1 college football. He'd wanted to be on TV on Saturday. So he had written letters to every college football coach in the NCAA Division 1 field. Only one had written back. Fortunately for him, he'd performed at least well enough academically to be looked at by the US Air Force Academy in Colorado Springs. They'd said that he could fly jets after graduation. He had only cared that they were a D1 football program.

He had had no idea what he was in for.

He thought about his first few months at the Academy all those years ago. Upperclassmen screaming at him, the high altitude of the mountain air starving him of oxygen, and the rigorous football practices and engineering classes sucking away all his energy each night. By his second year in Colorado Springs, he had hit his stride. Hightower had hit the books and made solid marks. He'd found that he was prouder of being part of the US Air Force team than of being a football player, although that was great too.

Now, looking back on it, he knew that all that hard work was just so that he could get here. Graduating the Academy was just the start. The years of grueling flight school studies. Rigorous survival training out in the desert. Combat missions around the world. Studying and putting up with the everyday bullshit of the military.

It was all for this.

His one moment to stand up and answer the call. To write his sentence in a history book. He just hoped to God that the following paragraph would be a good one.

Hightower climbed up the ten-step ladder situated underneath the aircraft cabin. It was like climbing into a spaceship, the jet was so huge. The South Pacific breeze was a steady fifteen knots off the flight line, whipping the pant legs of his green flight suit as he climbed, grabbing hold of the metal rails, his helmet bag in his gloved hand.

Today would be routine, but different. The two combat systems officers were hopping up onto their elevated seats in the rear of the cabin. Dozens of green-lit screens and gray buttons. They were setting everything up for the mission, making sure there would be no surprises. Checking ordnance status, communications frequencies, electronic measures, and probably saying a few prayers while they were at it.

Hightower slipped into the left pilot seat. His copilot was already sitting in the right. They began their own preflight checklists. The copilot would read what to do, and Hightower would flip the switch and confirm that it had been done.

Before long, they had clearance from ground control and were moving the throttles forward. The plane captain in front of his nose, wearing an orange vest and ear protection, moving his arms and then signaling to brake. Brakes checked, and they taxied on until they arrived at the hold short line. Takeoff clearance from tower, and then the power of the ancient gods revealed itself—the four General Electric turbofan engines, each one capable of producing more than seventeen thousand pounds of thrust, propelled them down the runway.

Hightower pulled back on the yoke, and they began their rapid climb out.

"Landing gear up. Time to go bomb North Korea."

* * *

The mission was scheduled to take ten hours.

Navigation was a bitch. While they always had carried charts and backed themselves up with the navigational beacons of the past, the truth was that the entire military had grown overly reliant on global positioning systems.

GPS had been the greatest thing ever in the 1990s and 2000s. Laser-guided bombs allowed them to place munitions on the rooftop of a vehicle. GPS integration allowed them to place munitions on target without having the hassle of a laser designator involved. And GPS allowed for precise timing and navigation. It wasn't just a matter of being in the right place. Precise navigation would mean more efficient fuel use, which would extend range, decrease refueling, and increase the non-fuel payload.

Then the 2010s had come, and people had begun seriously worrying about the overreliance on GPS. What about the *next* war? What about GPS spoofing? For less than fifty dollars, one could purchase a cheap GPS jamming device that would block the signal around a vehicle. For a few hundred dollars, a person could purchase a GPS jammer that would extend for several city blocks.

The military planners began worrying about the need for antijammers to augment their GPS navigation and GPS-guided munitions.

Now, flying over the Pacific at just under the speed of sound, Hightower shook his head at that tactic. They didn't need to worry about someone jamming the GPS *signal*. They needed to worry about a nation-state destroying the entire GPS *network*.

Which was exactly what China had done. Their cyber warriors had used—ironically—an American-made worm to hack into the GPS and military communications satellites. From there, they had been able to render many of them useless.

"Compton, how we doing?" Compton was only a first lieutenant, the junior of their two combat systems officers on board. This was his first deployment. But he was a sharp kid. Asked good questions when appropriate, but also knew when to keep his mouth shut. He was doing a lot of the navigating for this mission and coordinating with the refueling plane.

"Good, Hightower. Tanker should be about one hundred miles to the north."

"Roger." The senior combat systems officer was giving him pointers, he knew. And probably double-checking everything he did. No room for error today.

The KC-135 was right where it was supposed to be. None of the normal communications were made during today's refueling. They were being covert. They used lights to signal when they were ready. The refueling probe came down from the tanker, and Hightower carefully maneuvered his large, sleek bomber into position. Aerial refueling was extremely difficult. His aircraft was blown around by strong wind gusts as well as slices of wake turbulence from the tanker. He had to make constant tiny adjustments with his yoke and throttle to get into the right position. A crewman aboard the KC-135 saw Hightower's copilot flash his light, the signal to lower the probe the rest of the way. In it went, and thousands of pounds of jet fuel began streaming into his aircraft.

Minutes later, they were back on their own. The other B-1B trailing them was now taking its turn refueling. Then the two aircraft continued on their way, north over the East China Sea, and on into the Yellow Sea.

"Sir, we have good link with the RAMROD." RAMROD was the

callsign for the US Navy destroyer that would be jamming the North Korean coastline during their mission.

"Roger." Hightower turned to his copilot. "You have the controls."

"I have the controls."

"Be right back. Gonna use the little boys' room before we start."

Hightower unclipped his seat harness and communication cord and began walking aft through the aircraft, careful to always maintain hold of something. The last thing he needed was to hit some turbulence and knock himself out before they dropped bombs. He patted both of his combat systems officers on the back, making a few jokes to keep them loose. Smiles all around. But he knew that they were nervous.

After relieving himself in the latrine, he walked back up to the cockpit and strapped back in. As soon as he plugged in his comms, he said, "I'm back. Anything happen while I was gone?"

"Nope."

"Roger. I've got the controls."

"You have controls."

"Alright, we're about twenty minutes out. Let's start with the checklists." The crew began going through all the final preparations before releasing their weapons.

"Sniper POD is ready."

"Roger."

The senior combat systems officer said, "RAMROD just started jamming."

"Copy."

They flew for another ten minutes before the real action began. The B-1B used its laser designator to guide its slew of bunker-busting bombs to the target. Theirs was a coastal underground missile launch site on the western edge of North Korea. The second aircraft did the same, on a nearby mobile missile launcher. The targets were close enough to the Yellow Sea that neither aircraft had to go over land. They dropped their payload of bombs and held the laser designation on the target until impact.

The missile sites exploded in a cloud of grayish smoke, the

shockwaves shattering the windows of nearby buildings and vehicles.

"Good hit on target."

"Roger, coming around. Let's get back to Guam and have some beer."

21

That week, Natesh worked from seven in the morning until eight in the evening each day. Then he met with David and Tetsuo each night. Natesh was still planning logistics for Jinshan. But he also used his network access to identify and bring back crucial bits of intelligence that the CIA needed to pass on.

Tetsuo's countersurveillance team provided constant support for their meetings, always on the lookout for any pair of eyes that might be watching them. Natesh was staying in a penthouse room at the top of his hotel. Tetsuo secured a room several blocks away, at the Conrad Tokyo. Each night, Natesh would take a different route, prescribed by Tetsuo, and arrive at the hotel. He would walk into one of its several lounge bars and have a drink for a few minutes, giving Tetsuo and his team time to watch out for any of Jinshan's operatives. Then he would leave and take the stairs to Tetsuo's floor.

Tetsuo walked into tonight's meeting room on the twentieth floor. The luxurious Conrad Tokyo suite had an impressive view of the Hamarikyu Gardens and the Sumida River below. The floor-to-ceiling windows gave a glimpse of deep blue and city lights before the shades were permanently shut. Tetsuo ordered a variety of food, now spread out on a white-cloth-covered tray. Stir-fried shrimp and scallops with chili sauce. Braised noodles with duck. And deep-fried Japanese beef with a green salad.

David waited until Natesh and Tetsuo began eating before following suit. The smell and sight of the food gave the meeting the feel of a gathering of friends. It was all part of the charade, David realized. The painting of the picture for the agent. Tetsuo wanted him comfortable and happy. He wanted his asset to trust him, and to work hard for him. So far, it seemed to be working.

"A convoy of merchant vessels left China ten days ago," Natesh said as he used chopsticks to take a bite of duck.

"A convoy?"

"Yes. They're transiting the Pacific together. I don't know what's on them. But they have specially modified containers. I stumbled onto this. But I think it's important."

Tetsuo sat on the sofa, a white cloth napkin in his lap, barely touching what was on his small plate. "How did you acquire this information, and what do you mean specially modified?"

"I'm overseeing much of the logistics planning. I'm helping Jinshan's operation to plan the entire supply chain for his Pacific war. I have a small team here that's analyzing and optimizing everything they set up. It's complicated. But I discovered something in the data. Certain units in the Chinese military have been planning to use cargo ships—specially designed—to transport a massive number of Chinese troops and military equipment across the Pacific. It's a shortcut that we came up with in the Red Cell. I actually observed one of the shipping container factories with Lena a few weeks ago." Natesh looked at David briefly, shame in his eyes. "Instead of using their military transport ships, which are too few in number, or building new ones, which could take years, the Chinese are using what they already have."

"Merchant ships?"

"Yes. And they have a *lot* of them. There are factories in Guangzhou and Shanghai that are already working on these shipping containers. They create hundreds of them every day. These ones have special cutouts for piping and cables to run through them. They put bunks and lighting inside. Some of them are bathrooms. Some of them are little kitchens. It's like one big Lego ship. They can mix and match the specially made shipping containers to transport thousands of personnel. It turns a merchant ship into a giant troop transport."

David said, "Natesh, we've heard about these specially made shipping containers and cargo ships. Are you saying that some of them already left? In this convoy?"

Natesh nodded quickly. "Yes and no. A few of them left ten days ago. Six ships, I think. I traced the serial numbers of the shipping containers back to the factories that were making them. We have thousands of these specially made containers stored in ports in Shanghai and Guangzhou. But several hundred of them made their way onto these now-departed ships."

David said, "So how many people is that?"

"That's the weird part. They aren't loaded with enough of the specially made containers. Instead of one of these merchant ships having thousands of troops each, they only have a few hundred each. I don't know why they did it this way. It's very inefficient. So maybe a thousand troops, across all six ships. But some of these shipping containers have a reference number that's different than the troop transport containers. That's the part I don't know about. I don't know what those are used to transport."

"Where are the ships headed?"

"Ecuador, I think. That was their destination from the internal documentation I observed."

David looked at Tetsuo, concerned.

Tetsuo said, "When are they due to arrive in Ecuador?"

"In a few weeks. I'm not sure exactly, but that's not what's important. You see, these merchants went off the grid five days ago, right before their track was supposed to veer southeast. That's what triggered me to look at them more closely. They've all turned off their transponders, so even I can't see their location, course, or speed."

"What do you mean, before the track went southeast?"

"The intended track was available in our network archives. They looked to be taking a southerly route across the Pacific, towards

South America. I would guess this is to stay away from any American sensors."

David signaled Tetsuo. Tetsuo then turned to Natesh and said, "Can you excuse us a moment?"

David and Tetsuo walked into the bedroom of the suite and spoke softly. David said, "He's a computer expert and somewhat of a genius. He's seen how Jinshan's hackers and intelligence operatives work. He's got access to PLA military networks. Tetsuo, if we can trust him, he's our key to defeating the Chinese."

Tetsuo glanced back into the other room. Natesh was sitting on the couch, looking through the thin white drapes at the Tokyo cityscape. Tetsuo said, "What information would you want?"

"The SILVERSMITH team is trying to collect exact tracking data on Chinese military units, for one. Of particular interest are these specially outfitted merchant vessels. If Natesh has access to logistics networks, they would need to have locations on all PLA military units, right?"

Tetsuo nodded. "Makes sense, yes. Let's talk to him and then bring this information back to Langley. In my experience, they'll have the best resources to assist. If we just tell Natesh to go find out this information by himself, his snooping might attract unwanted attention. But if NSA and CIA assets are involved…"

David finished the thought. "Then we might get a lot of information without the Chinese knowing that we're in."

"Right. And who knows, NSA might already have this stuff. Our hackers and theirs are at war every day. But now it seems like the gloves are coming off."

The two men sat down across from Natesh.

Tetsuo asked a few more questions and was then anxious to leave. "Natesh, this is very helpful. Thank you." Tetsuo had placed his plate on the table and was writing notes down in a black binder. He looked back up. "Does a military base in Liaoning have any special significance to you?"

David watched Natesh's head bob. "Yes. Yes. They're conducting some special forces training there. I wasn't brought into what they were working on, however. Lena knew about it, but I only heard snippets of information about the project. I heard that there were PLA special forces teams headed there to train. And I know Jinshan was extremely interested in the success of that project. I once overhead him say that it was vitally important to the long-term strategy."

"But you don't know what they were working on?"

Natesh shifted in his seat, his forehead wrinkling as he thought. His eyes darted from side to side. "Jinshan hired me for a reason." He looked down as he spoke. "He believed, as I do, that the key to business and war is the same. Uninterrupted flow. In business, one must have an uninterrupted flow of profits, which will enable bigger and better things in the future, allowing firms to dominate their competition. In war, it's the same. The uninterrupted and cost-controlled flow of supplies—of fuel, weapons, people, and parts—enables a nation to wage war over long distances, for prolonged periods, and at scale. It's the key to overwhelming one's enemy. Jinshan knows this. So, my guess is that whatever his secret projects involve, they'll give him a strategic advantage over the United States."

They spoke for a while longer, and then Tetsuo wrapped up the meeting for the evening, reminding Natesh of what to look for and to be careful about not being detected. Natesh left, and David and Tetsuo waited another five minutes to do the same.

David walked out of the hotel, following close behind Tetsuo. Once on the street, they passed a sedan with tinted windows. The driver's-side sun visor was down, a green piece of paper barely visible between it and the windshield.

"We're clear?"

"Yup. See? You're getting the hang of this." Tetsuo smiled slightly, keeping his eyes on the street.

Inside the sedan were a pair of CIA employees. Locals who were trained in countersurveillance. Not an easy task in a city as busy and modern as Tokyo.

Tetsuo said, "We'll need to move him if things get too hot. It's risky, us meeting him here. Cities like this are horrible for this kind of thing. Too many cameras and casuals. I'm worried that they'll know where to look, and they'll find out he's been giving us information. At our next meeting, I'm going to brief him on an exfiltration plan."

"Okay. What do you want to do about the intel we just got?"

"We need to go straight to the embassy. I'm going to brief the station chief while I type it up. Langley needs that information yesterday. It's probably going to make the President's Daily Briefing. I liked your plan—let's let the SILVERSMITH folks figure out how they want Natesh to proceed with extracting the data from Jinshan's network." Tetsuo looked at David as they walked. "Your sister still on a Navy ship in the Pacific?"

"Yeah. Why?"

"Because if I had to guess, I'd say she's about to get new orders."

* * *

The next day, David worked from the CIA trailer on Yokota Air Base. Tetsuo entered the high-security facility, his jet-black hair wet from a late-winter rain.

"Susan wants us to join her on a video call."

"Now?"

"Yup."

He showed David to a closed room at the end of the trailer and set up the call. A moment later, David was looking at Susan and General Schwartz in the SILVERSMITH operations room, surrounded by a half dozen analysts.

"David, Tetsuo, glad you could join us. That was great intelligence that you provided us from Natesh—he could be a home run asset, if we do this right. We spoke with our partners at NSA. They're sending a few experts to you this morning. They'll have a device for you to give to Natesh—he'll need training. It is crucial that we get access to the Chinese military movements. With our reconnaissance networks degraded, and with them having switched their crypto on their own GPS network, we're getting very shaky data. Everyone's getting nervous in Washington."

"We're on it."

Susan went over the details of how they were to use Natesh to gain information on Chinese military movements. Then she turned to the screen. "David, catch the next flight back here. Tetsuo can manage things there."

"Will do."

A few hours later, David was flying back across the Pacific, headed home. As he flew, he couldn't help but wonder where his father and sister were, underway somewhere below. He prayed that they would be alright.

* * *

Tetsuo met with Natesh that night. He provided Natesh with training on a special watch. It looked just like a normal Timex piece. Nothing fancy—not even a smart watch. But that was just the exterior. Underneath, it was quite a sophisticated piece of equipment.

Tetsuo said, "You'll wear it to work. Make sure you're signed in to your computer and logged in to your network. Does your computer at work have Bluetooth or Wi-Fi?"

"There is a Wi-Fi network for the office. But that's not the secure network that the work computers are on. There are separate desktop units that we use to access the Chinese logistics network. I'm pretty sure they've disconnected any other connectivity. I can check, though."

"No, don't worry about it. We'll just use the alternate technique. You'll need to access one of those secure network computers at least twice a day. When you do, aim the face of the watch towards the computer's hard drive. Press the night-light button like this. Don't make it look obvious. Let's practice."

Natesh did it a few times.

"Good. Just like that. You'll feel a little vibration when it has established its connection. It is important that you hold it there for a full minute. I know that seems like a long time. But when it's complete with the data transfer, you'll feel another vibration. Again, try not to make it look too conspicuous. Just pretend you're scratching your shoulder or something. Like this." Tetsuo demonstrated. Natesh imitated it. "Good. Yes, just like that. A full minute, okay? You do that twice per day. Once in the morning when you get to work, then once right before you leave in the evening. We'll meet at a different location tomorrow night. Bring the watch. Actually, just start wearing it all the time. It's waterproof, in case you're wondering."

Natesh said, "I'm a little nervous about this."

Perhaps you shouldn't have betrayed your country and you wouldn't be in this position. Tetsuo said, "You'll do great."

"What are you hoping to get from this? I don't want to hurt anyone. That's why I'm going to do this. Because I want to avoid violence."

Tetsuo kept it vague. "Just information that will be helpful to keep the peace. Things that will help bring forth a peaceful resolution. Ship movements, manifest and cargo information." *Targeting coordinates.*

Natesh took a deep breath. "Okay. When will we meet next?"

22

Victoria was enjoying her run on the hangar treadmill. Today was one of those rare days when the sea state was so calm that the ship barely moved at all. Normally the ship's rolls simulated enormous hills on the treadmill.

The hangar was open, providing her with a nice breeze. The blue sky and the Pacific had a calming effect on her. Victoria had a little longer to go before she got to three miles. Sweat ran down her tee shirt and face.

Since Plug had crashed their other bird, this hangar had become a makeshift gym. Most of the ship's crew praised the transformation. Apparently, most felt that since the shooting was over, a gym was vastly preferable to a lousy helicopter.

But in the past few days, the intel reports Victoria was reading suggested that hostilities were anything but over.

"Boss!" Caveman shouted from the hangar door.

"What's up?" She was breathing heavily, trying to appear as if she was in better shape than she really was.

"Captain asked for you. Something's up."

She hit pause on the machine, slightly annoyed at the early end to her workout. She dried off the treadmill handlebar and panel with her white hand towel. Then she wiped the sweat off her face and took a swig of water from her plastic bottle. "What do you mean something's up?"

"I don't know. The SWOs are running around, though. The XO and captain are with the COMMO. They asked me to get you. We're headed west now…"

"I saw us turn. You sure they aren't just running drills?"

Caveman shook his head. "I asked the navigator, but she said she wasn't allowed to say. But everyone's got this look on their face like it's a big deal."

Victoria frowned. "Thanks."

She walked through the wardroom and to her quarters. Grabbing the phone, she dialed the captain. "Sir, it's Airboss. I just finished working out and—"

"Please come up now, Airboss. This is important."

"Yes, sir."

She hung up and walked quickly down the passageway, up the ladder, and headed to his stateroom. His door was closed. She knocked and entered.

The master chief, XO, and communications officer were in there.

The captain nodded to her. "Please have a seat, Boss."

She sat in a small chair that was pressed up against the wall, using her white towel to attempt to dry off her sweaty shirt and face.

"COMMO just gave me this." The captain held up a sheet of paper. "Flash message. We're to rendezvous with the Ford CSG and proceed towards Pearl Harbor at best speed."

Victoria looked at the other men in the room. Their faces were somber. "I take it something has happened?"

"About an hour ago, we bombed North Korea. We've already contacted the Ford CSG and chopped back to them. The commodore wants me on board to attend a meeting this afternoon. I'll need you guys to take me. They're about one hundred miles away right now."

"Yes, sir."

The captain looked around the room. "COMMO, that will be all, thank you. Please contact me immediately if you get anything else. And let me know what you need."

The junior officer nodded and left the space, closing the door behind him.

The captain said, "Alright, let's hear it. What are you guys thinking?"

The XO said, "Captain, if North Korea starts shooting, it's going to be a mess. And I worry how China might respond, considering their recent leadership change."

Victoria said, "I agree."

The captain said, "Worst-case scenario, then, we have to consider the possibility that a Pacific war is about to begin."

No one replied.

He continued, "What I want to know from you all is what do we need to do to get ready?"

The XO said, "We need more personnel. We're still twelve short from where we were before the missile strike." His voice lowered a bit, out of respect for the deceased. "And we're supposed to have about fifty more on board, according to manning requirements."

Victoria said, "We could use another helicopter to maintain that capability. With one aircraft, we'll be limited on how often and how much we can fly. And we need to replenish some of our ASW stores. We used a lot of buoys last month, as well as a few torpedoes. We need to resupply."

The captain nodded. "Master Chief?"

"Captain, we need to continue to train. Some of our crew have just switched into new jobs. They need to improve their expertise in those areas. I recommend GQ at least once more per day. But while we need to keep on the alert, we also need to pace ourselves. If this thing really blows up, the crew is going to be bracing for immediate combat. And we might get it. But the Pacific is a big ocean. It could be weeks or more before we see combat. We need to be ready, but I don't want us to burn out before we meet the enemy."

The captain listened intently. "Alright. Let's start thinking about changes we can make. And make a list of everything we need. XO— you be on point for this. Make sure the supply officer has a request order for everything on your list. I want to see it on the next replenishment at sea. I expect them to schedule us for two of them on our way to Hawaii."

"Yes, sir."

"And, Boss, you work your magic with the carrier. I need a deck hit today, prior to the admiral's four o'clock briefing. Please work with whoever schedules that stuff."

"Yes, sir."

* * *

Commander Boyle was flown to the *Ford* by one of the carrier's MH-60 Sierra helicopters. It landed him on the flight deck in the early afternoon, in between the cycle of fixed-wing aircraft launching and recovering.

Commander Boyle was escorted from the helicopter and over the flight deck by one of the white shirts. They helped him into the interior of the carrier, where he knew his way around. He had been a part of the ship's crew until recently. The death of the *Farragut*'s former CO had created an urgent hole to fill. Commander Boyle was the answer.

Inside the skin of the ship, he walked through the O-3 level, where most of the officers lived, passing by several offices run by men the same rank as he.

As the captain of his own destroyer, the *Farragut*, Commander Boyle was the highest-ranking officer on his ship. But the moment he stepped onto the aircraft carrier, he was just one O-5 among dozens. There were also several O-6s—Navy captains—one of whom was his boss, the commodore. The highest-ranking person in the entire carrier strike group was Rear Admiral Arthur Louis Manning IV—by coincidence, father to Commander Boyle's new airboss. Almost all these officers would be at the meeting he was scheduled to attend.

Boyle walked through the maze of white passageways and blue linoleum flooring, stepping through opened watertight compartment hatches, and around a few poor young seamen who were chipping paint and cleaning. Arriving at his destination, he knocked on the commodore's door three times.

"Enter," a voice bellowed from within.

Boyle walked inside to see two Navy captains—the commodore and his deputy—as well as two lieutenants. The lieutenants were sitting on a worn blue fabric sofa. One of them typed on a computer, editing a PowerPoint presentation that appeared on a flat-screen monitor fixed to the wall.

"Ah, glad you could join us, Commander Boyle. Please have a seat," said the deputy.

The commodore nodded to acknowledge him and then resumed squinting at the PowerPoint.

"You misspelled *airborne*. There's no E at the end," grumbled the commodore.

"Sir, I think there is," replied the lieutenant in a nervous voice.

"Look it up, then. And change the font. Who put this in Calibri font? The admiral's staff has put out *specific* guidelines for all his briefs. We've been over this." He shook his head in disgust. "*Calibri*."

The baggy-eyed lieutenant typing at the computer mumbled something under his breath. Boyle didn't catch it, but the deputy smiled.

"What was that?" said the commodore.

"I'll fix it, sir." He made a few changes and began rearranging the words on the screen to fit better.

Commander Boyle smiled inwardly. Senior officers, during speeches to their junior officers, often liked to say that they envied them. But the truth was that Boyle didn't miss this staff officer bull-shit one little bit.

Boyle's career was a winding road. He had stepped on and off the golden path towards admiral too many times to count. There was one unbreakable commandment known to all military personnel organizations. Thou shalt not have a gap in thy service record. And James Boyle didn't just have a gap.

He had a chasm.

A 1990 graduate of the University of Notre Dame, Boyle had served honorably for eight years as a surface warfare officer. His first assignment as a junior officer had been aboard the USS *Missouri*, one of the last of the US Navy battleships. He had stood watch on the bridge in 1991, the night they had begun firing their sixteen-inch guns into Kuwait, the booming of which still reverberated in his chest cavity.

After eight years as an overachieving junior officer, James Boyle had decided—against all advice from his chain of command—to get out and go civilian. The choice for him had been about family. His kids had barely seen him, and his wife was tired and stressed out from raising them alone for months on end.

Things had gone well in the private sector. He'd excelled at his job and had been rewarded with rapid promotions and generous bonuses. His wife and he had decided to purchase a new car—a BMW, which delighted his mother-in-law. They'd joined a country club. He'd begun networking more—playing rounds of golf with company executives and getting calls from high-end headhunters.

But something was missing.

Behind the smiles and raised glasses of congratulations was an emptiness that James Boyle couldn't make go away.

But he missed the brotherhood, and he missed the sense of fulfillment that came with a life of military service. His corporate friends were often awed by his stories—but he no longer wanted to tell them. Boyle was barely thirty years old in 2001, and he felt like he was already turning into an old man—reminiscing about the good old days, when he was miserable aboard a ship.

After long talks with his wife—some featuring her wiping teary eyes—she'd agreed to support him in his quest to go back to active duty. It wasn't quick or easy. The Navy personnel weenies had made him go through all sorts of medical screenings and jump through paperwork hoops. But eventually, James Boyle had been recommissioned back into active-duty Navy service.

That was in August of 2001. Just before the world had changed overnight.

Within weeks, he was underway, and sailing toward the Middle East. His ship was sortied in response to the September 11th attacks, and by October he was standing watch while his destroyer fired Tomahawk missiles at targets in Afghanistan.

As it turned out, getting out of the Navy had only hurt his career so much. He was promoted to commander, and he was even selected for a coveted commanding officer billet. He wouldn't make admiral. There were too many holes in his record for that. But he might just make captain someday. More importantly, he was happy. His time in corporate America had given him a new appreciation for everything that the military had to offer.

After his recent change of command six months ago, Boyle had been temporarily assigned to the USS *Ford* as she went through sea trials, and while he awaited his next set of orders. Then the call came a few weeks ago. The *Farragut* needed a captain. And like any good officer, Boyle was more than happy to take another command.

Now, he stood on board America's newest aircraft carrier, with a new command and a new challenge on the horizon, watching two junior officers squirm under the scrutiny of his new boss.

At times like this, when he watched young junior officers as they tried to appease the nitpickings of their senior officers, all he could do was laugh to himself. To the JOs, their whole world was right here on this ship. The commodore was their god. And thus, two of the best and brightest that the United States had to offer were held in brutal misery over which font must be used in the daily PowerPoint brief. These two junior officers would go on to do great things. But for now, this was their penance for having that privilege.

"Sir, I just checked—airborne has an E at the end."

"That's what I said," came the commodore. The lieutenant glanced up but didn't say anything. He just made the change. The commodore said, "Easy there, Lieutenant. It takes a big man to admit when he's wrong."

The lieutenant looked back up.

The commodore said, "I'm not a big man." Then a large grin broke out on his face.

The lieutenant smiled nervously back at him and resumed typing. Boyle stifled a laugh. At least the commodore had a sense of humor.

Both of these young officers were on the commodore's staff. One was the Destroyer Squadron (Desron)'s operations officer. The other was the future operations officer. There must have been fifty people on board the aircraft carrier with the term *operations officer* in their job title, each one working for a different staff or squadron. The operations officers were essentially the managers who planned things like ship movements and aircraft missions.

In a lot of ways, working on the carrier reminded Boyle of working in a large corporation. There were dozens of silos, each one filled with personnel that were very experienced in their own function, but had much less understanding of what lay in the other silos. In a business, there might be separate departments for IT, human resources, sales, marketing, finance, manufacturing, and R&D, each silo filled with people dedicated to performing their specific task.

On the aircraft carrier, it was the same thing. The different groups formed their own cultures. The nuclear engineers who operated deep within the bowels of the carrier hadn't seen sunlight in two weeks and had strict safety schedules about how many minutes they could stay in their hot duty spaces. But they would be like a deer on a highway if they went topside onto the carrier's flight deck. The flight deck crew who spent all day launching and recovering aircraft, on the other hand, were highly attuned to that environment, but they probably couldn't tell you the first thing about nuclear power. The junior officers on the commodore's staff, who spent all day meticulously planning what each ship was going to be doing for the next six weeks, were flabbergasted when they met some of the F-18 pilots who didn't even know the name of the destroyer only ten miles away. Everyone had a job to do, and they became experts at those jobs. The carrier environment was so complex that few, if any, were experts in everything.

That's why men like the commodore, the CAG, and the admiral got the big bucks.

There were significant differences between life on the carrier and in corporate America, however. When Boyle had worked in the business world, he had often heard his colleagues complain of never being able to detach from work. They were always answering emails and many times had to work at night after putting the kids to bed. Boyle laughed at that sentiment. On deployment, work *really* was constant. You *lived* with your fellow employees. You often ate with

—or at least in sight of—your boss at every meal. The phone often rang at all hours of the night because there was something that the watch standers needed you to know about. Work was *literally* 24/7. And there was no family, video chat, or phone calls. Not until you pulled into port every eight weeks. And the "time off" during port visits was spent with none other than your fellow employees. Eat, sleep, drink, work, play. It made no matter. Military life was all-consuming. And that was just the Navy. It was nothing compared to what some of the ground troops in Iraq and Afghanistan had to go through.

That wasn't to say that it was all bad. Sometimes separation made the heart grow fonder. Sometimes separation lead to... well...*permanent* separation. Relationship details were the subject of many conversations between shipmates. Not Boyle, though. His happy marriage was a private one. He missed his wife and kids dearly, and he had planned on seeing them soon. Would that still happen?

The *Ford*'s excursion was only supposed to last a few days. But a lot had changed in the past few weeks. Now, Boyle had a different boss, a new command, and no clue when he would next see his wife and kids.

The commodore said, "Commander, I'm sorry for keeping you waiting. The admiral's brief is in thirty-five minutes. We just need to put the finishing touches on this, and then I'll be with you."

"No problem, sir."

The commodore was in charge of all of the ships in the carrier strike group, with several notable exceptions. He was not in charge of the shotgun ship—in this case, the USS *Michael Monsoor*. And he was not in charge of the carrier itself—the USS *Ford*. Both of those were commanded by men who were equal in rank to him—O-6s, or US Navy captains. The commodore *was* in charge of all of the other warships in company—the destroyers and littoral combat ships, the Navy's newest version of frigates. Were they calling them frigates now, or were they still littoral combat ships? Boyle couldn't keep it straight anymore.

Boyle kept his mouth shut for now, but what he saw surprised him. The carrier strike group was headed towards Pearl Harbor, just like he'd expected. But there were two paths. A contingent of ships labeled SAG 131 was headed on a southwestern course.

There were several three-letter identifiers underneath the SAG 131 symbol. One of them had the letters FAR. *Farragut*. James watched carefully as the commodore, his deputy, and the two lieutenants walked through the brief. It looked like their surface action group was to be made up of destroyers and littoral combat ships, and one supply ship. They were headed to the South Pacific.

For what, he wasn't sure.

* * *

"Attention on deck!"

The members of the admiral's conference room on the USS *Ford* rose from their seats. Boyle stood just in front of one of the many seats lining the wall. Dozens of squadron COs and staff officers stood with him, surrounding the conference table. The seats at the center table were reserved for the most senior officers. Mostly O-6s. Admiral Manning marched in with his chief of staff and admiral's aide in tow, saying, "Seats."

The room sat in silent unison.

A Navy captain in digital utilities stood at the front of the room. His warfare pin hinted to Boyle that he was the admiral's new information warfare commander. This meant that he oversaw the collection and dissemination of intelligence for the strike group.

"Admiral Manning, good afternoon. As many of you now know, we have recently received specific intelligence that points to a growing Chinese naval threat. Over the past twenty-four hours, tensions have escalated in the Western Pacific theater. So far, North Korea's response to the bombing raid on their nuclear site has been merely verbal. But both North Korean military and Chinese military assets are on high alert. And there is now a Chinese naval unit that is suspected to be transiting east of the second island chain."

There were murmurs around the room. Some were hearing confirmation of these events for the first time.

Admiral Manning said, "This is the group of merchant ships?"

"Yes, sir."

"Continue, please." The room quieted.

The briefer began going through slides. A large map of the Pacific theater. Large gray circles overlaid parts of the map as a way to depict the ranges of surface-launched missiles.

"The Office of Naval Intelligence has indications that Chinese naval vessels are on high alert and may even now be intending open hostilities towards US naval forces in the Western Pacific. We believe that the merchant ships transiting the South Pacific are the first wave of a Chinese supply convoy."

"Do they have escorts?" asked the CAG.

"We don't believe so."

More murmurs throughout the room.

Admiral Manning pointed towards the screen on the far end of the conference table. "Do we have a more accurate update on Chinese submarine locations?"

"Sir, both ship and submarine locations are now at least twenty-four hours time-late." The information warfare commander's voice was painfully apologetic.

"Very well—Commodore, what's your plan for ASW?"

"Sir, we've asked for maritime air support round the clock from here on out once we get to Hawaii. And I'm working with HSM-74 to set up continuous helicopter support. The carrier strike group will also have a protective screen of destroyers looking for submarine threats at all times."

"You're about to take some of my destroyers from me, aren't you?"

The commodore gave an awkward smile. "Sir, the surface action group would be taking many of the destroyers south, but…"

"The carrier is the high-value unit, Scott. Let's make sure we prioritize it as such."

"Yes, sir."

"We can talk this when we get to your plans."

"Yes, sir." The commodore looked at his lieutenants sitting together on the wall. They were red-faced, realizing that they might have to rework all the plans they had just spent the past six hours making.

Admiral Manning turned to his left. "CAG, we're going to need to place a priority on over-the-horizon surveillance. If our satellites and drone support are diminished, we need organic capability to tell us where the bad guys are and what they're doing."

"Yes, sir. We've already begun planning for this."

"What's the status on plussing up the air wing to full strength?"

"Sir, the COD's been flying round the clock bringing in support personnel and parts. We have scheduled V-22 hits while we're in range of North Island. We have a squadron of F-35Cs aboard—as well as Growlers and the Screwtops. But we need more helicopters and super hornets, sir. We're about half strength compared to what our normal complement should be."

The admiral said, "What help is needed?"

"Sir, it might help if PACFLEET was encouraged..."

"Very well. I'll make the calls after we're done." The admiral looked at Captain Stewart. "Will you be able to fit in a day of taking on a few more squadrons over the next week?"

The CAG said, "Admiral, we'll need to get close to San Diego if we're going to take on more helicopters."

The admiral frowned. "We don't have time for that, I'm afraid. Remind me, what do we have aboard now?"

"We have exactly four Romeos and five Sierras, sir." The CAG looked along the wall of the room. He asked a commander in a flight suit, "If we can't get more helicopters, what do you need to conduct twenty-four-hour operations?"

Boyle realized that the commander in the flight suit must have been one of the helicopter squadron commanders. "Sir, we've made arrangements to pick up more personnel once we get near Hawaii. We're in talks with HSM-37 to detach one or two of their birds to us as well. They're out of Kanehoe Bay."

The admiral nodded. "Good. Gentlemen, we all saw how deadly just one Chinese submarine can be if not detected. We need to be vigilant. Do not sleep on the submarine threat. If the Chinese are moving on us, the carriers will be their number one target."

The officers at the central table nodded agreement. "Yes, sir."

The admiral turned. "Commodore, let's talk about your SAG now."

The commodore grabbed the clicker and switched the screen to show the map of ships that his lieutenants had worked on. "Sir, based on the intelligence we received earlier today, we intend to put a surface action group in a position to locate and interdict the Chinese convoy. We would plan to search the area our intel expects them to cross. If we make an average speed of eighteen knots, I'm confident that we can intercept them in the vicinity of the Marshall Islands."

"Who are you stealing from me, Commodore?"

The commodore did his best to look humble. "We had originally intended on taking four destroyers, three LCSs, and a supply ship."

The admiral stared at the map. As an afterthought, he said, "Remind the group who's with us now, Commodore. We have a lot of new faces with us."

"Sir, ships in company include one Arleigh Burke–class destroyer, the USS *Mason*. We have the latest Zumwalt-class destroyer riding shotgun—the USS *Michael Monsoor*. Our supply ship is the USNS *Henry J. Kaiser*, and we have two littoral combat ships: the *Detroit* and the *Fort Worth*."

"And the *Farragut*…"

"Yes, sir, the *Farragut* is steaming this way as we speak, and we actually have Commander Boyle, their new captain, with us here today."

"Welcome, Commander Boyle."

"Thank you, sir."

The admiral said, "Commodore, when do we meet up with the others?"

"Sir, we have three more destroyers, two LCSs, and a second supply ship steaming from San Diego now. They should join us the day after tomorrow based on my conversation with Captain Stewart and the navigator."

The navigator was in a flight suit, sitting against the wall. Boyle knew him to be a former P-3 squadron commanding officer, a mean poker player, and an overall good guy. He said, "That's right, sir. Around twenty hundred local time the day after tomorrow."

"And the strike group will pick up several more once we're closer to Pearl."

"How many?"

"Sir, we're still working that out."

"What's the issue?"

"Third and Seventh Fleet are trading pieces. No one wants to be shorted."

Admiral Manning frowned. "We can discuss that later. Tell me, are you planning on going with the destroyers when we break up?"

The room was uncomfortably quiet. This was probably not the best venue for the conversation. But Admiral Manning had a reputation for making his O-6s sweat it out during meetings like this. During one meeting Boyle had observed, when the information warfare commander had suggested that they take a conversation offline, Admiral Manning had replied, "What the hell was this meeting for, then? A show for all these junior officers to know that we're doing our job? Give me your damn answer, Captain." The O-6s had come prepared to discuss any and all agenda items after that.

The commodore cleared his throat. "I had planned to embark on the *Farragut*, sir..."

"And you'll leave the *Michael Monsoor* here?" The admiral looked down the table at the *Michael Monsoor*'s captain, who had also flown over for the meeting.

"Yes, sir, of course. Captain Hoblet on the *Monsoor* is the air defense commander. I assumed you would want to keep them as shotgun..."

Both the commodore and the admiral turned now to Captain Hoblet, who sat a few seats down from them at the center table. The air defense commander was normally the ship captain of the shotgun cruiser. Since this strike group had been thrown together in haste, and with units that were not scheduled to go on deployment for months or years, there weren't any cruisers to be given. The USS *Michael Monsoor* was a three-billion-dollar advancement in naval technology—or, depending on who you asked, a three-billion-dollar piece of junk.

Controversy had surrounded just about every new piece of military technology in recent years. Part of that was due to legitimate problems with the bureaucratic procurement machine that plagued the defense industry. Another part of it was the lobbyists of competitor defense firms, happy to run negative news campaigns if it might help their business. If one new military platform didn't get funding, the money wasn't saved by the taxpayers. It went to the competition, for a proven and ready piece of hardware that was battle-tested. Washington made Boyle sick, if he let himself think about it too much.

The Zumwalt-class destroyer was no exception to this. While much of the technology was state-of-the-art, it had several eye-popping problems—one of which was its air defense capability. The Zumwalt was unproven in this arena. Her systems were different than the AEGIS system that other Navy destroyers and cruisers used.

Admiral Manning said, "Should I be comfortable with a Zumwalt-class ship as my air defense commander?"

Captain Hoblet said, "Sir, the *Michael Monsoor* is fully capable of—"

"How much testing and training have you and your crew done? And how well integrated are you with the AEGIS destroyers?"

"Admiral, admittedly, the ship is brand-new. We haven't yet finished—"

"Let's be clinical in our decision making. The *Michael Monsoor* might be great at air defense. But I don't want to find out that there's some compatibility issue integrating with the other destroyers' AEGIS systems in the middle of a missile attack. Understood?"

"Yes, sir."

"From what I've read in your reports, you have tested some of the other weapons systems aboard, and she's more than adequate at the surface warfare mission."

"That's an accurate statement, sir."

"Very well. Commodore, when we're done here, let's look at sending the *Michael Monsoor* out as the SAG commander. Captain

Hoblet, you can delegate air defense duties to one of our escort destroyers that remains with *Ford*."

"Yes, sir." Hoblet's face betrayed no emotion.

"Commodore, what's the plan for the SAG?"

The commodore tried to maintain his composure while all eyes were on him after just getting shot down by his boss.

"Yes, sir, we'll have at least four detachments of helicopters embarked on those SAG ships. My intent"—he clicked the button to switch to the next slide—"is to create a giant line abreast formation —about one hundred miles of separation between each of the seven warships. We'll have the supply ship close to one of them. That gives us a seven-hundred-nautical-mile vertical line that we're covering each day, plus about two hundred more miles on each side that the helicopters can surveil."

"That's still a hell of a lot of open ocean to have to cover outside of that."

"Sir, there's a marine expeditionary unit embarked on the USS *America* in the vicinity of northern Australia. With your permission, sir, I'd like to ask PACFLEET to see if they can help them get some of the V-22s and F-35s to conduct a little surveillance in the South Pacific. That would help us narrow down the search area."

The admiral frowned. "You don't think PACCOM is going to want to use their Marines?"

"Sir, I'm sure they will. But other than spreading out my ships and…"

"What about the Australians?"

"Sir?"

"Have we reached out to the Royal Australian Air Force? Let's see if we can get some of their maritime surveillance aircraft to help out down there. Work with the IWC."

The information warfare commander said, "Sir, they already feed into our collection box—everything has just been disrupted over the past twenty-four hours. Actually, we may have an additional maritime reconnaissance tool soon. The Air Force has a few B-52s out of Guam that they're outfitting with Dragon's Eye sensors.

They'll be able to patrol large areas of ocean in the South Pacific around Guam."

"That's excellent news. Gentlemen, we need to look at the possibility that China is trying to do what Japan couldn't during World War II. North Korea may attack the South. China has threatened to retaliate against the United States if we attack North Korea. Now that we've bombed North Korea's missile site, we'll find out if China was bluffing. We may very well be at war this time next week. If that happens, China will be storming across the Pacific, trying to grab as much land as they can, as fast as possible. Then they'll arm it, and fortify that land so we can't take it back.

"All those battles you studied in World War II history—all those names you know—Midway, Wake Island, Tarawa, Iwo Jima—remember them. They are once again strategic land masses that we'll need to consider. Those islands are able to support runways that line up with the prevailing wind direction. There are only a handful. Once these islands are occupied by the Chinese military, it will be much harder for us to maintain control of the seas in the vicinity.

"Soon we'll send some of our ships off to be part of a surface action group to the south. Our carrier strike group will maintain tactical control of that SAG while they look for possible Chinese convoys that are trying to make it across the Pacific. Our strike group will head to Pearl Harbor to take on more people, parts, and aircraft. We'll be joined by more ships—preferably as many as possible." He looked at the commodore when he said that.

"We are working with Pacific Fleet on what our orders will be after we reach Hawaii. But for now, I need everyone in this room to start planning for war."

Determined nods from around the room.

"Whether it's China, North Korea, or both, our strike group may soon be in harm's way. Prepare. Train your people. Make sure they're in the right state of mind. Make sure they're keeping healthy. No more communications home. Operational security is paramount. That's all, gentlemen. Now get to work."

Everyone jumped to attention as the admiral stood and walked out of the room.

* * *

Commander Boyle caught the commodore's eye after the admiral left the conference room. Dozens of officers remained. Most were staff officers, huddled around their bosses, talking game plans and schedules.

The commodore smiled at Commander Boyle. "Well, you lucked out, Captain. Now you don't have to deal with me living on your ship."

Boyle gave a slight grin. "Did you want to talk, sir? My helicopter leaves in about forty minutes to take me back to *Farragut*."

"Yes, come back to my stateroom for a few minutes."

Boyle followed the commodore as he walked. The busy passageways of an aircraft carrier reminded Boyle of driving on a highway. It was crowded, with many bottlenecks. The people behind you always seemed to be in a rush to go faster, and the ones in front were always going too slow. But overall, the traffic moved fast. Every twenty feet or so, they stepped up and through the six-foot-tall open hatch of a watertight compartment. Boyle knew that if general quarters were called, all these watertight doors would be closed and sealed shut, increasing the chances that damage to the ship would be survivable.

Dark corridors branched off to either side of the main passageway. Doors lined the corridors. Some of the doors had name plates on them—living quarters for the officers. Some of the doors were office spaces. Heads—or bathrooms—were spaced throughout these living quarters. Boyle saw a man in a towel coming out of one of them, his flip-flops squeaking on the floor. Probably on the night watch, or a pilot with a night flight. Shipboard operations were twenty-four hours a day.

At last they reached the commodore's door. Unlike the other stateroom doors, which were plain gray plastic, his was a deep blue color, with a decorative wooden plaque on the outside. It read *Commander, Destroyer Squadron 22*. Underneath that, it read *Sea Combat Commander*. The man had many titles.

"Would you like a coffee? Coke?" The commodore opened up a mini fridge, holding up a can.

"Sure, I'll take a Coke, sir. Thank you."

They cracked open their soda cans and sat down, Boyle on the couch, and the commodore on a blue cushioned seat across from him. A small coffee table sat in the center. The room was cramped, but even these sparse quarters were considered luxurious living on board the carrier. The commodore was one of the highest-ranking members of the now-nine-thousand-person-strong carrier strike group. His reward was a couch and a Coke-stocked mini fridge, crammed together in a space the size of Boyle's wife's walk-in closet.

"Our conversation was going to be about how I planned to run the surface action group." He smiled. "But now that I won't be going…"

A knock at the door.

"Come in."

The door opened, and Captain Hoblet stuck his head in. "Scott… just wanted to chat for a second if you've got a chance. They're sending a helicopter over for me soon."

"Come in, come in." The commodore waved.

"Sir, I can leave."

"Jared, this is James Boyle, the new captain of the *Farragut*."

"Ah. Pleasure to meet you, James. It appears that we'll be working together." An amused look on the man's face. They shook hands.

"I'm sorry about the admiral's decision, Scott. If you like, I can talk to him about—"

"No. He's right, when I think about it from the perspective of air defense. Which I wasn't. It makes more sense to leave another AEGIS ship here with *Ford* and have you lead the SAG."

Hoblet nodded. "I tend to agree. I believe that *Michael Monsoor*'s air defense capabilities will exceed all expectations. But it's not worth the risk. Not if we have so many proven DDGs."

"Would you like to sit?"

"No, I just wanted to swing by to make sure you were good with all of this."

"We'll make it work. Hell, PACFLEET's staffers are rewriting everything we submit to them anyway."

Hoblet chuckled. "No doubt." He stuck out his hand, looking the commodore in the eye as they shook. "Godspeed." Then he looked at Boyle and said, "Commander. I'll be in touch." Captain Hoblet walked out, the door swinging shut behind him.

The commodore let out a long sigh. "How many pilots do they have on your ship?"

Boyle furrowed his brow. "Sir?" An odd question.

"Commander, I'm short one aviator on my staff. My air ops officer had a baby just before we put out to sea, and my team is struggling to speak aviator. I need a helicopter pilot who can help my staff work with the air wing. Pretty soon, we may be running round-the-clock surveillance and ASW flights from the carrier and all the ships in company. So, I need an air operations officer. I mentioned it to the CAG. The helicopter squadrons on board the carrier are short pilots, and he doesn't really want to steal from them if he can help it."

"We have five pilots aboard the *Farragut*, sir. But I would think that the helicopter squadron CO would have to sign off on that..."

The commodore picked up his phone and dialed a number. "CAG, Commodore. I want to steal one of the helicopter pilots on the *Farragut* and make him my new air ops officer. I'll bring him over here to the carrier. He can do double-duty and help relieve your helo bubbas if they need it. That okay with you?" The commodore grabbed a pen and paper. "Uh-huh. Okay. Yes, I'll have him do that. Thanks, CAG." He hung up.

Boyle looked at his watch. He needed to get ready to head back.

The commodore hung up the phone. "CAG gave his approval. Here, get in touch with the commanding officer of HSM-46 and figure out who you can send over. I'd like him here tomorrow, before you guys get out of range. We have a lot of work to do."

"Yes, sir."

* * *

Plug's mouth hung open. Victoria felt bad for him. He didn't deserve this. But it was slightly humorous to her that a man who had recently stared down death and danger in the cockpit had finally found his fear—paper pushing.

"There must be some mistake."

Victoria said, "The skipper said he talked to the CO of 74. You'll still get to fly with them on the carrier."

"Boss, I'm the maintenance officer for your det. I've done a good job, right? I was going to extend for another year. I was going try to be an instructor pilot—maybe see if I could get a slot in San Diego. This isn't even a job I'm supposed to have yet...and I can't roll now. How were they even able to cut orders so fast?"

"The Desron commodore wanted an air operations officer. He heard what a great job you've done here, and he personally selected you."

Plug glowered at her. "Really?"

"No. Any helicopter pilot would have done for him, probably. It was our skipper that chose you. He couldn't send one of the 2Ps, they don't have enough experience." Her face said she was sorry, but she was also amused.

"Is this punishment? Is it because I'm a wiseass?"

"No."

"Will this hurt my career?"

"It'll probably help it."

"Why?" His hands were in his face.

"Why will it help your career?"

"No." Plug let out a huge sigh as they sat on opposite sides of the empty wardroom table. "Why me? Never mind."

Victoria realized that Plug was just once again making his rapid transition through the different stages of grief. He didn't want to leave his ship, or his men. He didn't want to go work for SWOs. Didn't want to become a staff officer. It would mean less flying. More time in front of a computer, creating briefs and documents for senior officers to scour over.

Finally, acceptance.

"Fuck it. When do I leave?"

She said, "I want you to know that we'll really miss you. You did a great job here, Plug. I'm completely serious. Even if you did crash one of my helicopters."

"Don't get all mushy on me, old lady. And it was a landing. It just happened to be the case that I landed on water."

She smiled. "The deck hit is at fifteen hundred. Go break the news to your partners in crime and pack your stuff."

"Yes, Boss."

Victoria waited until he left and then picked up the phone next to her. It rang once.

"Spike, I'm in the wardroom. Please come see me." She hung up the phone without waiting for him to answer. He wasn't in trouble. But there were only a few things in life that could really entertain her right now. Messing with her junior officers by making them think they were in trouble was one of them.

Lieutenant Junior Grade Juan "Spike" Volonte crept through the wardroom door in a wrinkled flight suit, his eyes wide with apprehension. From the lines all over his face, she had interrupted a rare nap. "You wanted to see me, Boss?"

"Have a seat."

He walked over and sat in the seat that Plug had just been in. "Anything wrong?"

"I'm afraid that your performance as the detachment operations officer is no longer going to work for me."

"Boss, wait. What's wrong? If you need me to do something extra, I can do it. I…" Spike was as much of an overachiever as she was. He just wasn't as good at reading people.

"I'm making you the new MO."

A cloud of confusion formed on his face. "Me? Maintenance officer? Plug just walked by me in the hall. He looked…what's happening?"

"He's being sent over to the carrier. So is Murphy. We're down to one helicopter, and they apparently think that we can manage with just me and two 2Ps."

"Just three pilots?"

"Yes. It'll be me, you, and Caveman. Caveman will take over the scheduling from you. You'll take over the maintenance officer role from Plug. Think you can handle it?"

"Yes, ma'am."

"Good. Go down and talk to Senior Chief and let him know. Start spending all your free time there. From speaking with the captain, it sounds like we'll be doing a lot of surveillance flights over the next few weeks."

23

All three of the US Army Delta Force operators were Asian-American men. Two spoke fluent Mandarin and passable Cantonese. Chase would be their token white guy. Considering where they were headed, he hoped that wasn't one too many. They had been training together on Guam for the past week and had gelled as a team.

Chase had never heard of the "Bod Pod," as the US Air Force officer had referred to it. He stood next to a DARPA scientist who had flown halfway around the world to meet with them for thirty minutes, in the middle of the night, in Guam.

"This will be the first time we've ever used it operationally. But it *has* worked with the monkeys."

One of the Delta guys raised an eyebrow. "Monkeys?"

"Yup. Tested this sucker out with monkeys, just like the space program. I mean, they didn't have the oxygen masks or communications equipment like you guys will. So you'll be able to speak with the air crew. The monkeys couldn't."

Chase glanced at the Air Force officer and then at the spec ops guys. "I'm guessing that wasn't the only reason that the monkeys couldn't talk to the pilots."

The scientist said, "Quite right. Quite right." His eyes darted around nervously. "Anyhoo, you boys will each have your own pod. They're pressurized, so you won't need to wear or use your oxygen masks while flying. You won't be able to move around much. Pretty cramped in there. But try not to fall asleep. We set up a manual switch that you have to press. A fail-safe, so that the pilots can't eject you without you being ready."

"Well, that's nice. So what, we press the button and what...the bomb bay doors just open up and we fall out?"

"That's about it. Uh. Both you and the pilot have to press the button. And the pilot—"

The Air Force officer said, "It'll actually be the combat systems officer who you'll be speaking with. He'll press the button. And you'll be able to communicate with him, if you need to."

"Yes, right," said the scientist. "The combat systems officer will monitor the navigational track and make sure that the aircraft is set up at the appropriate course, speed, and altitude, and then press their release button. They can't press theirs until the aircraft's outer bomb bay is open. That will prevent you from falling three feet onto the closed metal doors of the B-2. That would hurt."

One of the Delta Force operators said, "And why do we need to do this again?"

"Well, this was the best way to covertly insert you into a modern military's denied area of operations."

The Delta operator replied, "This might be the most fucked-up thing I've ever heard of. I'm impressed. You want us to ride inside this little metal pod—the size and shape of *a bomb*—which is being carried in the bomb bay of a B-2 stealth bomber—and fly...how many hours?"

"Six hours' flight time," said one of the men wearing a black flight suit from the back of the room. Chase presumed he was the pilot who would actually be flying the stealthy aircraft.

"Six hours in this little metal canister, just waiting for you to open it up and drop us into China. Am I getting that right?"

Another one of the Deltas tapped him on the shoulder. "Yeah, but dude, *the monkeys didn't have comms*. We'll have comms. It'll be great. Maybe they can play us music."

The Delta operator shook his head and shrugged. "Yeah. Whatever. I'll be sleeping. Just yell really loud when we get there so that I wake up in time to open my chute."

The Air Force officer who was helping with the briefing suddenly looked worried. "Well, you really shouldn't sleep—it'll be a HALO drop. So actually, you'll need to put on your oxygen mask about thirty minutes before drop as well. And you probably need—"

Chase held up his hand. "I'm pretty sure he was just kidding."

One of the Delta Force men smiled and nodded, his eyes closed as if the conversation pained him. "We'll be awake, sir."

"*Monkeys*," said one of the others.

* * *

The B-2 Spirit took off from Anderson Air Force Base on Guam. It flew up the Yellow Sea and entered Chinese airspace over the Liuhe River delta.

The pilot said to his combat systems officer, "You know, I was just reading an article that says all this stealth technology is bullshit. The Chinese have radars that can pick us up no problem now."

The combat systems officer, who was also the mission commander, said, "That's fake news."

"No, *seriously*. Apparently, we shouldn't even call it stealth anymore."

"Feet dry," came the call from the combat systems officer as he monitored their progress on the navigational readout.

"Guess we'll find out," said the pilot, smiling. A single bead of sweat dripped down his forehead.

"Thirty minutes to drop zone. Hope those guys aren't suffocated or ice cubes when I press the button."

Both of the B-2 crewmembers knew that the NSA and US Air Force electronic and cyberattacks were now flooding Chinese air search radars with false contacts. Even if the B-2 Spirit was picked up, it would be one of dozens in its vicinity.

The B-2 barreled to the north at four hundred knots, its black wing-shaped body hidden inside a twenty-thousand-foot overcast cloud layer. Any fighters that were launched to explore the dozens of false tracks in the area would have a very hard time visually identifying them.

When they reached the drop zone, a mountainous rural region fifty miles to the northeast of a large city that the navigator couldn't begin to pronounce, he followed his checklist, and the outer bomb bay doors opened up. He triple-checked that all of his readouts were displaying the correct numbers and pressed DARPA's precious green button.

Chase and the three US Army tier one operators, having been cooped up in a torpedo-sized compartment for hours, each immediately pressed their own green buttons, which read "Release Consent."

Chase then quickly scrunched his arms close to his body and prepared himself for free fall.

But nothing happened.

Chase quickly depressed the button again, trying to control his anger. He could hear the voices of the other operators, yelling into their own pods' internal speakers. Chase was about to press his own call button to see if the Air Force crew had any idea what was going on when the floor opened up beneath him, the harness above him unlocked, and he fell into the black night sky, somewhere over China.

24

Two weeks later

Admiral Manning stood on vulture's row—the perch outside his towering bridge that overlooked the aircraft carrier's flight deck. They were headed into the wind, and their speed through the water added another fifteen knots. White caps dotted the dark blue ocean as far as the eye could see. A gray cloud layer blocked out the sun. He leaned forward, hands on the rail, squinting as he watched the scene below.

At the one o'clock position was the supply ship, the USNS *Matthew Perry*, inching closer by the second. Her flight deck was clear, but there were dozens of personnel scurrying about on her port deck. A female petty officer shot the line from the carrier to the supply ship. One of her companions patted her on the back when the line hit its mark.

Deckhands on both ships, on opposite sides of the deep blue river of water, were busy staging their work materials for the evolution, moving pushcarts, and forklifts, and stacking elevators with empty netting for pallets. The initial shot lines were replaced with thicker ones that were used to connect the two ships. Large black refueling hoses, looking like sea snakes, were carefully pulled from the supply ship across the water and attached to the aircraft carrier's fuel intake ports. Thousands of gallons of jet fuel began flowing from the supply ship to the aircraft carrier. Pallets of food and supplies began riding zip lines across to the carrier. The replenishment at sea had begun.

On the other side of the USNS *Matthew Perry*, the destroyer USS *Nitze* steamed into position. Soon it would be lined up in the exact opposite spot as the carrier, ready for her own replenishment at sea. The supply ship's personnel were incredibly skilled. Decades of experience had turned America's Navy into masters of underway logistics, able to move tons of material and countless gallons of fuel during transit.

The whole evolution took about two hours. MH-60 Sierra helicopters from the USS *Ford* flew back and forth among the three ships, ferrying pallets and munitions underneath them from one flight deck to another. In between the ships, the salt water sprayed up into the air as the close proximity of the ships caused the sea to swell into large waves.

"Admiral, you have a call from the SAG commander, sir."

He turned to see his aide standing in the bridge.

"Can I take it up here?"

"Yes, sir."

He followed the junior officer over to a section of the admiral's bridge that contained several communications devices.

"Captain Hoblet on HF secure, sir." He handed Admiral Manning the black plastic radio endpiece. It looked similar to an old landline phone, but without the rounded ends.

"This is Ford Strike Group actual, over."

"Ford CSG Actual, this is SAG 131 actual. Good morning, Admiral. We are on station in Box Bravo. We have all six of our ships in a line abreast, fifteen hundred miles long. Our helicopters and drones are running search patterns around the clock. And we have an Australian P-8 as well as a US Air Force B-52 set up for maritime search that should be providing us assistance beginning tomorrow morning. Over."

"SAG 131, this is Ford CSG. That is excellent news. Have you seen any sign of the Chinese merchant ships, over?"

"Ford CGS, this is SAG 131. Negative, over."

The admiral frowned.

"SAG 131, this is Ford CSG. Understood. Be safe, over."

"Ford CSG, SAG 131. Roger out."

He placed the receiver back in its holder. His personal aide, a lieutenant, walked in from the far end of the bridge.

"Admiral, you've got a call with CINCPAC in ten minutes, sir."

"Any luck with satcom?"

"I'm afraid not, sir. We'll still be using HF secure."

"Hope we get 'em this time. Okay. Lead the way, Suggs."

Admiral Manning followed the lieutenant out the hatch and down the ladder way, nine floors down. They were both huffing and puffing and trying not to show it when they reached the O-3 level. In every section of the ship where the admiral walked, someone called attention on deck. The officers and crew would then snap to attention until he told them to stand at ease.

They reached his stateroom, and he took a seat. His office had a plush blue carpet with the seal of the USS Ford Strike Group on the floor, a large oak desk, and traditional Navy pictures and memorabilia on the wall.

One of the pictures was of President Gerald Ford in his khaki uniform in 1944, aboard the USS *Monterey*, a light carrier. Admiral Manning had read up on Ford's military service before he was placed in charge of the carrier. President Ford's ship had participated in carrier strikes in the Marianas, New Guinea, and the Battle of Philippine Sea, among others.

A knock at the door as it opened, the admiral's chief of staff entering, followed by a lieutenant from the communications department, here to make sure that there were no issues with the HF transmission.

The admiral said, "We need to get better weather information, COS. We're blind out here without our satellites."

"Yes, sir, I agree."

He turned to his aide, who sat at the admiral's coffee table, taking notes. "Suggs, you see that picture over there?"

Lieutenant Suggs looked up. "The one of President Ford, sir?"

"Yes. His light carrier was knocked out of commission in 1944. Do you know what happened to it?"

"Yes, sir. A typhoon hit it. The USS *Monterey* was one of several ships that were damaged in the typhoon that hit Admiral Halsey's Third Fleet in 1944. Three destroyers were lost, and over eight hundred men died at sea. A fire erupted on the USS *Monterey*, Ford's ship. They declared it unfit for sea duty after that."

"Goddammit, Suggs. You're a lowly lieutenant. When a flag officer tries to teach you a lesson, sound like you know less than he does, okay? Remind me never to get an Oxford-educated loop again…"

The junior officer smiled. Suggs was a Rhodes Scholar and had studied at Oxford for two years after graduating from the Naval Academy.

"Sorry, sir. I'll try to sound less informed." The communications lieutenant shared a smile with Suggs.

The COS ignored the light-hearted humor, buried in his own notes. "Admiral, PACFLEET has announced the ships that will be joining us."

"Have they? How many has the good admiral decided to lend me?"

The COS brought down his reading glasses. "Seven."

"*Seven?*"

"Yes, sir. Four destroyers, two LCSs and a cruiser. Plus we'll have multiple SSNs underneath us."

The admiral sat back in his chair. "And they're still deploying others towards the WestPac?"

"Yes, sir. They're going to join up with the two other strike groups that are already on station."

Admiral Manning put his thumb and forefinger to his lip, looking off into space. "They must really be worried."

The radio squelched and the lieutenant from the comms department immediately turned up the volume. They could hear the voice of one of the Pacific Fleet duty officers initiating communication. The conversation lasted a little over ten minutes. Admiral Manning did most of the listening, while his four-star boss gave him his orders.

When it was over, Admiral Manning dismissed the lieutenants so that he could converse with his chief of staff. He also called in the CAG, the *Ford* CO, and the commodore, who each entered a few minutes later.

"Gentlemen, have a seat. We need to talk."

* * *

Plug took his tray through the salad bar line. He had already placed a plate of meat lasagna on the tray, with two garlic breadsticks and a glass of bug juice. The salad was good quality. Ripe cherry tomatoes and crisp baby carrots. Fresh vegetables almost every day on the carrier. He couldn't complain about that. It sure as hell beat the week-old brownish lettuce that seemed to always be served on board the smaller ships. Plus, he didn't have to worry about the food rolling off the table since the carrier barely rolled.

"Plug, you got a seat yet?"

He looked over to see Kevin Suggs sitting alone at one of the four-seater tables, next to a TV playing an Armed Forces Network replay of the Super Bowl. Because who didn't love watching the Cowboys lose again? America's team, his ass.

Plug slid his tray onto the table. "How is life as the loop?" Loop was the nickname given to flag officer aides. Admirals and generals were authorized to have an officer designated as their personal assistant. It was an extremely competitive assignment, as it combined great networking opportunities with the experience of witnessing how leaders operated at the highest levels of the military. The term *loop* referred to the gold embroidered braid that wrapped around the right shoulder of flag aides in certain uniform types.

"It's alright. Getting busy, though."

Another lieutenant sat down with them, this one wearing the blue working uniform with an information warfare pin on his chest. "You believe that shit?" he said to Suggs.

Suggs introduced Plug and the lieutenant, who worked in the carrier's communications department.

The lieutenant asked, "So, Plug, you room with Suggs now?"

"Yup."

He asked Plug, "How'd you get stuck with him?"

"Well, I needed a room, and the Desron stateroom was filled. So I guess they figured since we were both aviators without a squadron, why not stick us together? Even though he is an inferior pilot, having no idea how to hover and all."

"Last I checked, they didn't make *Top Gun* about helicopters, did they?"

"One word, my friend. Airwolf."

Suggs laughed. "Touché."

Plug waved off the mock-insults. "So what's wrong? Where were you guys coming from just now?"

Suggs's face grew serious. "We were in with the admiral while he was getting orders from PACFLEET. Some crazy stuff is going down, man. It appears that the Chinese have dispatched a strike group headed a lot farther east than normal. Lot of speculation on where they might be headed."

"What are you talking about? How many ships?"

"About six of them, including a carrier."

Plug shook his head. "No, hold up. I was just getting briefed on this before watch. You got it wrong. There are six Chinese *merchant* ships crossing the South Pacific. That's what the SAG is going to intercept. *Farragut* is only a few days from where they think they'll start catching them on FLIR with helicopter flights."

Suggs waved his finger. "No, my friend. Two separate groups of Chinese vessels now, both headed east. You have the correct information on the merchants. But there's another." His head cocked at an angle to emphasize his point. "And these ones are *warships*."

Plug frowned. "How the hell did they get six warships headed this way without us knowing about it?"

"We did notice it. That's why we're discussing it now."

"What do we think they are up to?"

Suggs frowned. "Two schools of thought. One, they might be headed towards Panama to resupply or reinforce their wounded ships there."

"And the second theory?"

"Some of the experts think that they might be heading in range of Pearl Harbor."

"Why?"

"Why do we send strike groups into the South China Sea? Power projection, my friend. This new Chinese president doesn't like the fact that we bombed North Korea, only fifty miles from his border."

"So what are we going to do?"

"Apparently, we're going to situate ourselves a few hundred miles west of Hawaii. We'll be making sure that these Chinese warships are in our crosshairs the entire time they're over there."

Plug shook his head. "Why do I get the feeling that things are escalating?"

"Because they are, my friend. They are."

* * *

Plug was living a constant reminder of why he didn't want a job out of the cockpit. He had been aboard the carrier for less than a week and felt like he was drinking through a surface warfare firehose. The days began at 0530. He woke up, walked down the dark passageway of the carrier in his tattered bathrobe, shaved in the men's room sink, and stood in line for one of the showers. After five minutes, he got in and took a Navy shower. A few seconds of water—playing Russian roulette with the temperature and pressure coming out of the spout— a few seconds of soap and shampoo, and then a few more seconds of water to wash it all off. The assembly line was done with him in less than a minute, and the next man was up. He squished in his sandals back down the passageway, retrieved his hotel-style key card from his shaving kit, inserted it in the door, and went back into his room.

His shit-hot roommate, Suggs, had been up for an hour already. His sweaty workout clothes were drying on a hanger in the corner of the room, swaying gently with the roll of the carrier. Suggs was slapping a thin layer of aftershave on his face. "Morning."

Plug grunted in reply. "You going to eat?"

Suggs gave him a sheepish look. "Yeah, but I gotta eat in the strike group wardroom."

Plug frowned. "And my kind isn't wanted there, is that it?"

"Sorry, man. If it makes you feel any better, my ancestors were slaves, so…you can look at this as reparations. I'll sneak you out some of the gourmet pastries."

"Are you serious?"

"About the slave thing?"

"No. Do they really have gourmet pastries?"

"No, but sometimes they have pretty good coffee cake in the morning. With those little sugary crumbles on it. Haven't seen that anywhere else on the boat. I'll snag you some."

"Awesome. Thanks."

"Later, bud."

The door opened and shut as Suggs left. Plug checked his watch again—0555. He threw on his flight suit, wrapped the laces of his Belleville boots twice around and double-knotted them, and grabbed his notebook and empty coffee thermos. He took a deep breath and walked out the door.

Marching down the p-way, eyes still adjusting to being awake after only four and a half hours of sleep, he headed towards the galley. He would have to hurry through breakfast. He had a lot of work to do. Another day of making PowerPoint briefs and white papers for his new boss, writing flight schedules, and standing hours of watch in some tiny computer-filled room the SWOs called Zulu.

Plug was pretty sure that there was a conspiracy aboard the carrier. Each meeting he had was located on opposite sides of the monstrous ship. It was a workout just marching along the miles of passageways all day and night. Of course, he had no idea whether it *was* day or night, because he never saw outside the skin of the ship anymore.

He stood in the buffet line in the aft wardroom. There were several wardrooms aboard the carrier. He had to admit that the food was better here. It was higher quality, more plentiful, and almost always available. Meals were always buffet-style—none of that antiquated "request permission to join the mess" BS with the ship captain at every meal. Plug still asked to join the table, and he would tack on a "sir" if there was an O-5 sitting there. But the carrier had so many aviator-types aboard, their "chill" factor permeated the culture. Meals were just more laid-back here.

It was ironic that on Plug's first tour in such an aviation-centric place, he—an aviator—was assigned to the only surface warfare–centric command. Plug was now the air operations officer for the commodore. The commodore had a staff of about twenty officers—almost all of them experienced surface warfare officers and senior enlisted who had served aboard ships. In addition to being in charge of the destroyers in company of the carrier, the commodore was also the sea combat commander. That meant that he was in charge of all the surface warfare missions and antisubmarine warfare missions that the carrier strike group would execute.

Plug piled two hard-boiled eggs, some sausage, and slices of fresh melon onto his plate. He then put a bagel into the assembly-line toaster, which spat out the blackened slices a few seconds later.

"Hey, Lieutenant McGuire." One of the Desron guys he was working with. An SWO. This one was the future operations officer.

"Just call me Plug, man." He placed his tray down at the table.

"Plug, got it. How's the new job treating you?"

Plug just gave him a look as he smeared cream cheese onto his bagel.

"That good, huh?"

"I have no idea what I'm doing. We go from meeting to meeting all day long, planning flight schedules and helicopter logistics flights for tomorrow, for the next week, and for the next month. Then around noon, everything changes, and I throw out my plans and start all over again. The commodore is pissed at me every time I talk to him. I think he thinks I'm an idiot."

"To be honest, we all kind of think that…"

Plug smiled. "I'm sorry, man. I'm awful with names. What'd you say yours was again?"

"John Herndon. I'm the Desron future operations officer. Don't worry. You'll get the hang of it. Hey, I think we're on watch together tonight. You're standing Zulu TAO-UI, right?"

"I don't even know what you just said."

"You're the tactical action officer under instruction in the Zulu cell tonight."

"Oh, yeah. Six o'clock, right?"

"Is that pilot for eighteen hundred?"

"Exactly."

"You got your slides for the commodore's brief this morning?"

"Yeah. But he'll probably shit all over it."

"I wouldn't sweat it. He's like that with everyone at first. Once he gets to know you, he'll warm up. The key is making him look good in front of the admiral. You do that, you'll be fine."

An hour later, the Desron staff sat around their small conference table, briefing the commodore. A flat-screen on the opposite side of the room displayed the brief that had been updated with everyone's slides only minutes before. Because the information in the brief— ship locations, status, and schedules—changed so frequently, this was the only way they could ensure that it would be accurate.

When it came time for Plug to go, he stood up, looking at the single slide that had taken him an hour to make. The slide had rows of ships and aircraft and depicted the surveillance coverage around the strike group and when the aircraft Plug had scheduled were set to take off and land.

"Commodore, good morning, sir. This shows the surveillance coverage we have for the next twenty-four hours before we pull into Hawaii."

"What is that?"

Plug followed his finger to the screen. "What, sir?"

"It looks like we have a thirty-minute break there around twenty hundred. That's unsat. Fix it."

Plug sighed, trying to maintain his bearing. Was a half hour really that important? Fixing it wasn't as easy as changing the slide. He was learning the painful truth about his new job. In order to make changes to the carrier strike group's flight schedule, Plug had to beg, borrow, and steal from people he was not in charge of. He would have to go around to the various groups that scheduled and planned the flights taking off on the carrier and surrounding ships. Then he would see if they were able to change their *own* flight schedules. The aviators in the air wing's operations department, the helicopter schedulers in the carrier's squadrons, and the individual operations officers on each ship would all be affected.

The strike group's flight schedule was like a giant puzzle. Everything had to fit perfectly together. The cycles of carrier-launched jet flights were almost always the limiting factor—the F-18s and F-35s were each a flying fuel emergency from the moment they took off. They had about ninety minutes to either land or refuel—after that, someone was in trouble. The multiengine cargo plane, the C-2 greyhound, flew on and off once or twice per day, and the first line of jets often launched after that. The radar control aircraft, the E-2C Hawkeye, was up before and after the jets. And a search-and-rescue helicopter was always airborne, staying close to the carrier, ready to retrieve anyone from the water in the unlikely event of a crash.

Around the carrier, floating single-spot runways—some referred to them as ships—perpetually changed their distances from each other and the carrier. That, in turn, changed the time it took to *fly* from one ship to the next, the fuel required, and the weight that could be transported. And because the ship's own schedules always changed—one destroyer might get sent fifty miles farther out to do a mission that was incompatible with conducting flight operations, for instance—the schedule never seemed to work.

The fixed-wing guys thought the helicopters messed everything up for them. The surface warfare officers thought the helicopters always messed everything up for *them*. The two communities didn't speak the same language *or* have a healthy appreciation for the other's challenges. But *Plug* was expected to be the liaison between the two worlds, and make it all work.

"Yes, sir," he replied. *No problem.*

* * *

Half a day and a dozen meetings later, Plug sat at one of the computer terminals in the back of the Zulu module, his eyes wanting to shut. There were six computers in the space that the staff members shared to get their work done when they weren't actually on watch. Because the staff had well over six people, someone was usually standing over Plug's shoulder, waiting for a computer to free up.

Plug had finally gotten one of the carrier-based helicopter squadrons to agree to extend one of their flights an extra thirty minutes and refuel after that particular cycle of fighter jets landed, not before. He had tomorrow's schedule written up and emailed out to the surrounding destroyers, giving their operations officers a chance to weigh in—which they always did.

"You look tired, man." It was John Herndon, standing over him. "Come on, let's go get a latte before we go on watch."

Plug shot him a look. "A coffee?"

"A *latte*."

"Are you messing with me?"

"Tell me you know what I'm talking about."

Plug shook his head, his eyes barely open. He checked his thermos. Empty. "I need a coffee refill anyway. I'll never be able to stay awake until midnight."

"You really don't know what I mean. Okay, come on. Follow me."

Plug got up and followed him out of Zulu, through the carrier's combat direction center, down several ladders, and onto the main deck. Here the passageway was extremely wide and was the busiest foot traffic corridor on board. Hundreds of officers and enlisted were headed to and from various places on the ship. A bright red, white and blue barbershop pole spun next to one door, with a line of men waiting outside. And then, finally...

"*No kidding.*"

A big green-and-white Starbucks sign.

"It's one of the most popular destinations on the ship. Don't ever come after zero nine thirty. Line gets too long."

They stood in line for about ten minutes but eventually were rewarded with hot, halfway decent cups of caramel macchiato.

Plug sipped his. "It's not bad."

"Nope. And all you had to do is walk half a mile up six flights of stairs, and spend five bucks."

Plug took another sip. "Alright, man, six hours of watch. Let's do this."

They walked up to the carrier's intelligence center and got a brief from the intel officer on duty. "The SAG is now about three hundred miles east of Guam, still searching for the Chinese merchant ships."

Lieutenant Herndon said, "Anything?"

"Negative. Not on those guys. But there's plenty of other stuff going on. Come here, I'll read off the brief I'm prepping for my boss." He scrolled through his computer screen, which showed a bunch of maps with various ships, submarines, and aircraft status reports on them. "We now have intel that a possible Chinese submarine is in the Eastern Pacific. And the aircraft carrier *Shang-dong* has left port with a few escort destroyers. That's the only activity going on in the Western Pacific that isn't North Korea–related."

Plug said, "What's going on there?"

"Typical North Korea stuff. They're saying they'll turn all Americans to fire and ash, yada yada yada. But the reason that we're concerned is because we're seeing their military more active than normal. So, we're keeping an eye on that."

They left the intelligence center and walked next door into the strike group's command and control center. The battle watch captain was a balding submariner lieutenant commander, and he didn't look like he was happy to be alive, let alone brief two junior officers.

The battle watch captain said, "Alright, listen up, because I'll only go through this once. We now have seven new ships in company for a grand total of ten surrounding the Ford. You knuckle-heads down in Zulu need to get your act together and put them in screen and tell them to keep up. Right now, they're all just jumbled up, and some are falling behind as we make our way to Hawaii."

"Sir, who's with us?" asked Lieutenant Herndon.

The battle watch captain rattled off several ship names, then said, "Flight operations are done for the day at twenty-one hundred, so we can make best speed to Pearl Harbor. The RAS for tomorrow just got canceled, as expected."

Plug made a few notes on the new ships that were joining them. He still needed to put some of them on his daily flight schedule email to all destroyers. There was too much to keep track of. He was going to lose his mind before this was all over.

Next, they walked aft and down towards the carrier's combat direction center, getting briefed by the duty officer there. It was very similar information to what they had already received during their previous two briefs, although this one included what the carrier's sensor operators were seeing.

Finally, they debriefed with the Desron watch standers who were coming off duty. Plug had finished his latte now and threw the empty cup in the trash. They sat down in the black swivel chairs in the Zulu watch space. Two large display screens in the front of the room showed the tactical picture. One side had a large-scale view of the area. The other was centered on everything within one hundred miles of the carrier. Small icons of different shape and color represented surface, air, and subsurface contacts in the vicinity.

When the debrief was done, the off-going duty section departed and Plug logged in on his computer. He joined a bunch of the tactical chat rooms and was able to message different people, both on the carrier and aboard other ships in the battle group—who were also on watch. Herndon showed him which messenger contacts he most needed to talk to and which ones he should let his enlisted watch standers talk to.

"Let them talk to their peers and the individual sensor operators. You should be talking to the TAOs on each ship. Tell them what you want them to do, and ask them questions when your own watch standers can't answer them for you. But remember, those ship TAOs are in charge of a lot of people and are fighting fires on their ships— figuratively speaking. So if they don't answer immediately, just be patient. They'll get to you. And don't piss them off. Because you can't do your job unless they answer."

Plug turned as he heard a squelch and hiss of static on the large black radio next to them. Then one of the enlisted watch standers, a chief, began speaking what sounded like a foreign language. Letters and numbers. He was reading from a large laminated binder. When he finished the carefully worded transmission, he said, "Execute."

"What was he just doing?" Plug asked Herndon.

"Placing the ships in screen. Not sure why the guys before us didn't do it. I swear, half the watch is just spent cleaning up the mess of the previous duty section." He turned to the chief. "Thanks, Chief."

"No problem, sir."

Herndon stood and walked up to the whiteboard on the wall. There was a big compass circle drawn in black erasable marker, with the carrier in the middle.

"We give each ship a designated section to hang out in—that's what we mean when we say that we're putting the ships in screen around the carrier. We make each ship's slice of the water big enough that it isn't too challenging for them to stay inside, but restrictive enough that it keeps them where we want them to be." Herndon began erasing and updating the different three-letter identifiers around the carrier. There were distances and compass radials that showed where each ship was located.

On the radio, each of the ships began responding. Plug recognized some of what they were saying, but not all.

"And the reason that we place them in screen?"

Herndon smiled. "You pilots really don't know anything, do you?"

"Be nice."

"It's like placing Secret Service agents in a circle around the president. It's the optimal way to protect the high-value unit—the carrier. We have rings of defense around us. Anti-air, anti-submarine, and airborne early warning, if you have enough assets."

"Huh. I mean, that makes total sense. I knew that the ships were protecting us in that way, but I guess I just never thought about someone actually placing them there. I just assumed that the ships knew where to go on their own."

"There are some things that the ships will do automatically. Like if someone fires at them, they'll automatically fire back. But it's our job to make sure we're allocating our resources in the most efficient way possible. The more you learn about this, the easier your job will get, too. You'll be able to influence which ships are in what part of the screen—that can make your flight schedule easier to execute. Or so I was told by the last guy that had your job."

"Nice."

"I gotta say, though, I've never seen it like this before." He thumbed over to the whiteboard.

"What do you mean?"

"Normally we have three or four ships to put in screen, tops. Today we have ten. I've never seen us place this many around a single carrier."

* * *

Victoria stood at attention on the flight deck of the *Farragut*. She faced aft, towards the ship's crew. The crew stood in formation opposite her, their backs to the ship's trailing white wake.

Hundreds swayed in silence as Captain Boyle pinned her Navy Cross medal on her uniform. Then he shook her hand, looking into her eyes and congratulating her. Proud smiles among the crew, and a few claps, which were immediately silenced by disciplined chiefs.

Juan stood next to her. He received a Distinguished Flying Cross with combat V. AWR1 got an air medal. And the entire ship received a Presidential Unit Citation.

The ship's galley had a celebratory meal of hot dogs and hamburgers—cooked out on the flight deck—and cold sodas in Rubbermaid trash bins filled with ice. The cooks had set up a few tables with napkins and sides. Sailors grabbed tiny bags of potato chips, and cookies, and scooped brown beans and potato salad onto their plates. Speakers blared rap music until the master chief came over and changed it to Jimmy Buffett.

Victoria stood sipping a canned Coke, watching some of her men eat and joke with each other.

Juan walked up next to her. "You alright, Boss?"

"Yeah, fine. You?"

"Just trying to wrap my mind around all this, you know?"

"You did a great job. You should wear that with pride." She pointed at the medal pinned to his service dress blues. The new captain had insisted that they wear their more formal uniforms for the ceremony today. Flight suits wouldn't do for a medal of this prominence.

"You've got to admit it's a little funny."

"What is?"

"Plug got one of these too. He intentionally crashed his helicopter into the water, and they give him a Distinguished Flying Cross."

She smiled. "I don't think that was the way we wrote it up…"

"Still. It's a better story if you tell it that way."

Victoria smiled. "You ready to fly tonight?"

"Yes, ma'am."

"We need to find these Chinese merchant ships. They'll want to board them when we find them. Could be military personnel on board that might resist that. I'm not sure what will happen."

Juan chewed on his hot dog and checked his watch. "How much longer should we give these guys before we start clearing off the flight deck for tonight?"

She took a deep breath. "Just a little bit longer. Everyone needs to chill out a bit before things get crazy again."

25

Langley, Virginia

David sat in the director's conference room on the seventh floor of the CIA headquarters.

"When did we get this information?" the director asked.

Susan said, "It came from the team's burst transmission over the past twenty-four hours."

"And you think that GIANT is our only option?"

"We think he's our best option," Susan said.

David and the SILVERSMITH team had just gotten a report from Chase and the Delta Force operatives who were embedded near the Chinese camp at Liaoning. Chase and the Deltas had been observing the Chinese special forces teams conduct mortar and small-arms training. Then, in the past two days, the Chinese teams had begun leaving the base via military air transport. Other CIA intelligence sources were reporting that those teams were being sent overseas. Possibly towards the United States. But no one knew how they were getting into the country, or where they would be going.

The director said, "So as it stands, we don't have confirmation that they are headed towards the US. But that's your best guess."

"Based on signals intel, yes. But we want to be sure."

"Is it worth sacrificing GIANT?"

Susan was silent. But she nodded.

"Okay. Let's contact Tetsuo and have him put this in motion with GIANT."

It took ten minutes to get Tetsuo on the secure line from Japan. He had been prepped by Susan and was waiting for the call.

Susan greeted Tetsuo over the speakerphone. Then she said, "Tetsuo, as you and I discussed, we've gotten some new information from Chase and his team. GIANT had previously offered to go to the camp at Liaoning. We have decided to take him up on that offer and make arrangements for him to inspect the camp after all."

The line was silent. David felt bad. Tetsuo was no doubt less than thrilled at the change of plans. Susan and Director Buckingham glanced at each other.

The director chimed in, "As you are aware, Tetsuo, the situation in China has become less and less stable. Anti-American sentiment is high. Jinshan is seen as a savior among his people, protecting them from Western religious fanatics like this American man they say killed their president. Jinshan is using his popularity and power to crack down on all political opposition. You know that Secretary Zhang, whom GIANT worked for, was the first one to go. GIANT's ability to provide us with valuable intelligence has likely come to an end. But we think we can get him access to the Liaoning base. If he can get target information there…if he can find out where those Chinese special operations teams are headed and pass it to Chase Manning's SOF team, that would be invaluable for us."

Tetsuo finally spoke. "I agree that GIANT's value as an agent has diminished, due to his affiliation with Secretary Zhang. But to send him to the Liaoning camp *now*, after all that's happened? How will he even be able to get there?"

"We're going to help him with that. One of our agents in China will help him get access as an inspector and arrange the flight. But he'll have a short window of opportunity before he's found out. We think he'll only have a day or two before it's discovered that he's inspecting the camp. So we'll have to coordinate with Chase

Manning's SOF team to make sure they know to grab him if that becomes necessary."

David knew that Chase's SOF team was supposed to be on an observation and reconnaissance mission. Extracting GIANT was considered a high-risk tertiary option.

Tetsuo said, "Sir, is this up for debate?"

"I'm afraid not. The president needs to know what's going on there. China is becoming too hostile towards American interests. We need to know if they're actually preparing for war, and what they're planning."

"Understood. What is the timing?"

"As soon as possible."

* * *

Jinshan had been traveling a lot in the past few days. He had just finished a meeting in Guangzhou. Final preparations with Admiral Song, who would soon be going to sea. Lena rode in his car to the airport. Jinshan looked at her with admiration. She was his most precious possession. A beautiful flower that he had cultivated and grown to perfection.

She looked at him with those dark eyes, waiting obediently to hear his bidding. He hoped he lived long enough to see her achieve victory in America. Lena was the closest thing to a daughter he would ever have, and he suspected she harbored a similar filial affection towards him. He could sense it when she spoke to him.

"What have you found out about Zhang?"

She was direct and to the point. "He is purged, as you wished."

Jinshan knew she meant dead. "And his assistant? Dr. Wang? The one we suspect may be a traitor?"

Jinshan had recently learned that Zhang's top advisor, an old economist who had been educated in America, might have been working with the CIA. Cyber penetrations into the CIA's clandestine archives and financial records had given his team at the Ministry of State Security almost enough information to be sure. But the MSS had decided to leave him in place in order to see who else he might try to contact.

"There is a problem with him. Somehow, he has arranged a flight toward one of our camps. The one at Liaoning."

"How is that possible?"

"We aren't sure."

"Why is he going there?"

"His orders say that the visit is a state inspection." She must have seen the surprise on his face. "I admit that I was too late in detecting and stopping the flight. I apologize. We are not sure how the flight or visit was arranged. But I have contacted the officer in charge of base security. He'll make sure that it doesn't become a problem."

Jinshan nodded. "Good."

26

Chase and his reconnaissance team were concealed on a ridgeline several miles from the Chinese military camp in Liaoning Province.

Their paradrop had been relatively uneventful, despite the unusual entry. They had landed on a flat dirt field only a few hundred feet from a forest.

The three Delta operators and Chase had quickly gathered up their parachutes and headed into the woods for concealment. The forest rose up into a small mountain. The terrain in this area was hilly. Where the rivers turned the mountainous land into valleys, towns and farms sprung up. By staying in the mountains, the four men were able to travel throughout the area with a low threat of discovery.

They had reached the first of their planned reconnaissance positions after a two-day hike. There was a source of water an hour away. The vegetation and rock formations at their location provided good cover from unwanted observers. But the position also allowed them to see deep into the next valley, where the Chinese military training was supposed to be.

Chase and the Deltas had been observing the Chinese military training for over a week now. They had watched the same routine day in and day out. Nighttime small-arms training and mortar fire. Some sort of exercise with four-wheel-drive trucks being parked in a certain way.

Then, two days ago, transport planes had begun flying in and picking up a few squads at a time.

The Chinese troops were leaving the camp. As far as Chase's team could tell, about two hundred men had left via military transport aircraft, and only one squad remained.

The final team looked like it was getting ready to go now. A group of twelve men, their gear prestaged near the flight line.

"Where you think they're all headed?"

Chase squeezed the brownish contents of his MRE through a tiny tear in the vacuum-sealed pouch while looking through his observation scope. This one was called chicken and rice, but they all tasted the same.

"Beats me. Maybe it's just a school, and they're just headed back to their normal base of operations." The tone in the man's voice told Chase that he didn't believe his own words.

Chase said, "Let's go over it again. The drone transmission is in thirty minutes. I need to have our report ready to go. It looked like they were training in teams."

Another one of the military transports flew low overhead, the sound of the engines rumbling through the hills. Chase and the Deltas were hidden by the thick mountain bush and had specially designed tarps over their gear that would reduce and break up their heat signatures from IR cameras. But the loud noise and close proximity of the aircraft still halted all conversation until it had passed.

The camp was a cluster of buildings, vehicles and a paved runway. One of the Deltas had named it Camp Kung Pao. As Chase bit into a tasteless protein bar, he thought about what he wouldn't give for some good Kung Pao chicken right now. He sighed, knowing that he needed to concentrate and document his findings. He tapped with one finger on the thin military-grade tablet strapped to his left forearm. He wrote short text reports that would be instantly encrypted and shot up in a burst transmission to an Air Force drone at precise times each day.

Chase had suggested that the Air Force just use the drone for the entire mission, but that idea had been rejected. The Chinese cyberattacks that had crippled their satellites had also infected many of the military datalink networks—particularly the ones that were used to control drones from long-range. While the Air Force was able to preprogram drones and retrieve information once the drones returned from their mission, they were no longer the real-time reaction platform that the military had grown accustomed to over the past two decades.

Too much reliance on technology, that was the lesson. And the US military was learning it the hard way.

Chase and the three Delta operators were able to react quickly, however. That was why General Schwartz had suggested that they go in. Their mission was to observe and report back. They were to find out what mission the Chinese special operators were training for—and what could be so important that Cheng Jinshan believed it could help China take the Pacific. They would send short updates each day and then provide a more detailed report once they were safely out of the lion's den.

"Definitely teams. And they only trained at night."

"We only observed them for a week. Could be that we just didn't see them training during the day."

"Nah. They were doing training at night for a reason. Whatever they're doing, they're doing it at night."

Another of the Deltas said, "Each team was set up the same way. Three vehicles, along a road. Two vehicles on the outside as a barricade road block, protecting the interior team. About ten, twelve guys per squad, tops. The ones in the middle were the mortar experts. The ones on the outside were providing perimeter coverage, security, and feedback with range-finding equipment."

Chase nodded. "That's what I saw, too. What was your evaluation of how well they operated?"

"They sucked compared to a US Tier One unit...but for the Chinese? Pretty okay. And I agree with the assessment that they're from special operations units—you see the uniforms? No patches or name tags. Really good equipment compared to what the PLA issues. And the way they're moving in unison through those shoot-houses? Quick and efficient. They're good. Much better than your average run-of-the-mill PLA regulars."

Chase knew that this was as good a compliment as these Deltas were likely to give to a foreign adversary. Compared to the elite US special operators, they were right. The Chinese soldiers they had spent the last few days observing didn't look exceptional. But that was like comparing a college football player to an NFL football player. Either one would score a touchdown when playing against a high school team—especially when the high school team didn't know that the game was about to begin.

"So, what do you guys think the target is?"

"Based on the attack coming from a mortar, about a mile away from its target? Don't know. Could be any number of things. But it's interesting the way that they trained."

"What about it?"

"The way they set up with the three vehicles every time. I think they intend on being in an urban or suburban area. Somewhere with a road, obviously. But somewhere that they think they will encounter resistance soon after they begin firing their mortar rounds."

"So, a military target? A base?" asked Chase.

"Could be."

Chase tapped a little black device with a thick rubber antenna that was placed on the ground next to him. It was the same device that would transfer information to and from the drone each day. Since the drone could only send and receive its transmission once per day without alerting Chinese signals intelligence, Chase's team needed to be the constant presence in the field.

Chase said, "All I know is that today's transmission should be our last. If there isn't any training going on here, they'll bring us home—"

The device began whirring, and Chase noticed flashes of text on the small digital readout.

"Drone?" one of the Deltas asked.

"Yeah. It's taking our daily report."

The drone was an Air Force RQ-180, one of the super-secret stealth projects created by Northrop Grumman out in the deserts of the American West. It was nearly invisible as it transited its preprogrammed route at thirty-seven thousand feet, taking high-resolution video of the camp and storing the encrypted data that Chase had spent the previous day typing on his armband. When the aircraft landed in South Korea in a few hours, it would quickly be taxied into a closed hangar. Personnel from three-letter agencies would extract and analyze the data that it collected and pass it up the chain, ending up on the SILVERSMITH desk an hour later.

The men listened as the transmission device stopped making noise. Chase tapped a few keys on his armband, inputting his code that allowed him to see what messages they had. He knew he would have less than two minutes to read it before the data was erased from the hard drive.

THIS ORDER CHANGES PREVIOUSLY COMMUNICATED PLAN. GIANT EN ROUTE TO BASE AT LIAONING, WHERE HE WILL ATTEMPT TO RETRIEVE VITAL INFORMATION. SUSPECT GIANT COMPROMISED AND IN DANGER. YOUR PRIORITY IS TO RECOVER DATA PROVIDED BY GIANT VIA BURST TRANSMISSION. IF POSSIBLE, SECONDARY OBJECTIVE IS TO EXTRACT GIANT FROM CAMP AND EVACUATE TO LZ.

Chase swore as he read the message.

"What is it?"

"You guys aren't going to believe this."

* * *

GIANT arrived on a small white passenger jet a few hours later. Chase and team watched as he entered the compound at the center of the camp, a handful of military personnel providing him escort. They were now only one mile from the camp—precariously close—as they had hustled to the nearest ridge immediately upon receiving their new orders.

"How many do you suppose are still on site?"

"Rotating shift in the guard tower. Couple dozen in the barracks. A rover team in the jeep about one mile to the north. My estimate is about fifty personnel in total, give or take. All lightly armed."

"Looks like his plane is all turned around and ready to go."

"Think he got what he needed yet?"

That was where the plan would get hairy, Chase knew. So did the Deltas. The message from the drone gave them no indication of when or how to extract GIANT. Just do it. They had decided to give him two hours inside. If he didn't come out, they were going to storm the camp and hope for the best. The word *covert* would no longer be a descriptor in their mission type.

But if he did come out before the two hours were up, they would have to grab him before they placed him back on the plane. If they placed him back on the plane...

Just how was GIANT compromised? And what kind of danger was he in? No. That wasn't the right question.

"This is FUBAR, man."

"Yup," replied Chase.

"*Wait*. Manning, you see that? That's our boy, right? Where are they taking him?"

Chase uncapped his observation scope and looked through the sight. It was GIANT, alright. They had just taken him out the back exit of the building he had been in. Now GIANT was in the rear seat of a military jeep, squished in between two uniformed PLA soldiers. The jeep was being driven by a third soldier up a dirt road, winding along the smaller mountain in between their position and the camp.

"Don't look like they're taking him for a joy ride, does it?"

Chase followed the dirt road, advancing ahead of the jeep to try and identify where they might stop. "Come on. We need to move. It'll wind around about a half mile from us. But we'll need to get there before they do. We may have just caught a big break."

The Delta operators took about one second to process the request and conduct the risk-reward ratio, then they quietly began their sprint down the thickly wooded mountainside. Chase weaved in between spruce trees, racing as fast as his legs would take him. Their boots plowed into hard packed dirt and tree roots, making way more noise than he wanted to as they headed towards the bend in the road that might be their only chance to intercept what he assumed was going to be an execution.

Upon arrival, the four men crouched low to the ground, hiding behind tree trunks and boulders a mere twenty feet from the bend in the road. Any second now...

The group didn't have time to confer on tactics. Two of the Deltas fired from silenced submachine guns, hitting the tires and the engine block. The smoking jeep ground to a halt on the gravel road. Confused by the noise and the sudden stop of their vehicle, the PLA soldiers began stepping out of their vehicle. One of them had his weapon out and was peering over the smoking holes on the hood.

Another rattle of silenced fire, and two of the three men were down. The third, the PLA soldier standing on the far side of the jeep, fired wildly back at them.

Chase placed the crosshairs of his weapon over the man's head with a controlled movement and pressed the trigger. His target's head snapped back in a burst of red, and his lifeless body fell down the wooded mountain on the far side of the road. Chase got up and ran forward.

The Deltas were pulling GIANT out of the rear seat.

"GIANT's hit," one of them said, opening up a medical kit. The Delta operator's experienced hands moved fast in an attempt to stop the bleeding and stabilize his patient.

"That gunfire was loud. You think they'll send others?"

"Maybe. Maybe not, if they were taking him out here to be shot."

GIANT tapped his breast pocket. His eyes were going in and out of focus, and his breathing came in shallow gasps. One of the Deltas reached where GIANT was tapping on his chest and pulled out a black object about the size of a quarter, handing it to Chase. GIANT nodded at him and whispered in English, "Answers. Plans." He took another rasping breath and looked at Chase. "They are going to invade."

Chase held the man's shoulder. "We know. What were they working on here?"

The man pointed to the black object, now in Chase's hand, saying, "Take it to CIA. But warn them. The attack begins very soon. Jinshan uses misdirection. He wants to take the Pacific in one blow."

The man let out a spasm of coughs, wincing in pain.

Chase looked around. Two of the Deltas were spread out and kneeling, looking through their rifle scopes, surveilling the surrounding countryside. The Delta operator who had been working on GIANT walked up to Chase, whispering, "He's gonna bleed out. We need to go. Nothing we can do for him, man."

Chase nodded.

The old man hadn't heard the exchange, but the look in his eye said he had arrived at the same conclusion. "You must leave." He grabbed Chase's arm. "*Hawaii and Guam.* Jinshan will attack each. You must warn..." He gripped Chase's arm in a final show of strength, emphasizing the importance of his message.

The old man shut his eyes, wheezed for a few more seconds, and then silence.

Chase signaled the Delta operators to rally on him. "We need to put the bodies in the vehicle and roll it down off the road. That'll buy us a little time. Extraction is in five hours."

The group of four elite special operators moved quickly, piling the bodies into the jeep, taking off the parking brake, placing it in neutral, and rolling it down the hill. It slammed unceremoniously into a large pine about one hundred feet down, far enough away from the road to make it difficult to see. Then they humped it up the mountainside, leaving the smoking jeep and dead bodies behind.

They spent the next half day traveling to their LZ. Finally, two hours after sunset, the shadowy figure of an Air Force Special Operations CV-22 Osprey hovered over an empty field, a dozen miles away from the nearest set of eyes.

NVG-equipped pilots landed the tilt rotor aircraft, and a pair of

Air Force PJs stepped onto Chinese soil, their weapons aimed into the tree line as the team of four jogged up the rear ramp.

A joint Air Force and NSA electronic and cyberattack had crippled radar and electrical power throughout much of the region during the hour that the Osprey was over land. The Chinese systems came back online just as the Osprey went feet wet, headed to Osan Air Base in Korea.

27

C heng Jinshan arrived at the remote mountain base early in the morning. This underground fortress was located fifty miles to the west of Beijing. He had arrived by convoy of helicopters, along with dozens of his staff and military generals. Caravans of vehicles were also headed this way and would be there in a matter of hours.

The secretive mountain bunker fortress was originally built in the 1960s. Construction had been ordered by Chairman Mao Zedong, fearful of a Soviet nuclear attack. Many such bunkers had been created, scattered throughout the Chinese countryside. But *this* one was for leadership. By Jinshan's order, the cavernous concrete halls and passageways were filled with LED lighting, high-tech security systems, ventilation systems, and communications networks. Surface-to-air missile batteries were set up on the surrounding mountaintops, and a battalion of highly trained PLA troops had been deployed to the area, guaranteeing his protection.

This was to be Jinshan's wartime headquarters. Remote, heavily fortified, and highly secure. It was designed to withstand a direct nuclear attack, and arrangements had been made to transport him away to one of several other locations in the event that such a catastrophe occurred.

During the first half of the day, Jinshan listened to updates from his generals on the status of forces. He received a brief on the timeline of events, asking very few questions, since he had helped to tailor the plans to his specifications. Things were going well. Everyone was where they needed to be, before the curtain went up.

"Mr. Jinshan, we have a call for you from the island."

He picked up the phone and heard Lena's voice. "Is everything ready?"

"Yes, Mr. Jinshan. We are standing by."

There was something in her voice. "What is it? What's wrong?"

"I was informed by one of my cyber experts that Natesh Chaudry may have seen something that he wasn't supposed to."

"What did he see?"

"He accessed files on the South Sea Fleet plans, and the merchant fleet…"

Jinshan lifted his head, thinking. "How was he able to access that information?"

"Our cyber team is looking into it."

"I'm afraid it is time for us to dispose of him. Would you mind taking care of that?"

"Of course, Mr. Jinshan. We are in our no-fly window right now, but—"

"Wait until the day's activities are over. I don't want to risk you getting injured. And I need you to oversee things on the island. Make sure no one makes any mistakes, Lena. I wish every one of my employees was as talented and reliable as you. Good luck." He hung up the phone and walked into the chamber where his most senior military leaders were waiting for him.

The battlefield was a quiet forest, with the scent of smoke in the air. Fire was coming. The Americans no doubt suspected that something was about to begin. But it would be too late for them to respond. His life's work was about to be realized. There was only one final thing to do. Cheng Jinshan raised his hand, his eyes cold. His generals each stared down the long table back at him.

"Attack."

* * *

Chase's V-22 landed at Osan Air Base just after 0800 local time. A dark blue sedan waited for him. A tall Asian man in sunglasses and a green canvas jacket stood next to the driver's door, beckoning Chase to get in. He bid the Delta operators farewell and got respectful nods in return.

The driver was young—he couldn't have been more than twenty-six or twenty-seven. Chase figured that he must have worked for the Agency out of Seoul Station.

"Tetsuo here yet?"

"Just arrived. He's with the analysts in the trailer."

The tires squeaked as they pulled into a hangar on the other side of the airfield. Chase and the young CIA operative walked to the CIA trailer inside the hangar. It was propped up on cinderblocks, with two armed guards standing outside the door. The guards watched carefully as the CIA agent who was escorting Chase used both his fingerprint and an eye scanner to gain access. A guard checked Chase's ID before they were allowed any further.

Tetsuo stood inside, shaking hands with Chase as he entered. "Glad you made it out okay. We were worried about you." He raised his eyebrows. "Whoa. Buddy, you smell."

"Yeah, well. Wasn't my idea to go in the field for a couple weeks."

"Everything go okay?"

"Got a bit rough at the end. Listen, I need to get information up the chain as soon as possible."

Tetsuo handed him a corded phone connected to the trailer's secure communications network. Within minutes, Chase was speaking with members of the SILVERSMITH team while Tetsuo listened in.

Susan's voice sounded strained. It was late at night there in Langley. "Let's hear your report."

Chase gave her the summary of events over the past week. He started with the most crucial information—China was indeed planning to attack the United States. Per GIANT's verbal communication, the time of the attack could be as soon as today. He didn't yet know what data he had transferred in the small data device.

Upon hearing this, General Schwartz interrupted. "Excuse me one moment. I'm going to put out an emergency message to our forces. I want to make sure I have the relevant information. Is there anything else he said?"

"He said that the entire Pacific was in play and emphasized that Guam and Hawaii would be among the first hit."

"Did he get information on where the Chinese special operations teams were headed? What are their targets? Are they really going to the US? Were they going to Guam and Hawaii?"

"I don't know. That was all he said."

"How is that possible? Our confidence on Chinese positions is lower than normal, but it isn't that bad," someone on the phone said. Chase didn't recognize the voice.

"I don't know," answered Chase.

More voices began offering explanations. Chase thought he heard someone say something about "missing group of merchants, and a recently activated group of Chinese surface ships."

Susan said, "Gentlemen, please. General, I think it would be appropriate to include the Hawaii and Guam information in your message. And I don't think we should wait any longer to send it."

"Just sent to the folks that manage the emergency warning messages out to the military," replied the general. "When we're done here, I'll go down the hall and double-check that there weren't any issues. But all our military units and government partners should get that broadcast within minutes."

Susan said, "Chase, what else can you tell us?"

He continued recounting the details of his mission, from his insertion and reconnaissance of the PLA special operations training, to GIANT's arrival and death. When he told them that GIANT had perished, everyone was silent. Tetsuo looked away. GIANT was his agent, and he was visibly upset.

Susan said, "Our techs just got the downloaded files from the device that GIANT passed you. They tell me it is an audio recording, with no other data. We're going to listen to it on our side with our

China analysts. Chase, Tetsuo, we'll call you back in thirty minutes after we finish our initial review."

The screen went dark.

Chase looked at Tetsuo. "Sorry about your man."

Tetsuo nodded. "Thanks," he sighed, then said, "Hey, your brother said to say hi. I was working with him in Tokyo. Nice guy." Tetsuo filled Chase in on everything that had transpired with Natesh.

"He's working for you now?"

"Yup."

"No kidding." Chase rubbed his chin. "Seems a little odd, don't you think? Them sending him to Tokyo right as all this is going down."

"Yeah. I'm with you. We've had discussions about that. But so far, the information he's given us has checked out. So he appears to be a reliable source. And those are getting hard to come by."

Chase said, "Anywhere I can shower around here while we're waiting?"

"Yeah, actually. There are locker rooms in the back of the hangar. We threw your stuff in one of them. It's unlocked, but it has your name on it."

"Awesome. Thanks, man. I'll be right back."

Chase hit the showers and was back in ten minutes. He was still exhausted but felt a million times better after getting two weeks' worth of dirt and grime off him. He went back through security and reentered the secure CIA trailer.

"They just sent me an email," Tetsuo said. "They're calling us back now."

The light on the phone flickered and the words "call connecting" appeared on the digital readout. Then Susan's voice. "Chase, Tetsuo, it was an audio recording. GIANT recorded himself speaking for the first five minutes, and then he recorded a conversation between him and what we assume were some of the officers at the camp. We just had it translated, and our analysts are all in agreement. They were training special operations teams to come to America. Some type of strategic attack with mortars. We aren't sure what the target was."

Chase said, "We saw those teams training. But they left the base just before GIANT arrived."

Susan said, "That was two days ago, correct?"

"Correct. That's when they started leaving. They all left over the past forty-eight hours."

"Then we should assume that they are all about to enter the United States, if they aren't here already. We've alerted the FBI and Homeland Security to be on the lookout for groups of people entering the country that match their description."

General Schwartz spoke up. "Gentlemen, regarding GIANT's warning that the attacks are imminent, and the idea that the Chinese would attack Guam and Hawaii in a first strike—we were discussing that here, and we just don't see it. There aren't any obvious PLA Navy movements towards Hawaii or Guam. The only thing we have is a group of missing merchant ships, but we expect them to be located shortly."

"Don't forget the carrier group…"

"True, but the carrier group is still near the Philippines."

"That's correct."

Chase felt like they were thinking out loud as they spoke. He also got the distinct feeling that they were panicked. That they felt like they were behind the eight ball. Which they very well might be.

General Schwartz continued, "That being said, if one or both of those locations—Guam and Hawaii—were to fall to the Chinese, that could be *devastating* to America's long-term success in a Pacific war. Both of those islands are of tremendous strategic importance. If they fell, it would be extremely difficult to support Western Pacific operations with air assets, given Korea and Japan's close proximity to China."

Susan said, "Tetsuo, you've been asking Natesh to get an update on the position of the special Chinese merchant ships. Any progress there?"

"I was due to meet with him tomorrow night."

"We need that information now. Our thinking here is that whatever is on those merchants must be related to an initial attack. Office of Naval Intelligence has told us that Chinese submarine activity has picked up in a big way. But it's those merchants that we're concerned about. Without satellite tracking, we need a way to locate them. Please get back to Japan. Contact Natesh, find out if he—"

The call went dead, and the lights in the trailer went out.

"What the hell?"

"Who turned the lights out?"

Chase heard a series of dull rumbles in the distance. Explosions.

* * *

The Chinese military has many islands in the Pacific—most notably the Spratley Islands, which have been developed from mere sandbars into static ocean-based military bases, complete with radars, air defense missiles, and surface-to-surface missile batteries. They also contain runways and fuel that can extend the range of land-based fighters and other military aircraft.

Several Chinese military bases, such as the submarine base at Yulin, and the Red Cell Island, had giant reinforced caverns that would shield ships and submarines from attack. The Yongning Air Base contained dozens of man-made caves that were used to shield fighters and bombers. These caves weren't just meant to protect against enemy bombs. They were designed to shield the PLA military assets from electromagnetic pulse weapons. *Chinese-launched* electromagnetic pulse weapons.

Those EMPs had just been launched.

Bursts of bright amber-white light were visible, even in daylight. But the EMP detonations went unseen by PLA eyes. Chinese soldiers, sailors, and airmen were underground and indoors, as ordered. They were making ready their weapons of war.

Soon after the great pulses of energy dispersed, disabling and disarming millions of electronic devices over the Western Pacific theater, the Chinese protective bunker doors opened, and their warriors began marching into battle.

Chinese unit commanders had been given clear instructions that morning. Prepare all units for EMP attack at exactly noon local time. Then, thirty minutes after the EMP detonation hundreds of miles above the earth, they were to begin deploying forces and attack all units not designated friendly.

Preplanned attacks were put into motion. Missiles began streaking towards military targets and utility nodes in Taiwan, South Korea, and Japan. Diplomats shot preapproved messages to nations around the world, which were designed to influence the political chess match in China's favor. Cyberattacks took down electrical grids and communications networks.

On the Red Cell Island, the giant coastal cave door opened. Within the hour, several warships emerged, switching on their radar and searching for prey.

On the Spratley Island military bases, which were unable to shelter underground, various preparations for the EMP attack had been made. Extra protection and coverings for their electronics. Quick checks that all systems were still operational. Then the radars were switched back on. Soon after, their missiles began firing off the rails at all unknown surface and air contacts. Aircraft were being shot out of the sky. Some were commercial jetliners, others were American fighters. But in war, expediency and effectiveness couldn't be sacrificed in the name of morality.

Dozens of Taiwanese, American, Korean, and Japanese ships were within range of PLA missiles. Central planning and coordination had taken months, with most of it conducted on the island. The Red Cell's input had been taken and used to improve the Chinese attack plans. But in truth, this was the masterpiece of only one man: Cheng Jinshan.

His goal for the opening round was to make thick the fog of war and use it as cover to take control of the Pacific.

28

Lena stood next to Admiral Song in the island's control center. The admiral sat in what would best be described as a captain's chair, elevated and in the rear of the dark command and control room. The duty officer didn't need the chair. He was too busy.

The interior of the island's mountain base was aflutter with Chinese soldiers and intelligence officers scurrying about. There was a buzz in the air like Lena had never felt before. The electric feeling of an epic conquest beginning.

"Ten minutes to the North American EMP detonation," said one of the men monitoring his computer screen. The man spoke calmly into his thin headset, blue light reflecting on his face. His voice was broadcast throughout the room for all to hear.

Another person said, "Sir, the Americans have activated their emergency warning alert notification—a national broadcast."

Lena knew that this description wasn't accurate. The *Americans* hadn't activated their emergency alert system. They couldn't. Not right now. Chinese cyberwarriors from the elite Third Department had seized control of it an hour before the attacks had begun.

A stroke of brilliant espionage and years of careful planning went into that operation. It required penetration of the Federal Communications Commission, FEMA, and many of the contractors whom they hired. But now, China would reap the rewards, as they controlled the Americans' own emergency alert system—at least for the time being. This gave them a window of opportunity to control the message.

The duty officer nodded. He looked behind at Lena and the admiral. "Our overlay to the emergency warning alert has been activated. The US national news stations have just received notification that the president of the United States will be addressing them shortly."

Lena knew that the real POTUS had done no such thing. With any luck, he was asleep in his bed. Or perhaps he had just been alerted to the beginnings of the attack.

Admiral Song said, "Understood. When will our video clip air?"

A woman looked up from her computer station. "Immediately, sir."

This was the most delicate part. Would the faux video footage of the American president be believable? Or would people suspect that it was doctored? It was a point of contention among the planners. Lena doubted that, in the madness that must be unfolding across the United States, many people would be able to tell that the man they were seeing on screen was only an actor.

The CGI alone had been incredibly expensive and complicated. Operatives had acted out the scene several months earlier in a specially made room. Then two trusted agents from one of Jinshan's media companies had edited the footage and changed the words.

Jinshan's inner circle of planners had argued back and forth in their strategy sessions about whether the Americans actually *would* respond with a nuclear weapon launch on North Korea. Perhaps the Chinese didn't *need* to rig it, so to speak.

Jinshan had disagreed.

This part of the plans couldn't be left to chance. Ever the master of political calculus and human psychology, Jinshan needed the American response to be disproportionate and inflammatory. The balance of power must be in his favor. And for that to be achieved, the United States must be portrayed as belligerent militaristic killers. Chinese-launched EMPs were now in flight. Soon, the *real* blackout began, and no one would get any other information to the contrary… until it was too late.

"The American presidential address video is running live on all major American TV networks."

Lena said, "All of them?" This was an indicator of whether the cyberwarriors had fully achieved their objective.

"Yes, they all took the bait."

"Excellent." Everything was going according to script.

Chinese cyberoperations teams and intelligence agents had spent months studying the exact method of communication between US federal agencies and the TV networks. The FCC and Department of Homeland Security had secure procedures and verification steps for this kind of thing. Encryption. Passwords. But the encryption had been easily broken by members of China's Third Department of the People's Liberation Army's General Staff Department—otherwise known as 3PLA. The Chinese equivalent of the NSA. Other intelligence operatives had uncovered a process to get the video signal uplinked to the news networks in a way that made it look like it was being live-streamed from the White House.

It was a complex deception, but it had worked. Now three hundred million Americans watched as their president told them on live TV that their nation was under nuclear attack from North Korea —*and that the United States had responded in kind.* That was the key. Once the world believed that the US had launched nuclear weapons on North Korea, the American political leverage would plunge. The tectonic plates of world diplomacy would shift, and the US would lose out in the realignment.

"Five minutes until the EMP device detonation."

People in the room looked up nervously at the ceiling. Some of the EMP detonations would be overhead, hundreds of miles up. They weren't in danger—that was what the nuclear scientists and weapons experts had said—but it was still a frightening thought. Nuclear detonations. Hundreds of miles overhead. They were shielded from the EMP effects in here, in the bunker built in to the island's mountain. In the cavernous underground shipyard, several destroyers waited.

The submarines were already underway, protected by a thousand feet of blue ocean.

Admiral Song got up and hobbled over to the corner of the room. He would need to leave soon after this. "Play the audio please," he said.

On the monitors, the masquerade began.

"My fellow Americans, our nation has come under attack. At one o'clock a.m. Eastern time, NORAD detected signs consistent with multiple ballistic missile launches originating from North Korea. While North Korea has conducted previous tests, these missiles continue to head east. As we realized that these missiles were headed towards the United States, we responded. Our ballistic missile defense was able to destroy many, but not all of these North Korean missiles.

"Moments ago, after conferring with the National Security Advisor, the Director of National Intelligence, and the Chairman of the Joint Chiefs of Staff, I have ordered a swift and proportionate response. The United States of America will not stand idly by while madmen plot treachery against our free and peace-loving nation.

"Due to the serious nature of the exchange between the United States and North Korea, the Department of Homeland Security has put out an alert urging all citizens to remain in their homes for the next twenty-four hours in order to decrease the potential impact of a retaliatory strike. We will put out more information over the next twenty-four hours.

"I urge all Americans to remain calm but alert. I assure you that we are taking every possible step to ensure the safety and security of the American people. We..."

Then Secret Service agents rushed into view of the camera, stealing the president away. The president yelled in confusion, and then the monitor switched to show the presidential seal, with a dark blue background. The show was over.

Lena knew that the part with the protective detail had been difficult to get right. Jinshan's producers had had to shoot that footage five times before they could be sure that the faces of the men in suits weren't in the frame. It made the editing process easier. It would have been suspicious if both Secret Service agents were seen to be of Asian descent.

The Americans would be thrown into chaos.

The last thing they viewed before the lights went out in their homes would be a disinformation campaign, designed to look like their own president had just launched a nuclear attack.

Then their world would go dark.

Several EMP weapons were now being deployed over major US cities. Most of them were being launched from submarines off the American coastline. Some of the EMP weapons were space-based, sitting dormant in satellites until the Chinese execute order was sent. Both methods gave the Americans almost no time to react.

A dozen nuclear detonations would soon be going off in outer space, at locations spread out over the United States.

Lena turned to the PLAN officer who was the liaison for Naval Operations. "What is the status of the submarine missile launches?"

The PLAN officer responded, "They are underway now, Ms. Chou."

"All of your vessels are away from the EMP impact zone?"

"Except for the ones identified to be in the zone, yes."

Admiral Song said, "What is the status of the American submarine cable operation?"

The PLAN officer turned to his computer screen and typed. "Getting an update now."

Lena thought of Cheng Jinshan and how he must be feeling right now. His decades of work were finally being realized. She knew that he was not well. How tired he had looked during their last meeting. Everyone could see that his health was failing him now, but no one dared to ask him specifics.

Still, there was another nagging feeling about Jinshan that Lena was holding inside. That girl. President Wu's daughter. She had seen herself in that poor child's eyes. Jinshan had ordered her execution. Had that really been necessary? It was one of the first times that she could remember that her penchant for violence hadn't flared. She had wanted to protect the girl, but had instead followed orders.

She didn't feel guilty. Just...what was it? Anger? Anger at

Jinshan and the other men who commanded her. Anger at her father for letting her go, all those years ago. She still hadn't seen or spoken to him. She knew what had motivated her father. She'd seen it when she was a girl but hadn't understood it then. General Chen was a narcissist. Jinshan wasn't like him. But both of them were more than willing to sacrifice innocents in the name of progress.

Lena had thought she was the same. But killing the girl had planted a seed of doubt in her mind. In that flash of gunfire and blood, she had snapped out of her spell. She hadn't felt her *needs* since that day, although it had only been a short time. But still…the thirst for killing came in frequent waves of intensity. She had always satisfied it through her work, when she could, and used her skills of deception to hide her violent output when she couldn't.

Now she was being told to finish off Natesh. How would she feel when that moment came? Standing in front of him with a cold blade or a silenced pistol? Would she finish him off, as Jinshan commanded? Would she feel the bloodlust well up in her bosom, as it always had? Or was her curse finally broken?

She wouldn't know until the time came.

Lena looked up at the tactical display showing the Western Pacific theater. The naval battles had begun. Getting to Japan would be near suicidal during this missile storm. But she felt no instinct of fear. If her personal jet was shot down, so be it. Let fate decide.

Admiral Song got up from his chair next to her. "I must go. Good luck, Miss Chou."

She nodded to him. "Thank you, Admiral. Good hunting."

He left through the door. She thought about how much respect these senior admirals and generals now showed her. It was all because of Jinshan, she knew.

Jinshan and Lena had grown close over the past two decades, since he had recruited her. He was her handler and mentor, although one she had rarely seen him in person. Sometimes it would be a year or more between their conversations. Cheng Jinshan was a billionaire business owner and a major player in the Chinese intelligence community. His success in each of those worlds only increased his success in the other. Jinshan's business influence and financial backing allowed him to influence Chinese politicians. Initially his business career had begun as a cover for his actual role in the Chinese intelligence apparatus. Then it had become too big for anyone to stop.

Lena thought about their relationship and the way that he complimented her and made her feel...what? Like a daughter? Ironically, it had been he who had removed her from her family. Sent to the United States to eventually be placed as a mole in the CIA. And now he had placed her real father in charge of China's military. It was a lot to process.

She wondered how much of Jinshan's affection was real. Was it part of his act, as a master manipulator? Did he care at all about her, or just appreciate how effective she had been as one of his agents?

When Jinshan had found Lena, she had been a young and innocent girl. She reminded herself that Natesh had been innocent too, when Jinshan had spotted him. He had only made one mistake when recruiting Natesh: assuming motive. Natesh was unlike many of the other rising stars Jinshan was used to working with. He had thought that the young man was interested in power. But it was not power he was after. Lena saw that after working with him.

Natesh was a gardener. He was addicted to growing things on a massive scale and improving them: companies, industries, technologies. He had confided in Lena over the past few weeks. Natesh had told her about his recruitment, and why he had been so excited to work for Jinshan.

When Jinshan had pitched Natesh the opportunity to change the world for the better, Natesh had seen the opportunity of a lifetime. The ultimate cultivation project. There were so many problems with the way governments were structured. Watching politicians lie their way into office frustrated him to no end. The world was collapsing, and at the mercy of the worst impulses of mankind. Greed. Fear. Treachery.

What Jinshan talked about was doing away with the systems of government that plagued the globe. He envisioned a single elite class of decision makers that were hand-picked to ensure the long-term success and well-being of mankind.

Natesh would have an important role to play, Jinshan had promised him. Lena recognized this for what it was. Classic recruitment. Jinshan was flattering Natesh, appealing to his ego and idealism.

Lena knew the truth. If he was to be with them, Natesh had to forfeit his high moral ground. The only way to remove the governments of the world and get to the utopia that Jinshan envisioned was through deception and violence.

The Chinese soldiers and intelligence operatives inside this room were under the impression that China would be attacking America. But that was merely the beginning. This wasn't about China. It was about the world. Jinshan had seen that China's government control and economic prosperity weren't sustainable. Not when the billions rose up from poverty and demanded better. But in order to achieve their goals, the millions of Chinese who were now conducting military operations needed to believe in the cause. That brainwashing was in progress. For now, they just needed to know what buttons to push.

But in the coming days, a flood of propaganda would be unleashed in Chinese media. The US would be accused of starting a nuclear war against North Korea. Chinese propaganda campaigns would convince the world that the unstable American leadership, now driven by religious zealots and political extremists, could no longer be ignored. China needed to act in order to keep the peace and protect the homeland.

None of this was true, but it didn't matter anymore. People believed what they read on their smartphones. If the state controlled the information, like it did in China, it could ignite public opinion and convince the masses to move towards any objective.

Lena kept wondering if she herself was susceptible to Jinshan's charms. Was she just his zombie assassin, following orders without thinking? Lena wasn't one to soul-search much, but she knew herself well enough to know that she had changed after she had killed President Wu and his family. Lena would have been fine if it had just been the president. Maybe even if it had just been the president and his wife. But she hadn't wanted to kill President Wu's daughter. The teenage girl had reminded Lena of herself.

So did Natesh, a little—due to his innocence upon recruitment, and his natural talent, however different his skill set might be from Lena's own. She admired his belief in Cheng Jinshan's vision for the future. Natesh wanted a better world, and he had been forced to sacrifice his integrity in an attempt to achieve it. Lena was in the same boat, in many ways.

She looked to the duty officer. "I'm headed to the other side of the island. Inform the air operations center to fuel my plane and have a pilot standing by. I will need to travel to Japan immediately."

The duty officer looked at her like she was crazy. "But Miss Chou…"

"Do it."

29

Chinese aircraft carrier Shangdong

Several hours later, Admiral Song stood on the bridge wing of China's newest aircraft carrier, the wind blowing in his face. He gazed out at the gray ocean, wondering what lay ahead.

After the EMP attack, he had boarded one of the destroyers just before it had departed the internal pier on the island. It had sailed out into the South China Sea. Within minutes, a pair of Chinese naval helicopters had approached, one landing on the destroyer. The helicopter had taken him fifty miles to the north to his small and nimble fleet, where his commanders were already preparing for their opening wave in the attack.

Now, he stood on the admiral's bridge on the magnificent aircraft carrier *Shangdong*—the flagship of his fleet. It was China's second aircraft carrier, but the first that had been built domestically. Their first aircraft carrier was an old Soviet-era carrier, refurbished by the Chinese some forty years later. But this…this was something special.

The *Shandong* carried three squadrons of Chinese fighters and sixteen helicopters. It had modern radars and armaments and was flanked by a dozen of China's most lethal warships. Two attack submarines protected her beneath the surface of the sea. Drones, reconnaissance aircraft, and satellite feed would allow Admiral Song to see and know everything that took place in the Pacific.

That was, if the satellites still worked after the EMP bursts—that was something that the scientists had argued about. And if the Americans hadn't begun taking out their networks. That was something that his planners had agreed on. All the more reason to strike while the iron was hot.

He walked inside the admiral's bridge, where his commanders and watch standers were able to give him instant updates.

"Do we still have GPS?"

"There have been some sporadic outages, Admiral Song, but right now it is still functional," a captain in charge of cyberoperations and communications replied.

"Very well." He turned to the captain of the aircraft carrier. "How long until we are ready to launch our aircraft?"

"A little over four hours, sir. We will be through the Luzon Strait at that time, and within range. The land-based tanker aircraft should be taking off shortly. But we anticipate American warships may be in the strike area. That could slow us down."

"Make best speed, Captain. And ensure that our escorts keep a tight screen around us. We will need protection from the American fast-attack submarines. They will have been unaffected by the EMPs, and we should assume that they will attack us if given the opportunity."

The captain nodded. Song knew that their own attack submarines and maritime patrol aircraft had spent the last twelve hours pinging away in the South China Sea. The maritime patrol aircraft had had to land during the EMP strike, for safety concerns. But the amount of active sonar activity throughout the Luzon Strait, and to the east, should have scared away most American submarines that could pose a problem to their launch.

Right now, the Americans were shell-shocked by the North Korean assault, timed to occur within hours of the Chinese-launched EMP and cyberattacks. With luck, the Americans wouldn't be sure that the EMP and cyberattacks were Chinese in origin. But they would strongly suspect it. The North Koreans simply weren't capable of that level of military sophistication. The confusion might mean that the Americans would be wary of taking retributive action against the Chinese. Jinshan had talked up "the fog of war" in his preparations. He was convinced that the Americans would suffer from confusion and indecision in the first few days.

This hesitation by the Americans was a key part of the Chinese strategy. Their desire for moral authority was their weakness. A strong leader should not wait until he had one hundred percent certainty that an enemy was responsible for an attack. If it was probable, then he should strike back. But the morally conservative American attitude demanded certainty. He had worked with them before in naval exercises and spoken to them at their diplomatic parties in China. If he had been in charge of their response, nuclear missiles would be flying toward Beijing right now. But Jinshan and his planners on the island had been certain that the Americans would not respond with nuclear weapons until it was their last possible option. And by then, it would be too late.

Admiral Song hoped to sail his fleet through the picket lines of a stunned American Pacific Fleet. There were two American aircraft carriers operating in the Western Pacific theater, and dozens of warships and submarines.

Song knew that the Chinese air force and missile force intended to strike the carriers and most warships within the next few hours. And while the military planners projected victory, in his mind, he knew that these were the optimistic presentations of eager young officers. Combat and experience would quickly season his men. Their bright looks and fearless attitudes would give way to realism and a thousand stoic stares. Blood and loss were a taste not easily forgotten.

But if China was to succeed, they must move swiftly, before the United States comprehended what was happening. And he fully intended to use the element of surprise to his advantage.

30

USS Lake Champlain
East China Sea

"Anything yet?" the captain asked.

"Radars are coming back up now, sir."

They had done a full restart of every air defense system that wasn't working properly. A flash like the sun, the lookout had said. That poor seaman was now down in sick bay, blind in one eye. The kid had been looking at some of the F-18s flying overhead when it happened. The captain shook his head.

A flash like the sun.

Inside the skin of the ship, many of the electronics had begun malfunctioning. Some didn't work at all. The captain had been in his stateroom, typing up an email, when it had started. His computer screen had gone dark. No blue screen of death. Just completely off, and it wouldn't turn back on.

He had walked into the combat information center, witnessing the chaos in there. Then the TAO had gotten word through the sound-powered phones of the "medical situation" with the forward lookout.

A flash like the sun.

The captain had read about the danger of electromagnetic pulse weapons while at the Pentagon. Thankfully, most of the military equipment on board the Ticonderoga-class cruiser was hardened against that sort of thing. But no one really *knew* what would happen if a real EMP went off above them. No one knew how powerful it would be, or how all the different systems might react. Would some of the "hardened military hardware" rely on weak links somewhere in the chain of electronics?

Another question was, *who* had fired the EMP weapons? The big stink this week was North Korea. But to his knowledge, North Korea didn't have that capability. China was the big kid on the block over here. The USS *Lake Champlain*'s officers and crew had received the recent messages about a sortied group of Chinese merchant ships, and an unusual Chinese surface action group deployment. Everyone was on edge after the exchanged fire between US and Chinese warships several weeks earlier. But they couldn't be completely sure who was responsible. The North Koreans had begun their attack on South Korea and Japan hours earlier. So, it made sense that they would launch EMPs out here—if they had them.

They needed intelligence, and they needed orders.

The USS *Carl Vinson* was off the starboard beam. The *Lake Champlain* was the shotgun cruiser in the Carl Vinson Carrier Strike Group. Two more destroyers were within twenty miles of their location. Between the destroyers and his cruiser, they were responsible for the defense from enemy air threats, whether they be fighters, bombers, or missiles. But for the last thirty minutes, the captain of the *Lake Champlain* hadn't been sure just what their air defense capability was. A pretty sad admission from the air defense commander.

He looked at the TAO. "Any orders from strike group?"

"No word from the carrier sir."

No one had responded to radio communications since the EMP. That was a bad sign. The captain had been scheduled to join a video conference with the carrier strike group. He had expected to discuss rules of engagement as they headed towards the Korean peninsula.

The last message that the *Lake Champlain* had received said that North Korea had attacked the South, and that North Korean forces should be considered hostile. But these widespread electronics and communications outages were greatly affecting their situational awareness.

Diagnostics on the air defense systems showed that technically, most of their equipment was unaffected by the EMP. But he could see with his own eyes that the display screens were not working properly.

A tech rep happened to be on board. He had been working on their SPY radar the week before and was due to leave for the carrier later in the day. Instead, he was removing panels and replacing parts, assisted by the ship's own enlisted radar experts. It took them twenty minutes, but they managed to get things working the way they were supposed to.

"What the hell are they doing over there?" The captain was pointing at the carrier.

"Not sure, sir. We now have them on bridge-to-bridge. But none of our other comms circuits are working yet."

"Nothing?"

"Not yet, sir."

"Then get someone up on bridge-to-bridge who knows what the hell's going on."

"Yes, sir."

The captain shook his head. He felt bad for raising his voice. He knew it wasn't the fault of the operations officer. But he needed information. They could be under attack, for God's sake. If he had to get the admiral to come up to the bridge of the carrier and speak to him there, he would do it. He left the combat information center to go to the bridge.

No sooner had the captain climbed up to the bridge than he heard a 1MC call asking him to return to CIC. "Captain, TAO, you're needed in combat. As soon as possible, sir."

Urgency in the woman's voice. No—fear. The woman was one of his best officers, and she didn't get rattled easily. Today was different.

The captain hurried back into the combat information center.

"Sir, AEGIS is now coming back online—we don't have everything operational yet, but we have enough to see multiple unknown air contacts inbound bearing two-six-zero for eighty miles."

"Altitude?"

"The system was having trouble..."

A loud aural warning tone went off.

"VAMPIRE! VAMPIRE! VAMPIRE!" a petty officer manning one of the air defense stations yelled. "TAO, enemy missiles inbound. Bearing two-four-zero for fifty miles. I show...forty...no, *sixty* inbound missiles headed towards our position."

The captain looked up at the screen. It was filled with little icons moving at a high rate of speed. "You know what to do, folks. Let's go!"

The combat information center erupted in organized shouts of information and rehearsed commands. The 1MC speaker said, "All hands stand by for heavy rolls." Then the alarm, followed by, "General quarters, general quarters, all hands man your battle stations..."

Sailors from the combat fire control division evaluated the information on their displays, their hands moving swiftly over buttons and keyboards. Sweaty palms and foreheads. Fast-beating hearts and dizzying levels of adrenaline. These sailors followed their years of training, trying not to think about the dozens of missiles skimming the surface of the water at just under the speed of sound, headed right towards them.

The cruiser shuddered as dozens of the ship's own surface-to-air missiles began launching up towards their targets, towers of flame shooting up from the vertical launch system, followed by smoke trails leading off towards the horizon.

"TAO, we now have an *additional* fifty missiles inbound from the same bearing line."

The captain gripped the armrests of his chair as the deck tilted. The bridge team was executing evasive maneuvers now. He gritted his teeth as he watched the little blue surface-to-air missile icons race towards the dozens of inbound missile tracks.

Something wasn't right.

"The destroyers aren't firing," the captain said. He turned to the TAO. "Have you been able to raise them?" A chill went down his spine. With this many inbound missiles, he desperately needed the other warships in company to help defend the carrier—and themselves.

"No, sir. Comms are down."

"There aren't enough." He was looking at the numbers, calculating and tapping his fingers on his armrest. The enemy simply had too many missiles. He wondered if the destroyers were still dealing with the effects of the EMP attack. Were their radars up? Did they even know that there were missiles overhead?

He wrung his sweaty hands together as dozens of the red missile symbols began to reach their battle group.

* * *

The first strike was with EMPs.

The second was with anti-ship missiles.

Hundreds of them. More than could be accounted for by air defense measures currently employed by the US Navy, let alone the slightly inferior technology of the Koreans and Japanese.

Most of the missiles were subsonic sea-skimming versions of the C-802. They sped along fifty feet above the water until the final stage of flight, when they began sprinting the last twenty-five miles at nearly *three times* the speed of sound—faster than many bullets travel.

Some of the missiles were the newly developed "carrier killers." Supersonic medium-range ballistic missiles—the DF-21D. Four of them were fired at the USS *Carl Vinson*. Those weren't among the sea-skimming missiles. The carrier killers launched up into space and then came back down with ferocious speed. The reentry vehicles traveled at Mach six and glided almost thirty miles towards their target. Two of them missed, hitting the water in between the USS *Carl Vinson* and her escorts.

Two of them hit.

Both reentry vehicles weighed more than a thousand pounds and carried warheads of over five hundred pounds. At six times the speed of sound, the damage was nothing short of catastrophic. The aft end of the USS *Carl Vinson* exploded as one of the missiles detonated upon impacting the flight deck, leaving a giant hole right where the jets normally landed. The second DF-21 hit triggered secondary explosions from stored fuel and munitions, turning huge portions of the carrier into a blazing inferno.

Miles to the west, the surface-to-air missiles fired from the USS *Lake Champlain* began intercepting the massive flock of subsonic anti-ship missiles. One of the destroyers was also firing now.

As some of the anti-ship missiles made it past the picket line of SAMs, the escort ships and aircraft carrier itself began firing their shorter-range defense weapons. Rolling airframe missiles began firing towards the incoming anti-ship missiles, hoping to score a kinetic kill. Then the Phalanx Close In Weapon System—a giant Gatling gun—fired thousands of tungsten penetrator rounds, the noise sounding like the giant zipper of an angry god.

Dozens of missiles made it through the defensive weapons, wisps of white shooting over the deep blue sea, and into the haze-gray Navy warships. Explosions of smoke and fire filled the air, and a rain of hot metal and ash, seawater and flesh, came down on the sea.

Scenes similar to this attack on the USS *Lake Champlain* and *Carl Vinson* battle group played out across the Western Pacific. Chinese satellites and ISR collection fed continuous tracking solutions into their military network.

And it was just the beginning.

* * *

The third wave. The cleanup crew.

The fifteen Chinese H-6K strategic bombers flew in a loose formation, each within twenty miles of the lead aircraft. Each bomber had a crew of four, a wingspan of 108 feet, and a cruise speed of just over 470 miles per hour. The planners had drawn up their route of flight to ensure that they were out of the way during the electromagnetic pulse attack. Their equipment was hardened against electromagnetic pulse weapons, but there was no need to test it. Takeoff was timed so that they were feet wet only one hour after the EMP.

"Target confirmed," came the voice of the flight commander over the encrypted radio. He had just received updated targeting information. "All aircraft cleared to fire."

The flight commander gave the internal instruction to his crew. Their grueling training over the past few weeks was about to be put to the test. They would strike at the heart of the great American Navy —the carrier strike groups in the Western Pacific—and cripple them within the opening hours of the war.

The cruise missiles began dropping from his aircraft. His heavy bomber weighed so much that he felt no indication that they had come off the rails. The missiles' boosters began igniting, and he saw trails of gray smoke shooting off into the distance, one by one. More of the missiles appeared in his peripheral vision outside his cockpit window. These were fired from the other aircraft. Soon the sky was filled with cruise missiles, heading off to the east.

Each of the Chinese bombers carried six anti-ship cruise missiles. The shore-based missiles were timed to launch just before the strategic bombers attacked, but the mission commander had no way of knowing whether that part of the plan had been executed properly.

Ten SU-30s, purchased from Russia in 2004, were on a similar mission up north. They were armed with the lethal KH-31 anti-ship cruise missile.

Reconnaissance aircraft and Chinese satellites had spent the last few hours identifying targets. Some of the satellites would likely be damaged from the EMP, but they would make do with backup collection sources. The intelligence officers on the island were gaining coordinates and passing them on to the shooters. The planners then assigned each bomber a list of targets in flight. Truth be told, they didn't even know which ships they were shooting at. It was just a latitude and longitude for the cruise missiles to aim for, until the missiles began their own active search.

The ocean was half ghost yard. Some of the ships had survived the EMP strikes without too much impact to their systems. Others hadn't been so lucky.

Miles away from the Chinese bomber aircraft, the USS *Lake Champlain* was now floating without power, having already been hit by several land-based anti-ship missiles. The men and women aboard were busy fighting fires and trying to stop the flooding. The radar and combat systems had been damaged in the attack. And they had no warning that another was now taking place.

Two anti-ship cruise missiles launched from the H-6K bomber ripped into the injured *Lake Champlain* within seconds of each other. The already bad flooding became worse as fuel and munitions ignited, creating secondary explosions.

The ship sank within minutes.

* * *

The Chinese radar plane flew high above the battle space, helping the now-attacking Chinese forces to maintain a clear picture of what was going on. The KJ-3000 was China's latest version of the American Air Force's AWACS—the Airborne early warning radar plane. It was a massive aircraft, and odd looking as most radar planes were. The giant airframe had a saucer-shaped radar fixed atop it.

"Surface-to-air missiles being launched from the Japanese warship *Myoko*, sir."

The Chinese air force officer who commanded the radar plane heard the call over his internal communications circuit. He watched his display screen as volleys of Japanese surface-to-air missiles began racing towards the Chinese anti-ship missiles. Decades of Chinese military modernization were about to be put to use. Would the advances in Chinese technology be as good as advertised? Would there be enough missiles to overcome the air defense systems?

The commander looked at his two groups of attacking air units. He said, "Vector two of the SU-30s towards the Japanese ship. I see multiple surface-to-air missiles originating from vicinity of the USS *Carl Vinson*, to the south. Send the rest of the SU-30s towards her. Those two carriers are our priority."

"Yes, sir."

The SU-30s, inbound from the north, received their new instructions from the KJ-3000 radar controllers. Two of them immediately turned towards the Japanese destroyer, firing their KH-31 anti-ship missiles. The KJ-3000 was using electronic attack measures to spoof the destroyer, tricking and confusing their radar picture.

The KH-31 missiles traveled only fifty feet over the ocean at nearly three times the speed of sound. The Japanese destroyer knew that they were coming but wasn't able to do anything about it. Their anti-air resources were no match for the electronic malfunctions from the EMP attack coupled with the electronic attack from the KJ-3000.

The missiles detonated on impact.

Two hundred pounds of high-explosive shaped charge collided with the steel hull at a speed of fifteen hundred miles per hour. The center of the Japanese destroyer exploded, and those who weren't killed in the blast either died in the fires that followed or went to the bottom of the ocean as it sank.

The commander of the Chinese radar aircraft zoomed out on his display. His datalink was being updated in real time by all the connected Chinese units. All over the Western Pacific, Chinese air and naval forces had begun their attacks. He looked at Taiwan—it was a jumble of red and blue air tracks. Most of them missiles launched from the Chinese mainland. Both Taiwan and Japan were being inundated by Chinese conventional missiles.

North Korea was invading the South. That would keep the Americans stationed there, and the South Korean military, more than busy.

31

Osan Air Base, South Korea

Chase and the other CIA employees were sitting in the pitch-black trailer.

"Why aren't the backup lights coming on?" someone asked.

"Must have been a transformer. You hear that boom outside?"

"Yeah, but the backup lights should still come back on."

Chase was as blind as a bat, feeling his way around the compartment. He could hear more cursing as one of the other CIA agents shuffled their way to the door. The ambient noise level of the room was eerily quiet without all the electronics and cooling fans running.

Then one of the guards opened the door from the outside, and a rush of light and air came in. "You guys okay?" They all walked outside of the trailer, the guard locking the door behind them.

"What's going on?"

"Don't know. Everyone's power just went out."

Chase didn't think that was it. "Anyone have a cell phone?"

One of the guards got his phone out of his bag. "Yeah, here. Hold on, the power's off. That's weird, I never turn it off." He kept pressing the power button. "Shit. It won't turn on. Sorry."

Chase said, "I don't think it's just you."

Another giant boom reverberated throughout the hangar. It sounded much closer. The group ducked in unison as the ground rumbled beneath their feet. Through the hangar doors, Chase could see clouds of yellow and black explosions billowing up on the far side of the runway.

Tetsuo said, "My God."

Chase watched as more smoke plumes rose from the runway and hangars. The sounds of explosions followed a second later. And there was a new sound. The ripping roar of fighter jets overhead.

"Come on." Tetsuo tapped him on the shoulder, and they cautiously walked out of the hangar. Dark aircraft silhouettes maneuvered thousands of feet above them, yellow tracer rounds shooting out ahead of them. Chase couldn't see what they were firing at.

He looked around the flight line. Base fire trucks sprayed water on burning buildings. Medical teams raced to help the wounded. But the wounded were everywhere, and the attack had just begun. All around him were chunks of metal, stone, and flesh.

"What is *that*?"

Chase looked to the north. Flying just a few dozen feet over the rooftops were a pair of large old biplanes—they looked like they were out of an old World War I movie.

"What the hell?"

The aircraft climbed up and turned to parallel the runway. Then tiny black figures began falling out the side of each aircraft, parachutes streaming open as they fell, their white canopies filling with air and then floating down to the ground. Floating down to the grass next to the runway, Chase realized.

"I think those are North Korean soldiers."

Chase shook his head in disbelief. There couldn't have been more than thirty of them, most still parachuting slowly to the ground. Chase now had a Sig Sauer P228 in a thigh holster, but he had put the carbine into a locker in the CIA trailer. He was about to tell Tetsuo that they should go get it when he saw movement on the far side of the runway.

The Delta operators were on it. The same three men that Chase had been in China with for the last week. They must have seen the North Korean paratroopers and were now taking up firing positions, two on rooftops and one in a jeep. Chase watched as the North Korean soldiers began going down, one by one.

A group of five North Koreans were running toward one of the base medical teams, who were working on an injured person. The five each hit the pavement within seconds of each other, courtesy of the Delta operators' quick shooting.

Some of the paratroopers hadn't even landed before they took rounds in the chest. Chase thought about whether that was an honorable way to kill, but he quickly shook off the thought. These North Korean soldiers had just invaded, and their missiles and artillery were now killing civilians in the area. This was about economics, not honor. They needed to kill as many of the invaders as possible before they could do damage.

The war had begun. And Chase was standing on the front lines.

He looked up and saw a cluster of dark green helicopters— Chinooks—flying north in formation. Those would be the South Korean or US Army helos, executing a preplanned response.

"Chase!" Tetsuo shouted at him as more explosions lit off nearby.

"What?" He could barely hear anything over the ringing in his ears.

"We need to get out of here and get to Natesh," Tetsuo yelled into his ear. "We need to see if we can get a flight out somewhere. But we're in a target zone. North Korean rockets and artillery are too close to take off here…"

Chase nodded. He was right. They had to assume that this North Korean attack coincided with Chinese plans. And if China was attacking…

Susan needed them to get to Japan. They had to find Natesh and see if he could provide intelligence on the location of Chinese merchants. Something was on those ships that was going to be a game changer for the Chinese, and they needed to stop it before it happened…if it wasn't already too late.

They found the young CIA operative who had driven Chase

earlier. He waved them to follow, and they jogged around the back of the hangar and got into a Humvee. They drove along the base perimeter and then turned to travel outside the gate.

Traffic was a mess. People were running and screaming in all directions. A drugstore had been hit by one of the missiles. A shell of the building was left, and the apartment complex next to it had caught fire.

They drove for what seemed an eternity, although it was more like an hour. Tetsuo drove on to the sidewalk in some cases to get around crashes and traffic jams. The heavily populated Korean towns were a mix of untouched urban areas and smoking rubble.

"Where are we going?"

The CIA operative said, "To another base. One farther south. I think you'll be able to get a flight out of there."

More helicopters flew overhead now. Dozens of them, all heading north. Chase caught sight of the words *United States Army* in black lettering on the side of one.

Rockets shot up into the air ahead of them. Bright yellow flashes in rapid succession, white trails of smoke following the rockets as they angled into the sky.

"What are those?"

"I think they're surface-to-air missiles."

"They're trying to shoot down the North Korean Scuds."

Chase said, "Are we going to be able to get out of here in this?"

"I don't know."

They took another turn, and then Chase saw that they were about to enter another base.

"What base is this? Will they fly us out in this?"

"Desiderio Army Airfield. It's one of the largest bases around. I've only been here once, but it was for a flight to Japan. So I know they do that here."

Chase could see smoke coming up from the ground near the runway. At least one missile had hit the base, although being this far south, they were far better off than Osan had been. Dark green helicopters were spinning on the pads everywhere he looked. Black-hawks. Apaches. Chinooks.

Every so often, a column of soldiers would jog into one of the helicopters. After several of the helicopters were filled with troops, a formation of them would take off and fly away to the north.

One of the base guards pointed his rifle at the car while they scanned their IDs. Behind a sandbag bunker, another gate guard, his eyes cold, aimed a heavy machine gun at them. Then the gate guard nodded and cleared them to enter. A minute later, they drove up to a white building in the center of the base.

A moment later, they stood in the air transfer office waiting area, trying to figure out if they would be able to get to Japan.

"That's the last flight. They have a high-priority passenger going to Yokota, but we haven't been able to clear them for takeoff with the Koreans. For obvious reasons." The man behind the counter at the base ops building kept looking out the window as he spoke. "Most of our electronics are fried. We think they used cyberattacks. Shit, I hope my wife is okay. I haven't been able to reach her. By the way, did you guys pass by…"

More rumbles as explosions went off outside and Chase couldn't hear the end of the man's sentence. His face was white, eyes wide.

"Look, the pilots are getting ready to go in case they get clearance. There's seats available. You talk to them if you want to get on. There's nothing else I can do here." He closed his window and headed back to the phone.

Chase and Tetsuo walked outside and over to a gray Army C-12 aircraft. Two big propellers on each side, with enough seats for about eight people, stuffed in like sardines. The doors were open and it looked like they were making preparations to start it up. Air crew and maintenance personnel ran around, removing tags and conducting preflight inspections.

Tetsuo and Chase jogged over to them. "Where are you guys headed?"

Another boom, and the group ducked. They looked over at the airfield tower, which had been hit with blast fragments. The windows were shattered, and no one was standing up inside. Medics and uniformed personnel ran towards the tower to help the wounded.

One of the pilots of the C-12 said, "We're headed to Yokota Air Base."

"Do you have room for two more?"

"Yeah, but that's all."

Tetsuo said, "We'll take it."

The pilot said, "Normally I would say you need a safety brief and to get your names on the manifest, but I think today's an exception. Just strap in. We're not waiting for clearance."

They did as instructed. Chase walked down the narrow airplane corridor as the cabin door was shut behind him. Nervous eyes of the other passengers watched him as he made his way in. Most of them wore Army fatigues. A few were in civilian clothing. Chase was still buckling his seat belt when they began rolling down the taxiway for takeoff.

Every few seconds, he heard another explosion outside, followed by a gasp from the passengers. He closed his eyes and said a quick prayer that the runway stayed clear long enough for them to take off safely. A prayer never hurt, he told himself.

Someone in a flight suit sitting in the forward-most seat yelled back to the passengers, "The pilots are going to fly low to the ground to stay out of trouble. Everyone, make sure you stay buckled in tight the whole time."

The small twin-engine prop plane taxied as fast as Chase could remember, practically getting airborne as they made their way to the runway. Then the familiar whine of the engines, the surge of power pushing Chase back into the cushions of his seat, and they were barreling down the runway.

The aircraft lifted off, flying over the Korean peninsula. Below, everywhere Chase looked were signs of a massive war beginning. There was hardly a street that didn't have a burning building or car.

"Look at that," someone said. "Dogfight."

Outside Chase's window, a twin-engine fighter jet was chasing another, turning hard and spewing yellow tracer rounds towards its prey. A second later, the wing came off the lead aircraft, and then the fuselage erupted in flames. The fireball fell towards the ground, trailing the thick black smoke of ignited jet fuel. No chute.

"Was that ours or theirs?" someone asked.

"Theirs. It was an F-15 that shot it down. I think that was a MIG-29."

The remains of the shot-down aircraft crashed into a cluster of one-story homes below. The last thing Chase saw before the image was no longer in view was a woman running out of the home next door, clutching her baby to her chest.

It took them thirty minutes before their aircraft was over water. Chase could feel his stomach flutter as the plane jolted up and down in the low altitude turbulence.

Tetsuo looked out the window in the seat ahead of him. "What is wrong with that ship?"

Chase saw what he was looking at. A cargo vessel maybe five miles away. There was something funny about the angle it was sitting on the water. As they got closer, he realized that its bow was much closer to the waterline than it should have been.

"They must have gotten that one."

"Yeah, it's sinking alright. I don't see any obvious damage up top. Must be a big hole below the waterline. Maybe a contact mine?" An orange lifeboat ejected into the sea behind it.

"There they go. Good luck, boys."

Their voices sounded detached. Like they were analyzing a sports team that they had no interest in.

The passengers shouted as the aircraft suddenly banked hard left. Chase felt his head being pressed back into his seat as a strong G-force came over them. Then the aircraft rolled wings level, and Chase felt a flutter in his stomach as the nose aimed down and they began diving towards the water. A white trail of smoke shot underneath them and continued on off the right side of the aircraft.

"Holy shit, was that a SAM?"

"Yup," replied a disinterested voice.

Chase looked at the man who'd said it. Army uniform. Ranger patch. Chase recognized the look of a man who'd been in combat before. The eyes of a man resigned to whatever fate might come, knowing that up here, he couldn't control it.

A uniformed woman in the rear of the aircraft was crying. One of the men in civilian clothes kept his head in between his knees, cursing over and over again like he had Tourette syndrome.

The aircraft leveled off, and the lurching maneuvers ceased. A few moments later, Chase watched as they passed a large gray warship on his right side. It looked like an American destroyer, a DDG, a long white wake behind it.

Chase could make out the crew members on the bridge wing looking up at his plane. Each of them wore the white masks and gloves known as anti-flash gear. Other crew members were manning machine guns along the ship. They were at battle stations.

32

J inshan sat behind the Chinese presidential desk. It was the first time he had actually operated from the office, but the symbolism was important today.

"They are here, Mr. Jinshan."

"Show him in."

In walked the ambassador of Japan. He did not look happy.

"Mr. Jinshan, the people of Japan strenuously object to the abhorrent attacks that have occurred over the past twenty-four hours. We demand that—"

Jinshan held up his hand. "Please, Mr. Ambassador. If you will allow me to speak."

The ambassador went silent, although he was visibly upset. His body language was, even in these dire circumstances, carefully calculated to convey just the amount of visual displeasure that his nation wanted to communicate.

"I understand that Japan must be very worried about what is happening. I could offer you reasons for why we have taken this course of action. But I will refrain from that conversation for now. It would be a waste of time. Something I have little of, I am afraid." Jinshan sipped tea from his cup. He was tired. He knew that he could have had someone else do this part. But he didn't trust anyone enough to get it right.

Jinshan continued, "Japan will be left alone."

"China has already *attacked* us." The ambassador did his best to control the volume of his voice.

"Mr. Ambassador, if you were to study the targets that we have attacked, you will note that they fall into one of two categories. The first category is any location that supports the American military. They are our true enemy in this fight. We cannot allow US military forces to inhabit a position in such close proximity to our own. The Americans have shown hostility towards us, and it would be strategic malpractice to allow them to continue this military presence unimpeded."

The Japanese ambassador said, "I disagree with this assessment. The Americans showed no hostility to China. They have been a peaceful—"

"Please, Mr. Ambassador. Hear me out first. Then we may have a short discussion. The second category of targets in Japan were, in fact, Japanese military targets. We regret that this was necessary, but it was. We have and will continue to destroy any weapons or systems that could hurt our own military progress in the region. I suggest you immediately convey this information to your superiors in Japan. Tell them to abandon all military assets while our campaign progresses. If you like, we can even have our military coordinate with yours to let you know when it is safe to proceed back onto your bases."

The ambassador fumed. "This is insulting and ridiculous. You can't expect us to agree to this. What gives you the right?"

Jinshan looked at his diplomatic team, who sat quietly on the couch beside the ambassador. Then he turned back to the ambassador. "Our *military power* gives us the right. It gives me no pleasure to say this, Mr. Ambassador. You must understand that. But if we wanted to, we could bomb your island nation into oblivion. We could coat it with fire. We could launch weapons of mass destruction that would make Hiroshima and Nagasaki look like child's play. The firebombing of World War II would be nothing to what China could unleash. But this will not happen—not as long as you agree to terms."

"What terms?" The ambassador looked squeamish. "Not surrender."

"No. I wouldn't ask that. It is undignified. *Neutrality*. I want Japan to remain neutral. To retain their honor and be at peace with China." He looked into the ambassador's eyes, knowing how important honor was in the Japanese culture. "We are speaking to the political leaders in South Korea and Taiwan today as well. We will make them the same offer. Promise neutrality, and we will not bomb your people. We will not invade your nations. We will allow you to live in peace and prosperity. But you must renounce any partnership with the United States and agree to terms. You must promise to stand idle while we wage war upon America. Do not sacrifice the well-being of your people for a bunch of *gaijin*." Jinshan used the Japanese word for foreigner.

The ambassador's face betrayed his shock at Jinshan's blunt words. When he regained his composure, his tone was hushed. "How is what you ask not to be considered surrender?"

Jinshan gave a slight grin. "Surrender will occur if you *decline* this proposition, Mr. Ambassador. And many lives will be lost before I offer terms of surrender. Surrender will come with a Chinese military occupation of your homeland. These terms contain no such caveat. This is an opportunity. I suggest you take it."

All pretense of shock and anger was gone from the ambassador's face. He was, after all, a professional diplomat, and Japanese to boot. His stoicism and discipline won the day. "I will provide you an answer soon."

Jinshan's face was impassive. "That is all, Mr. Ambassador. Please have an answer for me by tomorrow. Our military operations will proceed as described."

The ambassador rose and left the room, escorted by one of Jinshan's security guards and a member of his diplomatic team.

When the door closed, Jinshan turned to the others sitting on the couch. "Summon the South Korean ambassador next." They nodded. One of them hurried off to get the Korean ambassador, who was already waiting in the building. The ambassadors were probably alarmed at the notion of being brought hours away from Beijing to the Chinese leadership bunker in the mountains. But these were unusual times.

The roar of supersonic jets could be heard overhead. They would be the fighters, standing guard against any possible strikes on Beijing.

"Do you need any lunch, sir?" an assistant asked from the side door.

"No, thank you." He saw the way she looked at him, concern in her eyes. He must look dreadful. Jinshan sighed. He just needed to get through these first few months. After that, he could rest, for however long he had left.

The door swung open. "Mr. Jinshan, the ambassador from South Korea."

The ambassador walked in. She was an older woman, experience and intelligence in her eyes. Unlike the Japanese ambassador, she made no effort to display anger or shock at recent events. She stood until Jinshan offered her a seat, then sat quietly, waiting for him to start.

"Madame Ambassador, I wish to express my most sincere condolences at the loss of so many of your countrymen. I hoped that this day of North Korean aggression would never come."

The woman didn't miss a beat. "I don't believe it is unassisted, Mr. Jinshan. Or should I call you Mr. President?"

He shrugged. "Whatever pleases you."

"What do you want to ask me, Mr. Jinshan?"

"I can make it stop."

She stared back at him, her nostrils flaring. "How?"

"We will instruct the North Koreans to cease fire and return north of the DMZ. But no retaliatory strikes can be made."

"I can't say that I have knowledge, due to my communications restrictions that your guards imposed on me, but I believe that retaliatory strikes must be ongoing, Mr. Jinshan."

"I understand. But they must come to a stop."

"So, you are negotiating a cease-fire? Is that all?"

"No." He shook his head.

"I thought as much." She turned to look at his diplomatic team, listening along the wall. "I am told that many of the weapons launched towards the South may not have been North Korean in origin. I have heard rumors that China has attacked American military positions in Asia today. Although it is hard to know what the truth is, with all this confusion."

"The fog of war can be very confusing."

She hummed in agreement.

Jinshan placed his fingers together, hands resting on the table before him. "Madame Ambassador, here is my offer. A cease-fire with North Korea. And a treaty with China. We have, as you have been informed, begun our attack on American forces in the area. My time with you here is limited. But the people of South Korea are friends to the Chinese. We wish to maintain peace. I understand that you have agreements with the Americans. But their presence in the region has become untenable."

She raised her eyebrows. "Has it?"

"And it would be advantageous for you to align yourselves with us now. We can stop the fighting on the Korean peninsula. But there are tens of thousands of US troops and their families there. We do not want any Korean-based military units to attack Chinese interests. That includes the Americans. So—we have a few potential solutions. Either the Americans agree to leave immediately, or they are made to stop military operations from Korea. If the latter is the option, it does not matter to us whether the South Korean military enforces this new policy or whether the Chinese military does it. But my guess is that you would prefer that Chinese military forces were not deployed on Korean soil?"

The woman's eyes stared at Jinshan's own. "I understand what you are asking. And I will relay the message. But the Americans have a saying, Mr. Jinshan."

"And what is that?"

She rose. "Don't hold your breath."

Jinshan frowned as she left the building. In truth, he hadn't counted much on South Korea being cooperative. But soon enough, that wouldn't matter. The Korean strategic landscape was about to change dramatically.

* * *

The Chinese Type 094 ballistic missile submarine had been preparing for their launch for the past twelve hours. When the time finally came, it ejected two JL-2 missiles from its vertical launch tubes. Each missile was over thirty feet in height. Their booster rockets fired soon after they broke the surface of the deep blue ocean. The missiles had almost identical paths, their trajectories taking them over North Korea before they broke into a total of six independent reentry vehicles, each one carrying its own ninety-kiloton warheads. Hiroshima was sixteen kilotons.

The target each MIRV was aimed at had been chosen based on two factors: the likelihood that the US military would pick it, and the desire to minimize potential radioactive fallout on Chinese territory.

In six brilliant flashes of light, China attacked North Korea with nuclear weapons. The weapons had been programmed to detonate near ground level. At each target, all people and buildings in the immediate vicinity were vaporized, the bursts leaving craters almost two hundred meters in diameter. Thick mushroom clouds of radioactive ash and dust bloomed up over forty thousand feet into the air, and the winds pushed them east to spread their slow rain of poison.

Three of the targets were military bases with clusters of North Korea's most capable weaponry. The other three nuclear detonations were decapitation attempts. Locations where the *Great Leader* was thought to be. *Because*, Jinshan decided, *that's what America would do*. Fortified military bunkers, deep underground. One of them was a correct guess. That particular bunker location turned out to be ten meters *above* the bottom of the nuclear crater, when all was said and done.

Six locations in North Korea were now uninhabitable radioactive wastelands. Giant burning pockmarks on the earth. The surrounding populations to these detonation sites that hadn't already been killed in the initial attack would suffer radiation sickness and dramatically increased rates of cancer.

But Jinshan's ruse could now go on.

His cyber warriors and intelligence operatives around the world began information campaigns that spread the word.

The United States was responsible.

The only country to have ever used nuclear weapons in a war had done so again. America should be considered a pariah state. Jinshan would call upon all nations around the world to stand with China and against the US, or stand clear.

33

Lieutenant Ping and his team had become more familiar with how to navigate the US over the past week. At first, they had remained in hiding, at a remote Ministry of State Security safe house in America's heartland. There were a dozen teams like his, each now hidden throughout the United States. Most of the teams had just recently entered the country, having finished their specialized mortar training in the mountains of China.

Each team had an MSS agent who helped them to manage their affairs. The MSS agents were the babysitters, Ping knew. There to ensure that none of his men did anything that got them noticed. No phone calls, no computers, no communications. No walking out in town with a submachine gun slung over their shoulder. Phones weren't even allowed on the premises of the safe houses. Inconspicuous vehicles were used—aged pickup trucks, mostly. Just like they had trained with.

Ping's team received two sets of orders. The first was to PRESTAGE. To head to their attack point and prepare for orders to execute. The drive to New Jersey took his team twelve hours. Every time they passed a police car, the hair on the back of Ping's neck stood up. But they finally reached the house near the outskirts of Trenton, New Jersey, and he was confident that they would be ready.

The MSS operative showed him the cache in the garage, and Lieutenant Ping was impressed. He didn't ask how they were able to get military weaponry of this size and lethality into the United States. It didn't matter now.

When the EXECUTE order came that night, a familiar rush of adrenaline filled his veins. The order contained a specific time, only hours away. A wave of excitement shot through his men. Then everyone flipped a switch and moved with deliberate, controlled motions. They had been well trained, and they would conduct themselves with professionalism.

Two of them—the mortar experts—loaded up the equipment in to the pickup truck, which was backed into the three-car garage. The mortars were heavy, as were the cases of mortar rounds. The deadly cargo weighed the heavy-duty vehicles down enough that he worried it might attract attention. But that was what the rest of their weapons were for. Light machine guns with modern scopes, and two heavy machine guns with tripods that were now mounted to the pickup trucks.

It was late at night when they arrived on the empty road just north of McGuire Air Force Base. The air was still, everything calm and quiet. No sign of trouble. Ping's special forces team quickly unloaded the mortars and set up a defensive perimeter around them, waiting for police or base security, whoever came first.

"Range?" one of the mortar men asked.

One of them was looking through binoculars, a laser range finder fixed to the top.

"Seven hundred meters to the first target. Seven fifty to the second. Eight hundred to the third."

"Wait until we take out the first three, then give me updates on the others."

"Yes, Sergeant."

The night air was cool, the beginning of spring not yet taking the bite away from winter's spell. Streetlights buzzed overhead, their yellow light flickering onto the pavement. Ping shoved earplugs into each ear, and the world went dull. He whistled to one of his men who had a silenced machine gun, pointing at the streetlights. The man nodded and fired several times, knocking out the nearest three lights, leaving them in the shadows.

The lead mortar operator looked at Ping for approval, which he gave in a nod. Then the first metallic scraping sound came as the round slid down the barrel, followed by a *thunk* from the first mortar. The second mortar fired in rapid succession.

The first mortar was being loaded again when the initial round ripped through its target, a US Air Force KC-135 refueling tanker. The quiet night turned into a deafening symphony of explosions, and the darkness gave way to inferno.

Some of the mortar rounds missed their mark, pummeling the concrete flight line. The explosions popped tires and punctured the surrounding aircraft with their metal fragments. Other rounds tore into the large aircraft. Every so often, one of the mortar rounds scored a direct hit on a filled fuel storage compartment, setting off a mushroom cloud explosion of fire that turned night into day.

Ping's men worked fast, checking ranges and making adjustments to their fire. Their orders had specifically called for the refueling planes to be prioritized. KC-135s and KC-10s. If possible, take out the transports as well. The C-5s and C-17s.

Ping could see a fire vehicle and what looked like a base security vehicle racing towards one of the burning aircraft. By this time, ten of the enormous jets had been destroyed.

"Sir, a police vehicle is approaching us from the west."

Ping looked to where his man was pointing and saw a sedan with flashing blue lights racing towards them.

"Wait until it gets close," Ping said.

The police cruiser skidded to a halt about fifty feet from their three cars. The doors did not open. The vehicle's occupant must have been trying to decide just what he was looking at.

Ping's team had two pickup trucks and a minivan. The two pickup trucks were parked perpendicular to the road, blocking traffic and forming a barricade. The minivan was in the center. For a moment, the police vehicle remained unmoving, the Chinese special forces men staring back at him, their weapons trained.

Did the policeman yet know what was about to transpire? Did he see the threat?

A bright white searchlight from the driver's side of the police vehicle illuminated the nearest pickup truck. Enough to unmask a large fifty-caliber machine gun on a tripod, which instantly began firing. Yellow tracer rounds shot into and around the police vehicle, destroying it and the lone police officer inside and extinguishing the lights. A small fire smoldered in the police car's rear seat. Ping's special forces men looked at the wreckage, and at each other.

"Keep firing our mortars," Ping said, reminding his men to concentrate on the mission. "There are another six aircraft untouched on the tarmac. Hit them all, and we will depart."

Ping knew that the success of their mission was more important than whether they survived the night. But if they lived, his team could be reused for more operations such as this in the coming days. Tomorrow would be chaos in the United States. The other teams like his would all be executing similar orders throughout the country. Locating his team would not be easy in such confusion. And even if the US government managed to track them down, his men were exceptional fighters. America was not equipped to deal with men like them. That was what they had been told.

Ten minutes later, their mission complete, Ping signaled his team to saddle up and head out. Their caravan dispersed, each driver having familiarized himself with separate routes back to their safe house. None of them were stopped.

* * *

Not all of the Chinese special forces teams were so successful.

Outside Seymour Johnson Air Force base in North Carolina, the PLA special forces had just begun firing mortar rounds when the noise alerted patrons at the local Veterans of Foreign Wars post. The VFW members had gathered that night to celebrate the seventieth birthday of one of their own.

The new septuagenarian was a man by the name of Norman Francis. His friends called him "Bud." Bud had enlisted in the US Army in 1969.

Bud was sitting at the bar, drinking a tonic water and lime (he had given up alcohol years earlier) and providing one of the new members—a young man in his thirties, who was a veteran of Afghanistan—a recap of his complete military history. The young man was a good southern boy and patriot and listened respectfully.

Bud said, "So let's see—I went to basic training in Fort Jackson, Signal School at Fort Gordon, and Army Ranger school at Fort Benning. Then I arrived in South Vietnam in the February of 1970…"

Someone piped up from down the bar, "I thought you said it was '71…"

Bud frowned. "Don't know where you heard that. It was '70. I think I would know my own history. So then where was I? The Army sent me to Quang Tri in Northern I Corps, where I was assigned to the 298th Signal Company of the First Brigade Fifth Infantry (Mechanized). But see, I'd been to Ranger School. I didn't want to be part of some signal company, no offense. I was a Ranger. So I talked to my platoon sergeant and requested a transfer. Two days later I was the only passenger on a Huey headed to Hill 950—it overlooked the old Khe Sanh combat base. You know Khe Sanh? The Marines fought some awfully hard battles there in '68. But that was before I got there. So I got to Hill 950. US Army Special Forces were there with about forty Nung mercenaries. The hill overlooked the Ho Chi Minh Trail. We'd watch daily airstrikes bomb the valley and surrounding mountains. But then I got transferred to P Company. Went on a lot of missions along the DMZ and Laos with P Company. Had to call in artillery several times and—say, you hear that? That booming noise? That kind of sounds a lot like artillery right there. Now what in the Sam Hill is that?"

Bud led his companions out to the parking lot to see what was making that loud booming noise. He was an avid hunter and gun collector and always kept his hunting rifle on the rack in his pickup truck. And he was still an expert marksman.

He reached for the rifle and looked through the scope, scanning the surrounding area.

He had seen the news over the past few weeks. Looking through the scope on his rifle, he identified the enemy group to his friends.

"The Chi-com bastards are coming to attack us."

As one of the men in his party called the police, the birthday boy was already firing from three hundred yards out. Some of his companions were also hunters and gun enthusiasts. Rifles were removed from racks in their pickup trucks as well, and the battle began. Three of the old men were killed by return fire, but not before the new seventy-year-old was able to take out two of the Chinese soldiers. The rest of them were also killed, once the police got involved.

At another attack site outside McConnell Air Force base near Wichita, Kansas, the Chinese special forces troops made the unfortunate mistake of picking a position located less than a mile from where the Wichita SWAT team was coincidentally training that night. The SWAT team had recently purchased two used mine-resistant ambush-protected vehicles (MRAPs) from the US military. Half of the SWAT team members were military veterans and also recognized the sound of mortars firing in the quiet night air. Their response was swift and deadly. Wichita SWAT team 10, PLA special operators 0.

But many of the Chinese attacks on Air Force bases succeeded in their mission to radically reduce the number of US aerial refueling tankers in inventory. Within a matter of hours, the number of airworthy tankers in the US Air Force inventory went from over four hundred to under one hundred and fifty. Cheng Jinshan had succeeded. The Chinese had greatly diminished the American military's ability to wage long-range aerial warfare.

34

Chase and Tetsuo's aircraft landed at Yokota Air Base outside of Tokyo, Japan, in the early afternoon. If they had any misconceptions that Japan would be a safe refuge from the war, those ideas quickly diminished upon arrival.

During the flight in, Chase could make out towers of black smoke to the east. Fuel depots next to the runway had been hit by missiles. So had the runway. Their aircraft had to land on the first quarter of the runway. A small prop plane like the C-12 could do that —barely. But the jets would be grounded until the holes were fixed.

Once the plane taxied into the flight line and shut down, Chase and Tetsuo headed to the CIA trailer. Tetsuo picked up two CIA-owned encrypted cell phones. Then he got the keys to one of the government cars and drove them both into the city.

They needed to get in touch with Natesh.

"Phones aren't working." Tetsuo stared down at the Agency phone he'd taken from the CIA equipment locker next to the trailer. He was driving with one hand, typing keys on the phone with the other, glancing back and forth at traffic.

Chase said, "Either a cyberattack or a missile strike on a telecom-munications node."

"I gave him instructions to follow if anything like this happens. Hopefully he remembers where to go."

Tetsuo drove through the streets of Tokyo, a surreal experience. The city was normally a galaxy of bright LED screens and mobs of businessmen and women dashing through the streets. Now, the power was off, and red-eyed Japanese citizens ran about in a state of chaos. As in Korea, car crashes were rampant, the drivers likely distracted by missiles, jets, and explosions overhead. The almost-bare aisles of a corner convenience store were being looted, the shopkeeper batting the desperate away with a folded-up newspaper. And a shell-shocked man in a suit stood still in the middle of the road, staring Chase in the eye as he drove by, crowds running and screaming around him.

"This is nuts."

They pulled up under the roof of an expansive drop-off area outside a luxury hotel. They got out and Tetsuo said, "Wait in the lobby. I need to run across the street."

Chase gave him a confused look. "What's the plan?"

Tetsuo nodded up to the hotel. "Natesh should be up there, if he followed the extraction procedure. I need to go to the post office across the street and check the drop box. He should have left the special watch that the NSA had him wearing, and his room number. Once I get that, I'll meet you back here. Keep an eye out for him or anyone suspicious in the lobby."

"Got it." Chase turned and headed in.

* * *

Tetsuo came running into the lobby of the hotel. Chase stood in the shadow of a large marble column, scanning the open atrium. The look in Tetsuo's eyes told him that something was wrong.

"What is it?"

Tetsuo came over to him holding a small white paper, which he stuffed in his jacket pocket. He whispered, "He left me a note and the watch. The note said that he got the location of the merchant ships, and the Chinese carrier fleet that went missing a few days ago. He actually *wrote it out* and left it in this envelope." He was shaking his head.

"I thought he wasn't supposed to look himself. That watch that the NSA gave him was supposed to plant malware, right?"

Tetsuo began walking towards the elevator, scanning the room. "Correct. He wasn't supposed to do anything himself. If he wasn't careful, he probably ran through 3PLA tripwires." Tetsuo stopped walking, turning his head back and forth, stuck between what to do next. He looked towards Chase.

"What, man?"

"I'm trying to decide—"

"Spit it out."

"The note Natesh left gave precise coordinates of the merchants and the carrier fleet. I need to get this information, and any data that's on the watch, back to the NSA and Langley guys ASAP. I don't have time to babysit Natesh. But if he isn't blown, I want to throw him back in the cooker and keep using him." The hotel lobby rose up into a towering glass ceiling, wrapping around the glass elevator that rose forty floors high. "Can you babysit?"

"Of course. I'll stay here with him. It'll be fine."

Tetsuo nodded. "Alright. I might be a while. Here's the room number. It looks like they still have power in this place, so I'd take the elevator. Pretty high up. I'll be back when I can. And Chase, be careful. If he did tip off Chinese agents that he's stealing information for us—they'll be after him."

"Understood." Chase patted his concealed sidearm.

35

Victoria shifted in her seat, trying to ease the pain in her back that had flared up from long hours strapped into the bird. They were logging over three hours per flight, and as she was the only aircraft commander on board right now, she was stuck flying back-to-back triple bags. Three flights in a row. The Pacific Fleet's thirst for surface surveillance was unquenchable with the reduced satellite capability. And while the P-8s out of Australia were supposed to be assisting, it was a lot of area to cover.

She looked over at Spike. His hands flicked a few buttons and manipulated the joystick that controlled the FLIR. On the display in the front of him, she could see his handiwork. The camera locked in on a barely visible speck on the horizon and then zoomed in a few times. The screen finally focused on what looked like another tanker.

"Farragut control, 471, we have another Group 3. Looks like it's seventy miles to your northwest, heading zero-eight-niner at sixteen knots. How copy?"

"471, Farragut control, copy all."

Juan was getting pretty good. She could tell that his confidence had improved as well. He was much more comfortable over the back of the boat now.

"You think we're really getting extended, Boss?"

"I think so, yes." She was done with pretense. "We're only a few hundred miles from Guam now. If the Navy wasn't going to extend our deployment, I don't think they would have sent us out here."

Victoria took out her pen, which was wedged into the metal spring on her kneeboard, and wrote down the fuel and time. She did some quick math, just like she had every fifteen minutes for the last two hours, and came out with a sufficient fuel burn rate. "If they do extend us, though, they'll probably give us another port stop."

AWR1 spoke into his helmet mike from the back of the aircraft, "Come on, Boss. Ain't no port stop gonna make up for another month of deployment. I just wish they'd tell us."

Victoria said, "That would take all of the fun out of it."

A garbled radio call came over the UHF frequency. "Mayday... five miles southeast of...on guard..."

"What the hell was that?" said Spike. "Did he say mayday?"

"Shh," said Victoria. They were still broadcasting. "Tune it up with the ADF. See if you can get a cut on where its coming from."

"Yes, ma'am."

The ship's controller came over the radio. "471, Farragut control, RTB as soon as possible. We just got new orders."

Victoria keyed her mike. "Farragut, be advised, we just heard what sounded like a mayday call on guard."

"471, roger, stand by." After a moment, the captain's voice came on the radio and said, "471, understand you heard a mayday call. We have something big going on here. Please make best speed back to us."

Victoria and Juan exchanged glances. She said, "Roger, returning to Mom."

Juan got out the checklist. "Landing checks." His hands flipped through the upper circuit breakers and switches, calling out a few challenge-reply items to the crew.

A moment later, they were on final, Victoria at the stick.

"471, Deck, ready for numbers?" came Caveman's voice, transmitting from the ship's LSO shack radio.

"Send 'em."

Caveman read off the ship's course and speed, winds, pitch, and roll, then said, "You have green deck for one and one." A device that looked like a traffic light stuck to the hangar emitted a flashing green light.

Victoria flew the helicopter smoothly over the deck of the destroyer and held it in place for a half second, waiting for her aircrewman's verbal signal.

"In position."

She waited for the ship's rolls to settle, then lowered the collective lever with her left hand. The now-eighteen-thousand-pound aircraft floated vertically downward and into the trap.

"Beams coming closed. Trapped," Caveman said. "Boss, Captain wants to see you." The deck crew ran out to the helicopter, the sound of chains dragging along the flight deck as they ran in from either side of the rotor, tying down the aircraft, and placing chocks around each of the wheels.

The hangar door opened and the senior chief in charge of Victoria's maintenance team appeared with a few of the ordnancemen next to him. He gave her a signal with his hand slicing across his neck —*shut down.*

"Something's going on. I'm guessing they want to load weapons and they want us to shut down while they do it."

The LSO confirmed her suspicions a second later. "Boss, Deck. Captain has them bringing torps your way. Senior's asking you to shut down while they work."

"Roger, Deck." Then she said over the internal comms, "Spike, you have the controls. Let me get out of the rotor arc, then you handle the shutdown."

"Roger, I have the controls."

She unstrapped and opened her door, stepping out onto the deck, careful to balance herself as the ship rolled at high speed, sea spray spitting up and over the side of the ship and covering her tinted helmet visor as she walked. Inside the hangar, she saw several personnel rolling two MK-50 lightweight torpedoes on a pushcart towards the hangar door.

She walked through the ship and into the combat information

center. The captain was there, chatting with the TAO as they looked at the tactical display in front of them.

The captain said, "Airboss, we need to catch you up. We just got a FLASH message. Here."

FROM: CHIEF OF NAVAL OPERATIONS

TO: PACCOM

SUBJ: FLASH WARNING OF IMMINENT THREAT TO ALL US FORCES

1. DPRK MILITARY INVADED SOUTH KOREA AT 1900Z. ALL DPRK FORCES SHALL BE CONSIDERED HOSTILE UFN.

2. HOSTILITIES BETWEEN CHINA AND UNITED STATES CONSIDERED IMMINENT. ALL UNIT COMMANDERS SHOULD PREPARE FOR POSSIBLE CHINESE ATTACKS ON PACIFIC MILITARY AND STRATEGIC TARGETS, TO INCLUDE HAWAII AND GUAM.

"Oh my God." Victoria read it twice. "Guam?"

The captain nodded his head. "We're about one hundred and seventy miles to the east of Guam right now, but heading there fast. We think that's where the mayday call came from." There was a forlorn look on his face.

Victoria looked back and forth between the TAO and the captain. "You think it's already begun?"

The captain said, "Yes. We think that the Chinese may have already begun their attack on Guam."

* * *

Admiral Song watched as the two squadrons of Chinese J-15 fighters took off from the ski-jump-style carrier deck in pairs. Based on the Russian Su-33 fighter, the J-15 was capable of speeds close to Mach 2, had a range of fifteen hundred kilometers, and carried various weapons. The J-15 was the Chinese version of the Americans' F-18 Hornet and was meant to perform the role of a fighter and attack aircraft.

Because of the ski-jump-style carrier deck, however, Chinese fighters had to take off with less fuel and ordnance in order to get airborne. This meant that they would need to refuel almost as soon as they took off, before continuing on their mission to Guam.

It was a gamble, Admiral Song knew. The fighters would have to travel a long distance, relegated to carrying a small payload. Because of the tight fuel constraints, any problem along the way could spell disaster. They wouldn't be able to bingo to land-based airfields, since the mission was so far to the east. The only option was to refuel with the land-launched HY-6D tankers. A caravan of those refueling aircraft were scheduled to be at rally points along the route of flight between the Philippines and Guam.

Only two of the J-15s were equipped with anti-air weapons, while the rest were outfitted with air-to-surface weapons. The fighters would shoot down any American aircraft over the skies near Guam, assuming they could catch them off guard. Admiral Song worried about the lethality of US combat air patrols, especially their newer-generation F-22s. But considering that the island of Guam would be under the effects of China's EMP, the Chinese fighters had a distinct advantage.

US anti-air batteries in the region had been targeted by submarine-launched cruise missiles over the past few hours, but battle damage would remain unknown prior to launch. Without American surface-to-air missiles, Song's J-15 fighters would be able to target the airfields, submarines, ships, and military facilities at Guam, rendering them inert. With South Korea, Japan, and Guam bases removed from the American arsenal, the Chinese hold on the Western Pacific would be strong.

His only worry was the American Navy ships that had shown up on satellite imagery over the past twenty-four hours. Several destroyers, including one of the new Zumwalt-class ships, were traveling west towards Guam. He had a pair of attack submarines in the area, but those submarines needed to stay close to Guam to launch their cruise missiles at air defense targets first.

Admiral Song's only hope was that his attack aircraft could hit their targets before the American Navy ships got in range with their surface-to-air missiles. For if they were close enough to the Guam airspace when his J-15 fighters were overhead, it would greatly jeopardize his mission success.

36

There were six Chinese-flagged merchant vessels in all. Each of them had departed from Guangzhou. They were filled with shipping containers. Steel rectangles of blue, red, green and white, neatly stacked several stories high. Most of them were empty.

Some held precious cargo.

The merchant vessels had formed up closer together as they approached the Hawaii island chain, each no farther than five nautical miles from the central ship. Dozens of men were out on the deck, moving fast. They had trained for this moment hundreds of times during their journey across the Pacific.

While an onlooker might mistake these men for typical merchant fleet deckhands, they were anything but. The members of a special-trained group of PLA missile men were opening a particularly impor-tant set of shipping containers. Each had removable ceilings, which were taken off and stowed for sea.

Inside of these shipping containers were specially modified mobile missile launchers. The launchers were normally attached to heavy-duty transport vehicles, but the front sections of these vehicles had been cut off so that the weapon systems could fit neatly into the shipping containers. There were dozens of different types of missiles on each of the merchants.

Some were WS-43 tactical cruise missiles, which could loiter for thirty minutes and receive a target while airborne. The launchers for these were actually *already* made to look like shipping containers and had needed minimal modification for sea transport.

Some were DF-12 ballistic missiles. These were the big ones. Most of these had large eleven-hundred-pound warheads installed, but a few were set up with cluster munitions. The latter would be used on runways.

But the merchants weren't just carrying surface-to-surface missiles. On the fore and aft end of each merchant vessel, crews were setting up SAMs as well.

Each of the missile crews had begun preparing for launch the day before, working tirelessly day and night. Timing was everything.

"Sir, our air search radars are set up. We have dozens of contacts that we are now tracking off the coast. We believe many of them to be commercial air traffic."

"Very well, thank you." The commander of the missile force on the lead ship was waiting to hear from all the other vessels in company. Each one would eventually check in, telling him that they were ready to attack. The sky was blue. The weather was warm. With any luck, they would get their payload off without so much as a bullet fired at them.

He checked his watch. "Launch the drones."

Two catapults from the ship launched medium-sized fixed-wing drones into the air, their propellers buzzing as they flew to the east. There was no way to retrieve them, but that didn't matter. Last-minute targeting updates were needed. Minutes earlier, their GPS signal and satellite datalink had stopped working. At first, his communications officer had thought it might be a momentary glitch in the system. But after a few minutes, the commander had doubted that was the case. The attack had begun, and the Americans were responding. The US cyber warriors were striking back and had shut down Chinese satellite capability.

But had the intelligence operations succeeded in tricking the

Americans into thinking that his fleet of merchant ships were thousands of miles to the south, near the Marianas? That was what the false navigational plans stored in the logistics network had said.

Soon they would find out. Within the hour, Chinese targeting drones would be circling high over Hickam and Kaneohe Bay. His men would make their final targeting updates, and a rain of more than two hundred missiles would fall down on Hawaii, crippling the US military capability on the base.

* * *

"Sir, are we sure about this? Merchant ships?"

"Admiral, that's affirmative."

Admiral Manning stood in his stateroom on the USS *Ford*, speaking on the HF secure line to the commander of the Pacific Fleet, who was sitting in Hawaii. The four-star admiral on the phone —his boss—had just informed him that six Chinese merchant ships were located only seventy miles to the west of Oahu and should now be considered hostile. Intelligence had just come in that weapons on board these merchants included surface-to-surface missiles, which could target US military bases in Hawaii.

The synapses fired in Admiral Manning's brain. "We'll launch sorties on them immediately, sir."

"Good. Coordinate with Air Force assets launching from Hickam. The 199th has a pair of F-22s ready for air defense, but I don't know how long it will take them to load anti-ship weapons."

"Yes, sir, we'll be sure to coordinate."

Admiral Manning practically ran to his tactical flag command center. The room was the size and shape of a small movie theater, with lighting to match, but the big screen in the front of the room was cut up into several different tactical displays and video images.

Admiral Manning said, "Are there a group of merchants to our west?"

"Yes, sir. The Zulu guys just had Ripper 612 roger up to getting eyes on them."

"What did they see?"

"Nothing, sir. Just a group of merchants that are oddly close together."

"Send him back. And get the CAG in here. And launch the alert swing-loaded aircraft, now!"

"Yes, sir."

The strike group's communications officer bolted into the room. "Admiral! Sir, this just came in…"

He handed the admiral a printout.

They had just received an Emergency Low Frequency message from the National Command Authority. The United States was going to DEFCON 1.

* * *

Plug couldn't believe they had him doing this shit. He had literally spent his whole day typing on a freaking instant messenger—albeit a classified one. What did he do on this instant messenger? Answer to the admiral's staff every five seconds, letting them know what had changed since the last time they'd asked. Which was, primarily, nothing.

The admiral's staff—otherwise known as the strike group—watch team sat in their big computer-screen-filled tactical flag command center several decks above him. Plug, meanwhile, sat in his tiny computer-screen-filled Zulu module, deep in the heart of the ship. Half the time Plug suspected that the strike group watch standers didn't even read what he typed. But when they did, and he didn't answer fast enough, they called him on the radio, like they were doing now.

"Foxtrot Zulu, this is Foxtrot Alpha, over."

Plug rolled his eyes. He was tired of this bullshit SWO radio etiquette. Was it really necessary to say, "this is" before you said your name every time, and "over," at the end of every transmission? You didn't do that on a phone call. And aviators didn't waste words like that when making their radio calls. As if strike group didn't know it was the new guy in Zulu, Plug, talking? Ridiculous.

Plug picked up the phone and dialed the number for the strike group guy who was trying to talk to him over the radio. "What's up, man?"

Plug could hear the disdain in his voice. "You should use the tactical radio to respond," replied the lieutenant commander who was standing duty.

"Okay, I will next time. Just, what's up?"

"Are you in control of the Ripper aircraft right now?"

"Yeah."

"Well, vector the F-18 back over to those merchant ships and tell him to send back video. The admiral is standing right next to me, and he wants to see it."

"No problem."

Was that so hard? Plug just didn't get why these people had to play these silly radio games. Sure, maybe back in World War II, when you only had the option of talking over HF radios, it had made sense. But especially when they were on the same freaking boat— just use the phone.

"Sir, chat is down," the chief standing duty with him said.

"What?"

"Chat's down, sir."

Plug looked at his computer. The instant messenger chat rooms were all displaying gibberish.

"This happen often?"

The chief shook his head. "Nope. I'll troubleshoot." The chief got on the phone.

Plug frowned, reaching for the radio so that he could contact the F-18 they were having perform surveillance for them. That had been one of the few parts of the job that was kind of fun. The F-18s were amazing. They could get from one side of the carrier's area of operations to the other in a flash and then send him pictures or video of what he wanted to see. It would take him an hour to do that in a helicopter.

He held down the radio transmit button. "Ripper 612, Zulu."

"Go, Zulu."

"Can you guys go back to those merchants and resend your video?"

"Wilco."

Short and sweet. Plug couldn't believe he'd been relegated to this surface warrior hell. He was the only aviator on the carrier who didn't get to fly. And he was slowly being brainwashed by the SWOs. He was starting to talk like them. Soon he would be hanging out with them. Then he'd be using black shoe polish. Aviators wore brown shoes, after all.

"Holy shit. What the hell is that?" Plug was looking at the video imagery being broadcast by the F-18 back to the *Ford*.

One of Plug's underling watch standers said, "Sir, is that a missile? Are—hey, there's another one."

The voice of the F-18 aviator came on the radio. "Zulu, you guys seeing this?"

* * *

The communications speaker blared next to Admiral Manning. "Foxtrot Bravo, this is Foxtrot Zulu, Ripper 612 reports what looks like missiles on deck of the merchant ships. Merchant ships not transmitting AIS transponder identification. Recommend classify as hostile, over."

* * *

Plug had just finished speaking into the radio when the F-18 aircrew began calling him on the radio, asking him for more input. Then the aircraft carrier's internal phone rang next to his computer station. The caller ID read "CSG BWC." It was the battle watch captain, the same duty officer on the admiral's staff that he'd been speaking with.

The chief who was on watch with Plug said, "Sir, I'll talk to the F-18 crew. You talk to the strike group staff."

"Got it. Thanks, Chief."

He grabbed the phone in one hand and handed the radio to the chief with the other.

The battle watch captain yelled something in his ear, but he was speaking so fast that Plug could hardly understand him.

Plug heard the chief say over the radio, "Ripper flight, we see your FLIR image and are getting input from the chain of command. Stand by."

The battle watch captain said, "What type of missiles...?"

On the tactical radio Plug heard, "Foxtrot Alpha, this is Foxtrot Whiskey, we have missile warnings bearing two-seven-zero..." The destroyer in charge of the strike group's air defense had just announced a missile launch.

Plug said, "He *is* over the merchants. How the hell do you think we're seeing this video feed?"

Then the screen that had displayed the FLIR went black. The F-18 was no longer broadcasting video.

The 1MC above them began emitting a gong-like sound. "General quarters, general quarters. All hands, man your battle stations..."

$$* * *$$

The pair of F-18s from VFA-11 waited on the catapult of the USS *Ford*'s flight deck. Neither crew expected to launch. They were the swing-loaded alert aircraft, ready for both air and surface combat, if needed.

Lieutenant Kevin Suggs had technically left the squadron two months ago for his job as an admiral's aide, but he was still current on many of his qualifications and had convinced Admiral Manning that he would be better able to serve him if he occasionally got time in the cockpit. Admiral Manning, surprisingly, had been supportive.

It had taken a few weeks of convincing, but since the Red Rippers were short on pilots for this cruise, their fighter squadron's skipper had finally relented. He probably just felt bad for Suggs being a loop. No self-respecting jet pilot ever wanted to take an assignment outside of the cockpit.

Suggs was thrilled. He would keep flying. And what did those jokers at the carrier air wing operations do? They put him on the *alert* schedule, so he could sit and bake in the sun.

At least he had a book to read. *The Red Sparrow*, by Jason Matthews. Freaking amazing book.

The first indication that something unusual was happening was when one of the ordnancemen ran from one end of the flight deck to the other, waving his arms and screaming, signaling to another ordnanceman near the elevator.

Then the speaker on the flight deck broadcast the voice of the carrier's airboss, an O-5 seasoned pilot who directed all flight operations launching and recovering from the carrier. "Let's go, *Ford*! Launch the Alert-15 swing-loaded aircraft. Get moving."

Yellow and green shirts began sprinting around the deck. Then the ship's general quarters alarm sounded, and the airflow through the open cockpit picked up as the carrier began increasing speed and turning into the winds.

Everything happened in a flash.

Their orders came over the radio. Targeting information was being beamed into his cockpit computers.

Suggs's rear-seater was a woman who had recently arrived at the squadron for her department head tour. She and Suggs began racing through the pre-takeoff checklists. He followed the direction of one of the yellow shirts, the heavy wind across the flight deck whipping his shirt and cargo pants. The canopy closed overhead. Suggs taxied into position on catapult number two. His wingman taxied onto the catapult next to him. The director then signaled to lower the launch bar, and the aircraft slowly taxied a bit further until the launch bar aligned with the catapult shuttle. Suggs held his hands up during this part of the process. An ordnanceman in a red shirt ran underneath, arming the aircraft, passing a hand signal to the aircraft when complete. Then the yellow shirt, one hand outstretched and one palm open, signaled to "take tension." The F-18 squatted into position and was ready to fire out of a cannon.

Now the "shooter," another yellow shirt on the flight deck, waved his hand in the air in a furious rhythm, giving the run-up signal. Suggs set his throttle forward into military power, the highest afterburner setting. Two cones of fire erupted from the F-18's exhaust, and the roar of his jet engines filled the ears of all four thousand men and women on the ship. Suggs and the Shooter saluted, then Suggs placed his hands on the handlebar above his head. His hands couldn't be on the controls for launch, as it was such a violent process.

The Shooter pointed to several spots around the flight deck, making his final checks, crouched low as he touched the flight deck, then leaned and pointed forward, signaling for the launch.

Suggs, engines still at afterburner, heart pounding, hands still on the bar above his head, braced himself for the...

The aircraft jolted forward.

His helmet pressed back into his seat as the USS *Ford*'s electromagnetic catapult accelerated his F-18 to over one hundred and fifty knots in two seconds. The Superhornet launched off the flight deck, and Suggs quickly placed his hands back on the controls as they became airborne.

Shaking off the familiar shock of a cat launch, he checked his instruments, turned the aircraft to the proper heading, and climbed up to five thousand feet. He pushed the throttle forward and accelerated to five hundred knots while the weapons systems officer in the rear seat began prepping for their attack.

37

Captain Hoblet stood in the balcony overlooking the dimly lit ship's mission center of the USS *Michael Monsoor*, designated the DDG-1001. It was the newest commissioned ship in the Zumwalt class of destroyers. And they were—hopefully—about to prove that it had been worth the nearly four billion taxpayer dollars spent to build it.

"TAO, hostile air tracts are now in range," he heard piped onto the balcony over the speaker.

Below, highly trained and hand-picked sailors worked feverishly at over a dozen individual three-screen workstations. There, they could control everything on the ship, using trackballs and special button panels on the common display system. Hoblet watched his team as they sucked in information from the sensors and radar and used it in conjunction with the information other ships were plugging in to the datalink.

Updated positions of Chinese air contacts, now identified as J-15 attack aircraft, were projected on the screen in front of him. By Hoblet's estimate, they would be in range to fire air-to-surface missiles any minute now. If they were going to drop bombs on Guam, it would be a while longer. It was time to respond.

The TAO looked up at the captain from the floor twenty feet below, speaking through his headset. "Captain, TAO, we've received unconfirmed reports of explosions on Guam. Initial indications are that they are under missile attack."

Captain Hoblet looked at the tactical display again. The column of Chinese fighters en route to Guam couldn't have fired missiles already. They were still too far away. "Do we know where the attack came from?"

"We think the attack may have been submarine-launched, sir."

Captain Hoblet knew that Anderson Air Force Base was a strategic air command base. As such, it would be well protected against missile and electronic attack. But would they be able to withstand a coordinated attack coming from submarine-launched missiles and fighter squadrons?

"Is Guam firing back?"

"Hard to tell from the information we're getting, sir."

"Understood. Have our SAG destroyers reported that they are ready?"

"Yes, sir, the last one—*Farragut*—just rogered up."

"Very well. You are weapons free."

Seconds later, surface-to-air missiles began shooting up from the vertical launch systems of the USS *Michael Monsoor*, the USS *Farragut*, and each of the other destroyers in their surface action group. The missiles traveled at nearly three times the speed of sound, zooming towards the Chinese fighter squadrons.

The first barrage of missiles destroyed eight of the aircraft. The Chinese fighters were performing evasive maneuvers in a panic, shooting flares and chaff in hopes that the SAMs would miss. But the American missiles were the latest-generation, with upgraded software to ensure that they did not bite off on countermeasures.

Some of the Chinese aircraft, seeing the destruction ahead, realized the futility of their task and began turning around to retreat. That was when the second barrage of American surface-to-air missiles hit. Each of the J-15s was destroyed.

38

Plug watched the tactical display on his screen. The F-18 that had been monitoring the merchant ships hadn't checked in for the past fifteen minutes. He presumed that it had been shot down.

After general quarters had sounded, the commodore had entered the Zulu cell and sat down.

"AIROPS, what's the status?" the commodore asked, referring to Plug by his job title.

"Sir, the F-18 that was flying a surveillance mission for us located the six Chinese merchant ships about one hundred miles to the west. FLIR imagery from the Ripper aircraft revealed multiple missile batteries being set up on the decks of the merchant ships. We informed strike group, and they launched the swing-loaded alert aircraft and set general quarters."

The commodore stared up at the tactical display. "Tell the ships to report any unusual sonar contacts. If the Chinese are attacking Hawaii, they'll have submarines here as well. Where's SUBS?"

The chief said, "Sir, I'll contact the destroyers."

"Sir, SUBS is in the Sierra cell." SUBS was the title of the submarine officer on the commodore's staff. He advised the commodore on all subsurface and anti-submarine warfare matters.

"He's coordinating with COMSUBPAC and the Romeo squadron on board to start a local area search."

The commodore nodded and rose. "I'm going to Sierra. Call me there immediately if anything changes, and update me when the alert F-18s reach the merchants."

"Yes, sir."

* * *

Chinese Han-class submarine

"Conn, Sonar, contact designated US aircraft carrier 78 bearing zero-nine-five for thirteen thousand meters and closing."

Captain Ning watched as his men conducted their work. They were diligent and professional, quietly performing each task just like they had trained. Except these would be real torpedoes that they would fire. And this was a real American supercarrier they were hunting.

The captain saw hints of the immense pressure taking its toll on his men. The pitch of his conning officer's voice upon replying to the sonar technician. The beads of sweat on the forehead of the navigator, and the way he didn't make eye contact with the executive officer who stood over him. But the officers and crew were doing everything right.

Things would become far more difficult the closer they came to the carrier. Technically, they were already within torpedo range. If his weapon traveled at low speed, it could get as far as thirty thousand meters. But at that velocity, the targets would have plenty of notice, as well as a speed advantage which they could use to escape.

A good submarine commander planned his attack so as to surprise the enemy and give them little to no chance to evade the incoming weapon. Captain Ning had taken his submarine very close to American aircraft carriers before, in the South China Sea. He had been undetected then, and he fully expected the same result here. By the time the Americans knew his submarine was near, it would be too late.

The problem was the escorts.

While Captain Ning would love to remove his risk by attacking the escort ships first, that would also give away his element of surprise.

"How many ships in company with the carrier now?" The escorts had been multiplying over the past week, getting reinforcements from Pearl Harbor.

"Eight ships in screen around the carrier, Captain."

"Status?"

"They're all traveling west at an average speed of ten knots, with the carrier in the center of the formation."

The captain nodded. His XO walked over to him, sensing that he wanted to discuss something. They spoke in low voices.

"We won't be able to get shots off at all of them."

The XO said, "I agree."

"We'll need to prioritize the aircraft carrier above all else. Including our escape." Their eyes met.

The XO nodded. "Yes, Captain."

"Let's close them deep and quiet. We will—"

"Conn, Sonar, transients! Torpedo bearing one-seven-zero!"

The captain of the USS *Hawaii*, a Virginia-class submarine out of Pearl Harbor, stood in the conn, knowing that a Chinese Han-class submarine was only a few thousand yards away.

"Solution ready," said the XO.

"Weapon ready," said the weapons officer.

"Ship ready."

The captain gave the order to fire, and the massive torpedo was ejected from the submarine.

"Own ship's unit in the water, running normally."

The officers and crew around him all waited as the Mark 48 torpedo hurtled through the ocean on its way to the Chinese submarine.

* * *

Captain Ning couldn't believe his ears. High-pitched pings echoed throughout the submarine. He turned and said, "All ahead flank. Come left to course two-seven-zero."

"All ahead flank," came the repeated command.

"Left two-seven-zero."

"Torpedo is homing, Captain!"

One of his officers yelled, "Who fired? Find us a target."

Captain Ning gripped the rails as he made his way to the other side of the space, the submarine rolling hard to the right as it began evasive maneuvers. He leaned over one of his sailors as he looked at the display. "Launch countermeasures."

But as the pinging of the torpedo increased in frequency, he knew it was too late.

The last thing that went through his mind was a feeling of helplessness as he realized how outmatched his submarine had been. His crew hadn't even identified who had fired the torpedo.

The torpedo's pump-jet propulsor took it to speeds over fifty knots as its seeker continued to ping, painting a picture of the target and surrounding ocean. Other onboard sensors on the Mark 48 detected the electrical and magnetic fields of the Chinese submarine. All this information was used to make the weapon more lethal.

The six-hundred-and-fifty-pound high-explosive warhead detonated a mere three feet from the Han-class submarine, ripping a hole in the bow and breaching the pressure hull. The vessel's forward speed and flooding caused it to dive downward into the ocean depths. Many of the officers and crew were killed on impact. Others died in the flooding. And the last of them died when the submarine reached crush depth, imploding into itself.

* * *

Plug could hear SUBS's announcement on the strike group's communications network.

"Foxtrot Bravo, this is Foxtrot Sierra. All known Chinese subsurface contacts in the vicinity have been destroyed, over."

Plug and the chief looked at each other in gleeful disbelief. "Did he just say what I think he said?"

The chief nodded, a look of surprised elation on his face.

"This is Foxtrot Bravo, roger out," answered the strike group battle watch captain on the radio.

The phone rang and Plug picked it up. It was SUBS, giving him the five-second version of events per the commodore's direction. "Two Los Angeles–class and one Virginia-class submarine are in the area. Their location is above the Secret level and that's why you weren't notified during your intel brief."

Plug rolled his eyes at that comment. "And what, they just sunk them all?"

"Yes. They had located four Chinese submarines and were silently tracking them for the past few days. When the F-18 was reported shot down, the commander of the Pacific Fleet told his forces to designate all Chinese military units as hostile. It didn't take our fast-attacks long to do the rest. I have to go, it's still busy here. We think we got all of the Chinese submarines in the area, but we can't be sure."

"SUBS, good job."

"Yup." He hung up the phone.

John Herndon, the Desron's future operations officer, entered the room, looking up at the tactical display.

"What happened with the submarines?"

"SUBS said that our fast-attacks sank four of them."

"Just like that?"

"That's what he said."

Herndon nodded up to the displays at the front of the room. "Looks like one of them was pretty close to us."

Plug followed his gaze and saw a new red icon labeled "Sunk SUB."

Herndon said, "That's less than five miles from us. We must have been his target."

No one spoke for a moment, and things just got a lot more real in Plug's mind. *Holy shit, he's right.*

"Commodore wants me to check on the F-18s going after the merchant ships."

Plug said, "They haven't reported in yet, but they should be in weapons range now."

"Have the F-18s updated the ship locations in datalink?"

"Yes, why?"

"What are you waiting for? Why haven't you directed fire on the merchants yet?"

"What do you mean? I thought that the F-18s—"

"What are the F-18s armed with?"

"I don't know..."

"What if they miss, or run out of munitions? Come on, Plug, you don't just use one weapon, use a bunch. If we have updated coordinates on the merchants, use everything at your disposal. Use the ships, man."

Plug felt like he was in over his head. "How?"

The young lieutenant said, "I suggest that you request permission for some of the destroyers to fire anti-ship missiles at the merchants."

"*I'm* supposed to do that?"

"My guess is that the captains of those ships are cursing us right now for wasting time."

Just then, the commodore barreled into the room, glaring at Plug, and snatched up the radio handset. He spoke fast and used terms that Plug wasn't familiar with.

A few seconds later, the tactical display began filling with high-speed air tracks. Anti-ship missiles, lifting off the four ships the commodore had just ordered to begin firing.

* * *

Suggs banked his aircraft to the left and dove to one thousand feet. He looked at his display just forward of his stick. They didn't have the ships on FLIR, but the data on his display told them that they had a targeting solution all set up. He wasn't totally sure. He had never fired one of these weapons before.

"It's okay," the duty officer told him. "*She* had the training," he said, pointing to his rear-seater at the woman who was in charge of the aircraft's weapons systems. "And besides, you're not really going to fly, you're just an alert." This deployment was totally screwed up.

He hoped that they were staying far enough away and low enough that they could avoid surface-to-air missiles. He had been told by the duty officer on the air wing's frequency that the Ripper flight ahead of him had been shot down. "Look for a chute or survivor in the water when you're done," he had said.

Suggs felt a swell of anger at the idea that some of his old squadron mates were now dead at the hands of Chinese missiles. But he quickly forced the thought out of his mind. He had to compartmentalize. To lock up his emotion into a box and set it aside. Now wasn't the time.

"Almost ready," said the naval flight officer in the rear seat. Suggs had only just met her earlier today. She outranked him, but she was also kind of cute. Why was he thinking about this now? Why couldn't he compartmentalize *that* thought? He checked his heading, making a minor correction. It wouldn't be fraternization. It wasn't like they were in the same squadron. Maybe...

"*Bruiser away*," she said, then a split second later, "Bruiser two away."

Dark, futuristic shapes dropped from each wing mount, ignited, and shot out down and ahead of the fighter, speeding towards their prey.

The Chinese missile commander on the lead merchant ship was nervous now. Things weren't going fast enough. His men still needed five more minutes before they were ready to launch the ballistic missiles, and another twenty before they were within range of the cruise missiles. One of the air defense teams aboard the ship next to him had fired at an American fighter jet overhead, hitting it. He was happy to see that their training had paid off, resulting in a kill. But now the Americans would know that they were here. It would only be a matter of time until…

"Sir, our air defense team reports *multiple* air contacts inbound. Two appear to be American fighters—we classify them as FA-18s. They're just outside our surface-to-air missile range. But…"

The man stopped speaking. His eyes widened as he pointed to the horizon.

The commander turned to look where he was pointing. The small dark shapes skimming the water were moving too fast to see as they ran into the northernmost merchant ship. But what was clearly visible was the enormous cargo vessel erupting into a geyser of water and metal.

* * *

The missiles that the F-18s had fired were the brand-new long-range anti-ship missiles developed by DARPA. With the modernization of the Chinese navy, the Pentagon had needed a new air-launched anti-ship missile. DARPA had been working on it for years, and the SILVERSMITH team had ensured that the USS *Ford* received some of these high-tech weapons.

The long black missiles were fired from over seventy miles away and skimmed the surface of the ocean as they headed to their targets at just under the speed of sound. Their stealthy design made them almost invisible to radar.

The pair of F-18s carried two of the weapons each. The four missiles raced along the ocean and targeted four separate ships. Each one impacted its target in the center of the hull, just above the water-line, and the one-thousand-pound warheads exploded on impact. The four massive merchant ships began filling with water, their hulls not designed to withstand military ordnance. Within minutes, they were sinking.

Suggs tuned up the frequency for his controller, asking if they wanted him to perform strafing runs on the remaining two merchant ships.

"Negative, Ripper flight, remain clear. Additional strike inbound from the surface ships. Request you make a high pass in five mikes to obtain BDA." Battle damage assessment. They wanted him to make sure all of the merchants had been destroyed.

"Wilco," he replied.

Five minutes later, he brought his fighter up in altitude and overflew the target zone as his weapons systems officer manipulated the FLIR to show the surface picture.

She said, "Negative SAM threat, I'd say."

"Negative *any* threat," Suggs replied.

The merchants that hadn't already sunk were burning and listing badly. Only three were visible above the water. The ship-launched missiles had finished the job. There was no way any of the missiles could be launched now.

39

C hase looked at Natesh, who was on his laptop computer. "Tetsuo wants me downstairs."

Natesh looked up, concern in his eyes. He was right to be afraid. The Chinese were attacking the city. So far, the civilian segments of the city didn't seem to be targeted on purpose. But errant missiles and wreckage from shot-down aircraft had turned Tokyo into a field of scattered fires. And that wasn't what he was afraid of...

"Is he really going to make me go back to them?"

"Tetsuo?" Chase asked.

"Yes. Is he going to send me back to Jinshan, after what I've told you?"

Chase didn't know what to say. Talking to assets wasn't his strength. He had no experience quelling the misgivings of double agents. He wanted to scream at Natesh, to tell him that he would do whatever they asked, that he deserved it for what he had done. He wanted to tell the Indian-American piece of shit that people were dying around the world right now because of his complicity in Jinshan's plans.

"I'm not sure what he'll say. I'm just here to make sure you stay put, and that you're safe."

Natesh pointed to his laptop. "But I hacked in to their network. Not just the logistics network, but the 3PLA system. Do you know who they are? That's China's version of the NSA. If you get the files on this computer to your people, they'll have a huge advantage. But they'll know that I took it. I can't go back. They'll know that I betrayed them."

"You weren't supposed to do that. We didn't tell you to do that."

"I thought that if the attacks had begun, this was over. Tetsuo gave me…"

Chase's phone buzzed in his hand. He looked down and frowned.

"Tetsuo's here. He's having trouble in the lobby. He needs a room key to use the elevator, and they won't give him one. Where's yours?"

Natesh held up his room key. Chase snatched it and said, "I'll be right back."

Natesh nodded.

Chase walked out the door and took the elevator down. The elevator was one of those glass numbers that let you see everything while it traveled. It moved fast, and Chase could feel it in his stomach. His ears popped, and he forced himself to yawn to clear them.

The elevator finally reached the ground floor and opened with a ring. He walked along the marble floor and down to the lobby of the hotel. Tetsuo was walking through the revolving door, a frown on his face.

Tetsuo said, "What the hell are you doing down here? I told you to watch him."

"What are you talking about?"

"Why'd you…"

Chase shook his head and took out his phone, holding it up for Tetsuo to see. "You just sent me this text. You told me to come down."

Then his expression changed as he realized what had happened. Tetsuo and he both sprinted towards the elevator area.

* * *

Lena Chou hadn't been back to Japan in years.

She had been raised to hate the Japanese people. The atrocities that Japan had committed against the Chinese during World War II still served to fuel anti-Japanese sentiment in China even to this day. Especially in Chinese government-sponsored propaganda. The Chinese government loved to remind its citizens that Japan had helped kill fifteen to twenty million people—their grandparents and great-grandparents—during the war. Japan was a nation of villains.

If there was one thing Lena had learned from her youth in China, and from her understudies with Jinshan, it was that propaganda *worked*.

When she had arrived in Tokyo for the first time, as part of her espionage training before she was implanted in to the United States, she'd half-expected to be spat on by angry Japanese citizens. But nothing could have been further from the truth. She walked the clean streets and met many friendly people. They complimented her on her Japanese, and she fell in love with the land. The cooking was excellent, and the countryside was beautiful.

Things were very different now.

Lena had walked the streets of Tokyo, sirens blaring all around her. Fires were scattered around the city, towers of smoke billowing up hundreds of feet into the air. Bloodstains and rubble on the sidewalk.

A part of her was sad at what war had brought to one of her favorite countries. But she shook off the feeling. She pulled her coat tight around her, a gray hood covering her hair and keeping most of her face hidden.

Lena had performed a mental exercise while on her walk. She had locked up all of her emotions, all of her questions and worry, deep inside her mind. There was no room for doubt or hesitation now. She had to be *on* now. She had to function at the highest level. Her American competitors would show her no mercy if they found her here.

Once again, Lena had transformed herself into a machine. An instrument of death, if need be.

She walked into the Hilton hotel, her eyes darting over the expansive lobby area, taking in every detail. Dozens of empty seats and coffee tables filled the atrium. Shattered glass lay unmoved in some places. A single hotel attendant stood behind one of the desks. He looked like he had been crying.

Lena asked him, "Are the elevators still working?"

He nodded. "Yes, but we recommend you take the stairs."

She ignored him, walking to the elevator area. She took out her mobile phone. The special one that the Ministry of State Security had provided. She sent a text. Civilian phone networks were down, but she had been assured that this message would go through. She didn't even know who would receive it. Some local CIA case officer. The Japanese section of the MSS had handled the technical details. Lena was just the operator. If the message went through and they left as instructed, they would live. If not, Lena would soon pay them a visit. Sure enough, the response came.

COMING DOWN NOW.

She watched the elevator floor buttons until the circle with "50" lit up. Then 49...48...

She quickly pressed the up button, and the second elevator door opened. A few seconds later, she was being lifted up in the glass-walled elevator, the coffee tables sinking beneath her view, replaced by an exterior panorama of the city of Tokyo. From this vantage point, the wreckage looked even worse. Although the smoky reddish haze looked beautiful backed by the setting sun.

Chinese missiles had done a number on this city. But the attack was over for now. Jinshan was claiming that only American and military assets were being targeted. But due to the volume of missiles needed, older ones were required, and their targeting systems were not so accurate. Civilian casualties were unavoidable. Still, the PLA had been ordered to cease fire on all Japanese ground targets for twenty-four hours. A special mission was being conducted, they were told.

She turned away just as the other glass-encased elevator zoomed down next to her. Lena doubted that anyone would see her since the elevators were moving so fast, but she didn't want to leave it to chance. A tug in her soul urged her to get a glimpse. To see if it was him...

The hallway on the fiftieth floor stood empty. Lena arrived outside the hotel door and removed her silenced pistol from her pack. She fired three times into the lock of the door and then opened it.

Natesh stood wide-eyed inside.

"Lena." His concentration pivoted from her face to her gun.

She was pleased that she hadn't accidentally shot him in the process. That would have been embarrassing. But there were multiple ways to proceed here. And it was her decision whether he lived or not. She closed the door behind her, flipping the latch to hold it in place.

"Hello, my dear. Have a seat." She flicked her weapon towards one of the chairs by the window. He did as he was commanded. Lena pulled back her hoodie. She had to be quick. Her internal clock ticked away.

"So, how has your progress been?"

He looked like he was trying to be brave, but his lower lip was quivering, eyes glancing at the gun.

"Things have been going according to plan."

"You gave the Americans false data on the ship locations? As you were instructed?"

"Yes." He kept looking at the gun.

"It's alright, Natesh, I'm not here to kill you."

He looked puzzled at that. "Then why the gun?"

"To ensure compliance. If I have to use it, I will. But I trust that we can come to a better arrangement."

His breathing was fast and heavy. "What do you want?"

"What did you give them?"

His eyes darted over to his laptop on the desk. She followed his glance. "You said you wanted me to pass them false information on ship movements. So I did."

"Show me. And no tricks. Otherwise—well, you know very well what will happen. And, Natesh?"

"What?"

"It doesn't have to be quick. I'm an excellent shot. I could just take out one of your legs and cripple you, then drag you outside to where my friends are waiting. They'll bring you into a dark room and go to work on you for weeks. Keeping you alive just to make sure that you feel pain." She smiled as she said it.

He stood, looking woozy. "Okay. Okay. I might have given them some data that was beyond what we had discussed. I'm sorry." He held up his hands. "Just tell me how to make this right."

She tilted her head. "There. There. Now that wasn't so hard, was it? A bit of honesty can go a long way. Now, just show me what you've already provided them."

"It's been erased."

"Fine, then you'll write it down from memory. I have people that will need that."

Natesh was sitting behind his laptop computer now, typing. "Okay."

Natesh had been hedging his bets. Lena had instructed him to come to Japan. She had arranged for the Americans to find out about him, hoping that they would recruit him. It would be a way to provide the Americans with false information. Things had worked well enough at first. But then Natesh had tried to get cute.

The American offer had sounded pretty good, it seemed. So he had been giving them access and information beyond what he was supposed to provide, without reporting it to the Chinese. Natesh had left a special CIA-made device, designed to look like a wristwatch, in a mail drop across the street. He had also copied a file onto his personal laptop. His intention, now that the attack had begun, was to take as much as he could and provide it to the Americans in exchange for his freedom.

He told all this to Lena and began showing her how to gain access to his computer, and which software program to use. She made him write everything down. It took five minutes.

"Were you going to tell the Americans that I sent you here? That you were still betraying them, even now?"

Natesh looked frightened. He didn't answer her question. He just looked up at her and shrugged. "So what now?"

She smiled. "Now you come with me, and we live happily ever after."

"Why did you have me show you all that? Write everything down?"

"In case I need to kill you." Her eyes were emotionless.

He started to tear up.

She sighed. "Look, Natesh, we've accomplished what we came for. Now they're listening to you. They believe you. They'll make decisions based on information that you give them. Natesh, you are what we called a verified asset. Do you know how hard it is to create one of those? You are a gold mine to them. And now, we will take over the messaging. We'll begin providing them information that is in our best interests."

"But—I already gave them information. I told them about the attacks coming from North Korea. I told them about the locations of the merchants and the Chinese carrier group. They've already—"

"Natesh, timing is everything. You told them about the attacks coming from North Korea *just* before they occurred. So the Americans couldn't do anything to *stop* them. The only purpose that served was to verify that you were providing *accurate* information."

"But the attacks on Guam and Hawaii…"

"Yes, well—in all truth, we did not expect you to realize the actual positions of those units. We thought you would provide them the intended navigational tracks to the south, as you were instructed, drawing their forces to the Marianas or even to South America. Turns out you are better than our hackers thought—or maybe you got lucky. But the fact that the Americans were able to gain a victory at Hawaii based on your information only serves to solidify their faith in you as a source.

"We will need to be very careful not to compromise that trust. And you will continue to provide them with a lot of useful information. Just not…*too* useful. And when the time is right, when we want them to bet all their chips on one big hand, you will feed them something erroneous. Something that will work spectacularly in our favor. You can't buy that kind of mole, Natesh. You have to grow it."

"So, you planned this all along? You planned for me to betray you?"

"No. Not until you showed signs of—how shall I put it—sensitivity. When you began expressing doubts. When you began showing signs of *weakness*. That's when I spoke to Jinshan and thought that this might be a good way to go. We were ready to go either way. I suspected that the American offer might be too tempting. So we kept a close eye on what you were doing. In case you decided to get creative."

He frowned. "You've been watching me this whole time."

She checked her watch and gestured to the door. "We monitor our people. It's the only way to operate. Constant verification of loyalty. Now come on. We need to leave."

* * *

"Is that Natesh?" Tetsuo asked.

"Yeah."

Chase saw the glass elevator traveling down towards them. As the passengers came into view, he couldn't believe what he was seeing.

"Who's next to him?"

There was a hooded figure, back to the elevator's glass window. Then the figure turned. And Chase saw the eyes of the last person he expected to be here.

"That's Lena Chou."

She was staring straight at him.

* * *

Lena froze. Her senses were already heightened; she knew that the CIA could have someone here. But as her eyes met those of Chase Manning, her pulse quickened.

She removed her hood, letting her long black hair flow down

over her shoulders. Lena gripped her pistol, grappling with a mix of emotions inside of her. The elevator was fast approaching the bottom floor.

Lena slapped the second-floor button on the elevator, and their descent slowed to a halt. The door rang as it opened.

* * *

Chase and Tetsuo saw the elevator lights stop at the second floor. They were crouched on opposite sides of the lobby-level elevator area, half-hidden with their weapons aimed at the closed elevator doors.

Chase signaled to Tetsuo, pointing towards the stairs.

"We need to go up."

He nodded and rose, but then paused when the elevator rang and the round floor indicator illuminated to indicate that it was moving again. The first-floor light went bright yellow, then dark. Then the lobby level went bright yellow.

Another ding. And the door opened.

Chase and Tetsuo both moved towards the opening elevator door, their weapons pointed forward.

Natesh's corpse lay inside, a scarlet bloodstain on his chest.

Tetsuo ran over to him, checking his pulse. "He's dead. Let's check up on the second floor, where it stopped." He pressed the emergency hold button on the elevator. Then Tetsuo and Chase raced up the stairs to the second floor.

They searched for thirty minutes before they called in more CIA help to investigate the room and area surrounding the hotel. But Lena, and Natesh's laptop, were nowhere to be found.

* * *

Lin Yu watched as another commercial aircraft landed on the runway. It was strange, seeing them fly in one after the other, unload their passengers right on the flight line—no terminal or anything.

Then they would get refueled and take off again immediately. Everything was so fast.

Lin Yu had never been to a big commercial airport, but he had seen them in movies. And he was pretty sure that the occupants of the aircraft weren't marched off to a tent city in a field, only a few miles from the runway.

Then again, how many commercial planes were filled with Chinese soldiers, flying across the ocean?

He was a changed person now. He knew that it was propaganda they had been pouring on him for the last two weeks, during his crash-course boot camp. He knew it, but it didn't matter.

Lin Yu had heard and seen enough of what the Americans had done that he believed his instructors. He has been brainwashed to hate Americans—and to detest religion, any religion. The Americans only wanted to kill Chinese. They hated everything that his people stood for. He believed that now. And a part of him was amazed at how quickly the transformation had occurred.

He sat in his tent, cleaning his weapon, tired and ready to sleep. The kid in the rack next to him asked, "What do you think will happen tomorrow? Will we start the invasion?"

Lin Yu just laughed.

"What's so funny?"

He shook his head. "The invasion has already begun. We're here."

"Where?"

"America."

"I thought we were in Siberia. To get ready? Then we fly to America soon after?"

"That was just some bullshit they put out. They wanted to throw the Americans off in case they found out."

"But how did the planes get over the United States without being detected or shot down?"

"They used electromagnetic pulse weapons. And they had special forces units who destroyed some radars or anti-aircraft missiles. We didn't go over America much anyway. We were over Canada for the most part, until just before landing."

"How do you know all that?"

"I work in the operations department. This is America. More planes will come in all night long. Tomorrow we will likely push south and begin splitting the country in two. They will bring more of us in each day."

40

Admiral Manning sat at the head of the Ford Carrier Strike Group conference table, the room filled with staff officers. These were the war planners. The men and women who worked tirelessly day and night to fit each length of the chain together. The ones who would gladly give their lives in defense of the United States. Who gave up holidays with family, who missed the births of their children and sacrificed time and again over long deployments.

They had just been battle-tested and won.

Six Chinese merchant ships, fitted with storage containers filled with missiles, had been sunk by a combination of ship and air power from the Ford Strike Group. Four Chinese submarines in the water space surrounding the Hawaiian Islands had also been sunk by American fast-attack subs. The Chinese surprise attack on Hawaii had been completely rebuked.

SAG-131—the surface action group that Admiral Manning had dispatched to Guam—had turned a surprise Chinese air strike from catastrophe to minor victory. While the runways and air defense sites on Guam were damaged, they could be repaired quickly. And the ample US air assets on Guam were unharmed. They would be crucial in an American military response in the Western Pacific.

And there would need to be a response. For Hawaii and Guam were some of the few American success stories during the day.

"Proceed with the brief," said Admiral Manning.

His intelligence officer nodded. "Sir, over the past twelve hours, our normal collection and dissemination of intelligence has ground to a halt. There has been some type of cyberattack on the continental US infrastructure, we know that. But we also suspect that some of the undersea cables that connect Internet and telecommunications across the Atlantic and Pacific have also been cut. The Chinese have begun launching anti-satellite weapons to shoot down our recently launched satellites that we have up, as well as the classified ones we didn't think they knew about. In short, sir, the flow of intelligence is not what we're used to getting. But we do know a few things…"

He continued painting the picture that Admiral Manning had already picked up bits and pieces of from the conversation he'd had with the commander of the Pacific Fleet moments ago. But he let him continue—this brief wasn't just for Admiral Manning. Everyone needed the information.

Nuclear explosions had been detected in North Korea. While the military had not confirmed it through official channels, news reports had stated that the American president had ordered the attack, a retaliation for North Korea invading South Korea. That seemed ludicrous to Admiral Manning. No sane US president would give that order, but that was the information they were getting. But good news sources were hard to come by today. Much of the United States had been attacked by EMP weapons. Only a day after the war had begun, the fog was still thick.

China had attacked US military assets in Japan, Diego Garcia, Guam, the Philippines, Australia, and South Korea. Taiwan was also being hit hard. The attacks farther from the Chinese mainland had been carried out mostly by submarine-launched cruise missiles. Japanese, Taiwanese, and South Korean targets had been hit mostly by land-launched missiles and Chinese bombers.

"Sir, we really don't know the results of the Chinese attacks on Western Pacific allied nations yet. But we do have unconfirmed reports that both US aircraft carriers in the region have been sunk."

A few people gasped. Someone cursed. Most of the attendees had clenched jaws, choosing to remain silent.

Admiral Manning listened for another fifteen minutes while the intelligence brief went on. When it was finished, he stood up, and the room stood at attention.

"We are once again a nation at war. If not for our victories at Guam and Hawaii, I fear that we would be at a great disadvantage. We should be thankful for what we have, and mourn those we have lost." He clenched his jaw, and he took a few deep breaths out of his nose.

Then he said, "Ladies and gentlemen, stay vigilant. This fight has just begun."

We hope you enjoyed the book. There are more in the series. Be sure to join the Andrew Watts Reader List at **andrewwattsauthor.com.**

THE NEXT BOOK IN THE SERIES...

Thank you for reading book 4 in The War Planners series, THE ELEPHANT GAME.

Book 5 is titled OVERWHELMING FORCE. Find out how to get your copy at Andrewwattsauthor.com.

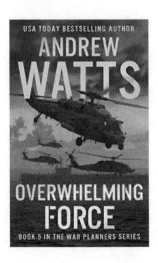

ABOUT THE AUTHOR

Andrew Watts graduated from the US Naval Academy in 2003 and served as a naval officer and helicopter pilot until 2013. During that time, he flew counter-narcotic missions in the Eastern Pacific and counter-piracy missions off the Horn of Africa. He was a flight instructor in Pensacola, FL, and helped to run ship and flight operations while embarked on a nuclear aircraft carrier deployed in the Middle East.

Today, he lives with his family in Ohio.

From Andrew: Thanks so much for reading my books. Be sure to join my Reader List! You'll be the first to know when I release a new book.

You can follow me or find out more here:
andrewwattsauthor.com

ALSO BY ANDREW WATTS

Books available for Kindle, print, and audiobook. To find out more about the books or Andrew Watts, go to andrewwattsauthor.com.

The War Planners Series

1. The War Planners
2. The War Stage
3. Pawns of the Pacific
4. The Elephant Game
5. Overwhelming Force

Max Fend Series

1. Glidepath
2. The Oshkosh Connection

Made in the USA
Middletown, DE
13 May 2019